THE BEST OF THE BEST

VOLUME 2

ALSO BY GARDNER DOZOIS

THE BEST OF THE BEST

VOLUME 2

20 Years of

THE BEST SHORT
SCIENCE FICTION

Novels

Gardner Dozois

st. martin's griffin ✠ new york

SF
Best of
v.2

www.stmartins.com

ISBN-13: 978-0-312-36341-3 (hc)
ISBN-10: 0-312-36341-9 (hc)
ISBN-13: 978-0-312-36342-0 (tpk)
ISBN-10: 0-312-36342-7 (tpk)

FIRST EDITION: FEBRUARY 2007

10 9 8 7 6 5 4 3 2 1

acknowledgment is made for permission to reprint the following materials:

"Sailing to Byzantium," by Robert Silverberg. Copyright © 1985 by Agberg, Ltd. First published in *Isaac Asimov's Science Fiction Magazine*, February 1985. Reprinted by permission of the author.

"Surfacing," by Walter Jon Williams. Copyright © 1988 by Davis Publications, Inc. First published in *Isaac Asimov's Science Fiction Magazine*, April 1988. Reprinted by permission of the author.

"The Hemingway Hoax," by Joe Haldeman. Copyright © 1990 by Joe Haldeman. First published in *Isaac Asimov's Science Fiction Magazine*, April 1990. Reprinted by permission of the author.

"Mr. Boy," by James Patrick Kelly. Copyright © 1990 by Davis Publications, Inc. First published in *Isaac Asimov's Science Fiction Magazine*, June 1990. Reprinted by permission of the author.

"Beggars in Spain," by Nancy Kress. Copyright © 1991 by Nancy Kress. First published as a chapbook by Axolotl Press. Reprinted by permission of the author.

"Griffin's Egg," by Michael Swanwick. Copyright © 1991 by Michael Swanwick. First published as a chapbook by Century Legend in 1991. Reprinted by permission of the author.

"Outnumbering the Dead," by Frederik Pohl. Copyright © 1991 by Frederik Pohl. First published as a chapbook by Century Legend in 1991. Reprinted by permission of the author.

"Forgiveness Day," by Ursula K. Le Guin. Copyright © 1994 by Ursula K. Le Guin. First published in *Asimov's Science Fiction*, November 1994. Reprinted by permission of the author and the author's agent, The Virgina Kidd Agency.

"The Cost to Be Wise," by Maureen F. McHugh. Copyright © 1996 by Maureen F. McHugh. First published in *Starlight 1* (Tor), edited by Patrick Nielsen Hayden. Reprinted by permission of the author.

"Oceanic," by Greg Egan. Copyright © 1998 by Dell Magazines. First published in *Asimov's Science Fiction*, August 1998. Reprinted by permission of the author.

"Tendeléo's Story," by Ian McDonald. Copyright © 2000 Ian McDonald. First published as a chapbook, *Tendeléo's Story* (PS Publishing). Reprinted by permission of the author.

"New Light on the Drake Equation," by Ian R. MacLeod. Copyright © 2001 by SCIFI.COM. First published electronically on SCI FICTION, May 23, 2001. Reprinted by permission of the author.

"Turquoise Days," by Alastair Reynolds. From *Diamond Dogs, Turquoise Days*, by Alastair Reynolds, copyright © 2002 by Alastair Reynolds. Used by permission of Ace Books, an imprint of The Berkeley Publishing Group, a division of Penguin Group (USA) Inc.

contents

preface

Since this series of Best-of-the-Year anthologies debuted, back in the dear, dim, vanished days of 1984, we've run through twenty-three annual collections, and 7,309,939 words of fiction by more than two hundred different authors.

A lot of those words took the form of short novels—or novellas, as they're usually referred to in the science fiction field. Outside of science fiction, the novella is rarely encountered these days, being, in fact, something of a literary endangered species. The novella is still alive and well in the science fiction world, though, and it's a rare year that doesn't see at least eight or ten of them published, often more.

Perhaps this is because, in many ways, the novella or short novel is a perfect length for a science fiction story: long enough to enable you to flesh out the details of a strange alien world or a bizarre future society, to give such a setting some depth, complexity, and *heft* . . . and yet, still short enough to pack a real punch, some power and elegance and bite, unblunted and unobscured by padding. Unlike many of today's novels, all too many of which strike me as novellas grossly padded-out to be five hundred pages long, there are rarely any wasted words in a good novella, a quality that they share with good short stories. A good novella is no longer than it *needs* to be. It does what it has to do, what it is designed to do, and then it *stops*. That novellas need to be as long as they are, long enough to justify the alternative term "short novels," is a measure of just how complicated and difficult are the tasks that they are designed to *do*: to create a whole fictional world, a universe that no one has ever explored before, to set that world forth in intricate detail, to people it with living characters, and then to use the tumbling interactions of that world and those people to tell a story that could not be told without *both* those elements being present. This is a formidable task to accomplish even in the space of a five-hundred-page novel, yet a good novella accomplishes it in the space of twenty or thirty thousand words—the novellas here are marvels of compression, in spite of the amount of ground they have to cover, and it would be hard to find a page of slack to cut out of any of them, or to end them one page earlier than they do.

As you can probably tell by now, I like novellas, and I've used a lot of them in my Best-of-the-Year anthologies over the past twenty-three years—more than a hundred of them, in fact. When I edited a retrospective look-back last year over the run of *The Year's Best Science Fiction* series, 2005's *The Best of the Best: 20 Years of the Year's Best Science Fiction*, I included as many novellas as I had room to use and still have space for anything *else* in the book—Nancy Kress's "Trinity," Brian Stableford's "Mortimer Gray's *History of Death*," Ted Chiang's "Story of Your Life," David Marusek's "The Wedding Album," Ian R. MacLeod's "Breathmoss"—but that left so many excellent novellas *un*used that I decided that there was justification for *another* retrospective anthology, the one that you're (presumptively; you might, I suppose, have telekinetic powers, and be floating the book in midair) holding in your hands at this moment, an anthology dedicated exclusively to the many first-rate novellas or short novels that have appeared in *The Year's Best Science Fiction* series over the years.

Or as many of them as we could fit in, anyway. Even with a huge anthology such as this one, there's no way that more than a small percentage of the more than a hundred (almost a hundred and twenty, actually) novellas that we've published in the *Best* could be made to fit into the amount of space that was physically possible. I quickly came to the realization that there was no list of deserving novellas that I could draw up that wouldn't exceed the space available by at least six or seven stories (and indeed, when I did finalize the line-up you see in this book, there were at least six or seven other novellas I wished I had room to use; we'll have to wait for the multidimensional, infinitely expansible version of this anthology to do the job *right*). I also quickly became aware, from talking to fans and readers on the *Asimov's* online forum and elsewhere, that there was no possible line-up I could come up with that was going to please everyone; no matter how many stories I included, since there wasn't room to include *all* of them, there was always *somebody* who was going to be disappointed that their favorite story was left out.

The brute fact was, though, that since there wasn't room for everything, or even everything that deserved to be in the *book*, that something was going to have to go. That called for hard decisions.

The first and in some ways most important decision I had to make was whether I should use novellas, such as Joe Haldeman's "The Hemingway Hoax" and Nancy Kress's "Beggars in Spain," that were later expanded into novels, or whether I should stick with less-famous stand-alone novellas that *weren't* subsequently turned into novels. After a great deal of soul-searching, I decided that to justify a title such as *The Best of the Best: 20 Years of the Year's Best Science Fiction Short Novels*, I *had* to include stories such as "The Hemingway Hoax" and "Beggars in Spain," even if they are available elsewhere in other forms—the anthology just wouldn't live up to its name otherwise. (Practical considerations did force a few exceptions: for instance, David Marusek's "We Were Out of Our Minds with Joy," otherwise a shoo-in, would be available on bookstore shelves at about the same time this anthology would be as the opening chapter of his excellent novel *Counting Heads* . . . and Tony Daniel's "Grist," another obvious choice, was being reprinted in a competing, big retrospective anthology that would also be on those same shelves at about the same time.) While I hoped to include lesser-known novellas that weren't as readily available and perhaps hadn't been seen or weren't findable by newer readers, it was clear that the only fair determining characteristic was literary quality: If it couldn't justifiably be called "The Best of the Best," it wasn't going to get in, all other practical and demographic considerations aside. (Don't bother to tell me that there are too many stories from *Asimov's* here; I know that already . . . and if I didn't have to give at least some consideration to demographics, there'd probably be more of them. In defense of that, though, *Asimov's* was one of the premier markets for novellas throughout the '80s and '90s, and, along with markets such as *The Magazine of Fantasy & Science Fiction, Interzone,* and *Analog,* remains one of the prime sources for novellas to this day . . . plus, not all the *Asimov's* stories here were bought by *me*. It also quickly became clear that there was no way that *every* year that the *Best* has been published could be represented; first-rate novellas tend to *clump*, for some reason, and thus there were inevitably going to be two or three novellas from the same year, and none from others.)

Having decided that everything was eligible (for symmetry with 2005's *The Best of the Best: 20 Years of the Year's Best Science Fiction*, I decided to limit myself to the first twenty volumes; in the unlikely event that I live long enough, maybe we'll get another retrospective out of the series ten years down the road), even the best-known stories and novellas that had been turned into novels, I then had to *re-read* everything, all hundred-plus novellas, a hefty percentage of those 7,309,939 words. Although a few of them turned out, unsurprisingly, to be too heavily dated to use after twenty years or more, most of them held up amazingly well, even some of the oldest stories. Eliminating most of them turned out to be one of the hardest editorial jobs I've ever undertaken; the quality of the available pool of novellas was so high that I drew up list after list after list (complicated by the fact that some authors had *two or three* excellent novellas that would have served my purposes just as well as the one I ended up actually using) right up until the last possible moment, and you could make as good an argument for most of them as for the one I ended up with; in fact, if I'd finalized on Tuesday rather than Monday, you'd have probably ended up with a different list altogether. Chances are, it still would probably have lived up to the title, though. The quality of the pool of novellas there was to draw upon was so high that, even if I'd closed my eyes, stabbed out a finger, and picked stories at random, you'd probably still be getting a pretty good anthology out of it.

In closing, I'd like to thank the often-unsung acquisitions editors who had the good taste to buy these stories in the first place: Ellen Datlow, Shawna McCarthy, Peter Crowther, Kristine Kathryn Rusch, Deborah Beale, Patrick Nielson Hayden, as well as all the editors over the last twenty years who bought all the stories in those twenty volumes that didn't happen to make the cut for this particular retrospective. I'd like to thank the *writers*, who labored long into the night over keyboards in lonely rooms to write all the stories in this anthology, and all the other stories in the twenty volumes of the *Best*, and all the good stories that didn't make it into any of them in the first place—because there've always been more good stories than we have room to use, every year from the beginning to now.

And lastly, I'd like to thank you, the readers, for buying and appreciating the volumes of this series, and thus making it a success. May you continue to enjoy future volumes, and may you enjoy this one as well!

—Gardner Dozois

THE BEST OF THE BEST

VOLUME 2

sailing to Byzantium

ROBERT SILVERBERG

Robert Silverberg is one of the most famous SF writers of modern times, with dozens of novels, anthologies, and collections to his credit. As both writer and editor (he was editor of the original anthology series *New Dimensions*, perhaps most acclaimed anthology series of its era), Silverberg was one of the most influential figures of the Post–New Wave era of the '70s, and continues to be at the forefront of the field to this very day, having won a total of five Nebula Awards and four Hugo Awards, plus SFWA's prestigious Grandmaster Award.

His novels include the acclaimed *Dying Inside, Lord Valentine's Castle, The Book of Skulls, Downward to the Earth, Tower of Glass, Son of Man, Nightwings, The World Inside, Born with the Dead, Shadrack in the Furnace, Thorns, Up the Line, The Man in the Maze, Tom O'Bedlam, Star of Gypsies, At Winter's End, The Face of the Waters, Kingdoms of the Wall, Hot Sky at Midnight, The Alien Years, Lord Prestimion, The Mountains of Majipoor,* and two novel-length expansions of famous Isaac Asimov stories, *Nightfall* and *The Ugly Little Boy*. His collections include *Unfamiliar Territory, Capricorn Games, Majipoor Chronicles, The Best of Robert Silverberg, The Conglomeroid Cocktail Party, Beyond the Safe Zone,* and a massive retrospective collection, *The Collected Stories of Robert Silverberg, Volume One: Secret Sharers*. His reprint anthologies are far too numerous to list here, but include *The Science Fiction Hall of Fame, Volume One* and the distinguished *Alpha* series, among dozens of others. His most recent books are the novel *The Longest Way Home,* the mosaic novel *Roma Eterna,* and a massive new retrospective collection, *Phases of the Moon: Six Decades of Masterpieces.* Coming up is a new collection, *In the Beginning.* He lives with his wife, writer Karen Haber, in Oakland, California.

Here, in the one of the most distinguished stories of a long and distinguished career, a story that won him both Hugo and Nebula awards, he takes us to the very far future, on tour with a twentieth-century man in a world where *everyone* is a tourist, and nothing is quite what it seems.

A t dawn he arose and stepped out onto the patio for his first look at Alexandria, the one city he had not yet seen. That year the five cities were Chang-an, Asgard, New Chicago, Timbuctoo, Alexandria: the usual mix of eras, cultures, realities. He and Gioia, making the long flight from Asgard in the distant north the night before, had arrived late, well after sundown, and had gone straight to bed. Now, by the gentle apricot-hued morning light, the fierce spires and battlements of Asgard seemed merely something he had dreamed.

The rumor was that Asgard's moment was finished anyway. In a little while, he had heard, they were going to tear it down and replace it, elsewhere, with Mohenjo-daro. Though there were never more than five cities, they changed constantly. He could remember a time when they had had Rome of the Caesars instead of Chang-an, and Rio de Janeiro rather than Alexandria. These people saw no point in keeping anything very long.

It was not easy for him to adjust to the sultry intensity of Alexandria after the frozen splendors of Asgard. The wind, coming off the water, was brisk and torrid both at once. Soft turquoise wavelets lapped at the jetties. Strong presences assailed his senses: the hot heavy sky, the stinging scent of the red lowland sand borne on the breeze, the sullen swampy aroma of the nearby sea. Everything trembled and glimmered in the early light. Their hotel was beautifully situated, high on the northern slope of the huge artificial mound known as the Paneium that was sacred to the goat-footed god. From here they had a total view of the city: the wide noble boulevards, the soaring obelisks and monuments, the palace of Hadrian just below the hill, the stately and awesome Library, the temple of Poseidon, the teeming marketplace, the royal lodge that Marc Antony had built after his defeat at Actium. And of course the Lighthouse, the wondrous many-windowed Lighthouse, the seventh wonder of the world, that immense pile of marble and limestone and reddish-purple Aswan granite rising in majesty at the end of its mile-long causeway. Black smoke from the beacon fire at its summit curled lazily into the sky. The city was awakening. Some temporaries in short white kilts appeared and began to trim the dense dark hedges that bordered the great public buildings. A few citizens wearing loose robes of vaguely Grecian style were strolling in the streets.

There were ghosts and chimeras and phantasies everywhere about. Two slim elegant centaurs, a male and a female, grazed on the hillside. A burly thick-thighed swordsman appeared on the porch of the temple of Poseidon holding a Gorgon's severed head and waved it in a wide arc, grinning broadly. In the street below the hotel gate three small pink sphinxes, no bigger than housecats, stretched and yawned and began to prowl the curbside. A larger one, lion-sized, watched warily from an alleyway: their mother, surely. Even at this distance he could hear her loud purring.

Shading his eyes, he peered far out past the Lighthouse and across the water. He hoped to see the dim shores of Crete or Cyprus to the north, or perhaps the great dark curve of Anatolia. *Carry me toward that great Byzantium*, he thought. *Where all is ancient, singing at the oars*. But he beheld only the endless empty sea, sun-bright and blinding though the morning was just beginning. Nothing was ever where he expected it to be. The continents did not seem to be in their proper places any longer. Gioia, taking him aloft long ago in her little flitterflitter, had shown him that. The tip of South America was canted far out into the Pacific, Africa was weirdly foreshortened; a broad tongue of ocean separated Europe and Asia. Australia did not appear to exist at all. Perhaps they had dug it up and used it for other things. There was no trace of the world he once had known. This was the fiftieth century. "The fiftieth century after *what*?" he had asked several times, but no one seemed to know, or else they did not care to say.

"Is Alexandria very beautiful?" Gioia called from within.

"Come out and see."

Naked and sleepy-looking, she padded out onto the white-tiled patio and nestled up beside him. She fit neatly under his arm. "Oh, yes, yes!" she said softly. "So very beautiful, isn't it? Look, there, the palaces, the Library, the Lighthouse! Where will we go first? The Lighthouse, I think. Yes? And then the marketplace—I want to see the Egyptian magicians—and the stadium, the races—will they be having races today, do you think? Oh, Charles, I want to see everything!"

"Everything? All on the first day?"

"All on the first day, yes," she said. "Everything."

"But we have plenty of time, Gioia."

"Do we?"

He smiled and drew her tight against his side.

"Time enough," he said gently.

He loved her for her impatience, for her bright bubbling eagerness. Gioia was not much like the rest in that regard, though she seemed identical in all other ways. She was short, supple, slender, dark-eyed, olive-skinned, narrow-hipped, with wide shoulders and flat muscles. They were all like that, each one indistinguishable from the rest, like a horde of millions of brothers and sisters—a world of small lithe childlike Mediterraneans, built for juggling, for bull-dancing, for sweet white wine at midday and rough red wine at night. They had the same slim bodies, the same broad mouths, the same great glossy eyes. He had never seen anyone who appeared to be younger than twelve or older than twenty. Gioia was somehow a little different, although he did not quite know how; but he knew that it was for that imperceptible but significant difference that he loved her. And probably that was why she loved him also.

He let his gaze drift from west to east, from the Gate of the Moon down broad Canopus Street and out to the harbor, and off to the tomb of Cleopatra at the tip of long slender Cape Lochias. Everything was here and all of it perfect, the obelisks, the statues and marble colonnades, the courtyards and shrines and groves, great Alexander himself in his coffin of crystal and gold: a splendid gleaming pagan city. But there were oddities—an unmistakable mosque near the public gardens, and what seemed to be a Christian church not far from the Library. And those ships in the harbor, with all those red sails and bristling masts—surely they were medieval, and late medieval at that. He had seen such anachronisms in other places before. Doubtless these people found them amusing. Life was a game for them. They played at it unceasingly. Rome, Alexandria, Timbuctoo—why not? Create an Asgard of translucent bridges and shimmering ice-girt palaces, then grow weary of it and take it away? Replace it with Mohenjo-daro? Why not? It seemed to him a great pity to destroy those lofty Nordic feasting halls for the sake of building a squat brutal sun-baked city of brown brick; but these people did not look at things the way he did. Their cities were only temporary. Someone in Asgard had said that Timbuctoo would be the next to go, with Byzantium rising in its place. Well, why not? Why not? They could have anything they liked. This was the fiftieth century, after all. The only rule was that there could be no more than five cities at once. "Limits," Gioia had informed him solemnly when they first began to travel together, "are very important." But she did not know why, or did not care to say.

He stared out once more toward the sea.

He imagined a newborn city congealing suddenly out of mists, far across the water: shining towers, great domed palaces, golden mosaics. That would be no great effort for them. They could just summon it forth whole out of time, the Emperor on his throne and the Emperor's drunken soldiery roistering in the streets, the brazen clangor of the cathedral gong rolling through the Grand Bazaar, dolphins leaping beyond the shoreside pavilions. Why not? They had Timbuctoo. They had Alexandria. Do you crave Constantinople? Then behold Constantinople! Or Avalon, or Lyonesse, or Atlantis. They could have anything they liked. It is pure Schopenhauer here: the world as will and imagination. Yes! These slender dark-eyed people journeying tirelessly from miracle to miracle. Why not Byzantium next? Yes! Why not? *That is no country for old men*, he thought. *The young in one another's arms, the birds in the trees*—yes! Yes! Anything they liked. They even had him. Suddenly he felt frightened. Questions he had not asked for a long time burst through into his consciousness. *Who am I? Why am I here? Who is this woman beside me?*

"You're so quiet all of a sudden, Charles," said Gioia, who could not abide silence for very long. "Will you talk to me? I want you to talk to me. Tell me what you're looking for out there."

He shrugged. "Nothing."

"Nothing?"

"Nothing in particular."

"I could see you seeing something."

"Byzantium," he said. "I was imagining that I could look straight across the water to Byzantium. I was trying to get a glimpse of the walls of Constantinople."

"Oh, but you wouldn't be able to see as far as that from here. Not really."

"I know."

"And anyway Byzantium doesn't exist."

"Not yet. But it will. Its time comes later on."

"Does it?" she said. "Do you know that for a fact?"

"On good authority. I heard it in Asgard," he told her. "But even if I hadn't, Byzantium would be inevitable, don't you think? Its time would have to come. How could we not do Byzantium, Gioia? We certainly will do Byzantium, sooner or later. I know we will. It's only a matter of time. And we have all the time in the world."

A shadow crossed her face. "Do we? Do we?"

He knew very little about himself, but he knew that he was not one of them. That he knew. He knew that his name was Charles Phillips and that before he had come to live among these people he had lived in the year 1984, when there had been such things as computers and television sets and baseball and jet planes, and the world was full of cities, not merely five but thousands of them, New York and London and Johannesburg and Paris and Liverpool and Bangkok and San Francisco and Buenos Aires and a multitude of others, all at the same time. There had been four and a half billion people in the world then; now he doubted that there were as many as four and a half million. Nearly everything had changed beyond comprehension. The moon still seemed the same, and the sun; but at night he searched in vain for familiar constellations. He had no idea how they had brought him from then to now, or why. It did no good to ask. No one had any answers for him; no one so much as appeared to understand what it was that he was trying to learn. After a time he had stopped asking; after a time he had almost entirely ceased wanting to know.

He and Gioia were climbing the Lighthouse. She scampered ahead, in a hurry as always, and he came along behind her in his more stolid fashion. Scores of other tourists, mostly in groups of two or three, were making their way up the wide flagstone ramps, laughing, calling to one another. Some of them, seeing him, stopped a moment, stared, pointed. He was used to that. He was so much taller than any of them; he was plainly not one of them. When they pointed at him he smiled. Sometimes he nodded a little acknowledgment.

He could not find much of interest in the lowest level, a massive square structure two hundred feet high built of huge marble blocks: within its cool musty arcades were hundreds of small dark rooms, the offices of the Lighthouse's keepers and mechanics, the barracks of the garrison, the stables for the three hundred donkeys that carried the fuel to the lantern far above. None of that appeared inviting to him. He forged onward without halting until he emerged on the balcony that led to the next level. Here the Lighthouse grew narrower and became octagonal: its face, granite now and handsomely fluted, rose in a stunning sweep above him.

Gioia was waiting for him there. "This is for you," she said, holding out a nugget of meat on a wooden skewer. "Roast lamb. Absolutely delicious. I had one while I was waiting for you." She gave him a cup of some cool green sherbet also, and darted off to buy a pomegranate. Dozens of temporaries were roaming the balcony, selling refreshments of all kinds.

He nibbled at the meat. It was charred outside, nicely pink and moist within. While he ate, one of the temporaries came up to him and peered blandly into his face. It was a stocky swarthy male wearing nothing but a strip of red and yellow cloth about its waist. "I sell meat," it said. "Very fine roast lamb, only five drachmas."

Phillips indicated the piece he was eating. "I already have some," he said.

"It is excellent meat, very tender. It has been soaked for three days in the juices of—"

"Please," Phillips said. "I don't want to buy any meat. Do you mind moving along?"

The temporaries had confused and baffled him at first, and there was still much about them that was unclear to him. They were not machines—they looked like creatures of flesh and blood—but they did not seem to be human beings, either, and no one treated them as if they were. He supposed they were artificial constructs, products of a technology so consummate that it was invisible. Some appeared to be more intelligent than others, but all of them behaved as if they had no more autonomy than characters in a play, which was essentially what they were. There were untold numbers of them in each of the five cities, playing all manner of roles: shepherds and swineherds, street-sweepers, merchants, boatmen, vendors of grilled meats and cool drinks, hagglers in the marketplace, schoolchildren, charioteers, policemen, grooms, gladiators, monks, artisans, whores and cutpurses, sailors— whatever was needed to sustain the illusion of a thriving, populous urban center. The darkeyed people, Gioia's people, never performed work. There were not enough of them to keep a city's functions going, and in any case they were strictly tourists, wandering with the wind, moving from city to city as the whim took them, Chang-an to New Chicago, New Chicago to Timbuctoo, Timbuctoo to Asgard, Asgard to Alexandria, onward, ever onward.

The temporary would not leave him alone. Phillips walked away and it followed him, cornering him against the balcony wall. When Gioia returned a few minutes later, lips prettily stained with pomegranate juice, the temporary was still hovering about him, trying with lunatic persistence to sell him a skewer of lamb. It stood much too close to him, almost nose to nose, great sad cowlike eyes peering intently into his as it extolled with mournful mooing urgency the quality of its wares. It seemed to him that he had had trouble like this with temporaries on one or two earlier occasions. Gioia touched the creature's elbow lightly and said, in a short sharp tone Phillips had never heard her use before, "He isn't interested. Get away from him." It went at once. To Phillips she said, "You have to be firm with them."

"I was trying. It wouldn't listen to me."

"You ordered it to go away, and it refused?"

"I asked it to go away. Politely. Too politely, maybe."

"Even so," she said. "It should have obeyed a human, regardless."

"Maybe it didn't think I was human," Phillips suggested. "Because of the way I look. My height, the color of my eyes. It might have thought I was some kind of temporary myself."

"No," Gioia said, frowning. "A temporary won't solicit another temporary. But it won't ever disobey a citizen, either. There's a very clear boundary. There isn't ever any confusion. I can't understand why it went on bothering you." He was surprised at how troubled she seemed: far more so, he thought, than the incident warranted. A stupid device, perhaps miscalibrated in some way, over-enthusiastically pushing its wares—what of it? What of it? Gioia, after a moment, appeared to come to the same conclusion. Shrugging, she said, "It's defective, I suppose. Probably such things are more common than we suspect, don't you think?" There was something forced about her tone that bothered him. She smiled and handed him her pomegranate. "Here. Have a bite, Charles. It's wonderfully sweet. They used to be extinct, you know. Shall we go on upward?"

The octagonal midsection of the Lighthouse must have been several hundred feet in height, a grim claustrophobic tube almost entirely filled by the two broad spiraling ramps that wound around the huge building's central well. The ascent was slow: a donkey team was a little way ahead of them on the ramp, plodding along laden with bundles of kindling for the lantern. But at last, just as Phillips was growing winded and dizzy, he and Gioia came out onto the second balcony, the one marking the transition between the octagonal section and the Lighthouse's uppermost story, which was cylindrical and very slender.

She leaned far out over the balustrade. "Oh, Charles, look at the view! Look at it!"

It was amazing. From one side they could see the entire city, and swampy Lake Mareotis and the dusty Egyptian plain beyond it, and from the other they peered far out into the gray and choppy Mediterranean. He gestured toward the innumerable reefs and shallows that infested the waters leading to the harbor entrance. "No wonder they needed a lighthouse here," he said. "Without some kind of gigantic landmark they'd never have found their way in from the open sea."

A blast of sound, a ferocious snort, erupted just above him. He looked up, startled. Immense statues of trumpet-wielding Tritons jutted from the corners of the Lighthouse at this level; that great blurting sound had come from the nearest of them. A signal, he thought. A warning to the ships negotiating that troubled passage. The sound was produced by some kind of steam-powered mechanism, he realized, operated by teams of sweating temporaries clustered about bonfires at the base of each Triton.

Once again he found himself swept by admiration for the clever way these people carried out their reproductions of antiquity. Or *were* they reproductions, he wondered? He still did not understand how they brought their cities into being. For all he knew, this place was the authentic Alexandria itself, pulled forward out of its proper time just as he himself had been. Perhaps this was the true and original Lighthouse, and not a copy. He had no idea which was the case, nor which would be the greater miracle.

"How do we get to the top?" Gioia asked.

"Over there, I think. That doorway."

The spiraling donkey-ramps ended here. The loads of lantern fuel went higher via a dumbwaiter in the central shaft. Visitors continued by way of a cramped staircase, so narrow at its upper end that it was impossible to turn around while climbing. Gioia, tireless, sprinted ahead. He clung to the rail and labored up and up, keeping count of the tiny window slits to ease the boredom of the ascent. The count was nearing a hundred when finally he stumbled into the vestibule of the beacon chamber. A dozen or so visitors were crowded into it. Gioia was at the far side, by the wall that was open to the sea.

It seemed to him he could feel the building swaying in the winds up here. How high were they? Five hundred feet, six hundred, seven? The beacon chamber was tall and narrow, divided by a catwalk into upper and lower sections. Down below, relays of temporaries carried wood from the dumbwaiter and tossed it on the blazing fire. He felt its intense heat from where he stood, at the rim of the platform on which the giant mirror of polished metal was hung. Tongues of flame leaped upward and danced before the mirror, which hurled its dazzling beam far out to sea. Smoke rose through a vent. At the very top was a colossal statue of Poseidon, austere, ferocious, looming above the lantern.

Gioia sidled along the catwalk until she was at his side. "The guide was talking before you came," she said, pointing. "Do you see that place over there, under the mirror? Someone standing there and looking into the mirror gets a view of ships at sea that can't be seen from here by the naked eye. The mirror magnifies things."

"Do you believe that?"

She nodded toward the guide. "It said so. And it also told us that if you look in a certain way, you can see right across the water into the city of Constantinople."

She is like a child, he thought. They all are. He said, "You told me yourself this very morning that it isn't possible to see that far. Besides, Constantinople doesn't exist right now."

"It will," she replied. "You said that to me, this very morning. And when it does, it'll be reflected in the Lighthouse mirror. That's the truth. I'm absolutely certain of it." She swung about abruptly toward the entrance of the beacon chamber. "Oh, look, Charles! Here come Nissandra and Aramayne! And there's Hawk! There's Stengard!" Gioia laughed and waved and called out names. "Oh, everyone's here! *Everyone!*"

They came jostling into the room, so many newcomers that some of those who had been there were forced to scramble down the steps on the far side. Gioia moved among them, hugging, kissing. Phillips could scarcely tell one from another—it was hard for him even to tell which were the men and which the women, dressed as they all were in the same sort of loose robes—but he recognized some of the names. These were her special friends, her set, with whom she had journeyed from city to city on an endless round of gaiety in the old days before he had come into her life. He had met a few of them before, in Asgard, in Rio, in Rome. The beacon-chamber guide, a squat wide-shouldered old temporary wearing a laurel wreath on its bald head, reappeared and began its potted speech, but no one listened to it; they were all too busy greeting one another, embracing, giggling. Some of them edged their way over to Phillips and reached up, standing on tiptoes, to touch their fingertips to his cheek in that odd hello of theirs. "Charles," they said gravely, making two syllables out of the name, as these people often did. "So good to see you again. Such a pleasure. You and Gioia—such a handsome couple. So well suited to each other."

Was that so? He supposed it was.

The chamber hummed with chatter. The guide could not be heard at all. Stengard and Nissandra had visited New Chicago for the water-dancing—Aramayne bore tales of a feast in Chang-an that had gone on for *days*—Hawk and Hekna had been to Timbuctoo to see the arrival of the salt caravan, and were going back there soon—a final party soon to celebrate the end of Asgard that absolutely should not be missed—the plans for the new city, Mohenjo-daro—we have reservations for the opening, we wouldn't pass it up for anything—and, yes, they were definitely going to do Constantinople after that, the planners were already deep into their Byzantium research—so good to see you, you look so beautiful all the time—have you been to the Library yet? The zoo? To the temple of Serapis?—

To Phillips they said, "What do you think of our Alexandria, Charles? Of course, you must have known it well in your day. Does it look the way you remember it?" They were always asking things like that. They did not seem to comprehend that the Alexandria of the Lighthouse and the Library was long lost and legendary by the time his twentieth century had been. To them, he suspected, all the places they had brought back into existence were more or less contemporary. Rome of the Caesars, Alexandria of the Ptolemies, Venice of the Doges, Chang-an of the T'angs, Asgard of the Aesir, none any less real than the next nor any less unreal, each one simply a facet of the distant past, the fantastic immemorial past, a plum plucked from that dark backward abysm of time. They had no contexts for separating one era from another. To them all the past was one borderless timeless realm. Why, then, should he not have seen the Lighthouse before, he who had leaped into this era from the New York of 1984? He had never been able to explain it to them. Julius Caesar and Hannibal, Helen of Troy and Charlemagne, Rome of the gladiators and New York of the Yankees and Mets, Gilgamesh and Tristan and Othello and Robin Hood and George Washington and Queen Victoria—to them, all equally real and unreal, none of them any more than bright figures moving about on a painted canvas. The past, the past, the elusive and fluid past—to them it was a single place of infinite accessibility and infinite connectivity. Of course, they would think he had seen the Lighthouse before. He knew better than to try again to explain things. "No," he said simply. "This is my first time in Alexandria."

They stayed there all winter long, and possibly some of the spring. Alexandria was not a place where one was sharply aware of the change of seasons, nor did the passage of time itself make itself very evident when one was living one's entire life as a tourist.

During the day there was always something new to see. The zoological garden, for instance: a wondrous park, miraculously green and lush in this hot dry climate, where astounding animals roamed in enclosures so generous that they did not seem like enclosures at all. Here were camels, rhinoceroses, gazelles, ostriches, lions, wild asses; and here, too, casually adjacent to those familiar African beasts, were hippogriffs, unicorns, basilisks, and fire-snorting dragons with rainbow scales. Had the original zoo of Alexandria had dragons and unicorns? Phillips doubted it. But this one did; evidently it was no harder for the backstage craftsmen to manufacture mythic beasts than it was for them to turn out camels and gazelles. To Gioia and her friends all of them were equally mythical, anyway. They were just as awed by the rhinoceros as by the hippogriff. One was no more strange—or any less—than the other. So far as Phillips had been able to discover, none of the mammals or birds of his era had survived into this one except for a few cats and dogs, though many had been reconstructed.

And then the Library! All those lost treasures, reclaimed from the jaws of time! Stupendous columned marble walls, airy high-vaulted reading rooms, dark coiling stacks stretching away to infinity. The ivory handles of seven hundred thousand papyrus scrolls bristling on the shelves. Scholars and librarians gliding quietly about, smiling faint scholarly smiles but plainly preoccupied with serious matters of the mind. They were all temporaries, Phillips realized. Mere props, part of the illusion. But were the scrolls illusions, too? "Here we have the complete dramas of Sophocles," said the guide with a blithe wave of its hand, indicating shelf upon shelf of texts. Only seven of his hundred twenty-three plays had survived the successive burnings of the library in ancient times by Romans, Christians, Arabs: were the lost ones here, the *Triptolemus*, the *Nausicaa*, the *Jason*, and all the rest? And would he find here, too, miraculously restored to being, the other vanished treasures of ancient literature—the memoirs of Odysseus, Cato's history of Rome, Thucidydes' life of Pericles, the missing volumes of Livy? But when he asked if he might explore the stacks, the guide smiled apologetically and said that all the librarians were busy just now. Another time, perhaps? Perhaps, said the guide. It made no difference, Phillips decided. Even if these people somehow had brought back those lost masterpieces of antiquity, how would he read them? He knew no Greek.

The life of the city buzzed and throbbed about him. It was a dazzlingly beautiful place: the vast bay thick with sails, the great avenues running rigidly east-west, north-south, the sunlight rebounding almost audibly from the bright walls of the palaces of kings and gods. They have done this very well, Phillips thought: very well indeed. In the marketplace hard-eyed traders squabbled in half a dozen mysterious languages over the price of ebony, Arabian incense, jade, panther skins. Gioia bought a dram of pale musky Egyptian perfume in a delicate tapering glass flask. Magicians and jugglers and scribes called out stridently to passersby, begging for a few moments of attention and a handful of coins for their labor. Strapping slaves, black and tawny and some that might have been Chinese, were put up for auction, made to flex their muscles, to bare their teeth, to bare their breasts and thighs to prospective buyers. In the gymnasium naked athletes hurled javelins and discuses, and wrestled with terrifying zeal. Gioia's friend Stengard came rushing up with a gift for her, a golden necklace that would not have embarrassed Cleopatra. An hour later she had lost it, or perhaps had given it away while Phillips was looking elsewhere. She bought another, even finer, the next day. Anyone could have all the money he wanted, simply by asking: it was as easy to come by as air for these people.

Being here was much like going to the movies, Phillips told himself. A different show every day: not much plot, but the special effects were magnificent and the detail work could hardly have been surpassed. A megamovie, a vast entertainment that went on all the time and was being played out by the whole population of Earth. And it was all so effortless, so spontaneous: just as when he had gone to a movie he had never troubled to think about the myriad technicians behind the scenes, the cameramen and the costume designers and the set builders and the electricians and the model makers and the boom operators, so, too, here he chose not to question the means by which Alexandria had been set before him. It felt real. It *was* real. When he drank the strong red wine it gave him a pleasant buzz. If he leaped from the beacon chamber of the Lighthouse he suspected he would die, though perhaps he would not stay dead for long: doubtless they had some way of restoring him as often as was necessary. Death did not seem to be a factor in these people's lives.

By day they saw sights. By night he and Gioia went to parties, in their hotel, in seaside villas, in the palaces of the high nobility. The usual people were there all the time, Hawk and Hekna, Aramayne, Stengard and Shelimir, Nissandra, Asoka, Afonso, Protay. At the parties there were five or ten temporaries for every citizen, some as mere servants, others as entertainers or even surrogate guests, mingling freely and a little daringly. But everyone knew, all the time, who was a citizen and who just a temporary. Phillips began to think his own status lay somewhere between. Certainly they treated him with a courtesy that no one ever would give a temporary, and yet there was a condescension to their manner that told him not simply that he was not one of them but that he was someone or something of an altogether different order of existence. That he was Gioia's lover gave him some standing in their eyes, but not a great deal: obviously he was always going to be an outsider, a primitive, ancient and quaint. For that matter he noticed that Gioia herself, though unquestionably a member of the set, seemed to be regarded as something of an outsider, like a tradesman's great-granddaughter in a gathering of Plantagenets. She did not always find out about the best parties in time to attend; her friends did not always reciprocate her effusive greetings with the same degree of warmth; sometimes he noticed her straining to hear some bit of gossip that was not quite being shared with her. Was it because she had taken him for her lover? Or was it the other way around: that she had chosen to be his lover precisely because she was *not* a full member of their caste?

Being a primitive gave him, at least, something to talk about at their parties. "Tell us about war," they said. "Tell us about elections. About money. About disease." They wanted to know everything, though they did not seem to pay close attention: their eyes were quick to glaze. Still, they asked. He described traffic jams to them, and politics, and deodorants, and vitamin pills. He told them about cigarettes, newspapers, subways, telephone directories, credit cards, and basketball. "Which was your city?" they asked. New York, he told them. "And when was it? The seventh century, did you say?" The twentieth, he told them. They exchanged glances and nodded. "We will have to do it," they said. "The World Trade Center, the Empire State Building, the Citicorp Center, the Cathedral of St. John the Divine: how fascinating! Yankee Stadium. The Verrazano Bridge. We will do it all. But first must come Mohenjo-daro. And then, I think, Constantinople. Did your city have many people?" Seven million, he said. Just in the five boroughs alone. They nodded, smiling amiably, unfazed by the number. Seven million, seventy million—it was all the same to them, he sensed. They would just bring forth the temporaries in whatever quantity was required. He wondered how well they would carry the job off. He was no real judge of Alexandrias and Asgards, after all. Here they could have unicorns and hippogriffs in the zoo, and live sphinxes prowling in the gutters, and it did not trouble him. Their fanciful Alexandria was as good as history's, or better. But how sad, how disillusioning it would be, if the New York that they conjured up had Greenwich Village uptown and Times Square in the Bronx, and the New Yorkers, gentle and polite, spoke with the honeyed accents of Savannah or New Orleans. Well, that was nothing he needed to brood about just now. Very likely they were only being courteous when they spoke of doing his New York. They had all the vastness of the past to choose from: Nineveh, Memphis of the Pharaohs, the London of Victoria or Shakespeare or Richard the Third, Florence of the Medici, the Paris of Abelard and Heloise or the Paris of Louis XIV, Moctezuma's Tenochtitlan and Atahuallpa's Cuzco; Damascus, St. Petersburg, Babylon, Troy. And then there were all the cities like New Chicago, out of time that was time yet unborn to him but ancient history to them. In such richness, such an infinity of choices, even mighty New York might have to wait a long while for its turn. Would he still be among them by the time they got around to it? By then, perhaps, they might have become bored with him and returned him to his own proper era. Or possibly he would simply have grown old and died. Even here, he supposed, he would eventually die, though no one else ever seemed to. He did not know. He realized that in fact he did not know anything.

The north wind blew all day long. Vast flocks of ibises appeared over the city, fleeing the heat of the interior, and screeched across the sky with their black necks and scrawny legs extended. The sacred birds, descending by the thousands, scuttered about in every crossroad, pouncing on spiders and beetles, on mice, on the debris of the meat shops and the bakeries. They were beautiful but annoyingly ubiquitous, and they splashed their dung over the marble buildings; each morning squadrons of temporaries carefully washed it off. Gioia said little to him now. She seemed cool, withdrawn, depressed; and there was something almost intangible about her, as though she were gradually becoming transparent. He felt it would be an intrusion upon her privacy to ask her what was wrong. Perhaps it was only restlessness. She became religious, and presented costly offerings at the temples of Serapis, Isis, Poseidon, Pan. She went to the necropolis west of the city to lay wreaths on the tombs in the catacombs. In a single day she climbed the Lighthouse three times without any sign of fatigue. One afternoon he returned from a visit to the Library and found her naked on the patio; she had anointed herself all over with some aromatic green salve. Abruptly she said, "I think it's time to leave Alexandria, don't you?"

She wanted to go to Mohenjo-daro, but Mohenjo-daro was not yet ready for visitors. Instead they flew eastward to Chang-an, which they had not seen in years. It was Phillips's suggestion: he hoped that the cosmopolitan gaudiness of the old T'ang capital would lift her mood.

They were to be guests of the Emperor this time: an unusual privilege, which ordinarily had to be applied for far in advance, but Phillips had told some of Gioia's highly placed friends that she was unhappy, and they had quickly arranged everything. Three endlessly bowing functionaries in flowing yellow robes and purple sashes met them at the Gate of Brilliant Virtue in the city's south wall and conducted them to their pavilion, close by the imperial palace and the Forbidden Garden. It was a light, airy place, thin walls of plastered brick braced by graceful columns of some dark, aromatic wood. Fountains played on the roof of green and yellow tiles, creating an unending cool rainfall of recirculating water. The balustrades were of carved marble, the door fittings were of gold.

There was a suite of private rooms for him, and another for her, though they would share the handsome damask-draped bedroom at the heart of the pavilion. As soon as they arrived, Gioia announced that she must go to her rooms to bathe and dress. "There will be a formal reception for us at the palace tonight," she said. "They say the imperial receptions are splendid beyond anything you could imagine. I want to be at my best." The Emperor and all his ministers, she told him, would receive them in the Hall of the Supreme Ultimate; there would be a banquet for a thousand people; Persian dancers would perform, and the celebrated jugglers of Chung-nan.

Afterward everyone would be conducted into the fantastic landscape of the Forbidden Garden to view the dragon races and the fireworks.

He went to his own rooms. Two delicate little maidservants undressed him and bathed him with fragrant sponges. The pavilion came equipped with eleven temporaries who were to be their servants: soft-voiced unobtrusive catlike Chinese, done with perfect verisimilitude, straight black hair, glowing skin, epicanthic folds. Phillips often wondered what happened to a city's temporaries when the city's time was over. Were the towering Norse heroes of Asgard being recycled at this moment into wiry dark-skinned Dravidians for Mohenjo-daro? When Timbuctoo's day was done, would its brightly robed black warriors be converted into supple Byzantines to stock the arcades of Constantinople? Or did they simply discard the old temporaries like so many excess props, stash them in warehouses somewhere, and turn out the appropriate quantities of the new model? He did not know; and once when he had asked Gioia about it she had grown uncomfortable and vague. She did not like him to probe for information, and he suspected it was because she had very little to give. These people did not seem to question the workings of their own world; his curiosities were very twentieth-century of him, he was frequently told, in that gently patronizing way of theirs. As his two little maids patted him with their sponges he thought of asking them where they had served before Chang-an. Rio? Rome? Haroun al-Raschid's Baghdad? But these fragile girls, he knew, would only giggle and retreat if he tried to question them. Interrogating temporaries was not only improper but pointless: it was like interrogating one's luggage.

When he was bathed and robed in rich red silks he wandered the pavilion for a little while, admiring the tinkling pendants of green jade dangling on the portico, the lustrous auburn pillars, the rainbow hues of the intricately interwoven girders and brackets that supported the roof. Then, wearying of his solitude, he approached the bamboo curtain at the entrance to Gioia's suite. A porter and one of the maids stood just within. They indicated that he should not enter; but he scowled at them and they melted from him like snowflakes. A trail of incense led him through the pavilion to Gioia's innermost dressing room. There he halted, just outside the door.

Gioia sat naked with her back to him at an ornate dressing table of some rare flame-colored wood inlaid with bands of orange and green porcelain. She was studying herself intently in a mirror of polished bronze held by one of her maids: picking through her scalp with her fingernails, as a woman might do who was searching out her gray hairs.

But that seemed strange. Gray hair, on Gioia? On a citizen? A temporary might display some appearance of aging, perhaps, but surely not a citizen. Citizens remained forever young. Gioia looked like a girl. Her face was smooth and unlined, her flesh was firm, her hair was dark: that was true of all of them, every citizen he had ever seen. And yet there was no mistaking what Gioia was doing. She found a hair, frowned, drew it taut, nodded, plucked it. Another. Another. She pressed the tip of her finger to her cheek as if testing it for resilience. She tugged at the skin below her eyes, pulling it downward. Such familiar little gestures of vanity; but so odd here, he thought, in this world of the perpetually young. Gioia, worried about growing old? Had he simply failed to notice the signs of age on her? Or was it that she worked hard behind his back at concealing them? Perhaps that was it. Was he wrong about the citizens, then? Did they age even as the people of less blessed eras had always done, but simply have better ways of hiding it? How old was she, anyway? Thirty? Sixty? Three hundred?

Gioia appeared satisfied now. She waved the mirror away; she rose; she beckoned for her banquet robes. Phillips, still standing unnoticed by the door, studied her with admiration: the small round buttocks, almost but not quite boyish, the elegant line of her spine, the surprising breadth of her shoulders. No, he thought, she is not aging at all. Her body is still like a girl's. She looks as young as on the day they first had met, however long ago that was—he could not say; it was hard to keep track of time here; but he was sure some years had passed since they had come together. Those gray hairs, those wrinkles and sags for which she had searched just now with such desperate intensity, must all be imaginary, mere artifacts of vanity. Even in this remote future epoch, then, vanity was not extinct. He wondered why she was so concerned with the fear of aging. An affectation? Did all these timeless people take some perverse pleasure in fretting over the possibility that they might be growing old? Or was it some private fear of Gioia's, another symptom of the mysterious depression that had come over her in Alexandria?

Not wanting her to think that he had been spying on her, when all he had really intended was to pay her a visit, he slipped silently away to dress for the evening. She came to him an hour later, gorgeously robed, swaddled from chin to ankles in a brocade of brilliant colors shot through with threads of gold, face painted, hair drawn up tightly and fastened with ivory combs: very much the lady of the court. His servants had made him splendid also, a lustrous black surplice embroidered with golden dragons over a sweeping floor-length gown of shining white silk, a necklace and pendant of red coral, a five-cornered gray felt hat that rose in tower upon tower like a ziggurat. Gioia, grinning, touched her fingertips to his cheek. "You look marvelous!" she told him. "Like a grand mandarin!"

"And you like an empress," he said. "Of some distant land: Persia, India. Here to pay a ceremonial visit on the Son of Heaven." An excess of love suffused his spirit, and, catching her lightly by the wrist, he drew her toward him, as close as he could manage it considering how elaborate their costumes were. But as he bent forward and downward, meaning to brush his lips lightly and affectionately against the tip of her nose, he perceived an unexpected strangeness, an anomaly: the coating of white paint that was her makeup seemed oddly to magnify rather than mask the contours of her skin, highlighting and revealing details he had never observed before. He saw a pattern of fine lines radiating from the corners of her eyes, and the unmistakable beginning of a quirk mark in her cheek just to the left of her mouth, and perhaps the faint indentation of frown lines in her flawless forehead. A shiver traveled along the nape of his neck. So it was not affectation, then, that had had her studying her mirror so fiercely. Age was in truth beginning to stake its claim on her, despite all that he had come to believe about these people's agelessness. But a moment later he was not so sure. Gioia turned and slid gently half a step back from him—she must have found his stare disturbing—and the lines he had thought he had seen were gone. He searched for them and saw only girlish smoothness once again. A trick of the light? A figment of an overwrought imagination? He was baffled.

"Come," she said. "We mustn't keep the Emperor waiting."

Five mustachioed warriors in armor of white quilting and seven musicians playing cymbals and pipes escorted them to the Hall of the Supreme Ultimate. There they found the full court arrayed: princes and ministers, high officials, yellow-robed monks, a swarm of imperial concubines. In a place of honor to the right of the royal thrones, which rose like gilded scaffolds high above all else, was a little group of stern-faced men in foreign costumes, the ambassadors of Rome and Byzantium, of Arabia and Syria, of Korea, Japan, Tibet, Turkestan. Incense smoldered in enameled braziers. A poet sang a delicate twanging melody, accompanying himself on a small harp. Then the Emperor and Empress entered: two tiny aged people, like waxen images, moving with infinite slowness, taking steps no greater than a child's. There was the sound of trumpets as they ascended their thrones. When the little Emperor was seated—he looked like a doll up there, ancient, faded, shrunken, yet still somehow a figure of extraordinary power—he stretched forth both his hands, and enormous gongs began to sound. It was a scene of astonishing splendor, grand and overpowering.

These are all temporaries, Phillips realized suddenly. He saw only a handful of citizens—eight, ten, possibly as many as a dozen—scattered here and there about the vast room. He knew them by their eyes, dark, liquid, knowing. They were watching not only the imperial spectacle but also Gioia and him; and Gioia, smiling secretly, nodding almost imperceptibly to them, was acknowledging their presence and their interest. But those few were the only ones in here who were autonomous living beings. All the rest—the entire splendid court, the great mandarins and paladins, the officials, the giggling concubines, the haughty and resplendent ambassadors, the aged Emperor and Empress themselves, were simply part of the scenery. Had the world ever seen entertainment on so grand a scale before? All this pomp, all this pageantry, conjured up each night for the amusement of a dozen or so viewers?

At the banquet the little group of citizens sat together at a table apart, a round onyx slab draped with translucent green silk. There turned out to be seventeen of them in all, including Gioia; Gioia appeared to know all of them, though none, so far as he could tell, was a member of her set that he had met before. She did not attempt introductions. Nor was conversation at all possible during the meal: there was a constant astounding roaring din in the room. Three orchestras played at once and there were troupes of strolling musicians also, and a steady stream of monks and their attendants marched back and forth between the tables loudly chanting sutras and waving censers to the deafening accompaniment of drums and gongs. The Emperor did not descend from his throne to join the banquet; he seemed to be asleep, though now and then he waved his hand in time to the music. Gigantic half-naked brown slaves with broad cheekbones and mouths like gaping pockets brought forth the food, peacock tongues and breast of phoenix heaped on mounds of glowing saffron-colored rice, served on frail alabaster plates. For chopsticks they were given slender rods of dark jade. The wine, served in glistening crystal beakers, was thick and sweet, with an aftertaste of raisins, and no beaker was allowed to remain empty for more than a moment. Phillips felt himself growing dizzy: when the Persian dancers emerged he could not tell whether there were five of them or fifty, and as they performed their intricate whirling routines it seemed to him that their slender muslin-veiled forms were blurring and merging one into another. He felt frightened by their proficiency, and wanted to look away, but he could not. The Chung-nan jugglers that followed them were equally skillful, equally alarming, filling the air with scythes, flaming torches, live animals, rare porcelain vases, pink jade hatchets, silver bells, gilded cups, wagon wheels, bronze vessels, and never missing a catch. The citizens applauded politely but did not seem impressed. After the jugglers, the dancers returned, performing this time on stilts; the waiters brought platters of steaming meat of a pale lavender color, unfamiliar in taste and texture: filet of camel, perhaps, or haunch of hippopotamus, or possibly some choice chop from a young dragon. There was more wine. Feebly Phillips tried to wave it away, but the servitors were implacable. This was a dryer sort, greenish-gold, austere, sharp on the tongue. With it came a silver dish, chilled to a polar coldness, that held shaved ice flavored with some potent smoky-flavored brandy. The jugglers were doing a second turn, he noticed. He thought he was going to be ill. He looked helplessly toward Gioia, who seemed sober but fiercely animated, almost manic, her eyes blazing like rubies. She touched his cheek fondly. A cool draft blew through the hall: they had opened one entire wall, revealing the garden, the night, the stars. Just outside was a colossal wheel of oiled paper stretched on wooden struts. They must have erected it in the past hour: it stood a hundred fifty feet high or even more, and on it hung lanterns by the thousands, glimmering like giant fireflies. The guests began to leave the hall. Phillips let himself be swept along into the garden, where under a yellow moon strange crook-armed trees with dense black needles loomed ominously. Gioia slipped her arm through his. They went down to a lake of bubbling crimson fluid and watched scarlet flamingolike birds ten feet tall fastidiously spearing angry-eyed turquoise eels. They stood in awe before a fat-bellied Buddha of gleaming blue tile-work, seventy feet high. A horse with a golden mane came prancing by, striking showers of brilliant red sparks wherever its hooves touched the ground. In a grove of lemon trees that seemed to have the power to wave their slender limbs about, Phillips came upon the Emperor, standing by himself and rocking gently back and forth. The old man seized Phillips by the hand and pressed something into his palm, closing his fingers tight about it; when he opened his fist a few moments later he found his palm full of gray irregular pearls. Gioia took them from him and cast them into the air, and they burst like exploding firecrackers, giving off splashes of colored light. A little later, Phillips realized that he was no longer wearing his sur-plice or his white silken undergown. Gioia was naked, too, and she drew him gently down into a carpet of moist blue moss, where they made love until dawn, fiercely at first, then slowly, languidly, dreamily. At sunrise he looked at her tenderly and saw that something was wrong.

"Gioia?" he said doubtfully.

She smiled. "Ah, no. Gioia is with Fenimon tonight. I am Belilala."

"With — Fenimon?"

"They are old friends. She had not seen him in years."

"Ah. I see. And you are — ?"

"Belilala," she said again, touching her fingertips to his cheek.

———

It was not unusual, Belilala said. It happened all the time; the only unusual thing was that it had not happened to him before now. Couples formed, traveled together for a while, drifted apart, eventually reunited. It did not mean that Gioia had left him forever. It meant only that just now she chose to be with Fenimon. Gioia would return. In the meanwhile he would not be alone. "You and I met in New Chicago," Belilala told him. "And then we saw each other again in Timbuctoo. Have you forgotten? Oh, yes, I see that you have forgotten!" She laughed prettily; she did not seem at all offended.

She looked enough like Gioia to be her sister. But, then, all the citizens looked more or less alike to him. And apart from their physical resemblance, so he quickly came to realize, Belilala and Gioia were not really very similar. There was a calmness, a deep reservoir of serenity, in Belilala, that Gioia, eager and volatile and ever impatient, did not seem to have. Strolling the swarming streets of Chang-an with Belilala, he did not perceive in her any of Gioia's restless feverish need always to know what lay beyond, and beyond, and beyond even that. When they toured the Hsing-ch'ing Palace, Belilala did not after five minutes begin—as Gioia surely would have done—to seek directions to the Fountain of Hsuan-tsung or the Wild Goose Pagoda. Curiosity did not consume Belilala as it did Gioia. Plainly she believed that there would always be enough time for her to see everything she cared to see. There were some days when Belilala chose not to go out at all, but was content merely to remain at their pavilion playing a solitary game with flat porcelain counters, or viewing the flowers of the garden.

He found, oddly, that he enjoyed the respite from Gioia's intense world-swallowing appetites; and yet he longed for her to return. Belilala—beautiful, gentle, tranquil, patient—was too perfect for him. She seemed unreal in her gleaming impeccability, much like one of those Sung celadon vases that appear too flawless to have been thrown and glazed by human hands. There was something a little soulless about her: an immaculate finish outside, emptiness within. Belilala might almost have been a temporary, he thought, though he knew she was not. He could explore the pavilions and palaces of Chang-an with her, he could make graceful conversation with her while they dined, he could certainly enjoy coupling with her; but he could not love her or even contemplate the possibility. It was hard to imagine Belilala worriedly studying herself in a mirror for wrinkles and gray hairs. Belilala would never be any older than she was at this moment; nor could Belilala ever have been any younger. Perfection does not move along an axis of time. But the perfection of Belilala's glossy surface made her inner being impenetrable to him. Gioia was more vulnerable, more obviously flawed—her restlessness, her moodiness, her vanity, her fears—and therefore she was more accessible to his own highly imperfect twentieth-century sensibility.

Occasionally he saw Gioia as he roamed the city, or thought he did. He had a glimpse of her among the miracle-vendors in the Persian Bazaar, and outside the Zoroastrian temple, and again by the goldfish pond in the Serpentine Park. But he was never quite sure that the woman he saw was really Gioia, and he never could get close enough to her to be certain: she had a way of vanishing as he approached, like some mysterious Lorelei luring him onward and onward in a hopeless chase. After a while he came to realize that he was not going to find her until she was ready to be found.

He lost track of time. Weeks, months, years? He had no idea. In this city of exotic luxury, mystery, and magic all was in constant flux and transition and the days had a fitful, unstable quality. Buildings and even whole streets were torn down of an afternoon and reerected, within days, far away. Grand new pagodas sprouted like toadstools in the night. Citizens came in from Asgard, Alexandria, Timbuctoo, New Chicago, stayed for a time, disappeared, returned. There was a constant round of court receptions, banquets, theatrical events, each one much like the one before. The festivals in honor of past emperors and empresses might have given some form to the year, but they seemed to occur in a random way, the ceremony marking the death of T'ai Tsung coming around twice the same year, so it seemed to him, once in a season of snow and again in high summer, and the one honoring the ascension of the Empress Wu being held twice in a single season. Perhaps he had misunderstood something. But he knew it was no use asking anyone.

One day Belilala said unexpectedly, "Shall we go to Mohenjo-daro?"

"I didn't know it was ready for visitors," he replied.

"Oh, yes. For quite some time now."

He hesitated. This had caught him unprepared. Cautiously he said, "Gioia and I were going to go there together, you know."

Belilala smiled amiably, as though the topic under discussion were nothing more than the choice of that evening's restaurant.

"Were you?" she asked.

"It was all arranged while we were still in Alexandria. To go with you instead—I don't know what to tell you, Belilala." Phillips sensed that he was growing terribly flustered. "You know that I'd like to go. With you. But on the other hand I can't help feeling that I shouldn't go there until I'm back with Gioia again. If I ever am." How foolish this sounds, he thought. How clumsy, how adolescent. He found that he was having trouble looking straight at her. Uneasily he said, with a kind of desperation in his voice, "I did promise her—there was a commitment, you understand—a firm agreement that we would go to Mohenjo-daro together—"

"Oh, but Gioia's already there!" said Belilala in the most casual way.

He gaped as though she had punched him.

"What?"

"She was one of the first to go, after it opened. Months and months ago. You didn't know?" she asked, sounding surprised, but not very. "You really didn't know?"

That astonished him. He felt bewildered, betrayed, furious. His cheeks grew hot, his mouth gaped. He shook his head again and again, trying to clear it of confusion. It was a moment before he could speak. "Already there?" he said at last. "Without waiting for me? After we had talked about going there together—after we had agreed—"

Belilala laughed. "But how could she resist seeing the newest city? You know how impatient Gioia is!"

"Yes. Yes."

He was stunned. He could barely think.

"Just like all short-timers," Belilala said. "She rushes here, she rushes there. She must have it all, now, now, right away, at once, instantly. You ought never expect her to wait for you for anything for very long: the fit seizes her, and off she goes. Surely you must know that about her by now."

"A short-timer?" He had not heard that term before.

"Yes. You knew that. You must have known that." Belilala flashed her sweetest smile. She showed no sign of comprehending his distress. With a brisk wave of her hand she said, "Well, then, shall we go, you and I? To Mohenjo-daro?"

"Of course," Phillips said bleakly.

"When would you like to leave?"

"Tonight," he said. He paused a moment. "What's a short-timer, Belilala?"

Color came to her cheeks. "Isn't it obvious?" she asked.

Had there ever been a more hideous place on the face of the earth than the city of Mohenjo-daro? Phillips found it difficult to imagine one. Nor could he understand why, out of all the cities that had ever been, these people had chosen to restore this one to existence. More than ever they seemed alien to him, unfathomable, incomprehensible.

From the terrace atop the many-towered citadel he peered down into grim claustrophobic Mohenjo-daro and shivered. The stark, bleak city looked like nothing so much as some prehistoric prison colony. In the manner of an uneasy tortoise it huddled, squat and compact, against the gray monotonous Indus River plain: miles of dark burnt-brick walls enclosing miles of terrifyingly orderly streets, laid out in an awesome, monstrous gridiron pattern of maniacal rigidity. The houses themselves were dismal and forbidding too, clusters of brick cells gathered about small airless courtyards. There were no windows, only small doors that opened not onto the main boulevards but onto the tiny mysterious lanes that ran between the buildings. Who had designed this horrifying metropolis? What harsh sour souls they must have had, these frightening and frightened folk, creating for themselves in the lush fertile plains of India such a Supreme Soviet of a city!

"How lovely it is," Belilala murmured. "How fascinating!"

He stared at her in amazement.

"Fascinating? Yes," he said. "I suppose so. The same way that the smile of a cobra is fascinating."

"What's a cobra?"

"Poisonous predatory serpent," Phillips told her. "Probably extinct. Or formerly extinct, more likely. It wouldn't surprise me if you people had recreated a few and turned them loose in Mohenjo to make things livelier."

"You sound angry, Charles."

"Do I? That's not how I feel."

"How do you feel, then?"

"I don't know," he said after a long moment's pause. He shrugged. "Lost, I suppose. Very far from home."

"Poor Charles."

"Standing here in this ghastly barracks of a city, listening to you tell me how beautiful it is, I've never felt more alone in my life."

"You miss Gioia very much, don't you?"

He gave her another startled look.

"Gioia has nothing to do with it. She's probably been having ecstasies over the loveliness of Mohenjo just like you. Just like all of you. I suppose I'm the only one who can't find the beauty, the charm. I'm the only one who looks out there and sees only horror, and then wonders why nobody else sees it, why in fact people would set up a place like this for *entertainment, for pleasure—*"

Her eyes were gleaming. "Oh, you are angry! You really are!"

"Does that fascinate you, too?" he snapped. "A demonstration of genuine primitive emotion? A typical quaint twentieth-century outburst?" He paced the rampart in short quick anguished steps. "Ah. Ah. I think I understand it now, Belilala. Of course: I'm part of your circus, the star of the sideshow. I'm the first experiment in setting up the next stage of it, in fact." Her eyes were wide. The sudden harshness and violence in his voice seemed to be alarming and exciting her at the same time. That angered him even more. Fiercely he went on, "Bringing whole cities back out of time was fun for a while, but it lacks a certain authenticity, eh? For some reason you couldn't bring the inhabitants, too; you couldn't just grab a few million prehistorics out of Egypt or Greece or India and dump them down in this era, I suppose because you might have too much trouble controlling them, or because you'd have the problem of disposing of them once you were bored with them. So you had to settle for creating temporaries to populate your ancient cities. But now you've got me. I'm something more real than a temporary, and that's a terrific novelty for you, and novelty is the thing you people crave more than anything else: maybe the *only* thing you crave. And here I am, complicated, unpredictable, edgy, capable of anger, fear, sadness, love, and all those other formerly extinct things. Why settle for picturesque architecture when you can observe picturesque emotion, too? What fun I must be for all of you! And if you decide that I was really interesting, maybe you'll ship me back where I came from and check out a few other ancient types—a Roman gladiator, maybe, or a Renaissance pope, or even a Neanderthal or two—"

"Charles," she said tenderly. "Oh, Charles, Charles, Charles, how lonely you must be, how lost, how troubled! Will you ever forgive me? Will you ever forgive us all?"

Once more he was astounded by her. She sounded entirely sincere, altogether sympathetic. Was she? Was she, really? He was not sure he had ever had a sign of genuine caring from any of them before, not even Gioia. Nor could he bring himself to trust Belilala now. He was afraid of her, afraid of all of them, of their brittleness, their slyness, their elegance. He wished he could go to her and have her take him in her arms; but he felt too much the shaggy prehistoric just now to be able to risk asking that comfort of her.

He turned away and began to walk around the rim of the citadel's massive wall.

"Charles?"

"Let me alone for a little while," he said.

He walked on. His forehead throbbed and there was a pounding in his chest. All stress systems going full blast, he thought: secret glands dumping gallons of inflammatory substances into his bloodstream. The heat, the inner confusion, the repellent look of this place—

Try to understand, he thought. Relax. Look about you. Try to enjoy your holiday in Mohenjo-daro.

He leaned warily outward, over the edge of the wall. He had never seen a wall like this; it must be forty feet thick at the base, he guessed, perhaps even more, and every brick perfectly shaped, meticulously set. Beyond the great rampart, marshes ran almost to the edge of the city, although close by the wall the swamps had been dammed and drained for agriculture. He saw lithe brown farmers down there, busy with their wheat and barley and peas. Cattle and buffaloes grazed a little farther out. The air was heavy, dank, humid. All was still. From somewhere close at hand came the sound of a droning, whining stringed instrument and a steady insistent chanting.

Gradually a sort of peace pervaded him. His anger subsided. He felt himself beginning to grow calm again. He looked back at the city, the rigid interlocking streets, the maze of inner lanes, the millions of courses of precise brickwork.

It is a miracle, he told himself, that this city is here in this place and at this time. And it is a miracle that I am here to see it.

Caught for a moment by the magic within the bleakness, he thought he began to understand Belilala's awe and delight, and he wished now that he had not spoken to her so sharply. The city was alive. Whether it was the actual Mohenjo-daro of thousands upon thousands of years ago, ripped from the past by some wondrous hook, or simply a cunning reproduction, did not matter at all. Real or not, this was the true Mohenjo-daro. It had been dead, and now, for the moment, it was alive again. These people, these *citizens*, might be trivial, but reconstructing Mohenjo-daro was no trivial achievement. And that the city that had been reconstructed was oppressive and sinister-looking was unimportant. No one was compelled to live in Mohenjo-daro any more. Its time had come and gone, long ago; those little dark-skinned peasants and craftsmen and merchants down there were mere temporaries, mere inanimate things, conjured up like zombies to enhance the illusion. They did not need his pity. Nor did he need to pity himself. He knew that he should be grateful for the chance to behold these things. Someday, when this dream had ended and his hosts had returned him to the world of subways and computers and income tax and television networks, he would think of Mohenjo-daro as he had once beheld it, lofty walls of tightly woven dark brick under a heavy sky, and he would remember only its beauty.

Glancing back, he searched for Belilala and could not for a moment find her. Then he caught sight of her carefully descending a narrow staircase that angled down the inner face of the citadel wall.

"Belilala!" he called.

She paused and looked his way, shading her eyes from the sun with her hand. "Are you all right?"

"Where are you going?"

"To the baths," she said. "Do you want to come?"

He nodded. "Yes. Wait for me, will you? I'll be right there." He began to run toward her along the top of the wall.

The baths were attached to the citadel: a great open tank the size of a large swimming pool, lined with bricks set on edge in gypsum mortar and waterproofed with asphalt, and eight smaller tanks just north of it in a kind of covered arcade. He supposed that in ancient times the whole complex had had some ritual purpose, the large tank used by common folk and the small chambers set aside for the private ablutions of priests or nobles. Now the baths were maintained, it seemed, entirely for the pleasure of visiting citizens. As Phillips came up the passageway that led to the main bath he saw fifteen or twenty of them lolling in the water or padding languidly about, while temporaries of the dark-skinned Mohenjo-daro type served them drinks and pungent little morsels of spiced meat as though this were some sort of luxury resort. Which was, he realized, exactly what it was. The temporaries wore white cotton loincloths; the citizens were naked. In his former life he had encountered that sort of casual public nudity a few times on visits to California and the south of France, and it had made him mildly uneasy. But he was growing accustomed to it here.

The changing rooms were tiny brick cubicles connected by rows of closely placed steps to the courtyard that surrounded the central tank. They entered one and Belilala swiftly slipped out of the loose cotton robe that she had worn since their arrival that morning. With arms folded she stood leaning against the wall, waiting for him. After a moment he dropped his own robe and followed her outside. He felt a little giddy, sauntering around naked in the open like this.

On the way to the main bathing area they passed the private baths. None of them seemed to be occupied. They were elegantly constructed chambers, with finely jointed brick floors and carefully designed runnels to drain excess water into the passageway that led to the primary drain. Phillips was struck with admiration for the cleverness of the prehistoric engineers. He peered into this chamber and that to see how the conduits and ventilating ducts were arranged, and when he came to the last room in the sequence he was surprised and embarrassed to discover that it was in use. A brawny grinning man, big-muscled, deep-chested, with exuberantly flowing shoulder-length red hair and a flamboyant, sharply tapering beard, was thrashing about merrily with two women in the small tank. Phillips had a quick glimpse of a lively tangle of arms, legs, breasts, buttocks.

"Sorry," he muttered. His cheeks reddened. Quickly he ducked out, blurting apologies as he went. "Didn't realize the room was occupied—no wish to intrude—"

Belilala had proceeded on down the passageway. Phillips hurried after her. From behind him came peals of cheerful raucous booming laughter and high-pitched giggling and the sound of splashing water. Probably they had not even noticed him.

He paused a moment, puzzled, playing back in his mind that one startling glimpse. Something was not right. Those women, he was fairly sure, were citizens: little slender elfin dark-haired girlish creatures, the standard model. But the man? That great curling sweep of red hair? Not a citizen. Citizens did not affect shoulder-length hair. And *red?* Nor had he ever seen a citizen so burly, so powerfully muscular. Or one with a beard. But he could hardly be a temporary, either. Phillips could conceive no reason why there would be so Anglo-Saxon-looking a temporary at Mohenjo-daro; and it was unthinkable for a temporary to be frolicking like that with citizens, anyway. "Charles?"

He looked up ahead. Belilala stood at the end of the passageway, outlined in a nimbus of brilliant sunlight. "Charles?" she said again. "Did you lose your way?"

"I'm right here behind you," he said. "I'm coming."

"Who did you meet in there?"

"A man with a beard."

"With a what?"

"A beard," he said. "Red hair growing on his face. I wonder who he is."

"Nobody I know," said Belilala. "The only one I know with hair on his face is you. And yours is black, and you shave it off every day." She laughed. "Come along, now! I see some friends by the pool!"

He caught up with her, and they went hand in hand out into the courtyard. Immediately a waiter glided up to them, an obsequious little temporary with a tray of drinks. Phillips waved it away and headed for the pool. He felt terribly exposed: he imagined that the citizens disporting themselves here were staring intently at him, studying his hairy primitive body as though he were some mythical creature, a Minotaur, a werewolf, summoned up for their amusement. Belilala drifted off to talk to someone and he slipped into the water, grateful for the concealment it offered. It was deep, warm, comforting. With swift powerful strokes he breaststroked from one end to the other.

A citizen perched elegantly on the pool's rim smiled at him. "Ah, so you've come at last, Charles!" *Char-less.* Two syllables. Someone from Gioia's set: Stengard, Hawk, Aramayne? He could not remember which one. They were all so much alike.

Phillips returned the man's smile in a halfhearted, tentative way. He searched for something to say and finally asked, "Have you been here long?"

"Weeks. Perhaps months. What a splendid achievement this city is, eh, Charles? Such utter unity of mood—such a total statement of a uniquely single-minded aesthetic—"

"Yes. Single-minded is the word," Phillips said dryly.

"Gioia's word, actually. Gioia's phrase. I was merely quoting."

Gioia. He felt as if he had been stabbed.

"You've spoken to Gioia lately?" he said.

"Actually, no. It was Hekna who saw her. You do remember Hekna, eh?" He nodded toward two naked women standing on the brick platform that bordered the pool, chatting, delicately nibbling morsels of meat. They could have been twins. "There is Hekna, with your Belilala." Hekna, yes. So this must be Hawk, Phillips thought, unless there has been some recent shift of couples. "How sweet she is, your Belilala," Hawk said. "Gioia chose very wisely when she picked her for you."

Another stab: a much deeper one. "Is that how it was?" he said. "Gioia *picked* Belilala for me?"

"Why, of course!" Hawk seemed surprised. It went without saying, evidently. "What did you think? That Gioia would merely go off and leave you to fend for yourself?"

"Hardly. Not Gioia."

"She's very tender, very gentle, isn't she?"

"You mean Belilala? Yes, very," said Phillips carefully. "A dear woman, a wonderful woman. But of course I hope to get together with Gioia again soon." He paused. "They say she's been in Mohenjo-daro almost since it opened."

"She was here, yes."

"*Was?*"

"Oh, you know Gioia," Hawk said lightly. "She's moved along by now, naturally."

Phillips leaned forward. "Naturally," he said. Tension thickened his voice. "Where has she gone this time?"

"Timbuctoo, I think. Or New Chicago. I forget which one it was. She was telling us that she hoped to be in Timbuctoo for the closing-down party. But then Fenimon had some pressing reason for going to New Chicago. I can't remember what they decided to do." Hawk gestured sadly. "Either way, a pity that she left Mohenjo before the new visitor came. She had such a rewarding time with you, after all: I'm sure she'd have found much to learn from him also."

The unfamiliar term twanged an alarm deep in Phillips's consciousness. "*Visitor?*" he said, angling his head sharply toward Hawk. "What visitor do you mean?"

"You haven't met him yet? Oh, of course, you've only just arrived."

Phillips moistened his lips. "I think I may have seen him. Long red hair? Beard like this?"

"That's the one! Willoughby, he's called. He's—what?—a Viking, a pirate, something like that. Tremendous vigor and force. Remarkable person. We should have many more visitors, I think. They're far superior to temporaries, everyone agrees. Talking with a temporary is a little like talking to one's self, wouldn't you say? They give you no significant illumination. But a visitor—someone like this Willoughby—or like you, Charles—a visitor can be truly enlightening, a visitor can transform one's view of reality—"

"Excuse me," Phillips said. A throbbing began behind his forehead. "Perhaps we can continue this conversation later, yes?" He put the flats of his hands against the hot brick of the platform and hoisted himself swiftly from the pool. "At dinner, maybe—or afterward—yes? All right?" He set off at a quick half-trot back toward the passageway that led to the private baths.

As he entered the roofed part of the structure his throat grew dry, his breath suddenly came short. He padded quickly up the hall and peered into the little bath chamber. The bearded man was still there, sitting up in the tank, breast-high above the water, with one arm around each of the women. His eyes gleamed with fiery intensity in the dimness. He was grinning in marvelous self-satisfaction; he seemed to brim with intensity, confidence, gusto.

Let him be what I think he is, Phillips prayed. I have been alone among these people long enough.

"May I come in?" he asked.

"Aye, fellow!" cried the man in the tub thunderously. "By my troth, come ye in, and bring your lass as well! God's teeth, I wot there's room aplenty for more folk in this tub than we!"

At that great uproarious outcry Phillips felt a powerful surge of joy. What a joyous rowdy voice! How rich, how lusty, how totally uncitizenlike!

And those oddly archaic words! *God's teeth? By my troth?* What sort of talk was that? What else but the good pure sonorous Elizabethan diction! Certainly it had something of the roll and fervor of Shakespeare about it. And spoken with—an Irish brogue, was it? No, not quite: it was English, but English spoken in no manner Phillips had ever heard. Citizens did not speak that way. But a *visitor* might. So it was true. Relief flooded Phillips's soul. Not alone, then! Another relic of a former age— another wanderer—a companion in chaos, a brother in adversity—a fellow voyager, tossed even farther than he had been by the tempests of time—

The bearded man grinned heartily and beckoned to Phillips with a toss of his head. "Well, join us, join us, man! Tis good to see an English face again, amidst all these Moors and rogue Portugals! But what have ye done with thy lass? One can never have enough wenches, d'ye not agree?"

The force and vigor of him were extraordinary: almost too much so. He roared, he bellowed, he boomed. He was so very much what he ought to be that he seemed more a character out of some old pirate movie than anything else, so blustering, so real, that he seemed unreal. A stage Elizabethan, larger than life, a boisterous young Falstaff without the belly.

Hoarsely Phillips said, "Who are you?"

"Why, Ned Willoughby's son Francis am I, of Plymouth. Late of the service of Her Most Protestant Majesty, but most foully abducted by the powers of darkness and cast away among these blackamoor Hindus, or whatever they be. And thyself?"

"Charles Phillips." After a moment's uncertainty he added, "I'm from New York."

"*New* York? What place is that? In faith, man, I know it not!"

"A city in America."

"A city in America, forsooth! What a fine fancy that is! In America, you say, and not on the Moon, or perchance underneath the sea?" To the women Willoughby said, "D'ye hear him? He comes from a city in America! With the face of an Englishman, though not the manner of one, and not quite the proper sort of speech. A city in America! A city. God's blood, what will I hear next?"

Phillips trembled. Awe was beginning to take hold of him. This man had walked the streets of Shakespeare's London, perhaps. He had clinked canisters with Marlowe or Essex or Walter Raleigh; he had watched the ships of the Armada wallowing in the Channel. It strained Phillips's spirit to think of it. This strange dream in which he found himself was compounding its strangeness now. He felt like a weary swimmer assailed by heavy surf, winded, dazed. The hot close atmosphere of the baths was driving him toward vertigo. There could be no doubt of it any longer. He was not the only primitive—the only visitor—who was wandering loose in this fiftieth century. They were conducting other experiments as well. He gripped the sides of the door to steady himself and said, "When you speak of Her Most Protestant Majesty, it's Elizabeth the First you mean, is that not so?"

"Elizabeth, aye! As to the First, that is true enough, but why trouble to name her thus? There is but one. First and Last, I do trow, and God save her, there is no other!"

Phillips studied the other man warily. He knew that he must proceed with care. A misstep at this point and he would forfeit any chance that Willoughby would take him seriously. How much metaphysical bewilderment, after all, could this man absorb? What did he know, what had anyone of his time known, of past and present and future and the notion that one might somehow move from one to the other as readily as one would go from Surrey to Kent? That was a twentieth-century idea, late nineteenth at best, a fantastical speculation that very likely no one had even considered before Wells had sent his time traveler off to stare at the reddened sun of the earth's last twilight. Willoughby's world was a world of Protestants and Catholics, of kings and queens, of tiny sailing vessels, of swords at the hip and oxcarts on the road: that world seemed to Phillips far more alien and distant than was this world of citizens and temporaries. The risk that Willoughby would not begin to understand him was great. But this man and he were natural allies against a world they had never made. Phillips chose to take the risk.

"Elizabeth the First is the queen you serve," he said. "There will be another of her name in England, in due time. Has already been, in fact."

Willoughby shook his head like a puzzled lion. "Another Elizabeth, d'ye say?"

"A second one, and not much like the first. Long after your Virgin Queen, this one. She will reign in what you think of as the days to come. That I know without doubt."

The Englishman peered at him and frowned. "You see the future? Are you a soothsayer, then? A necromancer, mayhap? Or one of the very demons that brought me to this place?"

"Not at all," Phillips said gently. "Only a lost soul, like yourself." He stepped into the little room and crouched by the side of the tank. The two citizen-women were staring at him in bland fascination. He ignored them. To Willoughby he said, "Do you have any idea where you are?"

The Englishman had guessed, rightly enough, that he was in India: "I do believe these little brown Moorish folk are of the Hindu sort," he said. But that was as far as his comprehension of what had befallen him could go.

It had not occurred to him that he was no longer living in the sixteenth century. And of course he did not begin to suspect that this strange and somber brick city in which he found himself was a wanderer out of an era even more remote than his own. Was there any way, Phillips wondered, of explaining that to him?

He had been here only three days. He thought it was devils that had carried him off. "While I slept did they come for me," he said. "Mephistophilis Sathanas his henchmen seized me—God alone can say why—and swept me in a moment out to this torrid realm from England, where I had reposed among friends and family. For I was between one voyage and the next, you must understand, awaiting Drake and his ship—you know Drake, the glorious Francis? God's blood, there's a mariner for ye! We were to go to the Main again, he and I, but instead here I be in this other place—" Willoughby leaned close and said, "I ask you, soothsayer, how can it be, that a man go to sleep in Plymouth and wake up in India? It is passing strange, is it not?"

"That it is," Phillips said.

"But he that is in the dance must needs dance on, though he do but hop, eh? So do I believe." He gestured toward the two citizen-women. "And therefore to console myself in this pagan land I have found me some sport among these little Portugal women—"

"Portugal?" said Phillips.

"Why, what else can they be, but Portugals? Is it not the Portugals who control all these coasts of India? See, the people are of two sorts here, the blackamoors and the others, the fair-skinned ones, the lords and masters who lie here in these baths. If they be not Hindus, and I think they are not, then Portugals is what they must be." He laughed and pulled the women against himself and rubbed his hands over their breasts as though they were fruits on a vine. "Is that not what you are, you little naked shameless Papist wenches? A pair of Portugals, eh?"

They giggled, but did not answer.

"No," Phillips said. "This is India, but not the India you think you know. And these women are not Portuguese."

"Not Portuguese?" Willoughby said, baffled.

"No more so than you. I'm quite certain of that."

Willoughby stroked his beard. "I do admit I found them very odd, for Portugals. I have heard not a syllable of their Portugee speech on their lips. And it is strange also that they run naked as Adam and Eve in these baths, and allow me free plunder of their women, which is not the way of Portugals at home, God wot. But I thought me, this is India, they choose to live in another fashion here—"

"No," Phillips said. "I tell you, these are not Portuguese, nor any other people of Europe who are known to you."

"Prithee, who are they, then?"

Do it delicately, now, Phillips warned himself. *Delicately.*

He said, "It is not far wrong to think of them as spirits of some kind—demons, even. Or sorcerers who have magicked us out of our proper places in the world." He paused, groping for some means to share with Willoughby, in a way that Willoughby might grasp, this mystery that had enfolded them. He drew a deep breath. "They've taken us not only across the sea," he said, "but across the years as well. We have both been hauled, you and I, far into the days that are to come."

Willoughby gave him a look of blank bewilderment.

"Days that are to come? Times yet unborn, d'ye mean? Why, I comprehend none of that!"

"Try to understand. We're both castaways in the same boat, man! But there's no way we can help each other if I can't make you see—"

Shaking his head, Willoughby muttered, "In faith, good friend, I find your words the merest folly. Today is today, and tomorrow is tomorrow, and how can a man step from one to t'other until tomorrow be turned into today?"

"I have no idea," said Phillips. Struggle was apparent on Willoughby's face; but plainly he could perceive no more than the haziest outline of what Phillips was driving at, if that much. "But this I know," he went on. "That your world and all that was in it is dead and gone. And so is mine, though I was born four hundred years after you, in the time of the second Elizabeth."

Willoughby snorted scornfully. "Four hundred—"

"You must believe me!"

"Nay! Nay!"

"It's the truth. Your time is only history to me. And mine and yours are history to *them*—ancient history. They call us visitors, but what we are is captives." Phillips felt himself quivering in the intensity of his effort. He was aware how insane this must sound to Willoughby. It was beginning to sound insane to him. "They've stolen us out of our proper times—seizing us like gypsies in the night—"

"Fie, man! You rave with lunacy!"

Phillips shook his head. He reached out and seized Willoughby tightly by the wrist. "I beg you, listen to me!" The citizen-women were watching closely, whispering to one another behind their hands, laughing. "Ask them!" Phillips cried. "Make them tell you what century this is! The sixteenth, do you think? Ask them!"

"What century could it be, but the sixteenth of our Lord?"

"They will tell you it is the fiftieth."

Willoughby looked at him pityingly. "Man, man, what a sorry thing thou art! The fiftieth, indeed!" He laughed. "Fellow, listen to me, now. There is but one Elizabeth, safe upon her throne in Westminster. This is India. The year is Anno 1591. Come, let us you and I steal a ship from these Portugals, and make our way back to England, and peradventure you may get from there to your America—"

"There is no England."

"Ah, can you say that and not be mad?"

"The cities and nations we knew are gone. These people live like magicians, Francis." There was no use holding anything back now, Phillips thought leadenly. He knew that he had lost. "They conjure up places of long ago, and build them here and there to suit their fancy, and when they are bored with them they destroy them, and start anew. There is no England. Europe is empty, featureless, void. Do you know what cities there are? There are only five in all the world. There is Alexandria of Egypt. There is Timbuctoo in Africa. There is New Chicago in America. There is a great city in China—in Cathay, I suppose you would say. And there is this place, which they call Mohenjo-daro, and which is far more ancient than Greece, than Rome, than Babylon."

Quietly Willoughby said, "Nay. This is mere absurdity. You say we are in some far tomorrow, and then you tell me we are dwelling in some city of long ago."

"A conjuration, only," Phillips said in desperation. "A likeness of that city. Which these folk have fashioned somehow for their own amusement. Just as we are here, you and I: to amuse them. Only to amuse them."

"You are completely mad."

"Come with me, then. Talk with the citizens by the great pool. Ask them what year this is; ask them about England; ask them how you come to be here." Once again Phillips grasped Willoughby's wrist. "We should be allies. If we work together, perhaps we can discover some way to get ourselves out of this place, and—"

"Let me be, fellow."

"Please—"

"Let me be!" roared Willoughby, and pulled his arm free. His eyes were stark with rage. Rising in the tank, he looked about furiously as though searching for a weapon. The citizen-women shrank back away from him, though at the same time they seemed captivated by the big man's fierce outburst. "Go to, get you to Bedlam! Let me be, madman! Let me be!"

———

Dismally Phillips roamed the dusty unpaved streets of Mohenjo-daro alone for hours. His failure with Willoughby had left him bleak-spirited and somber: he had hoped to stand back to back with the Elizabethan against the citizens, but he saw now that that was not to be. He had bungled things; or, more likely, it had been impossible ever to bring Willoughby to see the truth of their predicament.

In the stifling heat he went at random through the confusing congested lanes of flat-roofed windowless houses and blank featureless walls until he emerged into a broad marketplace. The life of the city swirled madly around him: the pseudo-life, rather, the intricate interactions of the thousands of temporaries who were nothing more than wind-up dolls set in motion to provide the illusion that pre-Vedic India was still a going concern. Here vendors sold beautiful little carved stone seals portraying tigers and monkeys and strange humped cattle, and women bargained vociferously with craftsmen for ornaments of ivory, gold, copper, and bronze. Weary-looking women squatted behind immense mounds of newly made pottery, pinkish red with black designs. No one paid any attention to him. He was the outsider here, neither citizen nor temporary. They belonged.

He went on, passing the huge granaries where workmen ceaselessly unloaded carts of wheat and others pounded grain on great circular brick platforms. He drifted into a public restaurant thronging with joyless silent people standing elbow to elbow at small brick counters, and was given a flat round piece of bread, a sort of tortilla or chapatti, in which was stuffed some spiced mincemeat that stung his lips like fire. Then he moved onward down a wide shallow timbered staircase into the lower part of the city, where the peasantry lived in cell-like rooms packed together as though in hives.

It was an oppressive city, but not a squalid one. The intensity of the concern with sanitation amazed him: wells and fountains and public privies everywhere, and brick drains running from each building, leading to covered cesspools. There was none of the open sewage and pestilent gutters that he knew still could be found in the India of his own time. He wondered whether ancient Mohenjo-daro had in truth been so fastidious. Perhaps the citizens had redesigned the city to suit their own ideals of cleanliness. No: most likely what he saw was authentic, he decided, a function of the same obsessive discipline that had given the city its rigidity of form. If Mohenjo-daro had been a verminous filthy hole, the citizens probably would have re-created it in just that way, and loved it for its fascinating reeking filth. Not that he had ever noticed an excessive concern with authenticity on the part of the citizens; and Mohenjo-daro, like all the other restored cities he had visited, was full of the usual casual anachronisms. Phillips saw images of Shiva and Krishna here and there on the walls of buildings he took to be temples, and the benign face of the mother-goddess Kali loomed in the plazas. Surely those deities had arisen in India long after the collapse of the Mohenjo-daro civilization. Were the citizens indifferent to such matters of chronology? Or did they take a certain naughty pleasure in mixing the eras—a mosque and a church in Greek Alexandria, Hindu gods in prehistoric Mohenjo-daro? Perhaps their records of the past had become contaminated with errors over the thousands of years. He would not have been surprised to see banners bearing portraits of Gandhi and Nehru being carried in procession through the streets. And there were phantasms and chimeras at large here again, too, as if the citizens were untroubled by the boundary between history and myth: little fat elephant-headed Ganeshas blithely plunging their trunks into water fountains, a six-armed three-headed woman sunning herself on a brick terrace. Why not? Surely that was the motto of these people: *Why not, why not, why not?* They could do as they pleased, and they did. Yet Gioia had said to him, long ago, "Limits are very important." In what, Phillips wondered, did they limit themselves, other than the number of their cities? Was there a quota, perhaps, on the number of "visitors" they allowed themselves to kidnap from the past? Until today he had thought he was the only one; now he knew there was at least one other; possibly there were more elsewhere, a step or two ahead or behind him, making the circuit with the citizens who traveled endlessly from New Chicago to Chang-an to Alexandria. We should join forces, he thought, and compel them to send us back to our rightful eras. *Compel?* How? File a class-action suit, maybe? Demonstrate in the streets? Sadly he thought of his failure to make common cause with Willoughby. We are natural allies, he thought. Together perhaps we might have won some compassion from these people. But to Willoughby it must be literally unthinkable that Good Queen Bess and her subjects were sealed away on the far side of a barrier hundreds of centuries thick. He would prefer to believe that England was just a few months' voyage away around the Cape of Good Hope, and that all he need do was commandeer a ship and set sail for home. Poor Willoughby: probably he would never see his home again.

The thought came to Phillips suddenly:

Neither will you.

And then, after it:

If you could go home, would you really want to?

One of the first things he had realized here was that he knew almost nothing substantial about his former existence. His mind was well stocked with details on life in twentieth-century New York, to be sure; but of himself he could say not much more than that he was Charles Phillips and had come from 1984. Profession? Age? Parents' names? Did he have a wife? Children? A cat, a dog, hobbies? No data: none. Possibly the citizens had stripped such things from him when they brought him here, to spare him from the pain of separation. They might be capable of that kindness. Knowing so little of what he had lost, could he truly say that he yearned for it? Willoughby seemed to remember much more of his former life, somehow, and longed for it all the more intensely. He was spared that. Why not stay here, and go on and on from city to city, sightseeing all of time past as the citizens conjured it back into being? Why not? Why not? The chances were that he had no choice about it, anyway.

He made his way back up toward the citadel and to the baths once more. He felt a little like a ghost, haunting a city of ghosts.

Belilala seemed unaware that he had been gone for most of the day. She sat by herself on the terrace of the baths, placidly sipping some thick milky beverage that had been sprinkled with a dark spice. He shook his head when she offered him some.

"Do you remember I mentioned that I saw a man with red hair and a beard this morning?" Phillips said. "He's a visitor. Hawk told me that."

"Is he?" Belilala asked.

"From a time about four hundred years before mine. I talked with him. He thinks he was brought here by demons." Phillips gave her a searching look. "I'm a visitor, too, isn't that so?"

"Of course, love."

"And how was I brought here? By demons also?"

Belilala smiled indifferently. "You'd have to ask someone else. Hawk, perhaps. I haven't looked into these things very deeply."

"I see. Are there many visitors here, do you know?"

A languid shrug. "Not many, no, not really. I've only heard of three or four besides you. There may be others by now, I suppose." She rested her hand lightly on his. "Are you having a good time in Mohenjo, Charles?"

He let her question pass as though he had not heard it.

"I asked Hawk about Gioia," he said.

"Oh?"

"He told me that she's no longer here, that she's gone on to Timbuctoo or New Chicago, he wasn't sure which."

"That's quite likely. As everybody knows, Gioia rarely stays in the same place very long."

Phillips nodded. "You said the other day that Gioia is a short-timer. That means she's going to grow old and die, doesn't it?"

"I thought you understood that, Charles."

"Whereas you will not age? Nor Hawk, nor Stengard, nor any of the rest of your set?"

"We will live as long as we wish," she said. "But we will not age, no."

"What makes a person a short-timer?"

"They're born that way, I think. Some missing gene, some extra gene—I don't actually know. It's extremely uncommon. Nothing can be done to help them. It's very slow, the aging. But it can't be halted."

Phillips nodded. "That must be very disagreeable," he said. "To find yourself one of the few people growing old in a world where everyone stays young. No wonder Gioia is so impatient. No wonder she runs around from place to place. No wonder she attached herself so quickly to the barbaric hairy visitor from the twentieth century, who comes from a time when *everybody* was a short-timer. She and I have something in common, wouldn't you say?"

"In a manner of speaking, yes."

"We understand aging. We understand death. Tell me: is Gioia likely to die very soon, Belilala?"

"Soon? Soon?" She gave him a wide-eyed childlike stare. "What is soon? How can I say? What you think of as soon and what I think of as soon are not the same things, Charles." Then her manner changed: she seemed to be hearing what he was saying for the first time. Softly she said, "No, no, Charles. I don't think she will die very soon."

"When she left me in Chang-an, was it because she had become bored with me?"

Belilala shook her head. "She was simply restless. It had nothing to do with you. She was never bored with you."

"Then I'm going to go looking for her. Wherever she may be, Timbuctoo, New Chicago, I'll find her. Gioia and I belong together."

"Perhaps you do," said Belilala. "Yes. Yes, I think you really do." She sounded altogether unperturbed, unrejected, unbereft. "By all means, Charles. Go to her. Follow her. Find her. Whatever she may be."

They had already begun dismantling Timbuctoo when Phillips got there. While he was still high overhead, his flitterflitter hovering above the dusty tawny plain where the River Niger met the sands of the Sahara, a surge of keen excitement rose in him as he looked down at the square gray flat-roofed mud brick buildings of the great desert capital. But when he landed he found gleaming metal-skinned robots swarming everywhere, a horde of them scuttling about like giant shining insects, pulling the place apart.

He had not known about the robots before. So that was how all these miracles were carried out, Phillips realized: an army of obliging machines. He imagined them bustling up out of the earth whenever their services were needed, emerging from some sterile subterranean storehouse to put together Venice or Thebes or Knossos or Houston or whatever place was required, down to the finest detail, and then at some later time returning to undo everything that they had fashioned. He watched them now, diligently pulling down the adobe walls, demolishing the heavy metal-studded gates, bulldozing the amazing labyrinth of alleyways and thoroughfares, sweeping away the market. On his last visit to Timbuctoo that market had been crowded with a horde of veiled Tuaregs and swaggering Moors, black Sudanese, shrewd-faced Syrian traders, all of them busily dickering for camels, horses, donkeys, slabs of salt, huge green melons, silver bracelets, splendid vellum Korans. They were all gone now, that picturesque crowd of swarthy temporaries. Nor were there any citizens to be seen. The dust of destruction choked the air. One of the robots came up to Phillips and said in a dry crackling insect-voice, "You ought not to be here. This city is closed."

He stared at the flashing, buzzing band of scanners and sensors across the creature's glittering tapered snout. "I'm trying to find someone, a citizen who may have been here recently. Her name is—"

"This city is closed," the robot repeated inexorably.

They would not let him stay as much as an hour. There is no food here, the robot said, no water, no shelter. This is not a place any longer. You may not stay. You may not stay. You may not stay.

This is not a place any longer.

Perhaps he could find her in New Chicago, then. He took to the air again, soaring northward and westward over the vast emptiness. The land below him curved away into the hazy horizon, bare, sterile. What had they done with the vestiges of the world that had gone before? Had they turned their gleaming metal beetles loose to clean everything away? Were there no ruins of genuine antiquity anywhere? No scrap of Rome, no shard of Jerusalem, no stump of Fifth Avenue? It was all so barren down there: an empty stage, waiting for its next set to be built. He flew on a great arc across the jutting hump of Africa and on into what he supposed was southern Europe: the little vehicle did all the work, leaving him to doze or stare as he wished. Now and again he saw another flitterflitter pass by, far away, a dark distant winged teardrop outlined against the hard clarity of the sky. He wished there was some way of making radio contact with them, but he had no idea how to go about it. Not that he had anything he wanted to say; he wanted only to hear a human voice. He was utterly isolated. He might just as well have been the last living man on Earth. He closed his eyes and thought of Gioia.

"Like this?" Phillips asked. In an ivory-paneled oval room sixty stories above the softly glowing streets of New Chicago he touched a small cool plastic canister to his upper lip and pressed the stud at its base. He heard a foaming sound; and then blue vapor rose to his nostrils.

"Yes," Cantilena said. "That's right."

He detected a faint aroma of cinnamon, cloves, and something that might almost have been broiled lobster. Then a spasm of dizziness hit him and visions rushed through his head: Gothic cathedrals, the Pyramids, Central Park under fresh snow, the harsh brick warrens of Mohenjo-daro, and fifty thousand other places all at once, a wild roller-coaster ride through space and time. It seemed to go on for centuries. But finally his head cleared and he looked about, blinking, realizing that the whole thing had taken only a moment. Cantilena still stood at his elbow. The other citizens in the room—fifteen, twenty of them—had scarcely moved. The strange little man with the celadon skin over by the far wall continued to stare at him.

"Well?" Cantilena asked. "What did you think?"

"Incredible."

"And very authentic. It's an actual New Chicagoan drug. The exact formula. Would you like another?"

"Not just yet," Phillips said uneasily. He swayed and had to struggle for his balance. Sniffing that stuff might not have been such a wise idea, he thought.

He had been in New Chicago a week, or perhaps it was two, and he was still suffering from the peculiar disorientation that that city always aroused in him. This was the fourth time that he had come here, and it had been the same every time. New Chicago was the only one of the reconstructed cities of this world that in its original incarnation had existed *after* his own era. To him it was an outpost of the incomprehensible future; to the citizens it was a quaint simulacrum of the archaeological past. That paradox left him aswirl with impossible confusions and tensions.

What had happened to *old* Chicago was of course impossible for him to discover. Vanished without a trace, that was clear: no Water Tower, no Marina City, no Hancock Center, no Tribune building, not a fragment, not an atom. But it was hopeless to ask any of the million-plus inhabitants of New Chicago about their city's predecessor. They were only temporaries; they knew no more than they had to know, and all that they had to know was how to go through the motions of whatever it was that they did by way of creating the illusion that this was a real city. They had no need of knowing ancient history.

Nor was he likely to find out anything from a citizen, of course. Citizens did not seem to bother much about scholarly matters. Phillips had no reason to think that the world was anything other than an amusement park to them. Somewhere, certainly, there had to be those who specialized in the serious study of the lost civilizations of the past—for how, otherwise, would these uncanny reconstructed cities be brought into being? "The planners," he had once heard Nissandra or Aramayne say, "are already deep into their Byzantium research." But who were the planners? He had no idea. For all he knew, they were the robots. Perhaps the robots were the real masters of this whole era, who created the cities not primarily for the sake of amusing the citizens but in their own diligent attempt to comprehend the life of the world that had passed away. A wild speculation, yes; but not without some plausibility, he thought.

He felt oppressed by the party gaiety all about him. "I need some air," he said to Cantilena, and headed toward the window. It was the merest crescent, but a breeze came through. He looked out at the strange city below.

New Chicago had nothing in common with the old one but its name. They had built it, at least, along the western shore of a large inland lake that might even be Lake Michigan, although when he had flown over it had seemed broader and less elongated than the lake he remembered. The city itself was a lacy fantasy of slender pastel-hued buildings rising at odd angles and linked by a webwork of gently undulating aerial bridges. The streets were long parentheses that touched the lake at their northern and southern ends and arched gracefully westward in the middle. Between each of the great boulevards ran a track for public transportation—sleek aquamarine bubble-vehicles gliding on soundless wheels—and flanking each of the tracks were lush strips of park. It was beautiful, astonishingly so, but insubstantial. The whole thing seemed to have been contrived from sunbeams and silk.

A soft voice beside him said, "Are you becoming ill?"

Phillips glanced around. The celadon man stood beside him: a compact, precise person, vaguely Oriental in appearance. His skin was of a curious gray-green hue like no skin Phillips had ever seen, and it was extraordinarily smooth in texture, as though he were made of fine porcelain.

He shook his head. "Just a little queasy," he said. "This city always scrambles me."

"I suppose it can be disconcerting," the little man replied. His tone was furry and veiled, the inflection strange. There was something feline about him. He seemed sinewy, unyielding, almost menacing. "Visitor, are you?"

Phillips studied him a moment. "Yes," he said.

"So am I, of course."

"Are you?"

"Indeed." The little man smiled. "What's your locus? Twentieth century? Twenty-first at the latest, I'd say."

"I'm from 1984. A.D. 1984."

Another smile, a self-satisfied one. "Not a bad guess, then." A brisk tilt of the head. "Y'ang-Yeovil."

"Pardon me?" Phillips said.

"Y'ang-Yeovil. It is my name. Formerly Colonel Y'ang-Yeovil of the Third Septentriad."

"Is that on some other planet?" asked Phillips, feeling a bit dazed.

"Oh, no, not at all," Y'ang-Yeovil said pleasantly. "This very world, I assure you. I am quite of human origin. Citizen of the Republic of Upper Han, native of the city of Port Ssu. And you—forgive me—your name—?"

"I'm sorry. Phillips. Charles Phillips. From New York City, once upon a time."

"Ah, New York!" Y'ang-Yeovil's face lit with a glimmer of recognition that quickly faded. "New York—New York—it was very famous, that I know—"

This is very strange, Phillips thought. He felt greater compassion for poor bewildered Francis Willoughby now. This man comes from a time so far beyond my own that he barely knows of New York—he must be a contemporary of the real New Chicago, in fact; I wonder whether he finds this version authentic—and yet to the citizens this Y'ang-Yeovil too is just a primitive, a curio out of antiquity—

"New York was the largest city of the United States of America," Phillips said.

"Of course. Yes. Very famous."

"But virtually forgotten by the time the Republic of Upper Han came into existence, I gather."

Y'ang-Yeovil said, looking uncomfortable, "There were disturbances between your time and mine. But by no means should you take from my words the impression that your city was—"

Sudden laughter resounded across the room. Five or six newcomers had arrived at the party. Phillips stared, gasped, gaped. Surely that was Stengard—and Aramayne beside him—and that other woman, half hidden behind them—

"If you'll pardon me a moment—" Phillips said, turning abruptly away from Y'ang-Yeovil. "Please excuse me. Someone just coming in—a person I've been trying to find ever since—"

He hurried toward her.

"Gioia?" he called. "Gioia, it's me! Wait! Wait!"

Stengard was in the way. Aramayne, turning to take a handful of the little vapor-sniffers from Cantilena, blocked him also. Phillips pushed through them as though they were not there. Gioia, halfway out the door, halted and looked toward him like a frightened deer.

"Don't go," he said. He took her hand in his. He was startled by her appearance. How long had it been since their strange parting on that night of mysteries in Chang-an? A year? A year and a half? So he believed. Or had he lost all track of time? Were his perceptions of the passing of the months in this world that unreliable? She seemed at least ten or fifteen years older. Maybe she really was; maybe the years had been passing for him here as in a dream, and he had never known it. She looked strained, faded, worn. Out of a thinner and strangely altered face her eyes blazed at him almost defiantly, as though saying, *See? See how ugly I have become?*

He said, "I've been hunting for you for—I don't know how long it's been, Gioia. In Mohenjo, in Timbuctoo, now here. I want to be with you again."

"It isn't possible."

"Belilala explained everything to me in Mohenjo. I know that you're a short-timer—I know what that means, Gioia. But what of it? So you're beginning to age a little. So what? So you'll only have three or four hundred years, instead of forever. Don't you think I know what it means to be a short-timer? I'm just a simple ancient man of the twentieth century, remember? Sixty, seventy, eighty years is all we would get. You and I suffer from the same malady, Gioia. That's what drew you to me in

the first place. I'm certain of that. That's why we belong with each other now. However much time we have, we can spend the rest of it together, don't you see?"

"You're the one who doesn't see, Charles," she said softly.

"Maybe. Maybe I still don't understand a damned thing about this place. Except
that you and I—that I love you—that I think you love me—"

"I love you, yes. But you don't understand. It's precisely because I love you that
you and I—you and I can't—"

With a despairing sigh she slid her hand free of his grasp. He reached for her
again, but she shook him off and backed up quickly into the corridor.

"Gioia?"

"Please," she said. "No. I would never have come here if I knew you were here.
Don't come after me. Please. Please."

She turned and fled.

He stood looking after her for a long moment. Cantilena and Aramayne appeared, and smiled at him as if nothing at all had happened. Cantilena offered him
a vial of some sparkling amber fluid. He refused with a brusque gesture. Where do I
go now, he wondered? What do I do? He wandered back into the party.

Y'ang-Yeovil glided to his side. "You are in great distress," the little man murmured.

Phillips glared. "Let me be."

"Perhaps I could be of some help."

"There's no help possible," said Phillips. He swung about and plucked one of the
vials from a tray and gulped its contents. It made him feel as if there were two of
him, standing on either side of Y'ang-Yeovil. He gulped another. Now there were
four of him. "I'm in love with a citizen," he blurted. It seemed to him that he was
speaking in chorus.

"Love. Ah. And does she love you?"

"So I thought. So I think. But she's a short-timer. Do you know what that means?
She's not immortal like the others. She ages. She's beginning to look old. And so
she's been running away from me. She doesn't want me to see her changing. She
thinks it'll disgust me, I suppose. I tried to remind her just now that I'm not immortal either, that she and I could grow old together, but she—"

"Oh, no," Y'ang-Yeovil said quietly. "Why do you think you will age? Have you
grown any older in all the time that you've been here?"

Phillips was nonplussed. "Of course I have. I—I—"

"Have you?" Y'ang-Yeovil smiled. "Here. Look at yourself." He did something intricate with his fingers and a shimmering zone of mirrorlike light appeared between
them.

Phillips stared at his reflection. A youthful face stared back at him. It was true,
then. He had simply not thought about it. How many years had he spent in this
world? The time had simply slipped by: a great deal of time, though he could not
calculate how much. They did not seem to keep close count of it here, nor had he.
But it must have been many years, he thought. All that endless travel up and down
the globe—so many cities had come and gone—Rio, Rome, Asgard, those were the
first three that came to mind—and there were others; he could hardly remember

every one. Years. His face had not changed at all. Time had worked its harshness on Gioia, yes, but not on him.

"I don't understand," he said. "Why am I not aging?"

"Because you are not real," said Y'ang-Yeovil. "Are you unaware of that?"

Phillips blinked. "Not—real?"

"Did you think you were lifted bodily out of your own time?" the little man asked. "Ah, no, no, there is no way for them to do such a thing. We are not actual time travelers: not you, not I, not any of the visitors. I thought you were aware of that. But perhaps your era is too early for a proper understanding of these things. We are very cleverly done, my friend. We are ingenious constructs, marvelously stuffed with the thoughts and attitudes and events of our own times. We are their finest achievement, you know: far more complex even than one of these cities. We are a step beyond the temporaries—more than a step, a great deal more. They do only what they are instructed to do, and their range is very narrow. They are nothing but machines, really. Whereas we are autonomous. We move about by our own will; we think, we talk, we even, so it seems, fall in love. But we will not age. How could we age? We are not real. We are mere artificial webworks of mental responses. We are mere illusions, done so well that we deceive even ourselves. You did not know that? Indeed, you did not know?"

He was airborne, touching destination buttons at random. Somehow he found himself heading back toward Timbuctoo. *This city is closed. This is not a place any longer.* It did not matter to him. Why should anything matter?

Fury and a choking sense of despair rose within him. I am software, Phillips thought. I am nothing but software.

Not real. Very cleverly done. An ingenious construct. A mere illusion.

No trace of Timbuctoo was visible from the air. He landed anyway. The gray sandy earth was smooth, unturned, as though there had never been anything there. A few robots were still about, handling whatever final chores were required in the shutting-down of a city. Two of them scuttled up to him. Huge bland gleaming silver-skinned insects, not friendly.

"There is no city here," they said. "This is not a permissible place."

"Permissible by whom?"

"There is no reason for you to be here."

"There's no reason for me to be anywhere," Phillips said. The robots stirred, made uneasy humming sounds and ominous clicks, waved their antennae about. They seemed troubled, he thought. They seem to dislike my attitude. Perhaps I run some risk of being taken off to the home for unruly software for debugging. "I'm leaving now," he told them. "Thank you. Thank you very much." He backed away from them and climbed into his flitterflitter. He touched more destination buttons.

We move about by our own will. We think, we talk, we even fall in love.

He landed in Chang-an. This time there was no reception committee waiting for him at the Gate of Brilliant Virtue. The city seemed larger and more resplendent: new pagodas, new palaces. It felt like winter: a chilly cutting wind was blowing. The sky was cloudless and dazzlingly bright. At the steps of the Silver Terrace he encountered Francis Willoughby, a great hulking figure in magnificent brocaded robes, with two dainty little temporaries, pretty as jade statuettes, engulfed in his arms. "Miracles and wonders! The silly lunatic fellow is here, too!" Willoughby roared. "Look, look, we are come to far Cathay, you and I!"

We are nowhere, Phillips thought. *We are mere illusions, done so well that we deceive even ourselves.*

To Willoughby he said, "You look like an emperor in those robes, Francis."

"Aye, like Prester John!" Willoughby cried. "Like Tamburlaine himself! Aye, am I not majestic?" He slapped Phillips gaily on the shoulder, a rough playful poke that spun him halfway about, coughing and wheezing. "We flew in the air, as the eagles do, as the demons do, as the angels do! Soared like angels! Like angels!" He came close, looming over Phillips. "I would have gone to England, but the wench Belilala said there was an enchantment on me that would keep me from England just now; and so we voyaged to Cathay. Tell me this, fellow, will you go witness for me when we see England again? Swear that all that has befallen us did in truth befall? For I fear they will say I am as mad as Marco Polo, when I tell them of flying to Cathay."

"One madman backing another?" Phillips asked. "What can I tell you? You still think you'll reach England, do you?" Rage rose to the surface in him, bubbling hot. "Ah, Francis, Francis, do you know your Shakespeare? Did you go to the plays? We aren't real. *We aren't real.* We are such stuff as dreams are made on, the two of us. That's all we are. O brave new world! What England? Where? There's no England. There's no Francis Willoughby. There's no Charles Phillips. What we are is—"

"Let him be, Charles," a cool voice cut in.

He turned. Belilala, in the robes of an empress, coming down the steps of the Silver Terrace.

"I know the truth," he said bitterly. "Y'ang-Yeovil told me. The visitor from the twenty-fifth century. I saw him in New Chicago."

"Did you see Gioia there, too?" Belilala asked.

"Briefly. She looks much older."

"Yes. I know. She was here recently."

"And has gone on, I suppose?"

"To Mohenjo again, yes. Go after her, Charles. Leave poor Francis alone. I told her to wait for you. I told her that she needs you, and you need her."

"Very kind of you. But what good is it, Belilala? I don't even exist. And she's going to die."

"You exist. How can you doubt that you exist? You feel, don't you? You suffer. You love. You love Gioia: is that not so? And you are loved by Gioia. Would Gioia love what is not real?"

"You think she loves me?"

"I know she does. Go to her, Charles. Go. I told her to wait for you in Mohenjo."

Phillips nodded numbly. What was there to lose?

"Go to her," said Belilala again. "Now."

"Yes," Phillips said. "I'll go now." He turned to Willoughby. "If ever we meet in London, friend, I'll testify for you. Fear nothing. All will be well, Francis."

He left them and set his course for Mohenjo-daro, half expecting to find the robots already tearing it down. Mohenjo-daro was still there, no lovelier than before. He went to the baths, thinking he might find Gioia there. She was not; but he came upon Nissandra, Stengard, Fenimon.

"She has gone to Alexandria," Fenimon told him. "She wants to see it one last time, before they close it."

"They're almost ready to open Constantinople," Stengard explained. "The capital of Byzantium, you know, the great city by the Golden Horn. They'll take Alexandria away, you understand, when Byzantium opens. They say it's going to be marvelous. We'll see you there for the opening, naturally?"

"Naturally," Phillips said.

He flew to Alexandria. He felt lost and weary. All this is hopeless folly, he told himself. I am nothing but a puppet jerking about on its strings. But somewhere above the shining breast of the Arabian Sea the deeper implications of something that Belilala had said to him started to sink in, and he felt his bitterness, his rage, his despair, all suddenly beginning to leave him. *You exist. How can you doubt that you exist? Would Gioia love what is not real?* Of course. Of course. Y'ang-Yeovil had been wrong: visitors were something more than mere illusions. Indeed, Y'ang-Yeovil had voiced the truth of their condition without understanding what he was really saying: *We think, we talk, we fall in love.* Yes. That was the heart of the situation. The visitors might be artificial, but they were not unreal. Belilala had been trying to tell him that just the other night. *You suffer. You love. You love Gioia. Would Gioia love what is not real?* Surely he was real, or at any rate real enough. What he was was something strange, something that would probably have been all but incomprehensible to the twentieth-century people whom he had been designed to simulate. But that did not mean that he was unreal. Did one have to be of woman born to be real? No. No. No. His kind of reality was a sufficient reality. He had no need to be ashamed of it. And, understanding that, he understood that Gioia did not need to grow old and die. There was a way by which she could be saved, if only she would embrace it. If only she would.

When he landed in Alexandria he went immediately to the hotel on the slopes of the Paneium where they had stayed on their first visit, so very long ago; and there she was, sitting quietly on a patio with a view of the harbor and the Lighthouse. There was something calm and resigned about the way she sat. She had given up. She did not even have the strength to flee from him any longer.

"Gioia," he said gently.

She looked older than she had in New Chicago. Her face was drawn and sallow and her eyes seemed sunken; and she was not even bothering these days to deal with the white strands that stood out in stark contrast against the darkness of her hair. He sat down beside her and put his hand over hers and looked out toward the obelisks, the palaces, the temples, the Lighthouse. At length he said, "I know what I really am now."

"Do you, Charles?" She sounded very far away.

"In my age we called it software. All I am is a set of commands, responses, cross-references, operating some sort of artificial body. It's infinitely better software than we could have imagined. But we were only just beginning to learn how, after all. They pumped me full of twentieth-century reflexes. The right moods, the right appetites, the right irrationalities, the right sort of combativeness. Somebody knows a lot about what it was like to be a twentieth-century man. They did a good job with Willoughby, too, all that Elizabethan rhetoric and swagger. And I suppose they got Y'ang-Yeovil right. *He* seems to think so: who better to judge? The twenty-fifth century, the Republic of Upper Han, people with gray-green skin, half Chinese and half Martian for all I know. *Somebody* knows. Somebody here is very good at programming, Gioia."

She was not looking at him.

"I feel frightened, Charles," she said in that same distant way.

"Of me? Of the things I'm saying?"

"No, not of you. Don't you see what has happened to me?"

"I see you. There are changes."

"I lived a long time wondering when the changes would begin. I thought maybe they wouldn't, not really. Who wants to believe they'll get old? But it started when we were in Alexandria that first time. In Chang-an it got much worse. And now— now—"

He said abruptly, "Stengard tells me they'll be opening Constantinople very soon."

"So?"

"Don't you want to be there when it opens?"

"I'm becoming old and ugly, Charles."

"We'll go to Constantinople together. We'll leave tomorrow, eh? What do you say? We'll charter a boat. It's a quick little hop, right across the Mediterranean. Sailing to Byzantium! There was a poem, you know, in my time. Not forgotten, I guess, because they've programmed it into me. All these thousands of years, and someone still remembers old Yeats. *The young in one another's arms, birds in the trees.* Come with me to Byzantium, Gioia."

She shrugged. "Looking like this? Getting more hideous every hour? While *they* stay young forever? While *you*—" She faltered; her voice cracked; she fell silent.

"Finish the sentence, Gioia."

"Please. Let me alone."

"You were going to say, 'While *you* stay young forever, too, Charles,' isn't that it? You knew all along that I was never going to change. I didn't know that, but you did."

"Yes. I knew. I pretended that it wasn't true—that as I aged, you'd age, too. It was very foolish of me. In Chang-an, when I first began to see the real signs of it—that was when I realized I couldn't stay with you any longer. Because I'd look at you, always young, always remaining the same age, and I'd look at myself, and—" She gestured, palms upward. "So I gave you to Belilala and ran away."

"All so unnecessary, Gioia."

"I didn't think it was."

"But you don't have to grow old. Not if you don't want to!"

"Don't be cruel, Charles," she said tonelessly. "There's no way of escaping what I have."

"But there is," he said.

"You know nothing about these things."

"Not very much, no," he said. "But I see how it can be done. Maybe it's a primitive simpleminded twentieth-century sort of solution, but I think it ought to work. I've been playing with the idea ever since I left Mohenjo. Tell me this, Gioia: Why can't you go to them, to the programmers, to the artificers, the planners, whoever they are, the ones who create the cities and the temporaries and the visitors. And have yourself made into something like me!"

She looked up, startled. "What are you saying?"

"They can cobble up a twentieth-century man out of nothing more than fragmentary records and make him plausible, can't they? Or an Elizabethan, or anyone else of any era at all, and he's authentic, he's convincing. So why couldn't they do an even better job with you? Produce a Gioia so real that even Gioia can't tell the difference? But a Gioia that will never age—a Gioia-construct, a Gioia-program, a visitor-Gioia! Why not? Tell me why not, Gioia."

She was trembling. "I've never heard of doing any such thing!"

"But don't you think it's possible?"

"How would I know?"

"Of course it's possible. If they can create visitors, they can take a citizen and duplicate her in such a way that—"

"It's never been done. I'm sure of it. I can't imagine any citizen agreeing to any such thing. To give up the body—to let yourself be turned into—into—"

She shook her head, but it seemed to be a gesture of astonishment as much as of negation.

He said, "Sure. To give up the body. Your natural body, your aging, shrinking, deteriorating short-timer body. What's so awful about that?"

She was very pale. "This is craziness, Charles. I don't want to talk about it any more."

"It doesn't sound crazy to me."

"You can't possibly understand."

"Can't I? I can certainly understand being afraid to die. I don't have a lot of trouble understanding what it's like to be one of the few aging people in a world where nobody grows old. What I can't understand is why you aren't even willing to consider the possibility that—"

"No," she said. "I tell you, it's crazy. They'd laugh at me."

"Who?"

"All of my friends. Hawk, Stengard, Aramayne—" Once again she would not look at him. "They can be very cruel, without even realizing it. They despise anything that seems ungraceful to them, anything sweaty and desperate and cowardly. Citizens don't do sweaty things, Charles. And that's how this will seem. Assuming it can be done at all. They'll be terribly patronizing. Oh, they'll be sweet to me, yes, dear Gioia, how wonderful for you, Gioia, but when I turn my back they'll laugh. They'll say the most wicked things about me. I couldn't bear that."

"They can afford to laugh," Phillips said. "It's easy to be brave and cool about dying when you know you're going to live forever. How very fine for them: but why should you be the only one to grow old and die? And they won't laugh, anyway. They're not as cruel as you think. Shallow, maybe, but not cruel. They'll be glad that you've found a way to save yourself. At the very least, they won't have to feel guilty about you any longer, and that's bound to please them. You can—"

"Stop it," she said.

She rose, walked to the railing of the patio, stared out toward the sea. He came up behind her. Red sails in the harbor, sunlight glittering along the sides of the Lighthouse, the palaces of the Ptolemies stark white against the sky. Lightly he rested his hand on her shoulder. She twitched as if to pull away from him, but remained where she was.

"Then I have another idea," he said quietly. "If you won't go to the planners, I will. Reprogram me, I'll say. Fix things so that I start to age at the same rate you do. It'll be more authentic, anyway, if I'm supposed to be playing the part of a twentieth-century man. Over the years I'll very gradually get some lines in my face, my hair will turn gray, I'll walk a little more slowly—we'll grow old together, Gioia. To hell with your lovely immortal friends. We'll have each other. We won't need them."

She swung around. Her eyes were wide with horror.

"Are you serious, Charles?"

"Of course."

"No," she murmured. "No. Everything you've said to me today is monstrous nonsense. Don't you realize that?"

He reached for her hand and enclosed her fingertips in his. "All I'm trying to do is find some way for you and me to—"

"Don't say any more," she said. "Please." Quickly, as though drawing back from a suddenly flaring flame, she tugged her fingers free of his and put her hand behind her. Though his face was just inches from hers he felt an immense chasm opening between them. They stared at one another for a moment; then she moved deftly to his left, darted around him, and ran from the patio.

Stunned, he watched her go, down the long marble corridor and out of sight. It was folly to give pursuit, he thought. She was lost to him: that was clear, that was beyond any question. She was terrified of him. Why cause her even more anguish? But somehow he found himself running through the halls of the hotel, along the winding garden path, into the cool green groves of the Paneium. He thought he saw her on the portico of Hadrian's palace, but when he got there the echoing stone halls were empty. To a temporary that was sweeping the steps he said, "Did you see a woman come this way?" A blank sullen stare was his only answer.

Phillips cursed and turned away.

"Gioia?" he called. "Wait! Come back!"

Was that her, going into the Library? He rushed past the startled mumbling librarians and sped through the stacks, peering beyond the mounds of double-handled scrolls into the shadowy corridors. "Gioia? *Gioia!*" It was a desecration, bellowing like that in this quiet place. He scarcely cared.

Emerging by a side door, he loped down to the harbor. The Lighthouse! Terror enfolded him. She might already be a hundred steps up that ramp, heading for the parapet from which she meant to fling herself into the sea. Scattering citizens and temporaries as if they were straws, he ran within. Up he went, never pausing for breath, though his synthetic lungs were screaming for respite, his ingeniously designed heart was desperately pounding. On the first balcony he imagined he caught a glimpse of her, but he circled it without finding her. Onward, upward. He went to the top, to the beacon chamber itself: no Gioia. Had she jumped? Had she gone down one ramp while he was ascending the other? He clung to the rim and looked out, down, searching the base of the Lighthouse, the rocks offshore, the causeway. No Gioia. I will find her somewhere, he thought. I will keep going until I find her. He went running down the ramp, calling her name. He reached ground level and sprinted back toward the center of town. Where next? The temple of Poseidon? The tomb of Cleopatra?

He paused in the middle of Canopus Street, groggy and dazed.

"Charles?" she said.

"Where are you?"

"Right here. Beside you." She seemed to materialize from the air. Her face was unflushed, her robe bore no trace of perspiration. Had he been chasing a phantom through the city? She came to him and took his hand, and said, softly, tenderly, "Were you really serious, about having them make you age?"

"If there's no other way, yes."

"The other way is so frightening, Charles."

"Is it?"

"You can't understand how much."

"More frightening than growing old? Than dying?"

"I don't know," she said. "I suppose not. The only thing I'm sure of is that I don't want you to get old, Charles."

"But I won't have to. Will I?"

He stared at her.

"No," she said. "You won't have to. Neither of us will."

Phillips smiled. "We should get away from here," he said after a while. "Let's go across to Byzantium, yes, Gioia? We'll show up in Constantinople for the opening. Your friends will be there. We'll tell them what you've decided to do. They'll know how to arrange it. Someone will."

"It sounds so strange," said Gioia. "To turn myself into — into a visitor? A visitor in my own world?"

"That's what you've always been, though."

"I suppose. In a way. But at least I've been *real* up to now."

"Whereas I'm not?"

"Are you, Charles?"

"Yes. Just as real as you. I was angry at first, when I found out the truth about myself. But I came to accept it. Somewhere between Mohenjo and here, I came to see that it was all right to be what I am: that I perceive things, I form ideas, I draw conclusions. I am very well designed, Gioia. I can't tell the difference between being what I am and being completely alive, and to me that's being real enough. I think, I feel, I experience joy and pain. I'm as real as I need to be. And you will be, too. You'll never stop being Gioia, you know. It's only your body that you'll cast away, the body that played such a terrible joke on you anyway." He brushed her cheek with his hand. "It was all said for us before, long ago:

> "Once out of nature I shall never take
> My bodily form from any natural thing,
> But such a form as Grecian goldsmiths make
> Of hammered gold and gold enameling
> To keep a drowsy Emperor awake—"

"Is that the same poem?" she asked.

"The same poem, yes. The ancient poem that isn't quite forgotten yet."

"Finish it, Charles."

> "—Or set upon a golden bough to sing
> To lords and ladies of Byzantium
> Of what is past, or passing, or to come."

"How beautiful. What does it mean?"

"That it isn't necessary to be mortal. That we can allow ourselves to be gathered into the artifice of eternity, that we can be transformed, that we can move on beyond the flesh. Yeats didn't mean it in quite the way I do—he wouldn't have begun to comprehend what we're talking about, not a word of it—and yet, and yet—the underlying truth is the same. Live, Gioia! With me!" He turned to her and saw color coming into her pallid cheeks. "It does make sense, what I'm suggesting, doesn't it? You'll attempt it, won't you? Whoever makes the visitors can be induced to remake you. Right? What do you think: can they, Gioia?"

She nodded in a barely perceptible way. "I think so," she said faintly. "It's very strange. But I think it ought to be possible. Why not, Charles? Why not?"

"Yes," he said. "Why not?"

In the morning they hired a vessel in the harbor, a low sleek pirogue with a blood-red sail, skippered by a rascally-looking temporary whose smile was irresistible. Phillips shaded his eyes and peered northward across the sea. He thought he could almost make out the shape of the great city sprawling on its seven hills, Constantine's New Rome beside the Golden Horn, the mighty dome of Hagia Sophia, the somber walls of the citadel, the palaces and churches, the Hippodrome, Christ in glory rising above all else in brilliant mosaic streaming with light.

"Byzantium," Phillips said. "Take us there the shortest and quickest way."

"It is my pleasure," said the boatman with unexpected grace.

Gioia smiled. He had not seen her looking so vibrantly alive since the night of the imperial feast in Chang-an. He reached for her hand—her slender fingers were quivering lightly—and helped her into the boat.

surfacing

WALTER JON WILLIAMS

Walter Jon Williams was born in Minnesota and now lives in Albuquerque, New Mexico. His short fiction has appeared frequently in *Asimov's Science Fiction*, as well as in *The Magazine of Fantasy & Science Fiction*, *Wheel of Fortune*, *Global Dispatches*, *Alternate Outlaws*, and in other markets, and has been gathered in the collections *Facets* and *Frankensteins and Foreign Devils*. His novels include *Ambassador of Progress*, *Knight Moves*, *Hardwired*, *The Crown Jewels*, *Voice of the Whirlwind*, *House of Shards*, *Days of Atonement*, *Aristoi*, *Metropolitan*, *City on Fire*, a huge disaster thriller, *The Rift*, and a *Star Trek* novel, *Destiny's Way*. His most recent books are the first two novels in his acclaimed modern space opera epic, Dread Empire's Fall, *Dread Empire's Fall: The Praxis* and *Dread Empire's Fall: The Sundering*. Coming up are two new novels, *Orthodox War* and *Conventions of War*. He won a long-overdue Nebula Award in 2001 for his story "Daddy's World," and took another Nebula in 2005 with his story "The Green Leopard Plague."

In the vivid adventure that follows, he takes us sailing on mysterious alien seas in distant alien worlds, in search of elusive and dangerous prey.

T here was an alien on the surface of the planet. A Kyklops had teleported into Overlook Station, and then flown down on the shuttle. Since, unlike humans, it could teleport without apparatus, presumably it took the shuttle just for the ride. The Kyklops wore a human body, controlled through an *n*-dimensional interface, and took its pleasures in the human fashion.

The Kyklops expressed an interest in Anthony's work, but Anthony avoided it: he stayed at sea and listened to aliens of another kind.

Anthony wasn't interested in meeting aliens who knew more than he did.

The boat drifted in a cold current and listened to the cries of the sea. A tall grey swell was rolling in from the southwest, crossing with a wind-driven easterly chop. The boat tossed, caught in the confusion of wave patterns.

It was a sloppy ocean, somehow unsatisfactory. Marking a sloppy day.

Anthony felt a thing twist in his mind. Something that, in its own time, would lead to anger.

The boat had been out here, both in the warm current and then in the cold, for three days. Each more unsatisfactory than the last.

The growing swell was being driven toward land by a storm that was breaking up fifty miles out to sea: the remnants of the storm itself would arrive by midnight and make things even more unpleasant. Spray feathered across the tops of the waves. The day was growing cold.

Spindrift pattered across Anthony's shoulders. He ignored it, concentrated instead on the long, grating harmonic moan picked up by the microphones his boat dangled into the chill current. The moan ended on a series of clicks and trailed off. Anthony tapped his computer deck. A resolution appeared on the screen. Anthony shaded his eyes from the pale sun and looked at it.

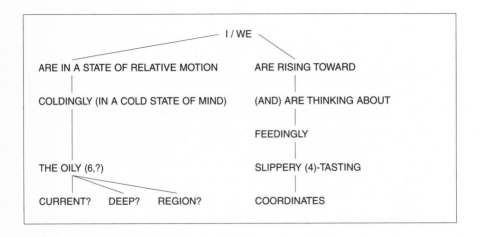

Anthony gazed stonily at the translation tree. "I am rising toward and thinking hungrily about the slippery-tasting coordinates" actually made the most objective sense, but the right-hand branch of the tree was the most literal and most of what Anthony suspected was context had been lost. "I and the oily current are in a state of motion toward one another" was perhaps more literal, but "We (the oily deep and I) are in a cold state of mind" was perhaps equally valid.

The boat gave a corkscrew lurch, dropped down the face of a swell, came to an abrupt halt at the end of its drogue. Water slapped against the stern. A mounting screw, come loose from a bracket on the bridge, fell and danced brightly across the deck.

The screw and the deck are in a state of relative motion, Anthony thought. The screw and the deck are in a motion state of mind.

Wrong, he thought, there is no Other in the Dwellers' speech.

We, I and the screw and the deck, are feeling cold.

We, I and the Dweller below, are in a state of mutual incomprehension.

A bad day, Anthony thought.

Inchoate anger burned deep inside him.

Anthony saved the translation and got up from his seat. He went to the bridge and told the boat to retrieve the drogue and head for Cabo Santa Pola at flank speed. He then went below and found a bottle of bourbon that had three good swallows left.

The trailing microphones continued to record the sonorous moans from below, the sound now mingled with the thrash of the boat's propellers.

The screw danced on the deck as the engines built up speed.

Its state of mind was not recorded.

The video news, displayed above the bar, showed the Kyklops making his tour of the planet. The Kyklops' human body, male, was tall and blue-eyed and elegant. He made witty conversation and showed off his naked chest as if he were proud of it. His name was Telamon.

His real body, Anthony knew, was a tenuous uncorporeal mass somewhere in n-dimensional space. The human body had been grown for it to wear, to move like a puppet. The nth dimension was interesting only to a mathematician: its inhabitants preferred wearing flesh.

Anthony asked the bartender to turn off the vid.

The yacht club bar was called the Leviathan, and Anthony hated the name. His creatures were too important, too much themselves, to be awarded a name that stank of human myth, of human resonance that had nothing to do with the creatures themselves. Anthony never called them Leviathans himself. They were Deep Dwellers.

There was a picture of a presumed Leviathan above the bar. Sometimes bits of matter were washed up on shore, thin tenuous membranes, long tentacles, bits of phosphorescence, all encrusted with the local equivalent of barnacles and infested with parasites. It was assumed the stuff had broken loose from the larger Dweller, or were bits of one that had died. The artist had done his best and painted something that looked like a whale covered with tentacles and seaweed.

The place had fake-nautical decor, nets, harpoons, flashing rods, and knicknacks made from driftwood, and the bar was regularly infected by tourists: that made it even worse. But the regular bartender and the divemaster and the steward were real sailors, and that made the yacht club bearable, gave him some company. His mail was delivered here as well.

Tonight the bartender was a substitute named Christopher: he was married to the owner's daughter and got his job that way. He was a fleshy, sullen man and no company.

We, thought Anthony, the world and I, are drinking alone. Anger burned in him, anger at the quality of the day and the opacity of the Dwellers and the storm that beat brainlessly at the windows.

"*Got* the bastard!" A man was pounding the bar. "Drinks on me." He was talking loudly, and he wore gold rings on his fingers. Raindrops sparkled in his hair. He wore a flashing harness, just in case anyone missed why he was here. Hatred settled in Anthony like poison in his belly.

"Got a thirty-foot flasher," the man said. He pounded the bar again. "Me and Nick got it hung up outside. Four hours. A four-hour fight!"

"Why have a fight with something you can't eat?" Anthony said.

The man looked at him. He looked maybe twenty, but Anthony could tell he was old, centuries old maybe. Old and vain and stupid, stupid as a boy. "It's a game fish," the man said.

Anthony looked into the fisherman's eyes and saw a reflection of his own contempt. "You wanna fight," he said, "you wanna have a *game*, fight something *smart*. Not a dumb animal that you can outsmart, that once you catch it will only rot and stink."

That was the start.

Once it began, it didn't take long. The man's rings cut Anthony's face, and Anthony was smaller and lighter, but the man telegraphed every move and kept leading with his right. When it was over, Anthony left him on the floor and stepped out into the downpour, stood alone in the hammering rain and let the water wash the blood from his face. The whiskey and the rage were a flame that licked his nerves and made them sing.

He began walking down the street. Heading for another bar.

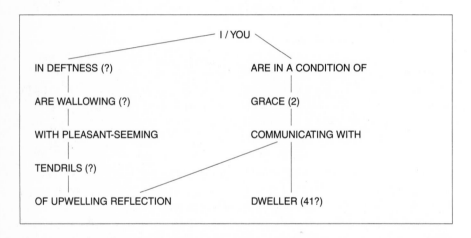

IN DEFTNESS (?)

ARE WALLOWING (?)

WITH PLEASANT-SEEMING

TENDRILS (?)

OF UPWELLING REFLECTION

I / YOU

ARE IN A CONDITION OF

GRACE (2)

COMMUNICATING WITH

DWELLER (41?)

GRACE(2) meant grace in the sense of physical grace, dexterity, harmony of motion, as opposed to spiritual grace, which was GRACE(1). The Dweller that Anthony was listening to was engaged in a dialogue with another, possibly the same known to the computer as 41, who might be named "Upwelling Reflection," but Deep Dweller naming systems seemed inconsistent, depending largely on a context that was as yet opaque, and "upwelling reflection" might have to do with something else entirely.

Anthony suspected the Dweller had just said hello.

Salt water smarted on the cuts on Anthony's face. His swollen knuckles pained him as he tapped the keys of his computer deck. He never suffered from hangover, and his mind seemed filled with an exemplary clarity; he worked rapidly, with burning efficiency. His body felt energized.

He was out of the cold Kirst Current today, in a warm, calm subtropical sea on the other side of the Las Madres archipelago. The difference of forty nautical miles was astonishing.

The sun warmed his back. Sweat prickled on his scalp. The sea sparkled under a violet sky.

The other Dweller answered.

Through his bare feet, Anthony could feel the subsonic overtones vibrating through the boat. Something in the cabin rattled. The microphones recorded the sounds, raised the subsonics to an audible level, played it back. The computer made its attempt.

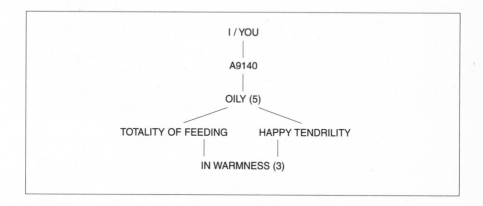

A9140 was a phrase that, as yet, had no translation.

The Dweller language, Anthony had discovered, had no separation of subject and object; it was a trait in common with the Earth cetaceans whose languages Anthony had first learned. "I swim toward the island" was not a grammatical possibility: "I and the island are in a condition of swimming toward one another" was the nearest possible approximation.

The Dwellers lived in darkness, and, like Earth's cetaceans, in a liquid medium. Perhaps they were psychologically unable to separate themselves from their environment, from their fluid surroundings. Never approaching the surface—it was presumed they could not survive in a nonpressurized environment—they had no idea of the upper limit of their world.

They were surrounded by a liquid three-dimensional wholeness, not an air-earth-sky environment from which they could consider themselves separate.

A high-pitched whooping came over the speakers, and Anthony smiled as he listened. The singer was one of the humpbacks that he had imported to this planet, a male called The One with Two Notches on His Starboard Fluke.

Two Notches was one of the brighter whales, and also the most playful. Anthony ordered his computer to translate the humpback speech.

Anthony, I and a place of bad smells have found one another, but this has not deterred our hunger.

The computer played back the message as it displayed the translation, and Anthony could understand more context from the sound of the original speech: that Two Notches was floating in a cold layer beneath the bad smell, and that the bad smell was methane or something like it—humans couldn't smell methane, but whales could. The overliteral translation was an aid only, to remind Anthony of idioms he might have forgotten.

Anthony's name in humpback was actually He Who Has Brought Us to the Sea of Rich Strangeness, but the computer translated it simply. Anthony tapped his reply.

What is it that stinks, Two Notches?

Some kind of horrid jellyfish. Were they-and-I feeding, they-and-I would spit one another out. I/They will give them/me a name: they/me are the jellyfish that smell like indigestion.

That is a good name, Two Notches.

I and a small boat discovered each other earlier today. We itched, so we scratched our back on the boat. The humans and I were startled. We had a good laugh together in spite of our hunger.

Meaning that Two Notches had risen under the boat, scratched his back on it, and terrified the passengers witless. Anthony remembered the first time this had happened to him back on Earth, a vast female humpback rising up without warning, one long scalloped fin breaking the water to port, the rest of the whale to starboard, thrashing in cetacean delight as it rubbed itself against a boat half its length. Anthony had clung to the gunwale, horrified by what the whale could do to his boat, but still exhilarated, delighted at the sight of the creature and its glorious joy.

Still, Two Notches ought not to play too many pranks on the tourists.

We should be careful, Two Notches. Not all humans possess our sense of humor, especially if they are hungry.

We were bored, Anthony. Mating is over, feeding has not begun. Also, it was Nick's boat that got scratched. In our opinion Nick and I enjoyed ourselves, even though we were hungry.

Hunger and food seemed to be the humpback subtheme of the day. Humpback songs, like the human, were made up of text and chorus, the chorus repeating itself, with variations, through the message.

I and Nick will ask each other and find out, as we feed.

Anthony tried to participate in the chorus/response about food, but he found himself continually frustrated at his clumsy phrasing. Fortunately the whales were tolerant of his efforts.

Have we learned anything about the ones that swim deep and do not breathe and feed on obscure things?

Not yet, Two Notches. Something has interrupted us in our hungry quest.

A condition of misfortune exists, like unto hunger. We must learn to be quicker.

We will try, Two Notches. After we eat.

We would like to speak to the Deep Dwellers now, and feed with them, but we must breathe.

We will speak to ourselves another time, after feeding.

We are in a condition of hunger, Anthony. We must eat soon.

We will remember our hunger and make plans.

The mating and calving season for the humpbacks was over. Most of the whales were already heading north to their summer feeding grounds, where they would do little but eat for six months. Two Notches and one of the other males had remained in the vicinity of Las Madres as a favor to Anthony, who used them to assist in locating the Deep Dwellers, but soon — in a matter of days — the pair would have to head north. They hadn't eaten anything for nearly half a year; Anthony didn't want to starve them.

But when the whales left, Anthony would be alone—again—with the Deep Dwellers. He didn't want to think about that.

The system's second sun winked across the waves, rising now. It was a white dwarf and emitted dangerous amounts of X-rays. The boat's falkner generator, triggered by the computer, snapped on a field that surrounded the boat and guarded it from energetic radiation. Anthony felt the warmth on his shoulders decrease. He turned his attention back to the Deep Dwellers.

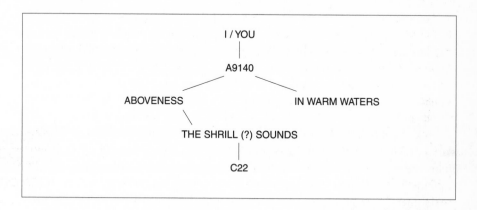

A blaze of delight rose in Anthony. The Dwellers, he realized, had overheard his conversation with Two Notches, and were commenting on it. Furthermore, he knew, A9140 probably was a verb form having to do with hearing—the Dwellers had a lot of them. "I/You hear the shrill sounds from above" might do as a working translation, and although he had no idea how to translate C22, he suspected it was a comment on the sounds. In a fever, Anthony began to work. As he bent over his keys he heard, through water and bone, the sound of Two Notches singing.

The Milky Way was a dim watercolor wash overhead. An odd twilight hung over Las Madres, a near-darkness that marked the hours when only the dwarf star was in the sky, providing little visible light but still pouring out X-rays. Cabo Santa Pola lay in a bright glowing crescent across the boat's path. Music drifted from a waterfront tavern, providing a counterpoint to the Deep Dweller speech that still rang in Anthony's head. A familiar figure waited on the dock, standing beneath the yellow lamp that marked Anthony's slip. Anthony waved and throttled the boat back.

A good day. Even after the yellow sun had set, Anthony still felt in a sunny mood. A9140 had been codified as "listen(14)," meaning listen solely in the sense of listening to a sound that originated from far outside the Dwellers' normal sphere—from outside their entire universe, in fact, which spoke volumes for the way the Dwellers saw themselves in relation to their world. They knew something else was up there, and their speech could make careful distinction between the world they knew and could perceive directly and the one they didn't. C22 was a descriptive term involving patterning: the Dwellers realized that the cetacean speech they'd been hearing wasn't simply random. Which spoke rather well for their cognition.

Anthony turned the boat and backed into the slip. Nick Kanellopoulos, whom the humpbacks called The One Who Chases Bad-Tasting Fish, took the sternline that Anthony threw him and tied it expertly to a cleat. Anthony shut off the engines, took a bowline, and hopped to the dock. He bent over the cleat and made his knot.

"You've gotta stop beating up my customers, Anthony," Nick said.

Anthony said nothing.

"You even send your damn whales to harass me."

Anthony jumped back into the boat and stepped into the cabin for a small canvas bag that held his gear and the data cubes containing the Dwellers' conversation. When he stepped back out of the cabin, he saw Nick standing on one foot, the other poised to step into the boat. Anthony gave Nick a look and Nick pulled his foot back. Anthony smiled. He didn't like people on his boat.

"Dinner?" he asked.

Nick gazed at him. A muscle moved in the man's cheek. He was dapper, olive-skinned, about a century old, the second-youngest human on the planet. He looked in his late teens. He wore a personal falkner generator on his belt that protected him from the dwarf's X-rays.

"Dinner. Fine." His brown eyes were concerned. "You look like hell, Anthony."

Anthony rubbed the stubble on his cheeks. "I feel on top of the world," he said.

"Half the time you don't even talk to me. I don't know why I'm eating supper with you."

"Let me clean up. Then we can go to the Villa Mary."

Nick shook his head. "Okay," he said. "But you're buying. You cost me a customer last night."

Anthony slapped him on the shoulder. "Least I can do, I guess."

A good day.

Near midnight. Winds beat at the island's old volcanic cone, pushed down the crowns of trees. A shuttle, black against the darkness of the sky, rose in absolute silence from the port on the other side of the island, heading toward the bright fixed star that was Overlook Station. The alien, Telamon, was aboard, or so the newscasts reported.

Deep Dwellers still sang in Anthony's head. Mail in hand, he let himself in through the marina gate and walked toward his slip. The smell of the sea rose around him. He stretched, yawned. Belched up a bit of the tequila he'd been drinking with Nick. He intended to get an early start and head back to sea before dawn.

Anthony paused beneath a light and opened the large envelope, pulled out page proofs that had been mailed, at a high cost, from the offices of the *Xenobiology Review* on Kemps. Discontent scratched at his nerves. He frowned as he glanced through the pages. He'd written the article over a year before, at the end of the first spring he'd spent here, and just glancing through it he now found the article over-tentative, overformal, and, worse, almost pleading in its attempt to justify his decision to move himself and the whales here. The palpable defensiveness made him want to squirm.

Disgust filled him. His fingers clutched at the pages, then tore the proofs across. His body spun full circle as he scaled the proofs out to the sea. The wind scattered thick chunks of paper across the dark waters of the marina.

He stalked toward his boat. Bile rose in his throat. He wished he had a bottle of tequila with him. He almost went back for one before he realized the liquor stores were closed.

"Anthony Maldalena?"

She was a little gawky, and her skin was pale. Dark hair in a single long braid, deep eyes, a bit of an overbite. She was waiting for him at the end of his slip, under the light. She had a bag over one shoulder.

Anthony stopped. Dull anger flickered in his belly. He didn't want anyone taking notice of the bruises and cuts on his face. He turned his head away as he stepped into his boat, dropped his bag on a seat.

"Mr. Maldalena. My name is Philana Telander. I came here to see you."

"How'd you get in?"

She gestured to the boat two slips down, a tall FPS-powered yacht shaped like a flat oval with a tall flybridge jutting from its center so that the pilot could see over wavetops. It would fly from place to place, but she could put it down in the water if she wanted. No doubt she'd bought a temporary membership at the yacht club.

"Nice boat," said Anthony. It would have cost her a fair bit to have it gated here. He opened the hatch to his forward cabin, tossed his bag onto the long couch inside.

"I meant," she said, "I came to this *planet* to see you."

Anthony didn't say anything, just straightened from his stoop by the hatch and looked at her. She shifted from one foot to another. Her skin was yellow in the light of the lamp. She reached into her bag and fumbled with something.

Anthony waited.

The clicks and sobs of whales sounded from the recorder in her hand.

"I wanted to show you what I've been able to do with your work. I have some articles coming up in *Cetology Journal* but they won't be out for a while."

"You've done very well," said Anthony. Tequila swirled in his head. He was having a hard time concentrating on a subject as difficult as whale speech.

Philana had specialized in communication with female humpbacks. It was harder to talk with the females: although they were curious and playful, they weren't vocal like the bulls; their language was deeper, briefer, more personal. They made no songs. It was almost as if, solely in the realm of speech, the cows were autistic. Their psychology was different and complicated, and Anthony had had little success in establishing any lasting communication. The cows, he had realized, were speaking a second tongue: the humpbacks were essentially bilingual, and Anthony had only learned one of their languages.

Philana had succeeded where Anthony had found only frustration. She had built from his work, established a structure and basis for communication. She still wasn't as easy in her speech with the cows as Anthony was with a bull like Two Notches, but she was far closer than Anthony had ever been.

Steam rose from the coffee cup in Philana's hand as she poured from Anthony's vacuum flask. She and Anthony sat on the cushioned benches in the stern of Anthony's boat. Tequila still buzzed in Anthony's head. Conflicting urges warred in him. He didn't want anyone else here, on his boat, this close to his work; but Philana's discoveries were too interesting to shut her out entirely. He swallowed more coffee.

"Listen to this," Philana said. "It's fascinating. A cow teaching her calf about life." She touched the recorder, and muttering filled the air. Anthony had difficulty understanding: the cow's idiom was complex, and bore none of the poetic repetition that made the males' language easier to follow. Finally he shook his head.

"Go ahead and turn it off," he said. "I'm picking up only one phrase in five. I can't follow it."

Philana seemed startled. "Oh. I'm sorry. I thought—"

Anthony twisted uncomfortably in his seat. "I don't know every goddamn thing about whales," he said.

The recorder fell silent. Wind rattled the canvas awning over the flybridge. Savage discontent settled into Anthony's mind. Suddenly he needed to get rid of this woman, get her off his boat and head to sea right now, away from all the things on land that could trip him up.

He thought of his father upside down in the smokehouse. Not moving, arms dangling.

He should apologize, he realized. We are, he thought, in a condition of permanent apology.

"I'm sorry," he said. "I'm just . . . not used to dealing with people."

"Sometimes I wonder," she said. "I'm only twenty-one, and . . ."

"Yes?" Blurted suddenly, the tequila talking. Anthony felt disgust at his own awkwardness.

Philana looked at the planks. "Yes. Truly. I'm twenty-one, and sometimes people get impatient with me for reasons I don't understand."

Anthony's voice was quiet. "I'm twenty-six."

Philana was surprised. "But. I thought." She thought for a long moment. "It seems I've been reading your papers for . . ."

"I was first published at twenty," he said. "The finback article."

Philana shook her head. "I'd never have guessed. Particularly after what I saw in your new XR paper."

Anthony's reaction was instant. "You saw that?" Another spasm of disgust touched him. Tequila burned in his veins. His stomach turned over. For some reason his arms were trembling.

"A friend on Kemps sent me an advance copy. I thought it was brilliant. The way you were able to codify your conceptions about a race of which you could really know nothing, and have it all pan out when you began to understand them. That's an incredible achievement."

"It's a piece of crap." Anthony wanted more tequila badly. His body was shaking. He tossed the remains of his coffee over his shoulder into the sea. "I've learned so much since. I've given up even trying to publish it. The delays are too long. Even if

I put it on the nets, I'd still have to take the time to write it, and I'd rather spend my time working."

"I'd like to see it."

He turned away from her. "I don't show my work till it's finished."

"I . . . didn't mean to intrude."

Apology. He could feel a knife twisting in his belly. He spoke quickly. "I'm sorry, Miss Telander. It's late, and I'm not used to company. I'm not entirely well." He stood, took her arm. Ignoring her surprise, he almost pulled her to her feet. "Maybe tomorrow. We'll talk again."

She blinked up at him. "Yes. I'd like that."

"Good night." He rushed her off the boat and stepped below to the head. He didn't want her to hear what was going to happen next. Acid rose in his throat. He clutched his middle and bent over the small toilet and let the spasms take him. The convulsions wracked him long after he was dry. After it was over he stood shakily, staggered to the sink, washed his face. His sinuses burned and brought tears to his eyes. He threw himself on the couch.

In the morning, before dawn, he cast off and motored out into the quiet sea.

The other male, The One Who Sings of Others, found a pair of Dwellers engaged in a long conversation and hovered above them. His transponder led Anthony to the place, fifty miles south into the bottomless tropical ocean. The Dwellers' conversation was dense. Anthony understood perhaps one word-phrase in ten. Sings of Others interrupted from time to time to tell Anthony how hungry he was.

The recordings would require days of work before Anthony could even begin to make sense of them. He wanted to stay on the site, but the Dwellers fell silent, neither Anthony nor Sings of Others could find another conversation, and Anthony was near out of supplies. He'd been working so intently he'd never got around to buying food.

The white dwarf had set by the time Anthony motored into harbor. Dweller mutterings did a chaotic dance in his mind. He felt a twist of annoyance at the sight of Philana Telander jumping from her big air yacht to the pier. She had obviously been waiting for him.

He threw her the bowline and she made fast. As he stepped onto the dock and fastened the sternline, he noticed sunburn reddening her cheeks. She'd spent the day on the ocean.

"Sorry I left so early," he said. "One of the humpbacks found some Dwellers, and their conversation sounded interesting."

She looked from Anthony to his boat and back. "That's all right," she said. "I shouldn't have talked to you last night. Not when you were ill."

Anger flickered in his mind. She'd heard him being sick, then.

"Too much to drink," he said. He jumped back into the boat and got his gear.

"Have you eaten?" she asked. "Somebody told me about a place called the Villa Mary."

He threw his bag over one shoulder. Dinner would be his penance. "I'll show you," he said.

"Mary was a woman who died," Anthony said. "One of the original Knight's Move people. She chose to die, refused the treatments. She didn't believe in living forever." He looked up at the arched ceiling, the moldings on walls and ceiling, the initials ML worked into the decoration. "Brian McGivern built this place in her memory," Anthony said. "He's built a lot of places like this, on different worlds."

Philana was looking at her plate. She nudged an ichthyoid exomembrane with her fork. "I know," she said. "I've been in a few of them."

Anthony reached for his glass, took a drink, then stopped himself from taking a second swallow. He realized that he'd drunk most of a bottle of wine. He didn't want a repetition of last night.

With an effort he put the glass down.

"She's someone I think about, sometimes," Philana said. "About the choice she made."

"Yes?" Anthony shook his head. "Not me. I don't want to spend a hundred years dying. If I ever decide to die, I'll do it quick."

"That's what people say. But they never do it. They just get older and older. Stranger and stranger." She raised her hands, made a gesture that took in the room, the decorations, the entire white building on its cliff overlooking the sea. "Get old enough, you start doing things like building Villa Marys all over the galaxy. McGivern's an oldest-generation immortal, you know. Maybe the wealthiest human anywhere, and he spends his time immortalizing someone who didn't want immortality of any kind."

Anthony laughed. "Sounds like you're thinking of becoming a Diehard."

She looked at him steadily. "Yes."

Anthony's laughter froze abruptly. A cool shock passed through him. He had never spoken to a Diehard before: the only ones he'd met were people who mumbled at him on street corners and passed out incoherent religious tracts.

Philana looked at her plate. "I'm sorry," she said.

"Why sorry?"

"I shouldn't have brought it up."

Anthony reached for his wine glass, stopped himself, put his hand down. "I'm curious."

She gave a little, apologetic laugh. "I may not go through with it."

"Why even think about it?"

Philana thought a long time before answering. "I've seen how the whales accept death. So graceful about it, so matter-of-fact—and they don't even have the myth of an afterlife to comfort them. If they get sick, they just beach themselves; and their friends try to keep them company. And when I try to give myself a reason for living beyond my natural span, I can't think of any. All I can think of is the whales."

Anthony saw the smokehouse in his mind, his father with his arms hanging, the fingers touching the dusty floor. "Death isn't nice."

Philana gave him a skeletal grin and took a quick drink of wine. "With any luck," she said, "death isn't anything at all."

Wind chilled the night, pouring upon the town through a slot in the island's volcanic cone. Anthony watched a streamlined head as it moved in the dark wind-
washed water of the marina. The head belonged to a cold-blooded amphibian
that lived in the warm surf of the Las Madres; the creature was known mislead-
ingly as a Las Madres seal. They had little fear of humanity and were curious
about the new arrivals. Anthony stamped a foot on the slip. Planks boomed. The
seal's head disappeared with a soft splash. Ripples spread in starlight, and Anthony smiled.

Philana had stepped into her yacht for a sweater. She returned, cast a glance at
the water, saw nothing.

"Can I listen to the Dwellers?" she asked. "I'd like to hear them."

Despite his resentment at her imposition, Anthony appreciated her being careful
with the term: she hadn't called them Leviathans once. He thought about her request, could think of no reason to refuse save his own stubborn reluctance. The
Dweller sounds were just background noise, meaningless to her. He stepped onto
his boat, took a cube from his pocket, put it in the trapdoor, pressed the PLAY button. Dweller murmurings filled the cockpit. Philana stepped from the dock to the
boat. She shivered in the wind. Her eyes were pools of dark wonder.

"So different."

"Are you surprised?"

"I suppose not."

"This isn't really what they sound like. What you're hearing is a computer-
generated metaphor for the real thing. Much of their communication is subsonic,
and the computer raises the sound to levels we can hear, and also speeds it up.
Sometimes the Dwellers take three or four minutes to speak what seems to be a
simple sentence."

"We would never have noticed them except for an accident," Philana said.
"That's how alien they are."

"Yes."

Humanity wouldn't know of the Dwellers' existence at all if it weren't for the subsonics confusing some automated sonar buoys, followed by an idiot computer assuming the sounds were deliberate interference and initiating an ET scan. Any
human would have looked at the data, concluded it was some kind of seismic interference, and programmed the buoys to ignore it.

"They've noticed *us*," Anthony said. "The other day I heard them discussing a
conversation I had with one of the humpbacks."

Philana straightened. Excitement was plain in her voice. "They can conceptualize something alien to them."

"Yes."

Her response was instant, stepping on the last sibilant of his answer. "And theo-
rize about our existence."

Anthony smiled at her eagerness. "I . . . don't think they've got around to that
yet."

"But they are intelligent."

"Yes."

"Maybe more intelligent than the whales. From what you say, they seem quicker to conceptualize."

"Intelligent in certain ways, perhaps. There's still very little I understand about them."

"Can you teach me to talk to them?"

The wind blew chill between them. "I don't," he said, "talk to them."

She seemed not to notice his change of mood, stepped closer. "You haven't tried that yet? That would seem to be reasonable, considering they've already noticed us."

He could feel his hackles rising, mental defenses sliding into place. "I'm not proficient enough," he said.

"If you could attract their attention, they could teach you." Reasonably.

"No. Not yet." Rage exploded in Anthony's mind. He wanted her off his boat, away from his work, his existence. He wanted to be alone again with his creatures, solitary witness to the lonely and wonderful interplay of alien minds.

"I never told you," Philana said, "why I'm here."

"No. You didn't."

"I want to do some work with the humpback cows."

"Why?"

Her eyes widened slightly. She had detected the hostility in his tone. "I want to chart any linguistic changes that may occur as a result of their move to another environment."

Through clouds of blinding resentment Anthony considered her plan. He couldn't stop her, he knew: anyone could talk to the whales if they knew how to do it. It might keep her away from the Dwellers. "Fine," he said. "Do it."

Her look was challenging. "I don't need your permission."

"I know that."

"You don't own them."

"I know that, too."

There was a splash far out in the marina. The Las Madres seal chasing a fish. Philana was still staring at him. He looked back.

"Why are you afraid of my getting close to the Dwellers?" she asked.

"You've been here two days. You don't know them. You're making all manner of assumptions about what they're like, and all you've read is one obsolete article."

"You're the expert. If my assumptions are wrong, you're free to tell me."

"Humans interacted with whales for centuries before they learned to speak with them, and even now the speech is limited and often confused. I've only been here two and a half years."

"Perhaps," she said, "you could use some help. Write those papers of yours. Publish the data."

He turned away. "I'm doing fine," he said.

"Glad to hear it." She took a long breath. "What did I do, Anthony? Tell me."

"Nothing," he said. Anthony watched the marina waters, saw the amphibian surface, its head pulled back to help slide a fish down its gullet. Philana was just standing there. We, thought Anthony, are in a condition of nonresolution.

"I work alone," he said. "I immerse myself in their speech, in their environment, for months at a time. Talking to a human breaks my concentration. I don't know *how* to talk to a person right now. After the Dwellers, you seem perfectly . . ."

"Alien?" she said. Anthony didn't answer. The amphibian slid through the water, its head leaving a short, silver wake.

The boat rocked as Philana stepped from it to the dock. "Maybe we can talk later," she said. "Exchange data or something."

"Yes," Anthony said. "We'll do that." His eyes were still on the seal.

Later, before he went to bed, he told the computer to play Dweller speech all night long.

Lying in his bunk the next morning, Anthony heard Philana cast off her yacht. He felt a compulsion to talk to her, apologize again, but in the end he stayed in his rack, tried to concentrate on Dweller sounds. I/We remain in a condition of solitude, he thought, the Dweller phrases coming easily to his mind. There was a brief shadow cast on the port beside him as the big flying boat rose into the sky, then nothing but sunlight and the slap of water on the pier supports. Anthony climbed out of his sleeping bag and went into town, provisioned the boat for a week. He had been too close to land for too long: a trip into the sea, surrounded by nothing but whales and Dweller speech, should cure him of his unease.

Two Notches had switched on his transponder: Anthony followed the beacon north, the boat rising easily over deep blue rollers. Desiring sun, Anthony climbed to the flybridge and lowered the canvas cover. Fifty miles north of Cabo Santa Pola there was a clear dividing line in the water, a line as clear as a meridian on a chart, beyond which the sea was a deeper, purer blue. The line marked the boundary of the cold Kirst current that had journeyed, wreathed in mist from contact with the warmer air, a full three thousand nautical miles from the region of the South Pole. Anthony crossed the line and rolled down his sleeves as the temperature of the air fell.

He heard the first whale speech through his microphones as he entered the cold current: the sound hadn't carried across the turbulent frontier of warm water and cold. The whales were unclear, distant and mixed with the sound of the screws, but he could tell from the rhythm that he was overhearing a dialogue. Apparently Sings of Others had joined Two Notches north of Las Madres. It was a long journey to make overnight, but not impossible.

The cooler air was invigorating. The boat plowed a straight, efficient wake through the deep blue sea. Anthony's spirits rose. This was where he belonged, away from the clutter and complication of humanity. Doing what he did best.

He heard something odd in the rhythm of the whale-speech; he frowned and listened more closely. One of the whales was Two Notches: Anthony recognized his speech patterns easily after all this time; but the other wasn't Sings of Others. There was a clumsiness in its pattern of chorus and response.

The other was a human. Annoyance hummed in Anthony's nerves. Back on Earth, tourists or eager amateur explorers sometimes bought cheap translation programs and tried to talk to the whales, but this was no tourist program: it was too eloquent, too knowing. Philana, of course. She'd followed the transponder signal and was busy gathering data about the humpback females. Anthony cut his engines and let the boat drift slowly to put its bow into the wind; he deployed the microphones from their wells in the hull and listened. The song was bouncing off a colder layer below, and it echoed confusingly.

Deep Swimmer and her calf, called The One That Nudges, are possessed of one another. I and that one am the father. We hunger for one another's presence.

Apparently hunger was once again the subtheme of the day. The context told Anthony that Two Notches was swimming in cool water beneath a boat. Anthony turned the volume up:

We hunger to hear of Deep Swimmer and our calf.

That was the human response: limited in its phrasing and context, direct and to the point.

I and Deep Swimmer are shy. We will not play with humans. Instead we will pretend we are hungry and vanish into deep waters.

The boat lurched as a swell caught it at an awkward angle. Water splashed over the bow. Anthony deployed the drogue and dropped from the flybridge to the cockpit. He tapped a message into the computer and relayed it.

I and Two Notches are pleased to greet ourselves. I and Two Notches hope we are not too hungry.

The whale's reply was shaded with delight. **Hungrily I and Anthony greet ourselves. We and Anthony's friend, Air Human, have been in a condition of conversation.**

Air Human, from the flying yacht. Two Notches went on.

We had found ourselves some Deep Dwellers, but some moments ago we and they moved beneath a cold layer and our conversation is lost. I starve for its return.

The words echoed off the cold layer that stood like a wall between Anthony and the Dwellers. The humpback inflections were steeped in annoyance.

Our hunger is unabated, Anthony typed. *But we will wait for the nonbreathers' return.*

We cannot wait long. Tonight we and the north must begin the journey to our feeding time.

The voice of Air Human rumbled through the water. It sounded like a distant, throbbing engine. *Our finest greetings, Anthony. I and Two Notches will travel north together. Then we and the others will feed.*

Annoyance slammed into Anthony. Philana had abducted his whale. Clenching his teeth, he typed a civil reply:

Please give our kindest greetings to our hungry brothers and sisters in the north.

By the time he transmitted his speech his anger had faded. Two Notches' departure was inevitable in the next few days, and he'd known that. Still, a residue of jealousy burned in him. Philana would have the whale's company on its journey north: he would be stuck here by Las Madres without the keen whale ears that helped him find the Dwellers.

Two Notches' reply came simultaneously with a programmed reply from Philana. Lyrics about greetings, hunger, feeding, calves, and joy whined through the water, bounced from the cold layer. Anthony looked at the hash his computer made of the translation and laughed. He decided he might as well enjoy Two Notches' company while it lasted.

That was a strange message to hear from our friend, Two Mouths, he typed. "Notch" and "mouth" were almost the same phrase: Anthony had just made a pun.

Whale amusement bubbled through the water. **Two Mouths and I belong to the most unusual family between surface and cold water. We-All and air breathe each other, but some of us have the bad fortune to live in it.**

The sun warmed Anthony's shoulders in spite of the cool air. He decided to leave off the pursuit of the Dwellers and spend the day with his humpback.

He kicked off his shoes, then stepped down to his cooler and made himself a sandwich.

The Dwellers never came out from beneath the cold layer. Anthony spent the afternoon listening to Two Notches tell stories about his family. Now that the issue of hunger was resolved by the whale's decision to migrate, the cold layer beneath them became the new topic of conversation, and Two Notches amused himself by harmonizing with his own echo. Sings of Others arrived in late afternoon and announced he had already begun his journey: he and Two Notches decided to travel in company.

Northward homing! Cold watering! Reunion joyous! The phrases dopplered closer to Anthony's boat, and then Two Notches broke the water thirty feet off the port beam, salt water pouring like Niagara from his black jaw, his scalloped fins spread like wings eager to take the air . . . Anthony's breath went out of him in surprise. He turned in his chair and leaned away from the sight, half in fear and half in awe . . . Even though he was used to the whales, the sight never failed to stun him, thrill him, freeze him in his tracks.

Two Notches toppled over backward, one clear brown eye fixed on Anthony. Anthony raised an arm and waved, and he thought he saw amusement in Two Notches' glance, perhaps the beginning of an answering wave in the gesture of a fin. A living creature the size of a bus, the whale struck the water not with a smack, but with a roar, a sustained outpour of thunder. Anthony braced himself for what was coming. Salt water flung itself over the gunwale, struck him like a blow. The cold was shocking: his heart lurched. The boat was flung high on the wave, dropped down its face with a jarring thud. Two Notches' flukes tossed high and Anthony could see the mottled pattern, grey and white, on the underside, distinctive as a fingerprint . . . and then the flukes were gone, leaving behind a rolling boat and a boiling sea.

Anthony wiped the ocean from his face, then from his computer. The boat's autobailing mechanism began to throb. Two Notches surfaced a hundred yards off, spouted a round cloud of steam, submerged again. The whale's amusement stung the water. Anthony's surprise turned to joy, and he echoed the sound of laughter.

I'm going to run my boat up your backside, Anthony promised; he splashed to the controls in his bare feet, withdrew the drogue and threw his engines into gear. Props thrashed the sea into foam. Anthony drew the microphones up into their wells, heard them thud along the hull as the boat gained way. Humpbacks usually took breath in a series of three: Anthony aimed ahead for Two Notches' second rising. Two Notches rose just ahead, spouted, and dove before Anthony could catch him. A cold wind cut through Anthony's wet shirt, raised bumps on his flesh. The boat increased speed, tossing its head on the face of a wave, and Anthony raced ahead, aiming for where Two Notches would rise for the third time.

The whale knew where the boat was and was able to avoid him easily; there was no danger in the game. Anthony won the race: Two Notches surfaced just aft of the boat, and Anthony grinned as he gunned his propellers and wrenched the rudder from side to side while the boat spewed foam into the whale's face. Two Notches gave a grunt of disappointment and sounded, tossing his flukes high. Unless he chose to rise early, Two Notches would be down for five minutes or more. Anthony raced the boat in circles, waiting. Two Notches' taunts rose in the cool water. The wind was cutting Anthony to the quick. He reached into the cabin for a sweater, pulled it on, ran up to the flybridge just in time to see Two Notches leap again half a mile away, the vast dark body silhouetted for a moment against the setting sun before it fell again into the welcoming sea.

Goodbye, goodbye. I and Anthony send fragrant farewells to one another.

White foam surrounded the slick, still place where Two Notches had fallen into the water. Suddenly the flybridge was very cold. Anthony's heart sank. He cut speed and put the wheel amidships. The boat slowed reluctantly, as if it, too, had been enjoying the game. Anthony dropped down the ladder to his computer.

Through the spattered windscreen, Anthony could see Two Notches leaping again, his long wings beating air, his silhouette refracted through seawater and rainbows. Anthony tried to share the whale's exuberance, his joy, but the thought of another long summer alone on his boat, beating his head against the enigma of the Dwellers, turned his mind to ice.

He ordered an infinite repeat of Two Notches' last phrase and stepped below to change into dry clothes. The cold layer echoed his farewells. He bent almost double and began pulling the sweater over his head.

Suddenly he straightened. An idea was chattering at him. He yanked the sweater back down over his trunk, rushed to his computer, tapped another message.

Our farewells need not be said just yet. You and I can follow one another for a few days before I must return. Perhaps you and the nonbreathers can find one another for conversation.

Anthony is in a condition of migration. Welcome, welcome. Two Notches' reply was jubilant.

For a few days, Anthony qualified. Before too long he would have to return to port for supplies, Annoyed at himself, he realized he could as easily have victualed for weeks.

Another voice called through the water, sounded faintly through the speakers. *Air Human and Anthony are in a state of tastiest welcome.*

In the middle of Anthony's reply, his fingers paused at the keys. Surprise rose quietly to the surface of his mind.

After the long day of talking in humpback speech, he had forgotten that Air Human was not a humpback. That she was, in fact, another human being sitting on a boat just over the horizon.

Anthony continued his message. His fingers were clumsy now, and he had to go back twice to correct mistakes. He wondered why it was harder to talk to Philana, now that he remembered she wasn't an alien.

He asked Two Notches to turn on his transponder, and, all through the deep shadow twilight when the white dwarf was in the sky, the boat followed the whale at a half-mile's distance. The current was cooperative, but in a few days a new set of north-west trade winds would push the current off on a curve toward the equator and the whales would lose its assistance.

Anthony didn't see Philana's boat that first day: just before dawn, Sings of Others heard a distant Dweller conversation to starboard. Anthony told his boat to strike off in that direction and spent most of the day listening. When the Dwellers fell silent, he headed for the whales' transponders again. There was a lively conversation in progress between Air Human and the whales, but Anthony's mind was still on Dwellers. He put on headphones and worked far into the night.

The next morning was filled with chill mist. Anthony awoke to the whooping cries of the humpbacks. He looked at his computer to see if it had recorded any announcement of Dwellers, and there was none. The whales' interrogation by Air Human continued. Anthony's toes curled on the cold, damp planks as he stepped on deck and saw Philana's yacht two hundred yards to port, floating three feet over the tallest swells. Cables trailed from the stern, pulling hydrophones and speakers on a subaquatic sled. Anthony grinned at the sight of the elaborate store-bought rig. He suspected that he got better acoustics with his homebuilt equipment, the translation softwear he'd programmed himself, and his hopelessly old-fashioned boat that couldn't even rise out of the water, but that he'd equipped with the latest-generation silent propellers.

He turned on his hydrophones. Sure enough, he got more audio interference from Philana's sled than he received from his entire boat.

While making coffee and an omelette of mossmoon eggs Anthony listened to the whales gurgle about their grandparents. He put on a down jacket and stepped onto the boat's stern and ate breakfast, watching the humpbacks as they occasionally broke surface, puffed out clouds of spray, sounded again with a careless, vast toss of their flukes. Their bodies were smooth and black: the barnacles that pebbled their skin on Earth had been removed before they gated to their new home.

Their song could be heard clearly even without the amplifiers. That was one change the contact with humans had brought: the males were a lot more vocal than once they had been, as if they were responding to human encouragement—or perhaps they now had more worth talking about. Their speech was also more terse than before, less overtly poetic; the humans' directness and compactness of speech, caused mainly by their lack of fluency, had influenced the whales to a degree.

The whales were adapting to communication with humans more easily than the humans were adapting to them. It was important to chart that change, be able to say how the whales had evolved, accommodated. They were on an entire new planet now, explorers, and the change was going to come fast. The whales were good at remembering, but artificial intelligences were better. Anthony was suddenly glad that Philana was here, doing her work.

As if on cue she appeared on deck, one hand pressed to her head, holding an earphone: she was listening intently to whalesong. She was bundled up against the chill, and gave a brief wave as she noticed him. Anthony waved back. She paused, beating time with one hand to the rhythm of whalespeech, then waved again and stepped back to her work.

Anthony finished breakfast and cleaned the dishes. He decided to say good morning to the whales, then work on some of the Dweller speech he'd recorded the day before. He turned on his computer, sat down at the console, typed his greetings. He waited for a pause in the conversation, then transmitted. The answer came back sounding like a distant buzzsaw.

We and Anthony wish one another a passage filled with splendid odors. We and Air Human have been scenting one another's families this morning.

We wish each other the joy of converse, Anthony typed.

We have been wondering. Two Notches said, **if we can scent whether we and Anthony and Air Human are in a condition of rut.**

Anthony gave a laugh. Humpbacks enjoyed trying to figure out human relationships: they were promiscuous themselves, and intrigued by ways different from their own.

Anthony wondered, sitting in his cockpit, if Philana was looking at him.

Air Human and I smell of aloneness, unpairness, he typed, and he transmitted the message at the same time that Philana entered the even more direct, *We are not.*

The state is not rut, apartness is the smell, Two Notches agreed readily — it was all one to him — and the lyrics echoed each other for a long moment, *aloneness, not, unpairness, not. Not.* Anthony felt a chill.

I and the Dwellers' speech are going to try to scent one another's natures, he typed hastily, and turned off the speakers. He opened his case and took out one of the cubes he'd recorded the day before.

Work went slowly.

By noon the mist had burned off the water. His head buzzing with Dweller sounds, Anthony stepped below for a sandwich. The message light was blinking on his telephone. He turned to it, pressed the play button.

"May I speak with you briefly?" Philana's voice. "I'd like to get some data, at your convenience." Her tone shifted to one of amusement. "The condition," she added, "is not that of rut."

Anthony grinned. Philana had been considerate enough not to interrupt him, just to leave the message for whenever he wanted it. He picked up the telephone, connected directory assistance in Cabo Santa Pola, and asked it to route a call to the phone on Philana's yacht. She answered.

"Message received," he said. "Would you join me for lunch?"

"In an hour or so," she said. Her voice was abstracted. "I'm in the middle of something."

"When you're ready. Bye." He rang off, decided to make a fish chowder instead of sandwiches, and drank a beer while preparing it. He began to feel buoyant, cheerful. Siren wailing sounded through the water.

Philana's yacht maneuvered over to his boat just as Anthony finished his second beer. Philana stood on the gunwale, wearing a pale sweater with brown zigzags on it. Her braid was undone, and her brown hair fell around her shoulders. She jumped easily from her gunwale to the flybridge, then came down the ladder. The yacht moved away as soon as it felt her weight leave. She smiled uncertainly as she stepped to the deck.

"I'm sorry to have to bother you," she said.

He offered a grin. "That's okay. I'm between projects right now."

She looked toward the cabin. "Lunch smells good." Perhaps, he thought, food equaled apology.

"Fish chowder. Would you like a beer? Coffee?"

"Beer. Thanks."

They stepped below and Anthony served lunch on the small foldout table. He opened another beer and put it by her place.

"Delicious. I never really learned to cook."

"Cooking was something I learned young."

Her eyes were curious. "Where was that?"

"Lees." Shortly. He put a spoonful of chowder in his mouth so that his terseness would be more understandable.

"I never heard the name."

"It's a planet." Mumbling through chowder. "Pretty obscure." He didn't want to talk about it.

"I'm from Earth."

He looked at her. "Really? Originally? Not just a habitat in the Sol system?"

"Yes. Truly. One of the few. The one and only Earth."

"Is that what got you interested in whales?"

"I've *always* been interested in whales. As far back as I can remember. Long before I ever saw one."

"It was the same with me. I grew up near an ocean, built a boat when I was a boy and went exploring. I've never felt more at home than when I'm on the ocean."

"Some people live on the sea all the time."

"In floating habitats. That's just moving a city out onto the ocean. The worst of both worlds, if you ask me."

He realized the beer was making him expansive, that he was declaiming and waving his free hand. He pulled his hand in.

"I'm sorry," he said, "about the last time we talked."

She looked away. "My fault," she said. "I shouldn't have—"

"You didn't do anything wrong." He realized he had almost shouted that, and could feel himself flushing. He lowered his voice. "Once I got out here I realized . . ." This was really hopeless. He plunged on. "I'm not used to dealing with people. There were just a few people on Lees and they were all . . . eccentric. And everyone I've met since I left seems at least five hundred years old. Their attitudes are so . . ." He shrugged.

"Alien." She was grinning.

"Yes."

"I feel the same way. Everyone's so much older, so much more . . . sophisticated, I suppose." She thought about it for a moment. "I *guess* it's sophistication."

"*They* like to think so."

"I can feel their pity sometimes." She toyed with her spoon, looked down at her bowl.

"And condescension." Bitterness striped Anthony's tongue. "The attitude of, oh, we went through that once, poor darling, but now we know better."

"Yes." Tiredly. "I know what you mean. Like we're not really people yet."

"At least my father wasn't like that. He was crazy, but he let me be a person. He—"

His tongue stumbled. He was not drunk enough to tell this story, and he didn't think he wanted to anyway.

"Go ahead," said Philana. She was collecting data, Anthony remembered, on families.

He pushed back from the table, went to the fridge for another beer. "Maybe later," he said. "It's a long story."

Philana's look was steady. "You're not the only one who knows about crazy fathers."

Then you tell me about yours, he wanted to say. Anthony opened the beer, took a deep swallow. The liquid rose again, acid in his throat, and he forced it down. Memories rose with the fire in Anthony's throat, burning him. His father's fine madness whirled in his mind like leaves in a hurricane. We are, he thought, in a condition of mutual distrust and permanent antagonism. Something therefore must be done.

"All right." He put the beer on the top of the fridge and returned to his seat. He spoke rapidly, just letting the story come. His throat burned. "My father started life with money. He became a psychologist and then a fundamentalist Catholic lay preacher, kind of an unlicensed messiah. He ended up a psychotic. Dad concluded that civilization was too stupid and corrupt to survive, and he decided to start over. He initiated an unauthorized planetary scan through a transporter gate, found a world that he liked, and moved his family there. There were just four of us at the time, dad and my mother, my little brother, and me. My mother was—is—she's not really her own person. There's a vacancy there. If you're around psychotics a lot, and you don't have a strong sense of self, you can get submerged in their delusions. My mother didn't have a chance of standing up to a full-blooded lunatic like my dad, and I doubt she tried. She just let him run things.

"I was six when we moved to Lees, and my brother was two. We were—" Anthony waved an arm in the general direction of the invisible Milky Way overhead. "—we were half the galaxy away. Clean on the other side of the hub. We didn't take a gate with us, or even instructions and equipment for building one. My father cut us off entirely from everything he hated."

Anthony looked at Philana's shocked face and laughed. "It wasn't so bad. We had everything but a way off the planet. Cube readers, building supplies, preserved food, tools, medical gear, wind and solar generators—Dad thought falkner generators were the cause of the rot, so he didn't bring any with him. My mother pretty much stayed pregnant for the next decade, but luckily the planet was benign. We settled down in a protected bay where there was a lot of food, both on land and in the water. We had a smokehouse to preserve the meat. My father and mother educated me pretty well. I grew up an aquatic animal. Built a sailboat, learned how to navigate. By the time I was fifteen I had charted two thousand miles of coast. I spent more than half my time at sea, the last few years. Trying to get away from my dad, mostly. He kept getting stranger. He promised me in marriage to my oldest sister after my eighteenth birthday." Memory swelled in Anthony like a tide, calm green water rising over the flat, soon to whiten and boil.

"There were some whale-sized fish on Lees, but they weren't intelligent. I'd seen recordings of whales, heard the sounds they made. On my long trips I'd imagine I was seeing whales, imagine myself talking to them."

"How did you get away?"

Anthony barked a laugh. "My dad wasn't the only one who could initiate a planetary scan. Seven or eight years after we landed some resort developers found our planet and put up a hotel about two hundred miles to the south of our settlement." Anthony shook his head. "Hell of a coincidence. The odds against it must have been incredible. My father frothed at the mouth when we started seeing their flyers and boats. My father decided our little settlement was too exposed and we moved farther inland to a place where we could hide better. Everything was camouflaged. He'd hold drills in which we were all supposed to grab necessary supplies and run off into the forest."

"They never found you?"

"If they saw us, they thought we were people on holiday."

"Did you approach them?"

Anthony shook his head. "No. I don't really know why."

"Well. Your father."

"I didn't care much about his opinions by that point. It was so *obvious* he was cracked. I think, by then, I had all I wanted just living on my boat. I didn't see any reason to change it." He thought for a moment. "If he actually tried to marry me off to my sister, maybe I would have run for it."

"But they found you anyway."

"No. Something else happened. The water supply for the new settlement was unreliable, so we decided to build a viaduct from a spring nearby. We had to get our hollow-log pipe over a little chasm, and my father got careless and had an accident. The viaduct fell on him. Really smashed him up, caused all sorts of internal injuries. It was very obvious that if he didn't get help, he'd die. My mother and I took my boat and sailed for the resort."

The words dried up. This was where things got ugly. Anthony decided he really couldn't trust Philana with it, and that he wanted his beer after all. He got up and took the bottle and drank.

"Did your father live?"

"No." He'd keep this as brief as he could. "When my mother and I got back, we found that he'd died two days before. My brothers and sisters gutted him and hung him upside down in the smokehouse." He stared dully into Philana's horrified face. "It's what they did to any large animal. My mother and I were the only ones who remembered what to do with a dead person, and we weren't there."

"My God. Anthony." Her hands clasped below her face.

"And then—" He waved his hands, taking in everything, the boat's comforts, Overlook, life over the horizon. "Civilization. I was the only one of the children who could remember anything but Lees. I got off the planet and got into marine biology. That's been my life ever since. I was amazed to discover that I and the family were rich—my dad didn't tell me he'd left tons of investments behind. The rest of the family's still on Lees, still living in the old settlement. It's all they know." He shrugged. "They're rich, too, of course, which helps. So they're all right."

He leaned back on the fridge and took another long drink. The ocean swell tilted the boat and rolled the liquid down his throat. Whale harmonics made the bottle cap dance on the smooth alloy surface of the refrigerator.

Philana stood. Her words seemed small after the long silence. "Can I have some coffee? I'll make it."

"I'll do it."

They both went for the coffee and banged heads. Reeling back, the expression on Philana's face was wide-eyed, startled, fawnlike, as if he'd caught her at something she should be ashamed of. Anthony tried to laugh out an apology, but just then the white dwarf came up above the horizon and the quality of light changed as the screens went up, and with the light her look somehow changed. Anthony gazed at her for a moment and fire began to lap at his nerves. In his head the whales seemed to urge him to make his move.

He put his beer down and grabbed her with an intensity that was made ferocious largely by Anthony's fear that this was entirely the wrong thing, that he was committing an outrage that would compel her shortly to clout him over the head with the coffee pot and drop him in his tracks. Whalesong rang frantic chimes in his head. She gave a strangled cry as he tried to kiss her and thereby confirmed his own worst suspicions about this behavior.

Philana tried to push him away. He let go of her and stepped back, standing stupidly with his hands at his sides. A raging pain in his chest prevented him from saying a word. Philana surprised him by stepping forward and putting her hands on his shoulders.

"Easy," she said. "It's all right, just take it easy."

Anthony kissed her once more, and was somehow able to restrain himself from grabbing her again out of sheer panic and desperation. By and by, as the kiss continued, his anxiety level decreased. I/You, he thought, are rising in warmness, in happy tendrils.

He and Philana began to take their clothes off. He realized this was the first time he had made love to anyone under two hundred years of age.

Dweller sounds murmured in Anthony's mind. He descended into Philana as if she were a midnight ocean, something that on first contact with his flesh shocked him into wakefulness, then relaxed around him, became a taste of brine, a sting in the eyes, a fluid vagueness. Her hair brushed against his skin like seagrass. She surrounded him, buoyed him up. Her cries came up to him as over a great distance, like the faraway moans of a lonely whale in love. He wanted to call out in answer. Eventually he did.

Grace (1), he thought hopefully. Grace(1).

Anthony had an attack of giddiness after Philana returned to her flying yacht and her work. His mad father gibbered in his memory, mocked him and offered dire warnings. He washed the dishes and cleaned the rattling bottle cap off the fridge, then he listened to recordings of Dwellers and eventually the panic went away. He had not, it seemed, lost anything.

He went to the double bed in the forepeak, which was piled high with boxes of food, a spool of cable, a couple spare microphones, and a pair of rusting Danforth anchors. He stowed the food in the hold, put the electronics in the compartment under the mattress, jammed the Danforths farther into the peak on top of the anchor chain where they belonged. He wiped the grime and rust off the mattress and realized he had neither sheets nor a second pillow. He would need to purchase supplies on the next trip to town.

The peak didn't smell good. He opened the forehatch and tried to air the place out. Slowly he became aware that the whales were trying to talk to him. **Odd scentings,** they said, **Things that stand in water**. Anthony knew what they meant. He went up on the flybridge and scanned the horizon. He saw nothing.

The taste is distant, he wrote. *But we must be careful in our movement.* After that he scanned the horizon every half hour.

He cooked supper during the white dwarf's odd half-twilight and resisted the urge to drink both the bottles of bourbon that were waiting in their rack. Philana dropped onto the flybridge with a small rucksack. She kissed him hastily, as if to get it over with.

"I'm scared," she said.

"So am I."

"I don't know why."

He kissed her again. "I do," he said. She laid her cheek against his woolen shoulder. Blind with terror, Anthony held on to her, unable to see the future.

After midnight Anthony stood unclothed on the flybridge as he scanned the horizon one more time. Seeing nothing, he nevertheless reduced speed to three knots and rejoined Philana in the forepeak. She was already asleep with his open sleeping bag thrown over her like a blanket. He raised a corner of the sleeping bag and slipped beneath it. Philana turned away from him and pillowed her cheek on her fist. Whale music echoed from a cold layer beneath. He slept.

Movement elsewhere in the boat woke him. Anthony found himself alone in the peak, frigid air drifting over him from the forward hatch. He stepped into the cabin and saw Philana's bare legs ascending the companion to the fly-bridge. He followed. He shivered in the cold wind.

Philana stood before the controls, looking at them with a peculiar intensity, as though she were trying to figure out which switch to throw. Her hands flexed as if to take the wheel. There was gooseflesh on her shoulders and the wind tore her hair around her face like a fluttering curtain. She looked at him. Her eyes were hard, her voice disdainful.

"Are we lovers?" she asked. "Is that what's going on here?" His skin prickled at her tone.

Her stiff-spined stance challenged him. He was afraid to touch her.

"The condition is that of rut," he said, and tried to laugh.

Her posture, one leg cocked out front, reminded him of a haughty water bird. She looked at the controls again, then looked aft, lifting up on her toes to gaze at the horizon. Her nostrils flared, tasted the wind. Clouds scudded across the sky. She looked at him again. The white dwarf gleamed off her pebble eyes.

"Very well," she said, as if this was news. "Acceptable." She took his hand and led him below. Anthony's hackles rose. On her way to the forepeak Philana saw one of the bottles of bourbon in its rack and reached for it. She raised the bottle to her lips and drank from the neck. Whiskey coursed down her throat. She lowered the bottle and wiped her mouth with the back of her hand. She looked at him as if he were something worthy of dissection.

"Let's make love," she said.

Anthony was afraid not to. He went with her to the forepeak. Her skin was cold. Lying next to him on the mattress she touched his chest as if she were unused to the feel of male bodies. "What's your name?" she asked. He told her. "Acceptable," she said again, and with a sudden taut grin raked his chest with her nails. He knocked her hands away. She laughed and came after him with the bottle. He parried the blow in time and they wrestled for possession, bourbon splashing everywhere. Anthony was surprised at her strength. She fastened teeth in his arm. He hit her in the face with a closed fist. She gave the bottle up and laughed in a cold metallic way and put her arms around him. Anthony threw the bottle through the door into the cabin. It thudded somewhere but didn't break. Philana drew him on top of her, her laugh brittle, her legs opening around him.

Her dead eyes were like stones.

In the morning Anthony found the bottle lying in the main cabin. Red clawmarks covered his body, and the reek of liquor caught at the back of his throat. The scend of the ocean had distributed the bourbon puddle evenly over the teak deck. There was still about a third of the whiskey left in the bottle. Anthony rescued it and swabbed the deck. His mind was full of cotton wool, cushioning any bruises. He was working hard at not feeling anything at all.

He put on clothes and began to work. After a while Philana unsteadily groped her way from the forepeak, the sleeping bag draped around her shoulders. There was a stunned look on her face and a livid bruise on one cheek. Anthony could feel his body tautening, ready to repel assault.

"Was I odd last night?" she asked.

He looked at her. Her face crumbled. "Oh no." She passed a hand over her eyes and turned away, leaning on the side of the hatchway. "You shouldn't let me drink," she said.

"You hadn't made that fact clear."

"I don't remember any of it," she said. "I'm sick." She pressed her stomach with her hands and bent over. Anthony narrowly watched her pale buttocks as she groped her way to the head. The door shut behind her.

Anthony decided to make coffee. As the scent of the coffee began to fill the boat, he heard the sounds of her weeping. The long keening sounds, desperate throat-tearing noises, sounded like a pinioned whale writhing helplessly on the gaff.

A vast flock of birds wheeled on the cold horizon, marking a colony of drift creatures. Anthony informed the whales of the creatures' presence, but the humpbacks already knew and were staying well clear. The drift colony was what they had been smelling for hours.

While Anthony talked with the whales, Philana left the head and drew on her clothes. Her movements were tentative. She approached him with a cup of coffee in her hand. Her eyes and nostrils were rimmed with red.

"I'm sorry," she said. "Sometimes that happens."

He looked at his computer console. "Jesus, Philana."

"It's something wrong with me. I can't control it." She raised a hand to her bruised cheek. The hand came away wet.

"There's medication for that sort of thing," Anthony said. He remembered she had a mad father, or thought she did.

"Not for this. It's something different."

"I don't know what to do."

"I need your help."

Anthony recalled his father's body twisting on the end of its rope, fingertips trailing in the dust. Words came reluctantly to his throat.

"I'll give what help I can." The words were hollow: any real resolution had long since gone. He had no clear notion to whom he was giving this message, the Philana of the previous night or this Philana or his father or himself.

Philana hugged him, kissed his cheek. She was excited.

"Shall we go see the drifters?" she asked. "We can take my boat."

Anthony envisioned himself and Philana tumbling through space. He had jumped off a precipice, just now. The two children of mad fathers were spinning in the updraft, waiting for the impact.

He said yes. He ordered his boat to circle while she summoned her yacht. She held his hand while they waited for the flying yacht to drift toward them. Philana kept laughing, touching him, stropping her cheek on his shoulder like a cat. They jumped from the flybridge to her yacht and rose smoothly into the sky. Bright sun warmed Anthony's shoulders. He took off his sweater and felt warning pain from the marks of her nails.

The drifters were colony creatures that looked like miniature mountains twenty feet or so high, complete with a white snowcap of guano. They were highly organized but unintelligent, their underwater parts sifting the ocean for nutrients or reaching out to capture prey—the longest of their gossamer stinging tentacles was up to two miles in length, and though they couldn't kill or capture a humpback, they were hard for the whale to detect and could cause a lot of stinging wounds be-fore the whale noticed them and made its escape. Perhaps they were unintelligent, distant relatives of the Deep Dwellers, whose tenuous character they resembled. Many different species of sea birds lived in permanent colonies atop the floating is-lands, thousands of them, and the drifters processed their guano and other waste. Above the water, the drifters' bodies were shaped like a convex lens set on edge, an aerodynamic shape, and they could clumsily tack into the wind if they needed to. For the most part, however, they drifted on the currents, a giant circular circumnav-igation of the ocean that could take centuries.

Screaming sea birds rose in clouds as Philana's yacht moved silently toward their homes. Philana cocked her head back, laughed into the open sky, and flew closer. Birds hurtled around them in an overwhelming roar of wings. Whistlelike cries is-sued from peg-toothed beaks. Anthony watched in awe at the profusion of colors, the chromatic brilliance of the evolved featherlike scales.

The flying boat passed slowly through the drifter colony. Birds roared and whis-tled, some of them landing on the boat in apparent hopes of taking up lodging: Feathers drifted down; birdshit spattered the windscreen. Philana ran below for a camera and used up several data cubes taking pictures. A trickle of optimism began to ease into Anthony at the sight of Philana in the bright morning sun, a broad smile gracing her face as she worked the camera and took picture after picture. He put an arm around Philana's waist and kissed her ear. She smiled and took his hand in her own. In the bright daylight the personality she'd acquired the previous night seemed to gather unto itself the tenebrous, unreal quality of a nightmare. The current Phi-lana seemed far more tangible.

Philana returned to the controls; the yacht banked and increased speed. Birds is-sued startled cries as they got out of the way. Wind tugged at Philana's hair. Anthony decided not to let Philana near his liquor again.

After breakfast, Anthony found both whales had set their transponders. He had to detour around the drifters—their insubstantial, featherlike tentacles could foul his state-of-the-art silent props—but when he neared the whales and slowed, he could hear the deep murmurings of Dwellers rising from beneath the cold current. There were half a dozen of them engaged in conversation, and Anthony worked the day and far into the night, transcribing, making hesitant attempts at translation. The Dweller speech was more opaque than usual, depending on a context that was un-stated and elusive. Comprehension eluded Anthony; but he had the feeling that the key was within his reach.

Philana waited for the Dwellers to end their converse before she brought her yacht near him. She had heated some prepared dinners and carried them to the fly-bridge in an insulated pouch. Her grin was broad. She put her pouch down and em-braced him. Abstracted Dweller subsonics rolled away from Anthony's mind. He was surprised at how glad he was to see her.

With dinner they drank coffee. Philana chattered bravely throughout the meal. While Anthony cleaned the dishes, she embraced him from behind. A memory of the other Philana flickered in his mind, disdainful, contemptuous, cold. Her father was crazy, he remembered again.

He buried the memory deliberately and turned to her. He kissed her and thought, I/We deny the Other. The Other, he decided, would cease to exist by a common act of will.

It seemed to work. At night his dreams filled with Dwellers crying in joy, his father warning darkly, the touch of Philana's flesh, breath, hands. He awoke hungry to get to work.

The next two days a furious blaze of concentration burned in Anthony's mind. Things fell into place. He found a word that, in its context, could mean nothing but light, as opposed to fluorescence—he was excited to find out the Dwellers knew about the sun. He also found new words for darkness, for emotions that seemed to have no human equivalents, but which he seemed nevertheless to comprehend. One afternoon a squall dumped a gallon of cold water down his collar and he looked up in surprise: he hadn't been aware of its slow approach. He moved his computer deck to the cabin and kept working. When not at the controls he moved dazedly over the boat, drinking coffee, eating what was at hand without tasting it. Philana was amused and tolerant; she buried herself in her own work.

On preparing breakfast the morning of the third day, Anthony realized he was running out of food. He was farther from the archipelago than he'd planned on going, and he had about two days' supply left; he'd have to return at flank speed, buy provisions, and then run out again. A sudden hot fury gripped him. He clenched his fists. He could have provisioned for two or three months—why hadn't he done it when he had the chance?

Philana tolerantly sipped her coffee. "Tonight I'll fly you into Cabo Santa Pola. We can buy a ton of provisions, have dinner at Villa Mary, and be back by midnight."

Anthony's anger floundered uselessly, looking for a target, then gave up. "Fine," he said.

She looked at him. "Are you ever going to talk to them? You must have built your speakers to handle it."

Now the anger had finally found a home. "Not yet," he said.

In late afternoon, Anthony set out his drogue and a homing transponder, then boarded Philana's yacht. He watched while she hauled up her aquasled and programmed the navigation computer. The world dimmed as the falkner field increased in strength. The transition to full speed was almost instantaneous. Waves blurred silently past, providing the only sensation of motion—the field cut out both wind and inertia. The green-walled volcanic islands of the Las Madres archipelago rolled over the horizon in minutes. Traffic over Cabo Santa Pola complicated the approach somewhat; it was all of six minutes before Philana could set the machine down in her slip.

A bright, hot sun brightened the white-and-turquoise waterfront. From a cold Kirst current to the tropics in less than half an hour.

Anthony felt vaguely resentful at this blinding efficiency. He could have easily equipped his own boat with flight capability, but he hadn't cared about speed when he'd set out, only the opportunity to be alone on the ocean with his whales and the

Dwellers. Now the very tempo of his existence had changed. He was moving at unaccustomed velocity, and the destination was still unclear.

After giving him her spare key, Philana went to do laundry—when one lived on small boats, laundry was done whenever the opportunity arose. Anthony bought supplies. He filled the yacht's forecabin with crates of food, then changed clothes and walked to the Villa Mary.

Anthony got a table for two and ordered a drink. The first drink went quickly and he ordered a second. Philana didn't appear. Anthony didn't like the way the waiter was looking at him. He heard his father's mocking laugh as he munched the last bread stick. He waited for three hours before he paid and left.

There was no sign of Philana at the laundry or on the yacht. He left a note on the computer expressing what he considered a contained disappointment, then headed into town. A brilliant sign that featured aquatic motifs called him to a cool, dark bar filled with bright green aquaria. Native fish gaped at him blindly while he drank something tall and cool. He decided he didn't like the way the fish looked at him and left.

He found Philana in his third bar of the evening. She was with two men, one of whom Anthony knew slightly as a charter boat skipper whom he didn't much like. He had his hand on her knee; the other man's arm was around her. Empty drinks and forsaken hors d'oeuvres lay on a table in front of them.

Anthony realized, as he approached, that his own arrival could only make things worse. Her eyes turned to him as he approached; her neck arched in a peculiar, balletic way that he had seen only once before. He recognized the quick, carnivorous smile, and a wash of fear turned his skin cold. The stranger whispered into her ear.

"What's your name again?" she asked.

Anthony wondered what to do with his hands. "We were supposed to meet."

Her eyes glittered as her head cocked, considering him. Perhaps what frightened him most of all was the fact there was no hostility in her look, nothing but calculation. There was a cigarette in her hand; he hadn't seen her smoke before.

"Do we have business?"

Anthony thought about this. He had jumped into space with this woman, and now he suspected he'd just hit the ground. "I guess not," he said, and turned.

"Qué pasó, hombre?"

"Nada."

Pablo, the Leviathan's regular bartender, was one of the planet's original Latino inhabitants, a group rapidly being submerged by newcomers. Pablo took Anthony's order for a double bourbon and also brought him his mail, which consisted of an inquiry from *Xenobiology Review* wondering what had become of their galley proofs. Anthony crumpled the note and left it in an ashtray.

A party of drunken fishermen staggered in, still in their flashing harnesses. Triumphant whoops assaulted Anthony's ears. His fingers tightened on his glass.

"Careful, Anthony," said Pablo. He poured another double bourbon. "On the house," he said.

One of the fishermen stepped to the bar, put a heavy hand on Anthony's shoulder. "Drinks on me," he said. "Caught a twelve-meter flasher today." Anthony threw the bourbon in his face.

He got in a few good licks, but in the end the pack of fishermen beat him severely and threw him through the front window. Lying breathless on broken glass, Anthony brooded on the injustice of his position and decided to rectify matters. He lurched back into the bar and knocked down the first person he saw.

Small consolation. This time they went after him with the flashing poles that were hanging on the walls, beating him senseless and once more heaving him out the window. When Anthony recovered consciousness he staggered to his feet, intending to have another go, but the pole butts had hit him in the face too many times and his eyes were swollen shut. He staggered down the street, ran face-first into a building, and sat down.

"You finished there, cowboy?" It was Nick's voice.

Anthony spat blood. "Hi, Nick," he said. "Bring them here one at a time, will you? I can't lose one-on-one."

"Jesus, Anthony. You're such an asshole."

Anthony found himself in an inexplicably cheerful mood. "You're lucky you're a sailor. Only a sailor can call me an asshole."

"Can you stand? Let's get to the marina before the cops show up."

"My boat's hundreds of miles away. I'll have to swim."

"I'll take you to my place, then."

With Nick's assistance Anthony managed to stand. He was still too drunk to feel pain, and ambled through the streets in a contented mood. "How did you happen to be at the Leviathan, Nick?"

There was weariness in Nick's voice. "They always call me, Anthony, when you fuck up."

Drunken melancholy poured into Anthony like a sudden cold squall of rain. "I'm sorry," he said.

Nick's answer was almost cheerful. "You'll be sorrier in the morning."

Anthony reflected that this was very likely true.

Nick gave him some pills that, by morning, reduced the swelling. When Anthony awoke he was able to see. Agony flared in his body as he staggered out of bed. It was still twilight. Anthony pulled on his bloody clothes and wrote an incoherent note of thanks on Nick's computer.

Fishing boats were floating out of harbor into the bright dawn. Probably Nick's was among them. The volcano above the town was a contrast in black stone and green vegetation. Pain beat at Anthony's bones like a rain of fists.

Philana's boat was still in its slip. Apprehension tautened Anthony's nerves as he put a tentative foot on the gunwale. The hatch to the cabin was still locked. Philana wasn't aboard. Anthony opened the hatch and went into the cabin just to be sure. It was empty.

He programmed the computer to pursue the transponder signal on Anthony's boat, then as the yacht rose into the sky and arrowed over the ocean, Anthony went into Philana's cabin and fell asleep on a pillow that smelled of her hair.

He awoke around noon to find the yacht patiently circling his boat. He dropped the yacht into the water, tied the two craft together, and spent half the afternoon transferring his supplies to his own boat. He programmed the yacht to return to Las Madres and orbit the volcanic spire until it was summoned by its owner or the police.

I and the sea greet one another, he tapped into his console, and as the call wailed out from his boat he hauled in the drogue and set off after the humpbacks. Apartness is the smell, he thought, aloneness is the condition. Spray shot aboard and spattered Anthony, and salt pain flickered from the cuts on his face. He climbed to the flybridge and hoped for healing from the sun and the glittering sea.

The whales left the cold current and suddenly the world was filled with tropic sunshine and bright water. Anthony made light conversation with the humpbacks and spent the rest of his time working on Dweller speech. Despite hours of concentrated endeavor he made little progress. The sensation was akin to that of smashing his head against a stone wall over and over, an act that was, on consideration, not unlike the rest of his life.

After his third day at sea his boat's computer began signaling him that he was receiving messages. He ignored this and concentrated on work.

Two days later he was cruising north with a whale on either beam when a shadow moved across his boat. Anthony looked up from his console and saw without surprise that Philana's yacht was eclipsing the sun. Philana, dark glasses over her deep eyes and a floppy hat over her hair, was peering down from the starboard bow.

"We have to talk," she said.

Joyously we greet Air Human, whooped Sings of Others.

I and Air Human are pleased to detect one another's presence, called Two Notches.

Anthony went to the controls and throttled up. Microphones slammed at the bottom of his boat. Two Notches poked one large brown eye above the waves to see what was happening, then cheerfully set off in pursuit.

Anthony and Air Human are in a state of excitement, he chattered. **I/We are pleased to join our race.**

The flying yacht hung off Anthony's stern. Philana shouted through cupped hands. "Talk to me, Anthony!"

Anthony remained silent and twisted the wheel into a fast left turn. His wake foamed over Two Notches' face and the humpback burbled a protest. The air yacht seemed to have little trouble following the turn. Anthony was beginning to have the sense of that stone wall coming up again, but he tried a few more maneuvers just in case one of them worked. Nothing succeeded. Finally he cut the throttle and let the boat slow on the long blue swells.

The trade winds had taken Philana's hat and carried it away. She ignored it and looked down at him. Her face was pale and beneath the dark glasses she looked drawn and ill.

"I'm not human, Anthony," she said. "I'm a Kyklops. That's what's really wrong with me."

Anthony looked at her. Anger danced in his veins. "You really are full of surprises."

"I'm Telamon's other body," she said. "Sometimes he inhabits me."

Whalesong rolled up from the sea. **We and Air Human send one another cheerful salutations and expressions of good will.**

"Talk to the whales first," said Anthony.

"Telamon's a scientist," Philana said. "He's impatient, that's his problem."

The boat heaved on an ocean swell. The trade wind moaned through the flybridge. "He's got a few more problems than that," Anthony said.

"He wanted me for a purpose but sometimes he forgets." A tremor of pain crossed Philana's face. She was deeply hung over. Her voice was ragged: Telamon had been smoking like a chimney and Philana wasn't used to it.

"He wanted to do an experiment on human psychology. He wanted to arrange a method of recording a person's memories, then transferring them to his own . . . sphere. He got my parents to agree to having the appropriate devices implanted, but the only apparatus that existed for the connection of human and Kyklops was the one the Kyklopes use to manipulate the human bodies that they wear when they want to enjoy the pleasures of the flesh. And Telamon is . . ." She waved a dismissive arm. "He's a decadent, the way a lot of the Kyklopes turn once they discover how much fun it is to be a human and that their real self doesn't get hurt no matter what they do to their clone bodies. Telamon likes his pleasures, and he likes to interfere. Sometimes, when he dumped my memory into the nth dimension and had a look at it, he couldn't resist the temptation to take over my body and rectify what he considered my errors. And occasionally, when he's in the middle of one of his binges, and his other body gives out on him, he takes me over and starts a party wherever I am."

"Some scientist," Anthony said.

"The Kyklopes are used to experimenting on pieces of themselves," Philana said. "Their own beings are tenuous and rather . . . detachable. Their ethics aren't against it. And he doesn't do it very often. He must be bored wherever he is—he's taken me over twice in a week." She raised her fist to her face and began to cough, a real smoker's hack. Anthony fidgeted and wondered whether to offer her a glass of water. Philana bent double and the coughs turned to cries of pain. A tear pattered on the teak.

A knot twisted in Anthony's throat. He left his chair and held Philana in his arms. "I've never told anyone," she said.

Anthony realized to his transient alarm that once again he'd jumped off a cliff without looking. He had no more idea of where he would land than last time.

Philana, Anthony was given to understand, was Greek for "lover of humanity." The Kyklopes, after being saddled with a mythological name by the first humans who had contacted them, had gone in for classical allusion in a big way. Telamon, Anthony learned, meant (among other things) "the supporter." After learning this, Anthony referred to the alien as Jockstrap.

"We should do something about him," Anthony said. It was late—the white dwarf had just set—but neither of them had any desire to sleep. He and Philana were standing on the flybridge. The falkner shield was off and above their heads the uninhibited stars seemed almost within reach of their questing fingertips. Overlook Station, fixed almost overhead, was bright as a burning brand.

Philana shook her head. "He's got access to my memory. Any plans we make, he can know in an instant." She thought for a moment. "If he bothers to look. He doesn't always."

"I'll make the plans without telling you what they are."

"It will take forever. I've thought about it. You're talking court case. He can sue me for breach of contract."

"It's your parents who signed the contract, not you. You're an adult now."

She turned away. Anthony looked at her for a long moment, a cold foreboding hand around his throat. "I hope," he said, "you're going to tell me that you signed that contract while Jockstrap was riding you."

Philana shook her head silently. Anthony looked up into the Milky Way and imagined the stone wall falling from the void, aimed right between his eyes, spinning slightly as it grew ever larger in his vision. Smashing him again.

"All we have to do is get the thing out of your head," Anthony said. "After that, let him sue you. You'll be free, whatever happens." His tone reflected a resolve that was absent entirely from his heart.

"He'll sue you, too, if you have any part of this." She turned to face him again. Her face pale and taut in the starlight. "All my money comes from him—how else do you think I could afford the yacht? I owe everything to him."

Bitterness sped through Anthony's veins. He could feel his voice turning harsh. "Do you want to get rid of him or not? Yes or no."

"He's not entirely evil."

"Yes or no, Philana."

"It'll take years before he's done with you. And he could kill you. Just transport you to deep space somewhere and let you drift. Or he could simply teleport me away from you."

The bright stars poured down rage. Anthony knew himself seconds away from violence. There were two people on this boat and one of them was about to get hurt. "*Yes or no!*" he shouted.

Philana's face contorted. She put her hands over her ears. Hair fell across her face. "Don't shout," she said.

Anthony turned and smashed his forehead against the control panel of the flybridge. Philana gave a cry of surprise and fear. Anthony drove himself against the panel again. Philana's fingers clutched at his shoulders. Anthony could feel blood running from his scalp. The pain drained his anger, brought a cold, brilliant clarity to his mind. He smashed himself a third time. Philana cried out. He turned to her. He felt a savage, exemplary satisfaction. If one were going to drive oneself against stone walls, one should at least take a choice of the walls available.

"Ask me," Anthony panted, "if I care what happens to me."

Philana's face was a mask of terror. She said his name.

"I need to know where you stand," said Anthony. Blood drooled from his scalp, and he suppressed the unwelcome thought that he had just made himself look ridiculous.

Her look of fear broadened.

"Am I going to jump off this cliff by myself, or what?" Anthony demanded.

"I want to get rid of him," she said.

Anthony wished her voice had contained more determination, even if it were patently false. He spat salt and went in search of his first aid kit. We are in a condition of slow movement through deep currents, he thought.

In the morning he got the keys to Philana's yacht and changed the passwords on the falkner controls and navigation comp. He threw all his liquor overboard. He figured that if Jockstrap appeared and discovered that he couldn't leave the middle of the ocean, and he couldn't have a party where he was, he'd get bored and wouldn't hang around for long.

From Philana's cabin he called an attorney who informed him that the case was complex but not impossible, and furthermore that it would take a small fortune to resolve. Anthony told him to get to work on it. In the meantime he told the lawyer to start calling neurosurgeons. Unfortunately there were few neurosurgeons capable of implanting, let alone removing, the rider device. The operation wasn't performed that often.

Days passed. A discouraging list of neurosurgeons either turned him down flat or wanted the legal situation clarified first. Anthony told the lawyer to start calling *rich* neurosurgeons who might be able to ride out a lawsuit.

Philana transferred most of her data to Anthony's computer and worked with the whales from the smaller boat. Anthony used her yacht and aquasled and cursed the bad sound quality. At least the yacht's flight capability allowed him to find the Dwellers faster.

As far as the Dwellers went, he had run all at once into a dozen blind alleys. Progress seemed measured in microns.

"What's B1971?" Philana asked once, looking over his shoulder as he typed in data.

"A taste. Perhaps a taste associated with a particular temperature striation. Perhaps an emotion." He shrugged. "Maybe just a metaphor."

"You could ask them."

His soul hardened. "Not yet." Which ended the conversation.

Anthony wasn't sure whether or not he wanted to touch her. He and Jockstrap were at war and Philana seemed not to have entirely made up her mind which side she was on. Anthony slept with Philana on the double mattress in the peak, but they avoided sex. He didn't know whether he was helping her out of love or something else, and while he figured things out, desire was on hold, waiting.

Anthony's time with Philana was occupied mainly by his attempt to teach her to cook. Anything else waited for the situation to grow less opaque. Anthony figured Jockstrap would clarify matters fairly soon.

Anthony's heart lurched as he looked up from lunch to see the taut, challenging grin on Philana's face. Anthony realized he'd been foolish to expect Telamon to show up only at night, as he always had before.

Anthony drew his lips into an answering grin. He was ready, no matter what the hour.

"Do I know you?" Anthony mocked. "Do we have business?"

Philana's appraisal was cold. "I've been called Jockstrap before," Telamon said.

"With good reason, I'm sure."

Telamon lurched to his feet and walked aft. He seemed not to have his sea legs yet. Anthony followed, his nerves dancing. Telamon looked out at the sea and curled Philana's lip as if to say that the water held nothing of interest.

"I want to talk about Philana," Telamon said. "You're keeping her prisoner here."

"She can leave me anytime she wants. Which is more than she can say about you."

"I want the codes to the yacht."

Anthony stepped up to Telamon, held Philana's cold gaze. "You're hurting her," he said.

Telamon stared at him with eyes like obsidian chips. He pushed Philana's long hair out of his face with an unaccustomed gesture. "I'm not the only one, Maldalena. I've got access to her mind, remember."

"Then look in her mind and see what she thinks of you."

A contemptuous smile played about Philana's lips. "I know very well what she thinks of me, and it's probably not what she's told you. Philana is a very sad and complex person, and she is not always truthful."

"She's what you made her."

"Precisely my next point." He waved his arm stiffly, unnaturally. The gesture brought him off balance, and Philana's body swayed for a moment as Telamon adjusted to the tossing of the boat. "I gave her money, education, knowledge of the world. I have corrected her errors, taught her much. She is, in many ways, my creation. Her feelings toward me are ambiguous, as any child's feelings would be toward her father."

"Daddy Jockstrap." Anthony laughed. "Do we have business, Daddy? Or are you going to take your daughter's body to a party first?"

Anthony jumped backward, arms flailing, as Philana disappeared, her place taken by a young man with curly dark hair and bright blue eyes. The stranger was dressed in a white cotton shirt unbuttoned to the navel and a pair of navy blue swimming trunks. He had seen the man before on vid, showing off his chest hairs. The grin stayed the same from one body to the next.

"She's gone, Maldalena. I teleported her to someplace safe." He laughed. "I'll buy her a new boat. Do what you like with the old one."

Anthony's heart hammered. He had forgotten the Kyklopes could do that, just teleport without the apparatus required by humans. And teleport other things as well.

He wondered how many centuries old the Kyklops' body was. He knew the mind's age was measured in eons.

"This doesn't end it," Anthony said.

Telamon's tone was mild. "Perhaps I'll find a nice planet for you somewhere, Maldalena. Let you play Robinson Crusoe, just as you did when you were young."

"That will only get you in trouble. Too many people know about this situation by now. And it won't be much fun holding Philana wherever you've got her."

Telamon stepped toward the stern, sat on the taffrail. His movements were fluid, far more confident than they had been when he was wearing the other, unaccustomed body. For a moment Anthony considered kicking Telamon into the drink, then decided against it. The possible repercussions had a cosmic dimension that Anthony preferred not to contemplate.

"I don't dislike you, Maldalena," the alien said. "I truly don't. You're an alcoholic, violent lout, but at least you have proven intelligence, perhaps a kind of genius."

"Call the kettle black again. I liked that part."

Two Notches' smooth body rose a cable's length to starboard. He exhaled with an audible hiss, mist drifting over his back. Telamon gave the whale a disinterested look, then turned back to Anthony.

"Being the nearest thing to a parent on the planet," he said, "I must say that I disapprove of you as a partner for Philana. However—" He gave a shrug. "Parents must know when to compromise in these matters." He looked up at Anthony with his blue eyes. "I propose we share her, Anthony. Formalize the arrangement we already seem to possess. I'll only occupy a little of her time, and for all the rest, the two of you can live out your lives with whatever sad domestic bliss you can summon. Till she gets tired of you, anyway."

Two Notches rolled under the waves. A cetacean murmur echoed off the boat's bottom. Anthony's mind flailed for an answer. He felt sweat prickling his scalp. He shook his head in feigned disbelief.

"Listen to yourself, Telamon. Is this supposed to be a scientist talking? A researcher?"

"You don't want to share?" The young man's face curled in disdain. "You want everything for yourself—the whole planet, I suppose, like your father."

"Don't be ridiculous."

"I know what Philana knows about you, and I've done some checking on my own. You brought the humpbacks here because you needed them. Away from *their* home, *their* kind. You *asked* them, I'm sure; but there's no way they could make an informed decision about this planet, about what they were doing. You needed them for your Dweller study, so you took them."

As if on cue, Two Notches rose from the water to take a breath. Telamon favored the whale with his taut smile. Anthony floundered for an answer while the alien spoke on.

"You've got data galore on the Dwellers, but do you publish? Do you share it with anybody, even with Philana? You hoard it all for yourself, all your specialized knowledge. You don't even talk to the Dwellers!" Telamon gave a scornful laugh. "You don't even want the *Dwellers* to know what Anthony knows!"

Anger poured through Anthony's veins like a scalding fire. He clenched his fists, considered launching himself at Telamon. Something held him back.

The alien stood, walked to Anthony, looked him up and down. "We're not so different," he said. "We both want what's ours. But *I'm* willing to share. Philana can be our common pool of data, if you like. Think about it."

Anthony swung, and in that instant Philana was back, horror in her eyes. Anthony's fist, aimed for the taller Telamon's chin, clipped Philana's temple and she fell back, flailing. Anthony caught her.

"It just happened, didn't it?" Her voice was woeful.

"You don't remember?"

Philana's face crumpled. She swayed and touched her temple. "I never do. The times when he's running me are just blank spots."

Anthony seated her on the port bench. He was feeling queasy at having hit her. She put her face in her hands. "I hate when that happens in front of people I know," she said.

"He's using you to hide behind. He was here in person, the son of a bitch." He took her hands in his own and kissed her. Purest desire flamed through him. He wanted to commit an act of defiance, make a statement of the nature of things. He put his arms around her and kissed her nape. She smelled faintly of pine, and there were needles in her hair. Telamon had put her on Earth, then, in a forest somewhere.

She strained against his tight embrace. "I don't know if this is a good idea," she said.

"I want to send a message to Telamon," Anthony said.

They made love under the sun, lying on the deck in Anthony's cockpit. Clear as a bell, Anthony heard Dweller sounds rumbling up the boat. Somewhere in the boat a metal mounting bracket rang to the subsonics. Philana clutched at him. There was desperation in her look, a search for affirmation, despair at finding none. The teak punished Anthony's palms. He wondered if Telamon had ever possessed her thus, took over her mind so that he could fuck her in his own body, commit incest with himself. He found the idea exciting.

His orgasm poured out, stunning him with its intensity. He kissed the moist juncture of Philana's neck and shoulder, and rose on his hands to stare down into Telamon's brittle grin and cold, knowing eyes.

"Message received, Anthony." Philana's throat convulsed in laughter. "You're taking possession. Showing everyone who's boss."

Horror galvanized Anthony. He jumped to his feet and backed away, heart pounding. He took a deep breath and mastered himself, strove for words of denial and could not find them. "You're sad, Telamon," he said.

Telamon threw Philana's arms over her head, parted her legs. "Let's do it again, Anthony." Taunting. "You're so masterful."

Anthony turned away. "Piss off, Telamon, you sick fuck." Bile rose in his throat.

"What happened?" Anthony knew Philana was back. He turned and saw her face crumple. "We were making love!" she wailed.

"A cheap trick. He's getting desperate." He squatted by her and tried to take her in his arms. She turned away from him.

"Let me alone for a while," she said. Bright tears filled her eyes.

Misplaced adrenaline ran charges through Anthony's body—no one to fight, no place to run. He picked up his clothes and went below to the main cabin. He drew on his clothing and sat on one of the berths, hands helpless on the seat beside him. He wanted to get blind drunk.

Half an hour later Philana entered the cabin. She'd braided her hair, drawn it back so tight from her temples it must have been painful. Her movements were slow, as if suddenly she'd lost her sea legs. She sat down at the little kitchen table, pushed away her half-eaten lunch.

"We can't win," she said.

"There's got to be some way," Anthony said tonelessly. He was clean out of ideas.

Philana looked at Anthony from reddened eyes. "We can give him what he wants," she said.

"No."

Her voice turned to a shout. "It's not *you* he does this to! It's not you who winks out of existence in the middle of doing laundry or making love, and wakes up somewhere else." Her knuckles were white as they gripped the table edge. "I don't know how long I can take this."

"All your life," said Anthony, "if you give him what he wants."

"At least then he wouldn't use it as a *weapon*!" Her voice was a shout. She turned away.

Anthony looked at her, wondered if he should go to her. He decided not to. He was out of comfort for the present.

"You see," Philana said, her head still turned away, "why I don't want to live forever."

"Don't let him beat you."

"It's not that. I'm afraid . . ." Her voice trembled. "I'm afraid that if I got old I'd *become* him. The Kyklopes are the oldest living things ever discovered. And a lot of the oldest immortals are a lot like them. Getting crazier, getting . . ." She shook her head. "Getting less human all the time."

Anthony saw a body swaying in the smokehouse. Philana's body, her fingernails trailing in the dust. Pain throbbed in his chest. He stood up, swayed as he was caught by a slow wave of vertigo. Somewhere his father was laughing, telling him he should have stayed on Lees for a life of pastoral incest.

"I want to think," he said. He stepped past her on the way to his computer. He didn't reach out to touch her as he passed. She didn't reach for him, either.

He put on the headphones and listened to the Dwellers. Their speech rolled up from the deep. Anthony sat unable to comprehend, his mind frozen. He was helpless as Philana. Whose was the next move? he wondered. His? Philana's?

Whoever made the next move, Anthony knew, the game was Telamon's.

At dinnertime Philana made a pair of sandwiches for Anthony, then returned to the cabin and ate nothing herself. Anthony ate one sandwich without tasting it, gave the second to the fish. The Dweller speech had faded out. He left his computer and stepped into the cabin. Philana was stretched out on one of the side berths, her eyes closed. One arm was thrown over her forehead.

Her body, Anthony decided, was too tense for this to be sleep. He sat on the berth opposite.

"He said you haven't told the truth," Anthony said.

Anthony could see Philana's eyes moving under translucent lids as she evaluated this statement, scanning for meaning. "About what," she said.

"About your relationship to him."

Her lips drew back, revealing teeth. Perhaps it was a smile.

"I've known him all my life. I gave you the condensed version."

"Is there more I should know?"

There was another pause. "He saved my life."

"Good for him."

"I got involved with this man. Three or four hundred years old, one of my professors in school. He was going through a crisis—he was a mess, really. I thought I could do him some good. Telamon disagreed, said the relationship was sick." Philana licked her lips. "He was right," she said.

Anthony didn't know if he really wanted to hear about this.

"The guy started making demands. Wanted to get married, leave Earth, start over again."

"What did you want?"

Philana shrugged. "I don't know. I hadn't made up my mind. But Telamon went into my head and confronted the guy and told him to get lost. Then he just took me out of there. My body was half the galaxy away, all alone on an undeveloped world. There were supplies, but no gates out."

Anthony gnawed his lip. This was how Telamon operated.

"Telamon kept me there for a couple weeks till I calmed down. He took me back to Earth. The professor had taken up with someone else, another one of his students. He married her, and six weeks later she walked out on him. He killed her, then killed himself."

Philana sighed, drew her hand over her forehead. She opened her eyes and sat up, swinging her legs off the berth. "So," she said. "That's one Telamon story. I've got more."

"When did this happen?"

"I'd just turned eighteen." She shook her head. "That's when I signed the contract that keeps him in my head. I decided that I couldn't trust my judgment about people. And Telamon's judgment of people is, well, quite good."

Resentment flamed in Anthony at this notion. Telamon had made his judgment of Anthony clear, and Anthony didn't want it to become a subject for debate. "You're older now," he said. "He can't have a veto on your life forever."

Philana drew up her legs and circled her knees with her arms. "You're violent, Anthony."

Anthony looked at her for a long moment of cold anger. "I hit you by accident. I was aiming at *him*, damn it."

Philana's jaw worked as she returned his stare. "How long before you aim at *me?*"

"I wouldn't."

"That's what my old professor said."

Anthony turned away, fury running through him like chill fire. Philana looked at him levelly for a moment, then dropped her forehead to her knees. She sighed. "I don't know, Anthony. I don't know anymore. If I ever did."

Anthony stared fixedly at the distant white dwarf, just arrived above the horizon and visible through the hatch. We are, he thought, in a condition of permanent bafflement. "What do you want, Philana?" he asked.

Her head came up, looked at him. "I want not to be a tennis ball in your game with Telamon, Anthony. I want to know I'm not just the prize given the winner."

"I wanted you before I ever met Telamon, Philana."

"Telamon changed a few things." Her voice was cold. "Before you met him, you didn't use my body to send messages to people."

Anthony's fists clenched. He forced them to relax.

Philana's voice was bitter. "Seems to me, Anthony, that's one of Telamon's habits you're all too eager to adopt."

Anthony's chest ached. He didn't seem able to breathe in enough air. He took a long breath and hoped his tension would ease. It didn't. "I'm sorry," he said. "It's not . . . a normal situation."

"For you, maybe."

Silence hung in the room, broken only by the whale clicks and mutters rising through the boat. Anthony shook his head. "What do we do, then?" he asked. "Surrender?"

"If we have to." She looked at him. "I'm willing to fight Telamon, but not to the point where one of us is destroyed." She leaned toward him, her expression intent. "And if Telamon wins, could you live with it?" she asked. "With surrender? If we had to give him what he wanted?"

"I don't know."

"I *have* to live with it. You don't. That's the difference."

"That's *one* difference." He took a breath, then rose from his place. "I have to think," he said.

He climbed into the cockpit. Red sunset was splattered like blood across the windscreen. He tried to breathe the sea air, clear the heaviness he felt in his chest, but it didn't work. Anthony went up onto the flybridge and stared forward. His eyes burned as the sun went down in flames.

The white dwarf was high overhead when Anthony came down. Philana was lying in the forepeak, covered with a sheet, her eyes staring sightlessly out the open hatch. Anthony took his clothes off and crawled in beside her.

"I'll surrender," he said. "If I have to, I'll surrender." She turned to him and put her arms around him. Hopeless desire burned in his belly.

He made love to Philana, his nerves numb to the possibility that Telamon might reappear. Her hungry mouth drank in his pain. He didn't know whether this was affirmation or not, whether this meant anything other than the fact there was nothing left to do at this point than stagger blindly into one another's embrace.

A Dweller soloed from below, the clearest Anthony had ever heard one. **We call to ourselves,** the Dweller said, **We speak of things as they are.** Anthony rose from bed and set his computer to record. Sings of Others, rising alongside to breathe, called a hello. Anthony tapped his keys, hit TRANSMIT.

Air Human and I are in a condition of rut, he said.

We congratulate Anthony and Air Human on our condition of rut, Sings of Others responded. The whooping whale cries layered atop the thundering Dweller noises. **We wish ourselves many happy copulations.**

Happy copulations, happy copulations, echoed Two Notches.

A pointless optimism began to resonate in Anthony's mind. He sat before the computer and listened to the sounds of the Deep Dwellers as they rumbled up his spine.

Philana appeared at the hatch. She was buttoning her shirt. "You told the whales about us?" she said.

"Why not?"

She grinned faintly. "I guess there's no reason not to."

Two Notches wailed a question. **Are Anthony and Air Human copulating now?**

Not at present, Anthony replied.

We hope you will copulate often.

Philana, translating the speech on her own, laughed. "Tell them we hope so, too," she said.

And then she stiffened. Anthony's nerves poured fire. Philana turned to him and regarded him with Telamon's eyes.

"I thought you'd see reason," Telamon said. *"I'll surrender.* I like that."

Anthony looked at the possessed woman and groped for a vehicle for his message. Words seemed inadequate, he decided, but would have to do. "You haven't won yet," he said.

Philana's head cocked to one side as Telamon viewed him. "Has it occurred to you," Telamon said, "that if she's free of me, she won't need you at all?"

"You forget something. I'll be rid of *you* as well."

"You can be rid of me any time."

Anthony stared at Telamon for a moment, then suddenly he laughed. He had just realized how to send his message. Telamon looked at him curiously. Anthony turned to his computer deck and flipped to the Dweller translation file.

I/We, he typed, *live in the warm brightness above. We are new to this world, and send good wishes to the Dwellers below.*

Anthony pressed TRANSMIT. Rolling thunder boomed from the boat's speakers. The grammar was probably awful, Anthony knew, but he was fairly certain of the words, and he thought the meaning would be clear.

Telamon frowned, stepped to gaze over Anthony's shoulder.

Calls came from below. A translation tree appeared on the screen.

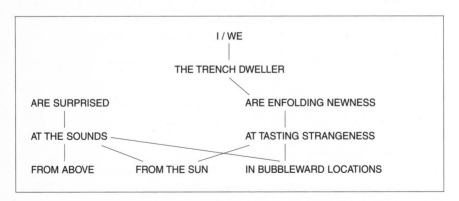

"Trench Dweller" was probably one of the Dwellers' names. "Bubbleward" was a phrase for "up," since bubbles rose to the surface. Anthony tapped the keys.

We are from far away, recently arrived. We are small and foreign to the world. We wish to brush the Dwellers with our thoughts. We regret our lack of clarity in diction.

"I wonder if you've thought this through," Telamon said.

Anthony hit TRANSMIT. Speakers boomed. The subsonics were like a punch in the gut.

"Go jump off a cliff," Anthony said.

"You're making a mistake," said Telamon.

The Dweller's answer was surprisingly direct.

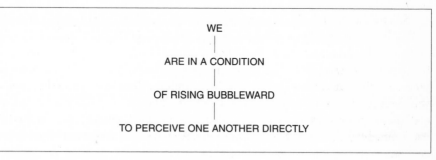

WE

|

ARE IN A CONDITION

|

OF RISING BUBBLEWARD

|

TO PERCEIVE ONE ANOTHER DIRECTLY

Anthony's heart crashed in astonishment. Could the Dwellers stand the lack of pressure on the surface? *I/We,* he typed, *Trench Dweller, proceed with consideration for safety. I/We recollect that we are small and weak.* He pressed TRANSMIT and flipped to the whalespeech file.

Deep Dweller rising to surface, he typed. *Run fast northward.*

The whales answered with cries of alarm. Flukes pounded the water. Anthony ran to the cabin and cranked the wheel hard to starboard. He increased speed to separate himself from the humpbacks. Behind him, Telamon stumbled in his unfamiliar body as the boat took the waves at a different angle.

Anthony returned to his computer console. *I/We are in a state of motion,* he reported. *Is living in the home of the light occasion for a condition of damage to us/Trench Dweller?*

"You're mad," said Telamon, and then Philana staggered. "He's done it *again,*" she said in a stunned voice. She stepped to the starboard bench and sat down. "What's happening?" she asked.

"I'm talking to the Dwellers. One of them is rising to say hello."

"Now?"

He gave her a skeletal grin. "It's what you wanted, yes?" She stared at him.

I'm going over cliffs, he thought. One after another.

That, Anthony concluded, is the condition of existence.

Subsonics rattled crockery in the kitchen.

BUBBLEWARD PLATEAU IS CONDITION FOR DAMAGE

|

DAMAGE IS ACCEPTABLE

Anthony typed, *I/We happily await greeting ourselves* and pressed TRANSMIT, then REPEAT. He would give the Dweller a sound to home in on.

"I don't understand," Philana said. He moved to join her on the bench, put his arm around her. She shrugged him off. "Tell me," she said. He took her hand.

"We're going to win."

"How?"

"I don't know yet."

She was too shaken to argue. "It's going to be a long fight," she said.

"I don't care."

Philana took a breath. "I'm scared."

"So am I," said Anthony.

The boat beat itself against the waves. The flying yacht followed, a silent shadow.

Anthony and Philana waited in silence until the Dweller rose, a green-grey mass that looked as if a grassy reef had just calved. Foam roared from its back as it broke water, half an ocean running down its sides. Anthony's boat danced in the sudden white tide, and then the ocean stilled. Bits of the Dweller were all around, spread over the water for leagues—tentacles, filters, membranes. The Dweller's very mass had calmed the sea. The Dweller was so big, Anthony saw, it constituted an entire ecosystem. Sea creatures lived among its folds and tendrils: some had died as they rose, their swim bladders exploding in the release of pressure; others leaped and spun and shrank from the brightness above.

Sunlight shone from the Dweller's form, and the creature pulsed with life.

Terrified, elated, Philana and Anthony rose to say hello.

The Hemingway Hoax

Joe Haldeman

Born in Oklahoma City, Oklahoma, Joe Haldeman took a B.S. degree in physics and astronomy from the University of Maryland, and did postgraduate work in mathematics and computer science. But his plans for a career in science were cut short by the U.S. Army, which sent him to Vietnam in 1968 as a combat engineer. Seriously wounded in action, Haldeman returned home in 1969 and began to write. He sold his first story to *Galaxy* in 1969, and by 1976 had garnered both the Nebula Award and the Hugo Award for his famous novel *The Forever War*, one of the landmark books of the '70s. He took another Hugo Award in 1977 for his story "Tricentennial," won the Rhysling Award in 1983 for the best science fiction poem of the year (although usually thought of primarily as a "hard-science" writer, Haldeman is, in fact, also an accomplished poet, and has sold poetry to most of the major professional markets in the genre), and won both the Nebula and the Hugo Award in 1991 for the novella version of "The Hemingway Hoax." His story "None So Blind" won the Hugo Award in 1995. His other books include two mainstream novels, *War Year* and *1969*, the SF novels *Mindbridge*, *All My Sins Remembered*, *There Is No Darkness* (written with his brother, SF writer Jack C. Haldeman II), *Worlds*, *Worlds Apart*, *Worlds Enough and Time*, *Buying Time*, *The Hemingway Hoax*, *Tool of the Trade*, *The Coming*, and *Camouflage*, which won the prestigious James Tiptree, Jr. Award. His short work has been gathered in the collections *Infinite Dreams*, *Dealing in Futures*, *Vietnam and Other Alien Worlds*, and *None So Blind*. As editor, he has produced the anthologies *Study War No More*, *Cosmic Laughter*, and *Nebula Award Stories Seventeen*. His most recent book is a new science fiction novel, *Old Twentieth*. Coming up are two new collections, *A Separate War and Other Stories*, and an omnibus of fiction and nonfiction, *War Stories*. Haldeman lives part of the year in Boston, where he teaches writing at the Massachusetts Institute of Technology, and the rest of the year in Florida, where he and his wife, Gay, make their home.

In the vivid and fast-moving novella that follows, Haldeman is at the very top of even his own high standard. What starts out as a relatively harmless literary hoax soon plunges us into an intricate maze of intrigue and murder and betrayal, as cosmic forces fight it out in a behind-the-scenes battle that may determine the fate of humanity itself.

1. THE TORRENTS OF SPRING

Our story begins in a run-down bar in Key West, not so many years from now. The bar is not the one Hemingway drank at, nor yet the one that claims to be the one he drank at, because they are both too expensive and full of tourists. This bar, in a more interesting part of town, is a Cuban place. It is neither clean nor well-lighted, but has cold beer and good strong Cuban coffee. Its cheap prices and rascally charm are what bring together the scholar and the rogue.

Their first meeting would be of little significance to either at the time, though the scholar, John Baird, would never forget it. John Baird was not capable of forgetting anything.

Key West is lousy with writers, mostly poor writers, in one sense of that word or the other. Poor people did not interest our rogue, Sylvester Castlemaine, so at first he didn't take any special note of the man sitting in the corner scribbling on a yellow pad. Just another would-be writer, come down to see whether some of Papa's magic would rub off. Not worth the energy of a con.

But Castle's professional powers of observation caught at a detail or two and focused his attention. The man was wearing jeans and a faded flannel shirt, but his shoes were expensive Italian loafers. His beard had been trimmed by a barber. He was drinking Heineken. The pen he was scribbling with was a fat Mont Blanc Diplomat, two hundred bucks on the hoof, discounted. Castle got his cup of coffee and sat at a table two away from the writer.

He waited until the man paused, set the pen down, took a drink. "Writing a story?" Castle said.

The man blinked at him. "No . . . just an article." He put the cap on the pen with a crisp snap. "An article about stories. I'm a college professor."

"Publish or perish," Castle said.

The man relaxed a bit. "Too true." He riffled through the yellow pad. "This won't help much. It's not going anywhere."

"Tell you what . . . bet you a beer it's Hemingway or Tennessee Williams."

"Too easy." He signaled the bartender. "Dos cervezas. Hemingway, the early stories. You know his work?"

"Just a little. We had to read him in school—*The Old Man and the Fish?* And then I read a couple after I got down here." He moved over to the man's table. "Name's Castle."

"John Baird." Open, honest expression; not too promising. You can't con somebody unless he thinks he's conning you. "Teach up at Boston."

"I'm mostly fishing. Shrimp nowadays." Of course Castle didn't normally fish, not for things in the sea, but the shrimp part was true. He'd been reduced to heading shrimp on the Catalina for five dollars a bucket. "So what about these early stories?"

The bartender set down the two beers and gave Castle a weary look.

"Well . . . they don't exist." John Baird carefully poured the beer down the side of his glass. "They were stolen. Never published."

"So what can you write about them?"

"Indeed. That's what I've been asking myself." He took a sip of the beer and settled back. "Seventy-four years ago they were stolen. December 1922. That's really what got me working on them; thought I would do a paper, a monograph, for the seventy-fifth anniversary of the occasion."

It sounded less and less promising, but this was the first imported beer Castle had had in months. He slowly savored the bite of it.

"He and his first wife, Hadley, were living in Paris. You know about Hemingway's early life?"

"Huh uh. Paris?"

"He grew up in Oak Park, Illinois. That was kind of a prissy, self-satisfied suburb of Chicago."

"Yeah, I been there."

"He didn't like it. In his teens he sort of ran away from home, went down to Kansas City to work on a newspaper.

"World War I started, and like a lot of kids, Hemingway couldn't get into the army because of bad eyesight, so he joined the Red Cross and went off to drive ambulances in Italy. Take cigarettes and chocolate to the troops.

"That almost killed him. He was just doing his cigarettes-and-chocolate routine and an artillery round came in, killed the guy next to him, tore up another, riddled Hemingway with shrapnel. He claims then that he picked up the wounded guy and carried him back to the trench, in spite of being hit in the knee by a machine gun bullet."

"What do you mean, 'claims'?"

"You're too young to have been in Vietnam."

"Yeah."

"Good for you. I was hit in the knee by a machine gun bullet myself, and went down on my ass and didn't get up for five weeks. He didn't carry anybody one step."

"That's interesting."

"Well, he was always rewriting his life. We all do it. But it seemed to be a compulsion with him. That's one thing that makes Hemingway scholarship challenging."

Baird poured the rest of the beer into his glass. "Anyhow, he actually was the first American wounded in Italy, and they made a big deal over him. He went back to Oak Park a war hero. He had a certain amount of success with women."

"Or so he says?"

"Right, God knows. Anyhow, he met Hadley Richardson, an older woman but quite a number, and they had a steamy courtship and got married and said the hell with it, moved to Paris to live a sort of Bohemian life while Hemingway worked on perfecting his art. That part isn't bullshit. He worked diligently and he did become one of the best writers of his era. Which brings us to the lost manuscripts."

"Do tell."

"Hemingway was picking up a little extra money doing journalism. He'd gone to

Switzerland to cover a peace conference for a news service. When it was over, he wired Hadley to come join him for some skiing.

"This is where it gets odd. On her own initiative, Hadley packed up all of Ernest's work. All of it. Not just the typescripts, but the handwritten first drafts and the carbons."

"That's like a Xerox?"

"Right. She packed them in an overnight bag, then packed her own suitcase. A porter at the train station, the Gare de Lyon, put them aboard for her. She left the train for a minute to find something to read—and when she came back, they were gone."

"Suitcase and all?"

"No, just the manuscripts. She and the porter searched up and down the train. But that was it. Somebody had seen the overnight bag sitting there and snatched it. Lost forever."

That did hold a glimmer of professional interest. "That's funny. You'd think they'd get a note then, like 'If you ever want to see your stories again, bring a million bucks to the Eiffel Tower' sort of thing."

"A few years later, that might have happened. It didn't take long for Hemingway to become famous. But at the time, only a few of the literary intelligentsia knew about him."

Castle shook his head in commiseration with the long-dead thief. "Guy who stole 'em probably didn't even read English. Dumped 'em in the river."

John Baird shivered visibly. "Undoubtedly. But people have never stopped looking for them. Maybe they'll show up in some attic someday."

"Could happen." Wheels turning.

"It's happened before in literature. Some of Boswell's diaries were recovered because a scholar recognized his handwriting on an old piece of paper a merchant used to wrap a fish. Hemingway's own last book, he put together from notes that had been lost for thirty years. They were in a couple of trunks in the basement of the Ritz, in Paris." He leaned forward, excited. "Then after he died, they found another batch of papers down here, in a back room in Sloppy Joe's. It could still happen."

Castle took a deep breath. "It could be made to happen, too."

"Made to happen?"

"Just speakin', you know, in theory. Like some guy who really knows Hemingway, suppose he makes up some stories that're like those old ones, finds some seventy-five-year-old paper and an old, what do you call them, not a word processor—"

"Typewriter."

"Whatever. Think he could pass 'em off for the real thing?"

"I don't know if he could fool me," Baird said, and tapped the side of his head. "I have a freak memory: eidetic, photographic. I have just about every word Hemingway ever wrote committed to memory." He looked slightly embarrassed. "Of course that doesn't make me an expert in the sense of being able to spot a phony. I just wouldn't have to refer to any texts."

"So take yourself, you know, or somebody else who spent all his life studyin' Hemingway. He puts all he's got into writin' these stories—he knows the people who are gonna be readin' 'em; knows what they're gonna look for. And he hires like an expert forger to make the pages look like they came out of Hemingway's machine. So could it work?"

Baird pursed his lips and for a moment looked professorial. Then he sort of laughed, one syllable through his nose. "Maybe it could. A man did a similar thing when I was a boy, counterfeiting the memoirs of Howard Hughes. He made millions."

"Millions?"

"Back when that was real money. Went to jail when they found out, of course."

"And the money was still there when he got out."

"Never read anything about it. I guess so."

"So the next question is, how much stuff are we talkin' about? How much was in that old overnight bag?"

"That depends on who you believe. There was half a novel and some poetry. The short stories, there might have been as few as eleven or as many as thirty."

"That'd take a long time to write."

"It would take forever. You couldn't just 'do' Hemingway; you'd have to figure out what the stories were about, then reconstruct his early style—do you know how many Hemingway scholars there are in the world?"

"Huh uh. Quite a few."

"Thousands. Maybe ten thousand academics who know enough to spot a careless fake."

Castle nodded, cogitating. "You'd have to be real careful. But then you wouldn't have to do all the short stories and poems, would you? You could say all you found was the part of the novel. Hell, you could sell that as a book."

The odd laugh again. "Sure you could. Be a fortune in it."

"How much? A million bucks?"

"A million . . . maybe. Well, sure. The last new Hemingway made at least that much, allowing for inflation. And he's more popular now."

Castle took a big gulp of beer and set his glass down decisively. "So what the hell are we waiting for?"

Baird's bland smile faded. "You're serious?"

2. IN OUR TIME

Got a ripple in the Hemingway channel.

Twenties again?

No, funny, this one's in the 1990s. See if you can track it down?

Sure. Go down to the armory first and—

Look—no bloodbaths this time. You solve one problem and start ten more.

Couldn't be helped. It's no tea party, twentieth century America.

Just use good judgment. That Ransom guy . . .

Manson. Right. That was a mistake.

3. A WAY YOU'LL NEVER BE

You can't cheat an honest man, as Sylvester Castlemaine well knew, but then again, it never hurts to find out just how honest a man is. John Baird refused his scheme, with good humor at first, but when Castle persisted, his refusal took on a sarcastic edge, maybe a tinge of outrage. He backed off and changed the subject, talking for a half hour about commercial fishing around Key West, and then said he had to run. He slipped his business card into John's shirt pocket on the way out. (Sylvester Castlemaine, Consultant, it claimed.)

John left the place soon, walking slowly through the afternoon heat. He was glad he hadn't brought the bicycle; it was pleasant to walk in the shade of the big aromatic trees, a slight breeze on his face from the Gulf side.

One could do it. One could. The problem divided itself into three parts: writing the novel fragment, forging the manuscript, and devising a suitable story about how one had uncovered the manuscript.

The writing part would be the hardest. Hemingway is easy enough to parody — one-fourth of the take-home final he gave in English 733 was to write a page of Hemingway pastiche, and some of his graduate students did a credible job — but parody was exactly what one would not want to do.

It had been a crucial period in Hemingway's development, those three years of apprenticeship the lost manuscripts represented. Two stories survived, and they were maddeningly dissimilar. "My Old Man," which had slipped down behind a drawer, was itself a pastiche, reading like pretty good Sherwood Anderson, but with an O. Henry twist at the end — very unlike the bleak understated quality that would distinguish the stories that were to make Hemingway's reputation. The other, "Up in Michigan," had been out in the mail at the time of the loss. It was a lot closer to Hemingway's ultimate style, a spare and, by the standards of the time, pornographic description of a woman's first sexual experience.

John riffled through the notes on the yellow pad, a talismanic gesture, since he could have remembered any page with little effort. But the sight of the words and the feel of the paper sometimes helped him think.

One would not do it, of course. Except perhaps as a mental exercise. Not to show to anybody. Certainly not to profit from.

You wouldn't want to use "My Old Man" as the model, certainly; no one would care to publish a pastiche of a pastiche of Anderson, now undeservedly obscure. So "Up in Michigan." And the first story he wrote after the loss, "Out of Season," would also be handy. That had a lot of the Hemingway strength.

You wouldn't want to tackle the novel fragment, of course, not just as an exercise, over a hundred pages. . . .

Without thinking about it, John dropped into a familiar fugue state as he walked through the run-down neighborhood, his freak memory taking over while his body ambled along on autopilot. This is the way he usually remembered pages. He transported himself back to the Hemingway collection at the JFK Library in Boston, last November, snow swirling outside the big picture windows overlooking the harbor, the room so cold he was wearing coat and gloves and could see his breath. They didn't normally let you wear a coat up there, afraid you might squirrel away a page out of the manuscript collection, but they had to make an exception because the heat pump was down.

He was flipping through the much-thumbed Xerox of Carlos Baker's interview with Hadley, page 52: "Stolen suitcase," Baker asked; "lost novel?"

The typescript of her reply appeared in front of him, more clear than the cracked sidewalk his feet negotiated: "This novel was a knockout, about Nick, up north in Michigan—hunting, fishing, all sorts of experiences—stuff on the order of 'Big Two-Hearted River,' with more action. Girl experiences well done, too." With an enigmatic addition, evidently in Hadley's handwriting, "Girl experiences too well done."

That was interesting. John hadn't thought about that, since he'd been concentrating on the short stories. Too well done? There had been a lot of talk in the eighties about Hemingway's sexual ambiguity—*gender* ambiguity, actually—could Hadley have been upset, sixty years after the fact, remembering some confidence that Hemingway had revealed to the world in that novel; something girls knew that boys were not supposed to know? Playful pillow talk that was filed away for eventual literary exploitation?

He used his life that way. A good writer remembered everything and then forgot it when he sat down to write, and reinvented it so the writing would be more real than the memory. Experience was important, but imagination was more important.

Maybe I would be a better writer, John thought, if I could learn how to forget. For about the tenth time today, like any day, he regretted not having tried to succeed as a writer, while he still had the independent income. Teaching and research had fascinated him when he was younger, a rich boy's all-consuming hobbies, but the end of this fiscal year would be the end of the monthly checks from the trust fund. So the salary from Boston University wouldn't be mad money any more, but rent and groceries in a city suddenly expensive.

Yes, the writing would be the hard part. Then forging the manuscript, that wouldn't be easy. Any scholar would have access to copies of thousands of pages that Hemingway typed before and after the loss. Could one find the typewriter Hemingway had used? Then duplicate his idiosyncratic typing style—a moment's reflection put a sample in front of him, spaces before and after periods and commas. . . .

He snapped out of the reverie as his right foot hit the first step on the back staircase up to their rented flat. He automatically stepped over the fifth step, the rotted one, and was thinking about a nice tall glass of iced tea as he opened the screen door.

"Scorpions!" his wife screamed, two feet from his face.

"What?"

"We have scorpions!" Lena grabbed his arm and hauled him to the kitchen.

"Look!" She pointed at the opaque plastic skylight. Three scorpions, each about six inches long, cast sharp silhouettes on the milky plastic. One was moving.

"My word."

"Your *word!*" She struck a familiar pose, hands on hips, and glared up at the creatures. "What are we going to do about it?"

"We could name them."

"John."

"I don't know." He opened the refrigerator. "Call the bug man."

"The bug man was just here yesterday. He probably flushed them out."

He poured a glass of cold tea and dumped two envelopes of artificial sweetener into it. "I'll talk to Julio about it. But you know they've been there all along. They're not bothering anybody."

"They're bothering the hell out of me!"

He smiled. "Okay. I'll talk to Julio." He looked into the oven. "Thought about dinner?"

"Anything you want to cook, sweetheart. I'll be damned if I'm going to stand there with three . . . poisonous . . . arthropods staring down at me."

"Poised to jump," John said, and looked up again. There were only two visible now, which made his skin crawl.

"Julio wasn't home when I first saw them. About an hour ago."

"I'll go check." John went downstairs and Julio, the landlord, was indeed home, but was not impressed by the problem. He agreed that it was probably the bug man, and they would probably go back to where they came from in a while, and gave John a flyswatter.

John left the flyswatter with Lena, admonishing her to take no prisoners, and walked a couple of blocks to a Chinese restaurant. He brought back a few boxes of takeout, and they sat in the living room and wielded chopsticks in silence, listening for the pitter-patter of tiny feet.

"Met a real live con man today." He put the business card on the coffee table between them.

"Consultant?" she read.

"He had a loony scheme about counterfeiting the missing stories." Lena knew more about the missing stories than ninety-eight percent of the people who Hemingway'ed for a living. John liked to think out loud.

"Ah, the stories," she said, preparing herself.

"Not a bad idea, actually, if one had a larcenous nature." He concentrated for a moment on the slippery Moo Goo Gai Pan. "Be millions of bucks in it."

He was bent over the box. She stared hard at his bald spot. "What exactly did he have in mind?"

"We didn't bother to think it through in any detail, actually. You go and find . . ." He got the slightly walleyed look that she knew meant he was reading a page of a book a thousand miles away. "Yes. A 1921 Corona portable, like the one Hadley gave him before they were married. Find some old paper. Type up the stories. Take them to Sotheby's. Spend money for the rest of your life. That's all there is to it."

"You left out jail."

"A mere detail. Also the writing of the stories. That could take weeks. Maybe you could get arrested first, write the stories in jail, and then sell them when you got out."

"You're weird, John."

"Well. I didn't give him any encouragement."

"Maybe you should've. A few million would come in handy next year."

"We'll get by."

" 'We'll get by.' You keep saying that. How do you know? You've never had to 'get by.'"

"Okay, then. We won't get by." He scraped up the last of the fried rice. "We won't be able to make the rent and they'll throw us out on the street. We'll live in a cardboard box over a heating grate. You'll have to sell your body to keep me in cheap wine. But we'll be happy, dear." He looked up at her, mooning. "Poor but happy."

"Slap-happy." She looked at the card again. "How do you know he's a con man?"

"I don't know. Salesman type. Says he's in commercial fishing now, but he doesn't seem to like it much."

"He didn't say anything about any, you know, criminal stuff he'd done in the past?"

"Huh uh. I just got the impression that he didn't waste a lot of time mulling over ethics and morals." John held up the Mont Blanc pen. "He was staring at this, before he came over and introduced himself. I think he smelled money."

Lena stuck both chopsticks into the half-finished carton of boiled rice and set it down decisively. "Let's ask him over."

"He's a sleaze, Lena. You wouldn't like him."

"I've never met a real con man. It would be fun."

He looked into the darkened kitchen. "Will you cook something?"

She followed his gaze, expecting monsters. "If you stand guard."

4. ROMANCE IS DEAD
SUBTITLE
THE HELL IT IS

"Be a job an' a half," Castle said, mopping up residual spaghetti sauce with a piece of garlic bread. "It's not like your Howard Hughes guy, or Hitler's notebooks."

"You've been doing some research." John's voice was a little slurred. He'd bought a half gallon of Portuguese wine, the bottle wrapped in straw like cheap Chianti, the wine not quite that good. If you could get past the first couple of glasses, it was okay. It had been okay to John for some time now.

"Yeah, down to the library. The guys who did the Hitler notebooks, hell, nobody'd ever seen a real Hitler notebook; they just studied his handwriting in letters and such, then read up on what he did day after day. Same with the Howard Hughes, but that was even easier, because most of the time nobody knew what the hell Howard Hughes was doing anyhow. Just stayed locked up in that room."

"The Hughes forgery nearly worked, as I recall," John said. "If Hughes himself hadn't broken silence . . ."

"Ya gotta know that took balls. 'Scuse me, Lena." She waved a hand and laughed. "Try to get away with that while Hughes was still alive."

"How did the Hitler people screw up?" she asked.

"Funny thing about that one was how many people they fooled. Afterwards everybody said it was a really lousy fake. But you can bet that before the newspapers bid millions of dollars on it, they showed it to the best Hitlerologists they could find, and they all said it was real."

"Because they wanted it to be real," Lena said.

"Yeah. But one of the pages had some chemical in it that wouldn't be in paper before 1945. That was kinda dumb."

"People would want the Hemingway stories to be real," Lena said quietly, to John. John's gaze stayed fixed on the center of the table, where a few strands of spaghetti lay cold and drying in a plastic bowl. "Wouldn't be honest."

"That's for sure," Castle said cheerily. "But it ain't exactly armed robbery, either."

"A gross misuse of intellectual . . . intellectual . . ."

"It's past your bedtime, John," Lena said. "We'll clean up." John nodded and pushed himself away from the table and walked heavily into the bedroom.

Lena didn't say anything until she heard the bedsprings creak. "He isn't always like this," she said quietly.

"Yeah. He don't act like no alky."

"It's been a hard year for him." She refilled her glass. "Me, too. Money."

"That's bad."

"Well, we knew it was coming. He tell you about the inheritance?" Castle leaned forward. "Huh uh."

"He was born pretty well off. Family had textile mills up in New Hampshire. John's grandparents died in an auto accident in the forties and the family sold off the mills—good timing, too. They wouldn't be worth much today.

"Then John's father and mother died in the sixties, while he was in college. The executors set up a trust fund that looked like it would keep him in pretty good shape forever. But he wasn't interested in money. He even joined the army, to see what it was like."

"Jesus."

"Afterwards, he carried a picket sign and marched against the war—you know, Vietnam.

"Then he finished his Ph.D. and started teaching. The trust fund must have been fifty times as much as his salary, when he started out. It was still ten times as much, a couple of years ago."

"Boy . . . howdy." Castle was doing mental arithmetic and algebra with variables like Porsches and fast boats.

"But he let his sisters take care of it. He let them reinvest the capital."

"They weren't too swift?"

"They were idiots! They took good solid blue-chip stocks and tax-free municipals, too 'boring' for them, and threw it all away gambling on commodities." She grimaced. "*Pork* bellies? I finally had John go to Chicago and come back with what was left of his money. There wasn't much."

"You ain't broke, though."

"Damned near. There's enough income to pay for insurance and eventually we'll be able to draw on an IRA. But the cash payments stop in two months. We'll have to live on John's salary. I suppose I'll get a job, too."

"What you ought to get is a typewriter."

Lena laughed and slouched back in her chair. "That would be something."

"You think he could do it? I mean if he would, do you think he could?"

"He's a good writer." She looked thoughtful. "He's had some stories published, you know, in the literary magazines. The ones that pay four or five free copies."

"Big deal."

She shrugged. "Pays off in the long run. Tenure. But I don't know whether being able to write a good literary story means that John could write a good Hemingway imitation."

"He knows enough, right?"

"Maybe he knows too much. He might be paralyzed by his own standards." She shook her head. "In some ways he's an absolute nut about Hemingway. Obsessed, I mean. It's not good for him."

"Maybe writing this stuff would get it out of his system."

She smiled at him. "You've got more angles than a protractor."

"Sorry; I didn't mean to—"

"No." She raised both hands. "Don't be sorry; I like it. I like you, Castle. John's a good man, but sometimes he's too good."

He poured them both more wine. "Nobody ever accused me of that."

"I suspect not." She paused. "Have you ever been in trouble with the police? Just curious."

"Why?"

"Just curious."

He laughed. "Nickel-and-dime stuff, when I was a kid. You know, jus' to see what you can get away with." He turned serious. "Then I pulled two months' hard time for somethin' I didn't do. Wasn't even in town when it happened."

"What was it?"

"Armed robbery. Then the guy came back an' hit the same goddamned store! I mean, he was one sharp cookie. He confessed to the first one and they let me go."

"Why did they accuse you in the first place?"

"Used to think it was somebody had it in for me. Like the clerk who fingered me." He took a sip of wine. "But hell. It was just dumb luck. And dumb cops. The guy was about my height, same color hair, we both lived in the neighborhood. Cops didn't want to waste a lot of time on it. Jus' chuck me in jail."

"So you do have a police record?"

"Huh uh. Girl from the ACLU made sure they wiped it clean. She wanted me to go after 'em for what? False arrest an' wrongful imprisonment. I just wanted to get out of town."

"It wasn't here?"

"Nah. Dayton, Ohio. Been here eight, nine years."

"That's good."

"Why the third degree?"

She leaned forward and patted the back of his hand. "Call it a job interview, Castle. I have a feeling we may be working together."

"Okay." He gave her a slow smile. "Anything else you want to know?"

5. THE DOCTOR AND THE DOCTOR'S WIFE

John trudged into the kitchen the next morning, ignored the coffeepot, and pulled a green bottle of beer out of the fridge. He looked up at the skylight. Four scorpions, none of them moving. Have to call the bug man today.

Red wine hangover, the worst kind. He was too old for this. Cheap red wine hangover. He eased himself into a soft chair and carefully poured the beer down the side of the glass. Not too much noise, please.

When you drink too much, you ought to take a couple of aspirin, and some vitamins, and all the water you can hold, before retiring. If you drink too much, of course, you don't remember to do that.

The shower turned off with a bass clunk of plumbing. John winced and took a long drink, which helped a little. When he heard the bathroom door open he called for Lena to bring the aspirin when she came out.

After a few minutes she brought it out and handed it to him. "And how is Dr. Baird today?"

"Dr. Baird needs a doctor. Or an undertaker." He shook out two aspirin and washed them down with the last of the beer. "Like your outfit."

She was wearing only a towel around her head. She simpered and struck a dancer's pose and spun daintily around. "Think it'll catch on?"

"Oh my yes." At thirty-five, she still had the trim model's figure that had caught his eye in the classroom, fifteen years before. A safe, light tan was uniform all over her body, thanks to liberal sunblock and the private sunbathing area on top of the house—private except for the helicopter that came low overhead every weekday at 1:15. She always tried to be there in time to wave at it. The pilot had such white teeth. She wondered how many sunbathers were on his route.

She undid the towel and rubbed her long blond hair vigorously. "Thought I'd cool off for a few minutes before I got dressed. Too much wine, eh?"

"Couldn't you tell from my sparkling repartee last night?" He leaned back, eyes closed, and rolled the cool glass back and forth on his forehead.

"Want another beer?"

"Yeah. Coffee'd be smarter, though."

"It's been sitting all night."

"Pay for my sins." He watched her swivel lightly into the kitchen and, more than ever before, felt the difference in their ages. Seventeen years; he was half again as old as she. A young man would say the hell with the hangover, go grab that luscious thing and carry her back to bed. The organ that responded to this meditation was his stomach, though, and it responded very audibly.

"Some toast, too. Or do you want something fancier?"

"Toast would be fine." Why was she being so nice? Usually if he drank too much, he reaped the whirlwind in the morning.

"Ugh." She saw the scorpions. "Five of them now."

"I wonder how many it will hold before it comes crashing down. Scorpions everywhere, stunned. Then angry."

"I'm sure the bug man knows how to get rid of them."

"In Africa they claimed that if you light a ring of fire around them with gasoline or lighter fluid, they go crazy, run amok, stinging themselves to death in their frenzies. Maybe the bug man could do that."

"Castle and I came up with a plan last night. It's kinda screwy, but it might just work."

"Read that in a book called *Jungle Ways*. I was eight years old and believed every word of it."

"We figured out a way that it would be legal. Are you listening?"

"Uh huh. Let me have real sugar and some milk."

She poured some milk in a cup and put it in the microwave to warm. "Maybe we should talk about it later."

"Oh no. Hemingway forgery. You figured out a way to make it legal. Go ahead. I'm all ears."

"See, you tell the publisher first off what it is, that you wrote it and then had it typed up to look authentic."

"Sure, be a big market for that."

"In fact, there could be. You'd have to generate it, but it could happen." The toast sprang up and she brought it and two cups of coffee into the living room on a tray. "See, the bogus manuscript is only one part of a book."

"I don't get it." He tore the toast into strips, to dunk in the strong Cuban coffee.

"The rest of the book is in the nature of an exegesis of your own text."

"If that con man knows what exegesis is, then I can crack a safe."

"That part's my idea. You're really writing a book *about* Hemingway. You use your own text to illustrate various points — 'I wrote it this way instead of that way because. . . .'"

"It would be different," he conceded. "Perhaps the second most egotistical piece of Hemingway scholarship in history. A dubious distinction."

"You could write it tongue-in-cheek, though. It could be really amusing, as well as scholarly."

"God, we'd have to get an unlisted number, publishers calling us night and day. Movie producers. Might sell ten copies, if I bought nine."

"You really aren't getting it, John. You don't have a particle of larceny in your heart."

He put a hand on his heart and looked down. "Ventricles, auricles. My undying love for you, a little heartburn. No particles."

"See, you tell the publisher the truth . . . but the publisher doesn't have to tell the truth. Not until publication day."

"Okay. I still don't get it."

She took a delicate nibble of toast. "It goes like this. They print the bogus Hemingway up into a few copies of bogus bound galleys. Top secret."

"My exegesis carefully left off."

"That's the ticket. They send it out to a few selected scholars, along with Xeroxes of a few sample manuscript pages. All they say, in effect, is 'Does this seem authentic to you? Please keep it under your hat, for obvious reasons.' Then they sit back and collect blurbs."

"I can see the kind of blurbs they'd get from Scott or Mike or Jack, for instance. Some variation of 'What kind of idiot do you think I am?'"

"Those aren't the kind of people you send it to, dope! You send it to people who think they're experts, but aren't. Castle says this is how the Hitler thing almost worked—they knew better than to show it to historians in general. They showed it to a few people and didn't quote the ones who thought it was a fake. Surely you can come up with a list of people who would be easy to fool."

"Any scholar could. Be a different list for each one; I'd be on some of them."

"So they bring it out on April Fool's Day. You get the front page of the *New York Times Book Review*. *Publishers Weekly* does a story. Everybody wants to be in on the joke. Best-seller list, here we come."

"Yeah, sure, but you haven't thought it through." He leaned back, balancing the coffee cup on his slight potbelly. "What about the guys who give us the blurbs, those second-rate scholars? They're going to look pretty bad."

"We did think of that. No way they could sue, not if the letter accompanying the galleys is carefully written. It doesn't have to say—"

"I don't mean getting sued. I mean I don't want to be responsible for hurting other people's careers—maybe wrecking a career, if the person was too extravagant in his endorsement, and had people looking for things to use against him. You know departmental politics. People go down the chute for less serious crimes than making an ass of yourself and your institution in print."

She put her cup down with a clatter. "You're always thinking about other people. Why don't you think about yourself for a change?" She was on the verge of tears. "Think about *us*."

"All right, let's do that. What do you think would happen to my career at BU if I pissed off the wrong people with this exercise? How long do you think it would take me to make full professor? Do you think BU would make a full professor out of a man who uses his specialty to pull vicious practical jokes?"

"Just do me the favor of thinking about it. Cool down and weigh the pluses and minuses. If you did it with the right touch, your department would love it—and God, Harry wants to get rid of the chairmanship so bad he'd give it to an axe murderer. You know you'll make full professor about thirty seconds before Harry hands you the keys to the office and runs."

"True enough." He finished the coffee and stood up in a slow creak. "I'll give it some thought. Horizontally." He turned toward the bedroom.

"Want some company?"

He looked at her for a moment. "Indeed I do."

6. IN OUR TIME

Back already?

Need to find a meta-causal. One guy seems to be generating the danger flag in various timelines. John Baird, who's a scholar in some of them, a soldier in some, and a rich playboy in a few. He's always a Hemingway nut, though. He does something that starts off the ripples in '95, '96, '97; depending on which time line you're in—but I can't seem to get close to it. There's something odd about him, and it doesn't have to do with Hemingway specifically.

But he's definitely causing the eddy?

Has to be him.

All right. Find a meta-causal that all the doom lines have in common, and forget about the others. Then go talk to him.

There'll be resonance—

But who cares? Moot after A.D. 2006.

That's true. I'll hit all the doom lines at once, then: neutralize the meta-causal, then jump ahead and do some spot checks.

Good. And no killing this time.

I understand. But—

You're too close to 2006. Kill the wrong person, and the whole thing could unravel.

Well, there are differences of opinion. We would certainly feel it if the world failed to come to an end in those lines.

As you say, differences of opinion. My opinion is that you better not kill anybody or I'll send you back to patrol the fourteenth century again.

Understood. But I can't guarantee that I can neutralize the meta-causal without eliminating John Baird.

Fourteenth century. Some people love it. Others think it was nasty, brutish, and long.

7. A CLEAN, WELL-LIGHTED PLACE

Most of the sleuthing that makes up literary scholarship takes place in settings either neutral or unpleasant. Libraries' old stacks, attics metaphorical and actual; dust and silverfish, yellowed paper and fading ink. Books and letters that appear in card files but not on shelves.

Hemingway researchers have a haven outside of Boston, the Hemingway Collection at the University of Massachusetts's John F. Kennedy Library. It's a triangular room with one wall dominated by a picture window that looks over Boston Harbor to the sea. Comfortable easy chairs surround a coffee table, but John had never seen them in use; worktables under the picture window provided realistic room for computer and clutter. Skins from animals the Hemingways had dispatched in Africa snarled up from the floor, and one wall was dominated by Hemingway memorabilia and photographs. What made the room Nirvana, though, was row upon row of boxes containing tens of thousands of Xerox pages of Hemingway correspondence, manuscripts, clippings—everything from a boyhood shopping list to all extant versions of every short story and poem and novel.

John liked to get there early so he could claim one of the three computers. He snapped it on, inserted a CD, and typed in his code number. Then he keyed in the database index and started searching.

The more commonly requested items would appear on screen if you asked for them—whenever someone requested a physical copy of an item, an electronic copy automatically was sent into the database—but most of the things John needed were obscure, and he had to haul down the letter boxes and physically flip through them, just like some poor scholar inhabiting the first nine-tenths of the twentieth century.

Time disappeared for him as he abandoned his notes and followed lines of instinct, leaping from letter to manuscript to note to interview, doing what was in essence the opposite of the scholar's job: a scholar would normally be trying to find out what these stories had been about. John instead was trying to track down every reference that might restrict what he himself could write about, simulating the stories.

The most confining restriction was the one he'd first remembered, walking away from the bar where he'd met Castle. The one-paragraph answer that Hadley had given to Carlos Baker about the unfinished novel; that it was a Nick Adams story about hunting and fishing up in Michigan. John didn't know anything about hunting, and most of his fishing experience was limited to watching a bobber and hoping it wouldn't go down and break his train of thought.

There was the one story that Hemingway had left unpublished, "Boys and Girls Together," mostly clumsy self-parody. It covered the right period and the right activities, but using it as a source would be sensitive business, tiptoeing through a minefield. Anyone looking for a fake would go straight there. Of course John could go up to the Michigan woods and camp out, see things for himself and try to recreate them in the Hemingway style. Later, though. First order of business was to make sure there was nothing in this huge collection that would torpedo the whole project—some postcard where Hemingway said "You're going to like this novel because it has a big scene about cleaning fish."

The short stories would be less restricted in subject matter. According to Hemingway, they'd been about growing up in Oak Park and Michigan and the battlefields of Italy.

That made him stop and think. The one dramatic experience he shared with Hemingway was combat—fifty years later, to be sure, in Vietnam, but the basic situations couldn't have changed that much. Terror, heroism, cowardice. The guns and grenades were a little more streamlined, but they did the same things to people. Maybe do a World War I story as a finger exercise, see whether it would be realistic to try a longer growing-up-in-Michigan pastiche.

He made a note to himself about that on the computer, oblique enough not to be damning, and continued the eye-straining job of searching through Hadley's correspondence, trying to find some further reference to the lost novel—damn!

Writing to Ernest's mother, Hadley noted that "the taxi driver broke his typewriter" on the way to the Constantinople conference—did he get it fixed, or just chuck it? A quick check showed that the typeface of his manuscripts did indeed change after July 1924. So they'd never be able to find it. There were typewriters in Hemingway shrines in Key West, Billings, Schruns; the initial plan had been to find which was the old Corona, then locate an identical one and have Castle arrange a swap.

So they would fall back on Plan B. Castle had claimed to be good with mechanical things, and thought if they could find a 1921 Corona, he could tweak the keys around so they would produce a convincing manuscript—lowercase "s" a hair low, "e" a hair high, and so forth.

How he could be so sure of success without ever having seen the inside of a manual typewriter, John did not know. Nor did he have much confidence.

But it wouldn't have to be a perfect simulation, since they weren't out to fool the whole world, but just a few reviewers who would only see two or three Xeroxed pages. He could probably do a close enough job. John put it out of his mind and moved on to the next letter.

But it was an odd coincidence for him to think about Castle at that instant, since Castle was thinking about him. Or at least asking.

8. THE COMING MAN

"How was he when he was younger?"

"He never was younger." She laughed and rolled around inside the compass of his arms to face him. "Than you, I mean. He was in his mid-thirties when we met. You can't be much over twenty-five."

He kissed the end of her nose. "Thirty this year. But I still get carded sometimes."

"I'm a year older than you are. So you have to do anything I say."

"So far so good." He'd checked her wallet when she'd gone into the bathroom to insert the diaphragm, and knew she was thirty-five. "Break out the whips and chains now?"

"Not till next week. Work up to it slowly." She pulled away from him and mopped her front with the sheet. "You're good at being slow."

"I like being asked to come back."

"How 'bout tonight and tomorrow morning?"

"If you feed me lots of vitamins. How long you think he'll be up in Boston?"

"He's got a train ticket for Wednesday. But he said he might stay longer if he got onto something."

Castle laughed. "Or into something. Think he might have a girl up there? Some student like you used to be?"

"That would be funny. I guess it's not impossible." She covered her eyes with the back of her hand. "The wife is always the last to know."

They both laughed. "But I don't think so. He's a sweet guy but he's just not real sexy. I think his students see him as kind of a favorite uncle."

"You fell for him once."

"Uh huh. He had all of his current virtues plus a full head of hair, no potbelly—and, hm, what am I forgetting?"

"He was hung like an elephant?"

"No, I guess it was the millions of dollars. That can be pretty sexy."

9. WANDERINGS

It was a good thing John liked to nose around obscure neighborhoods shopping; you couldn't walk into any old K mart and pick up a 1921 Corona portable. In fact, you couldn't walk into any typewriter shop in Boston and find one, not any. Nowadays they all sold self-contained word processors, with a few dusty electrics in the back room. A few had fancy manual typewriters from Italy or Switzerland; it had been almost thirty years since the American manufacturers had made a machine that wrote without electronic help.

He had a little better luck with pawnshops. Lots of Smith-Coronas, a few L. C. Smiths, and two actual Coronas that might have been old enough. One had too large a typeface and the other, although the typeface was the same as Hemingway's, was missing a couple of letters: Th quick b own fox jump d ov th lazy dog. The challenge of writing a convincing Hemingway novel without using the letters "e" and "r" seemed daunting. He bought the machine anyhow, thinking they might ultimately have two or several broken ones that could be concatenated into one reliable machine.

The old pawnbroker rang up his purchase and made change and slammed the cash drawer shut. "Now you don't look to me like the kind of man who would hold it against a man who . . ." He shrugged. "Well, who sold you something and then suddenly remembered that there was a place with lots of those somethings?"

"Of course not. Business is business."

"I don't know the name of the guy or his shop; I think he calls it a museum. Up in Brunswick, Maine. He's got a thousand old typewriters. He buys, sells, trades. That's the only place I know of you might find one with the missing whatever-you-call-ems."

"Fonts." He put the antique typewriter under his arm—the handle was missing—and shook the old man's hand. "Thanks a lot. This might save me weeks."

With some difficulty John got together packing materials and shipped the machine to Key West, along with Xeroxes of a few dozen pages of Hemingway's typed copy and a note suggesting Castle see what he could do. Then he went to the library and found a Brunswick telephone directory. Under "Office Machines & Supplies" was listed Crazy Tom's Typewriter Museum and Sales Emporium. John rented a car and headed north.

The small town had rolled up its sidewalks by the time he got there. He drove past Crazy Tom's and pulled into the first motel. It had a neon VACANCY sign but the innkeeper had to be roused from a deep sleep. He took John's credit card number and directed him to Room 14 and pointedly turned on the NO sign. There were only two other cars in the motel lot.

John slept late and treated himself to a full "trucker's" breakfast at the local diner: two pork chops and eggs and hash browns. Then he worked off ten calories by walking to the shop.

Crazy Tom was younger than John had expected, thirtyish with an unruly shock of black hair. A manual typewriter lay upside down on an immaculate worktable, but most of the place was definitely maculate. Thousands of peanut shells littered the floor. Crazy Tom was eating them compulsively from a large wooden bowl. When he saw John standing in the doorway, he offered some. "Unsalted," he said. "Good for you."

John crunched his way over the peanut-shell carpet. The only light in the place was the bare bulb suspended over the worktable, though two unlit high-intensity lamps were clamped on either side of it. The walls were floor-to-ceiling gloomy shelves holding hundreds of typewriters, mostly black.

"Let me guess," the man said as John scooped up a handful of peanuts. "You're here about a typewriter."

"A specific one. A 1921 Corona portable."

"Ah." He closed his eyes in thought. "Hemingway. His first. Or I guess the first after he started writing. A '27 Corona, now, that'd be Faulkner."

"You get a lot of calls for them?"

"Couple times a year. People hear about this place and see if they can find one like the master used, whoever the master is to them. Sympathetic magic and all that. But you aren't a writer."

"I've had some stories published."

"Yeah, but you look too comfortable. You do something else. Teach school." He looked around in the gloom. "Corona Corona." Then he sang the six syllables to the tune of "Corina, Corina." He walked a few steps into the darkness and returned with a small machine and set it on the table. "Newer than 1920 because of the way it says 'Corona' here. Older than 1927 because of the tab setup." He found a piece of paper and a chair. "Go on, try it."

John typed out a few quick foxes and aids to one's party. The typeface was identical to the one on the machine Hadley had given Hemingway before they'd been married. The up-and-down displacements of the letters were different, of course, but Castle should be able to fix that once he'd practiced with the backup machine.

John cracked a peanut. "How much?"

"What you need it for?"

"Why is that important?"

"It's the only one I got. Rather rent it than sell it." He didn't look like he was lying, trying to push the price up. "A thousand to buy, a hundred a month to rent."

"Tell you what, then. I buy it, and if it doesn't bring me luck, you agree to buy it back at a pro ratum. My one thousand dollars minus ten percent per month."

Crazy Tom stuck out his hand. "Let's have a beer on it."

"Isn't it a little early for that?"

"Not if you eat peanuts all morning." He took two long-necked Budweisers from a cooler and set them on paper towels on the table. "So what kind of stuff you write?"

"Short stories and some poetry." The beer was good after the heavy greasy breakfast. "Nothing you would've seen unless you read magazines like *Iowa Review* and *Triquarterly*."

"Oh yeah. Foldouts of Gertrude Stein and H.D. I might've read your stuff."

"John Baird."

He shook his head. "Maybe. I'm no good with names."

"If you recognized my name from *The Iowa Review* you'd be the first person who ever had."

"I was right about the Hemingway connection?"

"Of course."

"But you don't write like Hemingway for no *Iowa Review*. Short declarative sentences, truly this truly that."

"No, you were right about the teaching, too. I teach Hemingway up at Boston University."

"So that's why the typewriter? Play show-and-tell with your students?"

"That, too. Mainly I want to write some on it and see how it feels."

From the back of the shop, a third person listened to the conversation with great interest. He, it, wasn't really a "person," though he could look like one: he had never been born and he would never die. But then he didn't really exist, not in the down-home pinch-yourself-ouch! way that you and I do.

In another way, he did *more* than exist, since he could slip back and forth between places you and I don't even have words for.

He was carrying a wand that could be calibrated for heart attack, stroke, or metastasized cancer on one end; the other end induced a kind of aphasia. He couldn't use it unless he materialized. He walked toward the two men, making no crunching sounds on the peanut shells because he weighed less than a thought. He studied John Baird's face from about a foot away.

"I guess it's a mystical thing, though I'm uncomfortable with that word. See whether I can get into his frame of mind."

"Funny thing," Crazy Tom said; "I never thought of him typing out his stories. He was always sitting in some café writing in notebooks, piling up saucers."

"You've read a lot about him?" That would be another reason not to try the forgery. This guy comes out of the woodwork and says "I sold John Baird a 1921 Corona portable."

"Hell, all I do is read. If I get two customers a day, one of 'em's a mistake and the other just wants directions. I've read all of Hemingway's fiction and most of the journalism and I think all of the poetry. Not just the *Querschnitt* period; the more interesting stuff."

The invisible man was puzzled. Quite obviously John Baird planned some sort of Hemingway forgery. But then he should be growing worried over this man's dangerous expertise. Instead, he was radiating relief.

What course of action, inaction? He could go back a few hours in time and steal this typewriter, though he would have to materialize for that, and it would cause suspicions. And Baird could find another. He could kill one or both of them, now or last week or next, but that would mean duty in the fourteenth century for more than forever—when you exist out of time, a century of unpleasantness is long enough for planets to form and die.

He wouldn't have been drawn to this meeting if it were not a strong causal nexus. There must be earlier ones, since John Baird did not just stroll down a back street in this little town and decide to change history by buying a typewriter. But the earlier ones must be too weak, or something was masking them.

Maybe it was a good timeplace to get John Baird alone and explain things to him. Then use the wand on him. But no, not until he knew exactly what he was preventing. With considerable effort of will and expenditure of something like energy, he froze time at this instant and traveled to a couple of hundred adjacent realities that were all in this same bundle of doomed timelines.

In most of them, Baird was here in Crazy Tom's Typewriter Museum and Sales Emporium. In some, he was in a similar place in New York. In two, he was back in the Hemingway collection. In one, John Baird didn't exist: the whole planet was a lifeless blasted cinder. He'd known about that timeline; it had been sort of a dry run.

"He did both," John then said in most of the timelines. "Sometimes typing, sometimes fountain pen or pencil. I've seen the rough draft of his first novel. Written out in a stack of seven French schoolkids' copybooks." He looked around, memory working. A red herring wouldn't hurt. He'd never come across a reference to any other specific Hemingway typewriter, but maybe this guy had. "You know what kind of machine he used in Key West or Havana?"

Crazy Tom pulled on his chin. "Nope. Bring me a sample of the typing and I might be able to pin it down, though. And I'll keep an eye out—got a card?"

John took out a business card and his checkbook. "Take a check on a Boston bank?"

"Sure. I'd take one on a Tierra del Fuego bank. Who'd stiff you on a seventy-year-old typewriter?" Sylvester Castlemaine might, John thought. "I've had this business almost twenty years," Tom continued. "Not a single bounced check or bent plastic."

"Yeah," John said. "Why would a crook want an old typewriter?" The invisible man laughed and went away.

10. BANBAL STORY

Dear Lena & Castle,

Typing this on the new/old machine to give you an idea about what has to be modified to mimic EH's:

abcdefghijklmnopqrstuvwxyz

ABCDEFGHIJKLMNOPQRSTUVWXYZ234567890,./ "#%_&'()*?

Other mechanical things to think about—

1. Paper—One thing that made people suspicious about the Hitler forgery is that experts know that old paper smells old. And of course there was that fatal chemical-composition error that clinched it.

As we discussed, my first thought was that one of us would have to go to Paris and nose around in old attics and so forth, trying to find either a stack of 75-year-old paper or an old blank book we could cut pages out of. But in the JFK Library collection I found out that EH actually did bring some American-made paper along with him. A lot of the rough draft of in our time—written in Paris a year or two after our "discovery"—was typed on the back of 6 x 7" stationery from his parents' vacation place in Windemere, Xerox enclosed. It should be pretty easy to duplicate on a hand press, and of course it will be a lot easier to find 75-year-old American paper. One complication, unfortunately, is that I haven't really seen the paper; only a Xerox of the pages. Have to come up with some pretext to either visit the vault or have a page brought up, so I can check the color of the ink, memorise the weight and deckle of the paper, check to see how the edges are cut . . .

I'm starting to sound like a real forger. In for a penny, though, in for a pound. One of the critics who's sent the fragment might want to see the actual document, and compare it with the existing Windemere pages.

2. Inks. This should not be a problem. Here's a recipe for typewriter ribbon ink from a 1918 book of commercial formulas:

8 oz. lampblack

4 oz. gum arabic

1 quart methylated spirits

That last one is wood alcohol. The others ought to be available in Miami if you can't find them on the Rock.

Aging the ink on the paper gets a little tricky. I haven't been able to find anything about it in the libraries around here; no FORGERY FOR FUN & PROFIT. May check in New York before coming back.

(If we don't find anything, I'd suggest baking it for a few days at a temperature low enough not to greatly affect the paper, and then interleaving it with blank sheets of the old paper and pressing them together for a few days, to restore the old smell, and further absorb the residual ink solvents.)

Toyed with the idea of actually allowing the manuscript to mildew somewhat, but that might get out of hand and actually destroy some of it—or for all I know we'd be employing a species of mildew that doesn't speak French. Again, thinking like a true forger, which may be a waste of time and effort, but I have to admit is kind of fun. Playing cops and robbers at my age.

Well, I'll call tonight. Miss you, Lena.

Your partner in crime,

John.

11. A DIVINE GESTURE

When John returned to his place in Boston, there was a message on his answering machine: "John, this is Nelson Van Nuys. Harry told me you were in town. I left something in your box at the office and I strongly suggest you take it before somebody else does. I'll be out of town for a week, but give me a call if you're here next Friday. You can take me and Doris out to dinner at Panache."

Panache was the most expensive restaurant in Cambridge. Interesting. John checked his watch. He hadn't planned to go to the office, but there was plenty of time to swing by on his way to returning the rental car. The train didn't leave for another four hours.

Van Nuys was a fellow Hemingway scholar and sometimes drinking buddy who taught at Brown. What had he brought ninety miles to deliver in person, rather than mail? He was probably just in town and dropped by. But it was worth checking.

No one but the secretary was in the office, noontime, for which John was obscurely relieved. In his box were three interdepartmental memos, a textbook catalog, and a brown cardboard box that sloshed when he picked it up. He took it all back to his office and closed the door.

The office made him feel a little weary, as usual. He wondered whether they would be shuffling people around again this year. The department liked to keep its professors in shape by having them haul tons of books and files up and down the corridor every couple of years.

He glanced at the memos and pitched them, irrelevant since he wasn't teaching in the summer, and put the catalog in his briefcase. Then he carefully opened the cardboard box.

It was a half-pint Jack Daniel's bottle, but it didn't have bourbon in it. A cloudy greenish liquid. John unscrewed the top and with the sharp Pernod tang the memory came back. He and Van Nuys had wasted half an afternoon in Paris years ago, trying to track down a source of true absinthe. So he had finally found some.

Absinthe. Nectar of the gods, ruination of several generations of French artists, students, workingmen—outlawed in 1915 for its addictive and hallucinogenic qualities. Where had Van Nuys found it?

He screwed the top back on tightly and put it back in the box and put the box in his briefcase. If its effect really was all that powerful, you probably wouldn't want to drive under its influence. In Boston traffic, of course, a little lane weaving and a few mild collisions would go unnoticed.

Once he was safely on the train, he'd try a shot or two of it. It couldn't be all that potent. Child of the sixties, John had taken LSD, psilocybin, ecstasy, and peyote, and remembered with complete accuracy the quality of each drug's hallucinations. The effects of absinthe wouldn't be nearly as extreme as its modern successors. But it was probably just as well to try it first in a place where unconsciousness or Steve Allen imitations or speaking in tongues would go unremarked.

He turned in the rental car and took a cab to South Station rather than juggle suitcase, briefcase, and typewriter through the subway system. Once there, he nursed a beer through an hour of the Yankees murdering the Red Sox, and then rented a cart to roll his burden down to track 3, where a smiling porter installed him aboard the *Silver Meteor*, its range newly extended from Boston to Miami.

He had loved the train since his boyhood in Washington. His mother hated flying and so they often clickety-clacked from place to place in the snug comfort of first-class compartments. Eidetic memory blunted his enjoyment of the modern Amtrak version. This compartment was as large as the ones he had read and done puzzles in, forty years before—amazing and delighting his mother with his proficiency in word games—but the smell of good old leather was gone, replaced by plastic, and the fittings that had been polished brass were chromed steel now. On the middle of the red plastic seat was a Hospitality Pak, a plastic box encased in plastic wrap that contained a wedge of indestructible "cheese food," as if cheese had to eat, a small plastic bottle of cheap California wine, a plastic glass to contain it, and an apple, possibly not plastic.

John hung up his coat and tie in the small closet provided beside where the bed would fold down, and for a few minutes he watched with interest as his fellow passengers and their accompaniment hurried or ambled to their cars. Mostly old people, of course. Enough young ones, John hoped, to keep the trains alive a few decades more.

"Mr. Baird?" John turned to face a black porter, who bowed slightly and favored him with a blinding smile of white and gold. "My name is George, and I will be at your service as far as Atlanta. Is everything satisfactory?"

"Doing fine. But if you could find me a glass made of glass and a couple of ice cubes, I might mention you in my will."

"One minute, sir." In fact, it took less than a minute. That was one aspect, John had to admit, that had improved in recent years: The service on Amtrak in the sixties and seventies had been right up there with Alcatraz and the Hanoi Hilton.

He closed and locked the compartment door and carefully poured about two ounces of the absinthe into the glass. Like Pernod, it turned milky on contact with the ice.

He swirled it around and breathed deeply. It did smell much like Pernod, but with an acrid tang that was probably oil of wormwood. An experimental sip: the wormwood didn't dominate the licorice flavor, but it was there.

"Thanks, Nelson," he whispered, and drank the whole thing in one cold fiery gulp. He set down the glass and the train began to move. For a weird moment that seemed hallucinatory, but it always did, the train starting off so smoothly and silently.

For about ten minutes he felt nothing unusual, as the train did its slow tour of Boston's least attractive backyards. The conductor who checked his ticket seemed like a normal human being, which could have been a hallucination.

John knew that some drugs, like amyl nitrite, hit with a swift slap, while others creep into your mind like careful infiltrators. This was the way of absinthe; all he felt was a slight alcohol buzz, and he was about to take another shot, when it subtly began.

There were *things* just at the periphery of his vision, odd things with substance, but somehow without shape, that of course moved away when he turned his head to look at them. At the same time a whispering began in his ears, just audible over the train noise, but not intelligible, as if in a language he had heard before but not understood. For some reason the effects were pleasant, though of course they could be frightening if a person were not expecting weirdness. He enjoyed the illusions for a few minutes, while the scenery outside mellowed into woodsy suburbs, and the visions and voices stopped rather suddenly.

He poured another ounce and this time diluted it with water. He remembered the sad woman in "Hills Like White Elephants" lamenting that everything new tasted like licorice, and allowed himself to wonder what Hemingway had been drinking when he wrote that curious story.

Chuckling at his own—what? Effrontery?—John took out the 1921 Corona and slipped a sheet of paper into it and balanced it on his knees. He had earlier thought of the first two lines of the WWI pastiche; he typed them down and kept going:

The dirt on the sides of the trenches was never completely dry in the morning. If Nick could find an old newspaper he would put it between his chest and the dirt when he went out to lean on the side of the trench and wait for the light. First light was the best time. You might have luck and see a muzzle flash. But patience was better than luck. Wait to see a helmet or a head without a helmet.

Nick looked at the enemy line through a rectangular box of wood that went through the trench at about ground level. The other end of the box was covered by a square of gauze the color of dirt. A person looking directly at it might see the muzzle flash when Nick fired through the box. But with luck, the flash would be the last thing he saw.

Nick had fired through the gauze six times, perhaps killing three enemy, and the gauze now had a ragged hole in the center.

Okay, John thought, he'd be able to see slightly better through the hole in the center but staring that way would reduce the effective field of view, so he would deliberately try to look to one side or the other. How to type that down in a simple way? Someone cleared his throat.

John looked up from the typewriter. Sitting across from him was Ernest Hemingway, the weathered, wise Hemingway of the famous Karsh photograph.

"I'm afraid you must not do that," Hemingway said.

John looked at the half-full glass of absinthe and looked back. Hemingway was still there. "Jesus Christ," he said.

"It isn't the absinthe." Hemingway's image rippled and he became the handsome teenager who had gone to war, the war John was writing about. "I am quite real. In a way, I am more real than you are." As it spoke it aged: the mustachioed leading-man-handsome Hemingway of the twenties; the slightly corpulent, still magnetic media hero of the thirties and forties; the beard turning white, the features hard and sad and then twisting with impotence and madness, and then a sudden loud report and the cranial vault exploding, the mahogany veneer of the wall splashed with blood and brains and imbedded chips of skull. There was a strong smell of cordite and blood. The almost-headless corpse shrugged, spreading its hands. "I can look like anyone I want." The mess disappeared and it became the young Hemingway again.

John slumped and stared.

"This thing you just started must never be finished. This Hemingway pastiche. It will ruin something very important."

"What could it ruin? I'm not even planning to—"

"Your plans are immaterial. If you continue with this project, it will profoundly affect the future."

"You're from the future?"

"I'm from the future and the past and other temporalities that you can't comprehend. But all you need to know is that you must not write this Hemingway story. If you do, I or someone like me will have to kill you."

It gestured and a wand the size of a walking stick, half-black and half-white, appeared in its hand. It tapped John's knee with the white end. There was a slight tingle.

"Now you won't be able to tell anybody about me, or write anything about me down. If you try to talk about me, the memory will disappear—and reappear moments later, along with the knowledge that I will kill you if you don't cooperate." It turned into the bloody corpse again. "Understood?"

"Of course."

"If you behave, you will never have to see me again." It started to fade.

"Wait. What do you really look like?"

"This...." For a few seconds John stared at an ebony presence deeper than black, at once points and edges and surfaces and volume and hints of further dimensions. "You can't really see or know," a voice whispered inside his head. He reached into the blackness and jerked his hand back, rimed with frost and numb. The thing disappeared.

He stuck his hand under his armpit and feeling returned. That last apparition was the unsettling one. He had Hemingway's appearance at every age memorized, and had seen the corpse in his mind's eye often enough. A drug could conceivably have brought them all together and made up this fantastic demand—which might actually be nothing more than a reasonable side of his nature trying to make him stop wasting time on this silly project.

But that thing. His hand was back to normal. Maybe a drug could do that, too; make your hand feel freezing. LSD did more profound things than that. But not while arguing about a manuscript.

He considered the remaining absinthe. Maybe take another big blast of it and see whether ol' Ernie comes back again. Or no—there was a simpler way to check.

The bar was four rocking and rolling cars away, and bouncing his way from wall to window helped sober John up. When he got there, he had another twinge for the memories of the past. Stained Formica tables. No service; you had to go to a bar at the other end. Acrid with cigarette fumes. He remembered linen tablecloths and endless bottles of Coke with the names of cities from everywhere stamped on the bottom and, when his father came along with them, the rich sultry smoke of his Havanas. The fat Churchills from Punch that emphysema stopped just before Castro could. "A Coke, please." He wondered which depressed him more, the red can or the plastic cup with miniature ice cubes.

The test. It was not in his nature to talk to strangers on public conveyances. But this was necessary. There was a man sitting alone who looked about John's age, a Social Security-bound hippy with wire-rimmed John Lennon glasses, white hair down to his shoulders, bushy grey beard. He nodded when John sat down across from him, but didn't say anything. He sipped beer and looked blankly out at the gathering darkness.

"Excuse me," John said, "but I have a strange thing to ask you."

The man looked at him. "I don't mind strange things. But please don't try to sell me anything illegal."

"I wouldn't. It may have something to do with a drug, but it would be one I took."

"You do look odd. You tripping?"

"Doesn't feel like it. But I may have been . . . slipped something." He leaned back and rubbed his eyes. "I just talked to Ernest Hemingway."

"The writer?"

"In my roomette, yeah."

"Wow. He must be pretty old."

"He's dead! More than thirty years."

"Oh wow. Now that is something weird. What he say?"

"You know what a pastiche is?"

"French pastry?"

"No, it's when you copy . . . when you create an imitation of another person's writing. Hemingway's, in this case."

"Is that legal? I mean, with him dead and all."

"Sure it is, as long as you don't try to foist it off as Hemingway's real stuff."

"So what happened? He wanted to help you with it?"

"Actually, no . . . he said I'd better stop."

"Then you better stop. You don't fuck around with ghosts." He pointed at the old brass bracelet on John's wrist. "You in the 'Nam."

"Sixty-eight," John said. "Hue."

"Then you oughta know about ghosts. You don't fuck with ghosts."

"Yeah." What he'd thought was aloofness in the man's eyes, the set of his mouth, was aloneness, something slightly different. "You okay?"

"Oh yeah. Wasn't for a while, then I got my shit together." He looked out the window again, and said something weirdly like Hemingway: "I learned to take it a day at a time. The day you're in's the only day that's real. The past is shit and the future, hell, some day your future's gonna be that you got no future. So fuck it, you know? One day at a time."

John nodded. "What outfit were you in?"

"Like I say, man, the past is shit. No offense?"

"No, that's okay." He poured the rest of his Coke over the ice and stood up to go.

"You better talk to somebody about those ghosts. Some kinds shrink, you know? It's not that they're not real. But just you got to deal with 'em."

"Thanks. I will." John got a little more ice from the barman and negotiated his way down the lurching corridor back to his compartment, trying not to spill his drink while also juggling fantasy, reality, past, present, memory. . . .

He opened the door and Hemingway was there, drinking his absinthe. He looked up with weary malice. "Am I going to have to kill you?"

What John did next would have surprised Castlemaine, who thought he was a nebbish. He closed the compartment door and sat down across from the apparition. "Maybe you can kill me and maybe you can't."

"Don't worry. I can."

"You said I wouldn't be able to talk to anyone about you. But I just walked down to the bar car and did."

"I know. That's why I came back."

"So if one of your powers doesn't work, maybe another doesn't. At any rate, if you kill me, you'll never find out what went wrong."

"That's very cute, but it doesn't work." It finished off the absinthe and then ran a finger around the rim of the glass, which refilled out of nowhere.

"You're making assumptions about causality that are necessarily naïve, because you can't perceive even half of the dimensions that you inhabit."

"Nevertheless, you haven't killed me yet."

"And assumptions about my 'psychology' that are absurd. I am no more a human being than you are a paramecium."

"I'll accept that. But I would make a deal with a paramecium if I thought I could gain an advantage from it."

"What could you possibly have to deal with, though?"

"I know something about myself that you evidently don't, that enables me to overcome your don't-talk restriction. Knowing that might be worth a great deal to you."

"Maybe something."

"What I would like in exchange is, of course, my life, and an explanation of why I must not do the Hemingway pastiche. Then I wouldn't do it."

"You wouldn't do it if I killed you, either."

John sipped his Coke and waited.

"All right. It goes something like this. There is not just one universe, but actually uncountable zillions of them. They're all roughly the same size and complexity as this one and they're all going off in a zillion different directions, and it is one hell of a job to keep things straight."

"You do this by yourself? You're God?"

"There's not just one of me. In fact, it would be meaningless to assign a number to us, but I guess you could say that altogether, we are God . . . and the Devil, and the Cosmic Puppet Master, and the Grand Unification Theory, the Great Pumpkin and everything else. When we consider ourselves as a group, let me see, I guess a human translation of our name would be the Spatio-Temporal Adjustment Board."

"STAB?"

"I guess that is unfortunate. Anyhow, what STAB does is more the work of a scalpel than a knife." The Hemingway scratched its nose leaving the absinthe suspended in midair. "Events are supposed to happen in certain ways, in certain sequences. You look at things happening and say cause and effect, or coincidence, or golly, that couldn't have happened in a million years—but you don't even have a clue. Don't even try to think about it. It's like an ant trying to figure out General Relativity."

"It wouldn't have a clue. Wouldn't know where to start."

The apparition gave him a sharp look and continued. "These universes come in bundles. Hundreds of them, thousands, that are pretty much the same. And they affect each other. Resonate with each other. When something goes wrong in one, it resonates and screws up all of them."

"You mean to say that if I write a Hemingway pastiche, hundreds of universes are going to go straight to hell?"

The apparition spread its hands and looked to the ceiling. "Nothing is simple. The only thing that's simple is that nothing is simple.

"I'm a sort of literature specialist. American literature of the nineteenth and twentieth centuries. Usually. Most of my timespace is taken up with guys like Hemingway, Teddy Roosevelt, Heinlein, Bierce. Crane, Spillane, Twain."

"Not William Dean Howells?"

"Not him or James or Carver or Coover or Cheever or any of those guys. If everybody gave me as little trouble as William Dean Howells, I could spend most of my timespace on a planet where the fishing was good."

"Masculine writers?" John said. "But not all hairy-chested macho types."

"I'll give you an A—on that one. They're writers who have an accumulating effect on the masculine side of the American national character. There's no one word for it, though it is a specific thing: individualistic, competence-worshiping, short-term optimism and long-term existentialism. 'There may be nothing after I die but I sure as hell will do the job right while I'm here, even though I'm surrounded by idiots.' You see the pattern?"

"Okay. And I see how Hemingway fits in. But how could writing a pastiche interfere with it?"

"That's a limitation I have. I don't know specifically. I do know that the accelerating revival of interest in Hemingway from the seventies through the nineties is vitally important. In the Soviet Union as well as the United States. For some reason, I can feel your pastiche interfering with it." He stretched out the absinthe glass into a yard-long amber crystal, and it changed into the black-and-white cane. The glass reappeared in the drink holder by the window. "Your turn."

"You won't kill me after you hear what I have to say?"

"No. Go ahead."

"Well . . . I have an absolutely eidetic memory. Everything I've ever seen—or smelled or tasted or heard or touched, or even dreamed—I can instantly recall.

"Every other memory freak I've read about was limited—numbers, dates, calendar tricks, historical details—and most of them were *idiots savants*. I have at least normal intelligence. But from the age of about three, I have never forgotten anything."

The Hemingway smiled congenially. "Thank you. That's exactly it." It fingered the black end of the cane, clicking something. "If you had the choice, would you rather die of a heart attack, stroke, or cancer?"

"That's it?" The Hemingway nodded. "Well, you're human enough to cheat. To lie."

"It's not something you could understand. Stroke?"

"It might not work."

"We're going to find out right now." He lowered the cane.

"Wait! What's death? Is there . . . anything I should do, anything you know?"

The rod stopped, poised an inch over John's knee. "I guess you just end. Is that so bad?"

"Compared to not ending, it's bad."

"That shows how little you know. I and the ones like me can never die. If you want something to occupy your last moment, your last thought, you might pity me."

John stared straight into his eyes. "Fuck you."

The cane dropped. A fireball exploded in his head.

12. MARRIAGE IS A DANGEROUS GAME

"We'll blackmail him." Castle and Lena were together in the big antique bathtub, in a sea of pink foam, her back against his chest.

"Sure," she said. " 'If you don't let us pass this manuscript off as the real thing, we'll tell everybody you faked it.' Something wrong with that, but I can't quite put my finger on it."

"Here, I'll put mine on it."

She giggled. "Later. What do you mean, blackmail?"

"Got it all figured out. I've got this friend Pansy, she used to be a call girl. Been out of the game seven, eight years; still looks like a million bucks."

"Sure. We fix John up with this hooker—"

"Call girl isn't a hooker. We're talkin' class."

"In the first place, John wouldn't pay for sex. He did that in Vietnam and it still bothers him."

"Not talkin' about pay. Talkin' about fallin' in love. While she meanwhile fucks his eyeballs out"

"You have such a turn of phrase, Sylvester. Then while his eyeballs are out, you come in with a camera."

"Yeah, but you're about six steps ahead."

"Okay, step two; how do we get them together? Church social?"

"She moves in next door." There was another upstairs apartment, unoccupied. "You and me and Julio are conveniently somewhere else when she shows up with all these boxes and that big flight of stairs."

"Sure, John would help her. But that's his nature; he'd help her if she were an ugly old crone with leprosy. Carry a few boxes, sit down for a cup of coffee, maybe. But not jump into the sack."

"Okay, you know John." His voice dropped to a husky whisper and he cupped her breasts. "But I know men, and I know Pansy . . . and Pansy could give a hard-on to a corpse."

"Sure, and then fuck his eyeballs out. They'd come out easier."

"What?"

"Never mind. Go ahead."

"Well . . . look. Do you know what a call girl does?"

"I suppose you call her up and say you've got this eyeball problem."

"Enough with the eyeballs. What she does, she works for like an escort service. That part of it's legal. Guy comes into town, business or maybe on vacation, he calls up the service and they ask what kind of companion he'd like. If he says, like, give me some broad with a tight ass, can suck the chrome off a bumper hitch—the guy says like 'I'm sorry, sir, but this is not that kind of a service.' But mostly the customers are pretty hip to it, they say, oh, a pretty young blonde who likes to go dancing."

"Meanwhile they're thinking about bumper hitches and eyeballs."

"You got it. So it starts out just like a date, just the guy pays the escort service like twenty bucks for getting them together. Still no law broken.

"Now about one out of three, four times, that's it. The guy knows what's going on but he don't get up the nerve to ask, or he really doesn't know the score, and it's like a real dull date. I don't think that happened much with Pansy."

"In the normal course of things, though, the subject of bumper hitches comes up."

"Uh huh, but not from Pansy. The guy has to pop the question. That way if he's a cop it's, what, entrapment."

"Do you know whether Pansy ever got busted?"

"Naw. Mainly the cops just shake down the hookers, just want a blowjob anyhow. This town, half of 'em want a blow-job from guys.

"So they pop the question and Pansy blushes and says for you, I guess I could. Then, on the way to the motel or wherever she says, you know, I wouldn't ask this if we weren't really good friends, but I got to make a car payment by tomorrow, and I need like two hundred bucks before noon tomorrow?"

"And she takes MasterCard and VISA."

"No, but she sure as hell knows where every bank machine in town is. She even writes up an I.O.U." Castle laughed. "Told me a guy from Toledo's holdin' five grand of I.O.U.s from her."

"All right, but that's not John. She could suck the chrome off his eyeballs and he still wouldn't be interested in her if she didn't know Hemingway from hummingbirds."

Castle licked behind her ear, a weird gesture that made her shiver. "That's the trump card. Pansy reads like a son of a bitch. She's got like a thousand books. So this morning I called her up and asked about Hemingway."

"And?"

"She's read them all."

She nodded slowly. "Not bad, Sylvester. So we promote this love affair and sooner or later you catch them in the act. Threaten to tell me unless John accedes to a life of crime."

"Think it could work? He wouldn't say hell, go ahead and tell her?"

"Not if I do my part . . . starting tomorrow. I'm the best, sweetest, lovingest wife in this sexy town. Then in a couple of weeks Pansy comes into his life, and there he is, luckiest man alive. Best of both worlds. Until you accidentally catch them in *flagrante delicioso.*"

"So to keep both of you, he goes along with me."

"It might just do it. It might just." She slowly levered herself out of the water and smoothed the suds off her various assets.

"Nice."

"Bring me that bumper hitch, Sylvester. Hold on to your eyeballs."

13. IN ANOTHER COUNTRY

John woke up with a hangover of considerable dimension. The diluted glass of absinthe was still in the drink holder by the window. It was just past dawn, and a verdant forest rushed by outside. The rails made a steady hum; the car had a slight rocking that would have been pleasant to a person who felt well.

A porter knocked twice and inquired after Mr. Baird. "Come in," John said. A short white man, smiling, brought in coffee and Danish.

"What happened to George?"

"Pardon me, sir? George who?"

John rubbed his eyes. "Oh, of course. We must be past Atlanta."

"No, sir." The man's smile froze as his brain went into nutty-passenger mode. "We're at least two hours from Atlanta."

"George . . . is a tall back guy with gold teeth who—"

"Oh, you mean George Mason, sir. He does do this car, but he picks up the train in Atlanta, and works it to Miami and back. He hasn't had the northern leg since last year."

John nodded slowly and didn't ask what year it was. "I understand." He smiled up and read the man's name tag. "I'm sorry, Leonard. Not at my best in the morning." The man withdrew with polite haste.

Suppose that weird dream had not been a dream. The Hemingway creature had killed him—the memory of the stroke was awesomely strong and immediate—but all that death amounted to was slipping into another universe where George Mason was on a different shift. Or perhaps John had gone completely insane.

The second explanation seemed much more reasonable.

On the tray underneath the coffee, juice, and Danish was a copy of USA *Today*, a paper John normally avoided because, although it had its comic aspects, it didn't have any funnies. He checked the date, and it was correct. The news stories were plausible—wars and rumors of war—so at least he hadn't slipped into a dimension where Martians ruled an enslaved Earth or Barry Manilow was president. He turned to the weather map and stopped dead.

Yesterday the country was in the middle of a heat wave that had lasted weeks. It apparently had ended overnight. The entry for Boston, yesterday, was "72/58/sh." But it hadn't rained and the temperature had been in the nineties.

He went back to the front page and began checking news stories. He didn't normally pay much attention to the news, though, and hadn't seen a paper in several days. They'd canceled their *Globe* delivery for the six weeks in Key West and he hadn't been interested enough to go seek out a newsstand.

There was no mention of the garbage collectors' strike in New York; he'd overheard a conversation about that yesterday. A long obituary for a rock star he was sure had died the year before.

An ad for DeSoto automobiles. That company had gone out of business when he was a teenager.

Bundles of universes, different from each other in small ways. Instead of dying, or maybe because of dying, he had slipped into another one. What would be waiting for him in Key West?

Maybe John Baird.

He set the tray down and hugged himself, trembling. Who or what was he in this universe? All of his memories, all of his personality, were from the one he had been born in. What happened to the John Baird that was born in this one? Was he an associate professor in American Literature at Boston University? Was he down in Key West wrestling with a paper to give at Nairobi—or working on a forgery? Or was he a Fitzgerald specialist snooping around the literary attics of St. Paul, Minnesota?

The truth came suddenly. Both John Bairds were in this compartment, in this body. And the body was slightly different.

He opened the door to the small washroom and looked in the mirror. His hair was a little shorter, less grey, beard better trimmed.

He was less paunchy and . . . something felt odd. There was feeling in his thigh. He lowered his pants and there was no scar where the sniper bullet had opened his leg and torn up the nerves there.

That was the touchstone. As he raised his shirt, the parallel memory flooded in. Puckered round scar on the abdomen; in this universe the sniper had hit a foot higher—and instead of the convalescent center in Cam Ranh Bay, the months of physical therapy and then back into the war, it had been peritonitis raging; surgery in Saigon and Tokyo and Walter Reed, and no more army.

But slowly they converged again. Amherst and U. Mass.—perversely using the G.I. Bill in spite of his access to millions—the doctorate on *The Sun Also Rises* and the instructorship at B.U., meeting Lena and virtuously waiting until after the semester to ask her out. Sex on the second date, and the third . . . but there they verged again. This John Baird hadn't gone back into combat to have his midsection sprayed with shrapnel from an American grenade that bounced off a tree; never had dozens of bits of metal cut out of his dick—and in the ensuing twenty-five years had made more use of it. Girlfriends and even one disastrous homosexual encounter with a stranger. As far as he knew, Lena was in the dark about this side of him; thought that he had remained faithful other than one incident seven years after they married. He knew of one affair she had had with a colleague, and suspected more.

The two Johns' personalities and histories merged, separate but one, like two vines from a common root, climbing a single support.

Schizophrenic but not insane.

John looked into the mirror and tried to address his new or his old self—John A, John B. There were no such people. There was suddenly a man who had existed in two separate universes and, in a way, it was no more profound than having lived in two separate houses.

The difference being that nobody else knows there is more than one house.

He moved over to the window and set his coffee in the holder, picked up the absinthe glass and sniffed it, considered pouring it down the drain, but then put it in the other holder, for possible future reference.

Posit this: is it more likely that there are bundles of parallel universes prevailed over by a Hemingway look-alike with a magic cane, or that John Baird was exposed to a drug that he had never experienced before and it had had an unusually disorienting effect?

He looked at the paper. He had not hallucinated two weeks of drought. The rock star had been dead for some time. He had not seen a DeSoto in twenty years, and that was a hard car to miss. Tail fins that had to be registered as lethal weapons.

But maybe if you take a person who remembers every trivial thing, and zap his brain with oil of wormwood, that is exactly the effect: perfectly recalled things that never actually happened.

The coffee tasted repulsive. John put on a fresh shirt and decided not to shave and headed for the bar car. He bought the last imported beer in the cooler and sat down across from the long-haired white-bearded man who had an earring that had escaped his notice before, or hadn't existed in the other universe.

The man was staring out at the forest greening by. "Morning," John said.

"How do." The man looked at him with no sign of recognition.

"Did we talk last night?"

He leaned forward. "What?"

"I mean did we sit in this car last night and talk about Hemingway and Vietnam and ghosts?"

He laughed. "You're on somethin', man. I been on this train since two in the mornin' and ain't said boo to nobody but the bartender."

"You were in Vietnam?"

"Yeah, but that's over; that's shit." He pointed at John's bracelet. "What, you got ghosts from over there?"

"I think maybe I have."

He was suddenly intense. "Take my advice, man; I been there. You got to go talk to somebody. Some shrink. Those ghosts ain't gonna go 'way by themself."

"It's not that bad."

"It ain't the ones you killed." He wasn't listening. "Fuckin' dinks, they come back but they don't, you know, they just stand around." He looked at John and tears came so hard they actually spurted from his eyes. "It's your fuckin' friends, man, they all died and they come back now. . . ." He took a deep breath and wiped his face. "They used to come back every night. That like you?" John shook his head, helpless, trapped by the man's grief. "Every fuckin' night, my old lady, finally she said you go to a shrink or go to hell." He fumbled with the button on his shirt pocket and took out a brown plastic prescription bottle and stared at the label. He shook out a capsule. "Take a swig?" John pushed the beer over to him. He washed the pill down without touching the bottle to his lips.

He sagged back against the window. "I musta not took the pill last night, sometimes I do that. Sorry." He smiled weakly. "One day at a time, you know? You get through the one day. Fuck the rest. Sorry." He leaned forward again suddenly and put his hand on John's wrist. "You come outa nowhere and I lay my fuckin' trip on you. You don' need it."

John covered the hand with his own. "Maybe I do need it. And maybe I didn't come out of nowhere." He stood up. "I will see somebody about the ghosts. Promise."

"You'll feel better. It's no fuckin' cure-all, but you'll feel better."

"Want the beer?"

He shook his head. "Not supposed to."

"Okay." John took the beer and they waved at each other and he started back.

He stopped in the vestibule between cars and stood in the rattling roar of it, looking out the window at the flashing green blur. He put his forehead against the cool glass and hid the blur behind the dark red of his eyelids.

Were there actually a zillion of those guys each going through a slightly different private hell? Something he rarely asked himself was "What would Ernest Hemingway have done in this situation?"

He'd probably have the sense to leave it to Milton.

14. THE DANGEROUS SUMMER

Castle and Lena met him at the station in Miami and they drove back to Key West in Castle's old pickup. The drone of the air conditioner held conversation to a minimum, but it kept them cool, at least from the knees down.

John didn't say anything about his encounter with the infinite, or transfinite, not wishing to bring back that fellow with the cane just yet. He did note that the two aspects of his personality hadn't quite become equal partners yet, and small details of this world kept surprising him. There was a monorail being built down to Pigeon Key, where Disney was digging an underwater park. Gasoline stations still sold Regular. Castle's car radio picked up TV as well as AM/FM, but sound only.

Lena sat between the two men and rubbed up against John affectionately. That would have been remarkable for John-one and somewhat unusual for John-two. It was a different Lena here, of course; one who had had more of a sex life with John, but there was something more than that, too. She was probably sleeping with Castle, he thought, and the extra attention was a conscious or unconscious compensation, or defense.

Castle seemed a little harder and more serious in this world than the last, not only from his terse moodiness in the pickup, but from recollections of parallel conversations. John wondered how shady he actually was, whether he'd been honest about his police record.

(He hadn't been. In this universe, when Lena had asked him whether he had ever been in trouble with the police, he'd answered a terse "no." In fact, he'd done eight hard years in Ohio for an armed robbery he hadn't committed—the real robber hadn't been so stupid, here—and he'd come out of prison bitter, angry, an actual criminal. Figuring the world owed him one, a week after getting out he stopped for a hitchhiker on a lonely country road, pulled a gun, walked him a few yards off the road into a field of high corn, and shot him point-blank at the base of the skull. It didn't look anything like the movies.)

(He drove off without touching the body, which a farmer's child found two days later. The victim turned out to be a college student who was on probation for dealing—all he'd really done was buy a kilo of green and make his money back by selling bags to his friends, and one enemy—so the papers said DRUG DEALER FOUND SLAIN IN GANGLAND-STYLE KILLING and the police pursued the matter with no enthusiasm. Castle was in Key West well before the farmer's child smelled the body, anyhow.)

As they rode along, whatever Lena had or hadn't done with Castle was less interesting to John than what *he* was planning to do with her. Half of his self had never experienced sex, as an adult, without the sensory handicaps engendered by scar tissue and severed nerves in the genitals, and he was looking forward to the experience with a relish that was obvious, at least to Lena. She encouraged him in not-so-subtle ways, and by the time they crossed the last bridge into Key West, he was ready to tell Castle to pull over at the first bush.

He left the typewriter in Castle's care and declined help with the luggage. By this time Lena was smiling at his obvious impatience; she was giggling by the time they were momentarily stalled by a truculent door key; laughed her delight as he carried her charging across the room to the couch, then clawing off a minimum of clothing and taking her with fierce haste, wordless, and keeping her on a breathless edge he drifted the rest of the clothes off her and carried her into the bedroom, where they made so much noise Julio banged on the ceiling with a broomstick.

They did quiet down eventually, and lay together in a puddle of mingled sweat, panting, watching the fan push the humid air around. "Guess we both get to sleep in the wet spot," John said.

"No complaints." She raised up on one elbow and traced a figure eight on his chest. "You're full of surprises tonight, Dr. Baird."

"Life is full of surprises."

"You should go away more often—or at least come back more often."

"It's all that Hemingway research. Makes a man out of you."

"You didn't learn this in a book," she said, gently taking his penis and pantomiming a certain motion.

"I did, though, an anthropology book." In another universe. "It's what they do in the Solomon Islands."

"Wisdom of Solomon," she said, lying back. After a pause: "They have anthropology books at JFK?"

"Uh, no." He remembered he didn't own that book in this universe. "Browsing at Wordsworth's."

"Hope you bought the book."

"Didn't have to." He gave her a long slow caress. "Memorized the good parts."

On the other side of town, six days later, she was in about the same position on Castle's bed, and even more exhausted.

"Aren't you overdoing the loving little wifey bit? It's been a week."

She exhaled audibly. "What a week."

"Missed you." He nuzzled her and made an unsubtle preparatory gesture.

"No, you don't." She rolled out of bed. "Once is plenty." She went to the mirror and ran a brush through her damp hair. "Besides, it's not me you missed. You missed *it*." She sat at the open window, improving the neighborhood's scenery. "It's gonna need a Teflon lining installed."

"Old boy's feelin' his oats?"

"Not feeling *his* anything. God, I don't know what's gotten into him. Four, five times a day; six."

"Screwed, blewed, and tattooed. You asked for it."

"As a matter of fact, I didn't. I haven't had a chance to start my little act. He got off that train with an erection, and he still has it. No woman would be safe around him. Nothing wet and concave would be safe."

"So does that mean it's a good time to bring in Pansy? Or is he so stuck on you he wouldn't even notice her?"

She scowled at the brush, picking hair out of it. "Actually, Castle, I was just about to ask you the same thing. Relying on your well-known expertise in animal behavior."

"Okay." He sat up. "I say we oughta go for it. If he's a walkin' talkin' hard-on like you say . . . Pansy'd pull him like a magnet. You'd have to be a fuckin' monk not to want Pansy."

"Like Rasputin."

"Like who?"

"Never mind." She went back to the brush. "I guess, I guess one problem is that I really am enjoying the attention. I guess I'm not too anxious to hand him over to this champion sexpot."

"Aw, Lena—"

"Really. I do love him in my way, Castle. I don't want to lose him over this scheme."

"You're not gonna lose him. Trust me. You catch him dickin' Pansy, get mad, forgive him. Hell, you'll have him wrapped around your finger."

"I guess. You make the competition sound pretty formidable."

"Don't worry. She's outa there the next day."

"Unless she winds up in love with him. That would be cute."

"He's almost twice her age. Besides, she's a whore. Whores don't fall in love."

"They're women, Castle. Women fall in love."

"Yeah, sure. Just like on TV."

She turned away from him; looked out the window. "You really know how to make a woman feel great, you know?"

"Come on." He crossed over and smoothed her hair. She turned around but didn't look up. "Don't run yourself down, Lena. You're still one hell of a piece of ass."

"Thanks." She smiled into his leer and grabbed him. "If you weren't such a poet, I'd trade you in for a vibrator."

15. IN PRAISE OF HIS MISTRESS

Pansy was indeed beautiful, even under normal conditions; delicate features, wasp waist combined with generous secondary sexual characteristics. The conditions under which John first saw her were calculated to maximize sexiness and vulnerability. Red nylon running shorts, tight and very short, and a white sleeveless T-shirt from a local bar that was stamped LAST HETEROSEXUAL IN KEY WEST—all clinging to her golden skin with a healthy sweat, the cloth made translucent enough to reveal no possibility of underwear.

John looked out the screen door and saw her at the other door, struggling with a heavy box while trying to make the key work. "Let me help you," he said through the screen, and stepped across the short landing to hold the box while she got the door open.

"You're too kind." John tried not to stare as he handed the box back. Pansy, of course, was relieved at his riveted attention. It had taken days to set up this operation, and would take more days to bring it to its climax, so to speak, and more days to get back to normal. But she did owe Castle a big favor and this guy seemed nice enough. Maybe she'd learn something about Hemingway in the process.

"More to come up?" John asked.

"Oh, I couldn't ask you to help. I can manage."

"It's okay. I was just goofing off for the rest of the day."

It turned out to be quite a job, even though there was only one load from a small rented truck. Most of the load was uniform and heavy boxes of books, carefully labeled LIT A—B, GEN REF, ENCY 1–12, and so forth. Most of her furniture, accordingly, was cinder blocks and boards, the standard student bookshelf arrangement.

John found out that despite a couple of dozen boxes marked LIT, Pansy hadn't majored in literature, but rather Special Education; during the school year, she taught third grade at a school for the retarded in Key Largo. She didn't tell him about the several years she'd spent as a call girl, but if she had, John might have seen a connection that Castle would never have made—that the driving force behind both of the jobs was the same, charity. The more or less easy forty dollars an hour for going on a date and then having sex was a factor, too, but she really did like making lonely men feel special, and had herself felt more like a social worker than a woman of easy virtue. And the hundreds of men who had fallen for her, for love or money, weren't responding only to her cheerleader's body. She had a sunny disposition and a natural, artless way of concentrating on a man that made him for a while the only man in the world.

John would not normally be an easy conquest. Twenty years of facing classrooms full of coeds had given him a certain wariness around attractive young women. He also had an impulse toward faithfulness, Lena having suddenly left town, her father ill. But he was still in the grip of the weird overweening horniness that had animated him since inheriting this new body and double-image personality. If Pansy had said "Let's do it," they would be doing it so soon that she would be wise to unwrap the condom before speaking. But she was being as indirect as her nature and mode of dress would allow.

"Do you and your wife always come down here for the summer?"

"We usually go somewhere. Boston's no fun in the heat."

"It must be wonderful in the fall."

And so forth. It felt odd for Pansy, probably the last time she would ever seduce a man for reasons other than personal interest. She wanted it to be perfect. She wanted John to have enough pleasure in her to compensate for the embarrassment of their "accidental" exposure, and whatever hassle his wife would put him through afterwards.

She was dying to know why Castle wanted him set up. How Castle ever met a quiet, kindly gentleman like John was a mystery, too—she had met some of Castle's friends, and they had other virtues.

Quiet and kindly, but horny. Whenever she contrived, in the course of their working together, to expose a nipple or a little beaver, he would turn around to adjust himself, and blush. More like a teenager, discovering his sexuality, than a middle-aged married man.

He was a pushover, but she didn't want to make it too easy. After they had finished putting the books up on shelves, she said thanks a million; I gotta go now, spending the night house-sitting up in Islamorada. You and your wife come over for dinner tomorrow? Oh, then come on over yourself. No, that's all right, I'm a big girl. Roast beef okay? See ya.

Driving away in the rented truck, Pansy didn't feel especially proud of herself. She was amused at John's sexiness and looking forward to trying it out. But she could read people pretty well, and sensed a core of deep sadness in John. Maybe it was from Vietnam; he hadn't mentioned it, but she knew what the bracelet meant.

Whatever the problem, maybe she'd have time to help him with it—before she had to turn around and add to it.

Maybe it would work out for the best. Maybe the problem was with his wife, and she'd leave, and he could start over. . . .

Stop kidding yourself. Just lay the trap, catch him, deliver him. Castle was not the kind of man you want to disappoint.

16. FIESTA

She had baked the roast slowly with wine and fruit juice, along with dried apricots and apples plumped in port wine, seasoned with cinnamon and nutmeg and cardamom. Onions and large cubes of acorn squash simmered in the broth. She served new potatoes steamed with parsley and dressed Italian style, with garlicky olive oil and a splash of vinegar. Small Caesar salad and air-light *pan de agua*, the Cuban bread that made you forget every other kind of bread.

The way to a man's heart, her mother had contended, was through his stomach, and although she was accustomed to aiming rather lower, she thought it was probably a good approach for a longtime married man suddenly forced to fend for himself. That was exactly right for John. He was not much of a cook, but he was an accomplished eater.

He pushed the plate away after three helpings. "God, I'm such a pig. But that was irresistible."

"Thank you." She cleared the table slowly, accepting John's offer to help. "My mother's 'company' recipe. So you think Hadley might have just thrown the stories away, and made up the business about the train?"

"People have raised the possibility. There she was, eight years older than this handsome hubby—with half the women on the Left Bank after him, at least in her mind—and he's starting to get published, starting to build a reputation. . . ."

"She was afraid he was going to 'grow away' from her? Or did they have that expression back then?"

"I think she was afraid he would start making money from his writing. She had an inheritance, a trust fund from her grandfather, that paid over two thousand a year. That was plenty to keep the two of them comfortable in Paris. Hemingway talked poor in those days, starving artist, but he lived pretty well."

"He probably resented it, too. Not making the money himself."

"That would be like him. Anyhow, if she chucked the stories to ensure his dependency, it backfired. He was still furious thirty years later—three wives later. He said the stuff had been 'fresh from the mint,' even if the writing wasn't so great, and he was never able to reclaim it."

She opened a cabinet and slid a bottle out of its burlap bag, and selected two small glasses. "Sherry?" He said why not? and they moved into the living room.

The living room was mysteriously devoid of chairs, so they had to sit together on the small couch. "You don't actually think she did it."

"No." John watched her pour the sherry. "From what I've read about her, she doesn't seem at all calculating. Just a sweet gal from St. Louis who fell in love with a cad."

"Cad. Funny old-fashioned word."

John shrugged. "Actually, he wasn't really a cad. I think he sincerely loved every one of his wives . . . at least until he married them."

They both laughed. "Of course it could have been something in between," Pansy said, "I mean, she didn't actually throw away the manuscripts, but she did leave them sitting out, begging to be stolen. Why did she leave the compartment?"

"That's one screwy aspect of it. Hadley herself never said, not on paper. Every biographer seems to come up with a different reason: she went to get a newspaper, she saw some people she recognized and stepped out to talk with them, wanted some exercise before the long trip . . . even Hemingway had two different versions—she went out to get a bottle of Evian water or to buy something to read. That one pissed him off, because she did have an overnight bag full of the best American writing since Mark Twain."

"How would you have felt?"

"Felt?"

"I mean, you say you've written stories, too. What if somebody, your wife, made a mistake and you lost everything?"

He looked thoughtful. "It's not the same. In the first place, it's just hobby with me. And I don't have that much that hasn't been published—when Hemingway lost it, he lost it for good. I could just go to a university library and make new copies of everything."

"So you haven't written much lately?"

"Not stories. Academic stuff."

"I'd love to read some of your stories."

"And I'd love to have you read them. But I don't have any here. I'll mail you some from Boston."

She nodded, staring at him with a curious intensity. "Oh hell," she said, and turned her back to him. "Would you help me with this?"

"What?"

"The zipper." She was wearing a clingy white summer dress. "Undo the zipper a little bit."

He slowly unzipped it a few inches. She did it the rest of the way, stood up and hooked her thumbs under the shoulder straps and shrugged. The dress slithered to the floor. She wasn't wearing anything else.

"You're blushing." Actually, he was doing a good imitation of a beached fish. She straddled him, sitting back lightly on his knees, legs wide, and started unbuttoning his shirt.

"Uh," he said.

"I just get impatient. You don't mind?"

"Uh . . . no?"

17. ON BEING SHOT AGAIN

John woke up happy but didn't open his eyes for nearly a minute, holding on to the erotic dream of the century. Then he opened one eye and saw it hadn't been a dream: the tousled bed in the strange room, unguents and sex toys on the nightstand, the smell of her hair on the other pillow. A noise from the kitchen; coffee and bacon smells.

He put on pants and went into the living room to pick up the shirt where it had dropped. "Good morning, Pansy."

"Morning, stranger." She was wearing a floppy terry cloth bathrobe with the sleeves rolled up to her elbows. She turned the bacon carefully with a fork. "Scrambled eggs okay?"

"Marvelous." He sat down at the small table and poured himself a cup of coffee. "I don't know what to say."

She smiled at him. "Don't say anything. It was nice."

"More than nice." He watched her precise motions behind the counter. She broke the eggs one-handed, two at a time, added a splash of water to the bowl, plucked some chives from a windowbox and chopped them with a small Chinese cleaver, rocking it in a staccato chatter; scraped them into the bowl, and followed them with a couple of grinds of pepper. She set the bacon out on a paper towel, with another towel to cover. Then she stirred the eggs briskly with the fork and set them aside. She picked up the big cast-iron frying pan and poured off a judicious amount of grease. Then she poured the egg mixture into the pan and studied it with alertness.

"Know what I think?" John said.

"Something profound?"

"Huh uh. I think I'm in a rubber room someplace, hallucinating the whole thing. And I hope they never cure me."

"I think you're a butterfly who's dreaming he's a man. I'm glad I'm in your dream." She slowly stirred and scraped the eggs with a spatula.

"You like older men?"

"One of them." She looked up, serious. "I like men who are considerate . . . and playful." She returned to the scraping. "Last couple of boyfriends I had were all dick and no heart. Kept to myself the last few months."

"Glad to be of service."

"You could rent yourself out as a service." She laughed. "You must have been impossible when you were younger."

"Different." Literally.

She ran hot water into a serving bowl, then returned to her egg stewardship. "I've been thinking."

"Yes?"

"The lost manuscript stuff we were talking about last night, all the different explanations." She divided the egg into four masses and turned each one. "Did you ever read any science fiction?"

"No. Vonnegut."

"The toast." She hurriedly put four pieces of bread in the toaster. "They write about alternate universes. Pretty much like our own, but different in one way or another. Important or trivial."

"What, uh, what silliness."

She laughed and poured the hot water out of the serving bowl, and dried it with a towel. "I guess maybe. But what if . . . what if all of those versions were equally true? In different universes. And for some reason they all came together here." She started to put the eggs into the bowl when there was a knock on the door.

It opened and Ernest Hemingway walked in. Dapper, just twenty, wearing the Italian army cape he'd brought back from the war. He pointed the black-and-white cane at Pansy. "Bingo."

She looked at John and then back at the Hemingway. She dropped the serving bowl; it clattered on the floor without breaking. Her knees buckled and she fainted dead away, executing a half turn as she fell so that the back of her head struck the wooden floor with a loud thump and the bathrobe drifted open from the waist down.

The Hemingway stared down at her frontal aspect. "Sometimes I wish I were human," it said. "Your pleasures are intense. Simple, but intense." It moved toward her with the cane.

John stood up. "If you kill her—"

"Oh?" It cocked an eyebrow at him. "What will you do?"

John took one step toward it and it waved the cane. A waist-high brick wall surmounted by needle-sharp spikes appeared between them. It gestured again and an impossible moat appeared, deep enough to reach down well into Julio's living room. It filled with water and a large crocodile surfaced and rested its chin on the parquet floor, staring at John. It yawned teeth.

The Hemingway held up its cane. "The white end. It doesn't kill, remember?" The wall and moat disappeared and the cane touched Pansy lightly below the navel. She twitched minutely but continued to sleep. "She'll have a headache," it said. "And she'll be somewhat confused by the uncommunicatable memory of having seen me. But that will all fade, compared to the sudden tragedy of having her new lover die here, just sitting waiting for his breakfast."

"Do you enjoy this?"

"I love my work. It's all I have." It walked toward him, footfalls splashing as it crossed where the moat had been. "You have not personally helped, though. Not at all."

It sat down across from him and poured coffee into a mug that said ON THE SIXTH DAY GOD CREATED MAN—SHE MUST HAVE HAD PMS.

"When you kill me this time, do you think it will 'take'?"

"I don't know. It's never failed before." The toaster made a noise. "Toast?"

"Sure." Two pieces appeared on his plate; two on the Hemingway's. "Usually when you kill people they stay dead?"

"I don't kill that many people." It spread margarine on its toast, gestured, and marmalade appeared. "But when I do, yeah. They die all up and down the Omniverse, every timespace. All except you." He pointed toast at John's toast. "Go ahead. It's not poison."

"Not my idea of a last meal."

The Hemingway shrugged. "What would you like?"

"Forget it." He buttered the toast and piled marmalade on it, determined out of some odd impulse to act as if nothing unusual were happening. Breakfast with Hemingway, big deal.

He studied the apparition and noticed that it was somewhat translucent, almost like a traditional TV ghost. He could barely see a line that was the back of the chair, bisecting its chest below shoulder-blade level. Was this something new? There hadn't been too much light in the train; maybe he had just failed to notice it before.

"A penny for your thoughts."

He didn't say anything about seeing through it. "Has it occurred to you that maybe you're not *supposed* to kill me? That's why I came back?"

The Hemingway chuckled and admired its nails. "That's a nearly content-free assertion."

"Oh really." He bit into the toast. The marmalade was strong, pleasantly bitter.

"It presupposes a higher authority, unknown to me, that's watching over my behavior, and correcting me when I do wrong. Doesn't exist, sorry."

"That's the oldest one in the theologian's book." He set down the toast and kneaded his stomach; shouldn't eat something so strong first thing in the morning. "You can only *assert* the nonexistence of something; you can't prove it."

"What you mean is *you* can't." He held up the cane and looked at it. "The simplest explanation is that there's something wrong with the cane. There's no way I can test it; if I kill the wrong person, there's hell to pay up and down the Omniverse. But what I can do is kill you without the cane. See whether you come back again, some timespace."

Sharp, stabbing pains in his stomach now. "Bastard." Heart pounding slow and hard: shirt rustled in time to its spasms.

"Cyanide in the marmalade. Gives it a certain *frisson*, don't you think?"

He couldn't breathe. His heart pounded once, and stopped. Vicious pain in his left arm, then paralysis. From an inch away, he could just see the weave of the white tablecloth. It turned red and then black.

18. THE SUN ALSO RISES

From blackness to brilliance: the morning sun pouring through the window at a flat angle. He screwed up his face and blinked.

Suddenly smothered in terry cloth, between soft breasts. "John, John."

He put his elbow down to support himself, uncomfortable on the parquet floor, and looked up at Pansy. Her face was wet with tears. He cleared his throat. "What happened?"

"You, you started putting on your foot and . . . you just fell over. I thought . . ."

John looked down over his body, hard ropy muscle and deep tan under white body hair, the puckered bullet wound a little higher on the abdomen. Left leg ended in a stump just above the ankle.

Trying not to faint. His third past flooding back. Walking down a dirt road near Kontum, the sudden loud bang of the mine and he pitched forward, unbelievable pain, rolled over and saw his bloody boot yards away; grey, jagged shinbone sticking through the bloody smoking rag of his pant leg, bright crimson splashing on the dry dust, loud in the shocked silence; another bloodstain spreading between his legs, the deep mortal pain there—and he started to buck and scream and two men held him while the medic took off his belt and made a tourniquet and popped morphine through the cloth and unbuttoned his fly and slowly worked his pants down: penis torn by shrapnel, scrotum ripped open in a bright red flap of skin, bloody grey-blue egg of a testicle separating, rolling out. He fainted, then and now.

And woke up with her lips against his, her breath sweet in his lungs, his nostrils pinched painfully tight. He made a strangled noise and clutched her breast.

She cradled his head, panting, smiling through tears, and kissed him lightly on the forehead. "Will you stop fainting now?"

"Yeah. Don't worry." Her lips were trembling. He put a finger on them. "Just a longer night than I'm accustomed to. An overdose of happiness."

The happiest night of his life, maybe of three lives. Like coming back from the dead.

"Should I call a doctor?"

"No. I faint every now and then." Usually at the gym, from pushing too hard. He slipped his hand inside the terry cloth and covered her breast. "It's been . . . do you know how long it's been since I . . . did it? I mean . . . three times in one night?"

"About six hours." She smiled. "And you can say 'fuck.' I'm no schoolgirl."

"I'll say." The night had been an escalating progression of intimacies, gymnastics, accessories. "Had to wonder where a sweet girl like you learned all that."

She looked away, lips pursed, thoughtful. With a light fingertip she stroked the length of his penis and smiled when it started to uncurl. "At work."

"What?"

"I was a prostitute. That's where I learned the tricks. Practice makes perfect."

"Prostitute. Wow."

"Are you shocked? Outraged?"

"Just surprised." That was true. He respected the sorority and was grateful to it for having made Vietnam almost tolerable, an hour or so at a time. "But now you've got to do something really mean. I could never love a prostitute with a heart of gold."

"I'll give it some thought." She shifted. "Think you can stand up?"

"Sure." She stood and gave him her hand. He touched it but didn't pull; rose in a smooth practiced motion, then took one hop and sat down at the small table. He started strapping on his foot.

"I've read about those new ones," she said, "the permanent kind."

"Yeah; I've read about them, too. Computer interface, graft your nerves onto sensors." He shuddered. "No, thanks. No more surgery."

"Not worth it for the convenience?"

"Being able to wiggle my toes, have my foot itch? No. Besides, the VA won't pay for it." That startled John as he said it: here, he hadn't grown up rich. His father had spent all the mill money on a photocopy firm six months before Xerox came on the market. "You say you 'were' a prostitute. Not anymore?"

"No, that was the truth about teaching. Let's start this egg thing over." She picked up the bowl she had dropped in the other universe. "I gave up whoring about seven years ago." She picked up an egg, looked at it, set it down. She half turned and stared out the kitchen window. "I can't do this to you."

"You . . . can't do what?"

"Oh, lie. Keep lying." She went to the refrigerator. "Want a beer?"

"Lying? No, no thanks. What lying?"

She opened a beer, still not looking at him. "I like you, John. I really like you. But I didn't just . . . spontaneously fall into your arms." She took a healthy swig and started pouring some of the bottle into a glass.

"I don't understand."

She walked back, concentrating on pouring the beer, then sat down gracelessly. She took a deep breath and let it out, staring at his chest. "Castle put me up to it."

"Castle?"

She nodded. "Sylvester Castlemaine, boy wonder."

John sat back stunned. "But you said you don't do that anymore," he said without too much logic. "Do it for money."

"Not for money," she said in a flat, hurt voice.

"I should've known. A woman like you wouldn't want . . ." He made a gesture that dismissed his body from the waist down.

"You do all right. Don't feel sorry for yourself." Her face showed a pinch of regret for that, but she plowed on. "If it were just the obligation, once would have been enough. I wouldn't have had to fuck and suck all night long to win you over."

"No," he said, "that's true. Just the first moment, when you undressed. That was enough."

"I owe Castle a big favor. A friend of mine was going to be prosecuted for involving a minor in prostitution. It was a setup, pure and simple."

"She worked for the same outfit you did?"

"Yeah, but this was freelance. I think it was the escort service that set her up, sort of delivered her and the man in return for this or that."

She sipped at the beer. "Guy wanted a three-way. My friend had met this girl a couple of days before at the bar where she worked part-time . . . she looked old enough, said she was in the biz."

"She was neither?"

"God knows. Maybe she got caught as a juvie and made a deal. Anyhow, he'd just slipped it to her and suddenly cops comin' in the windows. Threw the book at him. 'Two inches, twenty years,' my friend said. He was a county commissioner somewhere, with enemies. Almost dragged my friend down with him. I'm *sorry*." Her voice was angry.

"Don't be," John said, almost a whisper. "It's understandable. Whatever happens, I've got last night."

She nodded. "So two of the cops who were going to testify got busted for possession, cocaine. The word came down and everybody remembered the woman was somebody else."

"So what did Castle want you to do? With me?"

"Oh, whatever comes natural—or *un*-natural, if that's what you wanted. And later be doing it at a certain time and place, where we'd be caught in the act."

"By Castle?"

"And his trusty little VCR. Then I guess he'd threaten to show it to your wife, or the university."

"I wonder. Lena . . . she knows I've had other women."

"But not lately."

"No. Not for years."

"It might be different now. She might be starting to feel, well, insecure."

"Any woman who looked at you would feel insecure."

She shrugged. "That could be part of it. Could it cost you your job, too?"

"I don't see how. It would be awkward, but it's not as if you were one of my students—and even that happens, without costing the guy his job." He laughed. "Poor old Larry. He had a student kiss and tell, and had to run the Speakers' Committee for four or five years. Got allergic to wine and cheese. But he made tenure."

"So what is it?" She leaned forward. "Are you an addict or something?"

"Addict?"

"I mean how come you even *know* Castle? He didn't pick your name out of a phone book and have me come seduce you, just to see what would happen."

"No, of course not."

"So? I confess, you confess."

John passed a hand over his face and pressed the other hand against his knee, bearing down to keep the foot from tapping. "You don't want to be involved."

"What do you call last night, Spin the Bottle? I'm in*volved*!"

"Not the way I mean. It's illegal."

"Oh golly. Not really."

"Let me think." John picked up their dishes and limped back to the sink. He set them down there and fiddled with the straps and pad that connected the foot to his stump, then poured himself a cup of coffee and came back, not limping.

He sat down slowly and blew across the coffee. "What it is, is that *Castle* thinks there's a scam going on. He's wrong. I've taken steps to ensure that it couldn't work." His foot tapped twice.

"You think. You hope."

"No. I'm sure. Anyhow, I'm stringing Castle along because I need his expertise in a certain matter."

" 'A certain matter,' yeah. Sounds wholesome."

"Actually, that part's not illegal."

"So tell me about it."

"Nope. Still might backfire."

She snorted. "You know what might backfire. Fucking with Castle."

"I can take care of him."

"You don't know. He may be more dangerous than you think he is."

"He talks a lot."

"You men." She took a drink and poured the rest of the bottle into the glass. "Look, I was at a party with him, couple of years ago. He was drunk, got into a little coke, started babbling."

"In vino veritas?"

"Yeah, and Coke is It. But he said he'd killed three people, strangers, just to see what it felt like. He liked it. I more than halfway believe him."

John looked at her silently for a moment, sorting out his new memories of Castle. "Well . . . he's got a mean streak. I don't know about murder. Certainly not over this thing."

"Which is?"

"You'll have to trust me. It's not because of Castle that I can't tell you." He remembered her one universe ago, lying helpless while the Hemingway lowered its cane onto her nakedness. "Trust me?"

She studied the top of the glass, running her finger around it. "Suppose I do. Then what?"

"Business as usual. You didn't tell me anything. Deliver me to Castle and his video camera; I'll try to put on a good show."

"And when he confronts you with it?"

"Depends on what he wants. He knows I don't have much money." John shrugged. "If it's unreasonable, he can go ahead and show the tape to Lena. She can live with it."

"And your department head?"

"He'd give me a medal."

19. IN OUR TIME

So it wasn't the cane. He ate enough cyanide to kill a horse, but evidently only in one universe.

You checked the next day in all the others?

All 119. He's still dead in the one where I killed him on the train—

That's encouraging.

—but there's no causal resonance in the others.

Oh, but there is some resonance. He remembered you in the universe where you poisoned him. Maybe in all of them.

That's impossible.

Once is impossible. Twice is a trend. A hundred and twenty means something is going on that we don't understand.

What I suggest—

No. You can't go back and kill them all one by one.

If the wand had worked the first time, they'd all be dead anyhow. There's no reason to think we'd cause more of an eddy by doing them one at a time.

It's not something to experiment with. As you well know.

I don't know how we're going to solve it otherwise.

Simple. Don't kill him. Talk to him again. He may be getting frightened, if he remembers both times he died.

Here's an idea. What if someone else killed him?

I don't know. If you just hired someone—made him a direct agent of your will—it wouldn't be any different from the cyanide. Maybe as a last resort. Talk to him again first.

All right. I'll try.

20. OF WOUNDS AND OTHER CAUSES

Although John found it difficult to concentrate, trying not to think about Pansy, this was the best time he would have for the foreseeable future to summon the Hemingway demon and try to do something about exorcising it. He didn't want either of the women around if the damned thing went on a killing spree again. They might just do as he did, and slip over into another reality—as unpleasant as that was, it was at least living—but the Hemingway had said otherwise. There was no reason to suspect it was not the truth.

Probably the best way to get the thing's attention was to resume work on the Hemingway pastiche. He decided to rewrite the first page to warm up, typing it out in Hemingway's style:

ALONG WITH YOUTH

1. Mitraigliatrice

The dirt on the side of the trench was never dry in the morning. If Fever could find a dry newspaper he could put it between his chest and the dirt when he went out to lean on the side of the trench and wait for the light .First light was the best time . You might have luck and see a muzzle flash to aim at . But patience was better than luck. Wait to see a helmet or a head without a helmet.

Fever looked at the enemy trench line through a rectangular box of wood that pushed through the trench wall at about ground level. The other end of the box was covered with a square of gauze the color of dirt. A man looking directly at it might see the muzzel flash when Fever fired through the box. But with luck, the flash would be the last thing he saw.

Fever had fired through the gauze six times. He'd potted at least three Austrians. Now the gauze had a ragged hole in the center. One bullet had come in the other way, an accident, and chiseled a deep gouge in the floor of the wooden box. Fever knew that he would be able to see the splinters sticking up before he could see any detail at the enemy trench line.

That would be maybe twenty minutes. Fever wanted a cigarette. There was plenty of time to go down in the bunker and light one. But it would fox his night vision. Better to wait.

Fever heard movement before he heard the voice. He picked up one of the grenades on the plank shelf to his left and his thumb felt the ring on the cotter pin. Someone was crawling in front of his position. Slow crawling but not too quiet. He slid his left forefinger through the ring and waited.

—Help me, came a strained whisper.

Fever felt his shoulders tense. Of course many Austrians could speak Italian.

—I am wounded. Help me. I can go no farther.

—What is your name an unit, Fever whispered through the box.

—Jean-Franco Dante. Four forty-seventh.

That was the unit that had taken such a beating at the evening show.—At first light they will kill me.

—All right. But I'm coming over with a grenade in my hand. If you kill me, you die as well.

—I will commend this logic to your superior officer. Please hurry.

Fever slid his rifle into the wooden box and eased himself to the top of the trench. He took the grenade out of his pocket and carefully worked the pin out, the arming lever held secure. He kept the pin around his finger so he could replace it.

He inched his way down the slope, guided by the man's whispers.

After a few minutes his probing hand found the man's shoulder.—Thank God. Make haste, now.

The soldier's feet were both shattered by a mine. He would have to be carried.

—Don't cry out, Fever said. This will hurt.

—No sound, the soldier said. And when Fever raised him up onto his back there was only a breath. But his canteen was loose. It fell on a rock and made a loud hollow sound.

Firecracker pop above them and the night was all glare and bobbing shadow. A big machine gun opened up rong, cararong, rong, rong. Fever headed for the parapet above as fast as he could but knew it was hopeless. He saw dirt spray twice to his right and then felt the thud of the bullet into the Italian, who said "Jesus" as if only annoyed, and they almost made it then but on the lip of the trench a hard snowball hit Fever behind the kneecap and they both went down in a tumble. They fell two yards to safety but the Italian was already dead.

Fever had sprained his wrist and hurt his nose falling and they hurt worse than the bullet. But he couldn't move his toes and he knew that must be bad. Then it started to hurt.

A rifleman closed the Italian's eyes and with the help of another clumsy one dragged Fever down the trench to the medical bunker. It hurt awfully and his shoe filled up with blood and he puked. They stopped to watch him puke and then dragged him the rest of the way.

The surgeon placed him between two kerosene lanterns. He removed the puttee and shoe and cut the bloody pants leg with a straight razor. He rolled Fever onto his stomach and had four men hold him down while he probed for the bullet. The pain was great but Fever was insulted enough by the four men not to cry out. He heard the bullet clink into a metal dish. It sounded like the canteen.

"That's a little too pat, don't you think?" John turned around and there was the Hemingway, reading over his shoulder. " 'It sounded like the canteen,' indeed." Khaki army uniform covered with mud and splattered with bright blood. Blood dripped and pooled at its feet.

"So shoot me. Or whatever it's going to be this time. Maybe I'll rewrite the line in the next universe."

"You're going to run out soon. You only exist in eight more universes."

"Sure. And you've never lied to me." John turned back around and stared at the typewriter, tensed.

The Hemingway sighed. "Suppose we talk, instead."

"I'm listening."

The Hemingway walked past him toward the kitchen. "Want a beer?"

"Not while I'm working."

"Suit yourself." It limped into the kitchen, out of sight, and John heard it open the refrigerator and pry the top off of a beer. It came back out as the five-year-old

Hemingway, dressed up in girl's clothing, both hands clutching an incongruous beer bottle. It set the bottle on the end table and crawled up onto the couch with childish clumsiness.

"Where's the cane?"

"I knew it wouldn't be necessary this time," it piped. "It occurs to me that there are better ways to deal with a man like you."

"Do tell." John smiled. "What is 'a man like me'? One on whom your cane for some reason doesn't work?"

"Actually, what I was thinking of was curiosity. That is supposedly what motivates scholars. You *are* a real scholar, not just a rich man seeking legitimacy?"

John looked away from the ancient eyes in the boy's face. "I've sometimes wondered myself. Why don't you cut to the chase, as we used to say. A few universes ago."

"I've done spot checks on your life through various universes," the child said. "You're always a Hemingway buff, though you don't always do it for a living."

"What else do I do?"

"It's probably not healthy for you to know. But all of you are drawn to the missing manuscripts at about this time, the seventy-fifth anniversary."

"I wonder why that would be."

The Hemingway waved the beer bottle in a disarmingly mature gesture. "The Omniverse is full of threads of coincidence like that. They have causal meaning in a dimension you can't deal with."

"Try me."

"In a way, that's what I want to propose. You will drop this dangerous project at once, and never resume it. In return, I will take you back in time, back to the Gare de Lyon on December 14, 1921."

"Where I will see what happens to the manuscripts."

Another shrug. "I will put you on Hadley's train, well before she said the manuscripts were stolen. You will be able to observe for an hour or so, without being seen. As you know, some people have theorized that there never was a thief; never was an overnight bag; that Hadley simply threw the writings away. If that's the case, you won't see anything dramatic. But the absence of the overnight bag would be powerful indirect proof."

John looked skeptical. "You've never gone to check it out for yourself?"

"If I had, I wouldn't be able to take you back. I can't exist twice in the same time-space, of course."

"How foolish of me. Of course"

"Is it a deal?"

John studied the apparition. The couch's plaid upholstery showed through its arms and legs. It did appear to become less substantial each time. "I don't know. Let me think about it a couple of days."

The child pulled on the beer bottle and it stretched into a long amber stick. It turned into the black-and-white cane. "We haven't tried cancer yet. That might be the one that works." It slipped off the couch and sidled toward John. "It does take longer and it hurts. It hurts 'awfully.'"

John got out of the chair. "You come near me with that and I'll drop kick you into next Tuesday."

The child shimmered and became Hemingway in his mid-forties, a big-gutted barroom brawler. "Sure you will, Champ." It held out the cane so that the tip was inches from John's chest. "See you around." It disappeared with a barely audible pop, and a slight breeze as air moved to fill its space.

John thought about that as he went to make a fresh cup of coffee. He wished he knew more about science. The thing obviously takes up space, since its disappearance caused a vacuum, but there was no denying that it was fading away.

Well, not fading. Just becoming more transparent. That might not affect its abilities. A glass door is as much of a door as an opaque one, if you try to walk through it.

He sat down on the couch, away from the manuscript so he could think without distraction. On the face of it, this offer by the Hemingway was an admission of defeat. An admission, at least, that it couldn't solve its problem by killing him over and over. That was comforting. He would just as soon not die again, except for the one time.

But maybe he should. That was a chilling thought. If he made the Hemingway kill him another dozen times, another hundred . . . what kind of strange creature would he become? A hundred overlapping autobiographies, all perfectly remembered? Surely the brain has a finite capacity for storing information; he'd "fill up," as Pansy said. Or maybe it wasn't finite, at least in his case—but that was logically absurd. There are only so many cells in a brain. Of course he might be "wired" in some way to the John Bairds in all the other universes he had inhabited.

And what would happen if he died in some natural way, not dispatched by an interdimensional assassin? Would he still slide into another identity? That was a lovely prospect: sooner or later he would be 130 years old, on his deathbed, dying every fraction of a second for the rest of eternity.

Or maybe the Hemingway wasn't lying, this time, and he had only eight lives left. In context, the possibility was reassuring.

The phone rang; for a change, John was grateful for the interruption. It was Lena, saying her father had come home from the hospital, much better, and she thought she could come on home day after tomorrow. Fine, John said, feeling a little wicked; I'll borrow a car and pick you up at the airport. Don't bother, Lena said; besides, she didn't have a flight number yet.

John didn't press it. If, as he assumed, Lena was in on the plot with Castle, she was probably here in Key West, or somewhere nearby. If she had to buy a ticket to and from Omaha to keep up her end of the ruse, the money would come out of John's pocket.

He hung up and, on impulse, dialed her parents' number. Her father answered. Putting on his professorial tone, he said he was Maxwell Perkins, Blue Cross claims adjuster, and he needed to know the exact date when Mr. Monaghan entered the hospital for this recent confinement. He said you must have the wrong guy; I haven't been inside a hospital in twenty years, knock on wood. Am I not speaking to John Franklin Monaghan? No, this is John *Frederick* Monaghan. Terribly sorry, natural mistake. That's okay; hope the other guy's okay, good-bye, good night, sir.

So tomorrow was going to be the big day with Pansy. To his knowledge, John hadn't been watched during sex for more than twenty years, and never by a disinterested, or at least dispassionate, observer. He hoped that knowing they were being spied upon wouldn't affect his performance. Or knowing that it would be the last time.

A profound helpless sadness settled over him. He knew that the last thing you should do, in a mood like this, was go out and get drunk. It was barely noon, anyhow. He took enough money out of his wallet for five martinis, hid the wallet under a couch cushion, and headed for Duval Street.

21. DYING, WELL OR BADLY

John had just about decided it was too early in the day to get drunk. He had polished off two martinis in Sloppy Joe's and then wandered uptown because the tourists were getting to him and a band was setting up, depressingly young and cheerful. He found a grubby bar he'd never noticed before, dark and smoky and hot. In the other universes it was a yuppie boutique. Three Social Security drunks were arguing politics almost loudly enough to drown out the game show on the television. It seemed to go well with the headache and sour stomach he'd reaped from the martinis and the walk in the sun. He got a beer and some peanuts and a couple of aspirin from the bartender, and sat in the farthest booth with a copy of the local classified ad newspaper. Somebody had obscurely carved FUCK ANARCHY into the tabletop.

Nobody else in this world knows what anarchy *is*, John thought, and the helpless anomie came back, intensified somewhat by drunken sentimentality. What he would give to go back to the first universe and undo this all by just not . . .

Would that be possible? The Hemingway was willing to take him back to 1921; why not back a few weeks? Where the hell was that son of a bitch when you needed him, it, whatever.

The Hemingway appeared in the booth opposite him, an Oak Park teenager smoking a cigarette. "I felt a kind of vibration from you. Ready to make your decision?"

"Can the people at the bar see you?"

"No. And don't worry about appearing to be talking to yourself. A lot of that goes on around here."

"Look. Why can't you just take me back to a couple of weeks before we met on the train, back in the first universe? I'll just . . ." The Hemingway was shaking its head slowly. "You can't."

"No. As I explained, you already exist there—"

"You said that *you* couldn't be in the same place twice. How do you know I can't?"

"How do you know you can't swallow that piano? You just can't."

"You thought I couldn't talk about you, either, you thought your stick would kill me. I'm not like normal people."

"Except in that alcohol does nothing for your judgment."

John ate a peanut thoughtfully. "Try this on for size. At 11:46 on June 3, a man named Sylvester Castlemaine sat down in Dos Hermosas and started talking with me about the lost manuscripts. The forgery would never have occurred to me if I hadn't talked to him. Why don't you go back and keep him from going into that cafe? Or just go back to 11:30 and kill him."

The Hemingway smiled maliciously. "You don't like him much."

"It's more fear than like or dislike." He rubbed his face hard, remembering. "Funny how things shift around. He was kind of likable the first time I met him. Then you killed me on the train and in the subsequent universe, he became colder, more serious. Then you killed me in Pansy's apartment and in this universe, he has turned mean. Dangerously mean, like a couple of men I knew in Vietnam. The ones who really love the killing. Like you, evidently."

It blew a chain of smoke rings before answering. "I don't 'love' killing, or anything else. I have a complex function and I fulfill it, because that is what I do. That sounds circular because of the limitations of human language.

"I can't go killing people right and left just to see what happens. When a person dies at the wrong time it takes forever to clean things up. Not that it wouldn't be worth it in your case. But I can tell you with certainty that killing Castlemaine would not affect the final outcome."

"How can you say that? He's responsible for the whole thing." John finished off most of his beer and the Hemingway touched the mug and it refilled. "Not poison."

"Wouldn't work," it said morosely. "I'd gladly kill Castlemaine any way you want—cancer of the penis is a possibility—if there was even a fighting chance that it would clear things up. The reason I know it wouldn't is that I am not in the least attracted to that meeting. There's no probability nexus associated with it, the way there was with your buying the Corona or starting the story on the train, or writing it down here. You may think that you would never have come up with the idea for the forgery on your own, but you're wrong."

"That's preposterous."

"Nope. There are universes in this bundle where Castle isn't involved. You may find that hard to believe, but your beliefs aren't important."

John nodded noncommittally and got his faraway remembering look. "You know . . . reviewing in my mind all the conversations we've had, all five of them, the only substantive reason you've given me not to write this pastiche, and I quote, is that 'I or someone like me will have to kill you.' Since that doesn't seem to be possible, why don't we try some other line of attack?"

It put out the cigarette by squeezing it between thumb and forefinger. There was a smell of burning flesh. "All right, try this: give it up or I'll kill Pansy. Then Lena."

"I've thought of that, and I'm gambling that you won't, or can't. You had a perfect opportunity a few days ago—maximum dramatic effect—and you didn't do it. Now you say it's an awfully complicated matter."

"You're willing to gamble with the lives of the people you love?"

"I'm gambling with a lot. Including them." He leaned forward. "Take me into the future instead of the past. Show me what will happen if I succeed with the Hemingway hoax. If I agree that it's terrible, I'll give it all up and become a plumber."

The old, wise Hemingway shook a shaggy head at him. "You're asking me to please fix it so you can swallow a piano. I can't. Even I can't go straight to the future and look around; I'm pretty much tied to your present and past until this matter is cleared up."

"One of the first things you said to me was that you were from the future. And the past. And 'other temporalities,' whatever the hell that means. You were lying then?"

"Not really." It sighed. "Let me force the analogy. Look at the piano."

John twisted half around. "Okay."

"You can't eat it—but after a fashion, I can." The piano suddenly transformed itself into a piano-shaped mountain of cold capsules, which immediately collapsed and rolled all over the floor. "Each capsule contains a pinch of sawdust or powdered ivory or metal, the whole piano in about a hundred thousand capsules. If I take one with each meal, I will indeed eat the piano, over the course of the next three hundred-some years. That's not a long time for me."

"That doesn't prove anything."

"It's not a *proof*; it's a demonstration." It reached down and picked up a capsule that was rolling by, and popped it into its mouth. "One down, 99,999 to go. So how many ways could I eat this piano?"

"Ways?"

"I mean I could have swallowed any of the hundred thousand first. Next I can choose any of the remaining 99,999. How many ways can—"

"That's easy. One hundred thousand factorial. A huge number."

"Go to the head of the class. It's ten to the godzillionth power. That represents the number of possible paths—the number of futures—leading to this one guaranteed, preordained event: my eating the piano. They are all different, but in terms of whether the piano gets eaten, their differences are trivial.

"On a larger scale, every possible trivial action that you or anybody else in this universe takes puts us into a slightly different future than would have otherwise existed. An overwhelming majority of actions, even seemingly significant ones, make no difference in the long run. All of the futures bend back to one central, unifying event—except for the ones that you're screwing up!"

"So what is this big event?"

"It's impossible for you to know. It's not important, anyhow." Actually, it would take a rather cosmic viewpoint to consider the event unimportant: the end of the world.

Or at least the end of life on Earth. Right now there were two earnest young politicians, in the United States and Russia, who on 11 August 2006 would be President and Premier of their countries. On that day, one would insult the other beyond forgiveness, and a button would be pushed, and then another button, and by the time the sun set on Moscow, or rose on Washington, there would be nothing left alive on the planet at all—from the bottom of the ocean to the top of the atmosphere—not a cockroach, not a paramecium, not a virus, and all because there are some things a man just doesn't have to take, not if he's a real man.

Hemingway wasn't the only writer who felt that way, but he was the one with the most influence on this generation. The apparition who wanted John dead or at least not typing didn't know exactly what effect his pastiche was going to have on Hemingway's influence, but it was going to be decisive and ultimately negative. It would prevent or at least delay the end of the world in a whole bundle of universes, which would put a zillion adjacent realities out of kilter, and there would be hell to pay all up and down the Omniverse. Many more people than six billion would die—and it's even possible that all of Reality would unravel, and collapse back to the Primordial Hiccup from whence it came.

"If it's not important, then why are you so hell-bent on keeping me from preventing it? I don't believe you."

"*Don't* believe me, then!" At an imperious gesture, all the capsules rolled back into the corner and reassembled into a piano, with a huge crashing chord. None of the barflies heard it. "I should think you'd cooperate with me just to prevent the unpleasantness of dying over and over."

John had the expression of a poker player whose opponent has inadvertently exposed his hole card. "You get used to it," he said. "And it occurs to me that sooner or later I'll wind up in a universe that I really like. This one doesn't have a hell of a lot to recommend it." His foot tapped twice and then twice again.

"No," the Hemingway said. "It will get worse each time."

"You can't know that. This has never happened before."

"True so far, isn't it?"

John considered it for a moment. "Some ways. Some ways not."

The Hemingway shrugged and stood up. "Well. Think about my offer." The cane appeared. "Happy cancer." It tapped him on the chest and disappeared.

The first sensation was utter tiredness, immobility. When he strained to move, pain slithered through his muscles and viscera, and stayed. He could hardly breathe, partly because his lungs weren't working and partly because there was something in the way. In the mirror beside the booth he looked down his throat and saw a large white mass, veined, pulsing. He sank back into the cushion and waited. He remembered the young wounded Hemingway writing his parents from the hospital with ghastly cheerfulness: "If I should have died it would have been very easy for me. Quite the easiest thing I ever did." I don't know, Ernie; maybe it gets harder with practice. He felt something tear open inside and hot stinging fluid trickled through his abdominal cavity. He wiped his face and a patch of necrotic skin came off with a terrible smell. His clothes tightened as his body swelled.

"Hey buddy, you okay?" The bartender came around in front of him and jumped. "Christ, Harry, punch nine-one-one!"

John gave a slight ineffectual wave. "No rush," he croaked.

The bartender cast his eyes to the ceiling. "Always on my shift?"

22. DEATH IN THE AFTERNOON

John woke up behind a Dumpster in an alley. It was high noon and the smell of fermenting garbage was revolting. He didn't feel too well in any case; as if he'd drunk far too much and passed out behind a Dumpster, which was exactly what had happened in this universe.

In this universe. He stood slowly to a quiet chorus of creaks and pops, brushed himself off, and staggered away from the malefic odor. Staggered, but not limping—he had both feet again, in this present. There was a hand-sized numb spot at the top of his left leg where a .51 caliber machine gun bullet had missed his balls by an inch and ended his career as a soldier.

And started it as a writer. He got to the sidewalk and stopped dead. This was the first universe where he wasn't a college professor. He taught occasionally—sometimes creative writing; sometimes Hemingway—but it was only a hobby now, and a nod toward respectability.

He rubbed his fringe of salt-and-pepper beard. It covered the bullet scar there on his chin. He ran his tongue along the metal teeth the army had installed thirty years ago. Jesus. Maybe it does get worse every time. Which was worse, losing a foot or getting your dick sprayed with shrapnel, numb from severed nerves, plus bullets in the leg and face and arm? If you knew there was a Pansy in your future, you would probably trade a foot for a whole dick. Though she had done wonders with what was left.

Remembering furiously, not watching where he was going, he let his feet guide him back to the oldster's bar where the Hemingway had showed him how to swallow a piano. He pushed through the door and the shock of air-conditioning brought him back to the present.

Ferns. Perfume. Lacy underthings. An epicene sales clerk sashayed toward him, managing to look worried and determined at the same time. His nose was pierced, decorated with a single diamond button. "Si-i-r," he said in a surprisingly deep voice, "may I *help* you?"

Crotchless panties. Marital aids. The bar had become a store called The French Connection. "Guess I took a wrong turn. Sorry." He started to back out.

The clerk smiled. "Don't be shy. Everybody needs *some*thing here."

The heat was almost pleasant in its heavy familiarity. John stopped at a convenience store for a six-pack of greenies and walked back home.

An interesting universe; much more of a divergence than the other had been. Reagan had survived the Hinckley assassination and actually went on to a second term. Bush was elected rather than succeeding to the presidency, and the country had not gone to war in Nicaragua. The Iran/Contra scandal nipped it in the bud.

The United States was actually cooperating with the Soviet Union in a flight to Mars. There were no DeSotos. Could there be a connection?

And in this universe he had actually met Ernest Hemingway.

Havana, 1952. John was eight years old. His father, a doctor in this universe, had taken a break from the New England winter to treat his family to a week in the tropics. John got a nice sunburn the first day, playing on the beach while his parents tried the casinos. The next day they made him stay indoors, which meant tagging along with his parents, looking at things that didn't fascinate eight-year-olds.

For lunch they went to La Florida, on the off chance that they might meet the famous Ernest Hemingway, who supposedly held court there when he was in Havana.

To John it was a huge dark cavern of a place, full of adult smells. Cigar smoke, rum, beer, stale urine. But Hemingway was indeed there, at the end of the long dark wood bar, laughing heartily with a table full of Cubans.

John was vaguely aware that his mother resembled some movie actress, but he couldn't have guessed that that would change his life. Hemingway glimpsed her and then stood up and was suddenly silent, mouth open. Then he laughed and waved a huge arm. "Come on over here, daughter."

The three of them rather timidly approached the table, John acutely aware of the careful inspection his mother was receiving from the silent Cubans. "Take a look, Mary," he said to the small blond woman knitting at the table. "The Kraut."

The woman nodded, smiling, and agreed that John's mother looked just like Marlene Dietrich ten years before. Hemingway invited them to sit down and have a drink, and they accepted with an air of genuine astonishment. He gravely shook John's hand, and spoke to him as he would to an adult. Then he shouted to the bartender in fast Spanish, and in a couple of minutes his parents had huge daiquiris and he had a Coke with a wedge of lime in it, tropical and grown-up. The waiter also brought a tray of boiled shrimp. Hemingway even ate the heads and tails, crunching loudly, which impressed John more than any Nobel Prize. Hemingway might have agreed, since he hadn't yet received one, and Faulkner had.

For more than an hour, two Cokes, John watched as his parents sat hypnotized in the aura of Hemingway's famous charm. He put them at ease with jokes and stories and questions—for the rest of his life John's father would relate how impressed he was with the sophistication of Hemingway's queries about cardiac medicine—but it was obvious even to a child that they were in awe, electrified by the man's presence.

Later that night John's father asked him what he thought of Mr. Hemingway. Forty-four years later, John of course remembered his exact reply: "He has fun all the time. I never saw a grown-up who plays like that."

Interesting. That meeting was where his eidetic memory started. He could remember a couple of days before it pretty well, because they had still been close to the surface. In other universes, he could remember back well before grade school. It gave him a strange feeling. All of the universes were different, but this was the first one where the differentness was so tightly connected to Hemingway.

He was flabby in this universe, fat over old, tired muscle, like Hemingway at his age, perhaps, and he felt a curious anxiety that he realized was a real *need* to have a drink. Not just desire, not thirst. If he didn't have a drink, something very very bad would happen. He knew that was irrational. Knowing didn't help.

John carefully mounted the stairs up to their apartment, stepping over the fifth one, also rotted in this universe. He put the beer in the refrigerator and took from the freezer a bottle of icy vodka—that was different—and poured himself a double shot and knocked it back, medicine drinking.

That spiked the hangover pretty well. He pried the top off a beer and carried it into the living room, thoughtful as the alcoholic glow radiated through his body. He sat down at the typewriter and picked up the air pistol, a fancy Belgian target model. He cocked it and, with a practiced two-handed grip, aimed at a paper target across the room. The pellet struck less than half an inch low.

All around the room the walls were pocked from where he'd fired at roaches, and once a scorpion. Very Hemingwayish, he thought; in fact, most of the ways he was different from the earlier incarnations of himself were in Hemingway's direction.

He spun a piece of paper into the typewriter and made a list:

EH & me—

—both had doctor fathers

—both forced into music lessons

—in high school wrote derivative stuff that didn't show promise

—Our war wounds were evidently similar in severity and location. Maybe my groin one was worse; army doctor there said that in Korea (and presumably WWI), without helicopter dustoff, I would have been dead on the battlefield. (Having been wounded in the kneecap and foot myself, I know that H's story about carrying the wounded guy on his back is unlikely. It was a month before I could put any stress on the knee.) He mentioned genital wounds, possibly similar to mine, in a letter to Bernard Baruch, but there's nothing in the Red Cross report about them.

But in both cases, being wounded and surviving was the central experience of our youth. Touching death.

—We each wrote the first draft of our first novel in six weeks (but his was better and more ambitious).

—Both had unusual critical success from the beginning.

—Both shy as youngsters and gregarious as adults.

—Always loved fishing and hiking and guns; I loved the bullfight from my first corrida, but may have been influenced by H's books.

—Spain in general

—have better women than we deserve

—drink too much

—hypochondria

—accident proneness

—a tendency toward morbidity

—One difference. I will never stick a shotgun in my mouth and pull the trigger. Leaves too much of a mess.

He looked up at the sound of the cane tapping. The Hemingway was in the Karsh wise-old-man mode, but was nearly transparent in the bright light that streamed from the open door. "What do I have to do to get your attention?" it said. "Give you cancer again?"

"That was pretty unpleasant."

"Maybe it will be the last." It half sat on the arm of the couch and spun the cane around twice. "Today is a big day. Are we going to Paris?"

"What do you mean?"

"Something big happens today. In every universe where you're alive, this day glows with importance. I assume that means you've decided to go along with me. Stop writing this thing in exchange for the truth about the manuscripts."

As a matter of fact, he had been thinking just that. Life was confusing enough already, torn between his erotic love for Pansy and the more domestic, but still deep, feeling for Lena . . . writing the pastiche was kind of fun, but he did have his own fish to fry. Besides, he'd come to truly dislike Castle, even before Pansy had told him about the setup. It would be fun to disappoint him.

"You're right. Let's go."

"First destroy the novel." In this universe, he'd completed seventy pages of the Up-in-Michigan novel.

"Sure." John picked up the stack of paper and threw it into the tiny fireplace. He lit it several places with a long barbecue match, and watched a month's work go up in smoke. It was only a symbolic gesture, anyhow; he could retype the thing from memory if he wanted to.

"So what do I do? Click my heels together three times and say 'There's no place like the Gare de Lyon'?"

"Just come closer."

John took three steps toward the Hemingway and suddenly fell up down sideways—

It was worse than dying. He was torn apart and scattered throughout space and time, being nowhere and everywhere, everywhen, being a screaming vacuum forever—

Grit crunched underfoot and coalsmoke was choking thick in the air. It was cold. Grey Paris skies glowered through the long skylights, through the complicated geometry of the black steel trusses that held up the high roof. Bustling crowds chattering French. A woman walked through John from behind. He pressed himself with his hands and felt real.

"They can't see us," the Hemingway said. "Not unless I will it."

"That was awful."

"I hoped you would hate it. That's how I spend most of my timespace. Come on." They walked past vendors selling paper packets of roasted chestnuts, bottles of wine, stacks of baguettes and cheeses. There were strange resonances as John remembered the various times he'd been here more than a half century in the future. It hadn't changed much.

"There she is." The Hemingway pointed. Hadley looked worn, tired, dowdy. She stumbled, trying to keep up with the porter who strode along with her two bags. John recalled that she was just recovering from a bad case of the grippe. She'd probably still be home in bed if Hemingway hadn't sent the telegram urging her to come to Lausanne because the skiing was so good, at Chamby.

"Are there universes where Hadley doesn't lose the manuscripts?"

"Plenty of them," the Hemingway said. "In some of them he doesn't sell 'My Old Man' next year, or anything else, and he throws all the stories away himself. He gives up fiction and becomes a staff writer for the Toronto *Star*. Until the Spanish Civil War; he joins the Abraham Lincoln Battalion and is killed driving an ambulance. His only effect on American literature is one paragraph in *The Autobiography of Alice B. Toklas*."

"But in some, the stories actually do see print?"

"Sure, including the novel, which is usually called *Along With Youth*. There." Hadley was mounting the steps up into a passenger car. There was a microsecond of agonizing emptiness, and they materialized in the passageway in front of Hadley's compartment. She and the porter walked through them.

"*Merci*," she said, and handed the man a few sou. He made a face behind her back.

"*Along With Youth?*" John said.

"It's a pretty good book, sort of prefiguring *A Farewell To Arms*, but he does a lot better in universes where it's not published. *The Sun Also Rises* gets more attention."

Hadley stowed both the suitcase and the overnight bag under the seat. Then she frowned slightly, checked her wristwatch, and left the compartment, closing the door behind her.

"Interesting," the Hemingway said. "So she didn't leave it out in plain sight, begging to be stolen."

"Makes you wonder," John said. "This novel. Was it about World War I?"

"The trenches in Italy," the Hemingway said.

A young man stepped out of the shadows of the vestibule, looking in the direction Hadley took. Then he turned around and faced the two travelers from the future.

It was Ernest Hemingway. He smiled. "Close your mouth, John. You'll catch flies." He opened the door to the compartment, picked up the overnight bag, and carried it into the next car.

John recovered enough to chase after him. He had disappeared.

The Hemingway followed. "What *is* this?" John said. "I thought you couldn't be in two timespaces at once."

"That wasn't me."

"It sure as hell wasn't the real Hemingway. He's in Lausanne with Lincoln Steffens."

"Maybe he is and maybe he isn't."

"He knew my *name*!"

"That he did." The Hemingway was getting fainter as John watched.

"Was he another one of you? Another STAB agent?"

"No. Not possible." It peered at John. "What's happening to you?"

Hadley burst into the car and ran right through them, shouting in French for the conductor. She was carrying a bottle of Evian water.

"Well," John said, "that's what—"

The Hemingway was gone. John just had time to think *Marooned in 1922?* when the railroad car and the Gare de Lyon dissolved in an inbursting cascade of black sparks and it was no easier to handle the second time, spread impossibly thin across all those light years and millennia, wondering whether it was going to last forever this time, realizing that it did anyhow, and coalescing with an impossibly painful *snap*:

Looking at the list in the typewriter. He reached for the Heineken; it was still cold. He set it back down. "God," he whispered. "I hope that's that."

The situation called for higher octane. He went to the freezer and took out the vodka. He sipped the gelid syrup straight from the bottle, and almost dropped it when out of the corner of his eye he saw the overnight bag.

He set the open bottle on the counter and sleepwalked over to the dining room table. It was the same bag, slightly beat-up, monogrammed EHR, Elizabeth Hadley Richardson. He opened it and inside was a thick stack of manila envelopes.

He took out the top one and took it and the vodka bottle back to his chair. His hands were shaking. He opened the folder and stared at the familiar typing.

ERNEST M. HEMINGWAY

ONE-EYE FOR MINE

Fever stood up. In the moon light he could xx see blood starting on his hands. His pants were torn at the knee and he knew it would be bleeding ~~there~~ too. He watched the lights of the caboose disppear in the trees where the track curved.

That lousy crut of a brakeman. He would get him xxx~~day~~ some day.   scuffed

Fever xxxxxxx off the end of a tie and sat down to pick the cinders out of his hands and knee. He could use some water. The brakeman had his canteen.

He could smell a campfire. He wondered if it would be smart to go find it. He knew about the wolves, the human kind that lived along the rails and the disgusting things they liked. He wasn't afraid of them but you didn't look for trouble.

You don't have to look for trouble, his father would say. Trouble will find you. His father didn't tell him about wolves, though, ~~or about women~~.

There was a noise in the brush. Fever stood up and slipped his hand around the horn grip of the fat Buck clasp knife in his pocket.

The screen door creaked open and he looked up to see Pansy walk in with a strange expression on her face. Lena followed, looking even stranger. Her left eye was swollen shut and most of that side of her face was bruised blue and brown.

He stood up, shaking with the sudden collision of emotions. "What the hell—"

"Castle," Pansy said. "He got outta hand."

"Real talent for understatement." Lena's voice was tightly controlled but distorted.

"He went nuts. Slappin' Lena around. Then he started to rummage around in a closet, rave about a shotgun, and we split."

"I'll call the police."

"We've already been there," Lena said. "It's all over."

"Of course. We can't work with—"

"No, I mean he's a *criminal*. He's wanted in Mississippi for second-degree murder. They went to arrest him, hold him for extradition. So no more Hemingway hoax."

"What Hemingway?" Pansy said.

"We'll tell you all about it," Lena said, and pointed at the bottle. "A little early, don't you think? You could at least get us a couple of glasses."

John went into the kitchen, almost floating with vodka buzz and anxious confusion. "What do you want with it?" Pansy said oh-jay and Lena said ice. Then Lena screamed.

He turned around and there was Castle standing in the door, grinning. He had a pistol in his right hand and a sawed-off shotgun in his left.

"You cunts," he said. "You fuckin' cunts. Go to the fuckin' cops."

There was a butcher knife in the drawer next to the refrigerator, but he didn't think Castle would stand idly by and let him rummage for it. Nothing else that might serve as a weapon, except the air pistol. Castle knew that it wouldn't do much damage.

He looked at John. "You three're gonna be my hostages. We're gettin' outta here, lose 'em up in the Everglades. They'll have a make on my pickup, though."

"We don't have a car," John said.

"I know that, asshole! There's a Hertz right down on One. You go rent one and don't try nothin' cute. I so much as smell a cop, I blow these two cunts away."

He turned back to the women and grinned crookedly, talking hard-guy through his teeth. "Like I did those two they sent, the spic and the nigger. They said somethin' about comin' back with a warrant to look for the shotgun and I was just bein' as nice as could be, I said hell, come on in, don't need no warrant. I got nothin' to hide, and when they come in I take the pistol from the nigger and kill the spic with it and shoot the nigger in the balls. You shoulda heard him. Some nigger. Took four more rounds to shut him up."

Wonder if that means the pistol is empty, John thought. He had Pansy's orange juice in his hand. It was an old-fashioned Smith & Wesson .357 Magnum six-shot, but from this angle he couldn't tell whether it had been reloaded. He could try to blind Castle with the orange juice.

He stepped toward him. "What kind of car do you want?"

"Just a *car*, damn it. Big enough." A siren whooped about a block away. Castle looked wary. "Bitch. You told 'em where you'd be."

"No," Lena pleaded. "We didn't tell them anything."

"Don't do anything stupid," John said.

Two more sirens, closer. "I'll show you *stupid!*" He raised the pistols toward Lena. John dashed the orange juice in his face.

It wasn't really like slow motion. It was just that John didn't miss any of it. Castle growled and swung around and in the cylinder's chambers John saw five copper-jacketed slugs. He reached for the gun and the first shot shattered his hand, blowing off two fingers, and struck the right side of his chest. The explosion was deafening and the shock of the bullet was like being hit simultaneously in the hand and chest with baseball bats. He rocked, still on his feet, and coughed blood spatter on Castle's face. He fired again, and the second slug hit him on the other side of the chest, this time spinning him half around. Was somebody screaming? Hemingway said it felt like an icy snowball, and that was pretty close, except for the inside part, your body saying Well, time to close up shop. There was a terrible familiar radiating pain in the center of his chest, and John realized that he was having a totally superfluous heart attack. He pushed off from the dinette and staggered toward Castle again. He made a grab for the shotgun and Castle emptied both barrels into his abdomen. He dropped to his knees and then fell over on his side. He couldn't feel anything. Things started to go dim and red. Was this going to be the last time?

Castle cracked the shotgun and the two spent shells flew up in an arc over his shoulder. He took two more out of his shirt pocket and dropped one. When he bent over to pick it up, Pansy leaped past him. In a swift motion that was almost graceful—it came to John that he had probably practiced it over and over, acting out fantasies—he slipped both shells into their chambers and closed the gun with a flip of the wrist. The screen door was stuck. Pansy was straining at the knob with both hands. Castle put the muzzles up to the base of her skull and pulled one trigger. Most of her head covered the screen or went through the hole the blast made. The crown of her skull, a bloody bowl, bounced off two walls and went spinning into the kitchen. Her body did a spastic little dance and folded, streaming.

Lena was suddenly on his back, clawing at his face. He spun and slammed her against the wall. She wilted like a rag doll and he hit her hard with the pistol on the way down. She unrolled at his feet, out cold, and with his mouth wide open laughing silently he lowered the shotgun and blasted her point-blank in the crotch. Her body jackknifed and John tried with all his will not to die but blackness crowded in and the last thing he saw was that evil grin as Castle reloaded again, peering out the window, presumably at the police.

It wasn't the terrible sense of being spread infinitesimally thin over an infinity of pain and darkness; things had just gone black, like closing your eyes. If this is death, John thought, there's not much to it.

But it changed. There was a little bit of pale light, some vague figures, and then colors bled into the scene, and after a moment of disorientation he realized he was still in the apartment, but apparently floating up by the ceiling. Lena was conscious again, barely, twitching, staring at the river of blood that pumped from between her legs. Pansy looked unreal, headless but untouched from the neck down, lying in a relaxed, improbable posture like a knocked-over department store dummy, blood still spurting from a neck artery out through the screen door.

His own body was a mess, the abdomen completely excavated by buckshot. Inside the huge wound, behind the torn coils of intestine, the shreds of fat and gristle, the blood, the shit, he could see sharp splintered knuckles of backbone. Maybe it hadn't hurt so much because the spinal cord had been severed in the blast.

He had time to be a little shocked at himself for not feeling more. Of course most of the people he'd known who had died did die this way, in loud spatters of blood and brains. Even after thirty years of the occasional polite heart attack or stroke carrying off friend or acquaintance, most of the dead people he knew had died in the jungle.

He had been a hero there, in this universe. That would have surprised his sergeants in the original one. Congressional Medal of Honor, so-called, which hadn't hurt the sales of his first book. Knocked out the NVA machine gun emplacement with their own satchel charge, then hauled the machine gun around and wiped out their mortar and command squads. He managed it all with bullet wounds in the face and triceps. Of course without the bullet wounds he wouldn't have lost his cool and charged the machine gun emplacement, but that wasn't noted in the citation.

A pity there was no way to trade the medals in — melt them down into one big fat bullet and use it to waste that crazy motherfucker who was ignoring the three people he'd just killed, laughing like a hyena while he shouted obscenities at the police gathering down below.

Castle fires a shot through the lower window and then ducks and a spray of automatic weapon fire shatters the upper window, filling the air with a spray of glass; bullets and glass fly painlessly through John where he's floating and he hears them spatter into the ceiling and suddenly everything is white with plaster dust — it starts to clear and he is much closer to his body, drawing down closer and closer; he merges with it and there's an instant of blackness and he's looking out through human eyes again.

A dull noise and he looked up to see hundreds of shards of glass leap up from the floor and fly to the window; plaster dust in billows sucked up into bullet holes in the ceiling, which then disappeared.

The top windowpane reformed as Castle uncrouched, pointed the shotgun, then jerked forward as a blossom of yellow flame and white smoke rolled back into the barrel.

His hand was whole, the fingers restored. He looked down and saw rivulets of blood running back into the hole in his abdomen, then individual drops; then it closed and the clothing restored itself; then one of the holes in his chest closed up and then the other.

The clothing was unfamiliar. A tweed jacket in this weather? His hands had turned old, liver spots forming as he watched. Slow like a plant growing, slow like the moon turning, thinking slowly too, he reached up and felt the beard, and could see out of the corner of his eye that it was white and long. He was too fat, and a belt buckle bit painfully into his belly. He sucked in and pried out and looked at the buckle, yes, it was old brass and said GOTT MIT UNS, the buckle he'd taken from a dead German so long ago. The buckle Hemingway had taken.

John got to one knee. He watched fascinated as the stream of blood gushed back into Lena's womb, disappearing as Castle grinning jammed the barrels in between her legs, flinched, and did a complicated dance in reverse (while Pansy's decapitated body writhed around and jerked upright); Lena, sliding up off the floor, leaped up between the man's back and the wall, then fell off and ran backwards as he flipped the shotgun up to the back of Pansy's neck and seeming gallons of blood and tissue came flying from every direction to assemble themselves into the lovely head and face, distorted in terror as she jerked awkwardly at the door and then ran backwards, past Castle as he did a graceful pirouette, unloading the gun and placing one shell on the floor, which flipped up to his pocket as he stood and put the other one there.

John stood up and walked through some thick resistance toward Castle. Was it *time* resisting him? Everything else was still moving in reverse: Two empty shotgun shells sailed across the room to snick into the weapon's chambers; Castle snapped it shut and wheeled to face John—

But John wasn't where he was supposed to be. As the shotgun swung around, John grabbed the barrels—hot!—and pulled the pistol out of Castle's waistband. He lost his grip on the shotgun barrels just as he jammed the pistol against Castle's heart and fired. A spray of blood from all over the other side of the room converged on Castle's back and John felt the recoil sting of the Magnum just as the shotgun muzzle cracked hard against his teeth, mouthful of searing heat then blackness forever, back in the featureless infinite time-space hell that the Hemingway had taken him to, forever, but in the next instant, a new kind of twitch, a twist . . .

23. THE TIME EXCHANGED

What does that mean, you "lost" him?

We were in the railroad car in the Gare de Lyon, in the normal observation mode. This entity that looked like Hemingway walked up, greeted us, took the manuscripts, and disappeared.

Just like that.

No. He went into the next car. John Baird ran after him. Maybe that was my mistake. I translated instead of running.

That's when you lost him.

Both of them. Baird disappeared, too. Then Hadley came running in—

Don't confuse me with Hadleys. You checked the adjacent universes.

All of them, yes. I think they're all right.

Think?

Well . . . I can't quite get to that moment. When I disappeared. It's as if I were still there for several more seconds, so I'm excluded.

And John Baird is still there?

Not by the time I can insert myself. Just Hadley running around—

No Hadleys. No Hadleys. So naturally you went back to 1996.

Of course. But there is a period of several minutes there from which I'm excluded as well. When I can finally insert myself, John Baird is dead.

Ah.

In every doom line, he and Castlemaine have killed each other. John is lying there with his head blown off, Castle next to him with his heart torn out from a point-blank pistol shot, with two very distraught women screaming while police pile in through the door. And this.

The overnight bag with the stories.

I don't think anybody noticed it. With Baird dead, I could spot-check the women's futures; neither of them mentions the bag. So perhaps the mission is accomplished.

Well, Reality is still here. So far. But the connection between Baird and this Hemingway entity is disturbing. That Baird is able to return to 1996 without your help is *very* disturbing. He has obviously taken on some of your characteristics, your abilities, which is why you're excluded from the last several minutes of his life.

I've never heard of that happening before.

It never has. I think that John Baird is no more human than you and I.

Is?

I suspect he's still around somewhen.

24. ISLANDS IN THE STREAM

and the unending lightless desert of pain becomes suddenly one small bright spark and then everything is dark red and a taste, a bitter taste, Hoppe's No. 9 gun oil and the twin barrels of the fine Boss pigeon gun cold and oily on his tongue and biting hard against the roof of his mouth; the dark red is light on the other side of his eyelids, sting of pain before he bumps a tooth and opens his eyes and mouth and lowers the gun and with shaking hands unloads—no, *dis*-loads—both barrels and walks backwards, shuffling in the slippers, slumping, stopping to stare out into the Idaho morning dark, helpless tears coursing up from the snarled white beard, walking backwards down the stairs with the shotgun heavily cradled in his elbow, backing into the storeroom and replacing it in the rack, then back up the stairs and slowly put the keys there in plain sight on the kitchen windowsill, a bit of mercy from Miss Mary, then sit and stare at the cold bad coffee as it warms back to one acid sip—

A tiny part of the mind saying *wait! I am John Baird it is 1996*

and back to a spiritless shower, numb to the needle spray, and cramped constipation and a sleep of no ease; an evening with Mary and George Brown tiptoeing around the blackest of black-ass worse and worse each day, only one thing to look forward to

got to throw out an anchor

faster now, walking through the Ketchum woods like a jerky cartoon in reverse, fucking FBI and IRS behind every tree, because you sent Ezra that money, felt sorry for him because he was crazy, what a fucking joke, should have finished the *Cantos* and shot himself.

effect preceding cause but I can read or hear scraps of thought somehow speeding to a blur now, driving in reverse hundreds of miles per hour back from Ketchum to Minnesota, the Mayo Clinic, holding the madness in while you talk to the shrink, promise not to hurt myself have to go home and write if I'm going to beat this, figuring what he wants to hear, then the rubber mouthpiece and smell of your own hair and flesh slightly burnt by the electrodes then deep total blackness *sharp stabs of thought sometimes stretching*

hospital days blur by in reverse, cold chrome and starch white, a couple of mouthfuls of claret a day to wash down the pills that seem to make it worse and worse

what will happen to me when he's born?

When they came back from Spain was when he agreed to the Mayo Clinic, still all beat-up from the plane crashes six years before in Africa, liver and spleen shot to hell, brain, too, nerves, can't write or can't stop: all day on one damned sentence for the Kennedy book but a hundred thousand fast words, pure shit, for the bullfight article. Paris book okay but stuck. Great to find the trunks in the Ritz but none of the stuff Hadley lost.

Here it stops. A frozen tableau:

Afternoon light slanting in through the tall cloudy windows of the Cambon bar, where he had liberated, would liberate, the hotel in August 1944. A good large American-style martini gulped too fast in the excitement. The two small trunks unpacked and laid out item by item. Hundreds of pages of notes that would become the Paris book. But nothing before '23, of course. *the manuscripts* The novel and the stories and the poems still gone. One moment nailed down with the juniper sting of the martini and then time crawling rolling flying backwards again—

no control?

Months blurring by, Madrid Riviera Venice feeling sick and busted up, the plane wrecks like a quick one-two punch brain and body, blurry sick even before them at the Finca Vigia, can't get a fucking thing done after the Nobel Prize, journalists day and night, the prize bad luck and bullshit anyhow but need the $35,000

damn, had to shoot Willie, cat since the boat-time before the war, but winged a burglar too, same gun, just after the Pulitzer, now that was all right

slowing down again—Havana—the Floridita—

Even Mary having a good time, and the Basque jai alai players, too, though they don't know much English, most of them, interesting couple of civilians, the doctor and the Kraut look-alike, but there's something about the boy that makes it hard to take my eyes off him, looks like someone I guess, another round of Papa Dobles, that boy, what is it about him? and then the first round, with lunch, and things speeding up to a blur again.

out on the Gulf a lot, enjoying the triumph of *The Old Man and the Sea*, the easy good-paying work of providing fishing footage for the movie, and then back into 1951, the worst year of his life that far, weeks of grudging conciliation, uncontrollable anger, and black-ass depression from the poisonous critical slime that followed *Across the River*, bastards gunning for him, Harold Ross dead, mother Grace dead, son Gregory a dope addict hip-deep into the dianetics horseshit, Charlie Scribner dead but first declaring undying love for that asshole Jones

most of the forties an anxious blur, Cuba Italy Cuba France Cuba China found Mary kicked Martha out, thousand pages on the fucking *Eden* book wouldn't come together Bronze Star better than Pulitzer

Martha a chrome-plated bitch in Europe but war is swell otherwise, liberating the Ritz, grenades rifles pistols and bomb runs with the RAF, China boring compared to it and the Q-ship runs off Cuba, hell, maybe the bitch was right for once, just kid stuff and booze marrying the bitch was the end of my belle epoch, easy to see from here, the thirties all sunshine Key West Spain Key West Africa Key West, good hard writing with Pauline holding down the store, good woman but sorry I had to

sorry I had to divorce

stopping

Walking Paris streets after midnight:

I was never going to throw back at her losing the manuscripts. Told Steffens that would be like blaming a human for the weather, or death. These things happen. Nor say anything about what I did the night after I found out she really had lost them. But this one time we got to shouting and I think I hurt her. Why the hell did she have to bring the carbons what the hell did she think carbons were for stupid stupid stupid and she crying and she giving me hell about Pauline Jesus any woman who could fuck up Paris for you could fuck up a royal flush

it slows down around the manuscripts or me—

golden years the mid-twenties everything clicks Paris Vorarlburg Paris Schruns Paris Pamplona Paris Madrid Paris Lausanne

couldn't believe she actually

most of a novel dozens of poems stories sketches—*contes*, Kitty called them by God woman you show me your *conte* and I'll show you mine

so drunk that night I know better than to drink that much absinthe so drunk I was half crawling going up the stairs to the apartment I saw weird I saw God I saw *I saw myself standing there on the fourth landing with Hadley's goddamn bag*

I waited almost an hour, that seemed like no time or all time, and when he, when I, when he came crashing up the stairs he blinked twice, then I walked through me groping, shook my head without looking back and managed to get the door unlocked

flying back through the dead winter French countryside, standing in the bar car fighting hopelessness to Hadley crying so hard she can't get out what was wrong with Steffens standing gaping like a fish in a bowl

twisting again, painlessly inside out, I suppose through various dimensions, seeing the man's life as one complex chord of beauty and purpose and ugliness and chaos, my life on one side of the Möbius strip consistent through its fading forty-year span, starting, *starting*, here:

the handsome young man sits on the floor of the apartment holding himself, rocking racked with sobs, one short manuscript crumpled in front of him, the room a mess with drawers pulled out, their contents scattered on the floor, it's like losing an arm a leg (a foot a testicle), it's like losing your youth and along with youth

with a roar he stands up, eyes closed fists clenched, wipes his face dry and stomps over to the window

breathes deeply until he's breathing normally

strides across the room, kicking a brassiere out of his way

stands with his hand on the knob and thinks this:

life can break you but you can grow back strong at the broken places

and goes out slamming the door behind him, somewhat conscious of having been present at his own birth.

With no effort I find myself standing earlier that day in the vestibule of a train.

Hadley is walking away, tired, looking for a vendor. I turn and confront two aspects of myself.

"Close your mouth, John. You'll catch flies."

They both stand paralyzed while I slide open the door and pull the overnight bag from under the seat. I walk away and the universe begins to tingle and sparkle.

I spend forever in the black void between timespaces. I am growing to enjoy it.

I appear in John Baird's apartment and set down the bag. I look at the empty chair in front of the old typewriter, the green beer bottle sweating cold next to it, and John Baird appears, looking dazed, and I have business elsewhere, elsewhen. A train to catch. I'll come back for the bag in twelve minutes or a few millennia, after the bloodbath that gives birth to us all.

25. A MOVEABLE FEAST

He wrote the last line and set down the pencil and read over the last page sitting on his hands for warmth. He could see his breath. Celebrate the end with a little heat.

He unwrapped the bundle of twigs and banked them around the pile of coals in the brazier. Crazy way to heat a room, but it's France. He cupped both hands behind the stack and blew gently. The coals glowed red and then orange and with the third breath the twigs smoldered and a small yellow flame popped up. He held his hands over the fire, rubbing the stiffness out of his fingers, enjoying the smell of the birch as it cracked and spit.

He put a fresh sheet and carbon into the typewriter and looked at his penciled notes. Final draft? Worth a try:

Ernest M. Hemingway,
74 rue da Cardinal Lemoine,
Paris, France

))UP IN MICHIGAN))
Jim Gilmore came to Horton's Bay from Canada. He bought the blacksmith shop from old man Hortom

Shit, a typo. He flinched suddenly, as if struck, and shook his head to clear it. What a strange sensation to come out of nowhere. A sudden cold stab of grief. But larger somehow than grief for a person.

Grief for everybody, maybe. For being human.

From a typo?

He went to the window and opened it in spite of the cold. He filled his lungs with the cold damp air and looked around the familiar orange-and-grey mosaic of chimney pots and tiled roofs under the dirty winter Paris sky.

He shuddered and eased the window back down and returned to the heat of the brazier. He had felt it before, exactly that huge and terrible feeling. But where?

For the life of him he couldn't remember.

Mr. Boy

JAMES PATRICK KELLY

James Patrick Kelly made his first sale in 1975, and since has gone on to become one of the most respected and popular writers to enter the field in the last twenty years. Although Kelly has had some success with novels, especially with *Wildlife*, he has perhaps had more impact to date as a writer of short fiction, with stories such as "Solstice," "The Prisoner of Chillon," "Glass Cloud," "Pogrom," "Home Front," "Undone," and "Bernardo's House," and is often ranked among the best short story writers in the business. His story "Think Like a Dinosaur" won him a Hugo Award in 1996, as did his story "10^{16} to 1," in 2000. Kelly's first solo novel, the mostly ignored *Planet of Whispers*, came out in 1984. It was followed by *Freedom Beach*, a mosaic novel written in collaboration with John Kessel, and then by another solo novel, *Look into the Sun*. His short work has been collected in *Think Like a Dinosaur*, and, most recently, in a new collection, *Strange But Not a Stranger*. His most recent book is the chapbook novella, *Burn*, and coming up is an anthology co-edited with John Kessel, *Feeling Very Strange: The Slipstream Anthology*. Born in Minneola, New York, Kelly now lives with his family in Nottingham, New Hampshire. He has a Web site at www.JimKelly.net, and reviews Internet-related matters for *Asimov's Science Fiction*.

F. Scott Fitzgerald told us long ago that the rich were not like you and me, but it takes the pyrotechnic and wildly inventive story that follows, the first story to really put James Patrick Kelly on the map as one of the foremost writers of his generation, to demonstrate just how unlike us they could eventually become.

I was already twitching by the time they strapped me down. Nasty pleasure and beautiful pain crackled through me, branching and rebranching like lightning. Extreme feelings are hard to tell apart when you have endorphins spilling across your brain. Another spasm shot down my legs and curled my toes. I moaned. The stiffs wore surgical masks that hid their mouths, but I knew they were smiling. They hated me because my mom could afford to have me stunted. When I really was just a kid I did not understand that. Now I hated them back; it helped me get through the therapy. We had a very clean transaction going here. No secrets between us.

Even though it hurts, getting stunted is still the ultimate flash. As I unlived my life, I overdosed on dying feelings and experiences. My body was not big enough to hold them all; I thought I was going to explode. I must have screamed because I could see the laugh lines crinkling around the stiffs' eyes. You do not have to worry about laugh lines after they twank your genes and reset your mitotic limits. My face was smooth and I was going to be twelve years old forever, or at least as long as Mom kept paying for my rejuvenation.

I giggled as the short one leaned over me and pricked her catheter into my neck. Even through the mask, I could smell her breath. She reeked of dead meat.

Getting stunted always left me wobbly and thick, but this time I felt like last Tuesday's pizza. One of the stiffs had to roll me out of recovery in a wheelchair.

The lobby looked like a furniture showroom. Even the plants had been newly waxed. There was nothing to remind the clients that they were bags of blood and piss. You are all biological machines now, said the lobby, clean as space-station lettuce. A scattering of people sat on the hard chairs. Stennie and Comrade were fidgeting by the elevators. They looked as if they were thinking of rearranging the furniture—like maybe into a pile in the middle of the room. Even before they waved, the stiff seemed to know that they were waiting for me.

Comrade smiled. "Zdrast'ye."

"You okay, Mr. Boy?" said Stennie. Stennie was a grapefruit-yellow stenonychosaurus with a brown underbelly. His razor-clawed toes clicked against the slate floor as he walked.

"He's still a little weak," said the stiff, as he set the chair's parking brake. He strained to act nonchalant, not realizing that Stennie enjoys being stared at. "He needs rest. Are you his brother?" he said to Comrade.

Comrade appeared to be a teenaged spike neck with a head of silky black hair that hung to his waist. He wore a window coat on which twenty-three different talking heads chattered. He could pass for human, even though he was really a Panasonic. "Nyet," said Comrade. "I'm just another one of his hallucinations."

The poor stiff gave him a dry nervous cough that might have been meant as a chuckle. He was probably wondering whether Stennie wanted to take me home or eat me for lunch. I always thought that the way Stennie got reshaped was more funny-looking than fierce—a python that had rear-ended an ostrich. But even though he was a head shorter than me, he did have enormous eyes and a mouthful of serrated teeth. He stopped next to the wheelchair and rose up to his full height. "I appreciate everything you've done." Stennie offered the stiff his spindly three-fingered hand to shake. "Sorry if he caused any trouble."

The stiff took it gingerly, then shrieked and flew backward. I mean, he jumped almost a meter off the floor. Everyone in the lobby turned, and Stennie opened his hand and waved the joy buzzer. He slapped his tail against the slate in triumph. Stennie's sense of humor was extreme, but then he was only thirteen years old.

Stennie's parents had given him the Nissan Alpha for his twelfth birthday, and we had been customizing it ever since. We installed blue mirror glass, and Stennie painted scenes from the Late Cretaceous on the exterior body armor. We ripped out all the seats, put in a wall-to-wall gel mat and a fridge and a microwave and a screen and a minidish. Comrade had even done an illegal operation on the carbrain so that we could override in an emergency and actually steer the Alpha ourselves with a joystick. It would have been cramped, but we would have lived in Stennie's car if our parents had let us.

"You okay there, Mr. Boy?" said Stennie.

"Mmm." As I watched the trees whoosh past in the rain, I pretended that the car was standing still and the world was passing me by.

"Think of something to do, okay?" Stennie had the car and all and he was fun to play with, but ideas were not his specialty. He was probably smart for a dinosaur. "I'm bored."

"Leave him alone, will you?" Comrade said.

"He hasn't said anything yet." Stennie stretched and nudged me with his foot. "Say something." He had legs like a horse: yellow skin stretched tight over long bones and stringy muscle.

"*Prosrees!* He just had his genes twanked, you jack." Comrade always took good care of me. Or tried to. "Remember what that's like? He's in damage control."

"Maybe I should go to socialization," Stennie said. "Aren't they having a dance this afternoon?"

"You're talking to me?" said the Alpha. "You haven't earned enough learning credits to socialize. You're a quiz behind and forty-five minutes short of E-class. You haven't linked since . . ."

"Just shut up and drive me over." Stennie and the Alpha did not get along. He thought the car was too strict. "I'll make up the plugging quiz, okay?" He probed a mess of empty juice boxes and snack wrappers with his foot. "Anyone see my comm anywhere?"

Stennie's schoolcomm was wedged behind my cushion. "You know," I said, "I can't take much more of this." I leaned forward, wriggled it free, and handed it over.

"Of what, *poputchik?*" said Comrade. "Joyriding? Listening to the lizard here?"

"Being stunted."

Stennie flipped up the screen of his comm and went on-line with the school's computer. "You guys help me, okay?" He retracted his claws and tapped at the oversized keyboard.

"It's extreme while you're on the table," I said, "but now I feel empty. Like I've lost myself."

"You'll get over it," said Stennie. "First question: Brand name of the first wiseguys sold for home use?"

"NEC-Bots, of course," said Comrade.

"Geneva? It got nuked, right?"

"*Da.*"

"Haile Selassie was that king of Ethiopia who the Marleys claim is god, right?

Name the Cold Wars: Nicaragua, Angola . . . Korea was the first." Typing was hard work for Stennie; he did not have enough fingers for it. "One was something like Venezuela. Or something."

"Sure it wasn't Venice?"

"Or Venus?" I said, but Stennie was not paying attention.

"All right, I know that one. And that. The Sovs built the first space station. Ronald Reagan—he was the president who dropped the bomb?"

Comrade reached inside of his coat and pulled out an envelope. "I got you something, Mr. Boy. A get-well present for your collection."

I opened it and scoped a picture of a naked dead fat man on a stainless-steel table. The print had a DI verification grid on it, which meant this was the real thing, not a composite. Just above the corpse's left eye there was a neat hole. It was rimmed with purple that had faded to bruise blue. He had curly gray hair on his head and chest, skin the color of dried mayonnaise, and a wonderfully complicated penis graft. He looked relieved to be dead. "Who was he?" I liked Comrade's present. It was extreme.

"CEO of Infoline. He had the wife, you know, the one who stole all the money so she could download herself into a computer."

I shivered as I stared at the dead man. I could hear myself breathing and feel the blood squirting through my arteries. "Didn't they turn her off?" I said. This was the kind of stuff we were not even supposed to imagine, much less look at. Too bad they had cleaned him up. "How much did this cost me?"

"You don't want to know."

"Hey!" Stennie thumped his tail against the side of the car. "I'm taking a quiz here, and you guys are drooling over porn. When was the First World Depression?"

"Who cares?" I slipped the picture back into the envelope and grinned at Comrade.

"Well, let me see then." Stennie snatched the envelope. "You know what I think, Mr. Boy? I think this corpse jag you're on is kind of sick. Besides, you're going to get in trouble if you let Comrade keep breaking laws. Isn't this picture private?"

"Privacy is twentieth-century thinking. It's all information, Stennie, and information should be accessible." I held out my hand. "But if *glasnost* bothers you, give it up." I wiggled my fingers.

Comrade snickered. Stennie pulled out the picture, glanced at it, and hissed. "You're scaring me, Mr. Boy."

His schoolcomm beeped as it posted his score on the quiz, and he sailed the envelope back across the car at me. "Not Venezuela, Vietnam. Hey, *Truman* dropped the plugging bomb. Reagan was the one who spent all the money. What's wrong with you dumbscuts? Now I owe school another fifteen minutes."

"Hey, if you don't make it look good, they'll know you had help." Comrade laughed.

"What's with this dance anyway? You don't dance." I picked Comrade's present up and tucked it into my shirt pocket. "You find yourself a cush or something, lizard boy?"

"Maybe." Stennie could not blush, but sometimes when he was embarrassed the loose skin under his jaw quivered. Even though he had been reshaped into a dinosaur, he was still growing up. "Maybe I am getting a little. What's it to you?"

"If you're getting it," I said, "it's got to be microscopic." This was a bad sign. I was losing him to his dick, just like all the other pals. No way I wanted to start over with someone new. I had been alive for twenty-five years now. I was running out of things to say to thirteen-year-olds.

As the Alpha pulled up to the school, I scoped the crowd waiting for the doors to open for third shift. Although there was a handful of stunted kids, a pair of gorilla brothers who were football stars and Freddy the Teddy—a bear who had furry hands instead of real paws—the majority of students at New Canaan High looked more or less normal. Most working stiffs thought that people who had their genes twanked were freaks.

"Come get me at five-fifteen," Stennie told the Alpha. "In the meantime, take these guys wherever they want to go." He opened the door. "You rest up, Mr. Boy, okay?"

"What?" I was not paying attention. "Sure." I had just seen the most beautiful girl in the world.

She leaned against one of the concrete columns of the portico, chatting with a couple other kids. Her hair was long and nut-colored and the ends twinkled. She was wearing a loose black robe over mirror skintights. Her schoolcomm dangled from a strap around her wrist. She appeared to be seventeen, maybe eighteen. But of course, appearances could be deceiving.

Girls had never interested me much, but I could not help but admire this one. "Wait, Stennie! Who's that?" She saw me point at her. "With the hair?"

"She's new—has one of those names you can't pronounce." He showed me his teeth as he got out. "Hey, Mr. Boy, you're *stunted*. You haven't got what she wants."

He kicked the door shut, lowered his head, and crossed in front of the car. When he walked, he looked like he was trying to squash a bug with each step. His snaky tail curled high behind him for balance, his twiggy little arms dangled. When the new girl saw him, she pointed and smiled. Or maybe she was pointing at me.

"Where to?" said the car.

"I don't know." I sank low into my seat and pulled out Comrade's present again. "Home, I guess."

I was not the only one in my family with twanked genes. My mom was a three-quarter-scale replica of the Statue of Liberty. Originally she wanted to be full-sized, but then she would have been the tallest thing in New Canaan, Connecticut. The town turned her down when she applied for a zoning variance. Her lawyers and their lawyers sued and countersued for almost two years. Mom's claim was that since she was born human, her freedom of form was protected by the Thirtieth Amendment. However, the form she wanted was a curtain of reshaped cells that would hang on a forty-two-meter-high ferroplastic skeleton. Her structure, said the planning board, was clearly subject to building codes and zoning laws. Eventually they reached an out-of-court settlement, which was why Mom was only as tall as an eleven-story building.

She complied with the town's request for a setback of five hundred meters from Route 123. As Stennie's Alpha drove us down the long driveway, Comrade broadcast the recognition code that told the robot sentries that we were okay. One thing Mom and the town agreed on from the start: no tourists. Sure, she loved publicity, but she was also very fragile. In some places her skin was only a centimeter thick. Chunks of ice falling from her crown could punch holes in her.

The end of our driveway cut straight across the lawn to Mom's granite-paved foundation pad. To the west of the plaza, directly behind her, was a utility building faced in ashlar that housed her support systems. Mom had been bioengineered to be pretty much self-sufficient. She was green not only to match the real Statue of Liberty but also because she was photosynthetic. All she needed was a yearly truckload of fertilizer, water from the well, and 150 kilowatts of electricity a day. Except for emergency surgery, the only time she required maintenance was in the fall, when her outer cells tended to flake off and had to be swept up and carted away.

Stennie's Alpha dropped us off by the doorbone in the right heel and then drove off to do whatever cars do when nobody is using them. Mom's greeter was waiting in the reception area inside the foot.

"Peter." She tried to hug me, but I dodged out of her grasp. "How are you, Peter?"

"Tired." Even though Mom knew I did not like to be called that, I kissed the air near her cheek. Peter Cage was her name for me; I had given it up years ago.

"You poor boy. Here, let me see you." She held me at arm's length and brushed her fingers against my cheek. "You don't look a day over twelve. Oh, they do such good work—don't you think?" She squeezed my shoulder. "Are you happy with it?"

I think my mom meant well, but she never did understand me. Especially when she talked to me with her greeter remote. I wormed out of her grip and fell back onto one of the couches. "What's to eat?"

"Doboys, noodles, fries—whatever you want." She beamed at me and then bent over impulsively and gave me a kiss that I did not want. I never paid much attention to the greeter; she was lighter than air. She was always smiling and asking five questions in a row without waiting for an answer and flitting around the room. It wore me out just watching her. Naturally, everything I said or did was cute, even if I was trying to be obnoxious. It was no fun being cute. Today Mom had her greeter wearing a dark blue dress and a very dumb white apron. The greeter's umbilical was too short to stretch up to the kitchen. So why was she wearing an apron? "I'm really, really glad you're home," she said.

"I'll take some cinnamon doboys." I kicked off my shoes and rubbed my bare feet through the dense black hair on the floor. "And a beer."

All of Mom's remotes had different personalities. I liked Nanny all right; she was simple, but at least she listened. The lovers were a challenge because they were usually too busy looking into mirrors to notice me. Cook was as pretentious as a four-star menu; the housekeeper had all the charm of a vacuum cleaner. I had always wondered what it would be like to talk directly to Mom's main brain up in the head, because then she would not be filtered through a remote. She would be herself.

"Cook is making you some nice broth to go with your doboys," said the greeter. "Nanny says you shouldn't be eating dessert all the time."

"Hey, did I ask for broth?"

At first Comrade had hung back while the greeter was fussing over me. Then he slid along the wrinkled pink walls of the reception room toward the plug where the greeter's umbilical was attached. When she started in about the broth, I saw him lean against the plug. Carelessly, you know? At the same time he stepped on the greeter's umbilical, crimping the furry black cord. She gasped and the smile flattened horribly on her face, as if her lips were two ropes someone had suddenly yanked taut. Her head jerked toward the umbilical plug.

"E-Excuse me." She was twitching.

"What?" Comrade glanced down at his foot as if it belonged to a stranger. "Oh, sorry." He pushed away from the wall and strolled across the room toward us. Although he seemed apologetic, about half the heads on his window coat were laughing.

The greeter flexed her cheek muscles. "You'd better watch out for your toy, Peter," she said. "It's going to get you in trouble someday."

Mom did not like Comrade much, even though she had given him to me when I was first stunted. She got mad when I snuck him down to Manhattan a couple of years ago to have a chop job done on his behavioral regulators. For a while after the operation, he used to ask me before he broke the law. Now he was on his own. He got caught once, and she warned me he was out of control. But she still threw money at the people until they went away.

"Trouble?" I said. "Sounds like fun." I thought we were too rich for trouble. I was the trust baby of a trust baby; we had vintage money and lots of it. I stood and Comrade picked up my shoes for me. "And he's not a toy; he's my best friend." I put my arms around his shoulder. "Tell Cook I'll eat in my rooms."

I was tired after the long climb up the circular stairs to Mom's chest. When the roombrain sensed I had come in, it turned on all the electronic windows and blinked my message indicator. One reason I still lived in my mom was that she kept out of my rooms. She had promised me total security, and I believed her. Actually I doubted that she cared enough to pry, although she could easily have tapped my windows. I was safe from her remotes up here, even the housekeeper. Comrade did everything for me.

I sent him for supper, perched on the edge of the bed, and cleared the nearest window of army ants foraging for meat through some Angolan jungle. The first message in the queue was from a gray-haired stiff wearing a navy blue corporate uniform. "Hello, Mr. Cage. My name is Weldon Montross and I'm with Datasafe. I'd like to arrange a meeting with you at your convenience. Call my DI number, 408-966-3286. I hope to hear from you soon."

"What the hell is Datasafe?"

The roombrain ran a search. "Datasafe offers services in encryption and information security. It was incorporated in the state of Delaware in 2013. Estimated billings last year were three hundred and forty million dollars. Headquarters are in San Jose, California, with branch offices in White Plains, New York, and Chevy Chase, Maryland. Foreign offices . . ."

"Are they trying to sell me something or what?"

The room did not offer an answer. "Delete," I said. "Next?"

Weldon Montross was back again, looking exactly as he had before. I wondered if he were using a virtual image. "Hello, Mr. Cage. I've just discovered that you've been admitted to the Thayer Clinic for rejuvenation therapy. Believe me when I say that I very much regret having to bother you during your convalescence, and I would not do so if this were not a matter of importance. Would you please contact Department of Identification number 408-966-3286 as soon as you're able?"

"You're a pro, Weldon, I'll say that for you." Prying client information out of the Thayer Clinic was not easy, but then the guy was no doubt some kind of op. He was way too polite to be a salesman. What did Datasafe want with me? "Any more messages from him?"

"No," said the roombrain.

"Well, delete this one too, and if he calls back tell him I'm too busy unless he wants to tell me what he's after." I stretched out on my bed. "Next?" The gel mattress shivered as it took my weight.

Happy Lurdane was having a smash party on the twentieth, but Happy was a boring cush and there was a bill from the pet store for the iguanas that I paid and a warning from the SPCA that I deleted and a special offer for preferred customers from my favorite fireworks company that I saved to look at later and my dad was about to ask for another loan when I paused him and deleted and last of all there was a message from Stennie, time-stamped ten minutes ago.

"Hey, Mr. Boy, if you're feeling better I've lined up a VE party for tonight." He did not quite fit into the school's telelink booth; all I could see was his toothy face and the long yellow curve of his neck. "Bunch of us have reserved some time on Playroom. Come in disguise. That new kid said she'd link, so scope her yourself if you're so hot. I found out her name, but it's kind of unpronounceable. Tree-something Joplin. Anyway, it's at seven, meet on channel seventeen, password is *warhead*. Hey, did you send my car back yet? Later." He faded.

"Sounds like fun." Comrade kicked the doorbone open and backed through, balancing a tray loaded with soup and fresh doboys and a mug of cold beer. "Are we going?" He set it onto the nightstand next to my bed.

"Maybe." I yawned. It felt good to be in my own bed. "Flush the damn soup, would you?" I reached over for a doboy and felt something crinkle in my jacket pocket. I pulled out the picture of the dead CEO. About the only thing I did not like about it was that the eyes were shut. You feel dirtier when the corpse stares back. "This is one sweet hunk of meat, Comrade." I propped the picture beside the tray. "How did you get it, anyway? Must have taken some operating."

"Three days' worth. Encryption wasn't all that tough, but there was lots of it." Comrade admired the picture with me as he picked up the bowl of soup. "I ended up buying about ten hours from IBM to crack the file. Kind of pricey, but since you were getting stunted, I had nothing else to do."

"You see the messages from that security op?" I bit into a doboy. "Maybe you were a little sloppy." The hot cinnamon scent tickled my nose.

"*Ya v'rot ego ebal!*" He laughed. "So some stiff is cranky? Plug him if he can't take a joke."

I said nothing. Comrade could be a pain sometimes. Of course I loved the picture, but he really should have been more careful. He had made a mess and left it for me to clean up. Just what I needed. I knew I would only get mad if I thought about it, so I changed the subject. "Well, do you think she's cute?"

"What's-her-face Joplin?" Comrade turned abruptly toward the bathroom. "Sure, for a *perdunya*," he said over his shoulder. "Why not?" Talking about girls made him snippy. I think he was afraid of them.

I brought my army ants back onto the window; they were swarming over a lump with brown fur. Thinking about him hanging on my elbow when I met this Tree-something Joplin made me feel weird. I listened as he poured the soup down the toilet. I was not myself at all. Getting stunted changes you; no one can predict how. I chugged the beer and rolled over to take a nap. It was the first time I had ever thought of leaving Comrade behind.

"VE party, Mr. Boy." Comrade nudged me awake. "Are we going or not?"

"Huh?" My gut still ached from the rejuvenation, and I woke up mean enough to chew glass. "What do you mean *we*?"

"Nothing." Comrade had that blank look he always put on so I would not know what he was thinking. Still, I could tell he was disappointed. "Are you going then?" he said.

I stretched—*ouch!* "Yeah, sure, get my joysuit." My bones felt brittle as candy. "And stop acting sorry for yourself." This nasty mood had momentum; it swept me past any regrets. "No way I'm going to lie here all night watching you pretend you have feelings to hurt."

"*Tak tochno.*" He saluted and went straight to the closet. I got out of bed and hobbled to the bathroom.

"This is a costume party, remember," Comrade called. "What are you wearing?"

"Whatever." Even his efficiency irked me; sometimes he did too much. "You decide." I needed to get away from him for a while.

Playroom was a new virtual-environment service on our local net. If you wanted to throw an electronic party at Versailles or Monticello or San Simeon, all you had to do was link—if you could get a reservation.

I came back to the bedroom and Comrade stepped up behind me, holding the joysuit. I shrugged into it, velcroed the front seam, and eyed myself in the nearest window. He had synthesized some kid-sized armor in the German Gothic style. My favorite. It was made of polished silver, with great fluting and scalloping. He had even programmed a little glow into the image so that on the window I looked like a walking night-light. There was an armet helmet with a red ostrich plume; the visor was tipped up so I could see my face. I raised my arm, and the joysuit translated the movement to the window so that my armored image waved back.

"Try a few steps," he said.

Although I could move easily in the lightweight joysuit, the motion interpreter made walking in the video armor seem realistically awkward. Comrade had scored the sound effects, too. Metal hinges rasped, chain mail rattled softly, and there was a satisfying *clunk* whenever my foot hit the floor.

"Great." I clenched my fist in approval. I was awake now and in control of my temper. I wanted to make up, but Comrade was not taking the hint. I could never quite figure out whether he was just acting like a machine or whether he really did not care how I treated him.

"They're starting." All the windows in the room lit up with Playroom's welcome screen. "You want privacy, so I'm leaving. No one will bother you."

"Hey, Comrade, you don't have to go . . ."

But he had already left the room. Playroom prompted me to identify myself. "Mr. Boy," I said, "Department of Identification number 203-966-2445. I'm looking for channel seventeen; the password is *warhead*."

A brass band started playing "Hail to the Chief" as the title screen lit the windows:

The White House
1600 Pennsylvania Avenue
Washington, DC, USA
© 2096, Playroom Presentations
REPRODUCTION OR REUSE STRICTLY PROHIBITED

and then I was looking at a wraparound view of a VE ballroom. A caption bar opened at the top of the windows and a message scrolled across. *This is the famous East Room, the largest room in the main house. It is used for press conferences, public receptions, and entertainments.* I lowered my visor and entered the simulation.

The East Room was decorated in bone white and gold; three chandeliers hung like cut-glass mushrooms above the huge parquet floor. A band played skitter at one end of the room, but no one was dancing yet. The band was Warhead, according to their drum set. I had never heard of them. Someone's disguise? I turned, and the joy-suit changed the view on the windows. Just ahead Satan was chatting with a forklift and a rhinoceros. Beyond, some blue cartoons were teasing Johnny America. There was not much furniture in the room, a couple of benches, an ugly piano, and some life-sized paintings of George and Martha. George looked like he had just been peeled off a cash card. I stared at him too long, and the closed-caption bar informed me that the painting had been painted by Gilbert Stuart and was the only White House object dating from the mansion's first occupancy in 1800.

"Hey," I said to a girl who was on fire. "How do I get rid of the plugging tour guide?"

"Can't," she said. "When Playroom found out we were kids, they turned on all their educational crap and there's no override. I kind of don't think they want us back."

"Dumbscuts." I scoped the room for something that might be Stennie. No luck. "I like the way your hair is burning." Now that it was too late, I was sorry I had to make idle party chat.

"Thanks." When she tossed her head, sparks flared and crackled. "My mom helped me program it."

"So, I've never been to the White House. Is there more than this?"

"Sure," she said. "We're supposed to have pretty much the whole first floor. Unless they shorted us. You wouldn't be Stone Kinkaid in there, would you?"

"No, not really." Even though the voice was disguised, I could tell this was Happy Lurdane. I edged away from her. "I'm going to check the other rooms now. Later."

"If you run into Stone, tell him I'm looking for him."

I left the East Room and found myself in a long marble passageway with a red carpet. A dog skeleton trotted toward me. Or maybe it was supposed to be a sheep. I waved and went through a door on the other side.

Everyone in the Red Room was standing on the ceiling; I knew I had found Stennie. Even though what they see is only a simulation, most people lock into the perceptual field of a VE as if it were real. Stand on your head long enough—even if only in your imagination—and you get airsick. It took kilohours of practice to learn to compensate. Upside down was one of Stennie's trademark ways of showing off.

The Red Room is an intimate parlor in the American Empire style of 1815–20 . . .

"Hi," I said. I hopped over the wainscoting and walked up the silk-covered wall to join the three of them.

"You're wearing German armor." When the boy in blue grinned at me, his cheeks dimpled. He was wearing shorts and white knee socks, a navy sweater over a white shirt. "Augsburg?" said Little Boy Blue. Fine blond hair drooped from beneath his tweed cap.

"Try Wolf of Landshut," I said. Stennie and I had spent a lot of time fighting VE wars in full armor. "Nice shorts." Stennie's costume reminded me of Christopher Robin. Terminally cute.

"It's not fair," said the snowman, who I did not recognize. "He says this is what he actually looks like." The snowman was standing in a puddle that was dripping onto the rug below us. Great effect.

"No," said Stennie, "what I said was I *would* look like this if I hadn't done something about it, okay?"

I had not known Stennie before he was a dinosaur. "No wonder you got twanked." I wished I could have saved this image, but Playroom was copy-protected.

"You've been twanked? No joke?" The great horned owl ruffled in alarm. She had a girl's voice. "I know it's none of my business, but I don't understand why anyone would do it. Especially a kid. I mean, what's wrong with good old-fashioned surgery? And you can be whoever you want in a VE." She paused, waiting for someone to agree with her. No help. "Okay, so I don't understand. But when you mess with your genes, you change who you are. I mean, don't you like who you are? I do."

"We're so happy for you." Stennie scowled. "What is this, mental health week?"

"We're rich," I said. "We can afford to hate ourselves."

"This may sound rude"—the owl's big blunt head swiveled from Stennie to me—"but I think that's sad."

"Yeah well, we'll try to work up some tears for you, birdie," Stennie said.

Silence. In the East Room, the band turned the volume up.

"Anyway, I've got to be going." The owl shook herself. "Hanging upside down is fine for bats, but not for me. Later." She let go of her perch and swooped out into the hall. The snowman turned to watch her go.

"You're driving them off, young man." I patted Stennie on the head. "Come on now, be nice."

"Nice makes me puke."

"You *do* have a bit of an edge tonight." I had trouble imagining this dainty little brat as my best friend. "Better watch out you don't cut someone."

The dog skeleton came to the doorway and called up to us. "We're supposed to dance now."

"About time." Stennie fell off the ceiling like a drop of water and splashed head-first onto the beige Persian rug. His image went all muddy for a moment and then he re-formed, upright and unharmed. "Going to skitter, tin man?"

"I need to talk to you for a moment," the snowman murmured.

"You *need* to?" I said.

"Dance, dance, dance," sang Stennie. "Later." He swerved after the skeleton out of the room.

The snowman said, "It's about a possible theft of information."

Right then was when I should have slammed it into reverse. Caught up with Stennie or maybe faded from Playroom altogether. But all I did was raise my hands over my head. "You got me, snowman; I confess. But society is to blame, too, isn't it? You will tell the judge to go easy on me? I've had a tough life."

"This is serious."

"You're Weldon—what's your name?" Down the hall, I could hear the thud of Warhead's bass line. "Montross."

"I'll come to the point, Peter." The only acknowledgment he made was to drop the kid voice. "The firm I represent provides information security services. Last week someone operated on the protected database of one of our clients. We have reason to believe that a certified photograph was accessed and copied. What can you tell me about this?"

"Not bad, Mr. Montross, sir. But if you were as good as you think you are, you'd know my name isn't Peter. It's Mr. Boy. And since nobody invited you to this party, maybe you'd better tell me now why I shouldn't just go ahead and have you deleted?"

"I know that you were undergoing genetic therapy at the time of the theft, so you could not have been directly responsible. That's in your favor. However, I also know that you can help me clear this matter up. And you need to do that, son, just as quickly as you can. Otherwise there's big trouble coming."

"What are you going to do, tell my mommy?" My blood started to pump; I was coming back to life.

"This is my offer. It's not negotiable. You let me sweep your files for this image. You turn over any hardcopies you've made and you instruct your wiseguy to let me do a spot reprogramming, during which I will erase his memory of this incident. After that, we'll consider the matter losed."

"Why don't I just drop my pants and bend over while I'm at it?"

"Look, you can pretend if you want, but you're not a kid anymore. You're twenty-five years old. I don't believe for a minute that you're as thick as your friends out there. If you think about it, you'll realize that you can't fight us. The fact that I'm here and I know what I know means that all your personal information systems are already tapped. I'm an op, son. I could wipe your files clean any time and I will, if it comes to that. However, my orders are to be thorough. The only way I can be sure I have everything is if you cooperate."

"You're not even real, are you, Montross? I'll bet you're nothing but cheesy old code. I've talked to elevators with more personality."

"The offer is on the table."

"Stick it!"

The owl flew back into the room, braked with outstretched wings, and caught onto the armrest of the Dolley Madison sofa. "Oh, you're still here," she said, noticing us. "I didn't mean to interrupt. . . ."

"Wait there," I said. "I'm coming right down."

"I'll be in touch," said the snowman. "Let me know just as soon as you change your mind." He faded.

I flipped backward off the ceiling and landed in front of her; my video armor rang from the impact. "Owl, you just saved the evening." I knew I was showing off, but just then I was willing to forgive myself. "Thanks."

"You're welcome, I guess." She edged away from me, moving with precise little birdlike steps toward the top of the couch. "But all I was trying to do was escape the band."

"Bad?"

"And loud." Her ear tufts flattened. "Do you think shutting the door would help?"

"Sure. Follow me. We can shut lots of doors." When she hesitated, I flapped my arms like silver wings. Actually, Montross had done me a favor; when he threatened me, some inner clock had begun an adrenaline tick. If this was trouble, I wanted more. I felt twisted and dangerous and I did not care what happened next. Maybe that was why the owl flitted after me as I walked into the next room.

The sumptuous State Dining Room can seat about 130 for formal dinners. The white-and-gold decor dates from the administration of Theodore Roosevelt.

The owl glided over to the banquet table. I shut the door behind me. "Better?" Warhead still pounded on the walls.

"A little." She settled on a huge bronze doré centerpiece with a mirrored surface. "I'm going soon anyway."

"Why?"

"The band stinks, I don't know anyone, and I hate these stupid disguises."

"I'm Mr. Boy." I raised my visor and grinned at her. "All right? Now you know someone."

She tucked her wings into place and fixed me with her owlish stare. "I don't like VEs much."

"They take some getting used to."

"Why bother?" she said. "I mean, if anything can happen in a simulation, nothing matters. And I feel dumb standing in a room all alone jumping up and down and flapping my arms. Besides, this joysuit is hot and I'm renting it by the hour."

"The trick is not to look at yourself," I said. "Just watch the screens and use your imagination."

"Reality is less work. You look like a little kid."

"Is that a problem?"

"Mr. Boy? What kind of name is that anyway?"

I wished she would blink. "A made-up name. But then all names are made up, aren't they?"

"Didn't I see you at school Wednesday? You were the one who dropped off the dinosaur."

"My friend Stennie." I pulled out a chair and sat facing her. "Who you probably hate because he's twanked."

"That was him on the ceiling, wasn't it? Listen, I'm sorry about what I said. I'm new here. I'd never met anyone like him before I came to New Canaan. I mean, I'd heard of reshaping and all—getting twanked. But where I used to live, everybody was pretty much the same."

"Where was that, Squirrel Crossing, Nebraska?"

"Close." She laughed. "Elkhart; it's in Indiana."

The reckless ticking in my head slowed. Talking to her made it easy to forget about Montross. "You want to leave the party?" I said. "We could go into discreet."

"Just us?" She sounded doubtful. "Right now?"

"Why not? You said you weren't staying. We could get rid of these disguises. And the music."

She was silent for a moment. Maybe people in Elkhart, Indiana, did not ask one another into discreet unless they had met in Sunday school or the 4-H Club.

"Okay," she said finally, "but I'll enable. What's your DI?"

I gave her my number.

"Be back in a minute."

I cleared Playroom from my screens. The message Enabling discreet mode flashed. I decided not to change out of the joysuit; instead I called up my wardrobe menu and chose an image of myself wearing black baggies. The loose folds and padded shoulders helped hide the scrawny little boy's body.

The message changed. Discreet mode enabled. Do you accept, yes/no?

"Sure," I said.

She was sitting naked in the middle of a room filled with tropical plants. Her skin was the color of cinnamon. She had freckles on her shoulders and across her breasts. Her hair tumbled down the curve of her spine; the ends glowed like embers in a breeze. She clutched her legs close to her and gave me a curious smile. Teenage still life. We were alone and secure. No one could tap us while we were in discreet. We could say anything we wanted. I was too croggled to speak.

"You *are* a little kid," she said.

I did not tell her that what she was watching was an enhanced image, a virtual me. "Uh . . . well, not really." I was glad Stennie could not see me. Mr. Boy at a loss—a first. "Sometimes I'm not sure what I am. I guess you're not going to like me either. I've been stunted a couple of times. I'm really twenty-five years old."

She frowned. "You keep deciding I won't like people. Why?"

"Most people are against genetic surgery. Probably because they haven't got the money."

"Myself, I wouldn't do it. Still, just because you did doesn't mean I hate you." She gestured for me to sit. "But my parents would probably be horrified. They're realists, you know."

"No fooling?" I could not help but chuckle. "That explains a lot." Like why she had an attitude about twanking. And why she thought VEs were dumb. And why she was naked and did not seem to care. According to hard-core realists, first came clothes, then jewelry, fashion, makeup, plastic surgery, skin tints, and hey jack! here we are up to our eyeballs in the delusions of 2096. Gene twanking, VE addicts, people downloading themselves into computers—better never to have started. They wanted to turn back to worn-out twentieth-century modes. "But you're no realist," I said. "Look at your hair."

She shook her head and the ends twinkled. "You like it?"

"It's extreme. But realists don't decorate!"

"Then maybe I'm not a realist. My parents let me try lots of stuff they wouldn't do themselves, like buying hairworks or linking to VEs. They're afraid I'd leave otherwise."

"Would you?"

She shrugged. "So what's it like to get stunted? I've heard it hurts."

I told her how sometimes I felt as if there were broken glass in my joints and how my bones ached and—more showing off—about the blood I would find on the toilet paper. Then I mentioned something about Mom. She had heard of Mom, of course. She asked about my dad, and I explained how Mom paid him to stay away but that he kept running out of money. She wanted to know if I was working or still going to school, and I made up some stuff about courses in history I was taking from Yale. Actually I had faded after my first semester. Couple of years ago. I did not have time to link to some boring college; I was too busy playing with Comrade and Stennie. But I still had an account at Yale.

"So that's who I am." I was amazed at how little I had lied. "Who are you?"

She told me that her name was Treemonisha but her friends called her Tree. It was an old family name; her great-great-grandsomething-or-other had been a composer named Scott Joplin. *Treemonisha* was the name of his opera.

I had to force myself not to stare at her breasts when she talked. "You like *opera?*" I said.

"My dad says I'll grow into it." She made a face. "I hope not."

The Joplins were a franchise family; her mom and dad had just been transferred to the Green Dream, a plant shop in the Elm Street Mall. To hear her talk, you would think she had ordered them from the Good Fairy. They had been married for twenty-two years and were still together. She had a brother, Fidel, who was twelve. They all lived in the greenhouse next to the shop where they grew most of their food and where flowers were always in bloom and where everybody loved everyone else. Nice life for a bunch of mall drones. So why was she thinking of leaving?

"You should stop by sometime," she said.

"Sometime," I said. "Sure."

For hours after we faded, I kept remembering things about her I had not realized I had noticed. The fine hair on her legs. The curve of her eyebrows. The way her hands moved when she was excited.

It was Stennie's fault: after the Playroom party he started going to school almost every day. Not just linking to E-class with his comm, but actually showing up. We knew he had more than remedial reading on his mind, but no matter how much we teased, he would not talk about his mysterious new cush. Before he fell in love we used to joyride in his Alpha afternoons. Now Comrade and I had the car all to ourselves. Not as much fun.

We had already dropped Stennie off when I spotted Treemonisha waiting for the bus. I waved, she came over. The next thing I knew we had another passenger on the road to nowhere. Comrade stared vacantly out the window as we pulled onto South Street; he did not seem pleased with the company.

"Have you been out to the reservoir?" I said. "There are some extreme houses out there. Or we could drive over to Greenwich and look at yachts."

"I haven't been anywhere yet, so I don't care," she said. "By the way, you don't go to college." She was not accusing me or even asking—merely stating a fact.

"Why do you say that?" I said.

"Fidel told me."

I wondered how her twelve-year-old brother could know anything at all about me. Rumors maybe, or just guessing. Since she did not seem mad, I decided to tell the truth.

"He's right," I said, "I lied. I have an account at Yale, but I haven't linked for months. Hey, you can't live without telling a few lies. At least I don't discriminate. I'll lie to anyone, even myself."

"You're bad." A smile twitched at the corners of her mouth. "So what *do* you do then?"

"I drive around a lot." I waved at the interior of Stennie's car. "Let's see . . . I go to parties. I buy stuff and use it."

"Fidel says you're rich."

"I'm going to have to meet this Fidel. Does money make a difference?"

When she nodded, her hairworks twinkled. Comrade gave me a knowing glance, but I paid no attention. I was trying to figure out how she could make insults sound like compliments when I realized we were flirting. The idea took me by surprise. *Flirting*.

"Do you have any music?" Treemonisha said.

The Alpha asked what groups she liked, and so we listened to some mindless dance hits as we took the circle route around the Laurel Reservoir. Treemonisha told me about how she was sick of her parents' store and rude customers and especially the dumb Green Dream uniform. "Back in Elkhart, Daddy used to make me wear it to school. Can you believe that? He said it was good advertising. When we moved, I told him either the khakis went or I did."

She had a yellow-and-orange dashiki over midnight-blue skintights. "I like your clothes," I said. "You have taste."

"Thanks." She bobbed her head in time to the music. "I can't afford much because I can't get an outside job because I have to work for my parents. It makes me mad, sometimes. I mean, franchise life is fine for Mom and Dad; they're happy being tucked in every night by GD, Inc. But I want more. Thrills, chills—you know, adventure. No one has adventures in the mall."

As we drove, I showed her the log castle, the pyramids, the private train that pulled sleeping cars endlessly around a two-mile track, and the marble bunker where Sullivan, the assassinated president, still lived on in computer memory. Comrade kept busy acting bored.

"Can we go see your mom?" said Treemonisha. "All the kids at school tell me she's awesome."

Suddenly Comrade was interested in the conversation. I was not sure what the kids at school were talking about. Probably they wished they had seen Mom, but I had never asked any of them over—except for Stennie.

"Not a good idea." I shook my head. "She's more flimsy than she looks, you know, and she gets real nervous if strangers just drop by. Or even friends."

"I just want to look. I won't get out of the car."

"Well," said Comrade, "if she doesn't get out of the car, who could she hurt?"

I scowled at him. He knew how paranoid Mom was. She was not going to like Treemonisha anyway, but certainly not if I brought her home without warning. "Let me work on her, okay?" I said to Treemonisha. "One of these days. I promise."

She pouted for about five seconds and then laughed at my expression. When I saw Comrade's smirk, I got angry. He was just sitting there watching us. Looking to cause trouble. Later there would be wisecracks. I had had about enough of him and his attitude.

By that time the Alpha was heading up High Ridge Road toward Stamford. "I'm hungry," I said. "Stop at the 7-Eleven up ahead." I pulled a cash card out and flipped it at him. "Go buy us some doboys."

I waited until he disappeared into the store and then ordered Stennie's car to drive on.

"Hey!" Treemonisha twisted in her seat and looked back at the store. "What are you doing?"

"Ditching him."

"Why? Won't he be mad?"

"He's got my card; he'll call a cab."

"But that's mean."

"So?"

Treemonisha thought about it. "He doesn't say much, does he?" She did not seem to know what to make of me—which I suppose was what I wanted. "At first I thought he was kind of like your teddy bear. Have you seen those big ones that keep little kids out of trouble?"

"He's just a wiseguy."

"Have you had him long?"

"Maybe too long."

I could not think of anything to say after that, so we sat quietly listening to the music. Even though he was gone, Comrade was still aggravating me.

"Were you really hungry?" Treemonisha said finally. "Because I was. Think there's something in the fridge?"

I waited for the Alpha to tell us, but it said nothing. I slid across the seat and opened the refrigerator door. Inside was a sheet of paper. "Dear Mr. Boy," it said. "If this was a bomb, you and Comrade would be dead and the problem would be solved. Let's talk soon. Weldon Montross."

"What's that?"

I felt the warm flush that I always got from good corpse porn, and for a moment I could not speak. "Practical joke," I said, crumpling the paper. "Too bad he doesn't have a sense of humor."

Push-ups. *Ten, eleven.*

"Uh-oh. Look at this," said Comrade.

"I'm busy!" *Twelve, thirteen, fourteen, fifteen . . . sixteen . . . seven . . .* Dizzy, I slumped and rested my cheek against the warm floor. I could feel Mom's pulse beneath the tough skin. It was no good. I would never get muscles this way. There was only one fix for my skinny arms and bony shoulders. Grow up, Mr. Boy.

"*Ya yebou!* You really should scope this," said Comrade. "Very spooky."

I pulled myself onto the bed to see why he was bothering me; he had been pretty tame since I had stranded him at the 7-Eleven. Most of the windows showed the usual: army ants next to old war movies next to feeding time from the Bronx Zoo's reptile house. But Firenet, which provided twenty-four-hour coverage of killer fires from around the world, had been replaced with a picture of a morgue. There were three naked bodies, shrouds pulled back for identification: a fat gray-haired CEO with a purple hole over his left eye, Comrade, and me.

"You look kind of dead," said Comrade.

My tongue felt thick. "Where's it coming from?"

"Viruses all over the system," he said. "Probably Montross."

"You know about him?" The image on the window changed back to a *barrida* fire in Lima.

"He's been in touch." Comrade shrugged. "Made his offer."

Crying women watched as the straw walls of their huts peeled into flame and floated away.

"Oh." I did not know what to say. I wanted to reassure him, but this was serious. Montross was invading my life, and I had no idea how to fight back. "Well, don't talk to him anymore."

"Okay." Comrade grinned. "He's dull as a spoon anyway."

"I bet he's a simulation. What else would a company like Datasafe use? You can't trust real people." I was still thinking about what I would look like dead. "Whatever, he's kind of scary." I shivered, worried and aroused at the same time. "He's slick enough to operate on Playroom. And now he's hijacking windows right here in my own mom." I should probably have told Comrade then about the note in the fridge, but we were still not talking about that day.

"He tapped into Playroom?" Comrade fitted input clips to the spikes on his neck, linked and played back the house files. "*Zayebees.* He was already here then. He piggybacked on with you." Comrade slapped his leg. "I can't understand how he beat my security so easily."

The roombrain flicked the message indicator. "Stennie's calling," it said.

"Pick up," I said.

"Hi, it's that time again." Stennie was alone in his car. "I'm on my way over to give you jacks a thrill." He pushed his triangular snout up to the camera and licked at the lens. "Doing anything?"

"Not really. Sitting around."

"I'll fix that. Five minutes." He faded.

Comrade was staring at nothing.

"Look, Comrade, you did your best," I said. "I'm not mad at you."

"Too plugging easy." He shook his head as if I had missed the point.

"What I don't understand is why Montross is so cranky anyway. It's just a picture of meat."

"Maybe he's not really dead."

"Sure he is," I said. "You can't fake a verification grid."

"No, but you can fake a corpse."

"You know something?"

"If I did I wouldn't tell you," said Comrade. "You have enough problems already. Like how do we explain this to your mom?"

"We don't. Not yet. Let's wait him out. Sooner or later he's got to realize that we're not going to use his picture for anything. I mean, if he's that nervous, I'll even give it back. I don't care anymore. You hear that, Montross, you dumbscut? We're harmless. Get out of our lives!"

"It's more than the picture now," said Comrade. "It's me. I found the way in." He was careful to keep his expression blank.

I did not know what to say to him. No way Montross would be satisfied erasing only the memory of the operation. He would probably reconnect Comrade's regulators to bring him back under control. Turn him to pudding. He would be just another wiseguy, like anyone else could own. I was surprised that Comrade did not ask me to promise not to hand him over. Maybe he just assumed I would stand by him.

We did not hear Stennie coming until he sprang into the room.

"Have fun or die!" He was clutching a plastic gun in his spindly hand, which he aimed at my head.

"Stennie, *no.*"

He fired as I rolled across the bed. The jellybee buzzed by me and squished against one of the windows. It was a purple, and immediately I smelled the tang of artificial grape flavor. The splatter on the wrinkled wall pulsed and split in two, emitting a second burst of grapeness. The two halves oozed in opposite directions, shivered, and divided again.

"Fun extremist!" He shot Comrade with a cherry as he dove for the closet. "Dance!"

I bounced up and down on the bed, timing my move. He fired a green at me that missed. Comrade, meanwhile, gathered himself up as zits of red jellybee squirmed across his window coat. He barreled out of the closet into Stennie, knocking him sideways. I sprang on top of them and wrestled the gun away. Stennie was paralyzed with laughter. I had to giggle too, in part because now I could put off talking to Comrade about Montross.

By the time we untangled ourselves, the jellybees had faded. "Set for twelve generations before they all die out," Stennie said as he settled himself on the bed. "So what's this my car tells me, you've been giving free rides? Is this the cush with the name?"

"None of your business. You never tell me about your cush."

"Okay. Her name is Janet Hoyt."

"Is it?" He caught me off-guard again. Twice in one day, a record. "Comrade, let's see this prize."

Comrade linked to the roombrain and ran a search. "Got her." He called Janet Hoyt's DI file to screen, and her face ballooned across an entire window.

She was a tanned blue-eyed blonde with the kind of off-the-shelf looks that med students slapped onto rabbits in genoplasty courses. Nothing on her face said she was different from any other ornamental moron fresh from the OR—not a dimple or a mole, not even a freckle. "You're ditching me for her?" It took all the imagination of a potato chip to be as pretty as Janet Hoyt. "Stennie, she's generic."

"Now wait a minute," said Stennie. "If we're going to play critic, let's scope your cush, too."

Without asking, Comrade put Tree's DI photo next to Janet's. I realized he was still mad at me because of her; he was only pretending not to care. "She's not my cush," I said, but no one was listening.

Stennie leered at her for a moment. "She's a stiff, isn't she?" he said. "She has that hungry look."

Seeing him standing there in front of the two huge faces on the wall, I felt like I was peeping on a stranger—that I was a stranger, too. I could not imagine how the two of us had come to this: Stennie and Mr. Boy with cushes. We were growing up. A frightening thought. Maybe next Stennie would get himself untwanked and really look like he had on Playroom. Then where would I be?

"Janet wants me to plug her," Stennie said.

"Right, and I'm the queen of Brooklyn."

"I'm old enough, you know." He thumped his tail against the floor.

"You're a dinosaur!"

"Hey, just because I got twanked doesn't mean my dick fell off."

"So do it then."

"I'm going to. I will, okay? But . . . this is no good." Stennie waved impatiently at Comrade. "I can't think with them watching me." He nodded at the windows. "Turn them off already."

"N'ye pizdi!" Comrade wiped the two faces from the windows, cleared all the screens in the room to blood red, yanked the input clips from his neck spikes, and left them dangling from the roombrain's terminal. His expression empty, he walked from the room without asking permission or saying anything at all.

"What's his problem?" Stennie said.

"Who knows?" Comrade had left the door open; I shut it. "Maybe he doesn't like girls."

"Look, I want to ask a favor." I could tell Stennie was nervous; his head kept swaying. "This is kind of embarrassing, but . . . okay, do you think maybe your mom would maybe let me practice on her lovers? I don't want Janet to know I've never done it before, and there's some stuff I've got to figure out."

"I don't know," I said. "Ask her."

But I did know. She would be amused.

People claimed my mom did not have a sense of humor. Lovey was huge, an ocean of a woman. Her umbilical was as big around as my thigh. When she walked, waves of flesh heaved and rolled. She had beautiful skin, flawless and moist. It did not take much to make her sweat. Peeling a banana would do it. Lovey was as oral as a baby; she would put anything into her mouth. And when she did not have a mouthful, she would babble on about whatever came into Mom's head. Dear hardly ever talked, although he could moan and growl and laugh. He touched Lovey whenever he could and shot her long smoldering looks. He was not furry, exactly, but he was covered with fine silver hair. Dear was a little guy, about my size. Although he had one of Upjohn's finest penises, elastic and overloaded with neurons, he was one of the least convincing males I had ever met. I doubt Mom herself believed in him all that much.

Big chatty woman, squirrelly tongue-tied little man. It *was* funny in a bent sort of way to watch the two of them go at each other. Kind of like a tug churning against a supertanker. They did not get the chance that often. It was dangerous; Dear had to worry about getting crushed, and poor Lovey's heart had stopped two or three times. Besides, I think Mom liked building up the pressure. Sometimes, as the days without sex stretched, you could almost feel lust sparkling off them like static electricity.

That was how they were when I brought Stennie up. Their suite took up the entire floor at the hips, Mom's widest part. Lovey was lolling in a tub of warm oil. She liked it flowery and laced with pheromones. Dear was prowling around her with a desperate expression, like he might jam his plug into a wall socket if he did not get taken care of soon. Stennie's timing was perfect.

"Look who's come to visit, Dear," said Lovey. "Peter and Stennie. How nice of you boys to stop by." She let Dear mop her forehead with a towel. "What can we do for you?"

The skin under Stennie's jaw quivered. He glanced at me, then at Dear, and then at the thick red lips that served as the bathroom door. Never even looked at her. He was losing his nerve.

"Oh my, isn't this exciting, Dear? There's something going on." She sank into the bath until her chin touched the water. "It's a secret, isn't it, Peter? Share it with Lovey."

"No secret," I said. "He wants to ask a favor." And then I told her.

She giggled and sat up. "I love it." Honey-colored oil ran from her hair and slopped between her breasts. "Were you thinking of both of us, Stennie? Or just me?"

"Well, I . . ." Stennie's tail switched. "Maybe we just ought to forget it."

"No, no." She waved a hand at him "Come here, Stennie. Come close, my pretty little monster."

He hesitated, then approached the tub. She reached for his right leg and touched him just above the heelknob. "You know, I've always wondered what scales would feel like." Her hand climbed; the oil made his yellow hide glisten. His eyes were the size of eggs.

The bedroom was all mattress. Beneath the transparent skin was a screen implant, so that Mom could project images not only on the walls but on the surface of the bed itself. Under the window was a layer of heavily vascular flesh, which could be stiffened with blood or drained until it was as soft as raw steak. A window dome arched over everything and could show slo-mo or thermographic fx across its span. The air was warm and wet and smelled like a chemical engineer's idea of a rose garden.

I settled by the lips. Dear ghosted along the edges of the room, dragging his umbilical like a chain, never coming quite near enough to touch anyone. I heard him humming as he passed me, a low moaning singsong, as if to block out what was happening. Stennie and Lovey were too busy with each other to care. As Lovey knelt in front of Stennie, Dear gave a mocking laugh. I did not understand how he could be jealous. He was with her, part of it. Lovey and Dear were Mom's remotes, two nodes of her nervous system. Yet his pain was as obvious as her pleasure. At last he squatted and rocked back and forth on his heels. I glanced up at the fx dome; yellow scales slid across oily rolls of flushed skin.

I yawned. I had always found sex kind of dull. Besides, this was all on the record. I could have Comrade replay it for me anytime: Lovey stopped breathing—then came four or five shuddering gasps in a row. I wondered where Comrade had gone. I felt sorry for him. Stennie said something to her about rolling over. "Okay?" Feathery skin sounds. A grunt. The soft wet slap of flesh against flesh. I thought of my mother's brain, up there in the head where no one ever went. I had no idea how much attention she was paying. Was she quivering with Lovey and at the same time calculating insolation rates on her chloroplasts? Investing in soy futures on the Chicago Board of Trade? Fending off Weldon Montross's latest attack? *Plug Montross.* I needed to think about something fun. My collection. I started piling bodies up in my mind. The hangings and the open-casket funerals and the stacks of dead at the camps and all those muddy soldiers. I shivered as I remembered the empty rigid faces. I liked it when their teeth showed. "Oh, oh, *oh!*" My greatest hits dated from the late twentieth century. The dead were everywhere back then, in vids and the news and even on T-shirts. They were not shy. That was what made Comrade's photo worth having; it was hard to find modern stuff that dirty. Dear brushed by me, his erection bobbing in front of him. It was as big around as my wrist. As he passed, I could see Stennie's leg scratch across the mattress skin, which glowed with blood-blue light. Lovey giggled beneath him and her umbilical twitched and suddenly I found myself wondering whether Tree was a virgin.

I came into the mall through the Main Street entrance and hopped the westbound slidewalk headed up Elm Street toward the train station. If I caught the 3:36 to Grand Central, I could eat dinner in Manhattan, far from my problems with Montross and Comrade. Running away had always worked for me before. Let someone else clean up the mess while I was gone.

The slidewalk carried me past a real-estate agency, a flash bar, a jewelry store, and a Baskin-Robbins. I thought about where I wanted to go after New York. San Francisco? Montreal? Maybe I should try Elkhart, Indiana—no one would think to look for me there. Just ahead, between a drugstore and a take-out Russian restaurant, was the wiseguy dealership where Mom had bought Comrade.

I did not want to think about Comrade waiting for me to come home, so I stepped into the drugstore and bought a dose of Carefree for $4.29. Normally I did not bother with drugs. I had been stunted; no over-the-counter flash could compare to that. But the propyl dicarbamates were all right. I fished the cash card out of my pocket and handed it to the stiff behind the counter. He did a double take when he saw the denomination, then carefully inserted the card into the reader to deduct the cost of the Carefree. It had my mom's name on it; he must have expected it would trip some alarm for counterfeit plastic or stolen credit. He stared at me for a moment, as if trying to remember my face so he could describe me to a cop, and then gave the cash card back. The denomination readout said it was still good for $16,381.18.

I picked out a bench in front of a specialty shop called The Happy Hippo, hiked up my shorts, and poked Carefree into the widest part of my thigh. I took a short dreamy swim in the sea of tranquillity and when I came back to myself, my guilt had been washed away. But so had my energy. I sat for a while and scoped the display of glass hippos and plastic hippos and fuzzy stuffed hippos, hippo vids and sheets and candles. Down the bench from me a homeless woman dozed. It was still pretty early in the season for a weather gypsy to have come this far north. She wore red shorts and droopy red socks with plastic sandals and four long-sleeved shirts, all unbuttoned, over a Funny Honey halter top. Her hair needed vacuuming and she smelled old. All grown-ups smelled that way to me; it was something I had never gotten used to. No perfume or deodorant could cover up the leathery stink of adulthood. Kids could smell bad too, but usually from something they got on them. It did not come from a rotting body. I rubbed a finger in the dampness under my arm, slicked it, and sniffed. There was a sweetness to kid sweat. I touched the drying finger to my tongue. You could even taste it. If I gave up getting stunted, stopped being Mr. Boy, I would smell like the woman at the end of the bench. I would start to die. I had never understood how grown-ups could live with that.

The gypsy woke up, stretched, and smiled at me with gummy teeth. "You left Comrade behind?" she said.

I was startled. "What did you say?"

"You know what this is?" She twitched her sleeve, and a penlight appeared in her hand.

My throat tightened. "I know what it looks like."

She gave me a wicked smile, aimed the penlight, and burned a pinhole through the bench a few centimeters from my leg. "Maybe I could interest you in some free laser surgery?"

I could smell scorched plastic. "You're going to needle me here, in the middle of the Elm Street Mall?" I thought she was bluffing. Probably. I hoped.

"If that's the way you want it. Mr. Montross wants to know when you're delivering the wiseguy to us."

"Get away from me."

"Not until you do what needs to be done."

When I saw Happy Lurdane come out of The Happy Hippo, I waved. A desperation move, but then it was easy to be brave with a head full of Carefree.

"Mr. Boy." She veered over to us. "Hi!"

I scooted farther down the bench to make room for her between me and the gypsy. I knew she would stay to chat. Happy Lurdane was one of those chirpy lightweights who seemed to want lots of friends but did not really try to be one. We tolerated her because she did not mind being snubbed and she threw great parties.

"Where have you been?" She settled beside me. "Haven't seen you in ages." The penlight disappeared, and the gypsy fell back into drowsy character.

"Around."

"Want to see what I just bought?"

I nodded. My heart was hammering.

She opened the bag and took out a fist-sized bundle covered with shipping plastic. She unwrapped a statue of a blue hippopotamus. "Be careful." She handed it to me.

"Cute." The hippo had crude flower designs drawn on its body; it was chipped and cracked.

"Ancient Egyptian. That means it's even *before* antique." She pulled a slip from the bag and read. "Twelfth Dynasty, 1991–1786 B.C. Can you believe you can just buy something like that here in the mall? I mean, it must be like a thousand years old or something."

"Try four thousand."

"No wonder it cost so much. He wasn't going to sell it to me, so I had to spend some of next month's allowance." She took it from me and rewrapped it. "It's for the smash party tomorrow. You're coming, aren't you?"

"Maybe."

"Is something wrong?"

I ignored that.

"Hey, where's Comrade? I don't think I've ever seen you two apart before."

I decided to take a chance. "Want to get some doboys?"

"Sure." She glanced at me with delighted astonishment. "Are you sure you're all right?"

I took her arm, maneuvering to keep her between me and the gypsy. If Happy got needled, it would be no great loss to Western Civilization. She babbled on about her party as we stepped onto the westbound slidewalk. I turned to look back. The gypsy waved as she hopped the eastbound.

"Look, Happy," I said, "I'm sorry, but I changed my mind. Later, okay?"

"But . . ."

I did not stop for an argument. I darted off the slidewalk and sprinted through the mall to the station. I went straight to a ticket window, shoved the cash card under the grill, and asked the agent for a one-way to Grand Central. Forty thousand people lived in New Canaan; most of them had heard of me because of my mom. Nine million strangers jammed New York City; it was a good place to disappear. The agent had my ticket in her hand when the reader beeped and spat the card out.

"No!" I slammed my fist on the counter. "Try it again." The cash card was guaranteed by AmEx to be secure. And it had just worked at the drugstore.

She glanced at the card, then slid it back under the grill. "No use." The denomination readout flashed alternating messages: VOIDED and BANK RECALL. "You've got trouble, son."

She was right. As I left the station, I felt the Carefree struggle one last time with my dread—and lose. I did not even have the money to call home. I wandered around for a while, dazed, and then I was standing in front of the flower shop in the Elm Street Mall.

GREEN DREAM
CONTEMPORARY AND CONVENTIONAL PLANTS

I had telelinked with Tree every day since our drive, and every day she had asked me over. But I was not ready to meet her family; I suppose I was still trying to pretend she was not a stiff. I wavered at the door now, breathing the cool scent of damp soil in clay pots. The gypsy could come after me again; I might be putting these people in danger. Using Happy as a shield was one thing, but I liked Tree. A lot. I backed away and peered through a window fringed with sweat and teeming with bizarre plants with flame-colored tongues. Someone wearing khaki moved. I could not tell if it was Tree or not. I thought of what she had said about no one having adventures in the mall.

The front of the showroom was a green cave, darker than I had expected. Baskets dripping with bright flowers hung like stalactites; leathery-leaved understory plants formed stalagmites. As I threaded my way toward the back, I came upon the kid I had seen wearing the Green Dream uniform, a khaki nightmare of pleats and flaps and brass buttons and about six too many pockets. He was misting leaves with a pump bottle filled with blue liquid. I decided he must be the brother.

"Hi," I said. "I'm looking for Treemonisha."

Fidel was shorter than me and darker than his sister. He had a wiry plush of beautiful black hair that I was immediately tempted to touch.

"Are you?" He eyed me as if deciding how hard I would be to beat up, then he smiled. He had crooked teeth. "You don't look like yourself."

"No?"

"What are you, scared? You're whiter than rice, cashman. Don't worry, the stiffs won't hurt you." Laughing, he feinted a punch at my arm; I was not reassured.

"You're Fidel."

"I've seen your DI files," he said. "I asked around, I know about you. So don't be telling my sister any more lies, understand?" He snapped his fingers in my face. "Behave yourself, cashman, and we'll be fine." He still had the boyish excitability I had lost after the first stunting. "She's out back, so first you have to get by the old man."

The rear of the store was brighter; sunlight streamed through the clear krylac roof. There was a counter and behind it a glass-doored refrigerator filled with cut flowers. A side entrance opened to the greenhouse. Mrs. Schlieman, one of Mom's lawyers who had an office in the mall, was deciding what to buy. She was shopping with her wiseguy secretary, who looked like he had just stepped out of a vodka ad.

"Wait." Fidel rested a hand on my shoulder. "I'll tell her you're here."

"But how long will they last?" Mrs. Schlieman sniffed a frilly yellow flower. "I should probably get the duraroses."

"Whatever you want, Mrs. Schlieman. Duraroses are a good product, I sell them by the truckload," said Mr. Joplin with a chuckle. "But these carnations are real flowers, raised here in my greenhouse. So maybe you can't stick them in your dishwasher, but put some where people can touch and smell them and I guarantee you'll get compliments."

"Why, Peter Cage," said Mrs. Schlieman. "Is that you? I haven't seen you since the picnic. How's your mother?" She did not introduce her wiseguy.

"Extreme," I said.

She nodded absently. "That's nice. All right then, Mr. Joplin, give me a dozen of your carnations—and two dozen yellow duraroses."

Mrs. Schlieman chatted politely at me while Tree's father wrapped the order. He was a short, rumpled, balding man who smiled too much. He seemed to like wearing the corporate uniform. Anyone else would have fixed the hair and the wrinkles. Not Mr. Joplin; he was a museum-quality throwback. As he took Mrs. Schlieman's cash card from the wiseguy, he beamed at me over his glasses. Glasses!

When Mrs. Schlieman left, so did the smile. "Peter Cage?" he said. "Is that your name?"

"Mr. Boy is my name, sir."

"You're Tree's new friend." He nodded. "She's told us about you. She's doing chores just now. You know, we have to work for a living here."

Sure, and I knew what he left unsaid: *unlike you, you spoiled little freak.* It was always the same with these stiffs. I walked in the door and already they hated me. At least he was not pretending, like Mrs. Schlieman. I gave him two points for honesty and kept my mouth shut.

"What is it you want here, Peter?"

"Nothing, sir." If he was going to "Peter" me, I was going to "sir" him right back. "I just stopped by to say hello. Treemonisha did invite me, sir, but if you'd rather I left. . . ."

"No, no. Tree warned us you might come."

She and Fidel raced into the room as if they were afraid their father and I would already be at each other's throats. "Oh, hi, Mr. Boy," she said.

Her father snorted at the sound of my name.

"Hi." I grinned at her. It was the easiest thing I had done that day.

She was wearing her uniform. When she saw that I had noticed, she blushed. "Well, you asked for it." She tugged self-consciously at the waist of her fatigues. "You want to come in?"

"Just a minute." Mr. Joplin stepped in front of the door, blocking our escape. "You finished E-class?"

"Yes."

"Checked the flats?"

"I'm almost done."

"After that you'd better pick some dinner and get it started. Your mama called and said she wouldn't be home until six-fifteen."

"Sure."

"And you'll take orders for me on line two?"

She leaned against the counter and sighed. "Do I have a choice?"

He backed away and waved us through. "Sorry, sweetheart. I don't know how we would get along without you." He caught her brother by the shirt. "Not you, Fidel. You're misting, remember?"

A short tunnel ran from their mall storefront to the rehabbed furniture warehouse built over the Amtrak rails. Green Dream had installed a krylac roof and fans and a grolighting system; the Joplins squeezed themselves into the leftover spaces not filled with inventory. The air in the greenhouse was heavy and warm and it smelled like rain. No walls, no privacy other than that provided by the plants.

"Here's where I sleep." Tree sat on her unmade bed. Her space was formed by a cinder-block wall painted yellow and a screen of palms. "Chinese fan, bamboo, lady, date, kentia," she said, naming them for me like they were her pets. "I grow them myself for spending money." Her schoolcomm was on top of her dresser. Several drawers hung open; pink skintights trailed from one. Clothes were scattered like piles of leaves across the floor. "I guess I'm kind of a slob," she said as she stripped off the uniform, wadded it, and then banked it off the dresser into the top drawer. I could see her bare back in the mirror plastic taped to the wall. "Take your things off if you want."

I hesitated.

"Or not. But it's kind of muggy to stay dressed. You'll sweat."

I unvelcroed my shirt. I did not mind at all seeing Tree without clothes. But I did not undress for anyone except the stiffs at the clinic. I stepped out of my pants. Being naked somehow had got connected with being helpless. I had this puckery feeling in my dick, like it was going to curl up and die. I could imagine the gypsy popping out from behind a palm and laughing at me. No, I was not going to think about *that*. Not here.

"Comfortable?" said Tree.

"Sure." My voice was turning to dust in my throat. "Do all Green Dream employees run around the back room in the nude?"

"I doubt it." She smiled as if the thought tickled her. "We're not exactly your average mall drones. Come help me finish the chores."

I was glad to let her lead so that she was not looking at me, although I could still watch her. I was fascinated by the sweep of her buttocks, the curve of her spine. She strolled, flat-footed and at ease, through her private jungle. At first I scuttled along on the balls of my feet, ready to dart behind a plant if anyone came. But after a while I decided to stop being so skittish. I realized I would probably survive being naked.

Tree stopped in front of a workbench covered with potted seedlings in plastic trays and picked up a hose from the floor.

"What's this stuff?" I kept to the opposite side of the bench, using it to cover myself.

"Greens." She lifted a seedling to check the water level in the tray beneath.

"What are greens?"

"It's too boring." She squirted some water in and replaced the seedling.

"Tell me, I'm interested."

"In greens? You liar." She glanced at me and shook her head. "Okay." She pointed as she said the names. "Lettuce, spinach, pak choi, chard, kale, rocket—got that? And a few tomatoes over there. Peppers, too. GD is trying to break into the food business. They think people will grow more of their own if they find out how easy it is."

"Is it?"

"Greens are." She inspected the next tray. "Just add water."

"Yeah, sure."

"It's because they've been photosynthetically enhanced. Bigger leaves arranged better, low respiration rates. They teach us this stuff at GD Family Camp. It's what we do instead of vacation." She squashed something between her thumb and fore-finger. "They mix all these bacteria that make their own fertilizer into the soil—fix nitrogen right out of the air. And then there's this other stuff that sticks to the roots, rhizobacteria and mycorrhizae." She finished the last tray and coiled the hose. "These flats will produce under candlelight in a closet. Bored yet?"

"How do they taste?"

"Pretty bland, most of them. Some stink, like kale and rocket. But we have to eat them for the good of the corporation." She stuck her tongue out. "You want to stay for dinner?" Mrs. Joplin made me call home before she would feed me; she refused to understand that my mom did not care. So I linked, asked Mom to send a car to the back door at 8:30, and faded. No time to discuss the missing sixteen thousand.

Dinner was from the cookbook Tree had been issued at camp: a bowl of cold bean soup, fresh corn bread, and chard and cheese loaf. She let me help her make it, even though I had never cooked before. I was amazed at how simple corn bread was. Six ingredients: flour, cornmeal, baking powder, milk, oil, and ovobinder. Mix and pour into a greased pan. Bake twenty minutes at 220°C and serve! There is nothing magic or even very mysterious about homemade corn bread, except for the way its smell held me spellbound.

Supper was the Joplins' daily meal together. They ate in front of security windows near the tunnel to the store; when a customer came, someone ran out front. According to contract, they had to stay open twenty-four hours a day. Many of the sub-urban malls had gone to all-night operation; the competition from New York City was deadly. Mr. Joplin stood duty most of the time, but since they were a franchise family everybody took turns. Even Mrs. Joplin, who also worked part-time as a fact-finder at the mall's DataStop.

Tree's mother was plump and graying, and she had a smile that was almost bright enough to distract me from her naked body. She seemed harmless, except that she knew how to ask questions. After all, her job was finding out stuff for DataStop cus-tomers. She had this way of locking onto you as you talked; the longer the conversa-tion, the greater her intensity. It was hard to lie to her. Normally that kind of aggressiveness in grown-ups made me jumpy.

No doubt she had run a search on me; I wondered just what she had turned up. Factfinders had to obey the law, so they only accessed public-domain information—unlike Comrade, who would cheerfully operate on whatever I set him to. The Joplins' bank records, for instance. I knew that Mrs. Joplin had made about $11,000 last year at the Infomat in the Elkhart Mall, that the family borrowed $135,000 at 9.78 percent interest to move to their new franchise, and that they lost $213 in their first two months in New Canaan.

I kept my research a secret, of course, and they acted innocent too. I let them pump me about Mom was we ate. I was used to being asked; after all, Mom was famous. Fidel wanted to know how much it had cost her to get twanked, how big she was, what she looked like on the inside and what she ate, if she got cold in the winter. Stuff like that. The others asked more personal questions. Tree wondered if Mom ever got lonely and whether she was going to be the Statue of Liberty for the rest of her life. Mrs. Joplin was interested in Mom's remotes, of all things. Which ones I got along with, which ones I could not stand, whether I thought any of them was really her. Mr. Joplin asked if she liked being what she was. How was I supposed to know?

After dinner, I helped Fidel clear the table. While we were alone in the kitchen, he complained. "You think they eat this shit at GD headquarters?" He scraped his untouched chard loaf into the composter.

"I kind of liked the corn bread."

"If only he'd buy meat once in a while, but he's too cheap. Or doboys. Tree says you bought her doboys."

I told him to skip school sometime and we would go out for lunch; he thought that was a great idea.

When we came back out, Mr. Joplin actually smiled at me. He had been losing his edge all during dinner. Maybe chard agreed with him. He pulled a pipe from his pocket, began stuffing something into it, and asked me if I followed baseball. I told him no. Paintball? No. Basketball? I said I watched dino fights sometimes.

"His pal is the dinosaur that goes to our school," said Fidel.

"He may look like a dinosaur, but he's really a boy," said Mr. Joplin, as if making an important distinction. "The dinosaurs died out millions of years ago."

"Humans aren't allowed in dino fights," I said, just to keep the conversation going. "Only twanked dogs and horses and elephants."

Silence. Mr. Joplin puffed on his pipe and then passed it to his wife. She watched the glow in the bowl through half-lidded eyes as she inhaled. Fidel caught me staring.

"What's the matter? Don't you get twisted?" He took the pipe in his turn.

I was so croggled I did not know what to say. Even the Marleys had switched to THC inhalers. "But smoking is bad for you." It smelled like a dirty sock had caught fire.

"Hemp is ancient. Natural." Mr. Joplin spoke in a clipped voice as if swallowing his words. "Opens the mind to what's real." When he sighed, smoke poured out of his nose. "We grow it ourselves, you know."

I took the pipe when Tree offered it. Even before I brought the stem to my mouth, the world tilted and I watched myself slide into what seemed very much like an hallucination. Here I was sitting around naked, in the mall, with a bunch of stiffs, smoking antique drugs. And I was enjoying myself. Incredible. I inhaled and immediately the flash hit me; it was as if my brain were an enormous bud, blooming inside my head.

"Good stuff." I laughed smoke and then began coughing.

Fidel refilled my glass with ice water. "Have a sip, cashman."

"Customer." Tree pointed at the window.

"Leave!" Mr. Joplin waved impatiently at him. "Go away." The man on the screen knelt and turned over the price tag on a fern. "Damn." He jerked his uniform from the hook by the door, pulled on the khaki pants, and was slithering into the shirt as he disappeared down the tunnel.

"So is Green Dream trying to break into the flash market too?" I handed the pipe to Mrs. Joplin. There was a fleck of ash on her left breast.

"What we do back here is our business," she said. "We work hard so we can live the way we want." Tree was studying her fingerprints. I realized I had said the wrong thing, so I shut up. Obviously, the Joplins were drifting from the lifestyle taught at Green Dream Family Camp.

Fidel announced he was going to school tomorrow, and Mrs. Joplin told him no, he could link to E-class as usual, and Fidel claimed he could not concentrate at home, and Mrs. Joplin said he was trying to get out of his chores. While they were arguing, Tree nudged my leg and shot me a *let's leave* look. I nodded.

"Excuse us." She pushed back her chair. "Mr. Boy has got to go home soon."

Mrs. Joplin pointed for her to stay. "You wait until your father gets back," she said. "Tell me, Mr. Boy, have you lived in New Canaan long?"

"All my life," I said.

"How old did you say you were?"

"Mama, he's twenty-five," said Tree. "I told you."

"And what do you do for a living?"

"*Mama*, you promised."

"Nothing," I said. "I'm lucky, I guess. I don't need to worry about money. If you didn't need to work, would you?"

"Everybody needs work to do," Mrs. Joplin said. "Work makes us real. Unless you have work to do and people who love you, you don't exist."

Talk about twentieth-century humanist goop! At another time in another place, I probably would have snapped, but now the words would not come. My brain had turned into a flower; all I could think were daisy thoughts. The Joplins were such a strange combination of fast-forward and rewind. I could not tell what they wanted from me.

"Seventeen dollars and ninety-nine cents," said Mr. Joplin, returning from the storefront. "What's going on in here?" He glanced at his wife, and some signal that I did not catch passed between them. He circled the table, came up behind me, and laid his heavy hands on my shoulders. I shuddered; I thought for a moment he meant to strangle me.

"I'm not going to hurt you, Peter," he said. "Before you go, I have something to say."

"*Daddy*." Tree squirmed in her chair. Fidel looked uncomfortable too, as if he guessed what was coming.

"Sure." I did not have much choice.

The weight on my shoulders eased but did not entirely go away. "You should feel the ache in this boy, Ladonna."

"I know," said Mrs. Joplin.

"Hard as plastic." Mr. Joplin touched the muscles corded along my neck. "You get too hard, you snap." He set his thumbs at the base of my skull and kneaded with an easy circular motion. "Your body isn't some machine that you've downloaded into. It's alive. Real. You have to learn to listen to it. That's why we smoke. Hear these muscles? They're screaming." He let his hand slide down my shoulders. "Now listen." His fingertips probed along my upper spine. "Hear that? Your muscles stay tense because you don't trust anyone. You always have to be ready to take a hit, and you can't tell where it's coming from. You're rigid and angry and scared. Reality . . . your body is speaking to you."

His voice was as big and warm as his hands. Tree was giving him a look that could boil water, but the way he touched me made too much sense to resist.

"We don't mind helping you ease the strain. That's the way Mrs. Joplin and I are. That's the way we brought the kids up. But first you have to admit you're hurting. And then you have to respect us enough to take what we have to give. I don't feel that in you, Peter. You're not ready to give up your pain. You just want us poor stiffs to admire how hard it's made you. We haven't got time for that kind of shit, okay? You learn to listen to yourself and you'll be welcome around here. We'll even call you Mr. Boy, even though it's a damn stupid name."

No one spoke for a moment.

"Sorry, Tree," he said. "We've embarrassed you again. But we love you, so you're stuck with us." I could feel it in his hands when he chuckled. "I suppose I do get carried away sometimes."

"*Sometimes?*" said Fidel. Tree just smoldered.

"It's late," said Mrs. Joplin. "Let him go now, Jamaal. His mama's sending a car over."

Mr. Joplin stepped back, and I almost fell off my chair from leaning against him. I stood, shakily. "Thanks for dinner."

Tree stalked through the greenhouse to the rear exit, her hairworks glittering against her bare back. I had to trot to keep up with her. There was no car in sight, so we waited at the doorway and I put on my clothes.

"I can't take much more of this." She stared through the little wire-glass window in the door, like a prisoner plotting her escape. "I mean, he's not a psychologist or a great philosopher or whatever the hell he thinks he is. He's just a pompous mall drone."

"He's not that bad." Actually, I understood what her father had said to me; it was scary. "I like your family."

"You don't have to live with them!" She kept watching at the door. "They promised they'd behave with you; I should have known better. This happens every time I bring someone home." She puffed an imaginary pipe, imitating her father. "Think what you're doing to yourself, you poor fool, and say, isn't it just too bad about modern life? Love, love, love—*fuck!*" She turned to me. "I'm sick of it. People are going to think I'm as sappy and thickheaded as my parents."

"I don't."

"You're lucky. You're rich and your mom leaves you alone. You're New Canaan. My folks are Elkhart, Indiana."

"Being New Canaan is nothing to brag about. So what are you?"

"Not a Joplin." She shook her head. "Not much longer, anyway; I'm eighteen in February. I think your car's here." She held out her arms and hugged me good-bye.

"Sorry you had to sit through that. Don't drop me, okay? I like you, Mr. Boy." She did not let go for a while.

Dropping her had never occurred to me; I was not thinking of anything at all except the silkiness of her skin, the warmth of her body. Her breath whispered through my hair and her nipples brushed my ribs and then she kissed me. Just on the cheek, but the damage was done. I was stunted. I was not supposed to feel this way about anyone.

Comrade was waiting in the backseat. We rode home in silence; I had nothing to say to him. He would not understand—none of my friends would. They would warn me that all she wanted was to spend some of my money. Or they would make bad jokes about the nudity or the Joplin' mushy realism. No way I could explain the innocence of the way they touched one another. *The old man did what to you?* Yeah, and if I wanted a hug at home who was I supposed to ask? Comrade? Lovey? The greeter? Was I supposed to climb up to the head and fall asleep against Mom's doorbone, waiting for it to open, like I used to do when I was really a kid?

The greeter was her usual nonstick self when I got home. She was so glad to see me and she wanted to know where I had been and if I had a good time and if I wanted Cook to make me a snack? Around. Yes. No.

She said the bank had called about some problem with one of the cash cards she had given me, a security glitch that they had taken care of and were very sorry about. Did I know about it and did I need a new card and would twenty thousand be enough? Yes. Please. Thanks.

And that was it. I found myself resenting Mom because she did not have to care about losing sixteen or twenty or fifty thousand dollars. And she had reminded me of my problems when all I wanted to think of was Tree. She was no help to me, never had been. I had things so twisted around that I almost told her about Montross myself, just to get a reaction. Here some guy had tapped our files and threatened my life, and she asked if I wanted a snack. Why keep me around if she was going to pay so little attention? I wanted to shock her, to make her take me seriously.

But I did not know how.

The roombrain woke me. "Stennie's calling."

"Mmm."

"Talk to me, Mr. Party Boy." A window opened; he was in his car. "You dead or alive?"

"Asleep." I rolled over. "Time is it?"

"Ten-thirty and I'm bored. Want me to come get you now, or should I meet you there?"

"Wha . . . ?"

"Happy's. Don't tell me you forgot. They're doing a *piano*."

"Who cares?" I crawled out of bed and slouched into the bathroom..

"She says she's asking Tree Joplin," Stennie called after me.

"Asking her what?" I came out.

"To the party."

"Is she going?"

"She's your cush." He gave me a toothy smile. "Call back when you're ready. Later." He faded.

"She left a message," said the roombrain. "Half hour ago.".

"Tree? You got me up for Stennie and not for her?"

"He's on the list, she's not. Happy called, too."

"Comrade should've told you. Where is he?" Now I was grouchy. "She's on the list, okay? Give me playback."

Tree seemed pleased with herself. "Hi, this is me. I got myself invited to a smash party this afternoon. You want to go?" She faded.

"That's all? Call her!"

"Both her numbers are busy; I'll set redial. I found Comrade; he's on another line. You want Happy's message?"

"No. Yes."

"You promised, Mr. Boy." Happy giggled. "Look, you really, really don't want to miss this. Stennie's coming, and he said I should ask Joplin if I wanted you here. So you've got no excuse."

Someone tugged at her. "Stop that! Sorry, I'm being molested by a thick . . ." She batted at her assailant. "Mr. Boy, did I tell you that this Japanese reporter is coming to shoot a vid? What?" She turned off camera. "Sure, just like on the nature channel. Wildlife of America. We're all going to be famous. In Japan! This is history, Mr. Boy. And you're . . ."

Her face froze as the redial program finally linked to the Green Dream. The roombrain brought Tree up in a new window. "Oh, hi," she said. "You rich boys sleep late."

"What's this about Happy's?"

"She invited me." Tree was recharging her hairworks with a red brush. "I said yes. Something wrong?"

Comrade slipped into the room; I shushed him. "You sure you want to go to a smash party? Sometimes they get a little crazy."

She aimed the brush at me. "You've been to smash parties before. You survived."

"Sure, but . . ."

"Well, I haven't. All I know is that everybody at school is talking about this one, and I want to see what's it's about."

"You tell your parents you're going?"

"Are you kidding? They'd just say it was too dangerous. What's the matter, Mr. Boy, are you scared? Come on, it'll be extreme."

"She's right. You *should* go," said Comrade.

"Is that Comrade?" Tree said. "You tell him, Comrade!"

I glared at him. "Okay, okay, I guess I'm outnumbered. Stennie said he'd drive. You want us to pick you up?"

She did.

I flew at Comrade as soon as Tree faded. "Don't you ever do that again!" I shoved him, and he bumped up against the wall. "I ought to throw you to Montross."

"You know, I just finished chatting with him." Comrade stayed calm and made no move to defend himself. "He wants to meet—the three of us, face to face. He suggested Happy's."

"He suggested . . . I told you not to talk to him."

"I know." He shrugged. "Anyway, I think we should do it."

"Who gave you permission to think?"

"You did. What if we give him the picture back and open our files and then I grovel, say I'm sorry, it'll never happen again, *blah, blah, blah*. Maybe we can even buy him off. What have we got to lose?"

"You can't bribe software. And what if he decides to snatch us?" I told Comrade about the gypsy with the penlight. "You want Tree mixed up in this?"

All the expression drained from his face. He did not say anything at first, but I had watched his subroutines long enough to know that when he looked this blank, he was shaken. "So we take a risk, maybe we can get it over with," he said. "He's not interested in Tree, and I won't let anything happen to you. Why do you think your mom bought me?"

Happy Lurdane lived on the former estate of Philip Johnson, a notorious twentieth-century architect. In his will Johnson had arranged to turn his compound into the Philip Johnson Memorial Museum, but after he died his work went out of fashion. The glass skyscrapers in the cities did not age well; they started to fall apart or were torn down because they wasted energy. Nobody visited the museum, and it went bankrupt. The Lurdanes had bought the property and made some changes.

Johnson had designed all the odd little buildings on the estate himself. The main house was a shoebox of glass with no inside walls; near it stood a windowless brick guest house. On a pond below was a dock that looked like a Greek temple. Past the circular swimming pool near the houses were two galleries that had once held Johnson's art collection, long since sold off. In Johnson's day, the scattered buildings had been connected only by paths, which made the compound impossible in the frosty Connecticut winters. The Lurdanes had enclosed the paths in clear tubes and commuted in a golf cart.

Stennie told his Alpha not to wait, since the lot was already full and cars were parked well down the driveway. Five of us squeezed out of the car: me, Tree, Comrade, Stennie, and Janet Hoyt. Janet wore a Yankees jersey over pin-striped shorts, Tree was a little overdressed in her silver jaunts, I had on baggies padded to make me seem bigger, and Comrade wore his usual window coat. Stennie lugged a box with his swag for the party.

Freddy the Teddy let us in. "Stennie and Mr. Boy!" He reared back on his hindquarters and roared. "Glad I'm not going to be the only beastie here. Hi, Janet. Hi, I'm Freddy," he said to Tree. His pink tongue lolled. "Come in, this way. Fun starts right here. Some kids are swimming, and there's sex in the guest house. Everybody else is with Happy having lunch in the sculpture gallery."

The interior of the Glass House was bright and hard. Dark wood-block floor, some unfriendly furniture, huge panes of glass framed in black-painted steel. The few kids in the kitchen were passing an inhaler around and watching a microwave fill up with popcorn.

"I'm hot." Janet stuck the inhaler into her face and pressed. "Anybody want to swim? Tree?"

"Okay." Tree breathed in a polite dose and breathed out a giggle. "You?" she asked me.

"I don't think so." I was too nervous: I kept expecting someone to jump out and throw a net over me. "I'll watch."

"I'd swim with you," said Stennie, "but I promised Happy I'd bring her these party favors as soon as I arrived." He nudged the box with his foot. "Can you wait a few minutes?"

"Comrade and I will take them over." I grabbed the box and headed for the door, glad for the excuse to leave Tree behind while I went to find Montross. "Meet you at the pool."

The golf cart was gone, so we walked through the tube toward the sculpture gallery. "You have the picture?" I said.

Comrade patted the pocket of his window coat.

The tube was not air-conditioned, and the afternoon sun pounded us through the optical plastic. There was no sound inside; even our footsteps were swallowed by the astroturf. The box got heavier. We passed the entrance to the old painting gallery, which looked like a bomb shelter. Finally I had to break the silence. "I feel strange, being here," I said. "Not just because of the thing with Montross. I really think I lost myself last time I got stunted. Not sure who I am anymore, but I don't think I belong with these kids."

"People change, *tovarisch*," said Comrade. "Even you."

"Have I changed?"

He smiled. "Now that you've got a cush, your own mother wouldn't recognize you."

"You know what your problem is?" I grinned and bumped up against him on purpose. "You're jealous of Tree."

"Shouldn't I be?"

"Oh, I don't know. I can't tell if Tree likes who I was or who I might be. She's changing, too. She's so hot to break away from her parents, become part of this town. Except that what she's headed for probably isn't worth the trip. I feel like I should protect her, but that means guarding her from people like me, except I don't think I'm Mom's Mr. Boy anymore. Does that make sense?"

"Sure." He gazed straight ahead, but all the heads on his window coat were scoping me. "Maybe when you're finished changing, you won't need me."

The thought had occurred to me. For years he had been the only one I could talk to, but as we closed on the gallery, I did not know what to say. I shook my head. "I just feel strange."

And then we arrived. The sculpture gallery was designed for show-offs: short flights of steps and a series of stagy balconies descended around the white-brick exterior walls to the central exhibition area. The space was open so you could chat with your little knot of friends and, at the same time, spy on everyone else. About thirty kids were eating pizza and Crispix off paper plates. At the bottom of the stairs, as advertised, was a black upright piano. Piled beside it was the rest of the swag. A Boston rocker, a case of green Coke bottles, a Virgin Mary in half a blue bathtub, a huge conch shell, china and crystal and assorted smaller treasures, including a four-thousand-year-old ceramic hippo. There were real animals too, in cages near the gun rack: a turkey, some stray dogs and cats, turtles, frogs, assorted rodents.

I was threading my way across the first balcony when I was stopped by the Japanese reporter, who was wearing microcam eyes.

"Excuse me, please," he said, "I am Matsuo Shikibu, and I will be recording this event today for Nippon Hoso Kyokai. Public telelink of Japan." He smiled and bowed. When his head came up, the red light between his lenses was on. "You are . . . ?"

"Raskolnikov," said Comrade, edging between me and the camera. "Rodeo Raskolnikov." He took Shikibu's hand and pumped it. "And my associate here, Mr. Peter Pan." He turned as if to introduce me, but we had long since choreographed this dodge. As I sidestepped past, he kept shielding me from the reporter with his body. "We're friends of the bride," Comrade said, "and we're really excited to be making new friends in your country. Banzai, Nippon!"

I slipped by them and scooted downstairs. Happy was basking by the piano; she spotted me as I reached the middle landing.

"Mr. Boy!" It was not so much a greeting as an announcement. She was wearing a body mike, and her voice boomed over the sound system. "You made it."

The stream of conversation rippled momentarily, a few heads turned, and then the party flowed on. Shikibu rushed to the edge of the upper balcony and caught me with a long shot.

I set the box on the Steinway. "Stennie brought this."

She opened it eagerly. "Look, everyone!" She held up a stack of square cardboard albums, about thirty centimeters on a side. There were pictures of musicians on the front, words on the back. "What are they?" she asked me.

"Phonograph records," said the kid next to Happy. "It's how they used to play music before digital."

"Erroll Garner, *Soliloquy*," she read aloud. "What's this? D-j-a-n-g-o Reinhardt and the American Jazz Giants. Sounds scary." She giggled as she pawed quickly through the other albums. Handy, Ellington, Hawkins, Parker, three Armstrongs. One was *Piano Rags by Scott Joplin*. Stennie's bent idea of a joke? Maybe the lizard was smarter than he looked. Happy pulled a black plastic record out of one sleeve and scratched a fingernail across little ridges. "Oh, a nonslip surface."

The party had a limited attention span. When she realized she had lost her audience, she shut off the mike and put the box with the rest of the swag. "We have to start at four, no matter what. There's so much stuff." The kid who knew about records wormed into our conversation; Happy put her hand on his shoulder. "Mr. Boy, do you know my friend Weldon?" she said. "He's new."

Montross grinned. "We met on Playroom."

"Where *is* Stennie, anyway?" said Happy.

"Swimming," I said. Montross appeared to be in his late teens. Bigger than me—everyone was bigger than me. He wore green shorts and a window shirt of surfers at Waimea. He looked like everybody; there was nothing about him to remember. I considered bashing the smirk off his face, but it was a bad idea. If he was software, he could not feel anything and I would probably break my hand on his temporary chassis. "Got to go. I promised Stennie I'd meet him back at the pool. Hey, Weldon, want to tag along?"

"You come right back," said Happy. "We're starting at four. Tell everyone."

We avoided the tube and cut across the lawn for privacy. Comrade handed Montross the envelope. He slid the photograph out, and I had one last glimpse. This time the dead man left me cold. In fact, I was embarrassed. Although he kept a straight face, I knew what Montross was thinking about me. Maybe he was right. I wished he would put the picture away. He was not one of us; he could not understand. I wondered if Tree had come far enough yet to appreciate corpse porn.

"It's the only copy," Comrade said.

"All right." Finally Montross crammed it into the pocket of his shorts.

"You tapped our files; you know it's true."

"So?"

"So enough!" I said. "You have what you wanted."

"I've already explained." Montross was being patient. "Getting this back doesn't close the case. I have to take preventive measures."

"Meaning you turn Comrade into a carrot."

"Meaning I repair him. You're the one who took him to the chop shop. Deregulated wiseguys are dangerous. Maybe not to you, but certainly to property and probably to other people. It's a straightforward procedure. He'll be fully functional afterward."

"Plug your procedure, jack. We're leaving."

Both wiseguys stopped. "I thought you agreed," said Montross.

"Let's go, Comrade." I grabbed his arm, but he shook me off.

"Where?" he said.

"Anywhere! Just so I never have to listen to this again." I pulled again, angry at Comrade for stalling. Your wiseguy is supposed to anticipate your needs, do whatever you want.

"But we haven't even tried to . . ."

"Forget it then. I give up." I pushed him toward Montross. "You want to chat, fine, go right ahead. Let him rip the top of your head off while you're at it, but I'm not sticking around to watch."

I checked the pool, but Tree, Stennie, and Janet had already gone. I went through the Glass House and caught up with them in the tube to the sculpture gallery.

"Can I talk to you?" I put my arm around Tree's waist, just like I had seen grownups do. "In private." I could tell she was annoyed to be separated from Janet. "We'll catch up." I waved Stennie on. "See you over there."

She waited until they were gone. "What?" Her hair, slick from swimming, left dark spots where it brushed her silver jaunts.

"I want to leave. We'll call my mom's car." She did not look happy. "I'll take you anywhere you want to go."

"But we just got here. Give it a chance."

"I've been to too many of these things."

"Then you shouldn't have come."

Silence. I wanted to tell her about Montross—everything—but not here. Anyone could come along and the tube was so hot. I was desperate to get her away, so I lied. "Believe me, you're not going to like this. I know." I tugged at her waist. "Sometimes even I think smash parties are too much."

"We've had this discussion before," she said. "Obviously you weren't listening. I don't need you to decide for me whether I'm going to like something, Mr. Boy. I have two parents too many; I don't need another." She stepped away from me. "Hey, I'm sorry if you're having a bad time. But do you really need to spoil it for me?" She turned and strode down the tube toward the gallery, her beautiful hair slapping against her back. I watched her go.

"But I'm in trouble," I muttered to the empty tube—and then was disgusted with myself because I did not have the guts to say it to Tree. I was too scared she would not care. I stood there, sweating. For a moment the stink of doubt filled my nostrils. Then I followed her in. I could not abandon her to the extremists.

The gallery was jammed now; maybe a hundred kids swarmed across the balconies and down the stairs. Some perched along the edges, their feet scuffing the white brick. Happy had turned up the volume.

". . . according to *Guinness*, was set at the University of Oklahoma in Norman, Oklahoma, in 2012. Three minutes and fourteen seconds." The crowd rumbled in disbelief. "The challenge states each piece must be small enough to pass through a hole thirty centimeters in diameter."

I worked my way to an opening beside a rubber tree. Happy posed on the keyboard of the piano. Freddy the Teddy and the gorilla brothers, Mike and Bubba, lined up beside her. "No mechanical tools are allowed." She gestured at an armory of axes, sledgehammers, spikes, and crowbars laid out on the floor. A paper plate spun across the room. I could not see Tree.

"This piano is over two hundred years old," Happy continued, "which means the white keys are ivory." She plunked a note. "Dead elephants!" Everybody heaved a sympathetic *awww*. "The blacks are ebony, hacked from the rain forest." Another note, less reaction. "It deserves to die."

Applause. Comrade and I spotted each other at almost the same time. He and Montross stood toward the rear of the lower balcony. He gestured for me to come down; I ignored him.

"Do you boys have anything to say?" Happy said.

"Yeah." Freddy hefted an ax. "Let's make landfill."

I ducked around the rubber tree and heard the *crack* of splitting wood, the iron groan of a piano frame yielding its last music. The spectators hooted approval. As I bumped past kids, searching for Tree, the instrument's death cry made me think of taking a hammer to Montross. If fights broke out, no one would care if Comrade and I dragged him outside. I wanted to beat him until he shuddered and came unstrung and his works glinted in the thudding August light. It would make me feel extreme again. *Crunch!* Kids shrieked, "Go, go, go!" The party was lifting off and taking me with it.

"You are Mr. Boy Cage." Abruptly Shikibu's microcam eyes were in my face. "We know your famous mother." He had to shout to be heard. "I have a question."

"Go away."

"*Thirty seconds.*" A girl's voice boomed over the speakers.

"U.S. and Japan are very different, yes?" He pressed closer. "We honor ancestors, our past. You seem to hate so much." He gestured at the gallery. "Why?"

"Maybe we're spoiled." I barged past him.

I saw Freddy swing a sledgehammer at the exposed frame. *Clang!* A chunk of twisted iron clattered across the brick floor, trailing broken strings. Happy scooped the mess up and shoved it through a thirty-centimeter hole drilled in an upright sheet of particle board.

The timekeeper called out again. "*One minute.*" I had come far enough around the curve of the stairs to see her.

"Treemonisha!"

She glanced up, her face alight with pleasure, and waved. I was frightened for her. She was climbing into the same box I needed to break out of. So I rushed down the stairs to rescue her—little boy knight in shining armor—and ran right into Comrade's arms.

"I've decided," he said. "*Mnye vcyaw ostoyeblo.*"

"Great." I had to get to Tree. "Later, okay?" When I tried to go by, he picked me up. I started thrashing. It was the first fight of the afternoon and I lost. He carried me over to Montross. The gallery was in an uproar.

"All set," said Montross. "I'll have to borrow him for a while. I'll drop him off tonight at your mom. Then we're done."

"Done?" I kept trying to get free, but Comrade crushed me against him.

"It's what you want." His body was so hard. "And what your mom wants."

"Mom? She doesn't even know."

"She knows everything," Comrade said. "She watches you constantly. What else does she have to do all day?" He let me go. "Remember you said I was sloppy getting the picture? I wasn't; it was a clean operation. Only someone tipped Datasafe off."

"But she promised. Besides, that makes no . . ."

"*Two minutes,*" Tree called.

". . . but he threatened me," I said. "He was going to blow me up. Needle me in the mall."

"We wouldn't do that." Montross spread his hands innocently. "It's against the law."

"Yeah? Well, then, drop dead, jack." I poked a finger at him. "Deal's off."

"No, it's not," said Comrade. "It's too late. This isn't about the picture anymore, Mr. Boy; it's about you. You weren't supposed to change, but you did. Maybe they botched the last stunting, maybe it's Treemonisha. Whatever, you've outgrown me, the way I am now. So I have to change too, or else I'll keep getting in your way."

He always had everything under control; it made me crazy. He was too good at running my life. "You should have told me Mom turned you in." *Crash!* I felt like the crowd was inside my head, screaming.

"You could've figured it out, if you wanted to. Besides, if I had said anything, your mom wouldn't have bothered to be subtle. She would've squashed me. She still might, even though I'm being fixed. Only by then I won't care. *Rosproyebi tvayou mat!*"

I heard Tree finishing the count. ". . . *twelve, thirteen, fourteen!*" No record today. Some kids began to boo, others laughed. "Time's up, you losers!"

I glared at the two wiseguys. Montross was busy emulating sincerity. Comrade found a way to grin for me, the same smirk he always wore when he tortured the greeter. "It's easier this way."

Easier. My life was too plugging easy. I had never done anything important by myself. Not even grow up. I wanted to smash something.

"Okay," I said. "You asked for it."

Comrade turned to Montross and they shook hands. I thought next they might clap one another on the shoulder and whistle as they strolled off into the sunset together. I felt like puking. "Have fun," said Comrade. "*Da svedanya.*"

"Sure." Betraying Comrade, my best friend, brought me both pain and pleasure at once—but not enough to satisfy the shrieking wildness within me. The party was just starting.

Happy stood beaming beside the ruins of the Steinway. Although nothing of what was left was more than half a meter tall, Freddy, Mike, and Bubba had given up now that the challenge was lost. Kids were already surging down the stairs to claim their share of the swag. I went along with them.

"Don't worry," announced Happy. "Plenty for everyone. Come take what you like. Remember, guns and animals outside, if you want to hunt. The safeties won't release unless you go through the door. Watch out for one another, people, we don't want anyone shot."

A bunch of kids were wrestling over the turkey cage; one of them staggered backward and knocked into me. "Gobble, gobble," she said. I shoved her back.

"Mr. Boy! Over here." Tree, Stennie, and Janet were waiting on the far side of the gallery. As I crossed to them, Happy gave the sign and Stone Kinkaid hurled the four-thousand-year-old ceramic hippo against the wall. It shattered. Everybody cheered. In the upper balconies, they were playing catch with a frog.

"You see who kept time?" said Janet.

"Didn't need to see," I said. "I could hear. They probably heard in Elkhart. So you like it, Tree?"

"It's about what I expected: dumb but fun. I don't think they. . . ." The frog sailed from the top balcony and splatted at our feet. Its legs twitched and guts spilled from its open mouth. I watched Tree's smile turn brittle. She seemed slightly embarrassed, as if she had just been told the price of something she could not afford.

"This is going to be a war zone soon," Stennie said.

"Yeah, let's fade." Janet towed Stennie to the stairs, swerving around the three boys lugging Our Lady of the Bathtub out to the firing range.

"Wait." I blocked Tree. "You're here, so you have to destroy something. Get with the program."

"I have to?" She seemed doubtful. "Oh, all right—but no animals."

A hail of antique Coke bottles crashed around Happy as she directed traffic at the dwindling swag heap. "Hey, people, please be very careful where you throw things." Her amplified voice blasted us as we approached. The first floor was a graveyard of broken glass and piano bones and bloody feathers. Most of the good stuff was already gone.

"Any records left?" I said.

Happy wobbled closer to me. "What?" She seemed punchy, as if stunned by the success of her own party.

"The box I gave you. From Stennie." She pointed; I spotted it under some cages and grabbed it. Tree and the others were on the stairs. Outside I could hear the crackle of small-arms fire. I caught up.

"Sir! Mr. Dinosaur, please." The press still lurked on the upper balcony. "Matsuo Shikibu, Japanese telelink NHK. Could I speak with you for a moment?"

"Excuse me, but this jack and I have some unfinished business." I handed Stennie the records and cut in front. He swayed and lashed his tail upward to counterbalance their weight.

"Remember me?" I bowed to Shikibu.

"My apologies if I offended . . ."

"Hey, Matsuo—can I call you Matsuo? This is your first smash party, right? Please, eyes on me. I want to explain why I was rude before. Help you understand the local customs. You see, we're kind of self-conscious here in the U.S. We don't like it when someone just watches while we play. You either join in or you're not one of us."

My little speech drew a crowd. "What's he talking about?" said Janet. She was shushed.

"So if you drop by our party and don't have fun, people resent you," I told him. "No one came here today to put on a show. This is who we are. What we believe in."

"Yeah!" Stennie was cheerleading for the extreme Mr. Boy of old. "Tell him." Too bad he did not realize it was his final appearance. What was Mr. Boy without his Comrade? "Make him feel some pain."

I snatched an album from the top of the stack, slipped the record out, and held it close to Shikibu's microcam eyes. "What does this say?"

He craned his neck to read the label. "John Coltrane, *Giant Steps*."

"Very good." I grasped the record with both hands and raised it over my head for all to see. "We're not picky, Matsuo. We welcome everyone. Therefore today it is my honor to initiate you—and the home audience back on NHK. If you're still watching, you're part of this too." I broke the record over his head.

He yelped and staggered backward and almost tripped over a dead cat. Stone Kinkaid caught him and propped him up. "Congratulations," said Stennie, as he waved his claws at Japan. "You're all extremists now."

Shikibu gaped at me, his microcam eyes askew. A couple of kids clapped.

"There's someone else here who has not yet joined us." I turned on Tree. "Another spectator." Her smile faded.

"You leave her alone," said Janet. "What are you, crazy?"

"I'm not going to touch her." I held up empty hands. "No, I just want her to ruin something. That's why you came, isn't it, Tree? To get a taste?" I rifled through the box until I found what I wanted. "How about this?" I thrust it at her.

"Oh yeah," said Stennie, "I meant to tell you. . . ."

She took the record and scoped it briefly. When she glanced up at me, I almost lost my nerve.

"Matsuo Shikibu, meet Treemonisha Joplin." I clasped my hands behind my back so no one could see me tremble. "The great-great-great-granddaughter of the famous American composer, Scott Joplin. Yes, Japan, we're all celebrities here in New Canaan. Now please observe." I read the record for him. "*Piano Rags by Scott Joplin*, Volume III. Who knows, this might be the last copy. We can only hope. So, what are you waiting for, Tree? You don't want to be a Joplin anymore? Just wait until your folks get a peek at this. We'll even send GD a copy. Go ahead, enjoy."

"Smash it!" The kids around us took up the chant. "Smash it!" Shikibu adjusted his lenses.

"You think I won't?" Tree pulled out the disk and threw the sleeve off the balcony. "This is a piece of junk, Mr. Boy." She laughed and then shattered the album against the wall. She held on to a shard. "It doesn't mean anything to me."

I heard Janet whisper. "What's going on?"

"I think they're having an argument."

"You want me to be your little dream cush." Tree tucked the piece of broken plastic into the pocket of my baggies. "The stiff from nowhere who knows nobody and does nothing without Mr. Boy. So you try to scare me off. You tell me you're so rich, you can afford to hate yourself. Stay home, you say, it's too dangerous, we're all crazy. Well, if you're so sure this is poison, how come you've still got your wiseguy and your cash cards? Are you going to move out of your mom, leave town, stop getting stunted? You're not giving it up, Mr. Boy, so why should I?"

Shikibu turned his camera eyes on me. No one spoke.

"You're right," I said. "She's right." I could not save anyone until I saved myself. I felt the wildness lifting me to it. I leapt onto the balcony wall and shouted for everyone to hear. "Shut up and listen, everybody! You're all invited to my place, okay?"

There was one last thing to smash.

"Stop this, Peter." The greeter no longer thought I was cute. "What're you doing?" She trembled as if the kids spilling into her were an infection.

"I thought you'd like to meet my friends," I said. A few had stayed behind with Happy, who had decided to sulk after I hijacked her guests. The rest had followed me home in a caravan so I could warn off the sentry robots. It was already a hall-of-fame bash. "Treemonisha Joplin, this is my mom. Sort of."

"Hi," Tree held out her hand uncertainly.

The greeter was no longer the human doormat. "Get them out of me." She was too jumpy to be polite. "Right now!"

Someone turned up a boombox. Skitter music filled the room like a siren. Tree said something I could not hear. When I put a hand to my ear, she leaned close and said, "Don't be so mean, Mr. Boy. I think she's really frightened."

I grinned and nodded. "I'll tell Cook to make us some snacks."

Bubba and Mike carried boxes filled with the last of the swag and set them on the coffee table. Kids fanned out, running their hands along her wrinkled blood-hot walls, bouncing on the furniture. Stennie waved at me as he led a bunch upstairs for a tour. A leftover cat had gotten loose and was hissing and scratching underfoot. Some twisted kids had already stripped and were rolling in the floor hair, getting ready to have sex.

"Get dressed, you." The greeter kicked at them as she coiled her umbilical to keep it from being trampled. She retreated to her wall plug. "You're *hurting* me." Although her voice rose to a scream, only half a dozen kids heard her. She went limp and sagged to the floor.

The whole room seemed to throb, as if to some great heartbeat, and the lights went out. It took a while for someone to kill the sound on the boombox. "What's wrong?" Voices called out. "Mr. Boy? Lights."

Both doorbones swung open, and I saw a bughead silhouetted against the twilit sky. Shikibu in his microcams. "Party's over," Mom said over her speaker system. There was nervous laughter. "Leave before I call the cops. Peter, go to your room right now. I want to speak to you."

As the stampede began, I found Tree's hand. "Wait for me?" I pulled her close. "I'll only be a minute."

"What are you going to do?" She sounded frightened. It felt good to be taken so seriously.

"I'm moving out, chucking all this. I'm going to be a working stiff." I chuckled. "Think your dad would give me a job?"

"Look out, dumbscut! Hey, *hey*. Don't push!"

Tree dragged me out of the way. "You're crazy."

"I know. That's why I have to get out of Mom's."

"Listen," she said, "you've never been poor, you have no idea. . . . Only a rich kid would think it's easy being a stiff. Just go up, apologize, tell her it won't happen again. Then change things later on, if you want. Believe me, life will be a lot simpler if you hang on to the money."

"I can't. Will you wait?"

"You want me to tell you it's okay to be stupid, is that it? Well, I've *been* poor, Mr. Boy, and still am, and I don't recommend it. So don't expect me to stand around and clap while you throw away something I've always wanted." She spun away from me, and I lost her in the darkness. I wanted to catch up with her, but I knew I had to do Mom now or I would lose my nerve.

As I was fumbling my way upstairs, I heard stragglers coming down. "On your right," I called. Bodies nudged by me.

"Mr. Boy, is that you?" I recognized Stennie's voice.

"He's gone," I said.

Seven flights up, the lights were on. Nanny waited on the landing outside my rooms, her umbilical stretched nearly to its limit. She was the only remote that was physically able to get to my floor, and this was as close as she could come.

It had been a while since I had seen her; Mom did not use her much anymore and I rarely visited, even though the nursery was only one flight down. But this was the remote who used to pick me up when I cried and who had changed my diapers and who taught me how to turn on my roombrain. She had skin so pale you could almost see veins and long black hair piled high on her head. I never thought of her as having a body because she always wore dark turtlenecks and long woolen skirts and silky panty hose. Nanny was a smile and warm hands and the smell of fresh pillowcases. Once upon a time, I thought her the most beautiful creature in the world. Back then I would have done anything she said.

She was not smiling now. "I don't know how you expect me to trust you anymore, Peter." Nanny had never been a very good scold. "Those brats were out of control. I can't let you put me in danger this way."

"If you wanted someone to trust, maybe you shouldn't have had me stunted. You got exactly what you ordered, the never-ending kid. Well, kids don't have to be responsible."

"What do you mean, what I ordered? It's what you wanted, too."

"Is it? Did you ever ask? I was only ten, the first time, too young to know better. For a long time I did it to please you. Getting stunted was the only thing I did that seemed important to you. But *you* never explained. You never sat me down and said, 'This is the life you'll have and this is what you'll miss and this is how you'll feel about it.'"

"You want to grow up, is that it?" She was trying to threaten me. "You want to work and worry and get old and die someday?" She had no idea what we were talking about.

"I can't live this way anymore, Nanny."

At first she acted stunned, as if I had spoken in Albanian. Then her expression hardened when she realized she had lost her hold on me. She was ugly when she was angry. "They put you up to this." Her gaze narrowed in accusation. "That little black cush you've been seeing. Those realists!"

I had always managed to hide my anger from Mom. Right up until then. "How do you know about her?" I had never told her about Tree.

"Peter, they live in a mall!"

Comrade was right. "You've been spying on me." When she did not deny it, I went berserk. "You liar." I slammed my fist into her belly. "You said you wouldn't watch." She staggered and fell onto her umbilical, crimping it. As she twitched on the floor, I pounced. "You promised." I slapped her face. "Promised." I hit her again. Her hair had come undone and her eyes rolled back in their sockets and her face was slack. She made no effort to protect herself. Mom was retreating from this remote too, but I was not going to let her get away.

"Mom!" I rolled off Nanny. "I'm coming up, Mom! You hear? Get ready." I was crying; it had been a long time since I had cried. Not something Mr. Boy did.

I scrambled up to the long landing at the shoulders. At one end another circular stairway wound up into the torch; in the middle, four steps led into the neck. It was the only doorbone I had never seen open; I had no idea how to get through.

"Mom, I'm here." I pounded. "Mom! You hear me?"

Silence.

"Let me in, Mom." I smashed myself against the doorbone. Pain branched through my shoulder like lightning, but it felt great because Mom shuddered from the impact. I backed up and, in a frenzy, hurled myself again. Something warm dripped on my cheek. She was bleeding from the hinges. I aimed a vicious kick at the doorbone, and it banged open. I went through.

For years I had imagined that if only I could get into the head I could meet my real mother. Touch her. I had always wondered what she looked like; she got reshaped just after I was born. When I was little I used to think of her as a magic princess glowing with fairy light. Later I pictured her as one or another of my friends' moms, only better dressed. After I had started getting twanked, I was afraid she might be just a brain floating in nutrient solution, like in some pricey memory bank. All wrong.

The interior of the head was dark and absolutely freezing. There was no sound except for the hum of refrigeration units. "Mom?" My voice echoed in the empty space. I stumbled and caught myself against a smooth wall. Not skin, like everywhere else in Mom—metal. The tears froze on my face.

"There's nothing for you here," she said. "This is a clean room. You're compromising it. You must leave immediately."

Sterile environment, metal walls, the bitter cold that super-conductors needed. I did not need to see. No one lived here. It had never occurred to me that there was no Mom to touch. She had downloaded, become an electron ghost tripping icy logic gates. "How long have you been dead?"

"This isn't where you belong," she said.

I shivered. "How long?"

"Go away," she said.

So I did. I had to. I could not stay very long in her secret place, or I would die of the cold.

As I reeled down the stairs, Mom herself seemed to shift beneath my feet and I saw her as if she were a stranger. Dead—and I had been living in a tomb. I ran past Nanny; she still sprawled where I had left her. All those years I had loved her, I had been in love with death. Mom had been sucking life from me the way her refrigerators stole the warmth from my body.

Now I knew there was no way I could stay, no matter what anyone said. I knew it was not going to be easy leaving, and not just because of the money. For a long time Mom had been my entire world. But I could not let her use me to pretend she was alive, or I would end up like her.

I realized now that the door had always stayed locked because Mom had to hide what she had become. If I wanted, I could have destroyed her. Downloaded intelligences have no more rights than cars or wiseguys. Mom was legally dead and I was her only heir. I could have had her shut off, her body razed. But somehow it was enough to go, to walk away from my inheritance. I was scared, and yet with every step I felt lighter. Happier. Extremely free.

I had not expected to find Tree waiting at the doorbone, chatting with Comrade as if nothing had happened. "I just had to see if you were really the biggest fool in the world," she said.

"Out." I pulled her through the door. "Before I change my mind."

Comrade started to follow us. "No, not you." I turned and stared back at the heads on his window coat. I had not intended to see him again; I had wanted to be gone before Montross returned him. "Look, I'm giving you back to Mom. She needs you more than I do."

If he had argued, I might have given in. The old unregulated Comrade would have said something. But he just slumped a little and nodded and I knew that he was dead, too. The thing in front of me was another ghost. He and Mom were two of a kind. "Pretend you're her kid, maybe she'll like that." I patted his shoulder.

"*Prekrassnaya ideya*," he said. "*Spaceba*."

"You're welcome," I said.

Tree and I trotted together down the long driveway. Robot sentries crossed the lawn and turned their spotlights on us. I wanted to tell her she was right. I had probably just done the single most irresponsible thing of my life—and I had high standards. Still, I could not imagine how being poor could be worse than being rich and hating yourself. I had seen enough of what it was like to be dead. It was time to try living.

"Are we going someplace, Mr. Boy?" Tree squeezed my hand. "Or are we just wandering around in the dark?"

"Mr. Boy is a damn stupid name, don't you think?" I laughed. "Call me Pete." I felt like a kid again.

Beggars in Spain

NANCY KRESS

Nancy Kress began selling her elegant and incisive stories in the midseventies, and has since become a frequent contributor to *Asimov's Science Fiction*, *The Magazine of Fantasy and Science Fiction*, *Omni*, *SCI FICTION*, and elsewhere. Her books include the novel version of her Hugo and Nebula-winning story, *Beggars in Spain*, and a sequel, *Beggars and Choosers*, as well as *The Prince Of Morning Bells*, *The Golden Grove*, *The White Pipes*, *An Alien Light*, *Brain Rose*, *Oaths and Miracles*, *Stinger*, *Maximum Light*, *Probability Moon*, *Probability Sun*, *Probability Space*, *Crossfire*, and *Nothing Human*. Her short work has been collected in *Trinity and Other Stories*, *The Aliens of Earth*, and *Beaker's Dozen*. Her most recent book is the novel *Crucible*. In addition to the awards for "Beggars in Spain," she has also won Nebula Awards for her stories "Out of All Them Bright Stars" and "The Flowers of Aulit Prison."

Here, in what may well be her single most famous story, and perhaps her best as well (high praise indeed!), she takes us to the near future for a hard-hitting, provocative look at the uneasy social consequences of difference.

> With energy and sleepless vigilance go forward and give us victories.
> —Abraham Lincoln, to Major General Joseph Hooker, 1863

1

They sat stiffly on his antique Eames chairs, two people who didn't want to be here, or one person who didn't want to and one who resented the other's reluctance. Dr. Ong had seen this before. Within two minutes he was sure: the woman was the silently furious resister. She would lose. The man would pay for it later, in little ways, for a long time.

"I presume you've performed the necessary credit checks already," Roger Camden said pleasantly, "so let's get right on to details, shall we, doctor?"

"Certainly," Ong said. "Why don't we start by your telling me all the genetic modifications you're interested in for the baby."

The woman shifted suddenly on her chair. She was in her late twenties—clearly a second wife—but already had a faded look, as if keeping up with Roger Camden was wearing her out. Ong could easily believe that. Mrs. Camden's hair was brown, her eyes were brown, her skin had a brown tinge that might have been pretty if her cheeks had had any color. She wore a brown coat, neither fashionable nor cheap, and shoes that looked vaguely orthopedic. Ong glanced at his records for her name: Elizabeth. He would bet people forgot it often.

Next to her, Roger Camden radiated nervous vitality, a man in late middle age whose bullet-shaped head did not match his careful haircut and Italian-silk business suit. Ong did not need to consult his file to recall anything about Camden. A caricature of the bullet-shaped head had been the leading graphic of yesterday's on-line edition of the *Wall Street Journal*: Camden had led a major coup in cross-border data-atoll investment. Ong was not sure what cross-border data-atoll investment was.

"A girl," Elizabeth Camden said. Ong hadn't expected her to speak first. Her voice was another surprise: upper-class British. "Blonde. Green eyes. Tall. Slender."

Ong smiled. "Appearance factors are the easiest to achieve, as I'm sure you already know. But all we can do about 'slenderness' is give her a genetic disposition in that direction. How you feed the child will naturally—"

"Yes, yes," Roger Camden said, "that's obvious. Now: intelligence. *High* intelligence. And a sense of daring."

"I'm sorry, Mr. Camden—personality factors are not yet understood well enough to allow genet—"

"Just testing," Camden said, with a smile that Ong thought was probably supposed to be light-hearted.

Elizabeth Camden said, "Musical ability."

"Again, Mrs. Camden, a disposition to be musical is all we can guarantee."

"Good enough," Camden said. "The full array of corrections for any potential gene-linked health problem, of course."

"Of course," Dr. Ong said. Neither client spoke. So far theirs was a fairly modest list, given Camden's money; most clients had to be argued out of contradictory genetic tendencies, alteration overload, or unrealistic expectations. Ong waited. Tension prickled in the room like heat.

"And," Camden said, "no need to sleep."

Elizabeth Camden jerked her head sideways to look out the window.

Ong picked a paper magnet off his desk. He made his voice pleasant. "May I ask how you learned whether that genetic-modification program exists?"

Camden grinned. "You're not denying it exists. I give you full credit for that, Doctor."

Ong held onto his temper. "May I ask how you learned whether the program exists?"

Camden reached into an inner pocket of his suit. The silk crinkled and pulled; body and suit came from different social classes. Camden was, Ong remembered, a Yagaiist, a personal friend of Kenzo Yagai himself. Camden handed Ong hard copy: program specifications.

"Don't bother hunting down the security leak in your data banks, Doctor—you won't find it. But if it's any consolation, neither will anybody else. Now." He leaned suddenly forward. His tone changed. "I know that you've created twenty children so far who don't need to sleep at all. That so far nineteen are healthy, intelligent, and psychologically normal. In fact, better than normal—they're all unusually precocious. The oldest is already four years old and can read in two languages. I know you're thinking of offering this genetic modification on the open market in a few years. All I want is a chance to buy it for my daughter now. At whatever price you name."

Ong stood. "I can't possibly discuss this with you unilaterally, Mr. Camden. Neither the theft of our data—"

"Which wasn't a theft—your system developed a spontaneous bubble regurgitation into a public gate, have a hell of a time proving otherwise—"

"—nor the offer to purchase this particular genetic modification lies in my sole area of authority. Both have to be discussed with the Institute's Board of Directors."

"By all means, by all means. When can I talk to them, too?"

"You?"

Camden, still seated, looked at him. It occurred to Ong that there were few men who could look so confident eighteen inches below eye level. "Certainly. I'd like the chance to present my offer to whoever has the actual authority to accept it. That's only good business."

"This isn't solely a business transaction, Mr. Camden."

"It isn't solely pure scientific research, either," Camden retorted. "You're a for-profit corporation here. With certain tax breaks available only to firms meeting certain fair-practice laws."

For a minute Ong couldn't think what Camden meant. "Fair-practice laws . . ."

". . . are designed to protect minorities who are suppliers. I know, it hasn't ever been tested in the case of customers, except for red-lining in Y-energy installations. But it could be tested, Doctor Ong. Minorities are entitled to the same product offerings as non-minorities. I know the Institute would not welcome a court case, Doctor. None of your twenty genetic beta-test families are either Black or Jewish."

"A court . . . but you're not Black or Jewish!"

"I'm a different minority. Polish-American. The name was Kaminsky." Camden finally stood. And smiled warmly. "Look, it is preposterous. You know that, and I know that, and we both know what a grand time journalists would have with it anyway. And you know that I don't want to sue you with a preposterous case, just to use the threat of premature and adverse publicity to get what I want. I don't want to make threats at all, believe me I don't. I just want this marvelous advancement you've come up with for my daughter." His face changed, to an expression Ong wouldn't have believed possible on those particular features: wistfulness. "Doctor— do you know how much more I could have accomplished if I hadn't had to *sleep* all my life?"

Elizabeth Camden said harshly, "You hardly sleep now."

Camden looked down at her as if he had forgotten she was there. "Well, no, my dear, not now. But when I was young . . . college, I might have been able to finish college and still support . . . well. None of that matters now. What matters, Doctor, is that you and I and your board come to an agreement."

"Mr. Camden, please leave my office now."

"You mean before you lose your temper at my presumptuousness? You wouldn't be the first. I'll expect to have a meeting set up by the end of next week, whenever and wherever you say, of course. Just let my personal secretary, Diane Clavers, know the details. Anytime that's best for you."

Ong did not accompany them to the door. Pressure throbbed behind his temples. In the doorway Elizabeth Camden turned. "What happened to the twentieth one?"

"What?"

"The twentieth baby. My husband said nineteen of them are healthy and normal. What happened to the twentieth?"

The pressure grew stronger, hotter. Ong knew that he should not answer; that Camden probably already knew the answer even if his wife didn't; that he, Ong, was going to answer anyway; that he would regret the lack of self-control, bitterly, later.

"The twentieth baby is dead. His parents turned out to be unstable. They separated during the pregnancy, and his mother could not bear the twenty-four-hour crying of a baby who never sleeps."

Elizabeth Camden's eyes widened. "She killed it?"

"By mistake," Camden said shortly. "Shook the little thing too hard." He frowned at Ong. "Nurses, Doctor. In shifts. You should have picked only parents wealthy enough to afford nurses in shifts."

"That's horrible!" Mrs. Camden burst out, and Ong could not tell if she meant the child's death, the lack of nurses, or the Institute's carelessness. Ong closed his eyes.

When they had gone, he took ten milligrams of cyclobenzaprine-Ill. For his back — it was solely for his back. The old injury hurting again. Afterward he stood for a long time at the window, still holding the paper magnet, feeling the pressure recede from his temples, feeling himself calm down. Below him Lake Michigan lapped peacefully at the shore; the police had driven away the homeless in another raid just last night, and they hadn't yet had time to return. Only their debris remained, thrown into the bushes of the lakeshore park: tattered blankets, newspapers, plastic bags like pathetic trampled standards. It was illegal to sleep in the park, illegal to enter it without a resident's permit, illegal to be homeless and without a residence. As Ong watched, uniformed park attendants began methodically spearing newspapers and shoving them into clean self-propelled receptacles.

Ong picked up the phone to call the President of Biotech Institute's Board of Directors.

Four men and three women sat around the polished mahogany table of the conference room. *Doctor, lawyer, Indian chief*, thought Susan Melling, looking from Ong to Sullivan to Camden. She smiled. Ong caught the smile and looked frosty.

Pompous ass. Judy Sullivan, the Institute lawyer, turned to speak in a low voice to Camden's lawyer, a thin nervous man with the look of being owned. The owner, Roger Camden, the Indian chief himself, was the happiest-looking person in the room. The lethal little man—what did it take to become that rich, starting from nothing? She, Susan, would certainly never know—radiated excitement. He beamed, he glowed, so unlike the usual parents-to-be that Susan was intrigued. Usually the prospective daddies and mommies—especially the daddies—sat there looking as if they were at a corporate merger. Camden looked as if he were at a birthday party.

Which, of course, he was. Susan grinned at him, and was pleased when he grinned back. Wolfish, but with a sort of delight that could only be called innocent—what would he be like in bed? Ong frowned majestically and rose to speak.

"Ladies and gentlemen, I think we're ready to start. Perhaps introductions are in order. Mr. Roger Camden, Mrs. Camden, are of course our clients. Mr. John Jaworski, Mr. Camden's lawyer. Mr. Camden, this is Judith Sullivan, the Institute's head of Legal; Samuel Krenshaw, representing Institute Director Dr. Brad Marsteiner, who unfortunately couldn't be here today; and Dr. Susan Melling, who developed the genetic modification affecting sleep. A few legal points of interest to both parties—"

"Forget the contracts for a minute," Camden interrupted. "Let's talk about the sleep thing. I'd like to ask a few questions."

Susan said, "What would you like to know?" Camden's eyes were very blue in his blunt-featured face; he wasn't what she had expected. Mrs. Camden, who apparently lacked both a first name and a lawyer, since Jaworski had been introduced as her husband's but not hers, looked either sullen or scared, it was difficult to tell which.

Ong said sourly, "Then perhaps we should start with a short presentation by Dr. Melling."

Susan would have preferred a Q&A, to see what Camden would ask. But she had annoyed Ong enough for one session. Obediently she rose.

"Let me start with a brief description of sleep. Researchers have known for a long time that there are actually three kinds of sleep. One is 'slow-wave sleep,' characterized on an EEG by delta waves. One is 'rapid-eye-movement sleep,' or REM sleep, which is much lighter sleep and contains most dreaming. Together these two make up 'core sleep.' The third type of sleep is 'optional sleep,' so-called because people seem to get along without it with no ill effects, and some short sleepers don't do it at all, sleeping naturally only 3 or 4 hours a night."

"That's me," Camden said. "I trained myself into it. Couldn't everybody do that?"

Apparently they were going to have a Q&A after all. "No. The actual sleep mechanism has some flexibility, but not the same amount for every person. The raphe nuclei on the brain stem—"

Ong said, "I don't think we need that level of detail, Susan. Let's stick to basics."

Camden said, "The raphe nuclei regulate the balance among neurotransmitters and peptides that lead to a pressure to sleep, don't they?"

Susan couldn't help it; she grinned. Camden, the laser-sharp ruthless financier, sat trying to look solemn, a third-grader waiting to have his homework praised. Ong looked sour. Mrs. Camden looked away, out the window.

"Yes, that's correct, Mr. Camden. You've done your research."

Camden said, "This is my *daughter*," and Susan caught her breath. When was the last time she had heard that note of reverence in anyone's voice? But no one in the room seemed to notice.

"Well, then," Susan said, "you already know that the reason people sleep is because a pressure to sleep builds up in the brain. Over the last twenty years, research has determined that's the *only* reason. Neither slow-wave sleep nor REM sleep serve functions that can't be carried on while the body and brain are awake. A lot goes on during sleep, but it can go on awake just as well, if other hormonal adjustments are made.

"Sleep once served an important evolutionary function. Once Clem Pre-Mammal was done filling his stomach and squirting his sperm around, sleep kept him immobile and away from predators. Sleep was an aid to survival. But now it's a left-over mechanism, like the appendix. It switches on every night, but the need is gone. So we turn off the switch at its source, in the genes."

Ong winced. He hated it when she oversimplified like that. Or maybe it was the light-heartedness he hated. If Marsteiner were making this presentation, there'd be no Clem Pre-Mammal.

Camden said, "What about the need to dream?"

"Not necessary. A left-over bombardment of the cortex to keep it on semi-alert in case a predator attacked during sleep. Wakefulness does that better."

"Why not have wakefulness instead then? From the start of the evolution?"

He was testing her. Susan gave him a full, lavish smile, enjoying his brass. "I told you. Safety from predators. But when a modem predator attacks—say, a cross-border data-atoll investor—it's safer to be awake."

Camden shot at her, "What about the high percentage of REM sleep in fetuses and babies?"

"Still an evolutionary hangover. Cerebrum develops perfectly well without it."

"What about neural repair during slow-wave sleep?"

"That does go on. But it can go on during wakefulness, if the DNA is programmed to do so. No loss of neural efficiency, as far as we know."

"What about the release of human growth enzyme in such large concentrations during slow-wave sleep?"

Susan looked at him admiringly. "Goes on without the sleep. Genetic adjustments tie it to other changes in the pineal gland."

"What about the—"

"The *side effects*?" Mrs. Camden said. Her mouth turned down. "What about the bloody side effects?"

Susan turned to Elizabeth Camden. She had forgotten she was there. The younger woman stared at Susan, mouth turned down at the corners.

"I'm glad you asked that, Mrs. Camden. Because there *are* side effects." Susan paused; she was enjoying herself. "Compared to their age mates, the non-sleep children—who have *not* had IQ genetic manipulation—are more intelligent, better at problem-solving, and more joyous."

Camden took out a cigarette. The archaic, filthy habit surprised Susan. Then she saw that it was deliberate: Roger Camden drawing attention to an ostentatious display to draw attention away from what he was feeling. His cigarette lighter was gold, monogrammed, innocently gaudy.

"Let me explain," Susan said. "REM sleep bombards the cerebral cortex with random neural firings from the brainstem; dreaming occurs because the poor besieged cortex tries so hard to make sense of the activated images and memories. It spends a lot of energy doing that. Without that energy expenditure, non-sleep cerebrums save the wear-and-tear and do better at coordinating real-life input. Thus— greater intelligence and problem-solving.

"Also, doctors have known for sixty years that anti-depressants, which lift the mood of depressed patients, also suppress REM sleep entirely. What they have proved in the last ten years is that the reverse is equally true: suppress REM sleep and people don't *get* depressed. The non-sleep kids are cheerful, outgoing . . . *joyous*. There's no other word for it."

"At what cost?" Mrs. Camden said. She held her neck rigid, but the corners of her jaw worked.

"No cost. No negative side effects at all."

"So far," Mrs. Camden shot back.

Susan shrugged. "So far."

"They're only four years old! At the most!"

Ong and Krenshaw were studying her closely. Susan saw the moment the Camden woman realized it; she sank back into her chair, drawing her fur coat around her, her face blank.

Camden did not look at his wife. He blew a cloud of cigarette smoke. "Everything has costs, Dr. Melling."

She liked the way he said her name. "Ordinarily, yes. Especially in genetic modification. But we honestly have not been able to find any here, despite looking." She smiled directly into Camden's eyes. "Is it too much to believe that just once the universe has given us something wholly good, wholly a step forward, wholly beneficial? Without hidden penalties?"

"Not the universe. The intelligence of people like you," Camden said, surprising Susan more than anything else that had gone before. His eyes held hers. She felt her chest tighten.

"I think," Dr. Ong said dryly, "that the philosophy of the universe may be beyond our concerns here. Mr. Camden, if you have no further medical questions, perhaps we can return to the legal points Ms. Sullivan and Mr. Jaworski have raised. Thank you, Dr. Melling."

Susan nodded. She didn't look again at Camden. But she knew what he said; how he looked, that he was there.

The house was about what she had expected, a huge mock Tudor on Lake Michigan north of Chicago. The land heavily wooded between the gate and the house, open between the house and the surging water. Patches of snow dotted the dormant grass. Biotech had been working with the Camdens for four months, but this was the first time Susan had driven to their home.

As she walked toward the house, another car drove up behind her. No, a truck, continuing around the curved driveway to a service entry at the side of the house. One man rang the service bell; a second began to unload a plastic-wrapped playpen from the back of the truck. White, with pink and yellow bunnies. Susan briefly closed her eyes.

Camden opened the door himself. She could see the effort not to look worried. "You didn't have to drive out, Susan—I'd have come into the city!"

"No, I didn't want you to do that, Roger. Mrs. Camden is here?"

"In the living room." Camden led her into a large room with a stone fireplace. English country-house furniture; prints of dogs or boats, all hung eighteen inches too high: Elizabeth Camden must have done the decorating. She did not rise from her wing chair as Susan entered.

"Let me be concise and fast," Susan said, "I don't want to make this any more drawn-out for you than I have to. We have all the amniocentesis, ultrasound, and Langston test results. The fetus is fine, developing normally for two weeks, no problems with the implant on the uterus wall. But a complication has developed."

"What?" Camden said. He took out a cigarette, looked at his wife, put it back unlit.

Susan said quietly, "Mrs. Camden, by sheer chance both your ovaries released eggs last month. We removed one for the gene surgery. By more sheer chance the second fertilized and implanted. You're carrying two fetuses."

Elizabeth Camden grew still. "Twins?"

"No," Susan said. Then she realized what she had said. "I mean, yes. They're twins, but non-identical. Only one has been genetically altered. The other will be no more similar to her than any two siblings. It's a so-called 'normal' baby. And I know you didn't want a so-called normal baby."

Camden said, "No. I didn't."

Elizabeth Camden said, "I did."

Camden shot her a fierce look that Susan couldn't read. He took out the cigarette again, lit it. His face was in profile to Susan, thinking intently; she doubted he knew the cigarette was there, or that he was lighting it. "Is the baby being affected by the other one's being there?"

"No," Susan said. "No, of course not. They're just . . . co-existing."

"Can you abort it?"

"Not without risk of aborting both of them. Removing the unaltered fetus might cause changes in the uterus lining that could lead to a spontaneous miscarriage of the other." She drew a deep breath. "There's that option, of course. We can start the whole process over again. But as I told you at the time, you were very lucky to have the in vitro fertilization take on only the second try. Some couples take eight or ten tries. If we started all over, the process could be a lengthy one."

Camden said, "Is the presence of this second fetus harming my daughter? Taking away nutrients or anything? Or will it change anything for her later on in the pregnancy?"

"No. Except that there is a chance of premature birth. Two fetuses take up a lot more room in the womb, and if it gets too crowded, birth can be premature. But the—"

"How premature? Enough to threaten survival?"

"Most probably not."

Camden went on smoking. A man appeared at the door. "Sir, London calling. James Kendall for Mr. Yagai."

"I'll take it." Camden rose. Susan watched him study his wife's face. When he spoke, it was to her. "All right, Elizabeth. All right." He left the room.

For a long moment the two women sat in silence. Susan was aware of disappointment; this was not the Camden she had expected to see. She became aware of Elizabeth Camden watching her with amusement.

"Oh, yes, Doctor. He's like that."

Susan said nothing.

"Completely overbearing. But not this time." She laughed softly, with excitement. "Two. Do you . . . do you know what sex the other one is?"

"Both fetuses are female."

"I wanted a girl, you know. And now I'll have one."

"Then you'll go ahead with the pregnancy."

"Oh, yes. Thank you for coming, Doctor."

She was dismissed. No one saw her out. But as she was getting into her car, Camden rushed out of the house, coatless. "Susan! I wanted to thank you. For coming all the way out here to tell us yourself."

"You already thanked me."

"Yes. Well. You're sure the second fetus is no threat to my daughter?"

Susan said deliberately, "Nor is the genetically altered fetus a threat to the naturally conceived one."

He smiled. His voice was low and wistful. "And you think that should matter to me just as much. But it doesn't. And why should I fake what I feel? Especially to you?"

Susan opened her car door. She wasn't ready for this, or she had changed her mind, or something. But then Camden leaned over to close the door, and his manner held no trace of flirtatiousness, no smarmy ingratiation. "I better order a second playpen."

"Yes."

"And a second car seat."

"Yes."

"But not a second night-shift nurse."

"That's up to you."

"And you." Abruptly he leaned over and kissed her, a kiss so polite and respectful that Susan was shocked. Neither lust nor conquest would have shocked her; this did. Camden didn't give her a chance to react; he closed the car door and turned back toward the house. Susan drove toward the gate, her hands shaky on the wheel until amusement replaced shock: It *had* been a deliberately distant, respectful kiss, an engineered enigma. And nothing else could have guaranteed so well that there would have to be another.

She wondered what the Camdens would name their daughters.

Dr. Ong strode the hospital corridor, which had been dimmed to half-light. From the nurse's station in Maternity a nurse stepped forward as if to stop him—it was the middle of the night, long past visiting hours—got a good look at his face, and faded back into her station. Around a corner was the viewing glass to the nursery. To Ong's annoyance, Susan Melling stood pressed against the glass. To his further annoyance, she was crying.

Ong realized that he had never liked the woman. Maybe not any women. Even those with superior minds could not seem to refrain from being made damn fools by their emotions.

"Look," Susan said, laughing a little, swiping at her face. "Doctor—*look*."

Behind the glass Roger Camden, gowned and masked, was holding up a baby in white undershirt and pink blanket. Camden's blue eyes—theatrically blue, a man really should not have such garish eyes—glowed. The baby had a head covered with blond fuzz, wide eyes, pink skin. Camden's eyes above the mask said that no other child had ever had these attributes.

Ong said, "An uncomplicated birth?"

"Yes," Susan Melling sobbed. "Perfectly straightforward. Elizabeth is fine. She's asleep. Isn't she beautiful? He has the most adventurous spirit I've ever known." She wiped her nose on her sleeve; Ong realized that she was drunk. "Did I ever tell you that I was engaged once? Fifteen years ago, in med school? I broke it off because he grew to seem so ordinary, so boring. Oh, God, I shouldn't be telling you all this I'm sorry I'm sorry."

Ong moved away from her. Behind the glass Roger Camden laid the baby in a small wheeled crib. The nameplate said BABY GIRL CAMDEN #1. 5.9 POUNDS. A night nurse watched indulgently.

Ong did not wait to see Camden emerge from the nursery or to hear Susan Melling say to him whatever she was going to say. Ong went to have the OB paged. Melling's report was not, under the circumstances, to be trusted. A perfect, unprecedented chance to record every detail of gene-alteration with a non-altered control, and Melling was more interested in her own sloppy emotions. Ong would obviously have to do the report himself, after talking to the OB. He was hungry for every detail. And not just about the pink-cheeked baby in Camden's arms. He wanted to know everything about the birth of the child in the other glass-sided crib: BABY GIRL CAMDEN #2. 5.1 POUNDS. The dark-haired baby with the mottled red features, lying scrunched down in her pink blanket, asleep.

2

Leisha's earliest memory was of flowing lines that were not there. She knew they were not there because when she reached out her fist to touch them, her fist was empty. Later she realized that the flowing lines were light: sunshine slanting in bars between curtains in her room, between the wooden blinds in the dining room, between the criss-cross lattices in the conservatory. The day she realized the golden flow was light she laughed out loud with the sheer joy of discovery, and Daddy turned from putting flowers in pots and smiled at her.

The whole house was full of light. Light bounded off the lake, streamed across the high white ceilings, puddled on the shining wooden floors. She and Alice moved continually through light, and sometimes Leisha would stop and tip back her head and let it flow over her face. She could feel it, like water.

The best light, of course, was in the conservatory. That's where Daddy liked to be when he was home from making money. Daddy potted plants and watered trees, humming, and Leisha and Alice ran between the wooden tables of flowers with their wonderful earthy smells, running from the dark side of the conservatory where the big purple flowers grew to the sunshine side with sprays of yellow flowers, running back and forth, in and out of the light. "Growth," Daddy said to her, "flowers all fulfilling their promise. Alice, be careful! You almost knocked over that orchid!" Alice, obedient, would stop running for a while. Daddy never told Leisha to stop running.

After a while the light would go away. Alice and Leisha would have their baths, and then Alice would get quiet, or cranky. She wouldn't play nice with Leisha, even when Leisha let her choose the game or even have all the best dolls. Then Nanny would take Alice to "bed," and Leisha would talk with Daddy some more until Daddy said he had to work in his study with the papers that made money. Leisha always felt a moment of regret that he had to go do that, but the moment never lasted very long because Mamselle would arrive and start Leisha's lessons, which she liked. Learning things was so interesting! She could already sing twenty songs and write all the letters in the alphabet and count to fifty. And by the time lessons were done, the light had come back, and it was time for breakfast.

Breakfast was the only time Leisha didn't like. Daddy had gone to the office, and Leisha and Alice had breakfast with Mommy in the big dining room. Mommy sat in a red robe, which Leisha liked, and she didn't smell funny or talk funny the way she would later in the day, but still breakfast wasn't fun. Mommy always started with The Question.

"Alice, sweetheart, how did you sleep?"

"Fine, Mommy."

"Did you have any nice dreams?"

For a long time Alice said no. Then one day she said, "I dreamed about a horse. I was riding him." Mommy clapped her hands and kissed Alice and gave her an extra sticky bun. After that Alice always had a dream to tell Mommy.

Once Leisha said, "I had a dream, too. I dreamed light was coming in the window and it wrapped all around me like a blanket and then it kissed me on my eyes."

Mommy put down her coffee cup so hard that coffee sloshed out of it. "Don't lie to me, Leisha. You did not have a dream."

"Yes, I did," Leisha said.

"Only children who sleep can have dreams. Don't lie to me. You did not have a dream."

"Yes I did! I did!" Leisha shouted. She could see it, almost: The light streaming in the window and wrapping around her like a golden blanket.

"I will not tolerate a child who is a liar! Do you hear me, Leisha—I won't tolerate it!"

"You're a liar!" Leisha shouted, knowing the words weren't true, hating herself because they weren't true but hating Mommy more and that was wrong, too, and there sat Alice stiff and frozen with her eyes wide, Alice was scared and it was Leisha's fault.

Mommy called sharply, "Nanny! Nanny! Take Leisha to her room at once. She can't sit with civilized people if she can't refrain from telling lies!"

Leisha started to cry. Nanny carried her out of the room. Leisha hadn't even had her breakfast. But she didn't care about that; all she could see while she cried was Alice's eyes, scared like that, reflecting broken bits of light.

But Leisha didn't cry long. Nanny read her a story, and then played Data Jump with her, and then Alice came up and Nanny drove them both into Chicago to the zoo where there were wonderful animals to see, animals Leisha could not have dreamed—nor Alice *either*. And by the time they came back Mommy had gone to her room and Leisha knew that she would stay there with the glasses of funny-smelling stuff the rest of the day and Leisha would not have to see her.

But that night, she went to her mother's room.

"I have to go to the bathroom," she told Mamselle. Mamselle said, "Do you need any help?" maybe because Alice still needed help in the bathroom. But Leisha didn't, and she thanked Mamselle. Then she sat on the toilet for a minute even though nothing came, so that what she had told Mamselle wouldn't be a lie.

Leisha tiptoed down the hall. She went first into Alice's room. A little light in a wall socket burned near the "crib." There was no crib in Leisha's room. Leisha looked at her sister through the bars. Alice lay on her side, with her eyes closed. The lids of the eyes fluttered quickly, like curtains blowing in the wind. Alice's chin and neck looked loose.

Leisha closed the door very carefully and went to her parents' room.

They didn't "sleep" in a crib but in a huge enormous "bed," with enough room between them for more people. Mommy's eyelids weren't fluttering; she lay on her back making a hrrr-hrrr sound through her nose. The funny smell was strong on her. Leisha backed away and tiptoed over to Daddy. He looked like Alice, except that his neck and chin looked even looser, folds of skin collapsed like the tent that had fallen down in the backyard. It scared Leisha to see him like that. Then Daddy's eyes flew open so suddenly that Leisha screamed.

Daddy rolled out of bed and picked her up, looking quickly at Mommy. But she didn't move. Daddy was wearing only his underpants. He carried Leisha out into the hall, where Mamselle came rushing up saying, "Oh, sir, I'm sorry, she just said she was going to the bathroom—"

"It's all right," Daddy said. "I'll take her with me."

"No!" Leisha screamed, because Daddy was only in his underpants and his neck had looked all funny and the room smelled bad because of Mommy. But Daddy carried her into the conservatory, set her down on a bench, wrapped himself in a piece of green plastic that was supposed to cover up plants, and sat down next to her.

"Now, what happened, Leisha? What were you doing?"

Leisha didn't answer.

"You were looking at people sleeping, weren't you?" Daddy said, and because his voice was softer Leisha mumbled, "Yes." She immediately felt better; it felt good not to lie.

"You were looking at people sleeping because you don't sleep and you were curious, weren't you? Like Curious George in your book?"

"Yes," Leisha said. "I thought you said you made money in your study all night!"

Daddy smiled. "Not all night. Some of it. But then I sleep, although not very much." He took Leisha on his lap. "I don't need much sleep, so I get a lot more done at night than most people. Different people need different amounts of sleep. And a few, a very few, are like you. You don't need any."

"Why not?"

"Because you're special. Better than other people. Before you were born, I had some doctors help make you that way."

"Why?"

"So you could do anything you want to and make manifest your own individuality."

Leisha twisted in his arms to stare at him; the words meant nothing. Daddy reached over and touched a single flower growing on a tall potted tree. The flower had thick white petals like the cream he put in coffee, and the center was a light pink.

"See, Leisha—this tree made this flower. Because it can. Only this tree can make this kind of wonderful flower. That plant hanging up there can't, and those can't either. Only this tree. Therefore the most important thing in the world for this tree to do is grow this flower. The flower is the tree's individuality—that means just *it*, and nothing else—made manifest. Nothing else matters."

"I don't understand, Daddy."

"You will. Someday."

"But I want to understand *now*," Leisha said, and Daddy laughed with pure delight and hugged her. The hug felt good, but Leisha still wanted to understand.

"When you make money, is that your indiv . . . that thing?"

"Yes," Daddy said happily.

"Then nobody else can make money? Like only that tree can make that flower?"

"Nobody else can make it just the ways I do."

"What do you do with the money?"

"I buy things for you. This house, your dresses, Mamselle to teach you, the car to ride in."

"What does the tree do with the flower?"

"Glories in it," Daddy said, which made no sense. "Excellence is what counts, Leisha. Excellence supported by individual effort. And that's *all* that counts."

"I'm cold, Daddy."

"Then I better bring you back to Mamselle."

Leisha didn't move. She touched the flower with one finger. "I want to sleep, Daddy."

"No, you don't, sweetheart. Sleep is just lost time, wasted life. It's a little death."

"Alice sleeps."

"Alice isn't like you."

"Alice isn't special?"

"No. You are."

"Why didn't you make Alice special, too?"

"Alice made herself. I didn't have a chance to make her special."

The whole thing was too hard. Leisha stopped stroking the flower and slipped off

Daddy's lap. He smiled at her. "My little questioner. When you grow up, you'll find your own excellence, and it will be a new order, a specialness the world hasn't ever seen before. You might even be like Kenzo Yagai. He made the Yagai generator that powers the world."

"Daddy, you look funny wrapped in the flower plastic." Leisha laughed. Daddy did, too. But then she said, "When I grow up, I'll make my specialness find a way to make Alice special, too," and Daddy stopped laughing.

He took her back to Mamselle, who taught her to write her name, which was so exciting she forgot about the puzzling talk with Daddy. There were six letters, all different, and together they were *her name.* Leisha wrote it over and over, laughing, and Mamselle laughed too. But later, in the morning, Leisha thought again about the talk with Daddy. She thought of it often, turning the unfamiliar words over and over in her mind like small hard stones, but the part she thought about most wasn't a word. It was the frown on Daddy's face when she told him she would use her specialness to make Alice special, too.

Every week Dr. Melling came to see Leisha and Alice, sometimes alone, sometimes with other people. Leisha and Alice both liked Dr. Melling, who laughed a lot and whose eyes were bright and warm. Often Daddy was there, too. Dr. Melling played games with them, first with Alice and Leisha separately and then together. She took their pictures and weighed them. She made them lie down on a table and stuck little metal things to their temples, which sounded scary but wasn't because there were so many machines to watch, all making interesting noises, while you were lying there. Dr. Melling was as good at answering questions as Daddy. Once Leisha said, "Is Dr. Melling a special person? Like Kenzo Yagai?" And Daddy laughed and glanced at Dr. Melling and said, "Oh, yes, indeed."

When Leisha was five she and Alice started school. Daddy's driver took them every day into Chicago. They were in different rooms, which disappointed Leisha. The kids in Leisha's room were all older. But from the first day she adored school, with its fascinating science equipment and electronic drawers full of math puzzlers and other children to find countries on the map with. In half a year she had been moved to yet a different room, where the kids were still older, but they were nonetheless nice to her. Leisha started to learn Japanese. She loved drawing the beautiful characters on thick white paper. "The Sauley School was a good choice," Daddy said.

But Alice didn't like the Sauley School. She wanted to go to school on the same yellow bus as Cook's daughter. She cried and threw her paints on the floor at the Sauley School. Then Mommy came out of her room—Leisha hadn't seen her for a few weeks, although she knew Alice had—and threw some candlesticks from the mantlepiece on the floor. The candlesticks, which were china, broke. Leisha ran to pick up the pieces while Mommy and Daddy screamed at each other in the hall by the big staircase.

"She's my daughter, too! And I say she can go!"

"You don't have the right to say anything about it! A weepy drunk, the most rotten role model possible for both of them . . . and I thought I was getting a fine English aristocrat!"

"You got what you paid for! Nothing! Not that you ever needed anything from me or anybody else!"

"Stop it!" Leisha cried. "Stop it!" and there was silence in the hall. Leisha cut her fingers on the china; blood streamed onto the rug. Daddy rushed in and picked her up. "Stop it," Leisha sobbed, and didn't understand when Daddy said quietly, "You stop it, Leisha. Nothing *they* do should touch you at all. You have to be at least that strong."

Leisha buried her head in Daddy's shoulder. Alice transferred to Carl Sandburg Elementary School, riding there on the yellow school bus with Cook's daughter.

A few weeks later Daddy told them that Mommy was going away for a few weeks to a hospital, to stop drinking so much. When Mommy came out, he said, she was going to live somewhere else for a while. She and Daddy were not happy. Leisha and Alice would stay with Daddy and they would visit Mommy sometimes. He told them this very carefully, finding the right words for truth. Truth was very important, Leisha already knew. Truth was being true to your self, your specialness. Your individuality. An individual respected facts, and so always told the truth.

Mommy, Daddy did not say but Leisha knew, did not respect facts.

"I don't want Mommy to go away," Alice said. She started to cry. Leisha thought Daddy would pick Alice up, but he didn't. He just stood there looking at them both.

Leisha put her arms around Alice. "It's all right, Alice. It's all right! We'll make it all right! I'll play with you all the time we're not in school so you don't miss Mommy!"

Alice clung to Leisha. Leisha turned her head so she didn't have to see Daddy's face.

3

Kenzo Yagai was coming to the United States to lecture. The title of his talk, which he would give in New York, Los Angeles, Chicago, and Washington, with a repeat in Washington as a special address to Congress, was "The Further Political Implications of Inexpensive Power." Leisha Camden, eleven years old, was going to have a private introduction after the Chicago talk, arranged by her father.

She had studied the theory of cold fusion at school, and her Global Studies teacher had traced the changes in the world resulting from Yagai's patented, low-cost applications of what had, until him, been unworkable theory. The rising prosperity of the Third World, the last death throes of the old communist systems, the decline of the oil states, the renewed economic power of the United States. Her study group had written a news script, filmed with the school's professional-quality equipment, about how a 1985 American family lived with expensive energy costs and a belief in tax-supported help, while a 2019 family lived with cheap energy and a belief in the contract as the basis of civilization. Parts of her own research puzzled Leisha.

"Japan thinks Kenzo Yagai was a traitor to his own country," she said to Daddy at supper.

"No," Camden said. "*Some* Japanese think that. Watch out for generalizations, Leisha. Yagai patented and marketed Y-energy first in the United States because here there were at least the dying embers of individual enterprise. Because of his invention, our entire country has slowly swung back toward an individual meritocracy, and Japan has slowly been forced to follow."

"Your father held that belief all along," Susan said. "Eat your peas, Leisha." Leisha ate her peas. Susan and Daddy had only been married less than a year; it still felt a little strange to have her there. But nice. Daddy said Susan was a valuable addition to their household: intelligent, motivated, and cheerful. Like Leisha herself.

"Remember, Leisha," Camden said, "a man's worth to society and to himself doesn't rest on what he thinks other people should do or be or feel, but on himself. On what he can actually do, and do well. People trade what they do well, and everyone benefits. The basic tool of civilization is the contract. Contracts are voluntary and mutually beneficial. As opposed to coercion, which is wrong."

"The strong have no right to take anything from the weak by force," Susan said. "Alice, eat your peas, too, honey."

"Nor the weak to take anything by force from the strong," Camden said. "That's the basis of what you'll hear Kenzo Yagai discuss tonight, Leisha."

Alice said, "I don't like peas."

Camden said, "Your body does. They're good for you."

Alice smiled. Leisha felt her heart lift; Alice didn't smile much at dinner any more. "My body doesn't have a contract with the peas."

Camden said, a little impatiently, "Yes, it does. Your body benefits from them. Now eat."

Alice's smile vanished. Leisha looked down at her plate. Suddenly she saw a way out. "No, Daddy look—Alice's body benefits, but the peas don't! It's not a mutually beneficial consideration—so there's no contract! Alice is right!"

Camden let out a shout of laughter. To Susan he said, "Eleven years old . . . *eleven*." Even Alice smiled, and Leisha waved her spoon triumphantly, light glinting off the bowl and dancing silver on the opposite wall.

But even so, Alice did not want to go hear Kenzo Yagai. She was going to sleep over at her friend Julie's house; they were going to curl their hair together. More surprisingly, Susan wasn't coming either. She and Daddy looked at each other a little funny at the front door, Leisha thought, but Leisha was too excited to think about this. She was going to hear *Kenzo Yagai*.

Yagai was a small man, dark and slim. Leisha liked his accent. She liked, too, something about him that took her a while to name. "Daddy," she whispered in the half-darkness of the auditorium, "he's a joyful man."

Daddy hugged her in the darkness.

Yagai spoke about spirituality and economics. "A man's spirituality—which is only his dignity as a man—rests on his own efforts. Dignity and worth are not automatically conferred by aristocratic birth—we have only to look at history to see that. Dignity and worth are not automatically conferred by inherited wealth—a great heir may be a thief, a wastrel, cruel, an exploiter, a person who leaves the world much poorer than he found it. Nor are dignity and worth automatically conferred by existence itself—a mass murderer exists, but is of negative worth to his society and possesses no dignity in his lust to kill.

"No, the only dignity, the only spirituality, rests on what a man can achieve with his own efforts. To rob a man of the chance to achieve, and to trade what he achieves with others, is to rob him of his spiritual dignity as a man. This is why communism has failed in our time. All coercion—all force to take from a man his own efforts to achieve—causes spiritual damage and weakens a society. Conscription, theft, fraud, violence, welfare, lack of legislative representation—*all* rob a man of his chance to choose, to achieve on his own, to trade the results of his achievement with others. Coercion is a cheat. It produces nothing new. Only freedom—the freedom to achieve, the freedom to trade freely the results of achievement—creates the environment proper to the dignity and spirituality of man."

Leisha applauded so hard her hands hurt. Going backstage with Daddy, she thought she could hardly breathe. Kenzo Yagai!

But backstage was more crowded than she had expected. There were cameras everywhere. Daddy said, "Mr. Yagai, may I present my daughter Leisha," and the cameras moved in close and fast—on *her*. A Japanese man whispered something in Kenzo Yagai's ear, and he looked more closely at Leisha. "Ah, yes."

"Look over here, Leisha," someone called, and she did. A robot camera zoomed so close to her face that Leisha stepped back, startled. Daddy spoke very sharply to someone, then to someone else. The cameras didn't move. A woman suddenly knelt in front of Leisha and thrust a microphone at her. "What does it feel like to never sleep, Leisha?"

"What?"

Someone laughed. The laugh was not kind. "Breeding geniuses . . ."

Leisha felt a hand on her shoulder. Kenzo Yagai gripped her very firmly, pulled her away from the cameras. Immediately, as if by magic, a line of Japanese men formed behind Yagai, parting only to let Daddy through. Behind the line, the three of them moved into a dressing room, and Kenzo Yagai shut the door.

"You must not let them bother you, Leisha," he said in his wonderful accent. "Not ever. There is an old Oriental proverb: 'The dogs bark but the caravan moves on.' You must never let your individual caravan be slowed by the barking of rude or envious dogs."

"I won't," Leisha breathed, not sure yet what the words really meant, knowing there was time later to sort them out, to talk about them with Daddy. For now she was dazzled by Kenzo Yagai, the actual man himself who was changing the world without force, without guns, with trading his special individual efforts. "We study your philosophy at my school, Mr. Yagai."

Kenzo Yagai looked at Daddy. Daddy said, "A private school. But Leisha's sister also studies it, although cursorily, in the public system. Slowly, Kenzo, but it comes. It comes." Leisha noticed that he did not say why Alice was not here tonight with them.

Back home, Leisha sat in her room for hours, thinking over everything that had happened. When Alice came home from Julie's the next morning, Leisha rushed toward her. But Alice seemed angry about something.

"Alice—what is it?"

"Don't you think I have enough to put up with at school already?" Alice shouted. "Everybody knows, but at least when you stayed quiet it didn't matter too much! They'd stopped teasing me! Why did you have to do it?"

"Do what?" Leisha said, bewildered.

Alice threw something at her: a hard-copy morning paper, on newsprint flimsier than the Camden system used. The paper dropped open at Leisha's feet. She stared at her own picture, three columns wide, with Kenzo Yagai. The headline said YAGAI AND THE FUTURE: ROOM FOR THE REST OF US? Y-ENERGY INVENTOR CONFERS WITH 'SLEEP-FREE' DAUGHTER OF MEGA-FINANCIER ROGER CAMDEN.

Alice kicked the paper. "It was on TV last night too — on TV. I work hard not to look stuck-up or creepy, and you go and do this! Now Julie probably won't even invite me to her slumber party next week!" She rushed up the broad curving stairs toward her room.

Leisha looked down at the paper. She heard Kenzo Yagai's voice in her head: "The dogs bark but the caravan moves on." She looked at the empty stairs. Aloud she said, "Alice — your hair looks really pretty curled like that."

4

"I want to meet the rest of them," Leisha said. "Why have you kept them from me this long?"

"I haven't kept them from you at all," Camden said. "Not offering is not the same as denial. Why shouldn't you be the one to do the asking? You're the one who now wants it."

Leisha looked at him. She was 15, in her last year at the Sauley School. "Why didn't you offer?"

"Why should I?"

"I don't know," Leisha said. "But you gave me everything else."

"Including the freedom to ask for what you want."

Leisha looked for the contradiction, and found it. "Most things that you provided for my education I didn't ask for, because I didn't know enough to ask and you, as the adult, did. But you've never offered the opportunity for me to meet any of the other sleepless mutants —"

"Don't use that word," Camden said sharply.

" — so you must either think it was not essential to my education or else you had another motive for not wanting me to meet them."

"Wrong," Camden said. "There's a third possibility. That I think meeting them is essential to your education, that I do want you to, but this issue provided a chance to further the education of your self-initiative by waiting for *you* to ask."

"All right," Leisha said, a little defiantly; there seemed to be a lot of defiance between them lately, for no good reason. She squared her shoulders. Her new breasts thrust forward. "I'm asking. How many of the Sleepless are there, who are they, and where are they?"

Camden said, "If you're using that term — 'the Sleepless' — you've already done some reading on your own. So you probably know that there are 1,082 of you so far in the United States, a few more in foreign countries, most of them in major metropolitan areas. Seventy-nine are in Chicago, most of them still small children. Only nineteen anywhere are older than you."

Leisha didn't deny reading any of this. Camden leaned forward in his study chair to peer at her. Leisha wondered if he needed glasses. His hair was completely gray now, sparse and stiff, like lonely broomstraws. The *Wall Street Journal* listed him among the hundred richest men in America; *Women's Wear Daily* pointed out that he was the only billionaire in the country who did not move in the society of international parties, charity balls, and personal jets. Camden's jet ferried him to business meetings around the world, to the chairmanship of the Yagai Economics Institute, and to very little else. Over the years he had grown richer, more reclusive, and more cerebral. Leisha felt a rush of her old affection.

She threw herself sideways into a leather chair, her long slim legs dangling over the arm. Absently she scratched a mosquito bite on her thigh. "Well, then, I'd like to meet Richard Keller." He lived in Chicago and was the beta-test Sleepless closest to her own age. He was 17.

"Why ask me? Why not just go?"

Leisha thought there was a note of impatience in his voice. He liked her to explore things first, then report on them to him later. Both parts were important.

Leisha laughed. "You know what, Daddy? You're predictable."

Camden laughed, too. In the middle of the laugh Susan came in. "He certainly is not. Roger, what about that meeting in Buenos Aires Thursday? Is it on or off?" When he didn't answer, her voice grew shriller. "Roger? I'm talking to you!"

Leisha averted her eyes. Two years ago Susan had finally left genetic research to run Camden's house and schedule; before that she had tried hard to do both. Since she had left Biotech, it seemed to Leisha, Susan had changed. Her voice was tighter. She was more insistent that Cook and the gardener follow her directions exactly, without deviation. Her blonde braids had become stiff sculptured waves of platinum.

"It's on," Roger said.

"Well, thanks for at least answering. Am I going?"

"If you like."

"I like."

Susan left the room. Leisha rose and stretched. Her long legs rose on tiptoe. It felt good to reach, to stretch, to feel sunlight from the wide windows wash over her face. She smiled at her father, and found him watching her with an unexpected expression.

"Leisha—"

"What?"

"See Keller. But be careful."

"Of what?"

But Camden wouldn't answer.

The voice on the phone had been noncommittal. "Leisha Camden? Yes, I know who you are. Three o'clock on Thursday?" The house was modest, a thirty-year-old Colonial on a quiet suburban street where small children on bicycles could be watched from the front window. Few roofs had more than one Y-energy cell. The trees, huge old sugar maples, were beautiful.

"Come in," Richard Keller said.

He was no taller than she, stocky, with a bad case of acne. Probably no genetic alterations except sleep, Leisha guessed. He had thick dark hair, a low forehead, and bushy black brows. Before he closed the door Leisha saw his stare at her car and driver, parked in the driveway next to a rusty ten-speed bike.

"I can't drive yet," she said. "I'm still fifteen."

"It's easy to learn," Keller said. "So, you want to tell me why you're here?"

Leisha liked his directness. "To meet some other Sleepless."

"You mean you never have? Not any of us?"

"You mean the rest of you know each other?" She hadn't expected that.

"Come to my room, Leisha."

She followed him to the back of the house. No one else seemed to be home. His room was large and airy, filled with computers and filing cabinets. A rowing machine sat in one corner. It looked like a shabbier version of the room of any bright classmate at the Sauley School, except there was more space without a bed. She walked over to the computer screen.

"Hey—you working on Boesc equations?"

"On an application of them."

"To what?"

"Fish migration patterns."

Leisha smiled. "Yeah—that would work. I never thought of that."

Keller seemed not to know what to do with her smile. He looked at the wall, then at her chin. "You interested in Gaea patterns? In the environment?"

"Well, no," Leisha confessed. "Not particularly. I'm going to study politics at Harvard. Pre-law. But of course we had Gaea patterns at school."

Keller's gaze finally came unstuck from her face. He ran a hand through his dark hair. "Sit down, if you want."

Leisha sat, looking appreciatively at the wall posters, shifting green on blue, like ocean currents. "I like those. Did you program them yourself?"

"You're not at all what I pictured," Keller said.

"How did you picture me?"

He didn't hesitate. "Stuck-up. Superior. Shallow, despite your IQ."

She was more hurt than she had expected to be.

Keller blurted, "You're the only one of the Sleepless who's really rich. But you already know that."

"No, I don't. I've never checked."

He took the chair beside her, stretching his stocky legs straight in front of him, in a slouch that had nothing to do with relaxation. "It makes sense, really. Rich people don't have their children genetically modified to be superior—they think any offspring of theirs is already superior. By their values. And poor people can't afford it. We Sleepless are upper-middle class, no more. Children of professors, scientists, people who value brains and time."

"My father values brains and time," Leisha said. "He's the biggest supporter of Kenzo Yagai."

"Oh, Leisha, do you think I don't already know that? Are you flashing me or what?"

Leisha said with great deliberateness, "I'm *talking* to you." But the next minute she could feel the hurt break through on her face.

"I'm sorry," Keller muttered. He shot off his chair and paced to the computer, back. "I *am* sorry. But I don't . . . I don't understand what you're doing here."

"I'm lonely," Leisha said, astonished at herself. She looked up at him. "It's true. I'm lonely. I am. I have friends and Daddy and Alice—but no one really knows, really understands—what? I don't know what I'm saying."

Keller smiled. The smile changed his whole face, opened up its dark planes to the light. "I do. Oh, do I. What do you do when they say, 'I had such a dream last night!'?"

"Yes!" Leisha said. "But that's even really minor—it's when *I* say, 'I'll look that up for you tonight' and they get that funny look on their face that means 'She'll do it while I'm asleep.'"

"But that's even really minor," Keller said. "It's when you're playing basketball in the gym after supper and then you go to the diner for food and then you say 'Let's have a walk by the lake' and they say 'I'm really tired. I'm going home to bed now.'"

"But that's really minor," Leisha said, jumping up. "It's when you really are absorbed by the movie and then you get the point and it's so goddamn beautiful you leap up and say 'Yes! Yes!' and Susan says 'Leisha, really—you'd think nobody but you ever enjoyed anything before.'"

"Who's Susan?" Keller said.

The mood was broken. But not really; Leisha could say "My stepmother" without much discomfort over what Susan had promised to be and what she had become. Keller stood inches from her, smiling that joyous smile, understanding, and suddenly relief washed over Leisha so strong that she walked straight into him and put her arms around his neck, only tightening them when she felt his startled jerk. She started to sob—she, Leisha, who never cried.

"Hey," Richard said. "Hey."

"Brilliant," Leisha said, laughing. "Brilliant remark."

She could feel his embarrassed smile. "Wanta see my fish migration curves instead?"

"No," Leisha sobbed, and he went on holding her, patting her back awkwardly, telling her without words that she was home.

Camden waited up for her, although it was past midnight. He had been smoking heavily. Through the blue air he said quietly, "Did you have a good time, Leisha?"

"Yes."

"I'm glad," he said, and put out his last cigarette, and climbed the stairs—slowly, stiffly, he was nearly seventy now—to bed.

They went everywhere together for nearly a year: swimming, dancing, to the museums, the theater, the library. Richard introduced her to the others, a group of twelve kids between fourteen and nineteen, all of them intelligent and eager. All Sleepless.

Leisha learned.

Tony's parents, like her own, had divorced. But Tony, fourte, lived with his mother, who had not particularly wanted a Sleepless child, while his father, who had, acquired a red hovercar and a young girlfriend who designed ergonomic chairs in Paris. Tony was not allowed to tell anyone—relatives, schoolmates—that he was Sleepless. "They'll think you're a freak," his mother said, eyes averted from her son's face. The one time Tony disobeyed her and told a friend that he never slept, his mother beat him. Then she moved the family to a new neighborhood. He was nine years old.

Jeanine, almost as long-legged and slim as Leisha, was training for the Olympics in ice skating. She practiced twelve hours a day, hours no Sleeper still in high school could ever have. So far the newspapers had not picked up the story. Jeanine was afraid that, if they did, they would somehow not let her compete.

Jack, like Leisha, would start college in September. Unlike Leisha, he had already started his career. The practice of law had to wait for law school; the practice of investment required only money. Jack didn't have much, but his precise financial analyses parlayed $600 saved from summer jobs to $3000 through stock-market investing, then to $10,000, and then he had enough to qualify for information-fund speculation. Jack was fifteen, not old enough to make legal investments; the transactions were all in the name of Kevin Baker, the oldest of the Sleepless, who lived in Austin. Jack told Leisha, "When I hit 84 percent profit over two consecutive quarters, the data analysts logged onto me. They were just sniffing. Well, that's their job, even when the overall amounts are actually small. It's the patterns they care about. If they take the trouble to cross-reference data banks and come up with the fact that Kevin is a Sleepless, will they try to stop us from investing somehow?"

"That's paranoid," Leisha said.

"No, it's not," Jeanine said. "Leisha, you don't *know*."

"You mean because I've been protected by my father's money and caring," Leisha said. No one grimaced; all of them confronted ideas openly, without shadowy allusions. Without dreams.

"Yes," Jeanine said. "Your father sounds terrific. And he raised you to think that achievement should not be fettered—Jesus Christ, he's a Yagaiist. Well, good. We're glad for you." She said it without sarcasm. Leisha nodded. "But the world isn't always like that. They hate us."

"That's too strong," Carol said. "Not hate."

"Well, maybe," Jeanine said. "But they're different from us. We're better, and they naturally resent that."

"I don't see what's natural about it," Tony said. "Why shouldn't it be just as natural to admire what's better? We do. Does any one of us resent Kenzo Yagai for his genius? Or Nelson Wade, the physicist? Or Catherine Raduski?"

"We don't resent them because we *are* better," Richard said. "Q.E.D."

"What we should do is have our own society," Tony said. "Why should we allow their regulations to restrict our natural, honest achievements? Why should Jeanine be barred from skating against them and Jack from investing on their same terms just because we're Sleepless? Some of them are brighter than others of them. Some have greater persistence. Well, we have greater concentration, more biochemical stability, and more time. All men are not created equal."

"Be fair, Jack—no one has been barred from anything yet," Jeanine said.

"But we will be."

"*Wait*," Leisha said. She was deeply troubled by the conversation. "I mean, yes, in many ways we're better. But you quoted out of context, Tony. The Declaration of Independence doesn't say all men are created equal in ability. It's talking about rights and power—it means that all are created equal *under the law*. We have no more right to a separate society or to being free of society's restrictions than anyone else does. There's no other way to freely trade one's efforts, unless the same contractual rules apply to all."

"Spoken like a true Yagaiist," Richard said, squeezing her hand.

"That's enough intellectual discussion for me," Carol said, laughing. "We've been at this for hours. We're at the beach, for Chrissake. Who wants to swim with me?"

"I do," Jeanine said. "Come on, Jack."

All of them rose, brushing sand off their suits, discarding sunglasses. Richard pulled Leisha to her feet. But just before they ran into the water, Tony put his skinny hand on her arm. "One more question, Leisha. Just to think about. If we achieve better than most other people, and we trade with the Sleepers when it's mutually beneficial, making no distinction there between the strong and the weak—what obligation do we have to those so weak they don't have anything to trade with us? We're already going to give more than we get—do we have to do it when we get nothing at all? Do we have to take care of their deformed and handicapped and sick and lazy and shiftless with the products of our work?"

"Do the Sleepers have to?" Leisha countered.

"Kenzo Yagai would say no. He's a Sleeper."

"He would say they would receive the benefits of contractual trade even if they aren't direct parties to the contract. The whole world is better-fed and healthier because of Y-energy."

"Come on!" Jeanine yelled. "Leisha, they're dunking me! Jack, you stop that! Leisha, help me!"

Leisha laughed. Just before she grabbed for Jeanine, she caught the look on Richard's face, on Tony's: Richard frankly lustful, Tony angry. At her. But why? What had she done, except argue in favor of dignity and trade?

Then Jack threw water on her, and Carol pushed Jack into the warm spray, and Richard was there with his arms around her, laughing.

When she got the water out of her eyes, Tony was gone.

Midnight. "Okay," Carol said. "Who's first?"

The six teenagers in the brambled clearing looked at each other. A Y-lamp, kept on low for atmosphere, cast weird shadows across their faces and over their bare legs. Around the clearing Roger Camden's trees stood thick and dark, a wall between them and the closest of the estate's outbuildings. It was very hot. August air hung heavy, sullen. They had voted against bringing an air-conditioned Y-field because this was a return to the primitive, the dangerous; let it be primitive.

Six pairs of eyes stared at the glass in Carol's hand.

"Come *on*," she said. "Who wants to drink up?" Her voice was jaunty, theatrically hard. "It was difficult enough to get this."

"How *did* you get it?" said Richard, the group member—except for Tony—with the least influential family contacts, the least money. "In a drinkable form like that?"

"My cousin Brian is a pharmaceutical supplier to the Biotech Institute. He's curious." Nods around the circle; except for Leisha, they were Sleepless precisely because they had relatives somehow connected to Biotech. And everyone was curious. The glass held interleukin-1, an immune system booster, one of many substances which as a side effect induced the brain to swift and deep sleep.

Leisha stared at the glass. A warm feeling crept through her lower belly, not unlike the feeling when she and Richard made love.

Tony said, "Give it to me!"

Carol did. "Remember—you only need a little sip."

Tony raised the glass to his mouth, stopped, looked at them over the rim from his fierce eyes. He drank.

Carol took back the glass. They all watched Tony. Within a minute he lay on the rough ground; within two, his eyes closed in sleep.

It wasn't like seeing parents sleep, siblings, friends. It was Tony. They looked away, didn't meet each other's eyes. Leisha felt the warmth between her legs tug and tingle, faintly obscene.

When it was her turn, she drank slowly, then passed the glass to Jeanine. Her head turned heavy, as if it were being stuffed with damp rags. The trees at the edge of the clearing blurred. The portable lamp blurred, too—it wasn't bright and clean anymore but squishy, blobby; if she touched it, it would smear. Then darkness swooped over her brain, taking it away: *Taking away her mind.* "Daddy!" She tried to call, to clutch for him, but then the darkness obliterated her.

Afterward, they all had headaches. Dragging themselves back through the woods in the thin morning light was torture, compounded by an odd shame. They didn't touch each other. Leisha walked as far away from Richard as she could. It was a whole day before the throbbing left the base of her skull, or the nausea her stomach.

There had not even been any dreams.

"I want you to come with me tonight," Leisha said, for the tenth or twelfth time. "We both leave for college in just two days; this is the last chance. I really want you to meet Richard."

Alice lay on her stomach across her bed. Her hair, brown and lusterless, fell around her face. She wore an expensive yellow jumpsuit, silk by Ann Patterson, which rucked up in wrinkles around her knees.

"Why? What do you care if I meet Richard or not?"

"Because you're my sister," Leisha said. She knew better than to say "my twin." Nothing got Alice angry faster.

"I don't want to." The next moment Alice's face changed. "Oh, I'm sorry, Leisha—I didn't mean to sound so snotty. But . . . but I don't want to."

"It won't be all of them. Just Richard. And just for an hour or so. Then you can come back here and pack for Northwestern."

"I'm not going to Northwestern."

Leisha stared at her.

Alice said, "I'm pregnant."

Leisha sat on the bed. Alice rolled onto her back, brushed the hair out of her eyes, and laughed. Leisha's ears closed against the sound. "Look at you," Alice said. "You'd think it was *you* who was pregnant. But you never would be, would you, Leisha? Not until it was the proper time. Not you."

"How?" Leisha said. "We both had our caps put in . . ."

"I had the cap removed," Alice said.

"You wanted to get pregnant?"

"Damn flash I did. And there's not a thing Daddy can do about it. Except, of course, cut off all credit completely, but I don't think he'll do that, do you?" She laughed again. "Even to me?"

"But Alice . . . why? Not just to anger Daddy!"

"No," Alice said. "Although you would think of that, wouldn't you? Because I want something to love. Something of my *own*. Something that has nothing to do with this house."

Leisha thought of her and Alice running through the conservatory, years ago, her and Alice, darting in and out of the sunlight. "It hasn't been so bad growing up in this house."

"Leisha, you're stupid. I don't know how anyone so smart can be so stupid. Get out of my room! Get out!"

"But Alice . . . a *baby* . . ."

"Get out!" Alice shrieked. "Go to Harvard! Go be successful! Just get out!"

Leisha jerked off the bed. "Gladly! You're irrational, Alice! You don't think ahead, you don't plan a *baby* . . ." But she could never sustain anger. It dribbled away, leaving her mind empty. She looked at Alice, who suddenly put out her arms. Leisha went into them.

"You're the baby," Alice said wonderingly. "You *are*. You're so . . . I don't know what. You're a baby."

Leisha said nothing. Alice's arms felt warm, felt whole, felt like two children running in and out of sunlight. "I'll help you, Alice. If Daddy won't."

Alice abruptly pushed her away. "I don't need your help."

Alice stood. Leisha rubbed her empty arms, fingertips scraping across opposite elbows. Alice kicked the empty, open trunk in which she was supposed to pack for Northwestern, and then abruptly smiled, a smile that made Leisha look away. She braced herself for more abuse. But what Alice said, very softly, was, "Have a good time at Harvard."

5

She loved it.

From the first sight of Massachusetts Hall, older than the United States by a half century, Leisha felt something that had been missing in Chicago: Age. Roots. Tradition. She touched the bricks of Widener Library, the glass cases in the Peabody Museum, as if they were the grail. She had never been particularly sensitive to myth or drama; the anguish of Juliet seemed to her artificial, that of Willy Lòan merely wasteful. Only King Arthur, struggling to create a better social order, had interested her. But now, walking under the huge autumn trees, she suddenly caught a glimpse of a force that could span generations, fortunes left to endow learning and achievement the benefactors would never see, individual effort spanning and shaping centuries to come. She stopped, and looked at the sky through the leaves, at the buildings solid with purpose. At such moments she thought of Camden, bending the will of an entire genetic research Institute to create her in the image he wanted.

Within a month, she had forgotten all such mega-musings.

The work load was incredible, even for her. The Sauley School had encouraged individual exploration at her own pace; Harvard knew what it wanted from her, at its pace. In the last twenty years, under the academic leadership of a man who in his youth had watched Japanese economic domination with dismay, Harvard had become the controversial leader of a return to hard-edged learning of facts, theories, applications, problem-solving, intellectual efficiency. The school accepted one out of every two hundred applications from around the world. The daughter of England's Prime Minister had flunked out her first year and been sent home.

Leisha had a single room in a new dormitory, the dorm because she had spent so many years isolated in Chicago and was hungry for people, the single so she would not disturb anyone else when she worked all night. Her second day a boy from down the hall sauntered in and perched on the edge of her desk.

"So you're Leisha Camden."

"Yes."

"Sixteen years old."

"Almost seventeen."

"Going to out-perform us all, I understand, without even trying."

Leisha's smile faded. The boy stared at her from under lowered downy brows. He was smiling, his eyes sharp. From Richard and Tony and the others Leisha had learned to recognize the anger that presented itself as contempt.

"Yes," Leisha said coolly, "I am."

"Are you sure? With your pretty little-girl hair and your mutant little-girl brain?"

"Oh, leave her alone, Hannaway," said another voice. A tall blond boy, so thin his ribs looked like ripples in brown sand, stood in jeans and bare feet, drying his wet hair. "Don't you ever get tired of walking around being an asshole?"

"Do you?" Hannaway said. He heaved himself off the desk and started toward the door. The blond moved out of his way. Leisha moved into it.

"The reason I'm going to do better than you," she said evenly, "is because I have certain advantages you don't. Including sleeplessness. And then after I 'out-perform' you, I'll be glad to help you study for your tests so that you can pass, too."

The blond, drying his ears, laughed. But Hannaway stood still, and into his eyes came an expression that made Leisha back away. He pushed past her and stormed out.

"Nice going, Camden," the blond said. "He deserved that."

"But I meant it," Leisha said. "I will help him study."

The blond lowered his towel and stared. "You did, didn't you? You meant it."

"Yes! Why does everybody keep questioning that?"

"Well," the boy said, "I don't. You can help me if I get into trouble." Suddenly he smiled. "But I won't."

"Why not?"

"Because I'm just as good at anything as you are, Leisha Camden."

She studied him. "You're not one of us. Not Sleepless."

"Don't have to be. I know what I can do. Do, be, create, trade."

She said, delighted, "You're a Yagaiist!"

"Of course." He held out his hand. "Stewart Sutter. How about a fishburger in the Yard?"

"Great," Leisha said. They walked out together, talking excitedly. When people stared at her, she tried not to notice. She was here. At Harvard. With space ahead of her, time to learn, and with people like Stewart Sutter who accepted and challenged her.

All the hours he was awake.

She became totally absorbed in her classwork. Roger Camden drove up once, walking the campus with her, listening, smiling. He was more at home than Leisha would have expected: He knew Stewart Sutter's father, Kate Addams' grandfather. They talked about Harvard, business, Harvard, the Yagai Economics Institute, Harvard. "How's Alice?" Leisha asked once, but Camden said that he didn't know, she had moved out and did not want to see him. He made her an allowance through his attorney. While he said this, his face remained serene.

Leisha went to the Homecoming Ball with Stewart, who was also majoring in pre-law but was two years ahead of Leisha. She took a weekend trip to Paris with Kate Addams and two other girlfriends, taking the Concorde III. She had a fight with Stewart over whether the metaphor of superconductivity could apply to Yagaiism, a stupid fight they both knew was stupid but had anyway, and afterward they became lovers. After the fumbling sexual explorations with Richard, Stewart was deft, experienced, smiling faintly as he taught her how to have an orgasm both by herself and with him. Leisha was dazzled. "It's so *joyful*," she said, and Stewart looked at her with a tenderness she knew was part disturbance but didn't know why.

At mid-semester she had the highest grades in the freshman class. She got every answer right on every single question on her mid-terms. She and Stewart went out for a beer to celebrate, and when they came back Leisha's room had been destroyed. The computer was smashed, the data banks wiped, hardcopies and books smoldering in a metal wastebasket. Her clothes were ripped to pieces, her desk and bureau hacked apart. The only thing untouched, pristine, was the bed.

Stewart said, "There's no way this could have been done in silence. Everyone on the floor—hell, on the floor *below*—had to know. Someone will talk to the police." No one did. Leisha sat on the edge of the bed, dazed, and looked at the remnants of her Homecoming gown. The next day Dave Hannaway gave her a long, wide smile.

Camden flew east again, taut with rage. He rented her an apartment in Cambridge with E-lock security and a bodyguard named Toshio. After he left, Leisha fired the bodyguard but kept the apartment. It gave her and Stewart more privacy, which they used to endlessly discuss the situation. It was Leisha who argued that it was an aberration, an immaturity.

"There have always been haters, Stewart. Hate Jews, hate Blacks, hate immigrants, hate Yagaiists who have more initiative and dignity than you do. I'm just the latest object of hatred. It's not new, it's not remarkable. It doesn't mean any basic kind of schism between the Sleepless and Sleepers."

Stewart sat up in bed and reached for the sandwiches on the night stand. "Doesn't it? Leisha, you're a different kind of person entirely. More evolutionarily fit, not only to survive but to prevail. Those other 'objects of hatred' you cite except Yagaiists—they were all powerless in their societies. They occupied *inferior* positions. You, on the other hand—all three Sleepless in Harvard Law are on the *Law Review*. All of them. Kevin Baker, your oldest, has already founded a successful bio-interface software firm and is making money, a lot of it. Every Sleepless is making superb grades, none have psychological problems, all are healthy—and most of you aren't even adults yet. How much hatred do you think you're going to encounter once you hit the big-stakes world of finance and business and scarce endowed chairs and national politics?"

"Give me a sandwich," Leisha said. "Here's my evidence you're wrong: You yourself. Kenzo Yagai. Kate Addams. Professor Lane. My father. Every Sleeper who inhabits the world of fair trade, mutually beneficial contracts. And that's most of you, or at least most of you who are worth considering. You believe that competition among the most capable leads to the most beneficial trades for everyone, strong and weak. Sleepless are making real and concrete contributions to society, in a lot of fields. That has to outweigh the discomfort we cause. We're *valuable* to you. You know that."

Stewart brushed crumbs off the sheets. "Yes. I do. Yagaiists do."

"Yagaiists run the business and financial and academic worlds. Or they will. In a meritocracy, they *should*. You underestimate the majority of people, Stew. Ethics aren't confined to the ones out front."

"I hope you're right," Stewart said. "Because, you know, I'm in love with you."

Leisha put down her sandwich.

"Joy," Stewart mumbled into her breasts, "you are joy."

When Leisha went home for Thanksgiving, she told Richard about Stewart. He listened tight-lipped.

"A Sleeper."

"A *person*," Leisha said. "A good, intelligent, achieving person!"

"Do you know what your good intelligent achieving Sleepers have done, Leisha? Jeanine has been barred from Olympic skating. 'Genetic alteration, analogous to steroid abuse to create an unsportsmanlike advantage.' Chris Devereaux's left Stanford. They trashed his laboratory, destroyed two years' work in memory formation proteins. Kevin Baker's software company is fighting a nasty advertising campaign, all underground of course, about kids using software designed by 'non-human minds.' Corruption, mental slavery, satanic influences: the whole bag of witch-hunt tricks. Wake up, Leisha!"

They both heard his words. Moments dragged by. Richard stood like a boxer, forward on the balls of his feet, teeth clenched. Finally he said, very quietly, "Do you love him?"

"Yes," Leisha said. "I'm sorry."

"Your choice," Richard said coldly. "What do you do while he's asleep? Watch?"

"You make it sound like a perversion!"

Richard said nothing. Leisha drew a deep breath. She spoke rapidly but calmly, a controlled rush: "While Stewart is asleep I work. The same as you do. Richard—don't do this. I didn't mean to hurt you. And I don't want to lose the group. I believe the Sleepers are the same species as we are—are you going to punish me for that? Are you going to *add* to the hatred? Are you going to tell me that I can't belong to a wider world that includes all honest, worthwhile people whether they sleep or not? Are you going to tell me that the most important division is by genetics and not by economic spirituality? Are you going to force me into an artificial choice, 'us' or 'them'?"

Richard picked up a bracelet. Leisha recognized it: She had given it to him in the summer. His voice was quiet. "No. It's not a choice." He played with the gold links a minute, then looked up at her. "Not yet."

By spring break, Camden walked more slowly. He took medicine for his blood pressure, his heart. He and Susan, he told Leisha, were getting a divorce. "She changed, Leisha, after I married her. You saw that. She was independent and productive and happy, and then after a few years she stopped all that and became a shrew. A whining shrew." He shook his head in genuine bewilderment. "You saw the change."

Leisha had. A memory came to her: Susan leading her and Alice in "games" that were actually controlled cerebral-performance tests, Susan's braids dancing around her sparkling eyes. Alice had loved Susan, then, as much as Leisha had.

"Dad, I want Alice's address."

"I told you up at Harvard, I don't have it," Camden said. He shifted in his chair, the impatient gesture of a body that never expected to wear out. In January Kenzo Yagai had died of pancreatic cancer; Camden had taken the news hard. "I make her allowance through an attorney. By her choice."

"Then I want the address of the attorney."

The attorney, however, refused to tell Leisha where Alice was. "She doesn't want to be found, Ms. Camden. She wanted a complete break."

"Not from me," Leisha said.

"Yes," the attorney said, and something flickered behind his eyes, something she had last seen in Dave Hannaway's face.

She flew to Austin before returning to Boston, making her a day late for classes. Kevin Baker saw her instantly, canceling a meeting with IBM. She told him what she needed, and he set his best data-net people on it, without telling them why. Within two hours she had Alice's address from the attorney's electronic files. It was the first time, she realized, that she had ever turned to one of the Sleepless for help, and it had been given instantly. Without trade.

Alice was in Pennsylvania. The next weekend Leisha rented a hovercar and driver—she had learned to drive, but only groundcars as yet—and went to High Ridge, in the Appalachian Mountains.

It was an isolated hamlet, twenty-five miles from the nearest hospital. Alice lived with a man named Ed, a silent carpenter twenty years older than she, in a cabin in the woods. The cabin had water and electricity but no news net. In the early spring light the earth was raw and bare, slashed with icy gullies. Alice and Ed apparently worked at nothing. Alice was eight months pregnant.

"I didn't want you here," she said to Leisha. "So why are you?"

"Because you're my sister."

"God, look at you. Is that what they're wearing at Harvard? Boots like that? When did you become fashionable, Leisha? You were always too busy being intellectual to care."

"What's this all about, Alice? Why here? What are you doing?"

"Living," Alice said. "Away from dear Daddy, away from Chicago, away from drunken broken Susan—did you know she drinks? Just like Mom. He does that to people. But not to me. I got out. I wonder if you ever will."

"Got out? To *this*?"

"I'm happy," Alice said angrily. "Isn't that what it's supposed to be about? Isn't that the aim of your great Kenzo Yagai—happiness through individual effort?"

Leisha thought of saying that Alice was making no efforts that she could see. She didn't say it. A chicken ran through the yard of the cabin. Behind, the mountains rose in layers of blue haze. Leisha thought what this place must have been like in winter: cut off from the world where people strived towards goals, learned, changed.

"I'm glad you're happy, Alice."

"Are you?"

"Yes."

"Then I'm glad, too," Alice said, almost defiantly. The next moment she abruptly hugged Leisha, fiercely, the huge hard mound of her belly crushed between them. Alice's hair smelled sweet, like fresh grass in sunlight.

"I'll come see you again, Alice."

"Don't," Alice said.

6

SLEEPLESS MUTIE BEGS FOR REVERSAL OF GENE TAMPERING, screamed the headline in the Food Mart. "PLEASE LET ME SLEEP LIKE REAL PEOPLE!" CHILD PLEADS.

Leisha typed in her credit number and pressed the news kiosk for a printout, although ordinarily she ignored the electronic tabloids. The headline went on circling the kiosk. A Food Mart employee stopped stacking boxes on shelves and watched her. Bruce, Leisha's bodyguard, watched the employee.

She was twenty-two, in her final year at Harvard Law, editor of the Law Review, ranked first in her class. The next three were Jonathan Cocchiara, Len Carter, and Martha Wentz. All Sleepless.

In her apartment she skimmed the print-out. Then she accessed the Groupnet run from Austin. The files had more news stories about the child, with comments from other Sleepless, but before she could call them up Kevin Baker came on-line himself, on voice.

"Leisha. I'm glad you called. I was going to call you."

"What's the situation with this Stella Bevington, Kev? Has anybody checked it out?"

"Randy Davies. He's from Chicago but I don't think you've met him, he's still in high school. He's in Park Ridge, Stella's in Skokie. Her parents wouldn't talk to him—were pretty abusive, in fact—but he got to see Stella face-to-face anyway. It doesn't look like an abuse case, just the usual stupidity: parents wanted a genius child, scrimped and saved, and now they can't handle that she *is* one. They scream at her to sleep, get emotionally abusive when she contradicts them, but so far no violence."

"Is the emotional abuse actionable?"

"I don't think we want to move on it yet. Two of us will keep in close touch with Stella—she does have a modem, and she hasn't told her parents about the net—and Randy will drive out weekly."

Leisha bit her lip. "A tabloid shitpiece said she's seven years old."

"Yes."

"Maybe she shouldn't be left there. I'm an Illinois resident, I can file an abuse grievance from here if Candy's got too much in her briefcase. . . ." *Seven years old.*

"No. Let it sit a while. Stella will probably be all right. You know that."

She did. Nearly all of the Sleepless stayed "all right," no matter how much opposition came from the stupid segment of society. And it was only the stupid segment, Leisha argued—a small if vocal minority. Most people could, and would, adjust to the growing presence of the Sleepless, when it became clear that that presence included not only growing power but growing benefits to the country as a whole.

Kevin Baker, now twenty-six, had made a fortune in micro-chips so revolutionary that Artificial Intelligence, once a debated dream, was yearly closer to reality. Carolyn Rizzolo had won the Pulitzer Prize in drama for her play *Morning Light*. She was twenty-four. Jeremy Robinson had done significant work in superconductivity applications while still a graduate student at Stanford. William Thaine, *Law Review* editor when Leisha first came to Harvard, was now in private practice. He had never lost a case. He was twenty-six, and the cases were becoming important. His clients valued his ability more than his age.

But not everyone reacted that way.

Kevin Baker and Richard Keller had started the datanet that bound the Sleepless into a tight group, constantly aware of each other's personal fights. Leisha Camden financed the legal battles, the educational costs of Sleepless whose parents were unable to meet them, the support of children in emotionally bad situations. Rhonda Lavelier got herself licensed as a foster mother in California, and whenever possible the Group maneuvered to have small Sleepless who were removed from their homes assigned to Rhonda. The Group now had three ABA lawyers; within the next year they would gain four more, licensed to practice in five different states.

The one time they had not been able to remove an abused Sleepless child legally, they kidnapped him.

Timmy DeMarzo, four years old. Leisha had been opposed to the action. She had argued the case morally and pragmatically—to her they were the same thing—thus: If they believed in their society, in its fundamental laws and in their ability to belong to it as free-trading productive individuals, they must remain bound by the society's contractual laws. The Sleepless were, for the most part, Yagaiists. They should already know this. And if the FBI caught them, the courts and press would crucify them.

They were not caught.

Timmy DeMarzo—not even old enough to call for help on the datanet, they had learned of the situation through the automatic police-record scan Kevin maintained through his company—was stolen from his own backyard in Wichita. He had lived the last year in an isolated trailer in North Dakota; no place was too isolated for a modem. He was cared for by a legally irreproachable foster mother who had lived there all her life. The foster mother was second cousin to a Sleepless, a broad cheerful woman with a much better brain than her appearance indicated. She was a Yagaiist. No record of the child's existence appeared in any data bank: not the IRS, not any school's, not even the local grocery store's computerized check-out slips. Food specifically for the child was shipped in monthly on a truck owned by a Sleepless in State College, Pennsylvania. Ten of the Group knew about the kidnapping, out of the total 3,428 born in the United States. Of that total, 2,691 were part of the Group via the net. Another 701 were as yet too young to use a modem. Only 36 Sleepless, for whatever reason, were not part of the Group.

The kidnapping had been arranged by Tony Indivino.

"It's Tony I wanted to talk to you about," Kevin said to Leisha. "He's started again. This time he means it. He's buying land."

She folded the tabloid very small and laid it carefully on the table. "Where?"

"Allegheny Mountains. In southern New York State. A lot of land. He's putting in the roads now. In the spring, the first buildings."

"Jennifer Sharifi still financing it?" She was the American-born daughter of an Arab prince who had wanted a Sleepless child. The prince was dead and Jennifer, dark-eyed and multilingual, was richer than Leisha would one day be.

"Yes. He's starting to get a following, Leisha."

"I know."

"Call him."

"I will. Keep me informed about Stella."

She worked until midnight at the *Law Review*, then until four A.M. preparing her classes. From four to five she handled legal matters for the Group. At five A.M. she called Tony, still in Chicago. He had finished high school, done one semester at Northwestern, and at Christmas vacation he had finally exploded at his mother for forcing him to live as a Sleeper. The explosion, it seemed to Leisha, had never ended.

"Tony? Leisha."

"The answer is yes, yes, no, and go to hell."

Leisha gritted her teeth. "Fine. Now tell me the questions."

"Are you really serious about the Sleepless withdrawing into their own self-sufficient society? Is Jennifer Sharifi willing to finance a project the size of building a small city? Don't you think that's a cheat of all that can be accomplished by patient integration of the Group into the mainstream? And what about the contradictions of living in an armed restricted city and still trading with the Outside?"

"I would never tell *you* to go to hell."

"Hooray for you," Tony said. After a moment he added, "I'm sorry. That sounds like one of *them*."

"It's wrong for us, Tony."

"Thanks for not saying I couldn't pull it off."

She wondered if he could. "We're not a separate species, Tony."

"Tell that to the Sleepers."

"You exaggerate. There are haters out there, there are *always* haters, but to give up . . ."

"We're not giving up. Whatever we create can be freely traded: software, hardware, novels, information, theories, legal counsel. We can travel in and out. But we'll have a safe place to return *to*. Without the leeches who think we owe them blood because we're better than they are."

"It isn't a matter of owing."

"Really?" Tony said. "Let's have this out, Leisha. All the way. You're a Yagaiist—what do you believe in?"

"Tony . . ."

"Do *it*," Tony said, and in his voice she heard the fourteen-year-old Richard had introduced her to. Simultaneously, she saw her father's face: not as he was now, since the by-pass, but as he had been when she was a little girl, holding her on his lap to explain that she was special.

"I believe in voluntary trade that is mutually beneficial. That spiritual dignity comes from supporting one's life through one's own efforts, and trading the results of those efforts in mutual cooperation throughout the society. That the symbol of this is the contract. And that we need each other for the fullest, most beneficial trade."

"Fine," Tony bit off. "Now what about the beggars in Spain?"

"The what?"

"You walk down a street in a poor country like Spain and you see a beggar. Do you give him a dollar?"

"Probably."

"Why? He's trading nothing with you. He has nothing to trade."

"I know. Out of kindness. Compassion."

"You see six beggars. Do you give them all a dollar?"

"Probably," Leisha said.

"You would. You see a hundred beggars and you haven't got Leisha Camden's money—do you give them each a dollar?"

"No."

"Why not?"

Leisha reached for patience. Few people could make her want to cut off a comm link; Tony was one of them. "Too draining on my own resources. My life has first claim on the resources I earn."

"All right. Now consider this. At Biotech Institute—where you and I began, dear pseudo-sister—Dr. Melling has just yesterday—"

"*Who?*"

"Dr. Susan Melling. Oh, God, I completely forgot—she used to be married to your father!"

"I lost track of her," Leisha said. "I didn't realize she'd gone back to research. Alice once said . . . never mind. What's going on at Biotech?"

"Two crucial items, just released. Carla Dutcher has had first-month fetal genetic analysis. Sleeplessness is a dominant gene. The next generation of the Group won't sleep either."

"We all knew that," Leisha said. Carla Dutcher was the world's first pregnant Sleepless. Her husband was a Sleeper. "The whole world expected that."

"But the press will have a windfall with it anyway. Just watch. Muties Breed! New Race Set To Dominate Next Generation of Children!"

Leisha didn't deny it. "And the second item?"

"It's sad, Leisha. We've just had our first death."

Her stomach tightened. "Who?"

"Bernie Kuhn. Seattle." She didn't know him. "A car accident. It looks pretty straightforward—he lost control on a steep curve when his brakes failed. He had only been driving a few months. He was seventeen. But the significance here is that his parents have donated his brain and body to Biotech, in conjunction with the pathology department at the Chicago Medical School. They're going to take him apart to get the first good look at what prolonged sleeplessness does to the body and brain."

"They should," Leisha said. "That poor kid. But what are you so afraid they'll find?"

"I don't know. I'm not a doctor. But whatever it is, if the haters can use it against us, they will."

"You're paranoid, Tony."

"Impossible. The Sleepless have personalities calmer and more reality-oriented than the norm. Don't you read the literature?"

"Tony—"

"What if you walk down that street in Spain and a hundred beggars each want a dollar and you say no and they have nothing to trade you but they're so rotten with anger about what you have that they knock you down and grab it and then beat you out of sheer envy and despair?"

Leisha didn't answer.

"Are you going to say that's not a human scenario, Leisha? That it never happens?"

"It happens," Leisha said evenly. "But not all that often."

"Bullshit. Read more history. Read more *newspapers*. But the point is: What do you owe the beggars then? What does a good Yagaiist who believes in mutually beneficial contracts do with people who have nothing to trade and can only take?"

"You're not—"

"*What*, Leisha? In the most objective terms you can manage, what do we owe the grasping and non-productive needy?"

"What I said originally. Kindness. Compassion."

"Even if they don't trade it back? Why?"

"Because . . ." She stopped.

"Why? Why do law-abiding and productive human beings owe anything to those who neither produce very much nor abide by laws? What philosophical or economic or spiritual justification is there for owing them anything? Be as honest as I know you are."

Leisha put her head between her knees. The question gaped beneath her, but she didn't try to evade it. "I don't know. I just know we do."

"Why?"

She didn't answer. After a moment, Tony did. The intellectual challenge was gone from his voice. He said, almost tenderly, "Come down in the spring and see the site for Sanctuary. The buildings will be going up then."

"No," Leisha said.

"I'd like you to."

"No. Armed retreat is not the way."

Tony said, "The beggars are getting nastier, Leisha. As the Sleepless grow richer. And I don't mean in money."

"Tony—" she said, and stopped. She couldn't think what to say.

"Don't walk down too many streets armed with just the memory of Kenzo Yagai."

In March, a bitterly cold March of winds whipping down the Charles River, Richard Keller came to Cambridge. Leisha had not seen him for four years. He didn't send her word on the Groupnet that he was coming. She hurried up the walk to her townhouse, muffled to the eyes in a red wool scarf against the snowy cold, and he stood there blocking the doorway. Behind Leisha, her bodyguard tensed.

"Richard! Bruce, it's all right, this is an old friend."

"Hello, Leisha."

He was heavier, sturdier-looking, with a breadth of shoulder she didn't recognize. But the face was Richard's, older but unchanged: dark low brows, unruly dark hair. He had grown a beard.

"You look beautiful," he said.

She handed him a cup of coffee. "Are you here on business?" From the Groupnet she knew that he had finished his Master's and had done outstanding work in marine biology in the Caribbean, but had left that a year ago and disappeared from the net.

"No. Pleasure." He smiled suddenly, the old smile that opened up his dark face. "I almost forgot about that for a long time. Contentment, yes, we're all good at the contentment that comes from sustained work, but pleasure? Whim? Caprice? When was the last time you did something silly, Leisha?"

She smiled. "I ate cotton candy in the shower."

"Really? Why?"

"To see if it would dissolve in gooey pink patterns."

"Did it?"

"Yes. Lovely ones."

"And that was your last silly thing? When was it?"

"Last summer," Leisha said, and laughed.

"Well, mine is sooner than that. It's now. I'm in Boston for no other reason than the spontaneous pleasure of seeing you."

Leisha stopped laughing. "That's an intense tone for a spontaneous pleasure, Richard."

"Yup," he said, intensely. She laughed again. He didn't.

"I've been in India, Leisha. And China and Africa. Thinking, mostly. Watching. First I traveled like a Sleeper, attracting no attention. Then I set out to meet the Sleepless in India and China. There are a few, you know, whose parents were willing to come here for the operation. They pretty much are accepted and left alone. I tried to figure out why desperately poor countries—by our standards anyway, over there Y-energy is mostly available only in big cities—don't have any trouble accepting the superiority of Sleepless, whereas Americans, with more prosperity than any time in history, build in resentment more and more."

Leisha said, "Did you figure it out?"

"No. But I figured out something else, watching all those communes and villages and kampongs. We are too individualistic."

Disappointment swept Leisha. She saw her father's face: *Excellence is what counts, Leisha. Excellence supported by individual effort.* . . . She reached for Richard's cup. "More coffee?"

He caught her wrist and looked up into her face. "Don't misunderstand me, Leisha. I'm not talking about work. We are too much individuals in the rest of our lives. Too emotionally rational. Too much alone. Isolation kills more than the free flow of ideas. It kills joy."

He didn't let go of her wrist. She looked down into his eyes, into depths she hadn't seen before: It was the feeling of looking into a mine shaft, both giddy and frightening, knowing that at the bottom might be gold or darkness. Or both.

Richard said softly, "Stewart?"

"Over long ago. An undergraduate thing." Her voice didn't sound like her own.

"Kevin?"

"No, never—we're just friends."

"I wasn't sure. Anyone?"

"No."

He let go of her wrist. Leisha peered at him timidly. He suddenly laughed. "Joy, Leisha." An echo sounded in her mind, but she couldn't place it and then it was gone and she laughed too, a laugh airy and frothy as pink cotton candy in summer.

"Come home, Leisha. He's had another heart attack."

Susan Melling's voice on the phone was tired. Leisha said, "How bad?"

"The doctors aren't sure. Or say they're not sure. He wants to see you. Can you leave your studies?"

It was May, the last push toward her finals. The *Law Review* proofs were behind schedule. Richard had started a new business, marine consulting to Boston fishermen plagued with sudden inexplicable shifts in ocean currents, and was working twenty hours a day. "I'll come," Leisha said.

Chicago was colder than Boston. The trees were half-budded. On Lake Michigan, filling the huge east windows of her father's house, whitecaps tossed up cold spray. Leisha saw that Susan was living in the house: her brushes on Camden's dresser, her journals on the credenza in the foyer.

"Leisha," Camden said. He looked old. Gray skin, sunken cheeks, the fretful and bewildered look of men who accepted potency like air, indivisible from their lives. In the corner of the room, on a small eighteenth-century slipper chair, sat a short, stocky woman with brown braids.

"*Alice.*"

"Hello, Leisha."

"*Alice*. I've looked for you. . . ." The wrong thing to say. Leisha had looked, but not very hard, deterred by the knowledge that Alice had not wanted to be found. "How are you?"

"I'm fine," Alice said. She seemed remote, gentle, unlike the angry Alice of six years ago in the raw Pennsylvania hills. Camden moved painfully on the bed. He looked at Leisha with eyes which, she saw, were undimmed in their blue brightness.

"I asked Alice to come. And Susan. Susan came a while ago. I'm dying, Leisha."

No one contradicted him. Leisha, knowing his respect for facts, remained silent. Love hurt her chest.

"John Jaworski has my will. None of you can break it. But I wanted to tell you myself what's in it. The last few years I've been selling, liquidating. Most of my holdings are accessible now. I've left a tenth to Alice, a tenth to Susan, a tenth to Elizabeth, and the rest to you, Leisha, because you're the only one with the individual ability to use the money to its full potential for achievement."

Leisha looked wildly at Alice, who gazed back with her strange remote calm. "Elizabeth? My . . . mother? Is alive?"

"Yes," Camden said.

"You told me she was dead! Years and years ago!"

"Yes. I thought it was better for you that way. She didn't like what you were, was jealous of what you could become. And she had nothing to give you. She would only have caused you emotional harm."

Beggars in Spain . . .

"That was wrong, Dad. You were *wrong*. She's my *mother* . . ." She couldn't finish the sentence.

Camden didn't flinch. "I don't think I was. But you're an adult now. You can see her if you wish."

He went on looking at her from his bright, sunken eyes, while around Leisha the air heaved and snapped. Her father had lied to her. Susan watched her closely, a small smile on her lips. Was she glad to see Camden fall in his daughter's estimation? Had she all along been that jealous of their relationship, of Leisha . . .

She was thinking like Tony.

The thought steadied her a little. But she went on staring at Camden, who went on staring implacably back, unbudged, a man positive even on his death bed that he was right.

Alice's hand was on her elbow, Alice's voice so soft that no one but Leisha could hear. "He's done now, Leisha. And after a while you'll be all right."

Alice had left her son in California with her husband of two years, Beck Watrous, a building contractor she had met while waitressing in a resort on the Artificial Islands. Beck had adopted Jordan, Alice's son.

"Before Beck there was a real bad time," Alice said in her remote voice. "You know, when I was carrying Jordan I actually used to dream that he would be Sleepless? Like you. Every night I'd dream that, and every morning I'd wake up and have morning sickness with a baby that was only going to be a stupid nothing like me. I stayed with Ed—in Pennsylvania, remember? You came to see me there once—for two more years. When he beat me, I was glad. I wished Daddy could see. At least Ed was touching me."

Leisha made a sound in her throat.

"I finally left because I was afraid for Jordan. I went to California, did nothing but eat for a year. I got up to 190 pounds." Alice was, Leisha estimated, five-foot-four. "Then I came home to see Mother."

"You didn't tell me," Leisha said. "You knew she was alive and you didn't tell me."

"She's in a drying-out tank half the time," Alice said, with brutal simplicity. "She wouldn't see you if you wanted to. But she saw me, and she fell slobbering all over me as her 'real' daughter, and she threw up on my dress. And I backed away from her and looked at the dress and knew it *should* be thrown up on, it was so ugly. Deliberately ugly. She started screaming how Dad had ruined her life, ruined mine, all for *you*. And do you know what I did?"

"What?" Leisha said. Her voice was shaky.

"I flew home, burned all my clothes, got a job, started college, lost fifty pounds, and put Jordan in play therapy."

The sisters sat silent. Beyond the window the lake was dark, unlit by moon or stars. It was Leisha who suddenly shook, and Alice who patted her shoulder.

"Tell me . . ." Leisha couldn't think what she wanted to be told, except that she wanted to hear Alice's voice in the gloom, Alice's voice as it was now, gentle and remote, without damage any more from the damaging fact of Leisha's existence. Her very existence as damage. ". . . tell me about Jordan. He's five now? What's he like?"

Alice turned her head to look levelly into Leisha's eyes. "He's a happy, ordinary little boy. Completely ordinary."

Camden died a week later. After the funeral, Leisha tried to see her mother at the Brookfield Drug and Alcohol Abuse Center. Elizabeth Camden, she was told, saw no one except her only child, Alice Camden Watrous.

Susan Melling, dressed in black, drove Leisha to the airport. Susan talked deftly, determinedly, about Leisha's studies, about Harvard, about the *Review*. Leisha answered in monosyllables but Susan persisted, asking questions, quietly insisting on answers: When would Leisha take her bar exams? Where was she interviewing for jobs? Gradually Leisha began to lose the numbness she had felt since her father's casket was lowered into the ground. She realized that Susan's persistent questioning was a kindness.

"He sacrificed a lot of people," Leisha said suddenly.

"Not me," Susan said. She pulled the car into the airport parking lot. "Only for a while there, when I gave up my work to do his. Roger didn't respect sacrifice much."

"Was he wrong?" Leisha said. The question came out with a kind of desperation she hadn't intended.

Susan smiled sadly. "No. He wasn't wrong. I should never have left my research. It took me a long time to come back to myself after that."

He does that to people, Leisha heard inside her head. Susan? Or Alice? She couldn't, for once, remember clearly. She saw her father in the old conservatory, potting and repotting the dramatic exotic flowers he had loved.

She was tired. It was muscle fatigue from stress, she knew; twenty minutes of rest would restore her. Her eyes burned from unaccustomed tears. She leaned her head back against the car seat and closed them.

Susan pulled the car into the airport parking lot and turned off the ignition. "There's something I want to tell you, Leisha."

Leisha opened her eyes. "About the will?"

Susan smiled tightly. "No. You really don't have any problems with how he divided the estate, do you? It seems to you reasonable. But that's not it. The research team from Biotech and Chicago Medical has finished its analysis of Bernie Kuhn's brain."

Leisha turned to face Susan. She was startled by the complexity of Susan's expression. Determination, and satisfaction, and anger, and something else Leisha could not name.

Susan said, "We're going to publish next week, in the *New England Journal of Medicine*. Security has been unbelievably restricted—no leaks to the popular press. But I want to tell you now, myself, what we found. So you'll be prepared."

"Go on," Leisha said. Her chest felt tight.

"Do you remember when you and the other Sleepless kids took interleukin-1 to see what sleep was like? When you were sixteen?"

"How did you know about that?"

"You kids were watched a lot more closely than you think. Remember the headache you got?"

"Yes." She and Richard and Tony and Carol and Jeanine . . . after her rejection by the Olympic Committee, Jeanine had never skated again. She was a kindergarten teacher in Butte, Montana.

"Interleukin-1 is what I want to talk about. At least partly. It's one of a whole group of substances that boost the immune system. They stimulate the production of antibodies, the activity of white blood cells, and a host of other immunoenhancements. Normal people have surges of IL-1 released during the slow-wave phases of sleep. That means that they—we—are getting boosts to the immune system during sleep. One of the questions we researchers asked ourselves twenty-eight years ago was: Will Sleepless kids who don't get those surges of IL-1 get sick more often?"

"I've never been sick," Leisha said.

"Yes, you have. Chicken pox and three minor colds by the end of your fourth year," Susan said precisely. "But in general you were all a very healthy lot. So we researchers were left with the alternate theory of sleep-driven immunoenhancement: That the burst of immune activity existed as a counterpart to a greater vulnerability of the body in sleep to disease, probably in some way connected to the fluctuations in body temperature during REM sleep. In other words, sleep *caused* the immune vulnerability that endogenous pyrogens like IL-1 counteract. Sleep was the problem, immune system enhancements were the solution. Without sleep, there would be no problem. Are you following this?"

"Yes."

"Of course you are. Stupid question." Susan brushed her hair off her face. It was going gray at the temples. There was a tiny brown age spot beneath her right ear.

"Over the years we collected thousands—maybe hundreds of thousands—of Single Photon Emission Tomography scans of you and the other kids' brains, plus endless EEG's, samples of cerebrospinal fluid, and all the rest of it. But we couldn't really see inside your brains, really know what's going on in there. Until Bernie Kuhn hit that embankment."

"Susan," Leisha said, "give it to me straight. Without more build-up."

"You're not going to age."

"What?"

"Oh, cosmetically, yes. Gray hair, wrinkles, sags. But the absence of sleep peptides and all the rest of it affects the immune and tissue-restoration systems in ways we don't understand. Bernie Kuhn had a perfect liver. Perfect lungs, perfect heart, perfect lymph nodes, perfect pancreas, perfect medulla oblongata. Not just healthy, or young—*perfect*. There's a tissue regeneration enhancement that clearly derives from the operation of the immune system but is radically different from anything we ever suspected. Organs show no wear and tear—not even the minimal amount expected in a seventeen-year-old. They just repair themselves, perfectly, on and on . . . and on."

"For how long?" Leisha whispered.

"Who the hell knows? Bernie Kuhn was young—maybe there's some compensatory mechanism that cuts in at some point and you'll all just collapse, like an entire fucking gallery of Dorian Grays. But I don't think so. Neither do I think it can go on forever; no tissue regeneration can do that. But a long, long time."

Leisha stared at the blurred reflections in the car windshield. She saw her father's face against the blue satin of his casket, banked with white roses. His heart, unregenerated, had given out.

Susan said, "The future is all speculative at this point. We know that the peptide structures that build up the pressure to sleep in normal people resemble the components of bacterial cell walls. Maybe there's a connection between sleep and pathogen receptivity. We don't know. But ignorance never stopped the tabloids. I wanted to prepare you because you're going to get called supermen, *homo perfectus*, who-all-knows what. Immortal."

The two women sat in silence. Finally Leisha said, "I'm going to tell the others. On our datanet. Don't worry about the security. Kevin Baker designed Groupnet; nobody knows anything we don't want them to."

"You're that well organized already?"

"Yes."

Susan's mouth worked. She looked away from Leisha. "We better go in. You'll miss your flight."

"Susan . . ."

"What?"

"Thank you."

"You're welcome," Susan said, and in her voice Leisha heard the thing she had seen before in Susan's expression and not been able to name: It was longing.

Tissue regeneration. A *long, long time,* sang the blood in Leisha's ears on the flight to Boston. *Tissue regeneration.* And, eventually: *Immortal.* No, not that, she told herself severely. Not that. The blood didn't listen.

"You sure smile a lot," said the man next to her in first class, a business traveler who had not recognized Leisha. "You coming from a big party in Chicago?"

"No. From a funeral."

The man looked shocked, then disgusted. Leisha looked out the window at the ground far below. Rivers like micro-circuits, fields like neat index cards. And on the horizon, fluffy white clouds like masses of exotic flowers, blooms in a conservatory filled with light.

The letter was no thicker than any hard-copy mail, but hard-copy mail addressed by hand to either of them was so rare that Richard was nervous. "It might be explosive." Leisha looked at the letter on their hall credenza. MS. LIESHA CAMDEN. Block letters, misspelled.

"It looks like a child's writing," she said.

Richard stood with head lowered, legs braced apart. But his expression was only weary. "Perhaps deliberately like a child's. You'd be more open to a child's writing, they might have figured."

"'They'? Richard, are we getting that paranoid?"

He didn't flinch from the question. "Yes. For the time being."

A week earlier the *New England Journal of Medicine* had published Susan's careful, sober article. An hour later the broadcast and datanet news had exploded in speculation, drama, outrage, and fear. Leisha and Richard, along with all the Sleepless on the Groupnet, had tracked and charted each of four components, looking for a dominant reaction: speculation ("The Sleepless may live for centuries, and this might lead to the following events . . ."); drama ("If a Sleepless marries only Sleepers, he may have lifetime enough for a dozen brides—and several dozen children, a bewildering blended family . . ."); outrage ("Tampering with the law of nature has only brought among us unnatural so-called people who will live with the unfair advantage of time: time to accumulate more kin, more power, more property than the rest of us could ever know. . . ."); and fear ("How soon before the Super-race takes over?").

"They're all fear, of one kind or another," Carolyn Rizzolo finally said, and the Groupnet stopped their differentiated tracking.

Leisha was taking the final exams of her last year of law school. Each day comments followed her to the campus, along the corridors and in the classroom; each day she forgot them in the grueling exam sessions, all students reduced to the same status of petitioner to the great university. Afterward, temporarily drained, she walked silently back home to Richard and the Groupnet, aware of the looks of people on the street, aware of her bodyguard Bruce striding between her and them.

"It will calm down," Leisha said. Richard didn't answer.

The town of Salt Springs, Texas, passed a local ordinance that no Sleepless could obtain a liquor license, on the grounds that civil rights statutes were built on the "all men were created equal" clause of the Constitution, and Sleepless clearly were not covered. There were no Sleepless within a hundred miles of Salt Springs and no one had applied for a new liquor license there for the past ten years, but the story was picked up by United Press and by Datanet News, and within twenty-four hours heated editorials appeared, on both sides of the issue, across the nation.

More local ordinances appeared. In Pollux, Pennsylvania, the Sleepless could be denied apartment rental on the grounds that their prolonged wakefulness would increase both wear-and-tear on the landlord's property and utility bills. In Cranston Estates, California, Sleepless were barred from operating twenty-four hour businesses: "unfair competition." Iroquois County, New York, barred them from serving on county juries, arguing that a jury containing Sleepless, with their skewed idea of time, did not constitute "a jury of one's peers."

"All those statutes will be thrown out in superior courts," Leisha said. "But God! The waste of money and docket time to do it!" A part of her mind noticed that her tone as she said this was Roger Camden's.

The state of Georgia, in which some sex acts between consenting adults were still a crime, made sex between a Sleepless and a Sleeper a third-degree felony, classing it with bestiality.

Kevin Baker had designed software that scanned the newsnets at high speed, flagged all stories involving discrimination or attacks on Sleepless, and categorized them by type. The files were available on Groupnet. Leisha read through them, then called Kevin. "Can't you create a parallel program to flag defenses of us? We're getting a skewed picture."

"You're right," Kevin said, a little startled. "I didn't think of it."

"Think of it," Leisha said, grimly. Richard, watching her, said nothing.

She was most upset by the stories about Sleepless children. Shunning at school, verbal abuse by siblings, attacks by neighborhood bullies, confused resentment from parents who had wanted an exceptional child but had not bargained on one who might live centuries. The school board of Cold River, Iowa, voted to bar Sleepless children from conventional classrooms because their rapid learning "created feelings of inadequacy in others, interfering with their education." The board made funds available for Sleepless to have tutors at home. There were no volunteers among the teaching staff. Leisha started spending as much time on Groupnet with the kids, talking to them all night long, as she did studying for her bar exams, scheduled for July.

Stella Bevington stopped using her modem.

Kevin's second program catalogued editorials urging fairness towards Sleepless. The school board of Denver set aside funds for a program in which gifted children, including the Sleepless, could use their talents and build teamwork through tutoring even younger children. Rive Beau, Louisiana, elected Sleepless Danielle du

Chemey to the City Council, although Danielle was twenty-two and technically too young to qualify. The prestigious medical research firm of Halley-Hall gave much publicity to their hiring of Christopher Amren, a Sleepless with a Ph.D. in cellular physics.

Dora Clarq, a Sleepless in Dallas, opened a letter addressed to her and a plastic explosive blew off her arm.

Leisha and Richard stared at the envelope on the hall credenza. The paper was thick, cream-colored, but not expensive: the kind of paper made of bulky newsprint dyed the shade of vellum. There was no return address. Richard called Liz Bishop, a Sleepless who was majoring in Criminal Justice in Michigan. He had never spoken with her before—neither had Leisha—but she came on Groupnet immediately and told them how to open it, or she could fly up and do it if they preferred. Richard and Leisha followed her directions for remote detonation in the basement of the townhouse. Nothing blew up. When the letter was open, they took it out and read it:

Dear Ms. Camden,
  You been pretty good to me and I'm sorry to do this but I quit. They are making it pretty hot for me at the union not officially but you know how it is. If I was you I wouldn't go to the union for another bodyguard I'd try to find one privately. But be careful. Again I'm sorry but I have to live too.
                                                          Bruce

"I don't know whether to laugh or cry," Leisha said. "The two of us getting all this equipment, spending hours on this set-up so an explosive won't detonate . . ."

"It's not as if I at least had a whole lot else to do," Richard said. Since the wave of anti-Sleepless sentiment, all but two of his marine-consultant clients, vulnerable to the marketplace and thus to public opinion, had canceled their accounts.

Groupnet, still up on Leisha's terminal, shrilled in emergency override. Leisha got there first. It was Tony.

"Leisha. I'll need your legal help, if you'll give it. They're trying to fight me on Sanctuary. Please fly down here."

Sanctuary was raw brown gashes in the late-spring earth. It was situated in the Allegheny Mountains of southern New York State, old hills rounded by age and covered with pine and hickory. A superb road led from the closest town, Belmont, to Sanctuary. Low, maintenance-free buildings, whose design was plain but graceful, stood in various stages of completion. Jennifer Sharifi, looking strained, met Leisha and Richard. "Tony wants to talk to you, but first he asked me to show you both around."

"What's wrong?" Leisha asked quietly. She had never met Jennifer before but no Sleepless looked like that—pinched, spent, *weary*—unless the stress level was enormous.

Jennifer didn't try to evade the question. "Later. First look at Sanctuary. Tony respects your opinion enormously, Leisha; he wants you to see everything."

The dormitories each held fifty, with communal rooms for cooking, dining, relaxing, and bathing, and a warren of separate offices and studios and labs for work.

"We're calling them 'dorms' anyway, despite the etymology," Jennifer said, trying to smile. Leisha glanced at Richard. The smile was a failure.

She was impressed, despite herself, with the completeness of Tony's plans for lives that would be both communal and intensely private. There was a gym, a small hospital—"By the end of next year, we'll have eighteen AMA-certified doctors, you know, and four are thinking of coming here"—a daycare facility, a school, an intensive-crop farm. "Most of our food will come in from the outside, of course. So will most people's jobs, although they'll do as much of them as possible from here, over datanets. We're not cutting ourselves off from the world—only creating a safe place from which to trade with it." Leisha didn't answer.

Apart from the power facilities, self-supported Y-energy, she was most impressed with the human planning. Tony had Sleepless interested from virtually every field they would need both to care for themselves and to deal with the outside world. "Lawyers and accountants come first," Jennifer said. "That's our first line of defense in safeguarding ourselves. Tony recognizes that most modern battles for power are fought in the courtroom and boardroom."

But not all. Last, Jennifer showed them the plans for physical defense. She explained them with a mixture of defiance and pride: Every effort had been made to stop attackers without hurting them. Electronic surveillance completely circled the 150 square miles Jennifer had purchased—some *counties* were smaller than that, Leisha thought, dazed. When breached, a force field a half-mile within the E-gate activated, delivering electric shocks to anyone on foot—"But only on the *outside* of the field. We don't want any of our kids hurt." Unmanned penetration by vehicles or robots was identified by a system that located all moving metal above a certain mass within Sanctuary. Any moving metal that did not carry a special signaling device designed by Donna Pospula, a Sleepless who had patented important electronic components, was suspect.

"Of course, we're not set up for an air attack or an outright army assault," Jennifer said. "But we don't expect that. Only the haters in self-motivated hate." Her voice sagged.

Leisha touched the hard-copy of the security plans with one finger. They troubled her. "If we can't integrate ourselves into the world . . . free trade should imply free movement."

"Yeah. Well," Jennifer said, such an uncharacteristic Sleepless remark—both cynical and inarticulate—that Leisha looked up. "I have something to tell you, Leisha."

"What?"

"Tony isn't here."

"Where is he?"

"In Allegheny County jail. It's true we're having zoning battles about Sanctuary—zoning! In this isolated spot! But this is something else, something that just happened this morning. Tony's been arrested for the kidnapping of Timmy DeMarzo."

The room wavered. "FBI?"

"Yes."

"How . . . how did they find out?"

"Some agent eventually cracked the case. They didn't tell us how. Tony needs a lawyer, Leisha. Dana Monteiro has already agreed, but Tony wants you."

"Jennifer—I don't even take the bar exams until July!"

"He says he'll wait. Dana will act as his lawyer in the meantime. Will you pass the bar?"

"Of course. But I already have a job lined up with Morehouse, Kennedy, & Anderson in New York—" She stopped. Richard was looking at her hard, Jennifer gazing down at the floor. Leisha said quietly, "What will he plead?"

"Guilty," Jennifer said, "with—what is it called legally? Extenuating circumstances."

Leisha nodded. She had been afraid Tony would want to plead not guilty: more lies, subterfuge, ugly politics. Her mind ran swiftly over extenuating circumstances, precedents, tests to precedents. . . . They could use *Clements v. Voy* . . .

"Dana is at the jail now," Jennifer said. "Will you drive in with me?"

"Yes."

In Belmont, the county seat, they were not allowed to see Tony. Dana Monteiro, as his attorney, could go in and out freely. Leisha, not officially an attorney at all, could go nowhere. This was told them by a man in the D.A.'s office whose face stayed immobile while he spoke to them, and who spat on the ground behind their shoes when they turned to leave, even though this left him with a smear of spittle on his courthouse floor.

Richard and Leisha drove their rental car to the airport for the flight back to Boston. On the way Richard told Leisha he was leaving her. He was moving to Sanctuary, now, even before it was functional, to help with the planning and building.

She stayed most of the time in her townhouse, studying ferociously for the bar exams or checking on the Sleepless children through Groupnet. She had not hired another bodyguard to replace Bruce, which made her reluctant to go outside very much; the reluctance in turn made her angry with herself. Once or twice a day she scanned Kevin's electronic news clippings.

There were signs of hope. The New York *Times* ran an editorial, widely reprinted on the electronic news services:

Prosperity and Hatred: A Logic Curve We'd Rather Not See

The United States has never been a country that much values calm, logic, rationality. We have, as a people, tended to label these things "cold." We have, as a people, tended to admire feeling and action: We exalt in our stories and our memorials, not the creation of the Constitution but its defense at Iwo Jima; not the intellectual achievements of a Stephen Hawking but the heroic passion of a Charles Lindbergh; not the inventors of the monorails and computers that unite us but the composers of the angry songs of rebellion that divide us.

A peculiar aspect of this phenomenon is that it grows stronger in times of prosperity. The better off our citizenry, the greater their contempt for the calm reasoning that got them there, and the more passionate their indulgence in emotion. Consider, in the last century, the gaudy excesses of the Roaring Twenties and the anti-establishment contempt of the sixties. Consider, in our own century, the unprecedented prosperity brought about by Y-energy—and then consider that Kenzo Yagai, except to his followers, was seen as a greedy and bloodless logician, while our national adulation goes to neo-nihilist writer Stephen Castelli, to "feelie" actress Brenda Foss, and to daredevil gravity-well diver Jim Morse Luter.

But most of all, as you ponder this phenomenon in your Y-energy houses, consider the current outpouring of irrational feeling directed at the "Sleepless" since the publication of the joint findings of the Biotech Institute and the Chicago Medical School concerning Sleepless tissue regeneration.

Most of the Sleepless are intelligent. Most of them are calm, if you define that much-maligned word to mean directing one's energies into solving problems rather than to emoting about them. (Even Pulitzer Prize winner Carolyn Rizzolo gave us a stunning play of ideas, not of passions run amuck.) All of them show a natural bent toward achievement, a bent given a decided boost by the one-third more time in their days to achieve in. Their achievements lie, for the most part, in logical fields rather than emotional ones: Computers. Law. Finance. Physics. Medical research. They are rational, orderly, calm, intelligent, cheerful, young, and possibly very long-lived.

And, in our United States of unprecedented prosperity, increasingly hated.

Does the hatred that we have seen flower so fully over the last few months really grow, as many claim, from the "unfair advantage" the Sleepless have over the rest of us in securing jobs, promotions, money, success? Is it really envy over the Sleepless' good fortune? Or does it come from something more pernicious, rooted in our tradition of shoot-from-the-hip American action: Hatred of the logical, the calm, the considered? Hatred in fact of the superior mind?

If so, perhaps we should think deeply about the founders of this country: Jefferson, Washington, Paine, Adams—inhabitants of the Age of Reason, all. These men created our orderly and balanced system of laws precisely to protect the property and achievements created by the individual efforts of balanced and rational minds. The Sleepless may be our severest internal test yet of our own sober belief in law and order. No, the Sleepless were *not* "created equal," but our attitudes toward them should be examined with a care equal to our soberest jurisprudence. We may not like what we learn about our own motives, but our credibility as a people may depend on the rationality and intelligence of the examination.

Both have been in short supply in the public reaction to last month's research findings.

Law is not theater. Before we write laws reflecting gaudy and dramatic feelings, we must be very sure we understand the difference.

Leisha hugged herself, gazing in delight at the screen, smiling. She called the New York *Times*: Who had written the editorial? The receptionist, cordial when she answered the phone, grew brusque. The *Times* was not releasing that information, "prior to internal investigation."

It could not dampen her mood. She whirled around the apartment, after days of sitting at her desk or screen. Delight demanded physical action. She washed dishes, picked up books. There were gaps in the furniture patterns where Richard had taken pieces that belonged to him; a little quieter now, she moved the furniture to close the gaps.

Susan Melling called to tell her about the *Times* editorial; they talked warmly for a few minutes. When Susan hung up, the phone rang again.

"Leisha? Your voice still sounds the same. This is Stewart Sutter."

"Stewart." She had not seen him for years. Their romance had lasted two years and then dissolved, not from any painful issue so much as from the press of both their studies. Standing by the comm terminal, hearing his voice, Leisha suddenly felt again his hands on her breasts in the cramped dormitory bed: All those years before she had found a good use for a bed. The phantom hands became Richard's hands, and a sudden pain pierced her.

"Listen," Stewart said, "I'm calling because there's some information I think you should know. You take your bar exams next week, right? And then you have a tentative job with Morehouse, Kennedy, & Anderson."

"How do you know all that, Stewart?"

"Men's room gossip. Well, not as bad as that. But the New York legal community—that part of it, anyway—is smaller than you think. And, you're a pretty visible figure."

"Yes," Leisha said neutrally.

"Nobody has the slightest doubt you'll be called to the bar. But there is some doubt about the job with Morehouse, Kennedy. You've got two senior partners, Alan Morehouse and Seth Brown, who have changed their minds since this . . . flap. 'Adverse publicity for the firm,' 'turning law into a circus,' blah blah blah. You know the drill. But you've also got two powerful champions, Ann Carlyle and Michael Kennedy, the old man himself. He's quite a mind. Anyway, I wanted you to know all this so you can recognize exactly what the situation is and know whom to count on in the in-fighting."

"Thank you," Leisha said. "Stew . . . why do you care if I get it or not? Why should it matter to you?"

There was a silence on the other end of the phone. Then Stewart said, very low, "We're not all noodleheads out here, Leisha. Justice does still matter to some of us. So does achievement."

Light rose in her, a bubble of buoyant light.

Stewart said, "You have a lot of support here for that stupid zoning fight over Sanctuary, too. You might not realize that, but you do. What the Parks Commission crowd is trying to pull is . . . but they're just being used as fronts. You know that. Anyway, when it gets as far as the courts, you'll have all the help you need."

"Sanctuary isn't my doing. At all."

"No? Well, I meant the plural you."

"Thank you. I mean that. How are you doing?"

"Fine. I'm a daddy now."

"Really! Boy or girl?"

"Girl. A beautiful little bitch, drives me crazy. I'd like you to meet my wife sometime, Leisha."

"I'd like that," Leisha said.

She spent the rest of the night studying for her bar exams. The bubble stayed with her. She recognized exactly what it was: joy.

It was going to be all right. The contract, unwritten, between her and her society—Kenzo Yagai's society, Roger Camden's society—would hold. With dissent and strife and yes, some hatred: She suddenly thought of Tony's beggars in Spain, furious at the strong because they themselves were not. Yes. But it would hold.

She believed that.

She did.

7

Leisha took her bar exams in July. They did not seem hard to her. Afterward three classmates, two men and a woman, made a fakely casual point of talking to Leisha until she had climbed safely into a taxi whose driver obviously did not recognize her, or stop signs. The three were all Sleepers. A pair of undergraduates, clean-shaven blond men with the long faces and pointless arrogance of rich stupidity, eyed Leisha and sneered. Leisha's female classmate sneered back.

Leisha had a flight to Chicago the next morning. Alice was going to join her there. They had to clean out the big house on the lake, dispose of Roger's personal property, put the house on the market. Leisha had had no time to do it earlier.

She remembered her father in the conservatory, wearing an ancient flat-topped hat he had picked up somewhere, potting orchids and jasmine and passion flowers.

When the doorbell rang she was startled; she almost never had visitors. Eagerly, she turned on the outside camera—maybe it was Jonathan or Martha, back in Boston to surprise her, to celebrate—why hadn't she thought before about some sort of celebration?

Richard stood gazing up at the camera. He had been crying.

She tore open the door. Richard made no move to come in. Leisha saw that what the camera had registered as grief was actually something else: tears of rage.

"Tony's dead."

Leisha put out her hand, blindly. Richard did not take it.

"They killed him in prison. Not the authorities—the other prisoners. In the recreation yard. Murderers, rapists, looters, scum of the earth—and they thought they had the right to kill *him* because he was different."

Now Richard did grab her arm, so hard that something, some bone, shifted beneath the flesh and pressed on a nerve. "Not just different—*better*. Because he was better, because we all are, we goddamn just don't stand up and shout it out of some misplaced feeling for *their* feelings . . . God!"

Leisha pulled her arm free and rubbed it, numb, staring at Richard's contorted face.

"They beat him to death with a lead pipe. No one even knows how they got a lead pipe. They beat him on the back of the head and they rolled him over and—"

"Don't!" Leisha said. It came out a whimper.

Richard looked at her. Despite his shouting, his violent grip on her arm, Leisha had the confused impression that this was the first time he had actually seen her. She went on rubbing her arm, staring at him in terror.

He said quietly, "I've come to take you to Sanctuary, Leisha. Dan Walcott and Vernon Bulriss are in the car outside. The three of us will carry you out; if necessary. But you're coming. You see that, don't you? You're not safe here, with your high profile and your spectacular looks—you're a natural target if anyone is. Do we have to force you? Or do you finally see for yourself that we have no choice—the bastards have left us no choice—except Sanctuary?"

Leisha closed her eyes. Tony, at fourteen, at the beach. Tony, his eyes ferocious and alight, the first to reach out his hand for the glass of interleukin-1. Beggars in Spain.

"I'll come."

She had never known such anger. It scared her, coming in bouts throughout the long night, receding but always returning again. Richard held her in his arms, sitting with their backs against the wall of her library, and his holding made no difference at all. In the living room Dan and Vernon talked in low voices.

Sometimes the anger erupted in shouting, and Leisha heard herself and thought *I don't know you.* Sometimes it became crying, sometimes talking about Tony, about all of them. Not the shouting nor the crying nor the talking eased her at all.

Planning did, a little. In a cold dry voice she didn't recognize, Leisha told Richard about the trip to close the house in Chicago. She had to go; Alice was already there. If Richard and Dan and Vernon put Leisha on the plane, and Alice met her at the other end with union bodyguards, she should be safe enough. Then she would change her return ticket from Boston to Belmont and drive with Richard to Sanctuary.

"People are already arriving," Richard said. "Jennifer Sharifi is organizing it, greasing the Sleeper suppliers with so much money they can't resist. What about this townhouse here, Leisha? Your furniture and terminal and clothes?"

Leisha looked around her familiar office. Law books lined the walls, red and green and brown, although most of the same information was on-line. A coffee cup rested on a print-out on the desk. Beside it was the receipt she had requested from the taxi driver this afternoon, a giddy souvenir of the day she had passed her bar exams; she had thought of having it framed. Above the desk was a holographic portrait of Kenzo Yagai.

"Let it rot," Leisha said.

Richard's arm tightened around her.

"I've never seen you like this," Alice said, subdued. "It's more than just clearing out the house, isn't it?"

"Let's get on with it," Leisha said. She yanked a suit from her father's closet. "Do you want any of this stuff for your husband?"

"It wouldn't fit."

"The hats?"

"No," Alice said. "Leisha—what is it?"

"Let's just *do* it!" She yanked all the clothes from Camden's closet, piled them on the floor, scrawled FOR VOLUNTEER AGENCY on a piece of paper and dropped it on top of the pile. Silently, Alice started adding clothes from the dresser, which already bore a taped paper scrawled ESTATE AUCTION.

The curtains were already down throughout the house; Alice had done that yesterday. She had also rolled up the rugs. Sunset glared redly on the bare wooden floors.

"What about your old room?" Leisha said. "What do you want there?"

"I've already tagged it," Alice said. "A mover will come Thursday."

"Fine. What else?"

"The conservatory. Sanderson has been watering everything, but he didn't really know what needed how much, so some of the plants are—"

"Fire Sanderson," Leisha said curtly. "The exotics can die. Or have them sent to a hospital, if you'd rather. Just watch out for the ones that are poisonous. Come on, let's do the library."

Alice sat slowly on a rolled-up rug in the middle of Camden's bedroom. She had cut her hair; Leisha thought it looked ugly, jagged brown spikes around her broad face. She had also gained more weight. She was starting to look like their mother.

Alice said, "Do you remember the night I told you I was pregnant? Just before you left for Harvard?"

"Let's do the library!"

"Do you?" Alice said. "For God's sake, can't you just once listen to someone else, Leisha? Do you have to be so much like Daddy every single minute?"

"I'm not like Daddy!"

"The hell you're not. You're exactly what he made you. But that's not the point. Do you remember that night?"

Leisha walked over the rug and out the door. Alice simply sat. After a minute Leisha walked back in. "I remember."

"You were near tears," Alice said implacably. Her voice was quiet. "I don't even remember exactly why. Maybe because I wasn't going to college after all. But I put my arms around you, and for the first time in years—years, Leisha—I felt you really were my sister. Despite all of it—the roaming the halls all night and the show-off arguments with Daddy and the special school and the artificially long legs and golden hair—all that crap. You seemed to need me to hold you. You seemed to need me to hold you. You seemed to need me. You seemed to *need*."

"What are you saying?" Leisha demanded. "That you can only be close to someone if they're in trouble and need you? That you can only be a sister if I was in some kind of pain, open sores running? Is that the bond between you Sleepers? 'Protect me while I'm unconscious, I'm just as crippled as you are'?"

"No," Alice said. "I'm saying that *you* could be a sister only if you were in some kind of pain."

Leisha stared at her. "You're stupid, Alice."

Alice said calmly, "I know that. Compared to you, I am. I know that."

Leisha jerked her head angrily. She felt ashamed of what she had just said, and yet it was true, and they both knew it was true, and anger still lay in her like a dark void, formless and hot. It was the formless part that was the worst. Without shape, there could be no action; without action, the anger went on burning her, choking her.

Alice said, "When I was twelve Susan gave me a dress for our birthday. You were away somewhere, on one of those overnight field trips your fancy progressive school did all the time. The dress was silk, pale blue, with antique lace—very beautiful. I was thrilled, not only because it was beautiful but because Susan had gotten it for me and gotten software for you. The dress was mine. Was, I thought, *me*." In the gathering gloom Leisha could barely make out her broad, plain features. "The first time I wore it a boy said, 'Stole your sister's dress, Alice? Snitched it while she was *sleeping*?' Then he laughed like crazy, the way they always did.

"I threw the dress away. I didn't even explain to Susan, although I think she would have understood. Whatever was yours was yours, and whatever wasn't yours was yours, too. That's the way Daddy set it up. The way he hard-wired it into our genes."

"You, too?" Leisha said. "You're no different from the other envious beggars?"

Alice stood up from the rug. She did it slowly, leisurely, brushing dust off the back of her wrinkled skirt, smoothing the print fabric. Then she walked over and hit Leisha in the mouth.

"Now do you see me as real?" Alice asked quietly.

Leisha put her hand to her mouth. She felt blood. The phone rang. Camden's unlisted personal line. Alice walked over, picked it up, listened, and held it calmly out to Leisha. "It's for you."

Numb, Leisha took it.

"Leisha? This is Kevin. Listen, something's happened. Stella Bevington called me, on the phone not Groupnet, I think her parents took away her modem. I picked up the phone and she screamed, 'This is Stella! They're hitting me he's drunk—' and then the line went dead. Randy's gone to Sanctuary—hell, they've *all* gone. You're closest to her, she's still in Skokie. You better get there fast. Have you got bodyguards you trust?"

"Yes," Leisha said, although she hadn't. The anger—finally—took form. "I can handle it."

"I don't know how you'll get her out of there," Kevin said. "They'll recognize you, they know she called somebody, they might even have knocked her out . . ."

"I'll handle it," Leisha said.

"Handle what?" Alice said.

Leisha faced her. Even though she knew she shouldn't, she said, "What your people do. To one of ours. A seven-year-old kid who's getting beaten up by her parents because she's Sleepless—because she's *better* than you are—" She ran down the stairs and out to the rental car she had driven from the airport.

Alice ran right down with her. "Not your car, Leisha. They can trace a rental car just like that. My car."

Leisha screamed, "If you think you're—"

Alice yanked open the door of her battered Toyota, a model so old the Y-energy cones weren't even concealed but hung like drooping jowls on either side. She shoved Leisha into the passenger seat, slammed the door, and rammed herself behind the wheel. Her hands were steady. "Where?"

Blackness swooped over Leisha. She put her head down, as far between her knees as the cramped Toyota would allow. Two—no, three—days since she had eaten. Since the night before the bar exams. The faintness receded, swept over her again as soon as she raised her head.

She told Alice the address in Skokie.

"Stay way in the back," Alice said. "And there's a scarf in the glove compartment—put it on. Low, to hide as much of your face as possible."

Alice had stopped the car along Highway 42. Leisha said, "This isn't—"

"It's a union quick-guard place. We have to look like we have some protection, Leisha. We don't need to tell him anything. I'll hurry."

She was out in three minutes with a huge man in a cheap dark suit. He squeezed into the front seat beside Alice and said nothing at all. Alice did not introduce him.

The house was small, a little shabby, with lights on downstairs, none upstairs. The first stars shone in the north, away from Chicago. Alice said to the guard, "Get out of the car and stand here by the car door—no, more in the light—and don't do anything unless I'm attacked in some way." The man nodded. Alice started up the walk. Leisha scrambled out of the back seat and caught her sister two-thirds of the way to the plastic front door.

"Alice, what the hell are you doing? *I* have to—"

"Keep your voice down," Alice said, glancing at the guard. "Leisha, *think*. You'll be recognized. Here, near Chicago, with a Sleepless daughter—these people have looked at your picture in magazines for years. They've watched long-range holovids of you. They know you. They know you're going to be a lawyer. Me they've never seen. I'm nobody."

"Alice—"

"For Chrissake, get back in the car!" Alice hissed, and pounded on the front door.

Leisha drew off the walk, into the shadow of a willow tree. A man opened the door. His face was completely blank.

Alice said, "Child Protection Agency. We got a call from a little girl, this number. Let me in."

"There's no little girl here."

"This is an emergency, priority one," Alice said. "Child Protection Act 186. Let me in!"

The man, still blank-faced, glanced at the huge figure by the car. "You got a search warrant?"

"I don't need one in a priority-one child emergency. If you don't let me in, you're going to have legal snarls like you never bargained for."

Leisha clamped her lips together. No one would believe that, it was legal gobbledygook . . . Her lip throbbed where Alice had hit her.

The man stood aside to let Alice enter.

The guard started forward. Leisha hesitated, then let him. He entered with Alice. Leisha waited, alone, in the dark.

In three minutes they were out, the guard carrying a child. Alice's broad face gleamed pale in the porch light. Leisha sprang forward, opened the car door, and helped the guard ease the child inside. The guard was frowning, a slow puzzled frown shot with wariness.

Alice said, "Here. This is an extra hundred dollars. To get back to the city by yourself."

"Hey . . ." the guard said, but he took the money. He stood looking after them as Alice pulled away.

"He'll go straight to the police," Leisha said despairingly. "He has to, or risk his union membership."

"I know," Alice said. "But by that time we'll be out of the car."

"Where?"

"At the hospital," Alice said.

"Alice, we can't—" Leisha didn't finish. She turned to the back seat. "Stella? Are you conscious?"

"Yes," said the small voice.

Leisha groped until her fingers found the rear-seat illuminator. Stella lay stretched out on the back seat, her face distorted with pain. She cradled her left arm in her right. A single bruise colored her face, above the left eye.

"You're Leisha Camden," the child said, and started to cry.

"Her arm's broken," Alice said.

"Honey, can you . . ." Leisha's throat felt thick, she had trouble getting the words out ". . . can you hold on till we get you to a doctor?"

"Yes," Stella said. "Just don't take me back there!"

"We won't," Leisha said. "Ever." She glanced at Alice and saw Tony's face.

Alice said, "There's a community hospital about ten miles south of here."

"How do you know that?"

"I was there once. Drug overdose," Alice said briefly. She drove hunched over the wheel, with the face of someone thinking furiously. Leisha thought, too, trying to see a way around the legal charge of kidnapping. They probably couldn't say the child came willingly: Stella would undoubtedly cooperate but at her age and in her condition she was probably *non sui juris*, her word would have no legal weight . . .

"Alice, we can't even get her into the hospital without insurance information. Verifiable on-line."

"Listen," Alice said, not to Leisha but over her shoulder, toward the back seat, "here's what we're going to do, Stella. I'm going to tell them you're my daughter and you fell off a big rock you were climbing while we stopped for a snack at a roadside picnic area. We're driving from California to Philadelphia to see your grandmother. Your name is Jordan Watrous and you're five years old. Got that, honey?"

"I'm seven," Stella said. "Almost eight."

"You're a very large five. Your birthday is March 23. Can you do this, Stella?"

"Yes," the little girl said. Her voice was stronger.

Leisha stared at Alice. "Can *you* do this?"

"Of course I can," Alice said. "I'm Roger Camden's daughter."

Alice half-carried, half-supported Stella into the Emergency Room of the small community hospital. Leisha watched from the car: the short stocky woman, the child's thin body with the twisted arm. Then she drove Alice's car to the farthest corner of the parking lot, under the dubious cover of a skimpy maple, and locked it. She tied the scarf more securely around her face.

Alice's license plate number, and her name, would be in every police and rental-car databank by now. The medical banks were slower; often they uploaded from local precincts only once a day, resenting the governmental interference in what was still, despite a half-century of battle, a private-sector enterprise. Alice and Stella would probably be all right in the hospital. Probably. But Alice could not rent another car.

Leisha could.

But the data file that would flash to rental agencies on Alice Camden Watrous might or might not include that she was Leisha Camden's twin.

Leisha looked at the rows of cars in the lot. A flashy luxury Chrysler, an Ikeda van, a row of middle-class Toyotas and Mercedes, a vintage '99 Cadillac—she could imagine the owner's face if that were missing—ten or twelve cheap runabouts, a hovercar with the uniformed driver asleep at the wheel. And a battered farm truck.

Leisha walked over to the truck. A man sat at the wheel, smoking. She thought of her father.

"Hello," Leisha said.

The man rolled down his window but didn't answer. He had greasy brown hair.

"See that hovercar over there?" Leisha said. She made her voice sound young, high. The man glanced at it indifferently; from this angle you couldn't see that the driver was asleep. "That's my bodyguard. He thinks I'm in the hospital, the way my father told me to, getting this lip looked at." She could feel her mouth swollen from Alice's blow.

"So?"

Leisha stamped her foot. "So I don't want to be inside. He's a shit and so's Daddy. I want out. I'll give you 4,000 bank credits for your truck. Cash."

The man's eyes widened. He tossed away his cigarette, looked again at the hovercar. The driver's shoulders were broad, and the car was within easy screaming distance.

"All nice and legal," Leisha said, and tried to smirk. Her knees felt watery.

"Let me see the cash."

Leisha backed away from the truck, to where he could not reach her. She took the money from her arm clip. She was used to carrying a lot of cash; there had always been Bruce, or someone like Bruce. There had always been safety.

"Get out of the truck on the other side," Leisha said, "and lock the door behind you. Leave the keys on the seat, where I can see them from here. Then I'll put the money on the roof where you can see it."

The man laughed, a sound like gravel pouring. "Regular little Dabney Engh, aren't you? Is that what they teach you society debs at your fancy schools?"

Leisha had no idea who Dabney Engh was. She waited, watching the man try to think of a way to cheat her, and tried to hide her contempt. She thought of Tony.

"All right," he said, and slid out of the truck.

"Lock the door!"

He grinned, opened the door again, locked it. Leisha put the money on the roof, yanked open the driver's door, clambered in, locked the door, and powered up the window. The man laughed. She put the key into the ignition, started the truck, and drove toward the street. Her hands trembled.

She drove slowly around the block twice. When she came back, the man was gone, and the driver of the hovercar was still asleep. She had wondered if the man would wake him, out of sheer malice, but he had not. She parked the truck and waited.

An hour and a half later Alice and a nurse wheeled Stella out of the Emergency Entrance. Leisha leaped out of the truck and yelled, "Coming, Alice!" waving both her arms. It was too dark to see Alice's expression; Leisha could only hope that Alice showed no dismay at the battered truck, that she had not told the nurse to expect a red car.

Alice said, "This is Julie Bergadon, a friend that I called while you were setting Jordan's arm." The nurse nodded, uninterested. The two women helped Stella into the high truck cab; there was no back seat. Stella had a cast on her arm and looked drugged.

"How?" Alice said as they drove off.

Leisha didn't answer. She was watching a police hovercar land at the other end of the parking lot. Two officers got out and strode purposefully towards Alice's locked car under the skimpy maple.

"My God," Alice said. For the first time, she sounded frightened.

"They won't trace us," Leisha said. "Not to this truck. Count on it."

"Leisha." Alice's voice spiked with fear. "Stella's *asleep*."

Leisha glanced at the child, slumped against Alice's shoulder. "No, she's not. She's unconscious from painkillers."

"Is that all right? Normal? For . . . her?"

"We can black out. We can even experience substance-induced sleep." Tony and she and Richard and Jeanine in the midnight woods. . . . "Didn't you know that, Alice?"

"No."

"We don't know very much about each other, do we?"

They drove south in silence. Finally Alice said, "Where are we going to take her, Leisha?"

"I don't know. Any one of the Sleepless would be the first place the police would check—"

"You can't risk it. Not the way things are," Alice said. She sounded weary. "But all my friends are in California. I don't think we could drive this rust bucket that far before getting stopped."

"It wouldn't make it anyway."

"What should we do?"

"Let me think."

At an expressway exit stood a pay phone. It wouldn't be data-shielded, as Groupnet was. Would Kevin's open line be tapped? Probably.

There was no doubt the Sanctuary line would be.

Sanctuary. All of them going there or already there, Kevin had said. Holed up, trying to pull the worn Allegheny Mountains around them like a safe little den. Except for the children like Stella, who could not.

Where? With whom?

Leisha closed her eyes. The Sleepless were out; the police would find Stella within hours. Susan Melling? But she had been Alice's all-too-visible stepmother, and was co-beneficiary of Camden's will; they would question her almost immediately. It couldn't be anyone traceable to Alice. It could only be a Sleeper that Leisha knew, and trusted, and why should anyone at all fit that description? Why should she risk so much on anyone who did? She stood a long time in the dark phone kiosk. Then she walked to the truck. Alice was asleep, her head thrown back against the seat. A tiny line of drool ran down her chin. Her face was white and drained in the bad light from the kiosk. Leisha walked back to the phone.

"Stewart? Stewart Sutter?"

"Yes?"

"This is Leisha Camden. Something has happened." She told the story tersely, in bald sentences. Stewart did not interrupt.

"Leisha—" Stewart said, and stopped.

"I need help, Stewart." *'I'll help you, Alice.' 'I don't need your help.'* A wind whistled over the dark field beside the kiosk and Leisha shivered. She heard in the wind the thin keen of a beggar. In the wind, in her own voice.

"All right," Stewart said, "this is what we'll do. I have a cousin in Ripley, New York, just over the state line from Pennsylvania the route you'll be driving east. It has to be in New York, I'm licensed in New York. Take the little girl there. I'll call my cousin and tell her you're coming. She's an elderly woman, was quite an activist in her youth, her name is Janet Patterson. The town is—"

"What makes you so sure she'll get involved? She could go to jail. And so could you."

"She's been in jail so many times you wouldn't believe it. Political protests going all the way back to Vietnam. But no one's going to jail. I'm now your attorney of record. I'm privileged. I'm going to get Stella declared a ward of the state. That shouldn't be too hard with the hospital records you established in Skokie. Then she can be transferred to a foster home in New York, I know just the place, people who are fair and kind. Then Alice—"

"She's resident in Illinois. You can't—"

"Yes, I can. Since those research findings about the Sleepless life span have come out, legislators have been railroaded by stupid constituents scared or jealous or just plain angry. The result is a body of so-called 'law' riddled with contradictions, absurdities, and loopholes. None of it will stand in the long run—or at least I hope not—but in the meantime it can all be exploited. I can use it to create the most goddamn convoluted case for Stella that anybody ever saw, and in meantime she won't be returned home. But that won't work for Alice—she'll need an attorney licensed in Illinois."

"We have one," Leisha said. "Candace Holt."

"No, not a Sleepless. Trust me on this, Leisha. I'll find somebody good. There's a man in—are you crying?"

"No," Leisha said, crying.

"Ah, God," Stewart said. "Bastards. I'm sorry all this happened, Leisha."

"Don't be," Leisha said.

When she had directions to Stewart's cousin, she walked back to the truck. Alice was still asleep, Stella still unconscious. Leisha closed the truck door as quietly as possible. The engine balked and roared, but Alice didn't wake. There was a crowd of people with them in the narrow and darkened cab: Stewart Sutter, Tony Indivino, Susan Melling, Kenzo Yagai, Roger Camden.

To Stewart Sutter she said, You called to inform me about the situation at Morehouse, Kennedy. You are risking your career and your cousin for Stella. And you stand to gain nothing. Like Susan telling me in advance about Bernie Kuhn's brain. Susan, who lost her life to Daddy's dream and regained it by her own strength. A contract without consideration for each side is not a contract: Every first-year student knows that.

To Kenzo Yagai she said, Trade isn't always linear. You missed that. If Stewart gives me something, and I give Stella something, and ten years from now Stella is a different person because of that and gives something to someone else as yet unknown—it's an ecology. An *ecology* of trade, yes, each niche needed, even if they're not contractually bound. Does a horse need a fish? *Yes.*

To Tony she said, Yes, there are beggars in Spain who trade nothing, give nothing, do nothing. But there are *more* than beggars in Spain. Withdraw from the beggars, you withdraw from the whole damn country. And you withdraw from the possibility of the ecology of help. That's what Alice wanted, all those years ago in her bedroom. Pregnant, scared, angry, jealous, she wanted to help *me*, and I wouldn't let her because I didn't need it. But I do now. And she did then. Beggars need to help as well as be helped.

And finally, there was only Daddy left. She could see him, bright-eyed, holding thick-leaved exotic flowers in his strong hands. To Camden she said, You were wrong. Alice is special. Oh, Daddy—the specialness of Alice! You were *wrong.*

As soon as she thought this, lightness filled her. Not the buoyant bubble of joy, not the hard clarity of examination, but something else: sunshine, soft through the conservatory glass, where two children ran in and out. She suddenly felt light herself, not buoyant but translucent, a medium for the sunshine to pass clear through, on its way to somewhere else.

She drove the sleeping woman and the wounded child through the night, east, toward the state line.

griffin's egg
MICHAEL SWANWICK

Michael Swanwick made his debut in 1980, and in the twenty-five years that have followed has established himself as one of SF's most prolific and consistently excellent writers at short lengths, as well as one of the premier novelists of his generation. He has won the Theodore Sturgeon Award and the *Asimov's* Readers' Award poll. In 1991, his novel *Stations of the Tide* won him a Nebula Award as well, and in 1995 he won the World Fantasy Award for his story "Radio Waves." He's won the Hugo Award four times between 1999 and 2003, for his stories "The Very Pulse of the Machine," "Scherzo with Tyrannosaur," "The Dog Said Bow-Wow," and "Slow Life." His other books include the novels *In the Drift*, *Vacuum Flowers, The Iron Dragon's Daughter* (a finalist for the World Fantasy Award *and* the Arthur C. Clarke Award, a rare distinction!), *Jack Faust*, and, most recently, *Bones of the Earth*. His short fiction has been assembled in *Gravity's Angels, A Geography of Unknown Lands, Slow Dancing Through Time* (a collection of his collaborative short work with other writers), *Moon Dogs, Puck Aleshire's Abecedary, Tales of Old Earth*, *Cigar-Box Faust and Other Miniatures*, and *Michael Swanwick's Field Guide to the Mesozoic Megafauna*. He's also published a collection of critical articles, *The Postmodern Archipelago*, and a book-length interview, *Being Gardner Dozois*. His most recent book is a new collection, *The Periodic Table of SF*, and he is at work on a new novel. He's had stories in our second, third, fourth, sixth, seventh, tenth, and thirteenth through twenty-first annual collections. Swanwick lives in Philadelphia with his wife, Marianne Porter. He has a Web site at http://www.michaelswanwick .com.

In the complex and powerful novella that follows, Swanwick takes us to the Moon. In Swanwick's hands, the Moon is a surprising place, a vast industrial park of bewildering scale and complexity, home to many top-secret high-tech experimental projects, and home also to an intricate Lunar society with lifeways and customs of its own; a society that soon finds itself confronted with a bizarre and unsuspected menace that could spell not only its own doom, but that could inalterably change the whole human race . . . or wipe it out forever.

The sun cleared the mountains. Gunther Weil raised a hand in salute, then winced as the glare hit his eyes in the instant it took his helmet to polarize.

He was hauling fuel rods to Chatterjee Crater industrial park. The Chatterjee B reactor had gone critical forty hours before dawn, taking fifteen remotes and a microwave relay with it, and putting out a power surge that caused collateral damage to every factory in the park. Fortunately, the occasional meltdown was designed into the system. By the time the sun rose over the Rhaeticus highlands, a new reactor had been built and was ready to go online.

Gunther drove automatically, gauging his distance from Bootstrap by the amount of trash lining the Mare Vaporum road. Close by the city, discarded construction machinery and damaged assemblers sat in open-vacuum storage, awaiting possible salvage. Ten kilometers out, a pressurized van had exploded, scattering machine parts and giant worms of insulating foam across the landscape. At twenty-five kilometers, a poorly graded stretch of road had claimed any number of cargo skids and shattered running lights from passing traffic.

Forty kilometers out, though, the road was clear, a straight, clean gash in the dirt. Ignoring the voices at the back of his skull, the traffic chatter and automated safety messages that the truck routinely fed into his transceiver chip, he scrolled up the topographicals on the dash.

Right about here.

Gunther turned off the Mare Vaporum road and began laying tracks over virgin soil. "You've left your pre-scheduled route," the truck said. "Deviations from schedule may only be made with the recorded permission of your dispatcher."

"Yeah, well." Gunther's voice seemed loud in his helmet, the only physical sound in a babel of ghosts. He'd left the cabin unpressurized, and the insulated layers of his suit stilled even the conduction rumbling from the treads. "You and I both know that so long as I don't fall too far behind schedule, Beth Hamilton isn't going to care if I stray a little in between."

"You have exceeded this unit's linguistic capabilities."

"That's okay, don't let it bother you." Deftly he tied down the send switch on the truck radio with a twist of wire. The voices in his head abruptly died. He was completely isolated now.

"You said you wouldn't do that again." The words, broadcast directly to his trance chip, sounded as deep and resonant as the voice of God. "Generation Five policy expressly requires that all drivers maintain constant radio—"

"Don't whine. It's unattractive."

"You have exceeded this unit's linguistic—"

"Oh, shut up." Gunther ran a finger over the topographical maps, tracing the course he'd plotted the night before: Thirty kilometers over cherry soil, terrain no human or machine had ever crossed before, and then north on Murchison road. With luck he might even manage to be at Chatterjee early.

He drove into the lunar plain. Rocks sailed by to either side. Ahead, the mountains grew imperceptibly. Save for the trademarks dwindling behind him, there was nothing from horizon to horizon to show that humanity had ever existed. The silence was perfect.

Gunther lived for moments like this. Entering that clean, desolate emptiness, he experienced a vast expansion of being, as if everything he saw, stars, plain, craters and all, were encompassed within himself. Bootstrap City was only a fading dream, a distant island on the gently rolling surface of a stone sea. Nobody will ever be first here again, he thought. Only me.

A memory floated up from his childhood. It was Christmas eve and he was in his parents' car, on the way to midnight Mass. Snow was falling, thickly and windlessly, rendering all the familiar roads of Düsseldorf clean and pure under sheets of white. His father drove, and he himself leaned over the front seat to stare ahead in fascination into this peaceful, transformed world. The silence was perfect.

He felt touched by solitude and made holy.

The truck plowed through a rainbow of soft greys, submerged hues more hints than colors, as if something bright and festive held itself hidden just beneath a coating of dust. The sun was at his shoulder, and when he spun the front axle to avoid a boulder, the truck's shadow wheeled and reached for infinity. He drove reflexively, mesmerized by the austere beauty of the passing land.

At a thought, his peecee put music on his chip. *Stormy Weather* filled the universe.

He was coming down a long, almost imperceptible slope when the controls went dead in his hands. The truck powered down and coasted to a stop. "Goddamn you, you asshole machine!" he snarled. "What is it this time?"

"The land ahead is impassable."

Gunther slammed a fist on the dash, making the maps dance. The land ahead was smooth and sloping, any unruly tendencies tamed eons ago by the Mare Imbrium explosion. Sissy stuff. He kicked the door open and clambered down.

The truck had been stopped by a baby rille: a snakelike depression meandering across his intended route, looking for all the world like a dry streambed. He bounded to its edge. It was fifteen meters across, and three meters down at its deepest. Just shallow enough that it wouldn't show up on the topos. Gunther returned to the cab, slamming the door noiselessly behind him.

"Look. The sides aren't very steep. I've been down worse a hundred times. We'll just take it slow and easy, okay?"

"The land ahead is impassable," the truck said. "Please return to the originally scheduled course."

Wagner was on now. *Tannhäuser.* Impatiently, he thought it off.

"If you're so damned heuristic, then why won't you ever listen to reason?" He chewed his lip angrily, gave a quick shake of his head. "No, going back would put us way off schedule. The rille is bound to peter out in a few hundred meters. Let's just follow it until it does, then angle back to Murchison. We'll be at the park in no time."

Three hours later he finally hit the Murchison road. By then he was sweaty and smelly and his shoulders ached with tension. "Where are we?" he asked sourly. Then, before the truck could answer, "Cancel that." The soil had turned suddenly black. That would be the ejecta fantail from the Sony-Reinpfaltz mine. Their rail-gun was oriented almost due south in order to avoid the client factories, and so their tailings hit the road first. That meant he was getting close.

Murchison was little more than a confluence of truck treads, a dirt track crudely leveled and marked by blazes of orange paint on nearby boulders. In quick order Gunther passed through a series of landmarks: Harada Industrial fantail, Sea of Storms Macrofacturing fantail, Krupp fünfzig fantail. He knew them all. G5 did the robotics for the lot.

A light flatbed carrying a shipped bulldozer sped past him, kicking up a spray of dust that fell as fast as pebbles. The remote driving it waved a spindly arm in greeting. He waved back automatically, and wondered if it was anybody he knew.

The land hereabouts was hacked and gouged, dirt and boulders shoved into care-less heaps and hills, the occasional tool station or Oxytank Emergency Storage Plat-form chopped into a nearby bluff. A sign floated by: TOILET FLUSHING FACILITIES ½ KILOMETER. He made a face. Then he remembered that his ra-dio was still off and slipped the loop of wire from it. Time to rejoin the real world. Immediately his dispatcher's voice, harsh and static-y, was relayed to his trance chip.

"—ofabitch! Weil! Where the fuck are you?"

"I'm right here, Beth. A little late, but right where I'm supposed to be."

"Sonofa—" The recording shut off, and Hamilton's voice came on, live and mean. "You'd better have a real good explanation for this one, honey."

"Oh, you know how it is." Gunther looked away from the road, off into the dusty jade highlands. He'd like to climb up into them and never come back. Perhaps he would find caves. Perhaps there were monsters: vacuum trolls and moondragons with metabolisms slow and patient, taking centuries to move one body's-length, hy-perdense beings that could swim through stone as if it were water. He pictured them diving, following lines of magnetic force deep, deep into veins of diamond and plu-tonium, heads back and singing. "I picked up a hitchhiker, and we kind of got in-volved."

"Try telling that to E. Izmailova. She's mad as hornets at you."

"Who?"

"Izmailova. She's the new demolitions jock, shipped up here on a multicorporate contract. Took a hopper in almost four hours ago, and she's been waiting for you and Siegfried ever since. I take it you've never met her?"

"No."

"Well, I have, and you'd better watch your step with her. She's exactly the kind of tough broad who won't be amused by your antics."

"Aw, come on, she's just another tech on a retainer, right? Not in my line of com-mand. It's not like she can do anything to me."

"Dream on, babe. It wouldn't take much pull to get a fuckup like you sent down to Earth."

The sun was only a finger's breadth over the highlands by the time Chatterjee A loomed into sight. Gunther glanced at it every now and then, apprehensively. With his visor adjusted to the H-alpha wavelength, it was a blazing white sphere covered with slowly churning black specks: more granular than usual. Sunspot activity seemed high. He wondered that the Radiation Forecast Facility hadn't posted a surface advisory. The guys at the Observatory were usually right on top of things.

Chatterjee A, B, and C were a triad of simple craters just below Chladni, and while the smaller two were of minimal interest, Chatterjee A was the child of a meteor that had punched through the Imbrian basalts to as sweet a vein of aluminum ore as anything in the highlands. Being so convenient to Bootstrap made it one of management's darlings, and Gunther was not surprised to see that Kerr-McGee was going all out to get their reactor online again.

The park was crawling with walkers, stalkers and assemblers. They were all over the blister-domed factories, the smelteries, loading docks and vacuum garages. Constellations of blue sparks winked on and off as major industrial constructs were dismantled. Fleets of heavily-loaded trucks fanned out into the lunar plain, churning up the dirt behind them. Fats Waller started to sing *The Joint Is Jumping* and Gunther laughed.

He slowed to a crawl, swung wide to avoid a gas-plater that was being wrangled onto a loader, and cut up the Chatterjee B ramp road. A new landing pad had been blasted from the rock just below the lip, and a cluster of people stood about a hopper resting there. One human and eight remotes.

One of the remotes was speaking, making choppy little gestures with its arms. Several stood inert, identical as so many antique telephones, unclaimed by Earthside management but available should more advisors need to be called online.

Gunther unstrapped Siegfried from the roof of the cab and, control pad in one hand and cable spool in the other, walked him toward the hopper.

The human strode out to meet him. "You! What kept you?" E. Izmailova wore a jazzy red-and-orange Studio Volga boutique suit, in sharp contrast to his own company-issue suit with the G5 logo on the chest. He could not make out her face through the gold visor glass. But he could hear it in her voice: blazing eyes, thin lips.

"I had a flat tire." He found a good smooth chunk of rock and set down the cable spool, wriggling it to make sure it sat flush. "We got maybe five hundred yards of shielded cable. That enough for you?"

A short, tense nod.

"Okay." He unholstered his bolt gun. "Stand back." Kneeling, he anchored the spool to the rock. Then he ran a quick check of the unit's functions. "Do we know what it's like in there?"

A remote came to life, stepped forward and identified himself as Don Sakai, of G5's crisis management team. Gunther had worked with him before: a decent enough guy, but like most Canadians he had an exaggerated fear of nuclear energy. "Ms. Lang here, of Sony-Reinpfaltz, walked her unit in but the radiation was so strong she lost control after a preliminary scan." A second remote nodded confirmation, but the relay time to Toronto was just enough that Sakai missed it. "The remote just kept on walking." He coughed nervously, then added unnecessarily, "The autonomous circuits were too sensitive."

"Well, that's not going to be a problem with Siegfried. He's as dumb as a rock. On the evolutionary scale of machine intelligence he ranks closer to a crowbar than a computer." Two and a half seconds passed, and then Sakai laughed politely. Gunther nodded to Izmailova. "Walk me through this. Tell me what you want."

Izmailova stepped to his side, their suits pressing together briefly as she jacked a patch cord into his control pad. Vague shapes flickered across the outside of her visor like the shadows of dreams. "Does he know what he's doing?" she asked.

"Hey, I—"

"Shut up, Weil," Hamilton growled on a private circuit. Openly, she said, "He wouldn't be here if the company didn't have full confidence in his technical skills."

"I'm sure there's never been any question—" Sakai began. He lapsed into silence as Hamilton's words belatedly reached him.

"There's a device on the hopper," Izmailova said to Gunther. "Go pick it up."

He obeyed, reconfiguring Siegfried for a small, dense load. The unit bent low over the hopper, wrapping large, sensitive hands about the device. Gunther applied gentle pressure. Nothing happened. Heavy little bugger. Slowly, carefully, he upped the power. Siegfried straightened.

"Up the road, then down inside."

The reactor was unrecognizable, melted, twisted and folded in upon itself, a mound of slag with twisting pipes sprouting from the edges. There had been a coolant explosion early in the incident, and one wall of the crater was bright with sprayed metal. "Where is the radioactive material?" Sakai asked. Even though he was a third of a million kilometers away, he sounded tense and apprehensive.

"It's all radioactive," Izmailova said.

They waited. "I mean, you know. The fuel rods?"

"Right now, your fuel rods are probably three hundred meters down and still going. We are talking about fissionable material that has achieved critical mass. Very early in the process the rods will have all melted together in a sort of superhot puddle, capable of burning its way through rock. Picture it as a dense, heavy blob of wax, slowly working its way toward the lunar core."

"God, I love physics," Gunther said.

Izmailova's helmet turned toward him, abruptly blank. After a long pause, it switched on again and turned away. "The road down is clear at least. Take your unit all the way to the end. There's an exploratory shaft to one side there. Old one. I want to see if it's still open."

"Will the one device be enough?" Sakai asked. "To clean up the crater, I mean."

The woman's attention was fixed on Siegfried's progress. In a distracted tone she said, "Mr. Sakai, putting a chain across the access road would be enough to clean up this site. The crater walls would shield anyone working nearby from the gamma radiation, and it would take no effort at all to reroute hopper overflights so their passengers would not be exposed. Most of the biological danger of a reactor meltdown comes from alpha radiation emitted by particulate radioisotopes in the air or water. When concentrated in the body, alpha-emitters can do considerable damage; elsewhere, no. Alpha particles can be stopped by a sheet of paper. So long as you keep a reactor out of your ecosystem, it's as safe as any other large machine. Burying a destroyed reactor just because it is radioactive is unnecessary and, if you will forgive me for saying so, superstitious. But I don't make policy. I just blow things up."

"Is this the shaft you're looking for?" Gunther asked.

"Yes. Walk it down to the bottom. It's not far."

Gunther switched on Siegfried's chestlight, and sank a roller relay so the cable wouldn't snag. They went down. Finally Izmailova said, "Stop. That's far enough." He gently set the device down and then, at her direction, flicked the arming toggle. "That's done," Izmailova said. "Bring your unit back. I've given you an hour to put some distance between the crater and yourself." Gunther noticed that the remotes, on automatic, had already begun walking away.

"Um . . . I've still got fuel rods to load."

"Not today you don't. The new reactor has been taken back apart and hauled out of the blasting zone."

Gunther thought now of all the machinery being disassembled and removed from the industrial park, and was struck for the first time by the operation's sheer extravagance of scale. Normally only the most sensitive devices were removed from a blasting area. "Wait a minute. Just what kind of monster explosive are you planning to use?"

There was a self-conscious cockiness to Izmailova's stance. "Nothing I don't know how to handle. This is a diplomat-class device, the same design as saw action five years ago. Nearly one hundred individual applications without a single mechanical failure. That makes it the most reliable weapon in the history of warfare. You should feel privileged having the chance to work with one."

Gunther felt his flesh turn to ice. "Jesus Mother of God," he said. "You had me handling a briefcase nuke."

"Better get used to it. Westinghouse Lunar is putting these little babies into mass production. We'll be cracking open mountains with them, blasting roads through the highlands, smashing apart the rille walls to see what's inside." Her voice took on a visionary tone. "And that's just the beginning. There are plans for enrichment fields in Sinus Aestum. Explode a few bombs over the regolith, then extract plutonium from the dirt. We're going to be the fuel dump for the entire solar system."

His dismay must have shown in his stance, for Izmailova laughed. "Think of it as weapons for peace."

"You should've been there!" Gunther said. "It was unfuckabelievable. The one side of the crater just disappeared. It dissolved into nothing. Smashed to dust. And for a real long time everything glowed! Craters, machines, everything. My visor was so close to overload it started flickering. I thought it was going to burn out. It was nuts." He picked up his cards. "Who dealt this mess?"

Krishna grinned shyly and ducked his head. "I'm in."

Hiro scowled down at his cards. "I've just died and gone to Hell."

"Trade you," Anya said.

"No, I deserve to suffer."

They were in Noguchi Park by the edge of the central lake, seated on artfully scattered boulders that had been carved to look water-eroded. A knee-high forest of baby birches grew to one side, and somebody's toy sailboat floated near the impact cone at the center of the lake. Honeybees mazily browsed the clover.

"And then, just as the wall was crumbling, this crazy Russian bitch—"

Anya ditched a trey. "Watch what you say about crazy Russian bitches."

"—goes zooming up on her hopper . . ."

"I saw it on television," Hiro said. "We all did. It was news. This guy who works for Nissan told me the BBC gave it thirty seconds." He'd broken his nose in karate practice, when he'd flinched into his instructor's punch, and the contrast of square white bandage with shaggy black eyebrows gave him a surly, piratical appearance.

Gunther discarded one. "Hit me. Man, you didn't see anything. You didn't feel the ground shake afterwards."

"Just what was Izmailova's connection with the Briefcase War?" Hiro asked. "Obviously not a courier. Was she in the supply end or strategic?"

Gunther shrugged.

"You do remember the Briefcase War?" Hiro said sarcastically. "Half of Earth's military elites taken out in a single day? The world pulled back from the brink of war by bold action? Suspected terrorists revealed as global heroes?"

Gunther remembered the Briefcase War quite well. He had been nineteen at the time, working on a Finlandia Geothermal project when the whole world had gone into spasm and very nearly destroyed itself. It had been a major factor in his decision to ship off the planet. "Can't we ever talk about anything but politics? I'm sick and tired of hearing about Armageddon."

"Hey, aren't you supposed to be meeting with Hamilton?" Anya asked suddenly.

He glanced up at the Earth. The east coast of South America was just crossing the dusk terminator. "Oh, hell, there's enough time to play out the hand."

Krishna won with three queens. The deal passed to Hiro. He shuffled quickly, and slapped the cards down with angry little punches of his arm. "Okay," Anya said, "what's eating you?"

He looked up angrily, then down again and in a muffled voice, as if he had abruptly gone bashful as Krishna, said, "I'm shipping home."

"Home?"

"You mean to Earth?"

"Are you crazy? With everything about to go up in flames? Why?"

"Because I am so fucking tired of the Moon. It has to be the ugliest place in the universe."

"Ugly?" Anya looked elaborately about at the terraced gardens, the streams that began at the top level and fell in eight misty waterfalls before reaching the central pond to be recirculated again, the gracefully winding pathways. People strolled through great looping rosebushes and past towers of forsythia with the dreamlike skimming stride that made moonwalking so like motion underwater. Others popped in and out of the office tunnels, paused to watch the finches loop and fly, tended to beds of cucumbers. At the midlevel straw market, the tents where off-duty hobby capitalists sold factory systems, grass baskets, orange glass paperweights and courses in postinterpretive dance and the meme analysis of Elizabethan poetry were a jumble of brave silks, turquoise, scarlet and aquamarine. "I think it looks nice. A little crowded, maybe, but that's the pioneer aesthetic."

"It looks like a shopping mall, but that's not what I'm talking about. It's—" He groped for words. "It's like—it's what we're doing to this world that bothers me. I mean, we're digging it up, scattering garbage about, ripping the mountains apart, and for what?"

"Money," Anya said. "Consumer goods, raw materials, a future for our children. What's wrong with that?"

"We're not building a future, we're building weapons."

"There's not so much as a handgun on the Moon. It's an intercorporate development zone. Weapons are illegal here."

"You know what I mean. All those bomber fuselages, detonation systems, and missile casings that get built here, and shipped to low Earth orbit. Let's not pretend we don't know what they're for."

"So?" Anya said sweetly. "We live in the real world, we're none of us naive enough to believe you can have governments without armies. Why is it worse that these things are being built here rather than elsewhere?"

"It's the short-sighted, egocentric greed of what we're doing that gripes me! Have you peeked out on the surface lately and seen the way it's being ripped open, torn apart and scattered about? There are still places where you can gaze upon a harsh beauty unchanged since the days our ancestors were swinging in trees. But we're trashing them. In a generation, two at most, there will be no more beauty to the Moon than there is to any other garbage dump."

"You've seen what Earthbound manufacturing has done to the environment," Anya said. "Moving it off the planet is a good thing, right?"

"Yes, but the Moon—"

"Doesn't even have an ecosphere. There's nothing here to harm."

They glared at each other. Finally Hiro said, "I don't want to talk about it," and sullenly picked up his cards.

Five or six hands later, a woman wandered up and plumped to the grass by Krishna's feet. Her eye shadow was vivid electric purple, and a crazy smile burned on her face. "Oh hi," Krishna said. "Does everyone here know Sally Chang? She's a research component of the Center for Self-Replicating Technologies, like me."

The others nodded. Gunther said, Gunther said, "Gunther Weil. Blue-collar component of Generation Five."

She giggled.

Gunther blinked. "You're certainly in a good mood." He rapped the deck with his knuckles. "I'll stand."

"I'm on psilly," she said.

"One card."

"Psilocybin?" Gunther said. "I might be interested in some of that. Did you grow it or microfacture it? I have a couple of factories back in my room, maybe I could divert one if you'd like to license the software?"

Sally Chang shook her head, laughing helplessly. Tears ran down her cheeks.

"Well, when you come down we can talk about it." Gunther squinted at his cards. "This would make a great hand for chess."

"Nobody plays chess," Hiro said scornfully. "It's a game for computers."

Gunther took the pot with two pair. He shuffled, Krishna declined the cut, and he began dealing out cards. "So anyway, this crazy Russian lady—"

Out of nowhere, Chang howled. Wild gusts of laughter knocked her back on her heels and bent her forward again. The delight of discovery dancing in her eyes, she pointed a finger straight at Gunther. "You're a robot!" she cried.

"Beg pardon?"

"You're nothing but a robot," she repeated. "You're a machine, an automaton. Look at yourself! Nothing but stimulus-response. You have no free will at all. There's nothing there. You couldn't perform an original act to save your life."

"Oh yeah?" Gunther glanced around, looking for inspiration. A little boy—it might be Pyotr Nahfees, though it was hard to tell from here—was by the edge of the water, feeding scraps of shrimp loaf to the carp. "Suppose I pitched you into the lake? That would be an original act."

Laughing, she shook her head. "Typical primate behavior. A perceived threat is met with a display of mock aggression."

Gunther laughed.

"Then, when that fails, the primate falls back to a display of submission. Appeasement. The monkey demonstrates his harmlessness—you see?"

"Hey, this really isn't funny," Gunther said warningly. "In fact, it's kind of insulting."

"And so back to a display of aggression."

Gunther sighed and threw up both his hands. "How am I supposed to react? According to you, anything I say or do is wrong."

"Submission again. Back and forth, back and forth from aggression to submission and back again." She pumped her arm as if it were a piston. "Just like a little machine—you see? It's all automatic behavior."

"Hey, Kreesh—you're the neurobiowhatever here, right? Put in a good word for me. Get me out of this conversation."

Krishna reddened. He would not meet Gunther's eyes. "Ms. Chang is very highly regarded at the Center, you see. Anything she thinks about thinking is worth thinking about." The woman watched him avidly, eyes glistening, pupils small. "I think maybe what she means, though, is that we're all basically cruising through life. Like we're on autopilot. Not just you specifically, but all of us." He appealed to her directly. "Yes?"

"No, no, no, no." She shook her head. "Him specifically."

"I give up." Gunther put his cards down, and lay back on the granite slab so he could stare up through the roof glass at the waning Earth. When he closed his eyes, he could see Izmailova's hopper, rising. It was a skimpy device, little more than a platform-and-chair atop a cluster of four bottles of waste-gas propellant, and a set of smart legs. He saw it lofting up as the explosion blossomed, seeming briefly to hover high over the crater, like a hawk atop a thermal. Hands by side, the red-suited figure sat, watching with what seemed inhuman calm. In the reflected light she burned as bright as a star. In an appalling way, she was beautiful.

Sally Chang hugged her knees, rocking back and forth. She laughed and laughed.

Beth Hamilton was wired for telepresence. She flipped up one lens when Gunther entered her office, but kept on moving her arms and legs. Dreamy little ghost motions that would be picked up and magnified in a factory somewhere over the horizon. "You're late again," she said with no particular emphasis.

Most people would have experienced at least a twinge of reality sickness dealing with two separate surrounds at once. Hamilton was one of the rare few who could split her awareness between two disparate realities without loss of efficiency in either. "I called you in to discuss your future with Generation Five. Specifically, to discuss the possibility of your transfer to another plant."

"You mean Earthside."

"You see?" Hamilton said. "You're not as stupid as you like to make yourself out to be." She flipped the lens down again, stood very still, then lifted a metal-gauntleted hand and ran through a complex series of finger movements. "Well?"

"Well what?"

"Tokyo, Berlin, Buenos Aires—do any of these hold magic for you? How about Toronto? The right move now could be a big boost to your career."

"All I want is to stay here, do my job, and draw down my salary," Gunther said carefully. "I'm not looking for a shot at promotion, or a big raise, or a lateral career-track transfer. I'm happy right where I am."

"You've sure got a funny way of showing it." Hamilton powered down her gloves, and slipped her hands free. She scratched her nose. To one side stood her work table, a polished cube of black granite. Her peecee rested there, alongside a spray of copper crystals. At her thought, it put Izmailova's voice onto Gunther's chip.

"It is with deepest regret that I must alert you to the unprofessional behavior of one of your personnel components," it began. Listening to the complaint, Gunther experienced a totally unexpected twinge of distress and, more, of resentment that Izmailova had dared judge him so harshly. He was careful not to let it show.

"Irresponsible, insubordinate, careless, and possessed of a bad attitude." He faked a grin. "She doesn't seem to like me much." Hamilton said nothing. "But this isn't enough to . . ." His voice trailed off. "Is it?"

"Normally, Weil, it would be. A demo jock isn't 'just a tech on retainer,' as you so quaintly put it; those government licenses aren't easy to get. And you may not be aware of it, but you have very poor efficiency ratings to begin with. Lots of potential, no follow-through. Frankly, you've been a disappointment. However, lucky for you, this Izmailova dame humiliated Don Sakai, and he's let us know that we're under no particular pressure to accommodate her."

"Izmailova humiliated Sakai?"

Hamilton stared at him. "Weil, you're oblivious, you know that?"

Then he remembered Izmailova's rant on nuclear energy. "Right, okay. I got it now."

"So here's your choice. I can write up a reprimand, and it goes into your permanent file, along with Izmailova's complaint. Or you can take a lateral Earthside, and I'll see to it that these little things aren't logged into the corporate system."

It wasn't much of a choice. But he put a good face on it. "In that case it looks like you're stuck with me."

"For the moment, Weil. For the moment."

He was back on the surface the next two days running. The first day he was once again hauling fuel rods to Chatterjee C. This time he kept to the road, and the reactor was refueled exactly on schedule. The second day he went all the way out to Tries-necker to pick up some old rods that had been in temporary storage for six months while the Kerr-McGee people argued over whether they should be reprocessed or dumped. Not a bad deal for him, because although the sunspot cycle was on the wane, there was a surface advisory in effect and he was drawing hazardous duty pay.

When he got there, a tech rep telepresenced in from somewhere in France to tell him to forget it. There'd been another meeting, and the decision had once again been delayed. He started back to Bootstrap with the new a capella version of the *Threepenny Opera* playing in his head. It sounded awfully sweet and reedy for his tastes, but that was what they were listening to up home.

Fifteen kilometers down the road, the UV meter on the dash jumped.

Gunther reached out to tap the meter with his finger. It did not respond. With a freezing sensation at the back of his neck, he glanced up at the roof of the cab and whispered, "Oh, no."

"The Radiation Forecast Facility has just intensified its surface warning to a Most Drastic status," the truck said calmly. "This is due to an unanticipated flare storm, onset immediately. Everyone currently on the surface is to proceed with all haste to shelter. Repeat: Proceed immediately to shelter."

"I'm eighty kilometers from—"

The truck was slowing to a stop. "Because this unit is not hardened, excessive fortuitous radiation may cause it to malfunction. To ensure the continued safe operation of this vehicle, all controls will be frozen in manual mode and this unit will now shut off."

With the release of the truck's masking functions, Gunther's head filled with overlapping voices. Static washed through them, making nonsense of what they were trying to say:

```
****astic Status***epeat: We******his is
Beth. The****hail*** ***yo**** *ere? *C**
Su**ace adv***ry as********ve jus**issued
****ost***om**on **good**uddy****ve up**
****to Most**rast***rasticad*isory **Get
*off****me a**oot***Miko, Sabra**ic***
Sta**s. All unit* and* *the surfac*****d
damn**ou, Kangmei******your asse** per-
sonn*l are to find sh****are you lis*
***ng? Find undergrou***right now***
*elter immediately. Maxim*** shelter.
Do**t try to ge****don't want*to hear
you'***um exposure twenty minut***back to
Bootstrap. Too****tayed behind to turn
off****es. Repeat: Maximum exp****far,
it'll fry you. List***f the lights. Who
else***os*re twenty m*nutes. Fi*en, ther*
are thr*e facto****is out*ther*? Come in
ri******helter im***iatel****ries no****r
from***ur pr****ght n*w**Ev**yone! Anybo*
```

Th*****h***eco*ded*voi**ent**ocat*on***Are***u*dy
k*ow w**re*Mikhail is***ce of t*** Radi-
ati***Fore***li***ning**y***goofoff******C*mon,
Misha***on't yo*****cast Fa**lity. Due**o
an*Weisskopf*AG*is one, Niss****et coy on
us***ound u***unpre**c*ed solar flar*****
and**unar**acrostructyour voice,
hea***We g**** th***urfa***adviso****as
uralWeil******me kn*****ot word
Ezra's dug**nt*******upgrad******Most
Dr**if****'re listeni*****ome***a factory
out Chladn****

"Beth! The nearest shelter is back at Weisskopf—that's half an hour at top speed and I've got an advisory here of twenty minutes. Tell me what to do!"

But the first sleet of hard particles was coming in too hard to make out anything more. A hand, his apparently, floated forward and flicked off the radio relay. The voices in his head died.

The crackling static went on and on. The truck sat motionless, half an hour from nowhere, invisible death sizzling and popping down through the cab roof. He put his helmet and gloves on, double-checked their seals, and unlatched the door.

It slammed open. Pages from the op manual flew away, and a glove went tumbling gaily across the surface, chasing the pink fuzzy-dice that Eurydice had given him that last night in Sweden. A handful of wheat biscuits in an open tin on the dash turned to powder and were gone, drawing the tin after them. Explosive decompression. He'd forgotten to depressurize. Gunther froze in dismayed astonishment at having made so basic—so dangerous—a mistake.

Then he was on the surface, head tilted back, staring up at the sun. It was angry with sunspots, and one enormous and unpredicted solar flare.

I'm going to die, he thought.

For a long, paralyzing instant, he tasted the chill certainty of that thought. He was going to die. He knew that for a fact, knew it more surely than he had ever known anything before.

In his mind, he could see Death sweeping across the lunar plain toward him. Death was a black wall, featureless, that stretched to infinity in every direction. It sliced the universe in half. On this side were life, warmth, craters and flowers, dreams, mining robots, thought, everything that Gunther knew or could imagine. On the other side . . . Something? Nothing? The wall gave no hint. It was unreadable, enigmatic, absolute. But it was bearing down on him. It was so close now that he could almost reach out and touch it. Soon it would be here. He would pass through, and then he would know.

With a start he broke free of that thought, and jumped for the cab. He scrabbled up its side. His trance chip hissing, rattling and crackling, he yanked the magnetic straps holding Siegfried in place, grabbed the spool and control pad, and jumped over the edge.

He landed jarringly, fell to his knees, and rolled under the trailer. There was enough shielding wrapped around the fuel rods to stop any amount of hard radiation—

no matter what its source. It would shelter him as well from the sun as from his cargo. The trance chip fell silent, and he felt his jaws relaxing from a clenched tension.

Safe.

It was dark beneath the trailer, and he had time to think. Even kicking his re-breather up to full, and offlining all his suit peripherals, he didn't have enough oxygen to sit out the storm. So okay. He had to get to a shelter. Weisskopf was closest, only fifteen kilometers away and there was a shelter in the G5 assembly plant there. That would be his goal.

Working by feel, he found the steel supporting struts, and used Siegfried's magnetic straps to attach himself to the underside of the trailer. It was clumsy, difficult work, but at last he hung face-down over the road. He fingered the walker's controls, and sat Siegfried up.

Twelve excruciating minutes later, he finally managed to get Siegfried down from the roof unbroken. The interior wasn't intended to hold anything half so big. To get the walker in he had first to cut the door free, and then rip the chair out of the cab. Discarding both items by the roadside, he squeezed Siegfried in. The walker bent over double, reconfigured, reconfigured again, and finally managed to fit itself into the space. Gently, delicately, Siegfried took the controls and shifted into first.

With a bump, the truck started to move.

It was a hellish trip. The truck, never fast to begin with, wallowed down the road like a cast-iron pig. Siegfried's optics were bent over the controls, and couldn't be raised without jerking the walker's hands free. He couldn't look ahead without stopping the truck first.

He navigated by watching the road pass under him. To a crude degree he could align the truck with the treadmarks scrolling by. Whenever he wandered off the track, he worked Siegfried's hand controls to veer the truck back, so that it drifted slowly from side to side, zig-zagging its way down the road.

Shadows bumping and leaping, the road flowed toward Gunther with dangerous monotony. He jiggled and vibrated in his makeshift sling. After a while his neck hurt with the effort of holding his head back to watch the glaring road disappearing into shadow by the front axle, and his eyes ached from the crawling repetitiveness of what they saw.

The truck kicked up dust in passing, and the smaller particles carried enough of a static charge to cling to his suit. At irregular intervals he swiped at the fine grey film on his visor with his glove, smearing it into long, thin streaks.

He began to hallucinate. They were mild visuals, oblong patches of colored light that moved in his vision and went away when he shook his head and firmly closed his eyes for a concentrated moment. But every moment's release from the pressure of vision tempted him to keep his eyes closed longer, and that he could not afford to do.

It put him in mind of the last time he had seen his mother, and what she had said then. That the worst part of being a widow was that every day her life began anew, no better than the day before, the pain still fresh, her husband's absence a physical fact she was no closer to accepting than ever. It was like being dead, she said, in that nothing ever changed.

Ah God, he thought, this isn't worth doing. Then a rock the size of his head came bounding toward his helmet. Frantic hands jerked at the controls, and Siegfried skewed the truck wildly, so that the rock jumped away and missed him. Which put an end to that line of thought.

He cued his peecee. *Saint James' Infirmary* came on. It didn't help.

Come on, you bastard, he thought. You can do it. His arms and shoulders ached, and his back too, when he gave it any thought. Perversely enough, one of his legs had gone to sleep. At the angle he had to hold his head to watch the road, his mouth tended to hang open. After a while, a quivering motion alerted him that a small puddle of saliva had gathered in the curve of his faceplate. He was drooling. He closed his mouth, swallowing back his spit, and stared forward. A minute later he found that he was doing it again.

Slowly, miserably, he drove toward Weisskopf.

The G5 Weisskopf plant was typical of its kind: A white blister-dome to moderate temperature swings over the long lunar day, a microwave relay tower to bring in supervisory presence, and a hundred semiautonomous units to do the work.

Gunther overshot the access road, wheeled back to catch it, and ran the truck right up to the side of the factory. He had Siegfried switch off the engine, and then let the control pad fall to the ground. For well over a minute he simply hung there, eyes closed, savoring the end of motion. Then he kicked free of the straps, and crawled out from under the trailer.

Static skatting and stuttering inside his head, he stumbled into the factory.

In the muted light that filtered through the dome covering, the factory was dim as an undersea cavern. His helmet light seemed to distort as much as it illumined. Machines loomed closer in the center of its glare, swelling up as if seen through a fisheye lens. He turned it off, and waited for his eyes to adjust.

After a bit, he could see the robot assemblers, slender as ghosts, moving with unearthly delicacy. The flare storm had activated them. They swayed like seaweed, lightly out of sync with each other. Arms raised, they danced in time to random radio input.

On the assembly lines lay the remains of half-built robots, looking flayed and eviscerated. Their careful frettings of copper and silver nerves had been exposed to view and randomly operated upon. A long arm jointed down, electric fire at its tip, and made a metal torso twitch.

They were blind mechanisms, most of them, powerful things bolted to the floor in assembly logic paths. But there were mobile units as well, overseers and jacks-of-all-trades, weaving drunkenly through the factory with sun-maddened eye.

A sudden motion made Gunther turn just in time to see a metal puncher swivel toward him, slam down an enormous arm and put a hole in the floor by his feet. He felt the shock through his soles.

He danced back. The machine followed him, the diamond-tipped punch sliding nervously in and out of its sheath, its movements as trembling and dainty as a newborn colt's.

"Easy there, baby," Gunther whispered. To the far end of the factory, green arrows supergraffixed on the crater wall pointed to an iron door. The shelter. Gunther backed away from the punch, edging into a service aisle between two rows of machines that rippled like grass in the wind.

The punch press rolled forward on its trundle. Then, confused by that field of motion, it stopped, hesitantly scanning the ranks of robots. Gunther froze.

At last, slowly, lumberingly, the metal puncher turned away.

Gunther ran. Static roared in his head. Grey shadows swam among the distant machines, like sharks, sometimes coming closer, sometimes receding. The static loudened. Up and down the factory welding arcs winked on at the assembler tips, like tiny stars. Ducking, running, spinning, he reached the shelter and seized the airlock door. Even through his glove, the handle felt cold.

He turned it.

The airlock was small and round. He squeezed through the door and fit himself into the inadequate space within, making himself as small as possible. He yanked the door shut.

Darkness.

He switched his helmet lamp back on. The reflected glare slammed at his eyes, far too intense for such a confined area. Folded knees-to-chin into the roundness of the lock he felt a wry comradeship with Siegfried back in the truck.

The inner lock controls were simplicity itself. The door hinged inward, so that air pressure held it shut. There was a yank bar which, when pulled, would bleed oxygen into the airlock. When pressure equalized, the inner door would open easily. He yanked the bar.

The floor vibrated as something heavy went by.

The shelter was small, just large enough to hold a cot, a chemical toilet and a re-breather with spare oxytanks. A single overhead unit provided light and heat. For comfort there was a blanket. For amusement, there were pocket-sized editions of the Bible and the Koran, placed there by impossibly distant missionary societies. Even empty, there was not much space in the shelter.

It wasn't empty.

A woman, frowning and holding up a protective hand, cringed from his helmet lamp. "Turn that thing off," she said.

He obeyed. In the soft light that ensued he saw: stark white flattop, pink scalp visible through the sides. High cheekbones. Eyelids lifted slightly, like wings, by carefully sculpted eye shadow. Dark lips, full mouth. He had to admire the character it took to make up a face so carefully, only to hide it beneath a helmet. Then he saw her red and orange Studio Volga suit.

It was Izmailova.

To cover his embarrassment, he took his time removing his gloves and helmet. Izmailova moved her own helmet from the cot to make room, and he sat down beside her. Extending a hand, he stiffly said, "We've met before. My name is—"

"I know. It's written on your suit."

"Oh yeah. Right."

For an uncomfortably long moment, neither spoke. At last Izmailova cleared her throat and briskly said, "This is ridiculous. There's no reason we should—"

CLANG.

Their heads jerked toward the door in unison. The sound was harsh, loud, metallic. Gunther slammed his helmet on, grabbed for his gloves. Izmailova, also suiting up as rapidly as she could, tensely subvocalized into her trance chip: "What is it?"

Methodically snapping his wrist latches shut one by one, Gunther said, "I think it's a metal punch." Then, because the helmet muffled his words, he repeated them over the chip.

CLANG. This second time, they were waiting for the sound. Now there could be no doubt. Something was trying to break open the outer airlock door.

"A what?!"

"Might be a hammer of some type, or a blacksmith unit. Just be thankful it's not a laser jig." He held up his hands before him. "Give me a safety check."

She turned his wrists one way, back, took his helmet in her hands and gave it a twist to test its seal. "You pass." She held up her own wrists. "But what is it trying to do?"

Her gloves were sealed perfectly. One helmet dog had a bit of give in it, but not enough to breach integrity. He shrugged. "It's deranged—it could want anything. It might even be trying to repair a weak hinge."

CLANG.

"It's trying to get in here!"

"That's another possibility, yes."

Izmailova's voice rose slightly. "But even scrambled, there can't possibly be any programs in its memory to make it do that. How can random input make it act this way?"

"It doesn't work like that. You're thinking of the kind of robotics they had when you were a kid. These units are state of the art: They don't manipulate instructions, they manipulate concepts. See, that makes them more flexible. You don't have to program in every little step when you want one to do something new. You just give it a goal—"

CLANG.

"—like, to Disassemble a Rotary Drill. It's got a bank of available skills, like Cutting and Unbolting and Gross Manipulation, which it then fits together in various configurations until it has a path that will bring it to the goal." He was talking for the sake of talking now, talking to keep himself from panic. "Which normally works out fine. But when one of these things malfunctions, it does so on the conceptual level. See? So that—"

"So that it decides we're rotary drills that need to be disassembled."

"Uh . . . yeah."

CLANG.

"So what do we do when it gets in here?" They had both involuntarily risen to their feet, and stood facing the door. There was not much space, and what little there was they filled. Gunther was acutely aware that there was not enough room here to either fight or flee. "I don't know about you," he said, "but I'm going to hit that sucker over the head with the toilet."

She turned to look at him.

CLA—The noise was cut in half by a breathy, whooshing explosion. Abrupt, total silence. "It's through the outer door," Gunther said flatly.

They waited.

Much later, Izmailova said, "Is it possible it's gone away?"

"I don't know." Gunther undogged his helmet, knelt and put an ear to the floor. The stone was almost painfully cold. "Maybe the explosion damaged it." He could hear the faint vibrations of the assemblers, the heavier rumblings of machines roving the factory floor. None of it sounded close. He silently counted to a hundred. Nothing. He counted to a hundred again.

Finally he straightened. "It's gone."

They both sat down. Izmailova took off her helmet, and Gunther clumsily began undoing his gloves. He fumbled at the latches. "Look at me." He laughed shakily. "I'm all thumbs. I can't even handle this, I'm so unnerved."

"Let me help you with that." Izmailova flipped up the latches, tugged at his glove. It came free. "Where's your other hand?"

Then, somehow, they were each removing the other's suit, tugging at the latches, undoing the seals. They began slowly but sped up with each latch undogged, until they were yanking and pulling with frantic haste. Gunther opened up the front of Izmailova's suit, revealing a red silk camisole. He slid his hands beneath it, and pushed the cloth up over her breasts. Her nipples were hard. He let her breasts fill his hands and squeezed.

Izmailova made a low, groaning sound in the back of her throat. She had Gunther's suit open. Now she pushed down his leggings and reached within to seize his cock. He was already erect. She tugged it out and impatiently shoved him down on the cot. Then she was kneeling on top of him, and guiding him inside her.

Her mouth met his, warm and moist.

Half in and half out of their suits, they made love. Gunther managed to struggle one arm free, and reached within Izmailova's suit to run a hand up her long back and over the back of her head. The short hairs of her buzz cut stung and tickled his palm.

She rode him roughly, her flesh slippery with sweat against his. "Are you coming yet?" she murmured. "Are you coming yet? Tell me when you're about to come." She bit his shoulder, the side of his neck, his chin, his lower lip. Her nails dug into his flesh.

"Now," he whispered. Possibly he only subvocalized it, and she caught it on her trance chip. But then she clutched him tighter than ever, as if she were trying to crack his ribs, and her whole body shuddered with orgasm. Then he came too, riding her passion down into spiraling desperation, ecstasy and release.

It was better than anything he had ever experienced before.

Afterward, they finally kicked free of their suits. They shoved and pushed the things off the cot. Gunther pulled the blanket out from beneath them, and with Izmailova's help wrapped it about the both of them. They lay together, relaxed, not speaking.

He listened to her breathe for a while. The noise was soft. When she turned her face toward him, he could feel it, a warm little tickle in the hollow of his throat. The smell of her permeated the room. This stranger beside him.

Gunther felt weary, warm, at ease. "How long have you been here?" he asked. "Not here in the shelter, I mean, but . . ."

"Five days."

"That little." He smiled. "Welcome to the Moon, Ms. Izmailova."

"Ekatarina," she said sleepily. "Call me Ekatarina." Whooping, they soared high and south, over Herschel. The Ptolemaeus road bent and doubled below them, winding out of sight, always returning. "This is great!" Hiro crowed. "This is—I should've talked you into taking me out here a year ago."

Gunther checked his bearings and throttled down, sinking eastward. The other two hoppers, slaved to his own, followed in tight formation. Two days had passed since the flare storm and Gunther, still on mandatory recoup, had promised to guide his friends into the highlands as soon as the surface advisory was dropped. "We're coming in now. Better triplecheck your safety harnesses. You doing okay back there, Kreesh?"

"I am quite comfortable, yes."

Then they were down on the Seething Bay Company landing pad.

Hiro was the second down and the first on the surface. He bounded about like a collie off its leash, chasing upslope and down, looking for new vantage points. "I can't believe I'm here! I work out this way every day, but you know what? This is the first time I've actually been out here. Physically, I mean."

"Watch your footing," Gunther warned. "This isn't like telepresence—if you break a leg, it'll be up to Krishna and me to carry you out."

"I trust you. Man, anybody who can get caught out in a flare storm, and end up nailing—"

"Hey, watch your language, okay?"

"Everybody's heard the story. I mean, we all thought you were dead, and then they found the two of you asleep. They'll be talking about it a hundred years from now." Hiro was practically choking on his laughter. "You're a legend!"

"Just give it a rest." To change the subject, Gunther said, "I can't believe you want to take a photo of this mess." The Seething Bay operation was a strip mine. Robot bulldozers scooped up the regolith and fed it to a processing plant that rested on enormous skids. They were after the thorium here, and the output was small enough that it could be transported to the breeder reactor by hopper. There was no need for a railgun and the tailings were piled in artificial mountains in the wake of the factory.

"Don't be ridiculous." Hiro swept an arm southward, toward Ptolemaeus. "There!" The crater wall caught the sun, while the lowest parts of the surrounding land were still in shadow. The gentle slopes seemed to tower; the crater itself was a cathedral, blazing white.

"Where is your camera?" Krishna asked.

"Don't need one. I'll just take the data down on my helmet."

"I'm not too clear on this mosaic project of yours," Gunther said. "Explain to me one more time how it's supposed to work."

"Anya came up with it. She's renting an assembler to cut hexagonal floor tiles in black, white and fourteen intermediate shades of grey. I provide the pictures. We choose the one we like best, scan it in black and white, screen for values of intensity, and then have the assembler lay the floor, one tile per pixel. It'll look great—come by tomorrow and see."

"Yeah, I'll do that."

Chattering like a squirrel, Hiro led them away from the edge of the mine. They bounded westward, across the slope.

Krishna's voice came over Gunther's trance chip. It was an old ground-rat trick. The chips had an effective transmission radius of fifteen yards—you could turn off the radio and talk chip-to-chip, if you were close enough. "You sound troubled, my friend."

He listened for a second carrier tone, heard nothing. Hiro was out of range. "It's Izmailova. I sort of—"

"Fell in love with her."

"How'd you know that?"

They were spaced out across the rising slope, Hiro in the lead. For a time neither spoke. There was a calm, confidential quality to that shared silence, like the anonymous stillness of the confessional. "Please don't take this wrong," Krishna said.

"Take what wrong?"

"Gunther, if you take two sexually compatible people, place them in close proximity, isolate them and scare the hell out of them, they will fall in love. That's a given. It's a survival mechanism, something that was wired into your basic makeup long before you were born. When billions of years of evolution say it's bonding time, your brain doesn't have much choice but to obey."

"Hey, come on over here!" Hiro cried over the radio. "You've got to see this."

"We're coming," Gunther said. Then, over his chip, "You make me out to be one of Sally Chang's machines."

"In some ways we are machines. That's not so bad. We feel thirsty when we need water, adrenalin pumps into the bloodstream when we need an extra boost of aggressive energy. You can't fight your own nature. What would be the point of it?"

"Yeah, but . . ."

"Is this great or what?" Hiro was clambering over a boulder field. "It just goes on and on. And look up there!" Upslope, they saw that what they were climbing over was the spillage from a narrow cleft entirely filled with boulders. They were huge, as big as hoppers, some of them large as prefab oxysheds. "Hey, Krishna, I been meaning to ask you—just what is it that you do out there at the Center?"

"I can't talk about it."

"Aw, come on." Hiro lifted a rock the size of his head to his shoulder and shoved it away, like a shot-putter. The rock soared slowly, landed far downslope in a white explosion of dust. "You're among friends here. You can trust us."

Krishna shook his head. Sunlight flashed from the visor. "You don't know what you're asking."

Hiro hoisted a second rock, bigger than the first. Gunther knew him in this mood, nasty-faced and grinning. "My point exactly. The two of us know zip about neurobiology. You could spend the next ten hours lecturing us, and we couldn't catch enough to compromise security." Another burst of dust.

"You don't understand. The Center for Self-Replicating Technologies is here for a reason. The lab work could be done back on Earth for a fraction of what a lunar facility costs. Our sponsors only move projects here that they're genuinely afraid of."

"So what can you tell us about? Just the open stuff, the video magazine stuff. Nothing secret."

"Well . . . okay." Now it was Krishna's turn. He picked up a small rock, wound up like a baseball player and threw. It dwindled and disappeared in the distance. A puff of white sprouted from the surface. "You know Sally Chang? She has just finished mapping the neurotransmitter functions."

They waited. When Krishna added nothing further, Hiro dryly said, "Wow."

"Details, Kreesh. Some of us aren't so fast to see the universe in a grain of sand as you are."

"It should be obvious. We've had a complete genetic map of the brain for almost a decade. Now add to that Sally Chang's chemical map, and it's analogous to being given the keys to the library. No, better than that. Imagine that you've spent your entire life within an enormous library filled with books in a language you neither read nor speak, and that you've just found the dictionary and a picture reader."

"So what are you saying? That we'll have complete understanding of how the brain operates?"

"We'll have complete control over how the brain operates. With chemical therapy, it will be possible to make anyone think or feel anything we want. We will have an immediate cure for all non-traumatic mental illness. We'll be able to fine-tune aggression, passion, creativity—bring them up, damp them down, it'll be all the same. You can see why our sponsors are so afraid of what our research might produce."

"Not really, no. The world could use more sanity," Gunther said.

"I agree. But who defines sanity? Many governments consider political dissent grounds for mental incarceration. This would open the doors of the brain, allowing it to be examined from the outside. For the first time, it would be possible to discover unexpressed rebellion. Modes of thought could be outlawed. The potential for abuse is not inconsiderable.

"Consider also the military applications. This knowledge combined with some of the new nanoweaponry might produce a berserker gas, allowing you to turn the enemy's armies upon their own populace. Or, easier, to throw them into a psychotic frenzy and let them turn on themselves. Cities could be pacified by rendering the citizenry catatonic. A secondary, internal reality could then be created, allowing the conqueror to use the masses as slave labor. The possibilities are endless."

They digested this in silence. At last Hiro said, "Jeeze, Krishna, if that's the open goods, what the hell kind of stuff do you have to hide?"

"I can't tell you."

A minute later, Hiro was haring off again. At the foot of a nearby hill he found an immense boulder standing atilt on its small end. He danced about, trying to get good shots past it without catching his own footprints in them.

"So what's the problem?" Krishna said over his chip.

"The problem is, I can't arrange to see her. Ekatarina. I've left messages, but she won't answer them. And you know how it is in Bootstrap—it takes a real effort to avoid somebody who wants to see you. But she's managed it."

Krishna said nothing.

"All I want to know is, just what's going on here?"

"She's avoiding you."

"But why? I fell in love and she didn't, is that what you're telling me? I mean, is that a crock or what?"

"Without hearing her side of the story, I can't really say how she feels. But the odds are excellent she fell every bit as hard as you did. The difference is that you think it's a good idea, and she doesn't. So of course she's avoiding you. Contact would just make it more difficult for her to master her feelings for you."

"Shit!"

An unexpected touch of wryness entered Krishna's voice. "What do you want? A minute ago you were complaining that Sally Chang thinks you're a machine. Now you're unhappy that Izmailova thinks she's not."

"Hey, you guys! Come over here. I've found the perfect shot. You've got to see this."

They turned to see Hiro waving at them from the hilltop. "I thought you were leaving," Gunther grumbled. "You said you were sick of the Moon, and going away and never coming back. So how come you're upgrading your digs all of a sudden?"

"That was yesterday! Today, I'm a pioneer, a builder of worlds, a founder of dynasties!"

"This is getting tedious. What does it take to get a straight answer out of you?"

Hiro bounded high and struck a pose, arms wide and a little ridiculous. He staggered a bit on landing. "Anya and I are getting married!"

Gunther and Krishna looked at each other, blank visor to blank visor. Forcing enthusiasm into his voice, Gunther said, "Hey, no shit? Really! Congratu—"

A scream of static howled up from nowhere. Gunther winced and cut down the gain. "My stupid radio is—"

One of the other two—they had moved together and he couldn't tell them apart at this distance—was pointing upward. Gunther tilted back his head, to look at the Earth. For a second he wasn't sure what he was looking for. Then he saw it: a diamond pinprick of light in the middle of the night. It was like a small, bright hole in reality, somewhere in continental Asia. "What the hell is that?" he asked.

Softly, Hiro said, "I think it's Vladivostok."

By the time they were back over the Sinus Medii, that first light had reddened and faded away, and two more had blossomed. The news jockey at the Observatory was working overtime splicing together reports from the major news feeds into a montage of rumor and fear. The radio was full of talk about hits on Seoul and Buenos Aires. Those seemed certain. Strikes against Panama, Iraq, Denver and Cairo were disputed. A stealth missile had flown low over Hokkaido and been deflected into the Sea of Japan. The Swiss Orbitals had lost some factories to fragmentation satellites. There was no agreement as to the source aggressor, and though most suspicions trended in one direction, Tokyo denied everything.

Gunther was most impressed by the sound feed from a British video essayist, who said that it did not matter who had fired the first shot, or why. "Who shall we blame? The Southern Alliance, Tokyo, General Kim, or possibly some Grey terrorist group that nobody has ever heard of before? In a world whose weapons were wired to hair triggers, the question is irrelevant. When the first device exploded, it activated autonomous programs which launched what is officially labeled 'a measured response.' Gorshov himself could not have prevented it. His tactical programs chose this week's three most likely aggressors—at least two of which were certainly innocent—and launched a response. Human beings had no say over it.

"Those three nations in turn had their own reflexive 'measured responses.' The results of which we are just beginning to learn. Now we will pause for five days, while all concerned parties negotiate. How do we know this? Abstracts of all major defense programs are available on any public data net. They are no secret. Openness is in fact what deterrence is all about.

"We have five days to avert a war that literally nobody wants. The question is, in five days can the military and political powers seize control of their own defense programming? Will they? Given the pain and anger involved, the traditional hatreds, national chauvinism, and the natural reactions of those who number loved ones among the already dead, can those in charge overcome their own natures in time to pull back from final and total war? Our best informed guess is no. No, they cannot.

"Good night, and may God have mercy on us all."

They flew northward in silence. Even when the broadcast cut off in mid-word, nobody spoke. It was the end of the world, and there was nothing they could say that did not shrink to insignificance before that fact. They simply headed home.

The land about Bootstrap was dotted with graffiti, great block letters traced out in boulders: KARL OPS—EINDHOVEN '49 and LOUISE MCTIGHE ALBUQUERQUE N.M. An enormous eye in a pyramid. ARSENAL WORLD RUGBY CHAMPS with a crown over it. CORNPONE. Pi Lambda Phi. MOTORHEADS. A giant with a club. Coming down over them, Gunther reflected that they all referred to places and things in the world overhead, not a one of them indigenous to the Moon. What had always seemed pointless now struck him as unspeakably sad.

It was only a short walk from the hopper pad to the vacuum garage. They didn't bother to summon a jitney.

The garage seemed strangely unfamiliar to Gunther now, though he had passed through it a thousand times. It seemed to float in its own mystery, as if everything had been removed and replaced by its exact double, rendering it different and somehow unknowable. Row upon row of parked vehicles were slanted by type within painted lines. Ceiling lights strained to reach the floor, and could not.

"Boy, is this place still!" Hiro's voice seemed unnaturally loud.

It was true. In all the cavernous reaches of the garage, not a single remote or robot service unit stirred. Not so much as a pressure leak sniffer moved.

"Must be because of the news," Gunther muttered. He found he was not ready to speak of the war directly. To the back of the garage, five airlocks stood all in a row. Above them a warm, yellow strip of window shone in the rock. In the room beyond, he could see the overseer moving about.

Hiro waved an arm, and the small figure within leaned forward to wave back. They trudged to the nearest lock and waited.

Nothing happened.

After a few minutes, they stepped back and away from the lock to peer up through the window. The overseer was still there, moving unhurriedly. "Hey!" Hiro shouted over open frequency. "You up there! Are you on the job?"

The man smiled, nodded and waved again.

"Then open the goddamned door!" Hiro strode forward, and with a final, nodding wave, the overseer bent over his controls.

"Uh, Hiro," Gunther said, "There's something odd about . . ."

The door exploded open.

It slammed open so hard and fast the door was half torn off its hinges. The air within blasted out like a charge from a cannon. For a moment the garage was filled with loose tools, parts of vacuum suits and shreds of cloth. A wrench struck Gunther a glancing blow on his arm, spinning him around and knocking him to the floor.

He stared up in shock. Bits and pieces of things hung suspended for a long, surreal instant. Then, the air fled, they began to slowly shower down. He got up awkwardly, massaging his arm through the suit. "Hiro, are you all right? Kreesh?"

"Oh my God," Krishna said.

Gunther spun around. He saw Krishna crouched in the shadow of a flatbed, over something that could not possibly be Hiro, because it bent the wrong way. He walked through shimmering unreality and knelt beside Krishna. He stared down at Hiro's corpse.

Hiro had been standing directly before the door when the overseer opened the door without depressurizing the corridor within first. He had caught the blast straight on. It had lifted him and smashed him against the side of a flatbed, snapping his spine and shattering his helmet visor with the backlash. He must have died instantaneously.

"Who's there?" a woman said.

A jitney had entered the garage without Gunther's noticing it. He looked up in time to see a second enter, and then a third. People began piling out. Soon there were some twenty individuals advancing across the garage. They broke into two groups. One headed straight toward the locks and the smaller group advanced on Gunther and his friends. It looked for all the world like a military operation. "Who's there?" the woman repeated.

Gunther lifted his friend's corpse in his arms and stood. "It's Hiro," he said flatly. "Hiro."

They floated forward cautiously, a semicircle of blank-visored suits like so many kachinas. He could make out the corporate logos. Mitsubishi. Westinghouse. Holst Orbital. Izmailova's red-and-orange suit was among them, and a vivid Mondrian pattern he didn't recognize. The woman spoke again, tensely, warily. "Tell me how you're feeling, Hiro."

It was Beth Hamilton.

"That's not Hiro," Krishna said. "It's Gunther. That's Hiro. That he's carrying. We were out in the highlands and—" His voice cracked and collapsed in confusion.

"Is that you, Krishna?" someone asked. "There's a touch of luck. Send him up front, we're going to need him when we get in." Somebody else slapped an arm over Krishna's shoulders and led him away.

Over the radio, a clear voice spoke to the overseer. "Dmitri, is that you? It's Signe. You remember me, don't you, Dmitri? Signe Ohmstede. I'm your friend."

"Sure I remember you, Signe. I remember you. How could I ever forget my friend? Sure I do."

"Oh, good. I'm so happy. Listen carefully, Dmitri. Everything's fine."

Indignantly, Gunther chinned his radio to send. "The hell it is! That fool up there—!"

A burly man in a Westinghouse suit grabbed Gunther's bad arm and shook him. "Shut the fuck up!" he growled. "This is serious, damn you. We don't have the time to baby you."

Hamilton shoved between them. "For God's sake, Posner, he's just seen—" She stopped. "Let me take care of him. I'll get him calmed down. Just give us half an hour, okay?"

The others traded glances, nodded, and turned away.

To Gunther's surprise, Ekatarina spoke over his trance chip. "I'm sorry, Gunther," she murmured. Then she was gone.

He was still holding Hiro's corpse. He found himself staring down at his friend's ruined face. The flesh was bruised and as puffy-looking as an overboiled hot dog. He couldn't look away.

"Come on." Beth gave him a little shove to get him going. "Put the body in the back of that pick-up and give us a drive out to the cliff." At Hamilton's insistence, Gunther drove. He found it helped, having something to do. Hands afloat on the steering wheel, he stared ahead looking for the Mausoleum road cut-off. His eyes felt scratchy, and inhumanly dry.

"There was a preemptive strike against us," Hamilton said. "Sabotage. We're just now starting to put the pieces together. Nobody knew you were but on the surface or we would've sent somebody out to meet you. It's all been something of a shambles here."

He drove on in silence, cushioned and protected by all those miles of hard vacuum wrapped about him. He could feel the presence of Hiro's corpse in the back of the truck, a constant psychic itch between his shoulder blades. But so long as he didn't speak, he was safe; he could hold himself aloof from the universe that held the pain. It couldn't touch him. He waited, but Beth didn't add anything to what she'd already said.

Finally he said, "Sabotage?"

"A software meltdown at the radio station. Explosions at all the railguns. Three guys from Microspacecraft Applications bought it when the Boitsovij Kot railgun blew. I suppose it was inevitable. All the military industry up here, it's not surprising somebody would want to knock us out of the equation. But that's not all. Something's happened to the people in Bootstrap. Something really horrible. I was out at the Observatory when it happened. The newsjay called back to see if there was any backup software to get the station going again, and she got nothing but gibberish. Crazy stuff. I mean, really crazy. We had to disconnect the Observatory's remotes, because the operators were . . ." She was crying now, softly and insistently, and it was a minute before she could speak again. "Some sort of biological weapon. That's all we know."

"We're here."

As he pulled up to the foot of the Mausoleum cliff, it occurred to Gunther that they hadn't thought to bring a drilling rig. Then he counted ten black niches in the rockface, and realized that somebody had been thinking ahead.

"The only people who weren't hit were those who were working at the Center or the Observatory, or out on the surface. Maybe a hundred of us all told."

They walked around to the back of the pick-up. Gunther waited, but Hamilton didn't offer to carry the body. For some reason that made him feel angry and resentful. He unlatched the gate, hopped up on the treads, and hoisted the suited corpse. "Let's get this over with."

Before today, only six people had ever died on the Moon. They walked past the caves in which their bodies awaited eternity. Gunther knew their names by heart: Heisse, Yasuda, Spehalski, Dubinin, Mikami, Castillo. And now Hiro. It seemed incomprehensible that the day should ever come when there would be too many dead to know them all by name.

Daisies and tiger lilies had been scattered before the vaults in such profusion that he couldn't help crushing some underfoot.

They entered the first empty niche, and he laid Hiro down upon a stone table cut into the rock. In the halo of his helmet lamp the body looked piteously twisted and uncomfortable. Gunther found that he was crying, large hot tears that crawled down his face and got into his mouth when he inhaled. He cut off the radio until he had managed to blink the tears away. "Shit." He wiped a hand across his helmet. "I suppose we ought to say something."

Hamilton took his hand and squeezed.

"I've never seen him as happy as he was today. He was going to get married. He was jumping around, laughing and talking about raising a family. And now he's dead, and I don't even know what his religion was." A thought occurred to him, and he turned helplessly toward Hamilton. "What are we going to tell Anya?"

"She's got problems of her own. Come on, say a prayer and let's go. You'll run out of oxygen."

"Yeah, okay." He bowed his head. *"The Lord is my shepherd, I shall not want. . . ."*

Back at Bootstrap, the surface party had seized the airlocks and led the overseer away from the controls. The man from Westinghouse, Posner, looked down on them from the observation window. "Don't crack your suits," he warned. "Keep them sealed tight at all times. Whatever hit the bastards here is still around. Might be in the water, might be in the air. One whiff and you're out of here! You got that?"

"Yeah, yeah," Gunther grumbled. "Keep your shirt on."

Posner's hand froze on the controls. "Let's get serious here. I'm not letting you in until you acknowledge the gravity of the situation. This isn't a picnic outing. If you're not prepared to help, we don't need you. Is that understood?"

"We understand completely, and we'll cooperate to the fullest," Hamilton said quickly. "Won't we, Weil?"

He nodded miserably.

Only the one lock had been breached, and there were five more sets of pressurized doors between it and the bulk of Bootstrap's air. The city's designers had been cautious.

Overseen by Posner, they passed through the corridors, locks and changing rooms and up the cargo escalators. Finally they emerged into the city interior.

They stood blinking on the lip of Hell.

At first, it was impossible to pinpoint any source for the pervasive sense of wrongness nattering at the edge of consciousness. The parks were dotted with people, the fill lights at the juncture of crater walls and canopy were bright, and the waterfalls still fell gracefully from terrace to terrace. Button quail bobbed comically in the grass.

Then small details intruded. A man staggered about the fourth level, head jerking, arms waving stiffly. A plump woman waddled by, pulling an empty cart made from a wheeled microfactory stand, quacking like a duck. Someone sat in the knee-high forest by Noguchi Park, tearing out the trees one by one.

But it was the still figures that were on examination more profoundly disturbing. Here a man lay half in and half out of a tunnel entrance, as unselfconscious as a dog. There, three women stood in extreme postures of lassitude, bordering on despair. Everywhere, people did not touch or speak or show in any way that they were aware of one other. They shared an absolute and universal isolation.

"What shall we—" Something slammed onto Gunther's back. He was knocked forward, off his feet. Tumbling, he became aware that fists were striking him, again and again, and then that a lean man was kneeling atop his chest, hysterically shouting, "Don't do it! Don't do it!"

Hamilton seized the man's shoulders, and pulled him away. Gunther got to his knees. He looked into the face of madness: eyes round and fearful, expression full of panic. The man was terrified of Gunther.

With an abrupt wrench, the man broke free. He ran as if pursued by demons. Hamilton stared after him. "You okay?" she asked.

"Yeah, sure." Gunther adjusted his tool harness. "Let's see if we can find the others."

They walked toward the lake, staring about at the self-absorbed figures scattered about the grass. Nobody attempted to speak to them. A woman ran by, barefooted. Her arms were filled with flowers. "Hey!" Hamilton called after her. She smiled fleetingly over her shoulder, but did not slow. Gunther knew her vaguely, an executive supervisor for Martin Marietta.

"Is everybody here crazy?" he asked.

"Sure looks that way."

The woman had reached the shore and was flinging the blossoms into the water with great sweeps of her arm. They littered the surface.

"Damned waste." Gunther had come to Bootstrap before the flowers; he knew the effort involved getting permission to plant them and rewriting the city's ecologics. A man in a blue-striped Krupp suit was running along the verge of the lake.

The woman, flowers gone, threw herself into the water.

At first it appeared she'd suddenly decided to take a dip. But from the struggling, floundering way she thrashed deeper into the water it was clear that she could not swim.

In the time it took Gunther to realize this, Hamilton had leaped forward, running for the lake. Belatedly, he started after her. But the man in the Krupp suit was ahead of them both. He splashed in after the woman. An outstretched hand seized her shoulder and then he fell, pulling her under. She was red-faced and choking when he emerged again, arm across her chest.

By then Gunther and Beth were wading into the lake, and together they three got the woman to shore. When she was released, the woman calmly turned and walked away, as if nothing had happened.

"Gone for more flowers," the Krupp component explained. "This is the third time fair Ophelia there's tried to drown herself. She's not the only one. I've been hanging around, hauling 'em out when they stumble in."

"Do you know where everybody else is? Is there anyone in charge? Somebody giving out orders?"

"Do you need any help?" Gunther asked.

The Krupp man shrugged. "I'm fine. No idea where the others are, though. My friends were going on to the second level when I decided I ought to stay here. If you see them, you might tell 'em I'd appreciate hearing back from them. Three guys in Krupp suits."

"We'll do that," Gunther said.

Hamilton was already walking away.

On a step just beneath the top of the stairs sprawled one of Gunther's fellow G5 components. "Sidney," he said carefully. "How's it going?"

Sidney giggled. "I'm making the effort, if that's what you mean. I don't see that the 'how' of it makes much difference."

"Okay."

"A better way of phrasing that might be to ask why I'm not at work." He stood, and in a very natural manner accompanied Gunther up the steps. "Obviously I can't be two places at once. You wouldn't want to perform major surgery in your own absence, would you?" He giggled again. "It's an oxymoron. Like horses: Those classically beautiful Praxitelesian bodies excreting these long surreal turds."

"Okay."

"I've always admired them for squeezing so much art into a single image."

"Sidney," Hamilton said. "We're looking for our friends. Three people in blue-striped work suits."

"I've seen them. I know just where they went." His eyes were cool and vacant; they didn't seem to focus on anything in particular.

"Can you lead us to them?"

"Even a flower recognizes its own face." A gracefully winding gravel path led through private garden plots and croquet malls. They followed him down it.

There were not many people on the second terrace; with the fall of madness, most seemed to have retreated into the caves. Those few who remained either ignored or cringed away from them. Gunther found himself staring obsessively into their faces, trying to analyze the deficiency he felt in each. Fear nested in their eyes, and the appalled awareness that some terrible thing had happened to them coupled with a complete ignorance of its nature.

"God, these people!"

Hamilton grunted.

He felt he was walking through a dream. Sounds were muted by his suit, and colors less intense seen through his helmet visor. It was as if he had been subtly removed from the world, there and not-there simultaneously, an impression that strengthened with each new face that looked straight through him with mad, unseeing indifference.

Sidney turned a corner, broke into a trot and jogged into a tunnel entrance. Gunther ran after him. At the mouth of the tunnel, he paused to let his helmet adjust to the new light levels. When it cleared he saw Sidney dart down a side passage. He followed.

At the intersection of passages, he looked and saw no trace of their guide. Sidney had disappeared. "Did you see which way he went?" he asked Hamilton over the radio. There was no answer. "Beth?"

He started down the corridor, halted, and turned back. These things went deep. He could wander around in them forever. He went back out to the terraces. Hamilton was nowhere to be seen.

For lack of any better plan, he followed the path. Just beyond an ornamental holly bush he was pulled up short by a vision straight out of William Blake.

The man had discarded shirt and sandals, and wore only a pair of shorts. He squatted atop a boulder, alert, patient, eating a tomato. A steel pipe slanted across his knees like a staff or scepter, and he had woven a crown of sorts from platinum wire with a fortune's worth of hyper-conductor chips dangling over his forehead. He looked every inch a kingly animal.

He stared at Gunther, calm and unblinking.

Gunther shivered. The man seemed less human than anthropoid, crafty in its way, but unthinking. He felt as if he were staring across the eons at Grandfather Ape, crouched on the edge of awareness. An involuntary thrill of superstitious awe seized him. Was this what happened when the higher mental functions were scraped away? Did Archetype lie just beneath the skin, waiting for the opportunity to emerge?

"I'm looking for my friend," he said. "A woman in a G5 suit like mine? Have you seen her? She was looking for three—" He stopped. The man was staring at him blankly. "Oh, never mind."

He turned away and walked on.

After a time, he lost all sense of continuity. Existence fragmented into unconnected images: A man bent almost double, leering and squeezing a yellow rubber duckie. A woman leaping up like a jack-in-the-box from behind an air monitor, shrieking and flapping her arms. An old friend sprawled on the ground, crying, with a broken leg. When he tried to help her, she scrabbled away from him in fear. He couldn't get near to her without doing more harm. "Stay here," he said, "I'll find help." Five minutes later he realized that he was lost, with no slightest notion of how to find his way back to her again. He came to the stairs leading back down to the bottom level. There was no reason to go down them. There was no reason not to. He went down.

He had just reached the bottom of the stairs when someone in a lavender boutique suit hurried by.

Gunther chinned on his helmet radio.

"Hello!" The lavender suit glanced back at him, its visor a plate of obsidian, but did not turn back. "Do you know where everyone's gone? I'm totally lost. How can I find out what I should be doing?" The lavender suit ducked into a tunnel.

Faintly, a voice answered, "Try the city manager's office."

The city manager's office was a tight little cubby an eighth of a kilometer deep within the tangled maze of administrative and service tunnels. It had never been very important in the scheme of things. The city manager's prime duties were keeping the air and water replenished and scheduling airlock inspections, functions any computer could handle better than a man, had they dared trust them to a machine. The room had probably never been as crowded as it was now. Dozens of people suited for full vacuum spilled out into the hall, anxiously listening to Ekatarina confer with the city's Crisis Management Program. Gunther pushed in as close as he could; even so, he could barely see her.

"—the locks, the farms and utilities, and we've locked away all the remotes. What comes next?"

Ekatarina's peecee hung from her work harness, amplifying the CMP's silent voice. "Now that elementary control has been established, second priority must go to the industrial sector. The factories must be locked down. The reactors must be put to sleep. There is not sufficient human supervisory presence to keep them running. The factories have mothballing programs available upon request.

"Third, the farms cannot tolerate neglect. Fifteen minutes without oxygen, and all the tilapia will die. The calamari are even more delicate. Three experienced agricultural components must be assigned immediately. Double that number, if you only have inexperienced components. Advisory software is available. What are your resources?"

"Let me get back to you on that. What else?"

"What about the people?" a man asked belligerently. "What the hell are you worrying about factories for, when our people are in the state they're in?"

Izmailova looked up sharply. "You're one of Chang's research components, aren't you? Why are you here? Isn't there enough for you to do?" She looked about, as if abruptly awakened from sleep. "All of you! What are you waiting for?"

"You can't put us off that easily! Who made you the little brass-plated general? We don't have to take orders from you."

The bystanders shuffled uncomfortably, not leaving, waiting to take their cue from each other. Their suits were as good as identical in this crush, their helmets blank and expressionless. They looked like so many ambulatory eggs.

The crowd's mood balanced on the instant, ready to fall into acceptance or anger with a featherweight's push. Gunther raised an arm. "General!" he said loudly. "Private Weil here! I'm awaiting my orders. Tell me what to do."

Laughter rippled through the room, and the tension eased. Ekatarina said, "Take whoever's nearest you, and start clearing the afflicted out of the administrative areas. Guide them out toward the open, where they won't be so likely to hurt themselves. Whenever you get a room or corridor emptied, lock it up tight. Got that?"

"Yes, ma'am." He tapped the suit nearest him, and its helmet dipped in a curt nod. But when they turned to leave, their way was blocked by the crush of bodies.

"You!" Ekatarina jabbed a finger. "Go to the farmlocks and foam them shut; I don't want any chance of getting them contaminated. Anyone with experience running factories—that's most of us, I think—should find a remote and get to work shutting the things down. The CMP will help direct you. If you have nothing else to do, buddy up and work at clearing out the corridors. I'll call a general meeting when we've put together a more comprehensive plan of action." She paused. "What have I left out?"

Surprisingly, the CMP answered her: "There are twenty-three children in the city, two of them seven-year-old pre-legals and the rest five years of age or younger, offspring of registered-permanent lunar components. Standing directives are that children be given special care and protection. The third-level chapel can be converted to a care center. Word should be spread that as they are found, the children are to be brought there. Assign one reliable individual to oversee them."

"My God, yes." She turned to the belligerent man from the Center, and snapped, "Do it."

He hesitated, then saluted ironically and turned to go.

That broke the logjam. The crowd began to disperse. Gunther and his co-worker—it turned out to be Liza Nagenda, another ground-rat like himself—set to work.

In after years Gunther was to remember this period as a time when his life entered a dark tunnel. For long, nightmarish hours he and Liza shuffled from office to storage room, struggling to move the afflicted out of the corporate areas and into the light.

The afflicted did not cooperate.

The first few rooms they entered were empty. In the fourth, a distraught-looking woman was furiously going through drawers and files and flinging their contents away. Trash covered the floor. "It's in here somewhere, it's in here somewhere," she said frantically.

"What's in there, darling?" Gunther said soothingly. He had to speak loudly so he could be heard through his helmet. "What are you looking for?"

She tilted her head up with a smile of impish delight. Using both hands, she smoothed back her hair, elbows high, pushing it straight over her skull, then tucking in stray strands behind her ears. "It doesn't matter, because I'm sure to find it now. Two scarabs appear, and between them the blazing disk of the sun, that's a good omen, not to mention being an analogy for sex. I've had sex, all the sex anyone could want, buggered behind the outhouse by the lizard king when I was nine. What did I care? I had wings then and thought that I could fly."

Gunther edged a little closer. "You're not making any sense at all."

"You know, Tolstoy said there was a green stick in the woods behind his house that once found would cause all men to love one another. I believe in that green stick as a basic principle of physical existence. The universe exists in a matrix of four dimensions which we can perceive and seven which we cannot, which is why we experience peace and brotherhood as a seven-dimensional greenstick phenomenon."

"You've got to listen to me."

"Why? You gonna tell me Hitler is dead? I don't believe in that kind of crap."

"Oh hell," Nagenda said. "You can't reason with a flick. Just grab her arms and we'll chuck her out."

It wasn't that easy, though. The woman was afraid of them. Whenever they approached her, she slipped fearfully away.

If they moved slowly, they could not corner her, and when they both rushed her, she leaped up over a desk and then down into the knee-hole. Nagenda grabbed her legs and pulled. The woman wailed, and clutched at the knees of her suit. "Get offa me," Liza snarled. "Gunther, get this crazy woman off my damn legs."

"Don't kill me!" the woman screamed. "I've always voted twice—you know I did. I told them you were a gangster, but I was wrong. Don't take the oxygen out of my lungs!"

They got the woman out of the office, then lost her again when Gunther turned to lock the door. She went fluttering down the corridor with Nagenda in hot pursuit. Then she dove into another office, and they had to start all over again.

It took over an hour to drive the woman from the corridors and release her into the park. The next three went quickly enough by contrast. The one after that was difficult again, and the fifth turned out to be the first woman they had encountered, wandered back to look for her office. When they'd brought her to the open again, Liza Nagenda said, "That's four flicks down and three thousand, eight hundred fifty-eight to go."

"Look—" Gunther began. And then Krishna's voice sounded over his trance chip, stiffly and with exaggerated clarity. "Everyone is to go to the central lake immediately for an organizational meeting. Repeat: Go to the lake immediately. Go to the lake now." He was obviously speaking over a jury-rigged transmitter. The sound was bad and his voice boomed and popped on the chip.

"Alright, okay, I got that," Liza said. "You can shut up now."

"Please go to the lake immediately. Everyone is to go directly to the central—"

"Sheesh."

By the time they got out to the parklands again, the open areas were thick with people. Not just the suited figures of the survivors, either. All the afflicted were emerging from the caves and corridors of Bootstrap. They walked blindly, uncertainly, toward the lake, as if newly called from the grave. The ground level was filling with people.

"Sonofabitch," Gunther said wonderingly.

"Gunther?" Nagenda asked. "What's going on?"

"It's the trance chips! Sonofabitch, all we had to do was speak to them over the chips. They'll do whatever the voice in their heads tells them to do."

The land about the lake was so crowded that Gunther had trouble spotting any other suits.

Then he saw a suited figure standing on the edge of the second level waving broadly. He waved back and headed for the stairs.

By the time he got to level two, a solid group of the unafflicted had gathered. More and more came up, drawn by the concentration of suits. Finally Ekatarina spoke over the open channel of her suit radio.

"There's no reason to wait for us all to gather. I think everyone is close enough to hear me. Sit down, take a little rest, you've all earned it." People eased down on the grass. Some sprawled on their backs or stomachs, fully suited. Most just sat.

"By a fortunate accident, we've discovered a means of controlling our afflicted friends." There was light applause. "But there are still many problems before us, and they won't all be solved so easily. We've all seen the obvious. Now I must tell you of worse. If the war on Earth goes full thermonuclear, we will be completely and totally cut off, possibly for decades."

A murmur passed through the crowd.

"What does this mean? Beyond the immediate inconveniences—no luxuries, no more silk shirts, no new seed stock, no new videos, no way home for those of us who hadn't already decided to stay—we will be losing much that we require for survival. All our microfacturing capability comes from the Swiss Orbitals. Our water reserves are sufficient for a year, but we lose minute quantities of water vapor to rust and corrosion and to the vacuum every time somebody goes in or out an airlock, and those quantities are necessary for our existence.

"But we can survive. We can process raw hydrogen and oxygen from the regolith, and burn them to produce water. We already make our own air. We can do without most nanoelectronics. We can thrive and prosper and grow, even if Earth . . . even if the worst happens. But to do so we'll need our full manufacturing capability, and full supervisory capability as well. We must not only restore our factories, but find a way to restore our people. There'll be work and more for all of us in the days ahead."

Nagenda touched helmets with Gunther and muttered, "What a crock."

"Come on, I want to hear this."

"Fortunately, the Crisis Management Program has contingency plans for exactly this situation. According to its records, which may be incomplete, I have more military command experience than any other functional. Does anyone wish to challenge this?" She waited, but nobody said anything. "We will go to a quasimilitary structure for the duration of the emergency. This is strictly for organizational purposes. There will be no privileges afforded the officers, and the military structure will be dismantled immediately upon resolution of our present problems. That's paramount."

She glanced down at her peecee. "To that purpose, I am establishing beneath me a triumvirate of subordinate officers, consisting of Carlos Diaz-Rodrigues, Miiko Ezumi, and Will Posner. Beneath them will be nine officers, each responsible for a cadre of no more than ten individuals."

She read out names. Gunther was assigned to Cadre Four, Beth Hamilton's group. Then Ekatarina said, "We're all tired. The gang back at the Center have rigged up a decontamination procedure, a kitchen and sleeping spaces of sorts. Cadres One, Two and Three will put in four more hours here, then pull down a full eight hours sleep. Cadres Four through Nine may return now to the Center for a meal and four hours rest." She stopped. "That's it. Go get some shut-eye."

A ragged cheer arose, fell flat and died. Gunther stood. Liza Nagenda gave him a friendly squeeze on the butt and when he started to the right yanked his arm and pointed him left, toward the service escalators. With easy familiarity, she slid an arm around his waist.

He'd known guys who'd slept with Liza Nagenda, and they all agreed that she was

bad news, possessive, hysterical, ludicrously emotional. But what the hell. It was easier than not.

They trudged off.

There was too much to do. They worked to exhaustion—it was not enough. They
rigged a system of narrow-band radio transmissions for the CMP and ran a microwave patch back to the Center, so it could direct their efforts more efficiently—it
was not enough. They organized and rearranged constantly. But the load was too
great and accidents inevitably happened.

Half the surviving railguns—small units used to deliver raw and semiprocessed
materials over the highlands and across the bay—were badly damaged when the
noonday sun buckled their aluminum rails; the sunscreens had not been put in
place in time. An unknown number of robot bulldozers had wandered off from the
strip mines and were presumably lost. It was hard to guess how many because the
inventory records were scrambled. None of the food stored in Bootstrap could be
trusted; the Center's meals had to be harvested direct from the farms and taken out
through the emergency locks. An inexperienced farmer mishandled her remote,
and ten aquaculture tanks boiled out into vacuum, geysering nine thousand finger-
lings across the surface. On Posner's orders, the remote handler rigs were hastily
packed and moved to the Center. When uncrated, most were found to have damaged rocker arms.

There were small victories. On his second shift, Gunther found fourteen bales of
cotton in vacuum storage and set an assembler to sewing futons for the Center. That
meant an end to sleeping on bare floors and made him a local hero for the rest of
that day. There were not enough toilets in the Center; Diaz-Rodrigues ordered the
flare storm shelters in the factories stripped of theirs. Huriel Garza discovered a talent for cooking with limited resources.

But they were losing ground. The afflicted were unpredictable, and they were
everywhere. A demented systems analyst, obeying the voices in his head, dumped
several barrels of lubricating oil in the lake. The water filters clogged, and the
streams had to be shut down for repairs. A doctor somehow managed to strangle herself with her own diagnostic harness. The city's ecologics were badly stressed by random vandalism.

Finally somebody thought to rig up a voice loop for continuous transmission. "I
am calm," it said. "I am tranquil. I do not want to do anything. I am happy where
I am."

Gunther was working with Liza Nagenda trying to get the streams going again
when the loop came on. He looked up and saw an uncanny quiet spread over Bootstrap. Up and down the terraces, the flicks stood in postures of complete and utter
impassivity. The only movement came from the small number of suits scurrying like
beetles among the newly catatonic.

Liza put her hands on her hips. "Terrific. Now we've got to *feed* them."

"Hey, cut me some slack, okay? This is the first good news I've heard since I don't
know when."

"It's not good anything, sweetbuns. It's just more of the same."

She was right. Relieved as he was, Gunther knew it. One hopeless task had been traded for another.

He was wearily suiting up for his third day when Hamilton stopped him and said, "Weil! You know any electrical engineering?"

"Not really, no. I mean, I can do the wiring for a truck, or maybe rig up a microwave relay, stuff like that, but . . ."

"It'll have to do. Drop what you're on, and help Krishna set up a system for controlling the flicks. Some way we can handle them individually."

They set up shop in Krishna's old lab. The remnants of old security standards still lingered, and nobody had been allowed to sleep there. Consequently, the room was wonderfully neat and clean, all crafted-in-orbit laboratory equipment with smooth, anonymous surfaces. It was a throwback to a time before clutter and madness had taken over. If it weren't for the new-tunnel smell, the raw tang of cut rock the air carried, it would be possible to pretend nothing had happened.

Gunther stood in a telepresence rig, directing a remote through Bootstrap's apartments. They were like so many unconnected cells of chaos. He entered one and found the words BUDDHA = COSMIC INERTIA scrawled on its wall with what looked to be human feces. A woman sat on the futon tearing handfuls of batting from it and flinging them in the air. Cotton covered the room like a fresh snowfall. The next apartment was empty and clean, and a microfactory sat gleaming on a ledge. "I hereby nationalize you in the name of the People's Provisional Republic of Bootstrap, and of the oppressed masses everywhere," he said dryly. The remote gingerly picked it up. "You done with that chip diagram yet?"

"It will not be long now," Krishna said.

They were building a prototype controller. The idea was to code each peecee, so the CMP could identify and speak to its owner individually. By stepping down the voltage, they could limit the peecee's transmission range to a meter and a half so that each afflicted person could be given individualized orders. The existing chips, however, were high-strung Swiss Orbital thoroughbreds, and couldn't handle oddball power yields. They had to be replaced.

"I don't see how you can expect to get any useful work out of these guys, though. I mean, what we need are supervisors. You can't hope to get coherent thought out of them."

Bent low over his peecee, Krishna did not answer at first. Then he said, "Do you know how a yogi stops his heart? We looked into that when I was in grad school. We asked Yogi Premanand if he would stop his heart while wired up to our instruments, and he graciously consented. We had all the latest brain scanners, but it turned out the most interesting results were recorded by the EKG.

"We found that the yogi's heart did not, as we had expected, slow down, but rather went faster and faster, until it reached its physical limits and began to fibrillate. He had not slowed his heart; he had sped it up. It did not stop, but went into spasm.

"After our tests, I asked him if he had known these facts. He said no, that they were most interesting. He was polite about it, but clearly did not think our findings very significant."

"So you're saying . . . ?"

"The problem with schizophrenics is that they have too much going on in their heads. Too many voices. Too many ideas. They can't focus their attention on a single chain of thought. But it would be a mistake to think them incapable of complex reasoning. In fact, they're thinking brilliantly. Their brains are simply operating at such peak efficiencies that they can't organize their thoughts coherently.

"What the trance chip does is to provide one more voice, but a louder, more insistent one. That's why they obey it. It breaks through that noise, provides a focus, serves as a matrix along which thought can crystallize."

The remote unlocked the door into a conference room deep in the administrative tunnels. Eight microfactories waited in a neat row atop the conference table. It added the ninth, turned, and left, locking the door behind it. "You know," Gunther said, "all these elaborate precautions may be unnecessary. Whatever was used on Bootstrap may not be in the air anymore. It may never have been in the air. It could've been in the water or something."

"Oh, it's there all right, in the millions. We're dealing with an airborne schizomimetic engine. It's designed to hang around in the air indefinitely."

"A schizomimetic engine? What the hell is that?"

In a distracted monotone, Krishna said, "A schizomimetic engine is a strategic nonlethal weapon with high psychological impact. It not only incapacitates its target vectors, but places a disproportionately heavy burden on the enemy's manpower and material support caring for the victims. Due to the particular quality of the effect, it has a profoundly demoralizing influence on those exposed to the victims, especially those involved in their care. Thus, it is particularly desirable as a strategic weapon." He might have been quoting from an operations manual.

Gunther pondered that. "Calling the meeting over the chips wasn't a mistake, was it? You knew it would work. You knew they would obey a voice speaking inside their heads."

"Yes."

"This shit was brewed up at the Center, wasn't it? This is the stuff that you couldn't talk about."

"Some of it."

Gunther powered down his rig and flipped up the lens. "God damn you, Krishna! God damn you straight to Hell, you stupid fucker!"

Krishna looked up from his work, bewildered. "Have I said something wrong?"

"No! No, you haven't said a damned thing wrong—you've just driven four thousand people out of their fucking minds, is all! Wake up and take a good look at what you maniacs have done with your weapons research!"

"It wasn't weapons research," Krishna said mildly. He drew a long, involuted line on the schematic. "But when pure research is funded by the military, the military will seek out military applications for the research. That's just the way it is."

"What's the difference? It happened. You're responsible."

Now Krishna actually set his peecee aside. He spoke with uncharacteristic fire. "Gunther, we need this information. Do you realize that we are trying to run a technological civilization with a brain that was evolved in the neolithic? I am perfectly serious. We're all trapped in the old hunter-gatherer programs, and they are of no use to us anymore. Take a look at what's happening on Earth. They're hip-deep in a war that nobody meant to start and nobody wants to fight and it's even money that nobody can stop. The type of thinking that put us in this corner is not to our benefit. It has to change. And that's what we are working toward—taming the human brain. Harnessing it. Reining it in.

"Granted, our research has been turned against us. But what's one more weapon among so many? If neuroprogrammers hadn't been available, something else would have been used. Mustard gas maybe, or plutonium dust. For that matter, they could've just blown a hole in the canopy and let us all strangle."

"That's self-justifying bullshit, Krishna! Nothing can excuse what you've done."

Quietly, but with conviction, Krishna said, "You will never convince me that our research is not the most important work we could possibly be doing today. We must seize control of this monster within our skulls. We must change our ways of thinking." His voice dropped. "The sad thing is that we cannot change unless we survive. But in order to survive, we must first change."

They worked in silence after that.

Gunther awoke from restless dreams to find that the sleep shift was only half over. Liza was snoring. Careful not to wake her, he pulled his clothes on and padded barefoot out of his niche and down the hall. The light was on in the common room and he heard voices.

Ekatarina looked up when he entered. Her face was pale and drawn. Faint circles had formed under her eyes. She was alone.

"Oh, hi. I was just talking with the CMP." She thought off her peecee. "Have a seat."

He pulled up a chair and hunched down over the table. Confronted by her, he found it took a slight but noticeable effort to draw his breath. "So. How are things going?"

"They'll be trying out your controllers soon. The first batch of chips ought to be coming out of the factories in an hour or so. I thought I'd stay up to see how they work out."

"It's that bad, then?" Ekatarina shook her head, would not look at him. "Hey, come on, here you are waiting up on the results, and I can see how tired you are. There must be a lot riding on this thing."

"More than you know," she said bleakly. "I've just been going over the numbers. Things are worse than you can imagine."

He reached out and took her cold, bloodless hand. She squeezed him so tightly it hurt. Their eyes met and he saw in hers all the fear and wonder he felt.

Wordlessly, they stood.

"I'm niching alone," Ekatarina said. She had not let go of his hand, held it so tightly in fact, that it seemed she would never let it go.

Gunther let her lead him away.

They made love, and talked quietly about inconsequential things, and made love again. Gunther had thought she would nod off immediately after the first time, but she was too full of nervous energy for that.

"Tell me when you're about to come," she murmured. "Tell me when you're coming."

He stopped moving. "Why do you always say that?"

Ekatarina looked up at him dazedly, and he repeated the question. Then she laughed a deep, throaty laugh. "Because I'm frigid."

"Hah?"

She took his hand, and brushed her cheek against it. Then she ducked her head, continuing the motion across her neck and up the side of her scalp. He felt the short, prickly hair against his palm and then, behind her ear, two bumps under the skin where biochips had been implanted. One of those would be her trance chip and the other . . . "It's a prosthetic," she explained. Her eyes were grey and solemn. "It hooks into the pleasure centers. When I need to, I can turn on my orgasm at a thought. That way we can always come at the same time." She moved her hips slowly beneath him as she spoke.

"But that means you don't really need to have any kind of sexual stimulation at all, do you? You can trigger an orgasm at will. While you're riding on a bus. Or behind a desk. You could just turn that thing on and come for hours at a time."

She looked amused. "I'll tell you a secret. When it was new, I used to do stunts like that. Everybody does. One outgrows that sort of thing quickly."

With more than a touch of stung pride, Gunther said, "Then what am I doing here? If you've got that thing, what the hell do you need me for?" He started to draw away from her.

She pulled him down atop her again. "You're kind of comforting," she said. "In an argumentative way. Come here."

He got back to his futon and began gathering up the pieces of his suit. Liza sat up sleepily and gawked at him. "So," she said. "It's like that, is it?"

"Yeah, well. I kind of left something unfinished. An old relationship." Warily, he extended a hand. "No hard feelings, huh?"

Ignoring his hand, she stood, naked and angry. "You got the nerve to stand there without even wiping my smile off your dick first and say no hard feelings? Asshole!"

"Aw, come on now, Liza, it's not like that."

"Like hell it's not! You got a shot at that white-assed Russian ice queen, and I'm history. Don't think I don't know all about her."

"I was hoping we could still be, you know, friends."

"Nice trick, shithead." She balled her fist and hit him hard in the center of his chest. Tears began to form in her eyes. "You just slink away. I'm tired of looking at you."

He left.

But did not sleep. Ekatarina was awake and ebullient over the first reports coming in of the new controller system. "They're working!" she cried. "They're working!"

She'd pulled on a silk camisole, and strode back and forth excitedly, naked to the waist. Her pubic hair was a white flame, with almost invisible trails of smaller hairs reaching for her navel and caressing the sweet insides of her thighs. Tired as he was, Gunther felt new desire for her. In a weary, washed-out way, he was happy.

"Whooh!" She kissed him hard, not sexually, and called up the CMP. "Rerun all our earlier projections. We're putting our afflicted components back to work. Adjust all work schedules."

"As you direct."

"How does this change our long-range prospects?"

The program was silent for several seconds, processing. Then it said, "You are about to enter a necessary but very dangerous stage of recovery. You are going from a low-prospects high-stability situation to a high-prospects high-instability one. With leisure your unafflicted components will quickly grow dissatisfied with your government."

"What happens if I just step down?"

"Prospects worsen drastically."

Ekatarina ducked her head. "All right, what's likely to be our most pressing new problem?"

"The unafflicted components will demand to know more about the war on Earth. They'll want the media feeds restored immediately."

"I could rig up a receiver easily enough," Gunther volunteered. "Nothing fancy, but . . ."

"Don't you dare!"

"Hah? Why not?"

"Gunther, let me put it to you this way: What two nationalities are most heavily represented here?"

"Well, I guess that would be Russia and—oh."

"Oh is right. For the time being, I think it's best if nobody knows for sure who's supposed to be enemies with whom." She asked the CMP, "How should I respond?"

"Until the situation stabilizes, you have no choice but distraction. Keep their minds occupied. Hunt down the saboteurs and then organize war crime trials."

"That's out. No witch hunts, no scapegoats, no trials. We're all in this together."

Emotionlessly, the CMP said, "Violence is the left hand of government. You are rash to dismiss its potentials without serious thought."

"I won't discuss it."

"Very well. If you wish to postpone the use of force for the present, you could hold a hunt for the weapon used on Bootstrap. Locating and identifying it would involve everyone's energies without necessarily implicating anybody. It would also be widely interpreted as meaning an eventual cure was possible, thus boosting the general morale without your actually lying."

Tiredly, as if this were something she had gone over many times already, she said, "Is there really no hope of curing them?"

"Anything is possible. In light of present resources, though, it cannot be considered likely."

Ekatarina thought the peecee off, dismissing the CMP. She sighed. "Maybe that's what we ought to do. Donkey up a hunt for the weapon. We ought to be able to do something with that notion."

Puzzled, Gunther said, "But it was one of Chang's weapons, wasn't it? A schizomimetic engine, right?"

"Where did you hear that?" she demanded sharply.

"Well, Krishna said . . . He didn't act like . . . I thought it was public knowledge."

Ekatarina's face hardened. "Program!" she thought.

The CMP came back to life. "Ready."

"Locate Krishna Narasimhan, unafflicted, Cadre Five. I want to speak with him immediately." Ekatarina snatched up her panties and shorts, and furiously began dressing. "Where are my damned sandals? Program! Tell him to meet me in the common room. Right away."

"Received."

To Gunther's surprise, it took over an hour for Ekatarina to browbeat Krishna into submission. Finally, though, the young research component went to a lockbox, identified himself to it, and unsealed the storage areas. "It's not all that secure," he said apologetically. "If our sponsors knew how often we just left everything open so we could get in and out, they'd—well, never mind."

He lifted a flat, palm-sized metal rectangle from a cabinet. "This is the most likely means of delivery. It's an aerosol bomb. The biological agents are loaded here, and it's triggered by snapping this back here. It's got enough pressure in it to spew the agents fifty feet straight up. Air currents do the rest." He tossed it to Gunther who stared down at the thing in horror. "Don't worry, it's not armed."

He slid out a slim drawer holding row upon gleaming row of slim chrome cylinders. "These contain the engines themselves. They're off-the-shelf nanoweaponry. State-of-the-art stuff, I guess." He ran a fingertip over them. "We've programmed each to produce a different mix of neurotransmitters. Dopamine, phencylclidine, norepinephrine, acetylcholine, met-enkephalin, substance P, serotonin—there's a hefty slice of Heaven in here, and—" he tapped an empty space "—right here is our missing bit of Hell." He frowned, and muttered, "That's curious. Why are there two cylinders missing?"

"What's that?" Ekatarina said. "I didn't catch what you just said."

"Oh, nothing important. Um, listen, it might help if I yanked a few biological pathways charts and showed you the chemical underpinnings of these things."

"Never mind that. Just keep it sweet and simple. Tell us about these schizomimetic engines."

It took over an hour to explain.

The engines were molecule-sized chemical factories, much like the assemblers in a microfactory. They had been provided by the military, in the hope Chang's group would come up with a misting weapon that could be sprayed in an army's path to cause them to change their loyalty. Gunther dozed off briefly while Krishna was explaining why that was impossible, and woke up sometime after the tiny engines had made their way into the brain.

"It's really a false schizophrenia," Krishna explained. "True schizophrenia is a beautifully complicated mechanism. What these engines create is more like a bargain-basement knockoff. They seize control of the brain chemistry, and start pumping out dopamine and a few other neuromediators. It's not an actual disorder, *per se*. They just keep the brain hopping." He coughed. "You see."

"Okay," Ekatarina said. "Okay. You say you can reprogram these things. How?"

"We use what are technically called messenger engines. They're like neuromodulators—they tell the schizomimetic engines what to do." He slid open another drawer, and in a flat voice said, "They're gone."

"Let's keep to the topic, if we may. We'll worry about your inventory later. Tell us about these messenger engines. Can you brew up a lot of them, to tell the schizomimetics to turn themselves off?"

"No, for two reasons. First, these molecules were hand-crafted in the Swiss Orbitals; we don't have the industrial plant to create them. Secondly, you can't tell the schizomimetics to turn themselves off. They don't have off switches. They're more like catalysts than actual machines. You can reconfigure them to produce different chemicals, but . . ." He stopped, and a distant look came into his eyes. "Damn." He grabbed up his peecee, and a chemical pathways chart appeared on one wall. Then beside it, a listing of major neurofunctions. Then another chart covered with scrawled behavioral symbols. More and more data slammed up on the wall.

"Uh, Krishna . . . ?"

"Oh, go away," he snapped. "This is important."

"You think you might be able to come up with a cure?"

"Cure? No. Something better. Much better."

Ekatarina and Gunther looked at each other. Then she said, "Do you need anything? Can I assign anyone to help you?"

"I need the messenger engines. Find them for me."

"How? How do we find them? Where do we look?"

"Sally Chang," Krishna said impatiently. "She must have them. Nobody else had access." He snatched up a light pen, and began scrawling crabbed formulae on the wall.

"I'll get her for you. Program! Tell—"

"Chang's a flick," Gunther reminded her. "She was caught by the aerosol bomb." Which she must surely have set herself. A neat way of disposing of evidence that might've led to whatever government was running her. She'd have been the first to go mad.

Ekatarina pinched her nose, wincing. "I've been awake too long," she said. "All right, I understand. Krishna, from now on you're assigned permanently to research. The CMP will notify your cadre leader. Let me know if you need any support. Find me a way to turn this damned weapon off." Ignoring the way he shrugged her off, she said to Gunther, "I'm yanking you from Cadre Four. From now on, you report directly to me. I want you to find Chang. Find her, and find those messenger engines."

Gunther was bone-weary. He couldn't remember when he'd last had a good eight hours sleep. But he managed what he hoped was a confident grin. "Received."

A madwoman should not have been able to hide herself. Sally Chang could. Nobody should have been able to evade the CMP's notice, now that it was hooked into a growing number of afflicted individuals. Sally Chang did. The CMP informed Gunther that none of the flicks were aware of Chang's whereabouts. It accepted a directive to have them all glance about for her once every hour until she was found.

In the west tunnels, walls had been torn out to create a space as large as any factory interior. The remotes had been returned, and were now manned by almost two hundred flicks spaced so that they did not impinge upon each other's fields of instruction. Gunther walked by them, through the CMP's whispering voices: "Are all bulldozers accounted for? If so . . . Clear away any malfunctioning machines; they can be placed . . . for vacuum-welded dust on the upper surfaces of the rails . . . reduction temperature, then look to see that the oxygen feed is compatible . . ." At the far end a single suit sat in a chair, overseer unit in its lap.

"How's it going?" Gunther asked.

"Absolutely top-notch." He recognized Takayuni's voice. "Most of the factories are up and running, and we're well on our way to having the railguns operative too. You wouldn't believe the kind of efficiencies we're getting here."

"Good, huh?"

Takayuni grinned; Gunther could hear it in his voice. "Industrious little buggers!"

Takayuni hadn't seen Chang. Gunther moved on.

Some hours later he found himself sitting wearily in Noguchi Park, looking at the torn-up dirt where the kneehigh forest had been. Not a seedling had been spared; the silver birch was extinct as a lunar species. Dead carp floated belly-up in the oil-slicked central lake; a chain-link fence circled it now, to keep out the flicks. There hadn't been the time yet to begin cleaning up the litter, and when he looked about, he saw trash everywhere. It was sad. It reminded him of Earth.

He knew it was time to get going, but he couldn't. His head sagged, touched his chest, and jerked up. Time had passed.

A flicker of motion made him turn. Somebody in a pastel lavender boutique suit hurried by. The woman who had directed him to the city controller's office the other day. "Hello!" he called. "I found everybody just where you said. Thanks. I was starting to get a little spooked."

The lavender suit turned to look at him. Sunlight glinted on black glass. A still, long minute later, she said, "Don't mention it," and started away.

"I'm looking for Sally Chang. Do you know her? Have you seen her? She's a flick, kind of a little woman, flamboyant, used to favor bright clothes, electric makeup, that sort of thing."

"I'm afraid I can't help you." Lavender was carrying three oxytanks in her arms. "You might try the straw market, though. Lots of bright clothes there." She ducked into a tunnel opening and disappeared within.

Gunther stared after her distractedly, then shook his head. He felt so very, very tired.

The straw market looked as though it had been through a storm. The tents had been torn down, the stands knocked over, the goods looted. Shards of orange and green glass crunched underfoot. Yet a rack of Italian scarfs worth a year's salary stood untouched amid the rubble. It made no sense at all.

Up and down the market, flicks were industriously cleaning up. They stooped and lifted and swept. One of them was being beaten by a suit.

Gunther blinked. He could not react to it as a real event. The woman cringed under the blows, shrieking wildly and scuttling away from them. One of the tents had been re-erected, and within the shadow of its rainbow silks, four other suits lounged against the bar. Not a one of them moved to help the woman.

"Hey!" Gunther shouted. He felt hideously self-conscious, as if he'd been abruptly thrust into the middle of a play without memorized lines or any idea of the plot or notion of what his role in it was. "Stop that!"

The suit turned toward him. It held the woman's slim arm captive in one gloved hand. "Go away," a male voice growled over the radio.

"What do you think you're doing? Who are you?" The man wore a Westinghouse suit, one of a dozen or so among the unafflicted. But Gunther recognized a brown, kidney-shaped scorch mark on the abdomen panel. "Posner—is that you? Let that woman go."

"She's not a woman," Posner said. "Hell, look at her—she's not even human. She's a flick."

Gunther set his helmet to record. "I'm taping this," he warned. "You hit that woman again, and Ekatarina will see it all. I promise."

Posner released the woman. She stood dazed for a second or two, and then the voice from her peecee reasserted control. She bent to pick up a broom, and returned to work.

Switching off his helmet, Gunther said, "Okay. What did she do?"

Indignantly, Posner extended a foot. He pointed sternly down at it. "She peed all over my boot!"

The suits in the tent had been watching with interest. Now they roared. "Your own fault Will!" one of them called out. "I told you you weren't scheduling in enough time for personal hygiene."

"Don't worry about a little moisture. It'll boil off next time you hit vacuum!"

But Gunther was not listening. He stared at the flick Posner had been mistreating and wondered why he hadn't recognized Anya earlier. Her mouth was pursed, her face squinched up tight with worry, as if there were a key in the back of her head that had been wound three times too many. Her shoulders cringed forward now, too. But still.

"I'm sorry, Anya," he said. "Hiro is dead. There wasn't anything we could do."

She went on sweeping, oblivious, unhappy.

He caught the shift's last jitney back to the Center. It felt good to be home again. Miiko Ezumi had decided to loot the outlying factories of their oxygen and water surpluses, then carved a shower room from the rock. There was a long line for only three minutes' use, and no soap, but nobody complained. Some people pooled their time, showering two and three together. Those waiting their turns joked rowdily.

Gunther washed, grabbed some clean shorts and a Glavkosmos teeshirt, and padded down the hall. He hesitated outside the common room, listening to the gang sitting around the table, discussing the more colorful flicks they'd encountered.

"Have you seen the Mouse Hunter?"

"Oh yeah, and Ophelia!"

"The Pope!"

"The Duck Lady!

"Everybody knows the Duck Lady!"

They were laughing and happy. A warm sense of community flowed from the room, what Gunther's father would have in his sloppy-sentimental way called *Gemütlichkeit*. Gunther stepped within.

Liza Nagenda looked up, all gums and teeth, and froze. Her jaw snapped shut. "Well, if it isn't Izmailova's personal spy!"

"What?" The accusation took Gunther's breath away. He looked helplessly about the room. Nobody would meet his eye. They had all fallen silent.

Liza's face was grey with anger. "You heard me! It was you that ratted on Krishna, wasn't it?"

"Now that's way out of line! You've got a lot of fucking gall if—" He controlled himself with an effort. There was no sense in matching her hysteria with his own. "It's none of your business what my relationship with Izmailova is or is not." He looked around the table. "Not that any of you deserve to know, but Krishna's working on a cure. If anything I said or did helped put him back in the lab, well then, so be it."

She smirked. "So what's your excuse for snitching on Will Posner?"

"I never—"

"We all heard the story! You told him you were going to run straight to your precious Izmailova with your little helmet vids."

"Now, Liza," Takayuni began. She slapped him away.

"Do you know what Posner was doing?" Gunther shook a finger in Liza's face. "Hah? Do you? He was beating a woman—Anya! He was beating Anya right out in the open!"

"So what? He's one of us, isn't he? Not a zoned-out, dead-eyed, ranting, drooling flick!"

"You bitch!" Outraged, Gunther lunged at Liza across the table. "I'll kill you, I swear it!" People jerked back from him, rushed forward, a chaos of motion. Posner thrust himself in Gunther's way, arms spread, jaw set and manly. Gunther punched him in the face. Posner looked surprised, and fell back. Gunther's hand stung, but he felt strangely good anyway; if everyone else was crazy, then why not him?

"You just try it!" Liza shrieked. "I knew you were that type all along!"

Takayuni grabbed Liza away one way. Hamilton seized Gunther and yanked him the other. Two of Posner's friends were holding him back as well.

"I've had about all I can take from you!" Gunther shouted. "You cheap cunt!"

"Listen to him! Listen what he calls me!"

Screaming, they were shoved out opposing doors.

———

"It's all right, Gunther." Beth had flung him into the first niche they'd come to. He slumped against a wall, shaking, and closed his eyes. "It's all right now."

But it wasn't. Gunther was suddenly struck with the realization that with the exception of Ekatarina he no longer had any friends. Not real friends, close friends. How could this have happened? It was as if everyone had been turned into werewolves. Those who weren't actually mad were still monsters. "I don't understand."

Hamilton sighed. "What don't you understand, Weil?"

"The way people—the way we all treat the flicks. When Posner was beating Anya, there were four other suits standing nearby, and not a one of them so much as lifted a finger to stop him. Not one! And I felt it too, there's no use pretending I'm superior to the rest of them. I wanted to walk on and pretend I hadn't seen a thing. What's happened to us?"

Hamilton shrugged. Her hair was short and dark about her plain round face. "I went to a pretty expensive school when I was a kid. One year we had one of those exercises that're supposed to be personally enriching. You know? A life experience. We were divided into two groups—Prisoners and Guards. The Prisoners couldn't leave their assigned areas without permission from a guard, the Guards got better lunches, stuff like that. Very simple set of rules. I was a Guard.

"Almost immediately, we started to bully the Prisoners. We pushed 'em around, yelled at 'em, kept 'em in line. What was amazing was that the Prisoners let us do it. They outnumbered us five to one. We didn't even have authority for the things we did. But not a one of them complained. Not a one of them stood up and said No, you can't do this. They played the game.

"At the end of the month, the project was dismantled and we had some study seminars on what we'd learned: the roots of fascism, and so on. Read some Hannah Arendt. And then it was all over. Except that my best girlfriend never spoke to me again. I couldn't blame her either. Not after what I'd done.

"What did I really learn? That people will play whatever role you put them in. They'll do it without knowing that that's what they're doing. Take a minority, tell them they're special, and make them guards—they'll start playing Guard."

"So what's the answer? How do we keep from getting caught up in the roles we play?"

"Damned if I know, Weil. Damned if I know."

Ekatarina had moved her niche to the far end of a new tunnel. Hers was the only room the tunnel served, and consequently she had a lot of privacy. As Gunther stepped in, a static-y voice swam into focus on his trance chip. ". . . reported shock. In Cairo, government officials pledged . . ." It cut off.

"Hey! You've restored—" He stopped. If radio reception had been restored, he'd have known. It would have been the talk of the Center. Which meant that radio contact had never really been completely broken. It was simply being controlled by the CMP.

Ekatarina looked up at him. She'd been crying, but she'd stopped. "The Swiss Orbitals are gone!" she whispered. "They hit them with everything from softbombs to brilliant pebbles. They dusted the shipyards."

The scope of all those deaths obscured what she was saying for a second. He sank down beside her. "But that means—"

"There's no spacecraft that can reach us, yes. Unless there's a ship in transit, we're stranded here."

He took her in his arms. She was cold and shivering. Her skin felt clammy and mottled with gooseflesh. "How long has it been since you've had any sleep?" he asked sharply.

"I can't—"

"You're wired, aren't you?"

"I can't afford to sleep. Not now. Later."

"Ekatarina. The energy you get from wire isn't free. It's only borrowed from your body. When you come down, it all comes due. If you wire yourself up too tightly, you'll crash yourself right into a coma."

"I haven't been—" She stalled, and a confused, uncertain look entered her eyes. "Maybe you're right. I could probably use a little rest."

The CMP came to life. "Cadre Nine is building a radio receiver. Ezumi gave them the go-ahead."

"Shit!" Ekatarina sat bolt upright. "Can we stop it?"

"Moving against a universally popular project would cost you credibility you cannot afford to lose."

"Okay, so how can we minimize the—"

"Ekatarina," Gunther said. "Sleep, remember?"

"In a sec, babe." She patted the futon. "You just lie down and wait for me. I'll have this wrapped up before you can nod off." She kissed him gently, lingeringly. "All right?"

"Yeah, sure." He lay down and closed his eyes, just for a second.

When he awoke, it was time to go on shift, and Ekatarina was gone.

It was only the fifth day since Vladivostok. But everything was so utterly changed that times before then seemed like memories of another world. In a previous life I was Gunther Weil, he thought. I lived and worked and had a few laughs. Life was pretty good then.

He was still looking for Sally Chang, though with dwindling hope. Now, whenever he talked to suits he'd ask if they needed his help. Increasingly, they did not.

The third-level chapel was a shallow bowl facing the terrace wall. Tiger lilies grew about the chancel area at the bottom, and turquoise lizards skittered over the rock. The children were playing with a ball in the chancel. Gunther stood at the top, chatting with a sad-voiced Ryohei Iomato.

The children put away the ball and began to dance. They were playing London Bridge. Gunther watched them with a smile. From above they were so many spots of color, a flower unfolding and closing in on itself. Slowly, the smile faded. They were dancing too well. Not one of the children moved out of step, lost her place, or walked away sulking. Their expressions were intense, self-absorbed, inhuman. Gunther had to turn away.

"The CMP controls them," Iomato said. "I don't have much to do, really. I go through the vids and pick out games for them to play, songs to sing, little exercises to keep them healthy. Sometimes I have them draw."

"My God, how can you stand it?"

Iomato sighed. "My old man was an alcoholic. He had a pretty rough life, and at some point he started drinking to blot out the pain. You know what?"

"It didn't work."

"Yah. Made him even more miserable. So then he had twice the reason to get drunk. He kept on trying, though, I've got to give him that. He wasn't the sort of man to give up on something he believed in just because it wasn't working the way it should."

Gunther said nothing.

"I think that memory is the only thing keeping me from just taking off my helmet and joining them."

The Corporate Video Center was a narrow run of offices in the farthest tunnel reaches, where raw footage for adverts and incidental business use was processed before being squirted to better-equipped vid centers on Earth. Gunther passed from office to office, slapping off flatscreens left flickering since the disaster.

It was unnerving going through the normally busy rooms and finding no one. The desks and cluttered work stations had been abandoned in purposeful disarray, as though their operators had merely stepped out for a break and would be back momentarily. Gunther found himself spinning around to confront his shadow, and flinching at unexpected noises. With each machine he turned off, the silence at his back grew. It was twice as lonely as being out on the surface.

He doused a last light and stepped into the gloomy hall. Two suits with interwoven H-and-A logos loomed up out of the shadows. He jumped in shock. The suits did not move. He laughed wryly at himself, and pushed past. They were empty, of course—there were no Hyundai Aerospace components among the unafflicted. Someone had simply left these suits here in temporary storage before the madness.

The suits grabbed him.

"Hey!" He shouted in terror as they seized him by the arms and lifted him off his feet. One of them hooked the peecee from his harness and snapped it off. Before he knew what was happening he'd been swept down a short flight of stairs and through a doorway.

"Mr. Weil."

He was in a high-ceilinged room carved into the rock to hold air-handling equipment that hadn't been constructed yet. A high string of temporary work lamps provided dim light. To the far side of the room a suit sat behind a desk, flanked by two more, standing. They all wore Hyundai Aerospace suits. There was no way he could identify them.

The suits that had brought him in crossed their arms.

"What's going on here?" Gunther asked. "Who are you?"

"You are the last person we'd tell that to." He couldn't tell which one had spoken. The voice came over his radio, made sexless and impersonal by an electronic filter. "Mr. Weil, you stand accused of crimes against your fellow citizens. Do you have anything to say in your defense?"

"What?" Gunther looked at the suits before him and to either side. They were perfectly identical, indistinguishable from each other, and he was suddenly afraid of what the people within might feel free to do, armored as they were in anonymity. "Listen, you've got no right to do this. There's a governmental structure in place, if you've got any complaints against me."

"Not everyone is pleased with Izmailova's government," the judge said.

"But she controls the CMP, and we could not run Bootstrap without the CMP controlling the flicks," a second added.

"We simply have to work around her." Perhaps it was the judge; perhaps it was yet another of the suits. Gunther couldn't tell.

"Do you wish to speak on your own behalf?"

"What exactly am I charged with?" Gunther asked desperately. "Okay, maybe I've done something wrong, I'll entertain that possibility. But maybe you just don't understand my situation. Have you considered that?"

Silence.

"I mean, just what are you angry about? Is it Posner? Because I'm not sorry about that. I won't apologize. You can't mistreat people just because they're sick. They're still people, like anybody else. They have their rights."

Silence.

"But if you think I'm some kind of a spy or something, that I'm running around and ratting on people to Ek—to Izmailova, well that's simply not true. I mean, I talk to her, I'm not about to pretend I don't, but I'm not her spy or anything. She doesn't have any spies. She doesn't need any! She's just trying to hold things together, that's all.

"Jesus, you don't know what she's gone through for you! You haven't seen how much it takes out of her! She'd like nothing better than to quit. But she has to hang in there because—" An eerie dark electronic gabble rose up on his radio, and he stopped as he realized that they were laughing at him.

"Does anyone else wish to speak?"

One of Gunther's abductors stepped forward. "Your honor, this man says that flicks are human. He overlooks the fact that they cannot live without our support and direction. Their continued well-being is bought at the price of our unceasing labor. He stands condemned out of his own mouth. I petition the court to make the punishment fit the crime."

The judge looked to the right, to the left. His two companions nodded, and stepped back into the void. The desk had been set up at the mouth of what was to be the air intake duct. Gunther had just time enough to realize this when they reappeared, leading someone in a G5 suit identical to his own.

"We could kill you, Mr. Weil," the artificial voice crackled. "But that would be wasteful. Every hand, every mind is needed. We must all pull together in our time of need."

The G5 suit stood alone and motionless in the center of the room.

"Watch."

Two of the Hyundai suits stepped up to the G5 suit. Four hands converged on the helmet seals. With practiced efficiency, they flicked the latches and lifted the helmet. It happened so swiftly the occupant could not have stopped it if he'd tried.

Beneath the helmet was the fearful, confused face of a flick.

"Sanity is a privilege, Mr. Weil, not a right. You are guilty as charged. However, we are not cruel men. This once we will let you off with a warning. But these are desperate times. At your next offense—be it only so minor a thing as reporting this encounter to the Little General—we may be forced to dispense with the formality of a hearing." The judge paused. "Do I make myself clear?"

Reluctantly, Gunther nodded.

"Then you may leave."

On the way out, one of the suits handed him back his peecee.

Five people. He was sure there weren't any more involved than that. Maybe one or two more, but that was it. Posner had to be hip-deep in this thing, he was certain of that. It shouldn't be too hard to figure out the others.

He didn't dare take the chance.

At shift's end he found Ekatarina already asleep. She looked haggard and unhealthy. He knelt by her, and gently brushed her cheek with the back of one hand.

Her eyelids fluttered open.

"Oh, hey. I didn't mean to wake you. Just go back to sleep, huh?"

She smiled. "You're sweet, Gunther, but I was only taking a nap anyway. I've got to be up in another fifteen minutes." Her eyes closed again. "You're the only one I can really trust anymore. Everybody's lying to me, feeding me misinformation, keeping silent when there's something I need to know. You're the only one I can count on to tell me things."

You have enemies, he thought. They call you the Little General, and they don't like how you run things. They're not ready to move against you directly, but they have plans. And they're ruthless.

Aloud, he said, "Go back to sleep."

"They're all against me," she murmured. "Bastard sons of bitches."

The next day he spent going through the service spaces for the new air-handling system. He found a solitary flick's nest made of shredded vacuum suits, but after consultation with the CMP concluded that nobody had lived there for days. There was no trace of Sally Chang.

If it had been harrowing going through the sealed areas before his trial, it was far worse today. Ekatarina's enemies had infected him with fear. Reason told him they were not waiting for him, that he had nothing to worry about until he displeased them again. But the hindbrain did not listen.

Time crawled. When he finally emerged into daylight at the end of his shift, he felt light-headedly out of phase with reality from the hours of isolation. At first he noticed nothing out of the ordinary. Then his suit radio was full of voices, and people were hurrying about every which way. There was a happy buzz in the air. Somebody was singing.

He snagged a passing suit and asked, "What's going on?"

"Haven't you heard? The war is over. They've made peace. And there's a ship coming in!"

The *Lake Geneva* had maintained television silence through most of the long flight to the Moon for fear of long-range beam weapons. With peace, however, they opened direct transmission to Bootstrap.

Ezumi's people had the flicks sew together an enormous cotton square and hack away some hanging vines so they could hang it high on the shadowed side of the crater. Then, with the fill lights off, the video image was projected. Swiss spacejacks tumbled before the camera, grinning, all denim and red cowboy hats. They were talking about their escape from the hunter-seeker missiles, brash young voices running one over the other.

The top officers were assembled beneath the cotton square. Gunther recognized their suits. Ekatarina's voice boomed from newly erected loudspeakers. "When are you coming in? We have to make sure the spaceport field is clear. How many hours?"

Holding up five fingers, a blond woman said, "Forty-five!"

"No, forty-three!"

"Nothing like that!"

"Almost forty-five!"

Again Ekatarina's voice cut into the tumult. "What's it like in the orbitals? We heard they were destroyed."

"Yes, destroyed!"

"Very bad, very bad, it'll take years to—"

"But most of the people are—"

"We were given six orbits warning; most went down in lifting bodies, there was a big evacuation."

"Many died, though. It was very bad."

Just below the officers, a suit had been directing several flicks as they assembled a camera platform. Now it waved broadly, and the flicks stepped away. In the *Lake Geneva* somebody shouted, and several heads turned to stare at an offscreen television monitor. The suit turned the camera, giving them a slow, panoramic scan.

One of the spacejacks said, "What's it like there? I see that some of you are wearing space suits, and the rest are not. Why is that?"

Ekatarina took a deep breath. "There have been some changes here."

There was one hell of a party at the Center when the Swiss arrived. Sleep schedules were juggled, and save for a skeleton crew overseeing the flicks, everyone turned out to welcome the dozen newcomers to the Moon. They danced to skiffle, and drank vacuum-distilled vodka. Everyone had stories to tell, rumors to swap, opinions on the likelihood that the peace would hold.

Gunther wandered away midway through the party. The Swiss depressed him. They all seemed so young and fresh and eager. He felt battered and cynical in their presence. He wanted to grab them by the shoulders and shake them awake.

Depressed, he wandered through the locked-down laboratories. Where the Viral Computer Project had been, he saw Ekatarina and the captain of the *Lake Geneva* conferring over a stack of crated bioflops. They bent low over Ekatarina's peecee, listening to the CMP.

"Have you considered nationalizing your industries?" the captain asked. "That would give us the plant needed to build the New City. Then, with a few hardwired utilities, Bootstrap could be managed without anyone having to set foot inside it."

Gunther was too distant to hear the CMP's reaction, but he saw both women laugh. "Well," said Ekatarina. "At the very least we will have to renegotiate terms with the parent corporations. With only one ship functional, people can't be easily replaced. Physical presence has become a valuable commodity. We'd be fools not to take advantage of it."

He passed on, deeper into shadow, wandering aimlessly. Eventually, there was a light ahead, and he heard voices. One was Krishna's, but spoken faster and more forcefully than he was used to hearing it. Curious, he stopped just outside the door.

Krishna was in the center of the lab. Before him, Beth Hamilton stood nodding humbly. "Yes, sir," she said. "I'll do that. Yes." Dumbfounded, Gunther realized that Krishna was giving her orders.

Krishna glanced up. "Weil! You're just the man I was about to come looking for."

"I am?"

"Come in here, don't dawdle." Krishna smiled and beckoned, and Gunther had no choice but to obey. He looked like a young god now. The force of his spirit danced in his eyes like fire. It was strange that Gunther had never noticed before how tall he was. "Tell me where Sally Chang is."

"I don't—I mean, I can't, I—" He stopped and swallowed. "I think Chang must be dead." Then, "Krishna? What's happened to you?"

"He's finished his research," Beth said.

"I rewrote my personality from top to bottom," Krishna said. "I'm not half-crippled with shyness anymore—have you noticed?" He put a hand on Gunther's shoulder, and it was reassuring, warm, comforting. "Gunther, I won't tell you what it took to scrape together enough messenger engines from traces of old experiments to try this out on myself. But it works. We've got a treatment that among other things will serve as a universal cure for everyone in Bootstrap. But to do that, we need the messenger engines, and they're not here. Now tell me why you think Sally Chang is dead."

"Well, uh, I've been searching for her for four days. And the CMP has been looking too. You've been holed up here all that time, so maybe you don't know the flicks as well as the rest of us do. But they're not very big on planning. The likelihood one of them could actively evade detection that long is practically zilch. The only thing I can think is that somehow she made it to the surface before the effects hit her, got into a truck and told it to drive as far as her oxygen would take her."

Krishna shook his head and said, "No. It is simply not consistent with Sally Chang's character. With all the best will in the world, I cannot picture her killing herself." He slid open a drawer: row upon row of gleaming canisters. "This may help. Do you remember when I said there were canisters of mimetic engines missing, not just the schizomimetic?"

"Vaguely."

"I've been too busy to worry about it, but wasn't that odd? Why would Chang have taken a canister and not used it?"

"What was in the second canister?" Hamilton asked.

"Paranoia," Krishna said. "Or rather a good enough chemical analog. Now, paranoia is a rare disability, but a fascinating one. It's characterized by an elaborate but internally consistent delusional system. The paranoid patient functions well intellectually, and is less fragmented than a schizophrenic. Her emotional and social responses are closer to normal. She's capable of concerted effort. In a time of turmoil, it's quite possible that a paranoid individual could elude our detection."

"Okay, let's get this straight," Hamilton said. "War breaks out on Earth. Chang gets her orders, keys in the software bombs, and goes to Bootstrap with a canister full of madness and a little syringe of paranoia—no, it doesn't work. It all falls apart."

"How so?"

"Paranoia wouldn't inoculate her against schizophrenia. How does she protect herself from her own aerosols?"

Gunther stood transfixed. "Lavender!"

They caught up with Sally Chang on the topmost terrace of Bootstrap. The top level was undeveloped. Someday—so the corporate brochures promised—fallow deer would graze at the edge of limpid pools, and otters frolic in the streams. But the soil hadn't been built up yet, the worms brought in or the bacteria seeded. There were only sand, machines, and a few unhappy opportunistic weeds.

Chang's camp was to one side of a streamhead, beneath a fill light. She started to her feet at their approach, glanced quickly to the side and decided to brazen it out.

A sign reading EMERGENCY CANOPY MAINTENANCE STATION had been welded to a strut supporting the stream's valve stem. Under it were a short stacked pyramid of oxytanks and an aluminum storage crate the size of a coffin. "Very clever," Beth muttered over Gunther's trance chip. "She sleeps in the storage crate, and anybody stumbling across her thinks it's just spare equipment."

The lavender suit raised an arm and casually said, "Hiya, guys. How can I help you?"

Krishna strode forward and took her hands. "Sally, it's me—Krishna!"

"Oh, thank God!" She slumped in his arms. "I've been so afraid."

"You're all right now."

"I thought you were an Invader at first, when I saw you coming up. I'm so hungry—I haven't eaten since I don't know when." She clutched at the sleeve of Krishna's suit. "You do know about the Invaders, don't you?"

"Maybe you'd better bring me up to date."

They began walking toward the stairs. Krishna gestured quietly to Gunther and then toward Chang's worksuit harness. A canister the size of a hip flask hung there. Gunther reached over and plucked it off. The messenger engines! He held them in his hand.

To the other side, Beth Hamilton plucked up the near-full cylinder of paranoia-inducing engines and made it disappear.

Sally Chang, deep in the explication of her reasonings, did not notice.

". . . obeyed my orders, of course. But they made no sense. I worried and worried about that until finally I realized what was really going on. A wolf caught in a trap will gnaw off its leg to get free. I began to look for the wolf. What kind of enemy justified such extreme actions? Certainly nothing human."

"Sally," Krishna said, "I want you to entertain the notion that the conspiracy—for want of a better word—may be more deeply rooted than you suspect. That the problem is not an external enemy, but the workings of our own brains. Specifically that the Invaders are an artifact of the psychotomimetics you injected into yourself back when this all began."

"No. No, there's too much evidence. It all fits together! The Invaders needed a way to disguise themselves both physically, which was accomplished by the vacuum suits, and psychologically, which was achieved by the general madness. Thus, they can move undetected among us. Would a human enemy have converted all of Bootstrap to slave labor? Unthinkable! They can read our minds like a book. If we hadn't protected ourselves with the schizomimetics, they'd be able to extract all our knowledge, all our military research secrets . . ."

Listening, Gunther couldn't help imagining what Liza Nagenda would say to all of this wild talk. At the thought of her, his jaw clenched. Just like one of Chang's machines, he realized, and couldn't help being amused at his own expense.

Ekatarina was waiting at the bottom of the stairs. Her hands trembled noticeably, and there was a slight quaver in her voice when she said, "What's all this the CMP tells me about messenger engines? Krishna's supposed to have come up with a cure of some kind?"

"We've got them," Gunther said quietly, happily. He held up the canister. "It's over now, we can heal our friends."

"Let me see," Ekatarina said. She took the canister from his hand.

"No, wait!" Hamilton cried, too late. Behind her, Krishna was arguing with Sally Chang about her interpretations of recent happenings.

Neither had noticed yet that those in front had stopped.

"Stand back." Ekatarina took two quick steps backward. Edgily, she added, "I don't mean to be difficult. But we're going to sort this all out, and until we do, I don't want anybody too close to me. That includes you too, Gunther."

Flicks began gathering. By ones and twos they wandered up the lawn, and then by the dozen. By the time it was clear that Ekatarina had called them up via the CMP, Krishna, Chang and Hamilton were separated from her and Gunther by a wall of people.

Chang stood very still. Somewhere behind her unseen face, she was revising her theories to include this new event. Suddenly, her hands slapped at her suit, grabbing for the missing canisters. She looked at Krishna and with a trill of horror said, "You're one of them!"

"Of course I'm not—" Krishna began. But she was turning, stumbling, fleeing back up the steps.

"Let her go," Ekatarina ordered. "We've got more serious things to talk about." Two flicks scurried up, lugging a small industrial kiln between them. They set it down, and a third plugged in an electric cable. The interior began to glow. "This canister is all you've got, isn't it? If I were to autoclave it, there wouldn't be any hope of replacing its contents."

"Izmailova, listen," Krishna said.

"I am listening. Talk."

Krishna explained, while Izmailova listened with arms folded and shoulders tilted skeptically. When he was done, she shook her head. "It's a noble folly, but folly is all it is. You want to reshape our minds into something alien to the course of human evolution. To turn the seat of thought into a jet pilot's couch. This is your idea of a solution? Forget it. Once this particular box is opened, there'll be no putting its contents back in again. And you haven't advanced any convincing arguments for opening it."

"But the people in Bootstrap!" Gunther objected. "They—"

She cut him off. "Gunther, nobody likes what's happened to them. But if the rest of us must give up our humanity to pay for a speculative and ethically dubious rehabilitation . . . Well, the price is simply too high. Mad or not, they're at least human now."

"Am I inhuman?" Krishna asked. "If you tickle me, do I not laugh?"

"You're in no position to judge. You've rewired your neurons and you're stoned on the novelty. What tests have you run on yourself? How thoroughly have you mapped out your deviations from human norms? Where are your figures?" These were purely rhetorical questions; the kind of analyses she meant took weeks to run. "Even if you check out completely human—and I don't concede you will!— who's to say what the long-range consequences are? What's to stop us from drifting, step by incremental step, into madness? Who decides what madness is? Who programs the programmers? No, this is impossible. I won't gamble with our minds." Defensively, almost angrily, she repeated, "I won't gamble with our minds."

"Ekatarina," Gunther said gently, "how long have you been up? Listen to yourself. The wire is doing your thinking for you."

She waved a hand dismissively, without responding.

"Just as a practical matter," Hamilton said, "how do you expect to run Bootstrap without it? The setup now is turning us all into baby fascists. You say you're worried about madness—what will we be like a year from now?"

"The CMP assures me—"

"The CMP is only a program!" Hamilton cried. "No matter how much interactivity it has, it's not flexible. It has no hope. It cannot judge a new thing. It can only enforce old decisions, old values, old habits, old fears."

Abruptly Ekatarin a snapped. "Get out of my face!" she screamed. "Stop it, stop it, stop it! I won't listen to any more."

"Ekatarina—" Gunther began.

But her hand had tightened on the canister. Her knees bent as she began a slow genuflection to the kiln. Gunther could see that she had stopped listening. Drugs and responsibility had done this to her, speeding her up and bewildering her with conflicting demands, until she stood trembling on the brink of collapse. A good night's sleep might have restored her, made her capable of being reasoned with. But there was no time. Words would not stop her now. And she was too far distant for him to reach before she destroyed the engines. In that instant he felt such a strong outwelling of emotion toward her as would be impossible to describe.

"Ekatarina," he said. "I love you."

She half-turned her head toward him and in a distracted, somewhat irritated tone said, "What are you—"

He lifted the bolt gun from his work harness, leveled it, and fired.

Ekatarina's helmet shattered.

She fell.

"I should have shot to just breach the helmet. That would have stopped her. But I didn't think I was a good enough shot. I aimed right for the center of her head."

"Hush," Hamilton said. "You did what you had to. Stop tormenting yourself. Talk about more practical things."

He shook his head, still groggy. For the longest time, he had been kept on beta endorphins, unable to feel a thing, unable to care. It was like being swathed in cotton batting. Nothing could reach him. Nothing could hurt him. "How long have I been out of it?"

"A day."

"A day!" He looked about the austere room. Bland rock walls and laboratory equipment with smooth, noncommital surfaces. To the far end, Krishna and Chang were hunched over a swipeboard, arguing happily and impatiently overwriting each other's scrawls. A Swiss spacejack came in and spoke to their backs. Krishna nodded distractedly, not looking up. "I thought it was much longer."

"Long enough. We've already salvaged everyone connected with Sally Chang's group, and gotten a good start on the rest. Pretty soon it will be time to decide how you want yourself rewritten."

He shook his head, feeling dead. "I don't think I'll bother, Beth. I just don't have the stomach for it."

"We'll give you the stomach."

"Naw, I don't . . ." He felt a black nausea come welling up again. It was cyclic; it returned every time he was beginning to think he'd finally put it down. "I don't want the fact that I killed Ekatarina washed away in a warm flood of self-satisfaction. The idea disgusts me."

"We don't want that either." Posner led a delegation of seven into the lab. Krishna and Chang rose to face them, and the group broke into swirling halves. "There's been enough of that. It's time we all started taking responsibility for the consequences of—" Everyone was talking at once. Hamilton made a face.

"Started taking responsibility for—"

Voices rose.

"We can't talk here," she said. "Take me out on the surface."

They drove with the cabin pressurized, due west on the Seething Bay road. Ahead, the sun was almost touching the weary walls of Som-mering crater. Shadow crept down from the mountains and cratertops, yearning toward the radiantly lit Sinus Medii. Gunther found it achingly beautiful. He did not want to respond to it, but the harsh lines echoed the lonely hurt within him in a way that he found oddly comforting.

Hamilton touched her peecee. *Putting on the Ritz* filled their heads.

"What if Ekatarina was right?" he said sadly. "What if we're giving up everything that makes us human? The prospect of being turned into some kind of big-domed emotionless superman doesn't appeal to me much."

Hamilton shook her head. "I asked Krishna about that, and he said No. He said it was like . . . Were you ever nearsighted?"

"Sure, as a kid."

"Then you'll understand. He said it was like the first time you came out of the doctor's office after being lased. How everything seemed clear and vivid and distinct. What had once been a blur that you called 'tree' resolved itself into a thousand individual and distinct leaves. The world was filled with unexpected detail. There were things on the horizon that you'd never seen before. Like that."

"Oh." He stared ahead. The disk of the sun was almost touching Sommering. "There's no point in going any farther."

He powered down the truck.

Beth Hamilton looked uncomfortable. She cleared her throat and with brusque energy said, "Gunther, look. I had you bring me out here for a reason. I want to propose a merger of resources."

"A what?"

"Marriage."

It took Gunther a second to absorb what she had said. "Aw, no . . . I don't . . ."

"I'm serious. Gunther, I know you think I've been hard on you, but that's only because I saw a lot of potential in you, and that you were doing nothing with it. Well, things have changed. Give me a say in your rewrite, and I'll do the same for you."

He shook his head. "This is just too weird for me."

"It's too late to use that as an excuse. Ekatarina was right—we're sitting on top of something very dangerous, the most dangerous opportunity humanity faces today. It's out of the bag, though. Word has gotten out. Earth is horrified and fascinated. They'll be watching us. Briefly, very briefly, we can control this thing. We can help to shape it now, while it's small. Five years from now, it will be out of our hands.

"You have a good mind, Gunther, and it's about to get better. I think we agree on what kind of a world we want to make. I want you on my side."

"I don't know what to say."

"You want true love? You got it. We can make the sex as sweet or nasty as you like. Nothing easier. You want me quieter, louder, gentler, more assured? We can negotiate. Let's see if we can come to terms."

He said nothing.

Hamilton eased back in the seat. After a time, she said, "You know? I've never watched a lunar sunset before. I don't get out on the surface much."

"We'll have to change that," Gunther said.

Hamilton stared hard into his face. Then she smiled. She wriggled closer to him. Clumsily, he put an arm over her shoulder. It seemed to be what was expected of him. He coughed into his hand, then pointed a finger. "There it goes."

Lunar sunset was a simple thing. The crater wall touched the bottom of the solar disk. Shadows leaped from the slopes and raced across the lowlands. Soon half the sun was gone. Smoothly, without distortion, it dwindled. A last brilliant sliver of light burned atop the rock, then ceased to be. In the instant before the windshield adjusted and the stars appeared, the universe filled with darkness.

The air in the cab cooled. The panels snapped and popped with the sudden shift in temperature.

Now Hamilton was nuzzling the side of his neck. Her skin was slightly tacky to the touch, and exuded a faint but distinct odor. She ran her tongue up the line of his chin and poked it in his ear. Her hand fumbled with the latches of his suit.

Gunther experienced no arousal at all, only a mild distaste that bordered on disgust. This was horrible, a defilement of all he had felt for Ekatarina.

But it was a chore he had to get through. Hamilton was right. All his life his hindbrain had been in control, driving him with emotions chemically derived and randomly applied. He had been lashed to the steed of consciousness and forced to ride it wherever it went, and that nightmare gallop had brought him only pain and confusion. Now that he had control of the reins, he could make this horse go where he wanted.

He was not sure what he would demand from his reprogramming. Contentment, perhaps. Sex and passion, almost certainly. But not love. He was done with the romantic illusion. It was time to grow up.

He squeezed Beth's shoulder. One more day, he thought, and it won't matter. I'll feel whatever is best for me to feel. Beth raised her mouth to his. Her lips parted. He could smell her breath.

They kissed.

outnumbering the dead

FREDERIK POHL

Frederik Pohl is a seminal figure whose career spans almost the entire development of modern SF, having been one of the genre's major shaping forces—as writer, editor, agent, and anthologist—for more than fifty years. He was the founder of the *Star* series, SF's first continuing anthology series, and was the editor of the *Galaxy* group of magazines from 1960 to 1969, during which time *Galaxy*'s sister magazine, *Worlds of If*, won three consecutive Best Professional Magazine Hugos. As a writer, he won both Hugo and Nebula Awards for his novel *Gateway*, has also won the Hugo for his stories "The Meeting" (a collaboration with C. M. Kornbluth) and "Fermi and Frost," and won an additional Nebula for his novel *Man Plus*; he has also won the American Book Award and the French Prix Apollo. His many books include several written in collaboration with the late C. M. Kornbluth such as *The Space Merchants*, *Wolfbane*, and *Gladiator at Law*, as well as many solo novels, including *Beyond the Blue Event Horizon*, *The Coming of the Quantum Cats*, *Mining the Oort*, *O Pioneer!*, *The Siege of Eternity*, and *The Far Shore of Time*. Among his many collections are *The Gold at the Starbow's End*, *In the Problem Pit*, and *The Best of Frederik Pohl*. His most recent books are the novel *The Boy Who Would Live Forever*, and a massive retrospective collection, *Platinum Pohl*. He lives in Palatine, Illinois, with his wife, writer Elizabeth Ann Hull. He was named SFFWA Grand Master in 1993.

The novella that follows may well be one of the best pieces that Pohl has produced during his long career—a wise, funny, madly inventive, and ultimately quite moving look at what it's like to be the ultimate Have-Not in a high-tech future composed almost entirely of Haves.

1

*A*lthough the place is a hospital, or as much like a hospital as makes no difference, *it doesn't smell like one. It certainly doesn't look like one. With the flowering vines climbing its walls and the soothing, gentle* plink-tink *of the tiny waterfall at the head of the bed, it looks more like the de luxe suite in some old no-tell motel. Rafiel is now spruced up, replumbed and ready to go for another five years before he needs to come back to this place for more of the same, and so he doesn't look much like a hospital patient, either. He looks like a movie star, which he more or less is, who is maybe forty years old and has kept himself fit enough to pass for twenty-something. That part's wrong, though. After all the snipping and reaming and implanting they've done to him in the last eleven days, what he is a remarkably fit man of ninety-two.*

When Rafiel began to wake from his designer dream he was very hungry (that was due to the eleven days he had been on intravenous feeding) and quite horny, too (that was the last of the designer dream). "B'*jour*, Rafiel," said the soft, sweet voice of the nurser, intruding on his therapeutic dream as the last of it melted away. Rafiel felt the nurser's gentle touch removing the electrodes from his cheekbones, and, knowing very well just where he was and what he had been doing there, he opened his eyes.

He sat up in the bed, pushing away the nurser's velvety helping hand. While he was unconscious they had filled his room with flowers. There were great blankets of roses along one wall, bright red and yellow poppies on the windowsill that looked out on the deep interior court. "*Momento*, please," he said to the nurser, and experimentally stretched his naked body. They had done a good job. That annoying little pain in the shoulder was gone and, when he held one hand before him, he saw that so were the age spots on his skin. He was also pleased to find that he had awakened with a perfectly immense erection. "Seems okay," he said, satisfied.

"*Hai, claro*," the nurser said. That was the server's programmed all-purpose response to the sorts of sense-free or irrelevant things hospital patients said when they first woke up. "Your *amis* are waiting to come in."

"They can wait." Rafiel yawned, pleasantly remembering the last dream. Then, his tumescence subsiding, he slid his feet over the edge of the bed and stood up. He waved the nurser away and scowled in surprise. "Shit. They didn't fix this little dizziness I've been having."

"*Voulez* see your chart?" the nurser offered. But Rafiel didn't at all want to know what they'd done to him. He took an experimental step or two, and then the nurser would no longer be denied. Firmly it took his arm and helped him toward the sanitary room. It stood by as he used the toilet and joined him watchfully in the spray shower, the moisture rolling harmlessly down its metal flanks. As it dried him off, one of its hands caught his finger and held on for a moment—heartbeat, blood pressure, who knew what it was measuring? — before saying, "You may leave whenever you like, Rafiel."

"You're very kind," Rafiel said, because it was his nature to be polite even to machines. To human beings, too, of course. Especially to humans, as far as possible anyway, because humans were what became audiences and no sensible performer wanted to antagonize audiences. But with humans it was harder for Rafiel to be always polite, since his inner feelings, where all the resentments lay, were so frequently urging him to be the opposite — to be rude, insulting, even violent; to spit in some of these handsome young faces sometimes out of the anger that was always burning out of sight inside him. He had every right to that smouldering rage, since he was so terribly cheated in his life, but — he was a fair man — his special problem wasn't really their fault, was it? And besides, the human race in general had one trait that forgave them most others, they adored Rafiel. At least the surveys showed that 36.9 per cent of them probably did, a rating which only a handful of utter superstars could ever hope to beat.

That sort of audience devotion imposed certain obligations on a performer. Appearance was one, and so Rafiel considered carefully before deciding what to wear for his release from the hospital. From the limited selection his hospital closet offered he chose red pantaloons, a luminous blue blouse and silk cap to cover his unmade hair. On his feet he wore only moleskin slippers, but that was all right. He wouldn't be performing, and needed no more on the warm, soft, mossy flooring of his hospital room.

He time-stepped to the window, glancing out at the distant figures on the galleries of the hundred-meter atrium of the arcology he lived and worked in; and at the bright costumes of those strolling across the airy bridges, before he opaqued the window to study his reflection. That was satisfactory, though it would have been better if he'd had the closets in his condo to choose from. He was ready for the public who would be waiting for him — and for all the other things that would be waiting for him, too. He wondered if the redecoration of his condo had been completed, as it was supposed to have been while he was in the medical facility; he wondered if his agent had succeeded in rebooking the personal appearances he had had to miss, and whether the new show — what was it based on? Yes. *Oedipus Rex*. Whatever that was — had come together.

He was suddenly impatient to get on with his life, so he said, "All right, they can come in now" — and a moment later, when the nurser had signaled the receptionists outside that it was all right, in they all came, his friends and colleagues from the new show: pale, tiny Docilia flying over to him with a quick kiss, Mosay, his dramaturge, bearing still more flowers, a corsage to go on Rafiel's blouse, Victorium with his music box hung around his neck, all grinning and welcoming him back to life. "And *comment va* our Oedipus this morning?" Mosay asked, with pretend solicitude. Mosay didn't mean the solicitude to be taken seriously, of course, because there was really nothing for anyone to be solicitous about. The nursers wouldn't have awakened Rafiel if all the work hadn't been successfully done.

"*Tutto bene*," Rafiel answered as expected, letting Mosay press the bunch of little pink violets to his blouse and smelling their sweet scent appreciatively. "Ready for work. Oh, and having *faim*, too."

"But of course you are, after all *that*," said Docilia, hugging him, "and we have a lunch all set up for you. Can you go now?" she asked him, but looking at the nurser—which answered only by opening the door for them. Warmly clutching his arm and fondly chattering in his ear, Docilia led him out of the room where, for eleven days, he had lain unconscious while the doctors and the servers poked and cut and jabbed and mended him.

Rafiel didn't even look back as he entered this next serial installment of his life. There wasn't any nostalgia in the place for him. He had seen it all too often before.

2

The restaurant—well, call it that; it is like a restaurant—is located in the midzone of the arcology. There are a hundred or so floors rising above it and a couple of hundred more below. It is a place where famous vid stars go to be seen, and so at the entrance to the restaurant there is a sort of tearoomy, saloony, cocktail-loungy place, inhabited by ordinary people who hope to catch a glimpse of the celebrities who have come there to be glimpsed. As Rafiel and his friends pass through this warm, dim chamber heads gratifyingly turn. Mosay whispers something humorous to Docilia and Docilia, smiling in return, then murmurs something affectionate to Rafiel, but actually all of them are listening more to the people around them than to each other. "It's the short-time vid star," one overheard voice says, and Rafiel can't help glowing a little at the recognition, though he would have preferred, of course, to have been a celebrity only for his work and not for his problem. "I didn't know she was so tiny," says another voice—speaking of Docilia, of course; they often say that. And, though Mosay affects not to hear, when someone says; "He's got a grandissimo coming up," ils disent," his eyes twinkle a bit, knowing who that "he" is. But then the maître d' is coming over to guide them to their private table on an outside balcony.

Rafiel was the last out the door. He paused to give a general smile and wink to the people inside, then stepped out into the warm, diffused light of the balcony, quite pleased with the way things were going. His friends had chosen the right place for his coming-out meal. If it was important to be seen going to their lunch, it was also important to have their own private balcony set aside to eat it on. They wanted to be seen while eating, of course, because every opportunity to be seen was important to theater people—but from a proper distance. Such as on the balcony, where they were in view of all the people who chanced to be crossing the arcology atrium or looking out from the windows on the other side. The value of that was that then those people would say to the next persons they met, "*Senti*, guess who I saw at lunch today! Rafiel! And Docilia! And, *comme dît*, the music person." And their names would be refreshed in the public mind one more time.

So, though this was to be an agendaed lunch, the balcony was the right place to have it. It wasn't a business-looking place; it could have been more appropriate for lovers, with the soft, warm breezes playing on them and hummingbirds hovering by their juice glasses in the hope of a handout. Really, it would have been more comfortable for a couple; for the four of them, with their servers moving between them with their buffet trays, it was a pretty tight squeeze.

Rafiel ravened over the food, taking great heaps of everything as fast as the servers could bring it. His friends conspired to help. "Give him *pommes*," Mosay ordered, and Docilia whispered, "Try the *sushi ceveche*, it's *fine*." Mouth full and chewing, Rafiel let his friends fuss over him. From time to time he raised his eyes from his food to smile at jest or light line, but there was no need for him to take part in the talk. He was just out of the hospital, after all. (As well as being a star, even among these stars; but that was a given.) He knew that they would get down to business quickly enough. Docilia was always in a hurry to get on with the next production and Mosay, the dramaturge—was, well, a dramaturge. It was his *business* to get things moving. Meanwhile, it was Rafiel's right to satisfy one appetite and to begin to plan ahead for the pleasing prospect of relieving the other. When Docilia put a morsel of pickled fish between his lips he licked her fingertips affectionately and looked into her eyes.

He was beginning to feel at ease.

The eleven days in the medical facility had passed like a single night for Rafiel, since he had been peacefully unconscious for almost all of it. He saw, though, that time had passed for the others, because they had changed a little. Mosay was wearing a little waxed moustache now and Victorium was unexpectedly deeply tanned, right up to his *cache-sexe* and on the expanse of belly revealed by his short embroidered vest. Docilia had become pale blonde again. For that reason she was dressed all in white, or almost all: white bell-bottomed pants and a white halter top that showed her pale skin. The only touch of contrast was a patch of fuzzy peach-colored embroidery at the crotch of the slacks that, Rafiel was nearly sure he remembered, accurately matched the outlines of her pubic hair. It was a very Docilia kind of touch, Rafiel thought.

Of course, they were all very smartly dressed. They always were; like Rafiel they owed it to their public. The difference between Rafiel and the others was that every one of them looked to be about twenty years old—well, ageless, really, but certainly, at the most, no more than a beautifully fit thirtyish. They always had looked that way. All of them did. All ten *trillion* of them did, all over the world and the other worlds, or anyway nearly all. . . . Except, of course, for the handful of oddities like himself.

When Docilia saw Rafiel's gaze lingering on her—observing it at once, because Docilia was never unaware when someone was looking at her—she reached over and fondly patted his arm. He leaned to her ear to pop the question: "*Bitte*, are you free this afternoon?"

She gave him a tender smile. "For you," she said, almost sounding as though she meant it, "*siempre*." She picked up his hand and kissed the tip of his middle finger to show she was sincere. "*Mais* can we talk a little business first? Victorium's finished the score, and it's *belle*. We've got—"

"Can we play it over *casa tu*?"

Another melting smile. "*Hai*, we can. *Hai*, we will, as much as you like. But, listen, we've got a wonderful second-act duet, you and I. I love it, Rafiel! It's when you've just found out that the woman you've been shtupping, that's me, is your mother, that's me, too. Then I'm telling you that what you've done is a sin . . . and then at the end of the duet I run off to hang myself. Then you've got a solo dance. Play it for him, Victorium?"

Victorium didn't need to be begged; a touch of his fingers on his amulet recorder and the music began to pour out. Rafiel paused with his spoon in his juicy white sapote fruit to listen, not having much choice. It was a quick, tricky jazz tune coming out of Victorium's box, but with blues notes in it too, and a funny little hoppity-skippy syncopation to the rhythm that sounded Scottish to Rafiel.

"*Che? Che?*" Victorium asked anxiously as he saw the look on Rafiel's face. "Don't you like it?"

Rafiel said, "It's just that it sounds—gammy. *Pas* smooth. Sort of like a little limp in there."

"*Hai! Precisamente!*" cried Mosay. "You caught it at once!"

Rafiel blinked at him. "What did I catch?"

"What Victorium's music conveyed, of course! You're playing Oedipus Rex and he's *supposed* to be lame."

"Oh, *claro*," said Rafiel; but it wasn't really all that clear to him. He wiped the juice of the sapote off his lips while he thought it over. Then he asked the dramaturge, "Do you think it's a good idea for me to be dancing the part of somebody who's lame?" He got the answer when he heard Docilia's tiny giggle, and saw Victorium trying to smother one of his own. "Ah, *merde*," Rafiel grumbled as, once again, he confronted the unwelcome fact that it was not his talent but his oddity that delighted his audiences. Ageing had been slowed down for him, but it hadn't stopped. His reflexes were not those of a twenty-year-old; and it was precisely those amusing little occasional stumbles and slips that made him *Rafiel*. "I don't like it," he complained, knowing that didn't matter.

"But you *must* do it that way," cried the dramaturge, persuasive, forceful—being a dramaturge, in short, with a star to cajole into shape. "*C'est toi*, really! The part could have been made for you. Oedipus has a bit of a physical problem, but we see how he rises above his limitations and dances beautifully. As, always, do you yourself, Rafiel!"

"*D'accord*," Rafiel said, surrendering as he knew he must. He ate the fruit for a moment, thinking. When it was finished he pushed the shell aside and asked sourly, "How lame is this Oedipus supposed to be, exactly?"

"He's a *blessé*, a little bit. He has something wrong with his ankles. They were mutilated when he was a baby."

"Hum," said Rafiel, and gave Victorium a nod. The musician replayed the five bars of music.

"Can you dance to it?" Victorium asked anxiously.

"Of course I can. If I had my tap shoes—"

"Give him his tap shoes, Mosay," Docilia ordered, and then bent to help Rafiel slip them on, while the dramaturge clapped his hands for a server to bring a tap mat.

"Play from the end of the duet," Rafiel ordered, abandoning his meal to stand up in the narrow space of the balcony. He moved slightly, rocking back and forth, then began to tap, not on the beat of the music, but just off it—*step left, shuffle right*—while his friends nodded approvingly—*spank it back, scuff it forward*. But there wasn't really enough room. One foot caught another; he stumbled and almost fell, Victorium's strong hand catching him. "I'm clumsier than ever," he sighed resentfully.

"They'll love it," Mosay said, reassuring him, and not lying, either, Rafiel knew unhappily; for what was it but his occasional misstep, the odd quaver in his voice—to be frank about it, the peculiarly fascinating traits of his advancing age—that made him a superstar?

He finished his meal. "Come on, Docilia. I'm ready to go," he said, and although the others clearly wanted to stay and talk they all agreed that what Rafiel suggested was a good idea. They always did. It was one of the things that made Rafiel's life special—one of the good things. It came with being a superstar. He was used to being indulged by these people, because they needed him more than he needed them, although, as they all knew, the were going to live for ever and he was not.

3

All the worlds know the name of Rafiel, but, actually, "Rafiel" isn't all of his name. That name, in full, is Rafiel Gutmaker-Fensterborn, just as Docilia, in full, is Docilia Megareth-Morb, and Mosay is Mosay Koi Mosayus. But "Rafiel" is all he needs. Basically, that is the way you can tell when you've finally become a major vid star. You no longer need all those names to be identified or even to get your mail delivered. Even among a race of ten trillion separate, living, named human beings, when you have their kind of stardom a single name is quite enough.

Rafiel's difficulty at present was that he didn't happen to be in his own condo where his mail was. Instead he was in Docilia's, located fifty-odd stories above his own in the arcology. He really did want to know what messages were waiting for him.

On the other hand, this particular delay was worthwhile. Although Rafiel had been sleeping for eleven days, his glands had not. He was well charged up for the exertions of Docilia's bed. He came to climax in record time—the first time—with Docilia helpfully speeding him along. The second time was companionably hers. Then they lay pleasantly spooned, with Rafiel drowsily remembering now and then to kiss the back of her neck under the fair hair. It wasn't Alegretta's hair, he thought, though without any real pair (you couldn't actually go on aching all your life for a lost love, though sometimes he thought he was coming close); but it was nice hair, and it was always nice to make love to this tiny, active little body. But after a bit she stretched, yawned and left him, fondly promising to be quickly back, while she went to return her calls. He rolled over to gaze at the pleasing sight of her naked and youthfully sweet departing back.

It was a fact, Rafiel knew, that Docilia wasn't youthful in any chronological sense. In terms of life span she was certainly a good deal older than himself however she looked. But you couldn't ignore the way she looked, either, because the way she looked was what the audiences were going to see. As the story of *Oedipus Rex* began to come back to him, he began to wonder: Would any audience believe for one moment that this girlish woman could be his mother?

It was a silly thought. The audiences weren't going to worry about that sort of thing. If it registered with them at all it would be only another incongruity of the kind that they loved so well. Rafiel dismissed the worry, and then, as he lay there, pleasantly at ease, he at last became aware of the faint whisper of music from Docilia's sound system.

So it had been an agendaed tryst after all, he thought tolerantly. But a sweet one. If she had not forgotten to have Victorium's score playing from the moment they entered her flat, at least she had been quite serious about the lovemaking he had come there for. So Rafiel did what she wanted him to do; he lay there, letting the music tell its story to his ears. It wasn't a bad score at all, he thought critically. He was beginning to catch the rhythms in his throat and feet when Docilia came back.

She was glowing. "Oh Rafiel," she cried, "*look* at this!"

She was waving a tomograph, and when she handed it to him he was astonished to see that it was an image of what looked like a three-month fetus. He blinked at her in surprise. "Yours?"

She nodded ecstatically. "They just sent it from the crèche," she explained, nervous with pleasure. "Isn't it *très belle*?"

"Why, that's *molto bene*," he said warmly. "I didn't know you were *enceinte* at all. Who's the *padre*?"

She shrugged prettily. "Oh, his name is Charlus. I don't think you know him, but he's really good, isn't he? I mean, *look* at that gorgeous child."

In Rafiel's opinion, no first-trimester fetus could be called anything like "gorgeous," but he knew what was expected of him and was not willing to dampen her delight. "It's certainly a good-looking embryo, *senza dubito*," he told her with sincerity.

"His *always* are! He's fathered some of the best children I've ever seen—good-looking, and with his dark blue eyes, and oh, so tall and strong!" She hesitated for a moment, prettily almost blushing. Then, "We're going to share the *bambino* for a year," she confided proudly. "As a family, I mean. When the baby's born Charlus and I are going to start a home together. Don't you think that's a wonderful idea?"

There was only one possible answer to that, "Of course I do," said Rafiel, regardless of whether he did or not.

She gave him a fond pat. "That's what you ought to do too, Rafiel. Have a child with some nice *dama*, bring the baby up together."

"And when would I find time?" he asked. But that wasn't a true answer. The true answer was that, yes, he would have liked nothing better, provided that right woman was willing to donate the ovum . . . but the right woman had, long ago, firmly foreclosed that possibility.

Docilia had said something that he missed. When he asked for a repeat, she said, "I said, and it'll help my performance, won't it?"

He was puzzled. "Help how?"

She said, impatient with his lack of understanding. "Because Jocasta's a *Mutter*, don't you see? That's the whole point of the story, isn't it? And now I can get right into the part, because I'm being a *Mutter*, too."

Rafiel said sincerely, "You'll be fine." He meant it, too. He had assumed she would all along.

"Yes, *certo*," she said absently, thinking already of something else. "I think I ought to give a copy to the dad. He'll be so excited."

"*I* would be," Rafiel agreed. She blinked and returned her attention to him. She lifted the sheet and peered under it for a thoughtful moment. "I think," she said judiciously, "if you're not in a great hurry to leave, if we just give it a few more minutes. . . ."

"No hurry at all," he said, pulling her down to him and stroking her back in a no-hurry-at-all way. "Well," he said. "So what else have you been doing? Did they release your Inquisitor yet?"

"Three days ago," she said, rubbing her foot along his ankle. "God, those clothes were so *heavy*, and then the last scene—You didn't see it, of course?"

"How could I?"

"No, of course not. Well, try to, *si c'est* possible, because I'm really fine in the *auto-da-fé* scene."

"What scene?" Rafiel knew that Docilia had finished shooting something about the Spanish Inquisition, with lots of torture—torture stories always went well in this world that had so little personal experience of any kind of suffering, but he hadn't actually seen any part of it.

"Where they burn me at the stake. *Quelle horreur!* See, they spread the wood all around in a huge circle and light it at the edges, and I'm chained to the stake in the middle. *Che cosa!* I'm running from side to side, trying to get away from the fire as it burns toward me, and then I start burning myself, *capisce?* And then I just fall down on the burning coals."

"It sounds wonderful," Rafiel said, faintly envious. Maybe it was time for him to start looking for dramatic parts instead of all the song and dance?

"*I* was wonderful," she said absently, reaching under the covers to see what was happening. Then she turned her face to his. "And, guess what? You're getting to be kind of wonderful yourself, *galubka*, right now. . . ."

Three times was as far as Rafiel really thought he wanted to go. Anyway, Docilia was now in a hurry to send off the picture of her child. "Let yourself out?" she asked, getting up. Then, naked at her bedroom door, she stopped to look back at him.

"We'll all be fine in this *Oedipus*, Rafiel," she assured him. "You and me in the lead parts, and Mosay putting it all together, and that *merveilleux* score." Which was still repeating itself from her sound system, he discovered.

He blew her a kiss, laughing. "I'm listening, I'm listening," he assured her. And he did in fact listen for a few moments.

Yes, Rafiel told himself, it really was a good score. *Oedipus* would be a successful production, and when they had rehearsed it and revised it and performed it and recorded it, it would be flashed all over the solar system, over all Earth and the Moon and the capsule colonies on Mars and Triton and half a dozen other moons, and the orbiting habitats wherever they might be, and even to the distant voyagers well on their way to some other star—to all ten million million human beings, or as many of them as cared to watch it. And it would *last*. Recordings of it would survive for centuries, to be taken out and enjoyed by people not yet born, because anything that Rafiel appeared in became an instant classic.

Rafiel got up off Docilia's warm, shuddery bed and stood before her mirror, examining himself. Everything the mirror displayed looked quite all right. The belly was flat, the skin clear, the eyes bright—he looked as good as any hale and well-kept man of middle years would have looked, in the historically remote days when middle age could be distinguished from any other age. That was what those periodical visit to the hospital did for him. Though they couldn't make him immortal, like everyone else, they could at least do *that* much for his appearance and his general comity.

He sighed and rescued the red pantaloons from the floor. As he began to pull them on he thought: They can do all that, but they could not make him live for ever, like everyone else.

That wasn't an immediate threat. Rafiel was quite confident that he would live a while yet—well, quite a *long* while, if you measured it in days and seconds, perhaps another thirty years or so. But then he wouldn't live after that. And Docilia and Mosay and Victorium—yes, and lost Alegretta, too, and everyone else he had ever known—would perhaps take out the record of this new *Oedipus Rex* now and then and look at it and say to each other, "Oh, do you remember dear old Rafiel? How sweet he was. And what a pity." But dear old Rafiel would be *dead*.

4

The arcology Rafiel lives and works in rises 235 stories above central Indiana, and it has a population of 165,000 people. That's about average. From outside—apart from its size—the arcology looks more like something you'd find in a kitchen then a monolithic community. You might think of it as resembling the kind of utensil you would use to ream the juice out of an orange half (well, an orange half that had been stretched long and skinny), with its star-shaped cross section and its rounding taper to the top. Most of the dwelling units are in the outer ribs of the arcology's star. That gives a tenant a nice view, if he is the kind of person who really wants to look out on central Indiana. Rafiel isn't. As soon as he could afford it he moved to the more expensive inside condos overlooking the lively central atrium of the arcology, with all its glorious light and its graceful loops of flowering lianas and its wall-to-wall people—people on the crosswalks, people on their own balconies, even tiny, distant people moving about the floor level nearly two hundred stories below. To see all that is to see life. From the outer apartments, what can you see? Only farmlands, and the radiating troughs of the maglev trains, punctuated by the to-the-horizon stretch of all the other arcologies that rose from the plain like the stubble of a monster beard.

In spite of all Rafiel's assurances, Docilia insisted on getting dressed and escorting him back to his own place. She chattered all the way. "So this city you saved, *si chiama* Thebes," she was explaining to him as they got into the elevator, "was in a *hell* of a mess before you got there. Before Oedipus did, I mean. This Sphinx creature was just making *schrecklichkeit*. It was doing all kinds of rotten things—I don't know—like killing people, stealing their food, that sort of thing. I guess. Anyway, the whole city was just *desperate* for help, and then you came along to save them."

"And I killed the Sphinx, so they made me roi de Thebes out of gratitude?"

"*Certo!* Well, almost. You see, you don't have to *kill* it, exactly. It has this riddle that no one can figure out. You just have to solve its riddle, and then it I guess just goes kaput. So then you're their hero, Oedipus, but they don't exactly make you king. The way you get to be that is you marry the queen. That's me, Jocasta. I'm just a *pauvre petite* widow lady from the old dead king, but as soon as you marry me that makes you the *capo di tutti capi*. I'm still the queen, and I've got a brother, Creon, who's a kind of a king, too. But you're the boss." The elevator stopped, making her blink in slight surprise. "Oh, *siamo qui*," she announced, and led the way out of the car.

Rafiel halted her with a hand on her shoulder. "I can find my way home from here. You didn't need to come with me at all, *verstehen sie*?"

"I wanted to, *piccina*. I thought you might be a little, well, wobbly."

"I am wobbly, all right," he said, grinning, "*mais pas* from being in the hospital." He kissed her, and then turned her around to face the elevator. Before he released her he said, "Oh, listen. What's this riddle of the Sphinx I'm supposed to solve?"

She gave him an apologetic smile over her shoulder. "It's kind of dopey. 'What goes on four legs, two legs and three legs, and is strongest on two?' Can you imagine?"

He looked at her. "You mean you don't know the answer to that one?"

"Oh, but I do know the answer, Rafiel. Mosay told me what it was. It's—"

"Go on, Cele," he said bitterly. "*Auf wiedersehen*. The answer to the riddle is a 'man,' but I can see why it would be hard for somebody like you to figure it out."

Because, of course, he thought as he entered the lobby of his condo, none of these eternally youthful ones would ever experience the tottery, "three-legged," ancient-with-a-cane phase of life.

"Welcome back, Rafiel," someone called, and Rafiel saw for the first time that the lobby was full of paparazzi. They were buzzing at him in mild irritation, a little annoyed because they had missed him at the hospital, but nevertheless resigned to waiting on the forgivable whim of a superstar.

It was one of the things that Rafiel had had to resign himself to, long ago. It was a considerable nuisance. On the other hand, to be truthful, it didn't take much resignation. When the paps were lurking around for you, it proved your fame, and it was always nice to have renewed proof of that. He gave them a smile for the cameras, and a quick cut-and-point couple of steps of a jig—it was a number from his biggest success, the *Here's Hamlet!* of two years earlier. "Yes," he said, answering all their questions at once, "I'm out of the hospital, I'm back in shape, and I'm hot to trot on the new show that Mosay's putting together for me, *Oedipus Rex*." He started toward the door of his own flat. A woman put herself in his way.

"Raysia," she introduced herself, as though one name were enough for her, too. "I'm here for the interview."

He stopped dead. Then he recognized the face. Yes, one name was enough, for a top pap with her own syndicate. "Raysia, dear! *Cosi bella* to see you here, but—what interview are we talking about?"

"Your dramaturge set the appointment up last week," she explained. And, of course, that being so, there was nothing for Rafiel to do but to go through with it, making a mental note to get back to Mosay at the first opportunity to complain at not having been told.

But giving an interview was not a hard thing to do, after all, not with all the practice Rafiel had had. He fixed the woman up with a drink and a comfortable chair and took his place at the exercise barre in his study—he always liked to be working when he was interviewed, to remind them he was a dancer. First, though, he had a question. It might not have occurred to him if Docilia hadn't made him think of lost Alegretta, but now he had to ask it. He took a careful first position at the barre and swept one arm gracefully aloft as he asked, "Does your syndicate go to Mars?"

"Of course. I'm into *toutes les biospheres*," she said proudly, "not just Mars, but Mercury and the moons and nearly every orbiter. As well as, naturally, the whole planet Earth."

"That's wonderful," he said, intending to flatter her and doing his best to sound as though this sort of thing hadn't ever happened to him before. Slowly, carefully, he did his barre work, hands always graceful, getting full extension on the legs, her camera following automatically as he answered her questions. Yes, he felt fine. Yes, they were going to get into production on the new *Oedipus* right away—yes, he'd heard the score, and yes, he thought it was wonderful. "And the playwright," he explained, "is the greatest writer who ever lived. Wonderful old Sophocles, two thousand nearly seven hundred years old, and the play's as fresh as anything today."

She looked at him with a touch of admiration for an actor who had done his homework. "Have you read it?"

He hadn't done *that* much homework, though he fully intended to. "Well, not in the original," he admitted, since a non-truth was better than a lie.

"I have," she said absently, thinking about her next question—disconcertingly, too. Rafiel turned around at the barre to work on the right leg for a while. Hiding the sudden, familiar flash of resentment.

"*Vous êtes* terrible," he chuckled, allowing only rueful amusement to show. "All of you! You *know* so much." For they all did, and how unfair. Imagine! This child—this ancient twenty-year-old—reading a Greek play in the original, and not even Greek, he thought savagely, but whatever rough dialect had been spoken nearly three thousand years ago.

"*Mais pourquoi non*? We have time," she said, and got to her question. "How do you feel about the end of the play?" she asked.

"Where Oedipus blinds himself, you mean?" he tried, doing his best to sort out what he had been told of the story. "Yes, that's pretty bloody, isn't it? Stabbing out his own eyes, that's a very powerful—"

She was shaking her head. "No, *pas du tout*, I don't mean the blinding scene. I mean at the very end, where the chorus says"—her voice changed as she quoted—

> See proud Oedipus!
> He proves that no mortal
> Can ever be known to be happy
> Until he is allowed to leave this life,
> Until he is dead,
> And cannot suffer any more.

She paused, fixing him with her eye while the camera zeroed in to catch every fleeting shade of expression on his face. "I'm not a very good translator," she apologized, "but do you feel that way, Rafiel? I mean, as a mortal?"

Actors grow reflexes for situations like that—for the times when a fellow player forgets a line, or there's a disturbance from the audience—when something goes *wrong* and everybody's looking at you and you have to deal with it. He dealt with it. He gave her a sober smile and opened his mouth. "*Hai*, that's so true, in a way," he heard his mouth saying. "*N'est-ce pas?* I mean, not just for me but, credo, for all of us? It doesn't matter however long we live, there's always that big final question at the end that we call death, and all we have to confront it with is courage. And that's the lesson of the story, I think: courage! To face all our pains and fears and go on anyway!"

It wasn't good, he thought, but it was enough. Raysia shut off her camera, thanked him, asked for an autograph and left; and as soon as the door was closed behind her Rafiel was grimly on the phone.

But Mosay wasn't answering, had shut himself off. Rafiel left him a scorching message and sat down, with a drink in his hand, to go through his mail. He was not happy. He scrolled quickly through the easy part—requests for autographs, requests for personal appearances, requests for interviews. He didn't have to do anything about most of them; he rerouted them through Mosay's office and they would be dealt with there.

A note from a woman named Hillaree could not be handled in that way. She was a dramaturge herself—had he ever heard of her? He couldn't be sure; there were thousands of them, though few as celebrated as Mosay. Still, she had a proposition for Rafiel. She wanted to talk to him about a "wonderful" (she said) new script. The story took place on one of the orbiting space habitats, a place called *Hakluyt*, and she was, she said, convinced that Rafiel would be determined to do it, if only he would read the script.

Rafiel thought for a moment. He wasn't convinced at all. Still, on consideration, he copied the script to file without looking at it. Perhaps he would read the script, perhaps he wouldn't; but he could imagine that, in some future conversation with Mosay, it might be useful to be able to mention this other offer.

He sent a curt message to this Hillaree to tell her to contact his agent and then, fretful, stopped the scroll. He wasn't concentrating. Raysia's interview had bothered him. "We have time" indeed! Of course they did. They had endless time, time to learn a dead language, just for the fun of it, as Rafiel himself might waste an afternoon trying to learn how to bowl or paraglide at some beach. They *all* had time—all but Rafiel himself and a handful of other unfortunates like him—and it wasn't fair!

It did not occur to Rafiel that he had already had, in the nine decades since his birth, more lifetime than almost anyone in the long history of the human race before him. That was irrelevant. However much he had, everyone around him had so much *more*.

Still, in his ninety years of life Rafiel had learned a great deal—even actors could learn more than their lines, with enough time to do it in. He had learned to accept the fact that he was going to die, while everyone he knew lived on after him. He had even learned why this was so.

It was all a matter of the failings of the Darwinian evolution process.

In one sense, Darwinian evolution was one of the nicest things that had ever happened to life on Earth. In the selection of desirable traits to pass on to descendants—the famous "survival of the fittest"—virtue was rewarded. Traits that worked well for the organism were passed on, because the creatures that had them were more likely to reproduce than the ones lacking them.

Over the billions of years the process had produced such neat things—out of the unpromising single-celled creatures that began it all—as eyes, and anuses, and resistance to the diseases that other organisms wanted to give you, and ultimately even intelligence. That was the best development, in the rather parochial collective opinion of the intelligent human race. Smarts had turned out to be an evolutionary plus; that was why there were ten trillion human beings around, and hardly any of such things as the blue whale, the mountain gorilla and the elephant.

But there was one thing seriously wrong with the way the process works. From the point of view of the individual organism itself, evolution doesn't do a thing. Its benefits may be wonderful for the *next* generation, but it doesn't do diddly-squat for the organisms it is busily selecting, except to encourage the weaker ones to die before they get around to reproducing themselves.

That means that some very desirable traits that every human being would have liked to have—say, resistance to osteoporosis, or a wrinkle-free face—didn't get selected for in the Darwinian lottery. Longevity was not a survival feature. Once a person (or any other kind of animal) had its babies, the process switched itself off. Anything that benefited the organism after it was finished with its years of reproducing was a matter of pure chance. However desirable the new trait might have been, it wasn't passed on. Once the individual had passed the age of bearing young, the Darwinian score-keepers lost interest.

That didn't stop such desirable traits from popping up. Mutations appeared a million times which, if passed on, would have kept the lucky inheritors of subsequent generations hale for indefinite periods—avoiding, let us say, such inconveniences of age as going deaf at sixty, incontinent at eighty and mindless at the age of

a hundred. But such genes came and went and were lost. As they didn't have anything to do with reproductive efficiency, they didn't get preserved. There wasn't any
selective pass-through after the last babies were born.

So longevity was a do-it-yourself industry. There was no help from Darwin.
But . . .

But once molecular biology got itself well organized, there were things that *could*
be done. And were done. For most of the human population. But now and then,
there were an unfortunate flawed few who missed out on the wonders of modern
life-prolonging science because some undetectable and incurable quirks in their
systems rejected the necessary treatment. . . .

Like Rafiel. Who scrolled through, without actually seeing, the scores of trivial
messages—fan letters, requests for him to appear at some charitable function in
some impossible place, bank statements, bills—that had arrived for him while he
was away. And then, still fretful, turned off his communications and blanked his entertainment screen and even switched off the music as, out of habit and need, he
practiced his leaps and entrechats in the solitude of his home, while he wondered
bitterly what the point was in having a life at all, when you knew that it would sooner
or later *end*.

5

*People do still die now and then. It isn't just the unfortunates like Rafiel who do it,
either, though of course they are the ones for whom it is inevitable. Even normal
people sometimes die as well. They die of accident, of suicide, of murder, sometimes just of some previously unknown sickness or even of a medical blunder that
crashes the system. The normal people simply do not do that very often. Normal
people expect to live normally extended lives. How long those lives can be expected
to last is hard to say, because even the oldest persons around aren't yet much more
than bicentenarians (that's the time since the procedures first became available),
and they show no signs of old age yet. And, of course, since people do go on giving
birth to other people, all that longevity has added up to quite an unprecedented
population explosion. The total number of human beings living today is something
over ten trillion—that's a one followed by thirteen zeroes—which is far more than
the total number of previous members of the genus Homo in every generation since
the first Neanderthalers appeared. Now the living overwhelmingly outnumber the
dead.*

When Rafiel woke the next morning he found his good nature had begun to return.
Partly it was the lingering wisps of his last designer dream—Alegretta had starred in
it, as ordered, and that lost and cherished love of his life had never been more desirable and more desiring, for that matter, because that was the kind of dream he had
specified. So he woke up in a haze of tender reminiscence. Anyway, even the terminally mortal can't dwell on their approaching demise all the time, and Rafiel was
naturally a cheerful man.

Getting out of bed in the morning was a cheerful occasion, too, for he was surrounded with the many, many things he had to be cheerful about. As he breakfasted on what the servers brought him he turned on the vid tank and watched half a dozen tapes of himself in some of the highlights of his career. He was, he realized, quite good. In the tank his miniature self sang love ballads and jiving patter numbers and even arias, and his dancing—well, yes, now and then a bit trembly, he conceded to himself, but with *style*—was a delight to watch. Even for the person who had done it, but who, looking in the tank, could only see that imaged person as a separate and, really, very talented entity.

Cheerfully Rafiel moved to the barre to begin his morning warm-ups. He started gently, because he was still digesting his breakfast. There wasn't any urgency about it. Rehearsal call was more than an hour away, and he was contentedly aware that the person he had been looking at on the vid was a *star*.

In a world where the living far outnumbered the dead, space was precious. On the other hand, so was Rafiel, and stars were meant to be coddled. Mosay had taken a rehearsal room the size of a tennis court for Rafiel's own private use. The hall was high up in the arcology, and it wasn't just a big room. It was a very well-equipped one. It had bare powder-blue walls that would turn into any color Rafiel wanted them to be at the touch of a switch, a polished floor of real hardwood that clacked precisely to his taps, and, of course, full sound and light projection. Mosay, fussing over his star's accommodations, touched the keypad, and the obedient projectors transformed the bare walls into a glimmering throneroom.

"I'm afraid that it's the wrong period, of course," Mosay apologized, looking without pleasure at the palace of Versailles, "no *roi soleil* in Thebes, is there, but *I* want you to get the feel of the kingship thing, *sapete*? We don't have the programs for the Theban backdrops yet. Actually I don't know if we will, because as far as my research people can tell, the Thebans really didn't have any actual thronerooms anyway."

"It doesn't matter," Rafiel said absently, slipping into his tap shoes.

"It does to me! You know how I am about authenticity." Seeing what Rafiel was doing Mosay hastily turned to touch the control keys again. Victorium's overture began to tinkle from the hidden sound system. "*C'est beau, le son?* It's just a synthesizer arrangement so far."

"It's fine," said Rafiel.

"Are you sure? Well, *bon*. Now, *bitte*, do you want to think about how you want to do the first big scene? That's the one where you're onstage with all the townspeople. They'll be the chorus. You're waiting to find out what news your brother-in-law, Creon, has brought back from the Delphic oracle; he went to find out what you had to do to get things straightened out in Thebes. . . ."

"I've read the script, of course," said Rafiel, who had in fact finished scrolling through it at breakfast.

"Of course you have," said Mosay, rebuked. "So I'll let you alone while you try working out the scene, shall I? Because I want to start checking out shooting locations tomorrow, and so I've got a million things to do today."

"Go and do them," Rafiel bade him. When the dramaturge was gone Rafiel lifted his voice and commanded, "Display text, scene one, from the top. With music."

The tinkling began again at once, and so did the display of the lines. The words marched along the upper parts of the walls, all four walls at once so that wherever Rafiel turned he saw them. He didn't want to dance at this point, he thought. Perhaps just march back and forth—yes, remembering that the character was lame—yes, and a king too, all the same. . . . He began to pantomime the action and whisper the words of his part:

CHORUS: *Ecco* Creon, crowned with laurels.

"He's going to say," Rafiel half-sang in his turn, "what's wrong's our morals."

[ENTER CREON]

CREON: *D'accord*, but I've still worse to follow.
It's not me speaking. It's Apollo.

Rafiel stopped the crawl there and thought for a second. There were some doubts in his mind. How well was that superstitious mumbo-jumbo going to work? You couldn't expect a modern audience to take seriously some mumble from a priestess. On the other hand, and equally of course, Oedipus had not been a modern figure. Would *he* have taken it seriously? Yes, Rafiel decided, he had to, or else the story made no sense to begin with. In playing Oedipus, then, the most he could do was to show a little tolerant exasperation at the oracle's nagging. So he started the accompaniment again, and mimed a touch of amused patience at Creon's line, turning his head away—

And caught a glimpse of an intruder watching him rehearse from the doorway.

It was a small, unkempt-looking young man in a lavender kilt. He was definitely not anyone Rafiel had seen as a member of Mosay's troupe and therefore no one who had a right to be here. Rafiel gave him a cold stare and decided to ignore him.

He realized he'd missed a couple of Creon's lines, and his own response was coming up. He sang:

OEDIPUS: We'll take care of this hubble-bubble as
Soon as you tell us what the real trouble is.

But his concentration was gone. He clapped his hands to stop the music and turned to scowl at the intruder.

Who advanced to meet him, saying seriously, "I hope I'm not interfering. But on that line—"

Rafiel held up a forbidding hand. "Who are you?"

"Oh, sorry, I'm Charlus, your choreographer. Mosay said—"

"I do my own choreography!"

"Of course you do, Rafiel," the man said patiently. "You're *Rafiel*. I shouldn't have said choreographer, when all Mosay asked me to do was be your assistant. Do you remember me? From when you did *Make Mine Mars*, twenty years ago it must have been, and I tried out for the chorus line?"

Then Rafiel did identify him, but not from twenty years ago. "You sired Docilia's little one."

Charlus looked proud. "She told you, then? Evvero. We're both so happy—but, look, maestro, let me make a suggestion on that bubble-as, trouble-is bit. Suppose . . ."

And the man became Oedipus on the spot, as he performed a simultaneous obscene gesture and courtly bow, ending on one knee.

Rafiel pursed his lips, considering. It was an okay step. No, he admitted justly, it was more than that. It wasn't just an okay step, it was an okay *Rafiel* step, with just a little of Rafiel's well-known off-balance stagger as the right knee bumped the floor.

He made up his mind. "*Khorashaw*," he said. "I don't usually work with anybody else, but I'm willing to give it a try."

"*Spasibo*, Rafiel," the man said humbly.

"*De nada*. Have you got any ideas about the next line?"

Charlus looked embarrassed. "*Hai*, sure, but *est-ce* possible to go back a little bit, to where you come in?"

"My first entrance, at the beginning of the scene?"

Charlus nodded eagerly. "Right there, *pensez-vous* we might try something real macho? You are a king, after all—and you can enter like . . ."

He turned and repeated Oedipus's entrance to the hall, but slowly, s-l-o-w-l-y, with his head rocking and a ritualistic, high-stepping strut and turn before he descended sedately to a knee again. It was the same finish as the other step, but a world different in style and meaning.

Rafiel pursed his lips. "I like it," he said, meditating, "but do you think it really looks, well, Theban? I'd say it's *peut-être* basically Asian—maybe Thai?"

Charlus looked at him with new respect. "Close enough. It's *meno o mino* the Javanese' *patjak-kulu* movement. Am I getting too eclectic for you?"

Rafiel acknowledged, "Well, I guess I'm pretty eclectic myself."

"I know," said Charlus, smiling.

While Charlus was showing the mincing little *gedruk* step he thought would be good for Jocasta, Mosay looked in, eyebrows elevated in the obvious question.

Charlus was tactful. "I've got to make a trip to the *benjo*," he said, and Rafiel answered the unspoken question as soon as the choreographer was gone.

"Mind his helping out? No, I don't mind, Mosay. He's no performer himself, but as a choreographer, *hai*, he's *good*." Rafiel was just. The man was not only good, he was bursting with ideas. Better still, it was evident that he had watched every show Rafiel had ever done, and knew Rafiel's style better than Rafiel did himself.

"*Bene, bene*," Mosay said with absent-minded satisfaction. "When you hire the best people you get the best results. Oh, and *senti*, Rafiel"—remembering, as he was already moving toward the door—"those messages you forwarded to me? A couple of them were personal, so I routed them back to your machine. They'll be waiting for you. *Continuez, mes enfants.*" And a pat on the head for the returning Charlus and the dramaturge was gone, and they started again.

It was hard work, good work, with Rafiel happy with the way it was going, but long work, too; they barely stopped to eat a couple of sandwiches for lunch, and even then, though not actually dancing, Rafiel and Charlus were working with the formatting screen, moving computer-generated stick figures about in steps and groupings for the dance numbers of the show, Rafiel getting up every now and then to try a step, Charlus showing an arm gesture or a bob of the head to finish off a point.

By late afternoon Rafiel could see that Charlus was getting tired, but he himself was going strong. He had forgotten his hospital stay and was beginning to remember the satisfactions of collaboration. Having a second person help him find insights into the character and action was a great pleasure, particularly when that person was as unthreatening as the eager and submissive Charlus. "So now," Rafiel said, toweling some sweat away, "we're up to where we've found out that Thebes won't get straight until the assassin of the old king is found and punished, right? And this is where I sing my vow to the gods—"

"*Permesso?*" Charlus said politely. And took up a self-important strut, half tap, almost cakewalk, swinging his lavender kilt as he sang the lines: "I swear, without deceit or bias, We'll croak the rat who croaked King Laius."

"Yes?" said Rafiel, reserving judgment.

"And then Creon gives you the bad news. He tells you that, *corpo di bacco,* things are *bad*. The oracle says that the murderer is here in Thebes. I think right there is when you register the first suspicion that there's something funny going on. You know? Like . . ." miming someone suddenly struck by an unwanted thought.

"You don't think that's too early?"

"It's what you think that counts, Rafiel," Charlus said submissively, and looked up toward the door.

Mosay and Docilia were looking in, the dramaturge with a benign smile, Docilia with a quick kiss for Rafiel and another for Charlus. Although their appearance was a distraction, the kiss turned it into the kind of distraction that starts a new and pleasing line of thought; Docilia was in white again, but a minimum of white: a short white wrap-around skirt, a short wrap-around bolero on top, with bare flesh between and evidently nothing at all underneath. "Everything going all right?" the dramaturge asked, and answered himself: "Of course it is; it's going to be a *merveille du monde*. Dear ones, I just stopped by to tell you that I'm leaving you for a few days; I'm off to scout out some locations for shooting."

Rafiel took his eyes off Docilia and blinked at him. "We're going to make *Oedipus* on location?"

"I insist," said Mosay firmly. "No *faux* backgrounds; I want the real thing for *Oedipus*! We're going to have a Thebes that even the Thebans would admire, if there were any of them left."

Charlus cleared his throat. "Is Docilia going with you?" he asked.

That question had not occurred to Rafiel to ask, but once it was asked he wanted to know the answer, too. Mosay was looking thoughtfully at the choreographer. "Well," he said, "I thought she might have some ideas. . . . Why do you want to know that?"

Charlus had an answer ready. "Because we've started to work out some of the *pas de deux* routines, and Docilia ought to have a chance to try them out." Rafiel did not think it was a truthful one.

Evidently Mosay didn't either. He pursed his lips, considering, but Docilia answered for him. "Of course I should," she said. "You go on without me, Mosay. Have a nice trip; I'll see you when you get back. Only please, dear, try to find a place that isn't too *hot*. I sweat so when I'm dancing, you know."

Whatever plans Charlus had for Docilia, they were postponed. When at last they were through rehearsing, Docilia kissed the choreographer absently and pulled Rafiel along with her out of the room before Charlus could speak. "*J'ai molto faim*, dear," she said—but only to Rafiel, "and I've booked a table for us."

In the elevator, Rafiel looked at her thoughtfully. "Didn't Charlus want to see you?"

She smiled up at him, shrugging. "But he acted as though he didn't want you to go off with Mosay," Rafiel persisted. "Or with me either, for that matter. Is he, well, jealous?"

"Oh, Rafiel! What a terrible word that is, 'jealous.' Are you thinking of, what, the Othello thing?"

"He's the father of your child," Rafiel pointed out uncomfortably.

"*Mais oui*, but why should he be jealous if I'm shtupping you or Mosay, *Liebling*? I shtup him too, whenever he likes—when I don't have another date, of course. Come and eat a nice dinner, and stop *worrying*."

They walked together to their table—not on a balcony this time, but on a kind of elevated dais at the side of the room, so they could be well seen. It was the kind of place where theater people gathered, at the bottom of the atrium. Tables in the open surrounded the fiftieth-floor rooftop lake. There was a net overhead to catch any carelessly dropped objects, and from time to time they could hear the whine of the magnets pulling some bit of trash away. But nothing ever struck the diners. The place was full of children, and Docilia smiled at every one of them, practicing her upcoming motherhood. And swans floated in the lake, and stars were woven into the net overhead.

When the servers were bringing their monkey-orange juice Rafiel remembered. "Speaking of Charlus. He had an idea for your scene at the end. You know? Just before you go to hang yourself? As you're going out . . ."

He looked around to see who was looking at them, then decided to give the fans a treat. He stood up, and in the little cleared space between their table and the railing, did the step Charlus had called "*gedruk*," mincing and swaying his hips. It was not unnoticed. Soft chuckles sounded from around the dining room. "Oh, maybe yes," Docilia said, nodding, pleased. "It gets a laugh, doesn't it?"

"Yes," said Rafiel, "but that's the thing. Do we want *comedy* here? I mean, you're just about to die . . ."

"Exactly, dear," she said, not understanding. "That's why it will be twice as funny in the performance."

"*Aber a morceau* incongruous, don't you think? Comedy and death?"

She was more puzzled than ever. "*Hai*, that's what's funny, isn't it? I mean, *dying*. That's such a bizarre thing, it always makes the audience laugh." And then, when she saw his face, she bit her lip. "*Pas* all that funny for everybody, is it?" she said remorsefully. "You're *so normal*, dear Rafiel. Sometimes I just forget."

He shrugged and forgave her. "You know more about that than I do," he admitted, knowing that he sounded still grumpy—glad when a famous news comic came over to chat. Being the kind of place it was, table-hopping was, of course, compulsory. As pleased as Rafiel at the interruption, Docilia showed her tomographs of the baby to the comic and got the required words of praise.

Then it was Rafiel's turn to blunder. "What sort of surrogate are you using?" he asked, to make conversation, and she gave him a sharp look.

"Did somebody tell you? No? Well, it's cow," she said, and waited to see what his response would be. She seemed aggrieved. When all he did was nod non-comittally, she said, "Charlus wanted to use something fancier. Do you think I did the right thing, Rafiel? Insisting on an ordinary cow surrogate, I mean? So many people are using water buffalo now. . . ."

He laughed at her. "I wouldn't know, would I? I've never been a parent."

"Well, I have, and believe me, Rafiel, it isn't easy. What *difference* does it make, really, what kind of animal incubates your child for you? But Charlus says it's important and, oh, Rafiel, we had such a battle over it!"

She shook her head, mourning the obstinacy and foolishness of men. Then she decided to forgive. "It isn't altogether his fault, I suppose. He's worried. Especially now. Especially because it's almost *fin* the second trimester and that means it's time—"

She came to a quick halt, once more biting her lip. Rafiel knew why: it was more suddenly remembered tact. The end of the second trimester was when they had to do the procedure to make the child immortal, because at that point the fetal immune system wasn't developed yet and they could manipulate it in the ways that would make it live essentially for ever.

"That's a scary time, I know," said Rafiel, to be comforting, but of course he did know. Everyone knew he knew, and why he knew. The operation was serious for a little fetus. A lot of them died, when the procedure didn't work—or managed to survive, but with their natural immune systems mortally intact. Like Rafiel.

"Oh, *mon cher*," she said, "you know I didn't mean anything *personal* by that!"

"Of course you didn't," he said reassuringly; but all the same, the happy buzz of the day's good rehearsing was lost, the evening's edge was gone, and long before they had finished their leisurely supper, he had abandoned any plan of inviting her back to his condo for the night.

It did spoil the evening for him. Too early for sleep, too late to make any other arrangements, he wandered alone through his condo. He tried reading, but it seemed like a lot of effort. He glanced toward the barre, but his muscles were sore enough already from the day's work-out. He switched on the vid, roaming the channels to see if there was anything new and good, but there wasn't. A football series coming to its end in Katmandu, an election in Uruguay—who cared about such things? He paused over a story about a habitat now being fitted out with engines to leave the solar system: it was the one named *Hakluyt* and it held his interest for a moment because of that silly woman, Hillaree, with her script. It would be interesting, he thought, to take that final outward leap to another star. . . . Of course, not for him, who would be long dead before the expedition could hope to arrive. He switched to the obituaries—his favorite kind of news—but the sparse list held no names that interested him. He switched again to the entertainment channels. There was a new situation comedy that he had heard about. The name was *Dachau*, and he remembered that one of the parts was played by a woman he had slept with a few times, years ago. Now she was playing a—a what?—a concentration-camp guard in Germany in World War II, it seemed. It was a comic part; she was a figure of fun as the Jews and Gypsies and political enemies who were inmates constantly mocked and outwitted her. It did have its funny bits. Rafiel laughed as one of the inmates, having escaped to perform some heroic espionage feat for the Allies, was sneaked back into the camp under the very eyes of the commandant. Still, he wondered if things had really ever been that *jolly* in the real concentration camps of the time, where the real death ovens burned all day and all night.

It all depended on whether you were personally involved, he thought.

And then he switched it off, thinking of Docilia. He shouldn't have been so curt with her. She couldn't help being what she was. If death seemed comical to the deathless, was that her fault? Hadn't most of the world, for centuries on end, found fun in the antics of the dwarves and the deformed, even making them jesters at their courts? Perhaps the hunchbacks themselves hadn't found anything to laugh at—but that was *their* point of view.

As his attitude toward dying was his own.

He thought for a moment of calling Docilia to apologize—perhaps the evening might be salvaged yet. Then he remembered what Mosay had said about personal messages and scrolled them up.

The first one was personal, all right, and a surprise. It was a talking message, and as soon as the picture cleared he recognized the face of the man who happened to have been his biological father.

The man hadn't changed a bit. (Well, why would he, in a mere ninety-some years?) He was as youthful and as handsome as he had been when, on a rare visit, he had somewhat awkwardly taken young Rafiel on his knee. "I saw you were in the *Krankhaus* again," the man in the screen said, with the look of someone who was paying a duty call on an ailing friend—not a close one, though. "It reminded me we haven't heard from each other in a long time. I'm glad everything *fait bon*, Rafiel—son—and, really, you and I ought to have lunch together some *prossimo giorno*."

That was it. Rafiel froze the picture before it disappeared, to study the dark, well-formed face of the man whose genes he had carried. But the person behind the face eluded him. He sighed, shrugged and turned to the other message. . . .

And that one made him stiffen in his chair, with astonishment too sharp to be joy.

It wasn't an imaged message, or even a spoken one; it was a faxed note, in a crabbed, nearly illegible handwriting that he knew very well:

Dearest Rafiel, I was so glad to hear you got through another siege with the damned doctors. Mazel tov. I'm sending you a little gift to celebrate your recovery—and to remind you of me, because I think of you so very often.

What the gift was he could not guess, because it hadn't arrived yet, but the note was signed, most wonderfully signed:

For always, your Alegretta.

6

Naturally, all kinds of connections and antipathies appear among the Oedipus *troupe as they come together. Charlus is the sire of Docilia's unborn child. Andrev, who is to play the Creon, is the son of the composer of the score, Victorium. Ormeld, the Priest, and Andrev haven't acted together for thirty-five years, because of a nasty little firefight over billing in what happened to be the first production in which either got an acting credit. (They hug each other with effusive but wary joy when they come together in the rehearsal hall.) Sander, the Tiresias, studied acting under Mosay when Mosay had just abandoned his own dramatic career (having just discovered how sat- isfying the god-behind-the-scenes role of a dramaturge was). Sander is still just a little awed by his former teacher. All these interconnections are quite separate from the or- dinary who-had-been-sleeping-with-whom sort of thing. They had to be kept that way. If people dragged up that sort of ancient history they'd never get everything straight. Actually, nobody is dragging anything up—at least, not as far as the surface where it can be seen. On the contrary. Everybody is being overtly amiable to everybody else and conspicuously consecrated to the show, so far. True, they haven't yet had much chance to be anything else, since it's only the first day of full-cast rehearsal.*

Although Mosay was still off scouting for locations—somewhere in *Turkey*, some- body said, though why anybody would want to go to *Turkey* no one could imagine— he had taken time to talk to them all by grid on the first day. "Line up, everybody," he ordered, watching them through the monitor over his camera. "What I want you to do is just a quick run-through of the lines. Don't sing. Don't dance, don't even act—we just want to say the words and see each other. Docilia, please leave Charlus alone for a minute and pay attention. Victorium will proctor for me, while I"—a small but conspicuous sigh; Mosay had not forgotten his acting skills—"keep trying to find the *right* location for our production."

Actually it was Rafiel who was paying least attention, because his mind was full of lost Alegretta. Now, perhaps, found again? For you never forgot your first love . . .

Well, yes, you did, sometimes, but Rafiel never had. Never could have in spite of the sixty or seventy—could it have been eighty? a hundred?—other women he had loved, or at least made love to, in the years since then. Alegretta had been something very special in his life.

He was twenty years old then, a bright young certain-to-be-a-star song-and-dance man. Audiences didn't know that yet, because he was still doing the kind of thing you had to start out with, cheap simulations and interactives, where you never got to make your own dramatic statement. The trade was beginning to know him, though, and Rafiel was quite content to be working his way up in the positive knowledge that the big break was sure to come. (And it had come, no more than a year later.)

But just then he had, of all things, become sick. (No one got *sick*!) When the racking cough began to spoil his lines, he had to do something. He complained to his doctors about it. Somewhat startled (people didn't *have* coughs), the doctors put him in a clinic for observation, because they were as discomfited by it as Rafiel himself. And when all the tests were over, the head resident herself came to his hospital room to break the bad news.

Even all these decades later, Rafiel remembered exactly what she had looked like that morning. Striking. Sexy, too; he had noticed that right away, in spite of the circumstances. A tall woman, taller in fact than Rafiel himself; with reddish-brown hair, a nose with a bit of a bend in it that kept it from being perfect in any orthodox way, but a smile that made up for it all. He had looked at her, made suspicious by the smile, a little hostile because a little scared. She sat down next to him, no longer smiling. "Rafiel," she said directly, "I have some bad news for you."

"*Che c'e?* Can't you fix this damn cold?" he said, irritated.

She hesitated before she answered. "Oh, yes, we can cure *that*. We'll have it all cleared up by morning. But you see, you shouldn't have a cough at all now. It means . . ." she paused, obviously in some pain. "It means the procedure didn't work for you," she said at last, and that was how Alegretta told Rafiel that he was doomed to die in no more than another hundred years, at most.

When he understood what she was saying, he listened quietly and patiently to all the explanations that went with it. Queerly, he felt sorrier for her than for himself—just then he did, anyway; later on, when it had all sunk in, it was different. But as she was telling him that such failures were very rare, but still they came up now and then, and at least he had survived the attempt, which many unborn babies did not, he interrupted her. "I don't think you should be a doctor," he told her, searching her lovely face.

"Why not?" she asked.

"You take it too hard. You can't stand giving bad news."

She said soberly, "I haven't had much practice at it, have I?"

He laughed at her. She looked at him in surprise, but then, he was still in his twenties, and a promise of another hundred years seemed close enough to forever. "Practice on me," he urged. "When I'm released, let's have dinner."

They did. They had a dozen dinners, those first weeks, and breakfasts too, because that same night he moved into her flat above the hospital wing. They stayed together nearly two weeks; and there had never been another woman like her. "I'll never tell," she promised when they parted. "It's a medical confidence, you know. A secret." She never had told, either.

And his career did blossom. In those days, Rafiel didn't need to be an oddity to be a star, he became a star because he was so damn good.

It was only later on that he became an oddity as well because, though Alegretta had never told, there were a lot of other checkups, and ultimately somebody else had.

It had not mattered to Rafiel, then, that Alegretta was nearly a hundred to his twenty. Why should it? Such things made no difference in a world of eternal youth.

Alegretta did not look one minute older than himself . . . And it was only later, when she had left him, and he was miserably trying to figure out why, that he realized the meaning of the fact that she never would.

First run-throughs didn't matter much. All they were really for was to get the whole cast together, to get some idea of their lines and what the relationship of each character was to the others, who was what to whom. They didn't act, much less sing; they read their lines at half-voice, eyes on the prompter scroll on the wall more than each other. It didn't matter that Rafiel's mind was elsewhere. When others were onstage he took out the fax from Alegretta and read it again. And again. But he wasn't, he thought, any more inattentive than any of the others. The pretty young Antigone— what was her real name? Bruta? Something like that—was a real amateur, and amateurishly she kept trying to move toward stage front each time she spoke. Which was not often; and didn't matter, really, because when Mosay came back he would take charge of that sort of thing in his gentle, irresistible way. And Andrev, the Creon, had obviously never even looked at the script, while Sander, who was to play the blind prophet, Tiresias, complained that there wasn't any point in doing all this without the actual dramaturge being present. Victorium had his hands full.

But he was dealing with it. When they had finished the quick run-through he dispatched Charlus to start on the choreography of the first scene, where all the Thebans were reciting for the audience their opening misery under the Sphinx. Rafiel was reaching in his pocket for another look at the fax when Victorium came over. "*Sind Sie* okay, Rafiel?" he asked. "I thought you seemed just a little absent-minded."

"*Pas du tout*," Rafiel said, stuffing the letter away. Then, admitting it, "Well, just a little, *forse*. I, ah, had a letter from an old friend."

"Yes," Victorium said, nodding. "Mosay said something about it. Alegretta, was that her name?"

Rafiel shrugged, not letting his annoyance show. Of course Mosay had known all about Alegretta because Mosay made it a point to know everything there was to know about every one of his artists; but to pry into private mail, and then to discuss it with others, was going too far.

"Old lovers can still make the heart beat faster, can't they?" he said.

"Yes?" Victorium said, not meaning to sound skeptical, but obviously not troubled with any such emotions himself. "Has it been a long time? Will you be seeing her again?"

"Oh"—startled by the thought, almost afraid of it—"no, I don't think so. No, probably not—she's a long way away. She seems to be in one of the orbiters now. You know she used to be a doctor? But now she's given up medicine, doing some kind of science now."

"She sounds like a very interesting person," Victorium said neutrally—a little absent-minded himself, too, because in the center of the room Charlus had started showing the Thebans the dance parts, and Victorium had not failed to catch the sounds of his own music. Still looking at the Thebans, Victorium said, "Mosay asked me to show you the rough simulation for the opening. Let's go over to the small screen—oh, hell," he said interrupting himself, "can you *pardonnez-moi* a minute? *Verdammt*, Charlus has got them *hopping* when the music's obviously *con vivace*. I'll be right back."

Rafiel listened to the raised voices, giving them his full willed attention in order to avoid a repetition of the rush of feeling that Victorium's casual suggestion had provoked. Charlus seemed to be winning the argument, he thought, though the results would not be final until Mosay returned to ratify them. It was a fairly important scene. Antigone, Ismene, Polyneices, and Eteocles—the four children of Oedipus and Jocasta—were doing a sort of *pas de quatre* in tap, arms linked like the cygnets in *Swan Lake*, while they sang a recapitulation of how Oedipus came and saved them from the horrid Sphinx. The chorus was being a real chorus, in fact a chorus line, tapping in the background and, one by one, speaking up—a potter, a weaver, a soldier, a household slave—saying yes, but things are going badly now and something must be *done*. Then Rafiel would make his entrance as Oedipus and the story would roll on . . . but not today.

Victorium was breathing hard when he rejoined Rafiel. "You can ignore all that," he said grimly, "because I'm sure Mosay isn't going to let that *dummkopf* dance-teacher screw up the *grand ensemble*. Never mind." He snapped on the prompter monitor to show what he and Mosay had programmed for the under-the-credits opening. "Let's get down your part here. This is before the actual story begins, showing you and the Sphinx."

Rafiel gave it dutiful attention. Even in preliminary stick-figure simulation, he saw that the monster on the screen was particularly unpleasant-looking, like a winged reptile. "*Che* the hell *cosa* is that?"

"It's the Sphinx, of course. What else would it be?" Victorium said, stopping the computer simulation so Rafiel could study the creature.

"It doesn't look like a sphinx to me. It looks like a crocodile."

"Mosay," Victorium said with satisfaction, "looked it up. Thebes was a city on the Nile, you know. The Nile is *famous* for crocodiles. They sacrificed people to them."

"But this one has wings."

"*Perchè no?* You're probably thinking of that other Egyptian sphinx. The old one out of the desert? This one's different. It's a *Theban* sphinx, and it looks like whatever Mosay says it looks like." Victorium gave him the look of someone who would like to chide an actor for wasting time with irrelevant details—if the actor hadn't happened to be the star of the show. "The important thing is that it was terrorizing the whole city of Thebes, after their *ancien roi*, Laius, got murdered, until you came along and got rid of it for them. Which, of course, is why the Thebans let you marry Jocasta and be their *nouveau roi*." He thought for a moment. "I'll have to write some new music for the Sphinx to sing the riddle, but," he said wistfully, "Mosay says we don't want too much song and dance here because, see, *tutta qui* is just a kind of prologue. It isn't in the Sophocles play. We'll just run it under the credits to mise the scene—oh, *merde*. What's that?"

He was looking at the tel window on the screen, where Rafiel's name had begun to flash.

"Somebody's calling me, I guess," Rafiel said.

"You shouldn't be getting personal calls during rehearsal, should you?" he chided. Then he shrugged. "*San ferian.* See who it is, will you?"

But when Rafiel tapped out his acceptance no picture appeared on the screen, just a voice. It wasn't even the voice of a "who." It was the serene, impersonal voice of his household server, and it said:

"A living organism had been delivered to you. It is a gift. I have no program for caring for living creatures. Please instruct me."

"Now who in the world," Rafiel marveled, "would be sending me a *pet?*"

It wasn't anyone in the world—not the planet Earth, anyway; as soon as Rafiel saw the note pinned to the cage, where the snow-white kitten purred contentedly inside, he knew who it was from.

> This is my favorite cat's best kitten, dear Rafiel. I hope you'll love it as much as I do.

Rafiel found himself laughing out loud. How strange of Alegretta. How dear, too! Imagine anyone keeping a *pet.* It was not the kind of thing immortals were likely to do. Who wanted to get attached to some living thing that was sure to die in only a few years—only a moment, in the long lifetime of people now alive? (Most of them, anyway.) But it was a sweet thought, and a sweet little kitten, he found as he uneasily picked it up out of the cage and set it on his lap. The pretty little thing seemed comfortable there, still purring as it looked up at him out of sleepy blue eyes.

Most important, it was a gift from Alegretta. He was smiling as, careful not to disturb the little animal, he began searching his data bases for instructions on the care and feeding of kittens.

7

Rafiel has decided not to make love to Docilia again. He isn't sure why. He suspects it has something to do with the fact that the sire of her child is always nearby, which makes him uncomfortable. It isn't just that they've collaborated on creating a fetus that makes him shy off, it is more the fact that they intend to be a family. It is only later that he realizes that that means he can't bed any of the other members of the troupe, either. Not the Antigone, the little girl named Bruta, though she has asked him to—not even though she happens to have interested him at first, since she has auburn hair and her nose is not perfectly straight. (Perhaps it is because she looks a little bit like Alegretta that he especially doesn't want to make love to her.) Not any of them, in spite of the fact that, all through his performing life, Rafiel has seldom failed to make love in person to every female he was required to make love to in the performance, on the principle that it added realism to his art. (He wasn't particularly attracted to most of those women, either, only prepared to make sacrifices for his art.) This time, no. The only sen-

*sible reason he can give himself for his decision is that Docilia would surely find out,
and it would hurt her feelings to be passed over for the others.*

None of this inordinate chastity was because he didn't desire sexual intercourse. On
the contrary. He didn't need to program designer dreams of lovemaking. His subconscious did all the programming he needed. Almost every morning he woke from
dreams of hot and sweaty quick encounters and dreamily long-drawn-out ones. The
root of the problem was that, although he wanted to do it, he didn't want to do it *with*
anyone he knew. (One possible exception always noted, but always inaccessible.) So
he slept alone. When, one morning, some slight noise woke him with the scent of
perfumed woman in his nose he supposed it was a lingering dream. Then he opened
his eyes. A woman was there, in his room, standing by a chair and just stepping out
of the last of her clothing. "Who the hell are you?" he shouted as he sat up.

The woman was quite naked and entirely composed. She sat on the edge of his
bed and said, "I'm Hillaree. You looked so sexy there, I thought I might as well just
climb in."

"How the hell did you get into my condo?"

"I'm a dramaturge," she said simply. "How much would you respect me if I let
your doorwarden keep me out?"

Rafiel turned in the bed to look at her better. She was a curly-headed little thing,
with a wide, serious mouth, and he was quite sure he had never seen her before.

But he had heard her name, he realized. "Oh, *that* dramaturge," he said, faintly
remembering a long-ago message.

"The dramaturge who has a wonderful part for you," she confirmed, "if you
have intelligence enough to accept it." She patted his head in a friendly way, and
stood up.

"If you want me for a part, you should talk to my agent," he called after her.

"Oh, I did that, Rafiel. She threw me out." Hillaree was rummaging through the
heap of her discarded clothing on the bedside chair. She emerged with a lapcase,
which she carried back to the bed. "I admit this isn't going to be a *big* show," she told
him, squatting crosslegged on his bed as she opened the screen from the case. "I'm
not Mosay. I don't do *spectacoli*. But people are traveling out to the stars, Rafiel. The
newest one is a habitat called *Hakluyt*. The whole population has voted to convert
their habitat into an interstellar space vehicle—"

"I know about that!" he snapped, more or less truthfully. "Habitat people have
done that before—last year, wasn't it? Or a couple of years ago? I think one was going to Alpha Centauri or somewhere."

"You see? You don't even remember. No one else does, either, and yet it's a grand,
heroic story! These people are doing something hard and dangerous. No, Rafiel,"
she finished, wagging her pretty head, "it's the greatest story of our time and it needs
to be told *dramatically*, so people will *comprehend* it. And I'm the one to tell it, and
you're the one to play it. Oh, it won't be like a Mosay production, I'll give you that.
But you'll never again see anything as right for you as the part of the captain of the
kosmojet *Hakluyt*."

"I don't know anything about kosmojets, do I? Anyway, I can't. Mosay already had one cacafuega attack when he heard a rumor about it."

"*Fichtig* Mosay. He and I don't do the same kind of thing. This one will be *intimate*, and *personal. Pas* music, *pas* dancing, *pas* songs. It will be a whole new departure for your career."

"But a song-and-dance man is what I am!"

She sniffed at him. "You're a short-timer, Rafiel. You're going to get *old*. Listen to me. This is where you need to go. I've watched you. I'm willing to bet my reputation—"

"Your reputation!"

She ignored the interruption. "—that you're just as good an actor as you are a dancer and singer . . . and, just to make you understand what's involved here, you can have five points on the gross receipts, which you know you'll *jamais* get from Mosay."

"Five per cent of not very much is still very little," Rafiel said at once, grinning at her to show that he meant no hard feelings.

She nodded as though she had expected that. She opened her bag and fingered the keypad for her screen. "May I?" she said perfunctorily, not waiting for an answer. A scroll of legal papers began to roll up the screen. "This is the deal for the first broadcast," she said. "That's twenty million dollars from right here on Earth, plus another twenty million for the first-run remotes. Syndication: that's a contract with a guarantee of another forty million over a ten-year period. And all that's minimum, Rafiel; I'd bet anything that it'll double that. And there are the contracts for the sub rights—the merchandising, the music. Add it all up, and you'll see that the *guarantee* comes pretty close to a hundred million dollars. What's five per cent of that, Rafiel?"

The question was rhetorical. She wasn't waiting for an answer. She was already scrolling to the next display, not giving Rafiel a chance to order her out of his condo. "*Lá!*" she said, "*Voici!*"

What they were looking at on the screen was a habitat. It was not an impressive object to the casual view. As in all pictures from space, there was no good indication of size, and the thing might have been a beverage can, floating in orbit.

"There's where our story is," she said. "What you see there is habitat *Hakluyt*. It starts with a population of twenty thousand people, with room to expand to five times that. It's a whole small town, Rafiel. The kind of town they used to have in the old days before the arcologics, you know? A place with everybody knowing everybody else; interacting, loving, hating, dreaming—and totally cut off from everyone else. It's a microcosm of humanity, right there on *Hakluyt*, and we're going to tell its story."

Although Rafiel was looking at the woman's pictures, he didn't think them very interesting. As far as Rafiel could tell, *Hakluyt* was a perfectly ordinary habitat, a stubby cylinder with the ribs for the pion tracks circling its outer shell. What he could tell wasn't actually very much. He hadn't spent much time on habitats, only one two-week visit, once, with—with . . . ? No, he had long since forgotten the name of the companion of that trip, and indeed everything about the trip itself except that habitats were not particularly luxurious places to spend one's time.

"How much spin does this thing have?" he asked, out of technical curiosity. "I'm not used to dancing in light-G."

"When it's en route *pas* spin at all. The gravity effect will be along the line of thrust. But you're forgetting, Rafiel," she chided him. "There won't be any dancing anyway. That's why this is such a breakthrough for you. This is a dramatic *story*, and you'll act it!"

"Hum," said Rafiel, not pleased with this woman's continuing reminders that, in his special case, becoming older meant that it would become harder and harder for him to keep in dancer's kind of shape. "Why do you say they're cut off from the rest of the world? Habitats are a lot easier to get to than, *per esempio*, Mars. There's always a stream of ships going back and forth."

"Not to this habitat," Hillaree told him confidently. "You're missing the point, and that's the whole drama of our story. You see that cluster of motors on the base? *Hakluyt* isn't just going to stay in orbit. *Hakluyt* will be going all the way to the star Tau Ceti. They'll be cut off, all right. They aren't coming back to the Earth, ever."

As soon as the woman was out of his condo, unbedded but also unrejected, or at least not *finally* rejected in the way that most mattered to her, Rafiel was calling his agent to complain. Fruitlessly. It was a lot too early in the morning for Jeftha to be answering her tel. He tried again when he got to the rehearsal hall, with the same "No Incoming" icon appearing on the screen. "Bitch," he said to the screen, though without any real resentment—Jeftha was as good a talent agent as he had ever had—and joined the rest of the cast.

They had started without him. Charlus was drilling the chorus all over again and Victorium, with Docilia standing by, was impatiently waiting for Rafiel himself. "Now," he said, "If you're quite ready to go to work? Here's where we come to a tricky kind of place in *Oedipus*. You've ordered Creon banished, in spite of the fact that he's your brother-in-law. You think he lied to you about the prophecy from Apollo's priest, and you've just found out that your wife, Jocasta, is also your mother—"

"Victorium dear," Docilia began, "that's something I wanted to talk about. I don't have enough lines there, do I? Since it's *per certo* as big a shock to me too?"

"You'd have to talk to Mosay about that when he gets back, Docilia dear," Victorium said. "Can't we stick to the point? Besides the incest thing, Rafiel, you're the one who murdered her husband, who is also your real father—"

"I've read the script," Rafiel told him.

"Of course you have, Rafiel dear," Victorium said, sounding much less confident of it. "Then we follow you into Jocasta's room, and you see that she hung herself, out of shame."

"Can't I do that on-screen, Vic?" Docilia asked. "I mean, committing suicide's a really dramatic moment."

"I don't think so, dear, but that's another thing you'd have to talk to Mosay about. Anyway, it's not the point right now, is it? I'm talking about what Rafiel does when he sees you've committed suicide."

"I take the pins out of her hair and blind myself with them," said Rafiel, nodding.

"Right. You jab the gold hairpins into your eyes. That's what I'm thinking about. What's the best way for us to handle that?"

"How do you mean?" Rafiel asked, blinking at him.

"Well, we want it to look *real*, don't we?"

"Sure," Rafiel said, surprised, not understanding the point. That sort of thing was up to the computer synthesizers, which would produce any kind of effect anybody wanted.

Victorium was thoughtfully silent. Docilia cleared her throat. "On second thought," she said, "maybe it's better if I hang myself offstage after all."

Victorium stirred and gave her a serious look. Then he surrendered. "We'll talk about all this stuff later," he said. "Let me get Charlus off everybody's back and we'll try putting the scene after that together."

Rafiel was surprised to see Docilia give him a serious wink, but whatever she had on her mind had to wait. Victorium was calling them all together. "All right," he said, "let's run it through. All the bad stuff is out in the open now. Rafiel knows what he's done, and all four of you kids are onstage now in the forgiveness scene. Ket, you're the Polyneices, take it from the top."

Obediently the quartet formed and the boy began to sing

POLYNEICES: We forgive you. If you doubt it, ask that zany Antigone, or Eteocles, or sweet Ismene.
ETEOCLES: You can't be all that bad.
ISMENE: After all, *vous êtes* our dad.

"Now you, Rafiel," Victorium said, nodding, and Rafiel took up his lines.

OEDIPUS: Calm? *Come possible* for me to be calm? I've killed my pop and shtupped my dear old mom.
ANTIGONE: It's okay, dad, we're all with you. It'll be a lousy life, but we'll be true. Wherever you go—

"No, no," Charlus cried, breaking in. "Excuse me, Victorium, but no. Bruta, this is *tap*, not ballet. Keep your feet down on the floor, will you?"

"*Aspet!*" Victorium snapped. "I'm running this rehearsal, and if you keep interrupting—"

"But she's ruining it, don't you see?" the choreographer pleaded. "Just give me a minute with her. Please? Bruta, I want you to tap on the turn, and give us a little disco hip rotation when you sing. And I want to hear every tap all by itself, loud and clear . . ."

There was, naturally, more objection from Victorium. Rafiel backed away to watch, not directly involved, and turned when he felt Docilia plucking at his arm.

"Be real careful," she whispered. "Don't let Mosay push you into anything. I think he wants you to really do it. The blinding," she added impatiently when she saw that he hadn't understood.

Rafiel stared at her to see if she was joking. She wasn't. "Believe me, that's what he wants from you," she said, nodding. "No faking it. He wants real blood. Real pain. Pieces of eyeball hanging out on your cheek."

"Docilia!" he said, grimacing.

"*Was ist das* 'Docilia'? *Voi sapete* how Mosay is. Oh, maybe he wouldn't expect you to *permanently* blind yourself. After the shooting was over he'd pay so the doctors could graft in some new eyes for you—but still."

"Mosay wouldn't ask anybody to do that," Rafiel protested.

"Wouldn't he? Especially considering—Well, when he comes back, just ask him," she said, and stopped there.

Rafiel had grasped her meaning, anyway. Especially considering could only be that, in the long run, they were beginning to be looking on him as expendable.

When he finally did get through to his agent she was only perfunctorily apologetic. "*Mi scusi,*" Jeftha said. "I had a hard night." That was all the explanation she offered, but her dark and youthful face supported it. The skin was as unlined as always, but her eyes were red. "Acrobats," she said, wearily running one hand through her thick hedge of hair.

"You shouldn't sleep with your clients," Rafiel said, setting aside the historical fact that she had, on occasion, with himself. "Now, this woman Hillaree . . ."

When Jeftha heard about the dramaturge's surprise visit she was furious. "The *puta!* she snapped. "Going behind your agent's *back?* She'll never cast a client of mine again—but how could you, Rafiel? If Mosay finds out you've been dealing with a tuppenny tinhorn like Hillaree he'll go berserker!"

"I wasn't *dealing* with her," Rafiel began, but she cut him off.

"Pray he doesn't hear about it. He's in a bad enough mood already. When he got to look at his locations somebody told him that the Thebes he was trying to match was the wrong Thebes—two of them with the same name, Rafiel, can you imagine that? How stupid can they be? The Thebes in Egypt didn't count. The Thebes somewhere north of Athens was the one where Oedipus had been king, and it was an entirely different kind of territory."

"He's back?"

"He will be in the morning," she confirmed. "Now, was that what you were so *fou* to talk to me about?"

He hesitated, and then said, "Forget it now, anyway." Because he couldn't quite bring himself to ask her the question that was mostly on his mind, which was whether it was at all possible that Docilia's hints and implications could possibly be right.

8

The work of a dramaturge does not end with making sure a production is successfully performed. A major part of the job is making sure the audiences will want to spend their money to see it. In the furtherance of this endeavor, sweet are the uses of publicity; for which reason Mosay has arranged to do his first costumed rehearsals in a very conspicuous place. The place he has chosen is the public park on the roof of the ar-

cology, where there are plenty of loungers and strollers, and every one a sure word-of-mouth broadcaster when they get home. Nor has Mosay failed to alert the paparazzi to be present in force.

Rafiel thought seriously of taking the kitten with him to show off at the day's rehearsal—after all, who else in the troupe owned a live cat? But the park was half a kilometer square, with a lake and a woodsy area and sweet little gardens all around. There was even a boxwood maze, great for children to play in, but all too good a place for a little kitten to get lost in, he decided, and regretfully left it in the care of his server.

The trouble with the rooftop was that it was windy. They were nearly a kilometer above the ground, where the air was always blowing strong. Clever vanes deflected the worst of the gusts, but not all of them; Rafiel felt chilled and wished Mosay had chosen another workplace. Or that, at least, they hadn't been instructed to show up in costume: there wasn't much warmth in the short woolen tunic. The winds were stronger than usual that day, and there were thick black clouds rolling toward them over the arcologies to the west. Rafiel listened: had he heard the sound of distant thunder? Or just the wind?

He shivered and joined the other performers as they walked around to get used to their costumes. Although the rooftop was the common property of all the hundred-and-sixty-odd-thousand people who lived or worked in that particular arcology, Mosay had managed to persuade the arcology council to set one grassy sward aside for rehearsals. The council didn't object. They agreed that it would be a pleasing sort of entertainment for the tenants, and anyway Mosay was a first-rate persuader—after all, what other thing did a dramaturge really have to be?

The proof of his persuasive powers was that, astonishingly, everyone in the cast was there, and on time: Mosay himself, back from his fruitless quest but looking fresh and undaunted, and Victorium, and Charlus, the choreographer—no, *assistant* choreographer, Rafiel corrected himself resolutely—and all the eleven principal performers in the show and the dozen members of the chorus. Rafiel had practiced with the sandals and the sword in his condo, while the watching kitten purred approvingly; by now he was easy enough in the costume. Not Andrev, the Creon, who kept getting his sword caught between his knees. There weren't any costume problems for Sander, the Tiresias, since his costume was only a long featureless smock, and Sander, who was a tall, unkempt man with seal-colored hair that straggled down over his shoulders, wore the thing as though he was ignoring it, which was pretty much the way he wore all his clothes anyway. All the women wore simple white gowns, Docilia's Jocasta with flowers in her hair, the daughters unembellished.

But when Rafiel first saw Bruta, the Antigone, turn toward him his heart stopped for a moment, she was so like Alegretta. "*Che cosa*, Rafiel?" she asked in sudden worry at his expression, but he only shook his head. He kept watching her, thought. Apart from the chance resemblance to his life's lost love, Bruta struck him as a bit of puzzle. Bruta looked neither younger nor older than anyone else in the cast, of course—Rafiel himself always excepted—but it was obvious that she was a lot less experienced. That interested Rafiel. Mosay was not the kind who liked to bother with newcomers. He left the discovery of fresh talent to lesser dramaturges; he could afford to hire the best, who inevitably were also the ones who had long since made their reputations. Rafiel thought of asking Docilia, who would be sure to know everyone's reasons for everything they did, but there wasn't time. Mosay was already waving everyone to cluster around him.

"Company," said Mosay commandingly. "I'm glad to be back, but we've got a lot of work to do, so if I may have your attention?" He got it and said sunnily, "I do have one announcement before we begin. I've found our shooting location. *Wunderbar*, it has an existing set that we can use—oh, not *exactly* replicating old Thebes, in a technical sense, but close enough. And we'd better get on with it, so *if* you please. . . ." Rafiel concealed a grin at the way Mosay was making sure he looked every centimeter the staging genius as he played to the spectators behind the velvet ropes, and, of course, to the pointing cameras of the paparazzi. When he had everyone's attention he went on. "We aren't going to do the short fighting-the-Sphinx scene because we don't have a sphinx"—well, of course they didn't; they never would be a sphinx until the animation people put one in—"so we'll start with the *pas de quatre*, where you kids"—nodding to the four "children" of Oedipus and Jocasta—"sing your little song about how after Oedipus saved Thebes from the Sphinx he married your *maman*, the widowed Jocasta, whose husband had been mysteriously murdered and thus Oedipus became *koenig* himself—"

"Oh, hell, Mosay," said Docilia warmly, "that's a whole play right there. *Bisogniamo* say all that?"

"We must. We'll get it in, and anyway that's not your problem, Docilia, is it? In fact, you're not even in this scene, or the next scene either, except to stand around and look pretty, because this is where Creon makes his entrance and tells Oedipus what the oracle of Apollo said."

"I already know all the Creon lines," Andrev said proudly. He had the reputation of being a slow study.

"I certainly hope so, Andrev. Places, everybody? And now if we'll just take it from the last bars of Victorium's opening. . . ."

It wasn't a big scene for Rafiel. He didn't even get to make a real entrance, just ambled onstage to wait for Creon to show up. The scene belonged to the Creon. Victorium had written the music accordingly, with a background score full of dark and mystical dissonances—right enough for an oracle's pronouncements, Rafiel supposed.

What Creon brought was bad news, so Rafiel's responses had to be equally somber. Not just somber, though. Rafiel made sure all his gestures were, well, a trifle less *portentous* than the Creon's—after all, Rafiel was not merely playing an old, doomed Theban king, he was playing *himself* playing the king. That was what being a star was all about.

Rafiel flinched at a boom from the sky. Thunder was crashing somewhere in the distance, and Mosay agitatedly demanded of a watching arcology worker that they erect the dome. Just in time; rain was slashing down on the big transparent hood over the roof before the petaled sections had quite closed over them. Rafiel shuddered again. He found that he was feeling quite tired. He wondered if it was showing up in his performance . . . though of course it was only a dress rehearsal.

All the same, Rafiel didn't like the feeling that his dancing was not as lively—as bumptiously clumsy—as his audiences expected of him. He forced himself into the emotions of the part—easily enough, because Rafiel had all the ambiguity of any actor in his beliefs. Whatever he privately thought or felt, he could throw himself into the thoughts and feelings of the character he was playing; and if that character took silly oracular conundrums seriously, then for the duration of that role so would Rafiel. He worked so hard at it that at the end of the third run-through he was sweating as he finished his meditative *pas de seul*. So was the Creon, although he had no dancing to do. But it was Rafiel Mosay was watching, with a peculiar expression of concern on his face, and it was Rafiel he was looking at when he declared a twenty-minute break.

"*Comment ça va?*" Docilia asked, taking Rafiel's elbow.

He blinked at her. "Fine, fine," he assured her, though he didn't think he really was. Was it that obvious? He hadn't missed Mosay's watchful eyes, though now the dramaturge had forgotten him in the press of making quick calls on the communications monitor at the edge of the meadow. Rafiel made an effort and pressed Docilia's arm against his side amatively—well, maybe there was his problem right there, he thought. Deprivation. After all, why should any healthy person deliberately stop having sex, thus very possibly endangering not only his performance, but even his health?

"You don't *look* all right," Docilia told him, steering him through the park to a formal garden. "Except when you're looking at that Bruta."

"Oh, now really," Rafiel laughed—actually laughing, because the thought really amused him. "She's just so *young*."

"So amateurish, you mean."

"That too," he acknowledged, slipping his arm around her waist in a friendly way. "I'm surprised Mosay took her on."

"You don't know?"

"Know what?" Rafiel asked, proving that he did not.

"She's his latest daughter," Docilia informed him with pleasure. "So if you're shtupping her you're going to be part of the family."

Rafiel opened his mouth to deny that he was making love to Bruta, or indeed to anyone else since the last time with Docilia herself, but he closed it again. That, after all, was none of Docilia's business, not to mention that it did not comport well with the image of a lusty, healthy, *youthful* idol of every audience.

But she might have been reading his mind. "Oh, poor Rafiel," she said, tightening her grip on his waist. "You're just not getting enough, are you?" She looked around. There was hardly anyone near them, the casual spectators mostly still watching the performers in the rehearsal area. And they were near the maze.

"I have an idea," she murmured. "Can *we* go in the maze for a while?"

After all, why not? Rafiel surrendered. "I'd like nothing better," he said gallantly, knowing as well as she did that the best thing one did in the isolation of a maze was to do a little friendly fooling around with one's companion—on whom, in any case, Rafiel was beginning to feel he might as well be beginning to have sexual designs again, after all. They had no trouble finding a quiet dead end and, without discussion, Rafiel unhesitatingly put his hand on her.

"Are you sure you aren't too tired?" she asked, but turning toward him as she spoke; and, of course, that imposed on him the duty to prove that he wasn't tired at all. He realized he didn't have much time to demonstrate it in, so they wasted none. They were horizontal on the warm, grassy ground in a minute.

It was strange, he reflected, pumping away, that something you wanted to do could also be a wearisome chore. He was glad enough when they had finished. . . . And almost at that very moment, as though taking a quick cue, a voice from an unseen person, somewhere else in the maze, was thundering at them.

It was Mosay's voice. What he was saying—bawling—was: "Rafiel! Is that you I hear in there with Docilia? Come out this minute! We need to talk."

Rafiel was breathing hard, but he managed to grin at his partner and help her to her feet. "Can't it wait, Mosay?" he called, carefully conserving his breath.

"It can *not*," the dramaturge roared. "*Expliquez* yourself. Who's this woman who's claiming she's got you signed up for a new production?"

Rafiel groaned. Mosay had in fact found out. Docilia put an alarmed hand on his forearm.

"Oh, *paura*. You'd better pull yourself together," she whispered, doing the same for herself. "He's really *furioso* about something."

Rafiel gave in, tugging his underpants back on. "Well," he called to the featureless hedge, "we did talk a little bit, she and I—"

"She says you *agreed*!" snapped the invisible Mosay. "She's got a story about it in all the media, and I won't have it! Rafiel. You're making me look like a *Dummkopf*."

"I never actually agreed—"

"But you didn't say no, either, did you? That's not *cosi buono*. I won't have you making *any* commitments after this one," Mosay roared. "Now *vieni qui* and talk to me!"

His muttering died in the distance. Docilia turned to look into Rafiel's face. "What in the world have you done?" she asked.

"Nothing," he said positively, and then, thinking it over, "But I guess enough." He could have thrown the woman out of his home without any discussion at all, he thought. He hadn't. Resigned, he braced himself for the vituperation that was sure to come.

It came, all right, but not as pure vituperation. Mosay had switched to another mode. "Oh, *pauvre petit* Rafiel," he said sorrowfully, "haven't I always done everything I can for you? And now you're conspiring behind my back with some sleaze-ball for a cheap-and-dirty exploitation show?"

"It isn't really that cheap, Mosay, it's a hundred mil—"

"Cheap isn't just *money*, Rafiel. Cheap is cheap *people*. Second-raters. Do you want to wind up your career with the has-beens and never-wases? No, Rafiel," he said, shaking his head, "*non credo* you want that. And, anyway, I've talked to your agent, and Jeftha says the deal's already *kaput*." He allowed himself a forgiving smile, then turned away briskly.

"Now let's get some work done here, company," he called, clapping his hands. "One more time, from Creon's story about the oracle. . . ."

But they didn't actually get that far, and it was Rafiel's fault.

Rafiel started out well enough, rising in wrath to sing his attack on Creon's message from the oracle. Then something funny happened. Rafiel felt the ground sliding away underneath him. He didn't feel the impact of his head on the grassy lawn. He didn't know he had lost consciousness. He was only aware of beginning to come to, half dazed, as someone was—someones were—loading him on to a high-wheeled cart and hurrying him to an elevator, and walking beside him were people who were agitatedly talking about him as though he couldn't hear.

"You'll have to tell him, Mosay," said Docilia's voice, fuzzily registering in Rafiel's ears.

Then there was a mumble, of which all Rafiel could distinguish was when, at the end, someone raised his voice to say, "*Pas* me!"

"*Allora* who?" in Docilia's voice again, and a longer mumble mumble, and then once more Docilia: "I think it'd be better from *la donna* . . ."

And then he felt the quick chill spray of an anesthetic on the side of his neck. Rafiel fell asleep as the shot did its job. Deeply asleep. So deep that there was no need to worry about anything . . . and no desire to wonder just what it was that his friends had been talking about.

"Just fatigue," the doctor said reassuringly when Rafiel was conscious again. "You collapsed. *Probabilmente* you've just been working too hard."

"Probably?" Rafiel asked, challenging the woman, but she only shrugged.

"You're just as good as you were when you left here, basically," she said. "Your *ami*'s here to take you home."

The *ami* was Mosay, full of concern and sweetness. Rafiel was glad to see him.

"I'm sorry about being so silly, but I'll be ready to get back to work in the morning," Rafiel promised, leaning on the hard, strong form of the nurser.

"*Sans doute* you will," Mosay said worriedly. "Here, sit in the *chaise*, let the nurser give you a ride to the cars." And at the elevator, taking over the wheelchair himself: "Still," he added, "if you're at all tired, why shouldn't you take another day or two to rest? I've picked a location spot in Texas. . . ."

That roused Rafiel. "Texas? *Pas* Turkey?"

"Of course not Turkey," Mosay said severely. "There's just the right place out in the desert, hardly built up at all. Now, here we are at your place, and they've got your nice bed all ready for you—*Gesù Cristo!*" he interrupted himself, staring. "What's that?"

Weak as he was, Rafiel laughed out loud. His server was coming toward him welcomingly, and padding regally after, tail stiff in the air, was the kitten.

"It's just my cat, Mosay. A present from a friend."

"Does it bite?" When reassured, the dramaturge gave it a hostile look anyway, as though suspecting an attack or, worse, an excretion. "If that's what you like, Rafiel, why should I criticize? Anyway, I'll leave you now. You can join us when you're ready. We'll work around you for a bit. No, don't argue, it's no trouble. Just give me your word that you won't come out until you're *absolutely* ready . . ."

"I promise," said Rafiel, wondering why it felt so good to be undertaking to do nothing for a while. It never had before.

9

Rafiel, who loves to travel, seldom has time to do much of it. That seems a bit strange, since he is a famous presence in all the places where human beings live, on planet and off, but of course his presence in almost all of those places is only electronic. He is looking forward eagerly to the ride in the magnetrain, with no one for company but the little white kitten. When he finally embarks, after the obligate few days of loafing around his condo, it really is as great a pleasure for him as he had hoped—well, would have been, anyway, if he weren't continuing to be so unreasonably tired. Still he enjoys watching the scenery flash by at six hundred kilometers an hour— arcologies, fields, woods, rivers—and he enjoys doing nothing. He especially enjoys being alone. With his presence on the train unknown to the fans who might otherwise besiege him, with only the servers to bring his meals and make up his bed and tend to the kitten, he thinks he almost would not mind if the trip went on for ever. When they reach their destination at the edge of the Sonora Desert he is reluctant to get off.

Rafiel arrived at the Sonora arcology just in time to catch a few hours' sleep in a rented condo, not nearly as nice as his own, in an arcology an order of magnitude tinier. When he reported for work in the morning even Turkey began to seem more desirable. This desert was *hot.*

Mosay was there to greet him solicitously—proudly, too, as he waved around the set he had discovered. "*Wunderbar,* isn't it? And such *bonne chance* it was available. Of course, it's not an *exact* copy of the actual old Thebes, but I think it's quite *interessante,* don't you? And there's no sense casting great talents, is there, if you're going to ask them to play in front of a background of dried mud huts."

Wilting in the heat, Rafiel gazed around at Mosay's idea of an "interesting" Thebes. He was pretty sure that Thebes-in-Sonora didn't much resemble the old Thebes-in-Boeotia. So much marble! So much artfully concealed lighting inside the buildings—did the Greeks have artificial lighting at all? Would the Greeks have put that heroic-seized statue of Oedipus (actually, of Rafiel himself in his Oedipus suit) in the central courtyard? And, if they had, would they have surrounded it with banked white and yellow roses? Did they have *moats* around their castles? Well, did they have castles at all? Questions like that took Rafiel's mind off the merciless sun, but not enough.

"It's you and Docilia now, please," Mosay said—commanded, really. "Places!" And on cue Docilia began Jocasta's complaint about childbirth Rafiel reacted as the part called for as, shoulders swaying, head accusingly erect, she sang:

> *Che sapete,* husband? I did all the borning,
> Carrying those devils and puking every morning.

Never *peine* so *dur*, never agony so hot,
It was like pushing a pumpkin through —

"No, no, cut," Mosay shouted. "Oh, Rafiel! What do you think you're doing there, taking a little nap? Your wife's giving you hell about the kids she's borne for you and you're gaping around like some kind of *turista*. Get a little movement into it, will you?"

"Sorry," Rafiel said, as the cast relaxed. He saw Charlus coming, deferentially but with determination, toward him, as he turned his face to the server that came over to mop the sweat off his brow. There wasn't much of it, in spite of the heat; in the dry desert air it evaporated almost as fast as it formed.

"Do you mind, Rafiel?" Charlus offered, almost begging. "I was just thinking, you might want to wring your turn out and let the arms go all the way through when she starts the 'puking every morning' line."

"I didn't want to upstage her."

"No, of course not, but Mosay's got this idea that you have to be *interacting*, you see, and —"

"Sure," Rafiel said. "Let's get on with it." And he was able to keep his mind on his work, in spite of the heat, in spite of the fatigue, for nearly another hour. But by the time Mosay called a break for lunch he was feeling dizzy.

Instantly the sexy young Bruta was at his side. "Let me keep you company," she said, almost purring as she guided him to a seat in the shade. "What would you like? I'll bring you a plate."

"I'm not really hungry," he said, with utter truth. He didn't think he would ever be hungry again.

Bruta was all sympathy. "No, of course not. It is dreadfully hot, isn't it? But maybe just a plate of ice cream — do you like palmfruit?" He gave in, and watched her go for it with objective admiration. The girl was slim as an eel, with a tiny bum that any man would enjoy getting his hands on. But it was only objectively that the thought was interesting; nothing stirred in his groin, no pictures of an interesting figure developed in the crystal ball of his mind. Only —

His mouth was filling with thin, warm saliva.

It could not be possible that he was about to vomit, he thought, and then realized it was quite possible, in fact. He got briskly to his feet, prepared to give a close-lipped smile to anyone who was looking at him. No one was. He turned away from the direction of the buffet table, heading out into the desert. As he got behind Oedipus's castle he picked up his pace, pressing his palm of his hand against his involuntarily opening mouth, but he couldn't hold it. He bent forward and spewed a cupful of thin, colorless fluid on to the thirsty stand.

It wasn't painful to vomit. It was almost a pleasure, it happened so easily and quickly, and when it was over he felt quite a lot better — though puzzled, for he hadn't eaten enough that morning to have enough in his stomach to be worth vomiting.

He turned to see if any of the troupe had been looking in his direction. Apparently no human had, but a server was hurrying toward him across the desert. "Sir?" Its voice was humble but determined. "Sir, do you need assistance here?"

"No. *Hsieh-hsieh*," Rafiel added, remembering to be courteous as ever, even to machines.

"I must tell you that there is some risk to your safety here," the server informed him. "We have destroyed or removed fourteen small reptiles and other animals this morning, but others may come in. They are attracted by the presence of warm-blooded people. Please be careful where you step."

Rafiel almost forgot his distress, charmed by the interesting idea. "You mean rattlesnakes? I've heard of 'rattlesnakes.' They can bite a person and kill him."

"Oh, hardly kill one, sir, since we are equipped for quick medical attention. But it would be a painful experience, so if you don't mind rejoining the others? . . ."

And it paced him watchfully, all the way back.

It didn't seem that anyone had noticed, though Bruta was standing there with a tray in her hand. "Nothing to eat after all, please," Rafiel begged her. "It's just too hot."

"Whatever you say, Rafiel," she said submissively. But she stayed attentively by him all through the break, watchful as any serving machine. And when they started again, he saw the girl reporting to her father, and felt Mosay's eyes studying him.

He managed to keep his mind on what he was doing for that shot, and for the next. It was, he thought, a creditable enough performance, but it wasn't easy. They were shooting out of sequence, to take advantage of the lighting as the sun moved and for grouping the actors conveniently. Rafiel found that confusing. Worse, he discovered that he was feeling strangely detached. Docilia did not seem to be the Docilia he had so often bedded any more. She had become her role; Jocasta, the mother of his children and appallingly also of himself. When he reached the scene where he confronted her dead body, twisting as it hung in the throneroom, he felt an unconquerable need for reassurance. Without thinking, he reached out and touched her to make sure she was still warm.

"Oh, *merde*, Rafiel," she sighed, opening her eyes to stare at him, "what are you doing? You've wrecked the whole *drecklich* shot."

But Mosay was there already, soothing, a little apprehensive. "It's all right, Rafiel," he said. "I know this is hard on you, the first day's shooting, and all this heat. It's about time to quit for the day, anyway."

Rafiel nodded. "It'll be better in the morning," he promised.

But it wasn't.

It wasn't better the next day, or the day after that, or the day after that one. It didn't get better at all. "It's the heat, of course," Docilia told him, watching Charlus trying to perfect the chorus in their last appearance. ("Deeper *plié*, for God's sake—*use your legs!*"). "Imagine Mosay making us work in the *open*, for God's sake."

"Of course," Rafiel agreed. He had stopped trying to look as though he were all right when he was off camera. He just stood in the shade, with an air cooler blowing on him. And Charlus said the same thing.

"You'll be all right when we finish here," he promised, watching Bruta and the Ismene. "It's only another day or two—no, no! *Chassé* back now! Then a *pas de chat*, but throw your legs back and come down on the right foot—that's better. Don't you want to lie down, Rafiel?"

He did want that, of course. He wanted it a lot, but not enough to be seen doing it on the set. He did all his lying down when shooting was over for the day, back in the borrowed condo, where he slept almost all the free time he had, with the kitten curled up at his feet.

Even Docilia was mothering him, coming to tuck him in at night but making it clear that she was not intending, or even willing, to stay. She kissed him on the forehead and hesitated, looking at the purring kitten. "You got that from Alegretta, didn't you? *Permesso* ask you something?" And when he nodded, "No offense, Rafiel, but why are you so *verrückt* for this particular one?"

"You mean Alegretta? I don't know," he said, after thought. "*Forse* it's just because she's so different from us. She doesn't even talk like us. She's—serious."

"Oh, Rafiel! Aren't we serious? We work *hard*."

"Well, sure we do, but it's just—well—you know, we're just sort of making shadow pictures on a screen. Maybe it comes to what she's serious about," he offered. "You know, she started a whole new life for herself—quit medicine, took up science. . . ."

Docilia sniffed. "That's not so unusual. I could do that if I wanted to. Some day I probably will."

Rafiel smiled up at her, imagining this pale, tiny beauty becoming a scientist. "When?" he asked.

"What does it matter when? I've got plenty of time!"

And Rafiel fell asleep thinking about what "plenty of time" meant. It meant, among other things, that when you had forever to get around to *important* things, it gave you a good reason to postpone them—forever.

The shooting went faster than Rafiel had imagined, and suddenly they were at an end to it. As he waited in full make-up for his last scene, his face a ruin, himself unable to see through the wreck the make-up people had made of his eyes, Docilia came over. "You've been wonderful," she told him lovingly. "I'm glad it's over, though. I promise you I won't be sorry to leave here."

Rafiel nodded and said, more wistfully than not, "Still it's kind of nice to have a little solitude sometimes."

She gave him a perplexed look. "Solitude," she said, as though she'd never heard the word before.

Then Mosay was calling for him on the set . . . and then, before he had expected it, his part was done. Old Oedipus, blinded and helpless, was cast out of the city where he had reigned, and all that was left for the cast to shoot was the little come-on Mosay had prepared for the audiences, when the children and chorus got together to set up the sequel.

They didn't need Rafiel for that, but he lingered to watch, sweltering or not. A part of him was glad the ordeal was over. Another part was somberly wondering what would happen next in his life. Back to the hospital for more tinkering, most likely, he thought, but there was no pleasure in that. He decided not to think about it and watched the shooting of the final scene. One after another the minor actors were telling the audience they hoped they'd liked the show, and then, all together:

If so, we'll sure do more of these
Jazzy old soaps by Mr. Sophocles.

And that was it. They left the servers to strike the set. They got on the blessedly cool cast bus that took them back to the condo. Everyone was chattering, getting ready for the farewells. And Mosay came stumbling down the aisle to Rafiel, holding on to the seats. He leaned over, looking at Rafiel carefully. "Docilia says you wanted to stay here for a bit," he said.

That made Rafiel blink. What had she told him that for? "Well, I only said I kind of liked being alone here. . . ."

The dramaturge was shaking his head masterfully. "No, no. It's quite all right, there's nothing left but the technical stuff. I insist. You stay here. Rest. Take a few days here. I think you'll agree it's worth it, and—and—anyway, *ese*, after all, there's no real reason why you have to go back with us, is there?"

And, on thinking it over, Rafiel realized that there actually wasn't.

The trouble was that there wasn't any real reason to stay in the Sonora arcology, either. As far as Rafiel could see, there wasn't any reason for him to be anywhere at all, because—for the first time in how long?—he didn't have anything he had to do.

Since he'd had no practice at doing nothing, he made up things to do. He called people on the tel screen. Called old acquaintances—all of them proving to be kind, and solicitous, and quite unprecedently remote—called colleagues, even called a few paparazzi, though only to thank them for things they had already publicized for him and smilingly secretive about any future plans.

Future plans reminded him to call his agent. Jeftha, at least, seemed to feel no particular need to be kind. "I had the idea you were pretty sick," she said, studying him with care, and no more than half accepting his protestations that he was actually entirely well and ready for more work quite soon.

She shook her head at that. "I've called off all your appearances," she said. "Let them get hungry, then when you're ready to get back—"

"I'm ready now!"

The black and usually cheerful face froze. "No," she said.

It was the first time his agent had ever said a flat "no" to her best client. "Ay Jesus," he said, getting angry, "who the hell do you think you're talking to? I don't need *you*."

The expression on Jeftha's face became contrite. "I know you don't, *caro mio*, but I need you. I need you to be well. I—care about you, dear Rafiel."

That stopped the flooding anger in its tracks. He studied her suspiciously but, almost for the first time, she seemed to be entirely sincere. It was not a quality he had associated with agents.

"Anyway," she went on, the tone becoming more the one he was used to, "I can't let you make deals by yourself, *piccina*. You'll get involved with people like that stupid Hillaree and her dumb story ideas. Who wants to hear about *real* things like kosmojets going off to other stars? People don't care about now. They want the good old stories with lots of pain and torture and *dying*—excuse me, *carissimo*," she finished, flushing.

But she was right. Rafiel thought that he really ought to think about that: was that the true function of art, to provide suffering for people who were incapable of having any?

He probably would think seriously about that, he decided, but not just yet. So he did very little. He made his calls, and between calls he dozed, and loafed, and pulled a string across the carpeted floor to amuse the kitten, and now and then remembered to eat.

He began to think about an almost forgotten word that kept popping up in his mind. The word was "retirement."

It was a strange concept. He had never known anyone who had "retired." Still, he knew that people used to do it in the old days. It might be an interesting novelty. There was no practical obstacle in the way; he had long since accumulated all the money he could possibly need to last him out . . . for whatever time he had left to live. (After all, it wasn't as though he were going to live forever). Immortals had to worry about eternities, yes, but the cold fact was that no untreated human lasted much more than a hundred and twenty years, and Rafiel had already used up ninety of them.

He could even, he mused, be *like* an immortal in these declining years of his life. Just like an immortal, he could, if he liked, make a midcourse change. He could take up a new career and thus change what remained of his life entirely. He could be a writer, maybe; he was quite confident that any decent performer could do *that*. Or he could be a politician. Certainly enough people knew the name of the famous Rafiel to give him an edge over almost any other candidate for almost any office. In short, there was absolutely nothing to prevent him from trying something completely different with the rest of his life. He might fail at whatever he tried, of course. But what difference did that make, when he would be dead in a couple of decades anyway?

When the doorwarden rang he was annoyed at the interruption, since his train of thought had been getting interesting. He lifted his head in anger to the machine. "*Ho detto* positively no calls!"

The doorwarden was unperturbed. "There is always an exception," it informed him, right out of its basic programming, "in the case of visitors with special urgency, and I am informed this is one. The woman says she is from *Hakluyt* and she states that she is certain you will wish to see her."

"*Hakluyt*? Is it that *fou* dramaturge woman again? Well, she's wrong about that, I don't want to talk about her stupid show—"

But then the voice from the speaker changed. It wasn't the doorwarden's any more. It was a human voice, and a familiar, female human voice at that. "Rafiel," she said fondly, "what is this crap about a show? It's me, Alegretta. I came to visit you all the way from my ship *Hakluyt*, and I don't know anything about any stupid shows. Won't you please tell your doorwarden to let me in?"

10

Rafiel knows that Alegretta has come from somewhere near Mars, and he knows pretty well how far away Mars is from the Earth: many millions of kilometers. He knows how long even a steady-thrust spacecraft takes to cross that immense void between planets, and then how long it takes for a passenger to descend to a spaceport and get to this remote outpost on the edge of the Sonoran desert. And he is well able to count back the days and see that Alegretta must have started this trip to his side—at the very least—ten days or two weeks before, which is to say right around the time when he collapsed into the hospital back in Indiana. He knows all that, and understands its unpleasing implications. He just doesn't want to think about any of those implications at that moment.

When you have lost the love of your life and suddenly, without warning, she appears in it again, what do you do?

First, of course, there is kissing, and *It's been so longs*, and *How good it is to see yous* and of course Alegretta has to see how well the kitten she sent is doing, and Rafiel has to admire the fat white cat Alegretta has brought with her, a server carrying it for her in a great screened box (it has turned out to be the kitten's mother), and of course Rafiel has to offer food and drink, and Alegretta has to accept something . . . but then what? What—after half a century or more—do you *say* to each other? What Rafiel said, watching his love nibble on biscuits and monkey-orange and beer, was only, "I didn't expect you here."

"Well, I had to come," she said, diffident, smiling, stroking the snow-white cat that lay like a puddle in her lap, "because Nicolette here kept rubbing up against me to tell me that she really missed her baby kitten—and because, oh, Rafiel, I've been so damn much missing you." Which of course led to more kissing over the table, and while the server was cleaning up the beer that had got spilled in the process, Rafiel sank back to study her. She hadn't changed. The hair was a darker red now, but it was still Alegretta's unruly curly-mop hair, and the face and the body that went with the hair were not one hour older than they had been—sixty? seventy? however many years it had been since they last touched like this. Rafiel felt his heart trembling in his chest and said quickly, "What were you saying about *Hakluyt*?"

"My ship. Yes."

"You're going on that *ship*?"

"Of course I am, dear." And it turned out that she was, though such a thing had never occurred to him when he was talking to the dramaturge woman. There definitely was a *Hakluyt* habitat, and it really was, even now, being fitted with lukewarm-fusion drives and a whole congeries of pion generators that were there to produce the muons that would make the fusion reactor react.

"You know all this nuclear fusion stuff?" Rafiel asked, marveling.

"Certainly I do. I'm the head engineer on the ship, Rafiel," she said with pride, "and I'm afraid that means I can't stay here long. They're installing the drive engines right now, and I must be there before they finish."

He shook his head. "So now you've become a particle physicist."

"Well, an engineer, anyway. Why not? You get tired of one thing, after you've done it for ninety or a hundred years. I just didn't want to be a doctor any more; when things go right it's boring, and when they don't—"

She stopped, biting her lip, as though there were something she wanted to say. Rafiel headed her off. "But what will you find when you get to this distant what's-its-name star?"

"It's called Tau Ceti."

"This Tau Ceti. What do you expect? Will people be able to live there?"

She thought about that. "Well, yes, certainly they will—in the habitat, if nothing else. The habitat doesn't care what star it orbits. We do know there are planets there, too. We don't know, really, if any of them has life. . . ."

"But you're going anyway?"

"What else is there to do?" she asked, and he laughed.

"You haven't changed a bit," he said fondly.

"Of course not. Why should I?" She sounded almost angry—perhaps at Rafiel because, after all, he had. He shook his head, reached for her with loving hunger, and pulled her to him.

Of course they made love, with the cat and the kitten watching interestedly from the chaise lounge at the side of the room. Then they slept a while, or Alegretta did, because she was still tired from the long trip. Remarkably, Rafiel was not in the least tired. He watched over her tenderly, allowing himself to be happy in spite of the fact that he knew why she was there.

She didn't sleep long, and woke smiling up at him.

"I'm sorry, Rafiel," she said.

"What have you got to be sorry for?"

"I'm sorry I stayed away so long. I was afraid, you see." She sat up, naked. "I didn't know if I could handle seeing you, well, grow old."

Rafiel felt embarrassment. "It isn't pretty, I suppose."

"It's frightening," she said honestly. "I think you're the main reason I gave up medicine."

"It's all right," he said, soothing. "Anyway, I'm sure what you're doing now is more interesting. Going to another *star*! It takes a lot of courage, that."

"It takes a lot of hard work." Then she admitted, "It takes courage, too. It certainly took me a long time to make up my mind to do it. Sometimes I still wonder if I have the nerve to go through with it. We'll be thirty-five years en route, Rafiel. Nearly five thousand people, all packed together for that long."

He frowned. "I thought somebody said the *Hakluyt* was supposed to have twenty thousand to start."

"We were. We are. But there aren't that many volunteers for the trip, you see. That's why they made me chief engineer; the other experts didn't see any reason to leave the solar system, when they were doing so many interesting things here." She leaned forward to kiss him. "Do you know what my work is, Rafiel? Do you know anything about lukewarm-fusion?"

"Well," he began, and then honestly finished: "No."

She looked astonished, or perhaps it was just pitying. "But there are powerplants in every arcology. Haven't you ever visited one?" She didn't wait for an answer but began to tell him about her work, and how long she had had to study to master the engineering details. And in his turn he told her about his life as a star, with the personal appearances and the fans always showing up, wherever he went, with their love and excitement: and about the production of *Oedipus* they had just finished, and the members of the troupe. Alegretta was fascinated by the inside glimpse of the lives of the famous. Then, when he got to the point of telling her about Docilia and her decision to try monogamy with the father of her child, as soon as the child was born, anyway, Alegretta began to purse her lips again. She got up to stare out the window.

He called, "Is something wrong?"

She was silent for a moment, then turned to him seriously. "Rafiel, dear," she said. "There's something I have to tell you."

"I know," he said reluctantly.

"No, I don't think you do. I didn't come here by accident. Mosay—"

He was beside her by then, and closed her lips with a kiss. "But I do know," he said. "Mosay called you to tell you, didn't he? Why else would you come all the way back to Earth in such a great hurry? That little episode I had, it wasn't just fatigue, was it? It meant that they can't keep me going much longer, so the bad news is that I don't have much time left, do I? I'm going to die."

"Oh, Rafiel," she said, woebegone.

"But I've known that this was going to happen all my life," he said reasonably, "or at least since you told me. It's all right."

"It *isn't!*"

He shrugged, almost annoyed. "It has to be all right, because I'm mortal," he explained.

She was shaking her head. "Yes. But no." She seemed almost near tears as she plunged on. "Don't you see, that's why I came here like this. You don't have to die *completely*. There's a kind of immortality that even shot-timers have open to them if they want it. Like your Docilia."

He frowned at her, and she reached out and touched his lips. "Will you give me a baby?" she whispered. "A son? A boy who will look just like you when he grows up—around Tau Ceti?"

11

Although the Sonora arcology is far tinier and dingier than some of those in the busy, crowded north, it naturally does not lack any of the standard facilities—including a clinic for implanting a human fetus into a nurturing animal womb. On the fourth day after the donation the new parents (or, usually, at least one of them) may come up to the sunny brightly painted nursery to receive their fetus. It is true that the circumstances for Rafiel and Alegretta are a bit unusual. Most fetuses are implanted at once into the large mammal—a cow most often, or a large sow—that will bring them to term and deliver them. Their child has a more complicated incubation in store. He (it is definitely to be a boy, and they have spent a lot of time thinking of names for him) must go with Alegretta to the interstellar ship Hakluyt, *which means that the baby's host must go there too. Cows are not really very portable. So, just for now, for the sake of ease in transportation, their fetus has been temporarily implanted in a much smaller mammal, which is now spending as much time as it is allowed sitting purring in Alegretta's lap, a bit ruffled at recent indignities, but quite content.*

They didn't just talk and make love and babies. On the second day Alegretta announced she was temporarily going to be a doctor again.

"But you've probably forgotten how to do it," Rafiel said, half joking.

"The computer hasn't," she told him, not joking at all. She got his medical records from the datafile and studied them seriously for a long time. Then she sent the server out for some odds and ends. When they came she pressed sticky sensor buttons on his chest and belly—"I hope I remember how to do this without pulling all your hair off," she said—and pored over the readings on the screen. Then she had long conversations over the tel with someone, from which Rafiel was excluded and which wound up in the server bringing him new little bottles of spansules and syrups to take. "These will make you feel better," she told him.

But they both knew that even the best efforts of loving Alegretta could not possibly make him *be* better.

They were also both well aware that they could not stay long together in Sonora. If they hadn't known that, they would have been told so, because the callback lists kept piling up on the communications screen—Mosay and Jeftha and ten or twelve others for Rafiel, faxed messages from *Hakluyt* for Alegretta. Once a day they took time to read them, and occasionally to answer them. "They're putting the frozen stocks on board now," Alegretta announced to her lover, between callbacks.

"Frozen food for the trip? You must need a lot—"

"No, no. Not food—well, a little bit of frozen food, yes, but we couldn't carry enough to last out the trip. Most of the food we need we'll grow along the way. What I'm talking about is frozen sperm and ova—cats, dogs, livestock, birds—and frozen seeds and clones for planting. We'll need them when we get there."

"And what if there's no good planet there to plant them on?" he asked.

"Bite your tongue," she said absently, making him smile at her as she sat huddled over the manifest. He found himself smiling a good deal these days. His kitten, which had not let either of them out of its sight while its mother was off in the implantation clinic, was licking its left forepaw with concentrated attention. The lovers touched a lot, sometimes talking, sometimes just drowsing in the scents and warmths of each other. They looked at each other a lot, charmed to see in each other a prospective parent of a shared child.

Rafiel said meditatively, "It would have been fun to conceive it in the old-fashioned way."

She looked up. "It's safer when they do it in the laboratory. Not to mention this way we can be sure it's a boy." She came over and kissed him. "Anyway, we can—well, in a day or two we can—do all of that we want to."

Rafiel rubbed his ear against her cheek, quite content. It was a very minor inconvenience that sexual intercourse had to be postponed a bit, Alegretta's womb tender from the removal of the ovum.

"Are you getting restless?" she asked.

"Me? No, I'm happy to stay right here in the condo. Are you?"

She said, "Not really, but there is something I'd like to do outside."

"Name it."

"It's so you'll know what my work's like," she explained. "If you think you'd like to, I'd enjoy showing you what this arcology's powerplant looks like."

"Of course," he said.

He would have said the same to almost anything Alegretta proposed. Still, it wasn't the kind of "of course" he felt totally confident about, because one of Mosay's calls had been to warn him that the paparazzi knew he was still in the arcology. They somehow even knew that he and Alegretta had conceived a child. Someone in the clinic had let the news out. But Rafiel took what precautions he could to preserve their privacy. They chose their time—it was after midnight—and the doorwarden reported no one in the area when they stole out and down into the lowest reaches of the arcology.

It turned out that the powerplant wasn't particularly hot. It didn't look dangerous at all; everything was enameled white or glittering steel, no more worrisome in appearance than a kitchen. It was noisy, though; they both had to put on earplugs when the shift engineer, as a professional courtesy to his colleague, Alegretta, let them in. With all the roaring and whining around them they couldn't talk very well, but Alegretta had explained some of it on the way down, and pointed meaningfully to this great buzzing cylinder and that red-striped blank wall, and Rafiel was nearly sure he understood what he was seeing. He knew it was muon-catalysed fusion. He even knew that it was, in fact, the most desperately desired dream of powerplant designers for generations, a source of power that took its energy from the commonest of all elements: hydrogen, the same universal fuel that stoked the fires of the stars themselves, and delivered it in almost any form anyone could wish—heat, kinetic energy or electricity—without fuss or bother. Well, not entirely without *bother*. It had taken a long time and a lot of clever engineering to figure out how to get the pions to make the muons that would make the reaction go; but there it was. Lukewarm fusion operated without violent explosions, impossible containment or deadly radioactive contamination. It worked best at an optimal temperature of 700 degrees Celsius (instead of many thousands!), and so it was intrinsically both safe and convenient. It was, really, the fundamental reason why the living members of the human race now outnumbered the dead. The fetal procedures could extend life, but it was only the cheap and easy energy that would never run out that could keep all ten trillion human beings alive.

"Thanks," Alegretta said to the shift engineer as she collected their dosimeters and earplugs on the way out. Rafiel wasn't looking at the engineer as she checked the dosimeters and nodded to Alegretta to show they were all right. He was looking at Alegretta, so small and pretty and well, yes, so *young* to be the master of so much energy.

And so damned *intelligent*. She was explaining the system to him, pleased and flushed, as they moved toward the exit door. "It's not really hydrogen we burn; it's muonized deuterium; you know, the heavy isotope of hydrogen, but with a muon replacing its electron."

He didn't know, but he said, "Yes. Yes, I see."

She was going right on. "So, since the muon is heavier, it orbits closer to the nucleus. This means that two atoms of deuterium can come closer to each other than electron-hydrogen ever could, and thus they fuse very easily into helium — oh, *hell!*" she finished, looking out the door. "Who are *they?*"

He swore softly and took her arm. "Come on," he said, pushing their way through the swarm of paparazzi.

"We must have been seen going in," he told her, once they were safely back in the condo. "Or your friend the engineer called somebody."

"It is always like this, Rafiel?"

He wanted to be honest with her. "Sometimes we tip the paps off ourselves," he admitted. "I mean, I don't *personally* do it. I don't have to. Jeftha or Mosay or somebody will, because we *want* the paparazzi there, you know? They're good for business. They're the source of the publicity that makes us into stars."

"Did you?"

"Did I tip them off? No. No, this time they found us out on their own. They're good at that."

So he had no secrets any more; the paparazzi knew that his life was nearing its end and that he had started a child he would not live to see grow, all of which made him more newsworthy than ever, for the same reasons; because he was Rafiel, the short-timer; because he was going to do that black-comic thing, to die. Since hardly anybody really suffered, people like Rafiel filled a necessary niche in the human design: they did the suffering for everyone else to enjoy vicariously — and with the audience's inestimable privilege of turning the suffering off when they chose.

"Yes, but is it *always* like this?"

He picked up the kitten and cradled it in his arms, upside down, its blue eyes looking up warily at him.

"It will be as long as we're here together," he said.

She did not respond to that. She just walked silently over to the communications screen.

It seemed to Rafiel that his beloved wanted not to be beloved, or not actively beloved, right then. Her back was significantly turned toward him. She had taken some faxes from *Hakluyt* and was poring over them, not looking at him. He took his cue from her and went into the other room to deal with a couple of callbacks. He did not think he had satisfactorily explained the situation to her. On the other hand, he didn't think he had to.

When he came back she was sitting with a fax in her hand, purring Nicolette in her lap, her head down. He stood there for a moment, looking not at Alegretta but at the cat. The little animal showed no sign of the human gene splices that let her be a temporary incubator for their child. She was just a cat. But inside the cat was the child which would see such wonders, forever denied to himself—a new sun in the sky, planets (*perhaps* planets, anyway) where no human had ever set foot—all the things that were possible to someone with an endless life ahead of him.

He knew that the thing in the cat's belly was not actually a *child* yet, hardly even a real fetus; it was no larger than a grain of dust, but already it was richer in powers and prospects than its father would ever be.

Then, as Alegretta moved, he saw that she was weeping.

He stood staring at her, more embarrassed than he had ever been with Alegretta before. He couldn't remember ever seeing an adult cry before. Not even himself. He moved uncomfortably and must have made some small noise, because she looked up and saw him there.

She beckoned him over and put her hand on his. "My dear," she said, still weeping, "I can't put it off any longer. I have to be there for the final tests, so—I have to leave tomorrow."

"Come to bed," he said.

In the morning he was up before her. He woke her with a kiss. She smiled up at him as she opened her eyes, then let the smile slip away as she remembered, finally saw what he was holding in his hand. She looked at him in puzzlement. "What's that thing for?"

He held up the little cage. "I sent the server out for it first thing this morning," he said, "It's to put the kitten in for the trip. We don't want to break the family up again, do we?"

"We?"

He shrugged. "The you and me we. I decided I really wanted to see your *Hakluyt* before it takes you away from me."

"But Rafiel! It's such a long trip to *Hakluyt!*"

"Kosmojets go there, don't they?"

"Of course they do, but"—she hesitated, then plunged on—"but are you up to that kind of stress, Rafiel? I mean physically? Just to get into orbit is a strain, you know; you have to launch to orbit through the railgun, and that's a seven-gee acceleration. Can you stand seven gees?"

"I can," he said, "stand anything at all, except losing you so soon."

12

Rafiel is excited over the trip. Their first leg is an airplane flight. It's his first time in a plane in many years, and there's no choice about it; no maglev trains go to the Peruvian Andes. That's where the railgun is, on the westward slope of a mountain, pointing toward the stars. As the big turboprop settles in to its landing at the base of the railgun, Rafiel gets his first good look at the thing. It looks like a skijump in reverse: its traffic goes up. The scenery all around is spectacular. Off to the north of the railgun there's a huge waterfall which once was a hydroelectric dam supplying power to half

Peru and almost all of Bolivia. Lukewarm-fusion put the hydropower plants out of business and now it is just a decorative cataract. When they get out Rafiel finds his heart pounding and his breath panting, for even the base of the railgun in nearly 2500 meters above sea level, but he doesn't care. He is thrilled.

While they were dressing in their cushiony railgun suits, Rafiel paused to listen to the scream of a capsule accelerating up the rails to escape velocity. Alegretta stopped what she was doing, too, to look at him. "Are you *sure* you can handle this?" she asked. His offhand wave said that he was very, very sure. She checked him carefully as he got into each item of the railgun clothes. What they wore was important—no belts for either of them, no brassière for Alegretta, slippers rather than shoes, no heavy jewelry—because the seven-gee strain would cost them severely for any garment that pressed into their flesh or constrained their freedom. When Alegretta was satisfied about that, she got to the serious problem of fitting baskets to the cats.

"Will she be all right?" Rafiel asked anxiously, looking at Nicolette—meaning, really, will the almost-baby in her belly be all right?

"I'll make her be all right," Alegretta promised, checking the resilience of the padding with her knuckles. "That'll do. Anyway, cats stand high-gee better than people. You've heard stories of them falling out of tenth-story windows and walking away? They're true—sometimes true, anyway. Now let's get down to the loading platform."

That was busier than Rafiel had expected. Four or five other passengers were saying good-byes to friends on the platform, but it wasn't just people who were about to be launched into space. There were crates and cartons, all padded, being fitted carefully into place in the cargo section, and servers were strapping down huge Dewars of liquid gas. "Inside," a guard commanded, and when they were in the capsule a steward leaned over them to help with the straps and braces. "Just relax," he said, "and don't turn your heads." Then he bent to check the cat baskets. The kitten was already asleep, but her mother was obviously discontented with what was happening to her. However, there wasn't much she could do about it in the sweater-like restraint garment that held her, passive. . . . No, Rafiel thought, not a sweater; more like a straitjacket—

And then they were on their way.

The thrust squeezed all the breath out of Rafiel, who had not fully remembered what seven gees could do to him. The padded seat was memory plastic and it had molded itself to his body; the restraints were padded; the garments were without wrinkles or seams to cut into flesh. But still it was *seven gees*. The athletic dancer's body that had never gone over seventy-five kilograms suddenly and bruisingly weighed more than half a ton. Breathing was frighteningly difficult; his chest muscles were not used to expanding his ribcage against such force. When he turned his head, ever so minutely, he was instantly dizzied as the bones of the inner ear protested being twisted so viciously. He thought he was going to vomit; he forced himself to breathe.

It lasted only for a few minutes. Then they were free. The acceleration stopped.

The railgun had flung the capsule off its tip, and now they were simply thrown free into the sky, weightless. The only external force acting on the railgun launch capsule now was the dwindling friction of the outside air; that pressed Rafiel's body against the restraining straps at first, but then it, too, was gone.

"Congratulations, dear Rafiel," said Alegretta, smiling. "You're in space."

Once they had transhipped to a spacecraft it was eight days to Mars-orbit, where *Hakluyt* hung waiting for them. There were a few little sleeping cabins in the ship, in addition to the multi-bunk compartments. The cabins were expensive, but that was not a consideration for Rafiel, who was well aware that he had far more money than he would ever live to spend. So he and Alegretta and the cats had their own private space, just the four of them—or five, if you counted the little cluster of cells that was busily dividing in the white cat's belly, getting ready to become a person.

Their transport was a steady-thrust spacecraft, accelerating at a sizeable fraction of a gee all the way to turnaround, and decelerating from then on. It was possible to move around the ship quite easily. It was also pointless, because there was nothing much to do. There was no dining room, no cabaret, no swimming pool on the aft deck, no gym to work out in. The servers brought meals to the passengers where they were. Most of the passengers spent their time viewing vid programs, old and new, on their personal screens. Or sleeping. In the private cabin Rafiel and Alegretta had several other options, one of which was talking; but even they slept a lot.

More than a lot.

When, at their destination, they were docking with the habitat shuttlecraft Rafiel, puzzled, counted back and realized that he had only slept twice on the trip. They had to have been good long sleeps—two or three full twenty-four-hour days at a time; and that was when he realized that Alegretta had doped him to make him sleep as long as possible.

13

On board the Hakluyt, *Alegretta disappears as soon as Rafiel is settled in. She can't wait to see what damage her deputy may have done to her precious engines. This leaves Rafiel free to explore the habitat. There's no thrust on* Hakluyt's *engines yet, just the slow roll of the habitat to distinguish up from down. That's a bit of a problem for everybody. All habitats spin slowly so that centrifugal force will supply some kind of gravity. But when* Hakluyt *starts to move they'll stop the spin because they won't need it any more. The "down" the spin has provided them—radially outward from the central axis of the cylindrical habitat—will be replaced by a rearward "down," toward the thruster engines in the stern. Consequently, every last piece of furnishing will have to be rearranged as walls become floors and floors walls. Rafiel is having a lot of trouble with his orientation. Besides the fact that half the fittings have already been relocated, the light-gee pull is strange to him. Because he has spent so little time in low-gee environments he instinctively holds on to things as he walks, though really the feeling isn't much different from being on, say, the Moon. (But Rafiel hasn't been even there for nearly half a century.)*

Once he gets used to these things, though, he's fascinated. Everything so busy! Everyone in such a hurry! The whole ship's complement has turned out to finish loading, even small children—Rafiel is fascinated to see how many children there are. Young and old, they can't wait to start on their long interstellar journey—and aren't very patient with people (even very famous people) who happen to get in their way.

By the time Rafiel had been three days on *Hakluyt* he was beginning to get used to the fact that he didn't see much of Alegretta. Not when she was awake, at least. When she was awake all she seemed to have time for was to check on his vital signs and peer into her computer screen when she'd stuck sensors to his chest and make sure he was taking his spansules. Then she was off again, looking harried.

They did sleep together, of course, or at least they slept in the same bed. Not necessarily at the same times. Once or twice Rafiel came back to their tiny compartment and found her curled up there, out cold. When she felt him crawl in beside her she reached out to him. He was never quite certain she was awake even when they made love—awake enough to respond to him, certainly, and for a few pleased mumbles when they were through, but nothing that was actually articulate speech.

It was almost good enough, anyway, just to know that she was nearby. Not quite; but still it was fascinating to explore the ship, dodging the busy work teams, trying to be helpful when he could, to stay out of the way, at least, when he couldn't. The ship was full of marvels, not least the people who crewed it (busy, serious, plainly dressed and so *purposeful*). A special wonder was the vast central space that was a sort of sky as the habitat rotated (but what purpose would it serve when they were under way?). The greatest wonder of all was *Hakluyt* itself. It was going to go where no human had ever, *ever* gone before.

Everything about the ship delighted and astonished. Rafiel discovered that the couch in their room became a bed when they wanted it to, and if they didn't want either it disappeared entirely into a wall. There was a keypad in the room that controlled air, heat, lights, clock, messages—might run all of *Hakluyt*, Rafiel was amused to think, if he only knew what buttons to push. Or if all the things worked.

The fact was, they didn't all work. When Rafiel tried to get a news broadcast from Earth the screen produced a children's cartoon, and when he tried to correct it the whole screen dissolved into the snow of static. The water taps—hot, cold, potable—all ran merely cold.

When he woke to find exhausted Alegretta trying to creep silently into their bed, he said, making a joke, "I hope the navigation system works better than the rest of this stuff."

She took him seriously. "I'm sorry," she said, weary, covetously eyeing the bed. "It's the powerplant. It wasn't originally designed to drive a ship, only to supply power for domestic needs. Oh, it has plenty of power. But they located the thing midships instead of at the stem, and we had to brace everything against the drive thrust. That means relocating the water reservoirs—don't drink the water, by the way, dear; if you're thirsty, go to one of the kitchens—and—Well, hell," she finished remorsefully. "I should have been here."

Which added fuel to the growing guilt in Rafiel. He took a chance. "I want to help," he said.

"How?" she asked immediately—woundingly, just as he had feared she would.

He flinched and said, "They're loading more supplies—fresh wing-bean seeds this morning, I hear. At least I can help shift cargo!"

"You can *not*," she said in sudden alarm. "That's much too strenuous! I don't want you dying on me!" Then, relenting, she thought for a moment. "All right. I'll talk to Boretta, he's loadmaster. He'll find something for you—but now, please, let me come to bed."

Boretta did find something for him. Rafiel became a children's care-giver in one of the ship's nurseries, relieving for active duty the ten-year-old who had previously been charged with supervising the zero-to-three-year-olds.

It was not at all the kind of thing Rafiel had had in mind, but then he hadn't had much of anything very specifically in his mind, because what did *Hakluyt* need with a tap-dancer? But he was actually helping in the effort. (The ten-year-old he relieved was quite useful in bringing sandwiches and drinks to the sweating cargo handlers.) Rafiel found that he liked taking care of babies. Even the changing of diapers was a fairly constructive thing to do. Not exactly aesthetic, no. Extremely repetitious, yes, for the diapers never *stayed* clean. But while he was doing it he thought of the task as prepaying a debt he would owe to whomever, nine months later, would be changing the diapers of his own child.

The ten-year-old was nice enough to teach Rafiel the technical skills he needed for the work. More than that, he was nice enough to be acceptably impressed when he found out just who Rafiel was. ("But I've seen you on the screen! And you've got a new show coming out—when? Soon?") The boy even brought his older brother—a superior and taller version of the same, all of thirteen—around to meet this certified star. When Rafiel had a moment to think of it, between coaxing a two-year-old to take her nap and attempting to burp a younger one, it occurred to him that he was—yes, actually—quite happy. He liked all these strange, dedicated, space-faring people who shared the habitat with him. "Strange" was a good word for them, though. Unlike all the friends and colleagues he'd spent his life with, these *Hakluy*-tians spoke unornamented English, without loan words, without circumlocutions. They had basically unornamented bodies, too. Their clothes were simply functional, and even the youngest and best-looking wore no jewels.

When Rafiel had pondered over that for a while an explanation suddenly occurred to him. These people simply didn't have time for frills. Astonishing though the thought was, these *immortal* people were in such a hurry to *do* things that, even with eternities before them, they had no time to waste.

The day before *Hakluyt* was to leave, Alegretta somehow stole enough time from her duties to go with Rafiel to the birthing clinic, where they watched the transfer of their almost-child from Nicolette's tiny belly to the more than adequate one of a placid roan mare. It was a surgical spectacle, to be sure, but peaceful rather than gruesome. Even Nicolette did not seem to mind, as long as Alegretta's hand was on her head.

On the way back to their cabin, Alegretta was silent. Stranger still, she was dawdling, when always she was in a hurry to get to the work that she had to do.

Rafiel was aware of this, though he was continually distracted by passersby. The ten-year-old had spread the word of his fame. It seemed that every third person they passed, however busy, at least looked up and nodded or called a friendly greeting to him. After the twentieth or thirtieth exchange Rafiel said, "Sorry about all this, Alegretta."

She looked up at him curiously. "About what? About the fact that they like you? When's this *Oedipus* going to be released?"

"In about a week, I think."

"In about a week." It wasn't necessary for her to point out that in a week *Hakluyt* would be six days gone. "I think a lot of these people are going to want to watch it," she said, musing. "They'll be really sorry you aren't here so they can make a fuss over you when it's on."

Rafiel only nodded, though for some inexplicable reason internally he felt himself swelling with pleasure and pride. Then he bent close to her, puzzled at the low-pitched thing she had said. "What?"

"I said, you could be here," Alegretta repeated. "I mean, if you wanted to. If you didn't mind not going back to the Earth, ever, because—oh, God," she wailed, "how can you say 'Because you're going to be dead in a few weeks anyway so it doesn't really matter where you are' in a loving way?"

She stopped there, because Rafiel had put a gentle finger to her lips.

"You just did," he said. "And of course I'll come along. I was only waiting to be asked."

14

Fewer than thirty-six hours have passed since Hakluyt's launch, but all that time its stern thrusters were hard at their decades-long work of pushing the ship across interstellar space. By now it is already some fifteen million kilometers from its near-Martian orbit and, with every second that passes, Alegretta's lukewarm-fusion jets are thrusting it several hundred kilometers farther away. The reactors are performing perfectly. Still, Alegretta can hardly bear to let the controls and instruments that tell her so out of her sight. After the pre-launch frenzy Hakluyt's five thousand pioneers are beginning to catch up on their sleep. So is Alegretta.

Rafiel tried to make no noise as he pulled on his robe and started toward the sanitary, but he could see Alegretta beginning to stir in her sleep. Safely outside their room he was more relaxed—at least, *acted* relaxed, nodding brightly to the people he passed in the hall. It was only when he was looking in the mirror that the acting stopped and he let the fatigue and discomfort show in his face. There was more of it every day now. The body that had served him for ninety-odd years was wearing out. But, as there was absolutely nothing to be done about that fact, he put it out of his mind, showered quickly, dressed in the pink shorts and flowered tunic that was the closest he had to *Hakluyt*-style clothing and returned to their room. By then Alegretta was sitting dazedly on the edge of the bed, watching Nicolette, at the foot of the bed, dutifully licking her kitten.

"You should have slept a little longer," he said fondly.

She blinked up at him. "I can't. Anyway"—she paused for a yawn—"there's a staff meeting coming up. I ought to decide what I want to put in for."

Rafiel gently pushed the cats out of the way and sat down companionably next to her. They had talked about her future plans before. He knew that Alegretta would have to be reassigned to some other task for the long trip. Unless something went seriously wrong with the reactors there would be little for her to do there. (And if, most improbably, anything did go seriously wrong with them in the space between the stars, the ship would be in more trouble than its passengers could hope to survive.) "What kind of job are you looking for?"

"I'm not sure. I've been thinking of food control, maybe," she said frowning. "Or else waste recycling. Which do you think?"

He pretended to take the question seriously. He was aware that both jobs were full time, hands-on-assignments, like air and water control. If any of those vital services failed, the ship would be doomed in a different way. Therefore human crews would be assigned to them all the time the ship was in transit—and for longer still if they found no welcoming planet circling Tau Ceti. But he knew that there was nothing in his background to help Alegretta make a choice, so he said at random: "Food control sounds like more fun."

"Do you think so?" She thought that over. "Maybe it is, sort of, but I'd need a lot of retraining for aeroponics and trace-element management. The waste thing is easier. It's mostly plumbing, and I've got a good head start on that."

He kissed her. "Sleep on it," he advised, getting up.

She looked worriedly up at him, remembering to be a doctor. "You're the one who should be sleeping more."

"I've had plenty, and anyway I can't. Manfred will be waiting for me with the babies."

"Must you? I mean, should you? The boy can handle them by himself, and you look so tired. . . ."

"I'm fine," he said, trying to reassure the person who knew better than he.

She scolded, "You're *not* fine! You should be resting."

He shook his head. "No, dearest, I really am fine. It's only my body that's sick."

He hadn't lied to her. He was perfectly capable of helping with the babies, fine in every way—except for the body. That kept producing its small aches and pains, which would steadily become larger. That didn't matter, though, because they had not reached the point of interfering with tending the children. The work was easier than ever now, with the hectic last-minute labors all completed. The ten-year-old, Manfred Okasa-Pennyweight, had been allowed to return to the job, which meant that now there were two of them on the shift to share the diapering and feeding and playing.

Although Rafiel had been demoted to his assistant, Manfred deferred to him whenever possible. Especially because Manfred had decided that he might like to be a dancer himself—well, only for a *hobby*, he told Rafiel, almost apologizing. He was pretty sure his main work would be in construction, once they had found a planet to construct things on. And he was bursting with eagerness to see Rafiel perform. "We'll all going to watch the *Oedipus*," he told Rafiel seriously, looking up from the baby he was giving a bottle. "Everybody is. You're pretty famous here."

"That's nice," Rafiel said, touched and pleased, and when there was a momentary break he showed the boy how to do a cramp roll, left and right. The babies watched, interested, though Rafiel did not think it was one of his best performances. "It's hard to keep your feet down when you're tapping in a quarter-gee environment," he panted.

Manfred took alarm. "Don't do any more now, please. You shouldn't push yourself so hard," he said. Rafiel was glad enough to desist. He showed Manfred some of the less strenuous things, the foot positions that were basic to all ballet . . . though he wondered if ballet would be very interesting in this same environment. The grandest of leaps would fail of being impressive when the very toddlers in the nursery could jump almost as high.

When their shift was over, Manfred had a little time to himself before going to his schooling. Bashfully he asked if Rafiel would like to be shown anything on the ship, and Rafiel seized the chance. "I'd like to see where they do the waste recycling," he said promptly.

"You really want to go to the stink room? Well, of course, if you mean it." And on the way Manfred added chattily, "It probably doesn't smell too bad right now, because most of the recycled organics now are just chopped-up trees and things—they had to cut them all down before we launched, because they were growing the wrong way, you see?"

Rafiel saw. He smelled the processing stench, too: there was a definite odor in the waste-cycling chambers that wasn't just the piney smell of lumber, though the noise was even worse than the smell. Hammering and welding was going on noisily in the next compartment, where another batch of aeroponics trays were being resited for the new rearward orientation. "Plants want to grow *upward*, you see," Manfred explained. "That's why we had to chop down all those old trees."

"But you'll plant new ones, I suppose?"

"Oh, I don't think so. I mean, not pines and maples like these. They'll be planting some small ones—they help with the air recycling—and probably some fruit trees, I guess, but not any of these big old species. They wouldn't be fully grown until we got to Tau Ceti, and then they'd just have to come down again."

Rafiel peered into the digesting room, where the waste was broken down. "And everything goes into these tanks?"

"Everything organic that we don't want any more," Manfred said proudly. "All the waste, and everything that dies."

"Even people?" Rafiel asked, and was immediately sorry he had. Because of course they had probably never had a human corpse to recycle, so far.

"I've seen enough," he said, giving the boy a professional smile. He did not want to stay in this place where he would soon enough wind up. He would never make it to Tau Ceti, would never see his son born . . . but his body would at some fairly near time go into those reprocessing vats, along with the kitchen waste and the sewage and the bodies of whatever pets died en route, ultimately to be turned into food that would circulate in that closed ecosystem for ever. One way or another, Rafiel would never leave them.

While Alegretta was once again fussing over her diagnostic readouts Rafiel scrolled the latest batch of his messages from Earth.

The first few had been shocked, incredulous, reproachful; but now everyone he knew seemed at least resigned to their star's wild decision, and Mosay's letters were all but ecstatic. The paps were going crazy with the story of their dying Oedipus going off on his last great adventure. Even Docilia was delighted with the fuss the paps were making, though a little put out that the stories were all *him*, and Alegretta was pleased when the news said that another habitat had been stirred to vote for conversion to a ship; maybe Rafiel's example was going to get still others to follow them.

But she was less pleased with the vital signs readings on her screen. "You really should go into the sickbay," she said fretfully.

"So they could do what for me?" he asked, and of course she had no answer for that. There was no longer much that could be done. To change the subject Rafiel picked up the kitten. "Do you know what's funny here?" he asked. "These cats. And I've seen dogs and birds—all kinds of pets."

"Why not? We like pets." She was only half attentive, most of her concentration on the screen. "Actually, I may have started the fashion myself."

"Really? But on Earth people don't have them. You hardly ever see a pet animal in the arcologies. Aren't you afraid that they'll die on you?"

She turned to look at him, suddenly angry. "Like you, you mean?" she snapped, her eyes flashing. "Do you see what the screen is saying about your tests? There's blood in your urine sample, Rafiel!"

For once, he had known that before she did, because he had seen the color of what had gone into the little flask. He shrugged. "What do you expect? I guess my *rognons* are just wearing out. But, listen, what did you mean when you said you started the fashion—"

She cut him off. "Say kidneys when you mean kidneys," she said harshly, looking helpless and therefore angry because she was helpless. He recognized the look. It was almost the way she had looked when she first gave him the bad news about his mortality, so long and long ago, and it chased his vagrant question out of his mind.

"But I'm still feeling perfectly well," he said persuasively—and made the mistake of trying to prove it to her by walking a six-tap riff—a slow one, because of the light gravity.

He stopped, short of breath, after a dozen steps.

He looked at her. "That didn't feel so good," he panted. "Maybe I'd better go in after all."

15

Hakluyt's sickbay is just about as big as a hospital in an average Earthly arcology, and just about as efficient. Still, there is a limit to what any hospital can do for a short-timer nearing the end of his life expectancy. When, after four days, they wake Rafiel, he is in far from perfect health. His face is puffy. His skin is sallow. But he has left strict orders to wake him up so he can be on hand for the showing of Oedipus. As nothing they can do will make much difference anyhow, they do as he asks. They even fetch the clothes he requests from his room and when he is dressed he looks at himself in a mirror. He is wearing his fanciest and most theatrical outfit. It is a sunset-yellow full dress suit, with the hem of the tails outlined in stitches of luminous red and a diamond choker around his neck. The diamonds are real. With any luck at all, he thinks, people will look at his clothing and not at his face.

Probably not every one of *Hakluyt's* five thousand people were watching *Oedipus* as the pictures beamed from Earth caught up with the speeding interstellar ship. But those who were not were in a minority. There were twenty viewers keeping them company in the room where Rafiel and Alegretta sat hand in hand, along with Manfred and his brother and a good many people Rafiel didn't really know—but whom Manfred knew, or Alegretta did, and so they were invited to share.

It was a nice room. A room that might almost have been Rafiel's own old condo, open to the great central space within *Hakluyt*; they could look out and see hundreds of other lighted rooms like their own, all around the cylinder, some a quarter of a kilometer away. And most of the people in them were watching, too. When the four children of Jocasta and Oedipus did their comic little dance at the opening of the show, the people in the room laughed where Mosay wanted them to—and two seconds later along came the distant, delayed laughter from across the open space, amplified enough by the echo-focusing shape of the ship to reach their ears.

Rafiel hardly looked at the screen. He was content simply to sit there, pleased with the success of the show, comfortable with Alegretta's presence . . . at least, in a general sense comfortable, comfortable if you did not count the sometimes acute discomforts of his body. He didn't let the discomforts show. He was fondly aware that Alegretta's fingers slipped from hand to wrist from time to time, and knew that she was checking his pulse.

He was not at all in serious pain. Of course, the pain was there. Only the numbing medications they had been giving him were keeping it down to an inconvenience rather than agony. He accepted that, as he accepted the fact that his life expectancy was now measured in days. Neither fact preyed on his mind. There was an unanswered question somewhere in his mind, something he had wanted to ask Alegretta, but what it could have been he could not clearly say. He accepted the fact that his mind was confused. He even drowsed as he sat there, aware that he was drifting off for periods of time, waking only when there was laughter, or a sympathetic sound from the audience. He did not distinguish clearly between the half-dreams that filled his mind and the scene on the screens. When the audience murmured as he—as Oedipus—took his majestic oath to heal the sickness of the city, the murmur mingled in Rafiel's mind with a blurry vision of the first explorers from *Hakluyt* stepping out of a landing craft on to a green and lovely new planet, to the plaudits of an improbable welcoming committee. It wasn't until almost the end that he woke fully, because next to him there was a soft sound that had no relation to the performance on the screen.

Alegretta was weeping.

He looked at her in confusion, then at the screen. He had lost an hour or more of the performance. The play was now at the farewell of the chorus to the blinded and despairing Oedipus as, alone and disgraced, he went off to a hopeless future. And the chorus was singing:

> There goes old Oedipus.
> Once he was the best of us.
> Down from the top he is,
> Proof that all happiness
> Can't be known until you're dead.

Rafiel thought that over for some time. Then, blinking himself awake, he reached to touch Alegretta's cheek. "But I do know that now," he said, "and, look, I'm not dead yet."

"Know what, Rafiel?" she asked, huskily, not stopping what she was doing. Which, curiously, was pressing warm, sticky, metallic things to his temples and throat.

"Oh," he said, understanding, "the show's over now, isn't it?" For they weren't in the viewing room any more. He knew that, because he was in a bed — in their room? No, he decided, more likely back in the ship's sickbay. Another doctor was in the room, too, hunched over a monitor, and in the doorway Manfred was standing, looking more startled than grieving, but too grieving to speak.

Rafiel could see that the boy was upset and decided to say something reassuring, but he drifted off for a moment while he tried to think of what to say. When he looked again the boy was gone. So was the other doctor. Only Alegretta sat beside him, her eyes closed wearily and her hands folded in her lap; and at that moment Rafiel remembered the question on his mind. "The cats," he said.

Alegretta started. Her eyes flew open, guiltily turning to the monitor before they returned to him. "What? Oh, the cats. They're fine, Rafiel. Manfred's been taking care of them." Then, looking at the monitor again, "How do you feel?"

That struck Rafiel as a sensible question. It took him a while to answer it, though, because what he felt was almost nothing at all. There was no pain in the gut, nor anywhere else, only a sort of generalized numbness that made it hard for him to move.

He summed it all up in one word. "Fine. I feel fine." Then he paused to rehearse the question that had been on his mind. When it was clear he spoke. "Alegretta, didn't you say you started the fashion of having pets?"

"Pets? Yes, I was one of the first here on *Hakluyt*, years and years ago."

"Why?" he asked. And then, because he felt a need to hurry, he made his thickening tongue come out with it: "Did you do it so you could get used to things you loved dying? Things like me?"

"I didn't know you were a psychotherapist, dear Rafiel," she whispered. It was an admission, and she knew he understood it . . . though his eyes had closed and she could not tell whether he had heard the words. She did not need the confirmation of the screen or of the other doctor as he came running in to know that Rafiel had joined the minority of the dead. She kissed the unresponding lips and retired to the room they had shared, to weep, and to think of what, some day, she would tell their son about his father; that he had been famous, and loved, and brave . . . and most of all that, certainly, yes, Rafiel had after all been happy in his life, and known that to be true.

foɾɡiveness Day

uɾṣuʟA k. ʟE ɢuiN

Ursula K. Le Guin is probably one of the best-known and most universally respected SF writers in the world today. Her famous novel *The Left Hand of Darkness* may have been the most influential SF novel of its decade, and shows every sign of becoming one of the enduring classics of the genre. (Her 1968 fantasy novel, *A Wizard of Earthsea*, would be almost as influential on future generations of high fantasy and young adult writers.) *The Left Hand of Darkness* won both the Hugo and Nebula Awards, as did Le Guin's monumental novel *The Dispossessed* a few years later. Her novel *Tehanu* won her another Nebula in 1990, and she has also won three other Hugo Awards and a Nebula Award for her short fiction, as well as the National Book Award for children's literature for her novel *The Farthest Shore*, part of her Earthsea trilogy. Her other novels include *Planet of Exile*, *The Lathe of Heaven*, *City of Illusions*, *Rocannon's World*, *The Beginning Place*, *A Wizard of Earthsea*, *The Tombs of Atuan*, *Searoad*, *Always Coming Home*, and *The Telling*. She has had eight collections: *The Wind's Twelve Quarters*, *Orsinian Tales*, *The Compass Rose*, *Buffalo Gals and Other Animal Presences*, *A Fisherman of the Inland Sea*, *Four Ways to Forgiveness*, *Tales of Earthsea*, and *The Birthday of the World*. Her most recent books are a collection of her critical essays, *The Wave in the Mind: Talks and Essays on the Writer, the Reader, and the Imagination*, and a YA novel, *Gifts*. She lives with her husband in Portland, Oregon. She was named SFFWA Grand Master in 2003.

In the powerful novella that follows, Le Guin returned for the first time in a number of years to the star-spanning, Hainish-settled interstellar community known as the Ekumen, the same fictional universe as her famous novels *The Left Hand of Darkness* and *The Dispossessed*, for a thoughtful and passionate story of clashing cultural values, politics, violence, religion, and terror—and of the star-crossed relationship of a man and a woman who are literally worlds apart.

*S*olly had been a space brat, a Mobile's child, living on this ship and that, this world and that; she'd traveled five hundred light-years by the time she was ten. At twenty-five she had been through a revolution on Alterra, learned *aiji* on Terra and farthinking from an old hilfer on Rokanan, breezed through the Schools on Hain, and survived an assignment as Observer in murderous, dying Kheakh, skipping another half millennium at near-lightspeed in the process. She was young, but she'd been around.

She got bored with the Embassy people in Voe Deo telling her to watch out for this, remember that; she was a Mobile herself now, after all. Werel had its quirks—what world didn't? She'd done her homework, she knew when to curtsy and when not to belch, and vice versa. It was a relief to get on her own at last, in this gorgeous little city, on this gorgeous little continent, the first and only Envoy of the Ekumen to the Divine Kingdom of Gatay.

She was high for days on the altitude, the tiny, brilliant sun pouring vertical light into the noisy streets, the peaks soaring up incredibly behind every building, the dark blue sky where great near stars burned all day, the dazzling nights under six or seven lolloping bits of moon, the tall black people with their black eyes, narrow heads, long, narrow hands and feet, gorgeous people, her people! She loved them all. Even if she saw a little too much of them.

The last time she had had completely to herself was a few hours in the passenger cabin of the airskimmer sent by Gatay to bring her across the ocean from Voe Deo. On the airstrip she was met by a delegation of priests and officials from the King and the Council, magnificent in scarlet and brown and turquoise, and swept off to the Palace, where there was a lot of curtsying and no belching, of course, for hours—an introduction to his little shrunken old majesty, introductions to High Muckamucks and Lord Hooziwhats, speeches, a banquet—all completely predictable, no problems at all, not even the impenetrable giant fried flower on her plate at the banquet. But with her, from that first moment on the airstrip and at every moment thereafter, discreetly behind or beside or very near her, were two men: her Guide and her Guard.

The Guide, whose name was San Ubattat, was provided by her hosts in Gatay; of course he was reporting on her to the government, but he was a most obliging spy, endlessly smoothing the way for her, showing her with a bare hint what was expected or what would be a gaffe, and an excellent linguist, ready with a translation when she needed one. San was all right. But the Guard was something else.

He had been attached to her by the Ekumen's hosts on this world, the dominant power on Werel, the big nation of Voe Deo. She had promptly protested to the Embassy back in Voe Deo that she didn't need or want a bodyguard. Nobody in Gatay was out to get her and even if they were, she preferred to look after herself. The Embassy sighed. Sorry, they said. You're stuck with him. Voe Deo has a military presence in Gatay, which after all is a client state, economically dependent. It's in Voe Deo's interest to protect the legitimate government of Gatay against the native terrorist factions, and you get protected as one of their interests. We can't argue with that.

She knew better than to argue with the Embassy, but she could not resign herself to the Major. His military title, rega, she translated by the archaic word "Major," from a skit she'd seen on Terra. That Major had been a stuffed uniform, covered with medals and insignia. It puffed and strutted and commanded, and finally blew up into bits of stuffing. If only this Major would blow up! Not that he strutted, exactly, or even commanded, directly. He was stonily polite, woodenly silent, stiff and cold as rigor mortis. She soon gave up any effort to talk to him; whatever she said, he replied Yessum or Nomum with the prompt stupidity of a man who does not and will not actually listen, an officer officially incapable of humanity. And he was with her in every public situation, day and night, on the street, shopping, meeting with businessmen and officials, sightseeing, at court, in the balloon ascent above the mountains—with her everywhere, everywhere but bed.

Even in bed she wasn't quite as alone as she would often have liked; for the Guide and the Guard went home at night, but in the anteroom of her bedroom slept the Maid—a gift from His Majesty, her own private asset.

She remembered her incredulity when she first learned that word, years ago, in a text about slavery. "On Werel, members of the dominant caste are called *owners*; members of the serving class are called *assets*. Only owners are referred to as men or women; assets are called bondsmen, bondswomen."

So here she was, the owner of an asset. You don't turn down a king's gift. Her asset's name was Rewe. Rewe was probably a spy too, but it was hard to believe. She was a dignified, handsome woman some years older than Solly and about the same intensity of skin color, though Solly was pinkish brown and Rewe was bluish brown. The palms of her hands were a delicate azure. Rewe's manners were exquisite and she had tact, astuteness, an infallible sense of when she was wanted and when not. Solly of course treated her as an equal, stating right out at the beginning that she believed no human being had a right to dominate, much less own, another, that she would give Rewe no orders, and that she hoped they might become friends. Rewe accepted this, unfortunately, as a new set of orders. She smiled and said yes. She was infinitely yielding. Whatever Solly said or did sank into that acceptance and was lost, leaving Rewe unchanged: an attentive, obliging, gentle physical presence, just out of reach. She smiled, and said yes, and was untouchable.

And Solly began to think, after the first fizz of the first days in Gatay, that she needed Rewe, really needed her as a woman to talk with. There was no way to meet owner women, who lived hidden away in their bezas, women's quarters, "at home," they called it. All bondswomen but Rewe were somebody else's property, not hers to talk to. All she ever met was men. And eunuchs.

That had been another thing hard to believe, that a man would voluntarily trade his virility for a little social standing; but she met such men all the time in King Hotat's court. Born assets, they earned partial independence by becoming eunuchs, and as such often rose to positions of considerable power and trust among their owners. The eunuch Tayandan, majordomo of the palace, ruled the King, who didn't rule, but figureheaded for the Council. The Council was made up of various kinds of lord but only one kind of priest, Tualites. Only assets worshiped Kamye, and the original religion of Gatay had been suppressed when the monarchy became Tualite a century or so ago. If there was one thing she really disliked about Werel, aside from slavery and gender-dominance, it was the religions. The songs about Lady Tual were beautiful, and the statues of her and the great temples in Voe Deo were wonderful, and the *Arkamye* seemed to be a good story though long-winded; but the deadly self-righteousness, the intolerance, the stupidity of the priests, the hideous doctrines that justified every cruelty in the name of the faith! As a matter of fact, Solly said to herself, was there anything she *did* like about Werel?

And answered herself instantly: I love it, I love it. I love this weird little bright sun and all the broken bits of moons and the mountains going up like ice walls and the people—the people with their black eyes without whites like animals' eyes, eyes like dark glass, like dark water, mysterious—I want to love them, I want to know them, I want to reach them!

But she had to admit that the pissants at the Embassy had been right about one thing: being a woman was tough on Werel. She fit nowhere. She went about alone, she had a public position, and so was a contradiction in terms: proper women stayed at home, invisible. Only bondswomen went out in the streets, or met strangers, or worked at any public job. She behaved like an asset, not like an owner. Yet she was something very grand, an envoy of the Ekumen, and Gatay very much wanted to join the Ekumen and not to offend its envoys. So the officials and courtiers and businessmen she talked to on the business of the Ekumen did the best they could: they treated her as if she were a man.

The pretense was never complete and often broke right down. The poor old King groped her industriously, under the vague impression that she was one of his bedwarmers. When she contradicted Lord Gatuyo in a discussion, he stared with the blank disbelief of a man who has been talked back to by his shoe. He had been thinking of her as a woman. But in general the disgenderment worked, allowing her to work with them; and she began to fit herself into the game, enlisting Rewe's help in making clothes that resembled what male owners wore in Gatay, avoiding anything that to them would be specifically feminine. Rewe was a quick, intelligent seamstress. The bright, heavy, close-fitted trousers were practical and becoming, the embroidered jackets were splendidly warm. She liked wearing them. But she felt unsexed by these men who could not accept her for what she was. She needed to talk to a woman.

She tried to meet some of the hidden owner women through the owner men, and met a wall of politeness without a door, without a peephole. What a wonderful idea; we will certainly arrange a visit when the weather is better! I should be overwhelmed with the honor if the Envoy were to entertain Lady Mayoyo and my daughters, but my foolish, provincial girls are so unforgivably timid—I'm sure you understand. Oh, surely, surely, a tour of the inner gardens—but not at present, when the vines are not in flower! We must wait until the vines are in flower!

There was nobody to talk to, nobody, until she met Batikam the Makil.

It was an event: a touring troupe from Voe Deo. There wasn't much going on in Gatay's little mountain capital by way of entertainment, except for temple dancers—all men, of course—and the soppy fluff that passed as drama on the Werelian network. Solly had doggedly entered some of these wet pastels, hoping for a glimpse into the life "at home," but she couldn't stomach the swooning maidens who died of love while the stiff-necked jackass heroes, who all looked like the Major, died nobly in battle, and Tual the Merciful leaned out of the clouds smiling upon their deaths with her eyes slightly crossed and the whites showing, a sign of divinity. Solly had noticed that Werelian men never entered the network for drama. Now she knew why. But the receptions at the palace and the parties in her honor given by various lords and businessmen were pretty dull stuff: all men, always, because they wouldn't have the slave girls in while the Envoy was there; and she couldn't flirt even with the nicest men, couldn't remind them that they were men, since that would remind them that she was a woman not behaving like a lady. The fizz had definitely gone flat by the time the makil troupe came.

She asked San, a reliable etiquette advisor, if it would be all right for her to attend the performance. He hemmed and hawed and finally, with more than usual oily delicacy, gave her to understand that it would be all right so long as she went dressed as a man. "Women, you know, don't go in public. But sometimes, they want so much to see the entertainers, you know? Lady Amatay used to go with Lord Amatay, dressed in his clothes, every year; everybody knew, nobody said anything—you know. For you, such a great person, it would be all right. Nobody will say anything. Quite, quite all right. Of course, I come with you, the rega comes with you. Like friends, ha? You know, three good men friends going to the entertainment, ha? Ha?"

Ha, ha, she said obediently. What fun!—But it was worth it, she thought, to see the makils.

They were never on the network. Young girls at home were not to be exposed to their performances, some of which, San gravely informed her, were unseemly. They played only in theaters. Clowns, dancers, prostitutes, actors, musicians, the makils formed a kind of subclass, the only assets not personally owned. A talented slave boy bought by the Entertainment Corporation from his owner was thenceforth the property of the Corporation, which trained and looked after him the rest of his life.

They walked to the theater, six or seven streets away. She had forgotten that the makils were all transvestites, indeed she did not remember it when she first saw them, a troop of tall slender dancers sweeping out onto the stage with the precision and power and grace of great birds wheeling, flocking, soaring. She watched unthinking, enthralled by their beauty, until suddenly the music changed and the clowns came in, black as night, black as owners, wearing fantastic trailing skirts, with fantastic jutting jeweled breasts, singing in tiny, swoony voices, "Oh do not rape me please kind Sir, no no, not now!" They're men, they're men!Solly realized then, already laughing helplessly. By the time Batikam finished his star turn, a marvelous dramatic monologue, she was a fan. "I want to meet him," she said to San at a pause between acts. "The actor—Batikam."

San got the bland expression that signified he was thinking how it could be arranged and how to make a little money out of it. But the Major was on guard, as ever. Stiff as a stick, he barely turned his head to glance at San. And San's expression began to alter.

If her proposal was out of line, San would have signaled or said so. The Stuffed Major was simply controlling her, trying to keep her as tied down as one of "his" women. It was time to challenge him. She turned to him and stared straight at him.

"Rega Teyeo," she said, "I quite comprehend that you're under orders to keep me in order. But if you give orders to San or to me, they must be spoken aloud, and they must be justified. I will not be managed by your winks or your whims."

There was a considerable pause, a truly delicious and rewarding pause. It was difficult to see if the Major's expression changed; the dim theater light showed no detail in his blue-black face. But there was something frozen about his stillness that told her she'd stopped him. At last he said, "I'm charged to protect you, Envoy."

"Am I endangered by the makils? Is there impropriety in an envoy of the Ekumen congratulating a great artist of Werel?"

Again the frozen silence. "No," he said.

"Then I request you to accompany me when I go backstage after the performance to speak to Batikam."

One stiff nod. One stiff, stuffy, defeated nod. Score one! Solly thought, and sat back cheerfully to watch the lightpainters, the erotic dances, and the curiously touching little drama with which the evening ended. It was in archaic poetry, hard to understand, but the actors were so beautiful, their voices so tender that she found tears in her eyes and hardly knew why.

"A pity the makils always draw on the *Arkamye*," said San, with smug, pious disapproval. He was not a very high-class owner, in fact he owned no assets; but he was an owner, and a bigoted Tualite, and liked to remind himself of it. "Scenes from the *Incarnations of Tual* would be more befitting such an audience."

"I'm sure you agree, Rega," she said, enjoying her own irony.

"Not at all," he said, with such toneless politeness that at first she did not realise what he had said; and then forgot the minor puzzle in the bustle of finding their way and gaining admittance to the backstage and to the performers' dressing room.

When they realised who she was, the managers tried to clear all the other performers out, leaving her alone with Batikam (and San and the Major, of course); but she said no, no, no, these wonderful artists must not be disturbed, just let me talk a moment with Batikam. She stood there in the bustle of doffed costumes, half-naked people, smeared makeup, laughter, dissolving tension after the show, any backstage on any world, talking with the clever, intense man in elaborate archaic woman's costume. They hit it off at once. "Can you come to my house?" she asked. "With pleasure," Batikam said, and his eyes did not flick to San's or the Major's face:the first bondsman she had yet met who did not glance to her Guard or her Guide for permission to say or do anything, anything at all. She glanced at them only to see if they were shocked. San looked collusive, the Major looked rigid. "I'll come in a little while," Batikam said. "I must change."

They exchanged smiles, and she left. The fizz was back in the air. The huge close stars hung clustered like grapes of fire. A moon tumbled over the icy peaks, another jigged like a lopsided lantern above the curlicue pinnacles of the palace. She strode along the dark street, enjoying the freedom of the male robe she wore and its warmth, making San trot to keep up; the Major, long-legged, kept pace with her. A high, trilling voice called, "Envoy!" and she turned with a smile, then swung round, seeing the Major grappling momentarily with someone in the shadow of a portico. He broke free, caught up to her without a word, seized her arm in an iron grip, and dragged her into a run. "Let go!" she said, struggling; she did not want to use an aiji break on him, but nothing less was going to get her free.

He pulled her nearly off-balance with a sudden dodge into an alley; she ran with him, letting him keep hold on her arm. They came unexpectedly out into her street and to her gate, through it, into the house, which he unlocked with a word—how did he do that?—"What is all this?" she demanded, breaking away easily, holding her arm where his grip had bruised it.

She saw, outraged, the last flicker of an exhilarated smile on his face. Breathing hard, he asked, "Are you hurt?"

"Hurt? Where you yanked me, yes—what do you think you were doing?"

"Keeping the fellow away."

"What fellow?"

He said nothing.

"The one who called out? Maybe he wanted to talk to me!"

After a moment the Major said, "Possibly. He was in the shadow. I thought he might be armed. I must go out and look for San Ubattat: Please keep the door locked until I come back." He was out the door as he gave the order; it never occurred to him that she would not obey, and she did obey, raging. Did he think she couldn't look after herself? That she needed him interfering in her life, kicking slaves around, "protecting" her? Maybe it was time he saw what an aiji fall looked like. He was strong and quick, but had no real training. This kind of amateur interference was intolerable, really intolerable; she must protest to the Embassy again.

As soon she let him back in with a nervous, shamefaced San in tow, she said, "You opened my door with a password. I was not informed that you had right of entrance day and night."

He was back to his military blankness. "Nomum," he said.

"You are not to do so again. You are not to seize hold of me ever again. I must tell you that if you do, I will injure you. If something alarms you, tell me what it is and I will respond as I see fit. Now will you please go."

"With pleasure, mum," he said, wheeled, and marched out.

"Oh, Lady—Oh, Envoy," San said, "that was a dangerous person, extremely dangerous people, I am so sorry, disgraceful," and he babbled on. She finally got him to say who he thought it was, a religious dissident, one of the Old Believers who held to the original religion of Gatay and wanted to cast out or kill all foreigners and unbelievers. "A bondsman?" she asked with interest, and he was shocked—"Oh, no, no, a real person, a man—but most misguided, a fanatic, a heathen fanatic! Knifemen, they call themselves. But a man, Lady—Envoy, certainly a man!"

The thought that she might think that an asset might touch her upset him as much as the attempted assault. If such it had been.

As she considered it, she began to wonder if, since she had put the Major in his place at the theater, he had found an excuse to put her in her place by "protecting" her. Well, if he tried it again, he'd find himself upside down against the opposite wall.

"Rewe!" she called, and the bondswoman appeared instantly as always. "One of the actors is coming. Would you like to make us a little tea, something like that?"

Rewe smiled, said, "Yes," and vanished. There was a knock at the door. The Major opened it—he must be standing guard outside—and Batikam came in.

It had not occurred to her that the makil would still be in women's clothing, but it was how he dressed offstage too, not so magnificently, but with elegance, in the delicate, flowing materials and dark, subtle hues that the swoony ladies in the dramas wore. It gave considerable piquancy, she felt, to her own male costume. Batikam was not as handsome as the Major, who was a stunning-looking man till he opened his mouth; but the makil was magnetic, you had to look at him. He was a dark greyish brown, not the blue-black that the owners were so vain of (though there were plenty of black assets too, Solly had noticed: of course, when every bondswoman was her owner's sexual servant). Intense, vivid intelligence and sympathy shone in his face through the makil's stardust black makeup, as he looked around with a slow, lovely laugh at her, at San, and at the Major standing at the door. He laughed like a woman, a warm ripple, not the ha, ha of a man. He held out his hands to Solly, and she came forward and took them. "Thank you for coming, Batikam!" she said, and he said, "Thank you for asking me, Alien Envoy!"

"San," she said, "I think this is your cue?"

Only indecision about what he ought to do could have slowed San down till she had to speak. He still hesitated a moment, then smiled with unction and said, "Yes, so sorry, a very good night to you, Envoy! Noon hour at the Office of Mines, tomorrow, I believe?" Backing away, he backed right into the Major, who stood like a post in the doorway. She looked at the Major, ready to order him out without ceremony, how dare he shove back in!—and saw the expression on his face. For once his blank mask had cracked, and what was revealed was contempt. Incredulous, sickened contempt. As if he was obliged to watch someone eat a turd.

"Get out," she said. She turned her back on both of them. "Come on, Batikam; the only privacy I have is in here," she said, and led the makil to her bedroom.

He was born where his fathers before him were born, in the old, cold house in the foothills above Noeha. His mother did not cry out as she bore him, since she was a soldier's wife, and a soldier's mother, now. He was named for his great-uncle, killed on duty in the Sosa. He grew up in the stark discipline of a poor household of pure veot lineage. His father, when he was on leave, taught him the arts a soldier must know; when his father was on duty the old Asset-Sergeant Habbakam took over the lessons, which began at five in the morning, summer or winter, with worship, short-sword practice, and a cross-country run. His mother and grandmother taught him the other arts a man must know, beginning with good manners before he was two, and after his second birthday going on to history, poetry, and sitting still without talking.

The child's day was filled with lessons and fenced with disciplines; but a child's day is long. There was room and time for freedom, the freedom of the farmyard and the open hills. There was the companionship of pets, foxdogs, running dogs, spotted cats, hunting cats, and the farm cattle and the greathorses; not much companionship otherwise. The family's assets, other than Habbakam and the two housewomen, were sharecroppers, working the stony foothill land that they and their owners had lived on forever. Their children were light-skinned, shy, already stooped to their life-long work, ignorant of anything beyond their fields and hills. Sometimes they swam with Teyeo, summers, in the pools of the river. Sometimes he rounded up a couple of them to play soldiers with him. They stood awkward, uncouth, smirking when he shouted "Charge!" and rushed at the invisible enemy. "Follow me!" he cried shrilly, and they lumbered after him, firing their tree-branch guns at random, pow, pow. Mostly he went alone, riding his good mare Tasi or afoot with a hunting cat pacing by his side.

A few times a year visitors came to the estate, relatives or fellow officers of Teyeo's father, bringing their children and their housepeople. Teyeo silently and politely showed the child guests about, introduced them to the animals, took them on rides. Silently and politely, he and his cousin Gemat came to hate each other; at age fourteen they fought for an hour in a glade behind the house, punctiliously following the rules of wrestling, relentlessly hurting each other, getting bloodier and wearier and more desperate, until by unspoken consent they called it off and returned in silence to the house, where everyone was gathering for dinner. Everyone looked at them and said nothing. They washed up hurriedly, hurried to table. Gemat's nose leaked blood all through the meal; Teyeo's jaw was so sore he could not open it to eat. No one commented.

Silently and politely, when they were both fifteen, Teyeo and Rega Toebawe's daughter fell in love. On the last day of her visit they escaped by unspoken collusion and rode out side by side, rode for hours, too shy to talk. He had given her Tasi to ride. They dismounted to water and rest the horses in a wild valley of the hills. They sat near each other, not very near, by the side of the little quiet-running stream. "I love you," Teyeo said. "I love you," Emdu said, bending her shining black face down. They did not touch or look at each other. They rode back over the hills, joyous, silent.

When he was sixteen Teyeo was sent to the Officers' Academy in the capital of his province. There he continued to learn and practice the arts of war and the arts of peace. His province was the most rural in Voe Deo; its ways were conservative, and his training was in some ways anachronistic. He was of course taught the technologies of modern warfare, becoming a first-rate pod pilot and an expert in telereconnaissancee; but he was not taught the modern ways of thinking that accompanied the technologies in other schools. He learned the poetry and history of Voe Deo, not the history and politics of the Ekumen. The Alien presence on Werel remained remote, theoretical to him. His reality was the old reality of the veot class, whose men held themselves apart from all men not soldiers and in brotherhood with all soldiers, whether owners, assets, or enemies. As for women, Teyeo considered his rights over them absolute, binding him absolutely to responsible chivalry to women of his own class and protective, merciful treatment of bondswomen. He believed all foreigners to be basically hostile, untrustworthy heathens. He honored the Lady Tual, but worshiped the Lord Kamye. He expected no justice, looked for no reward, and valued above all competence, courage, and self-respect. In some respects he was utterly unsuited to the world he was to enter, in others well prepared for it, since he was to spend seven years on Yeowe fighting a war in which there was no justice, no reward, and never even an illusion of ultimate victory.

Rank among veot officers was hereditary. Teyeo entered active service as a rega, the highest of the three veot ranks. No degree of ineptitude or distinction could lower or raise his status or his pay. Material ambition was no use to a veot. But honor and responsibility were to be earned, and he earned them quickly. He loved service, loved the life, knew he was good at it, intelligently obedient, effective in command; he had come out of the Academy with the highest recommendations, and being posted to the capital, drew notice as a promising officer as well as a likable young man. At twenty-four he was absolutely fit, his body would do anything he asked of it. His austere upbringing had given him little taste for indulgence but an intense appreciation of pleasure, so the luxuries and entertainments of the capital were a discovery of delight to him. He was reserved and rather shy, but companionable and cheerful. A handsome young man, in with a set of other young men very like him, for a year he knew what it is to live a completely privileged life with complete enjoyment of it. The brilliant intensity of that enjoyment stood against the dark background of the war in Yeowe, the slave revolution on the colony planet, which had gone on all his lifetime, and was now intensifying. Without that background, he could not have been so happy. A whole life of games and diversions had no interest for him; and when his orders came, posted as a pilot and division commander to Yeowe, his happiness was pretty nearly complete.

He went home for his thirty-day leave. Having received his parents' approbation, he rode over the hills to Rega Toebawe's estate and asked for his daughter's hand in marriage. The rega and his wife told their daughter that they approved his offer and asked her, for they were not strict parents, if she would like to marry Teyeo. "Yes," she said. As a grown, unmarried woman, she lived in seclusion in the women's side of the house, but she and Teyeo were allowed to meet and even to walk together, the chaperone remaining at some distance. Teyeo told her it was a three-year posting; would she marry in haste now, or wait three years and have a proper wedding? "Now," she said, bending down her narrow, shining face. Teyeo gave a laugh of delight, and she laughed at him. They were married nine days later—it couldn't be sooner, there had to be some fuss and ceremony, even if it was a soldier's wedding—and for seventeen days Teyeo and Emdu made love, walked together, made love, rode together, made love, came to know each other, came to love each other, quarreled, made up, made love, slept in each other's arms. Then he left for the war on another world, and she moved to the women's side of her husband's house.

His three-year posting was extended year by year, as his value as an officer was recognised and as the war on Yeowe changed from scattered containing actions to an increasingly desperate retreat. In his seventh year of service an order for compassionate leave was sent out to Yeowe Headquarters for Rega Teyeo, whose wife was dying of complications of berlot fever. At that point, there was no headquarters on Yeowe; the Army was retreating from three directions towards the old colonial capital; Teyeo's division was fighting a rear-guard defense in the sea marshes; communications had collapsed.

Command on Werel continued to find it inconceivable that a mass of ignorant slaves with the crudest kind of weapons could be defeating the Army of Voe Deo, a disciplined, trained body of soldiers with an infallible communications network, skimmers, pods, every armament and device permitted by the Ekumenical Convention Agreement. A strong faction in Voe Deo blamed the setbacks on this submissive adherence to Alien rules. The hell with Ekumenical Conventions. Bomb the damned dusties back to the mud they were made of. Use the biobomb, what was it for, anyway? Get our men off the foul planet and wipe it clean. Start fresh. If we don't win the war on Yeowe, the next revolution's going to be right here on Werel, in our own cities, in our own homes! The jittery government held on against this pressure. Werel was on probation, and Voe Deo wanted to lead the planet to Ekumenical status. Defeats were minimised, losses were not made up, skimmers, pods, weapons, men were not replaced. By the end of Teyeo's seventh year, the Army on Yeowe had been essentially written off by its government. Early in the eighth year, when the Ekumen was at last permitted to send its Envoys to Yeowe, Voe Deo and the other countries that had supplied auxiliary troops finally began to bring their soldiers home.

It was not until he got back to Werel that Teyeo learned his wife was dead.

He went home to Noeha. He and his father greeted each other with a silent embrace, but his mother wept as she embraced him. He knelt to her in apology for having brought her more grief than she could bear.

He lay that night in the cold room in the silent house, listening to his heart beat like a slow drum. He was not unhappy, the relief of being at peace and the sweetness of being home were too great for that; but it was a desolate calm, and somewhere in it was anger. Not used to anger, he was not sure what he felt. It was as if a faint, sullen red flare colored every image in his mind, as he lay trying to think through the seven years on Yeowe, first as a pilot, then the ground war, then the long retreat, the killing and the being killed. Why had they been left there to be hunted down and slaughtered? Why had the government not sent them reinforcements? The questions had not been worth asking then, they were not worth asking now. They had only one answer: We do what they ask us to do, and we don't complain. I fought every step of the way, he thought without pride. The new knowledge sliced keen as a knife through all other knowledge—And while I was fighting, she was dying. All a waste, there on Yeowe. All a waste, here on Werel. He sat up in the dark, the cold, silent, sweet dark of night in the hills. "Lord Kamye," he said aloud, "help me. My mind betrays me."

During the long leave home he sat often with his mother. She wanted to talk about Emdu, and at first he had to force himself to listen. It would be easy to forget the girl he had known for seventeen days seven years ago, if only his mother would let him forget. Gradually he learned to take what she wanted to give him, the knowledge of who his wife had been. His mother wanted to share all she could with him of the joy she had had in Emdu, her beloved child and friend. Even his father, retired now, a quenched, silent man, was able to say, "She was the light of the house." They were thanking him for her. They were telling him that it had not all been a waste.

But what lay ahead of them? Old age, the empty house. They did not complain, of course, and seemed content in their severe, placid round of daily work; but for them the continuity of the past with the future was broken.

"I should remarry," Teyeo said to his mother. "Is there anyone you've noticed . . . ?"

It was raining, a grey light through the wet windows, a soft thrumming on the eaves. His mother's face was indistinct as she bent to her mending.

"No," she said. "Not really." She looked up at him, and after a pause asked, "Where do you think you'll be posted?"

"I don't know."

"There's no war now," she said, in her soft, even voice.

"No," Teyeo said. "There's no war."

"Will there be . . . ever? do you think?"

He stood up, walked down the room and back, sat down again on the cushioned platform near her; they both sat straight-backed, still except for the slight motion of her hands as she sewed; his hands lay lightly one in the other, as he had been taught when he was two.

"I don't know," he said. "It's strange. It's as if there hadn't been a war. As if we'd never been on Yeowe—the Colony, the Uprising, all of it. They don't talk about it. It didn't happen. We don't fight wars. This is a new age. They say that often on the net. The age of peace, brotherhood across the stars. So, are we brothers with Yeowe, now? Are we brothers with Gatay and Bambur and the Forty States? Are we brothers with our assets? I can't make sense of it. I don't know what they mean. I don't know where I fit in." His voice too was quiet and even.

"Not here, I think," she said. "Not yet."

After a while he said, "I thought . . . children . . ."

"Of course. When the time comes." She smiled at him. "You never could sit still for half an hour. . . . Wait. Wait and see."

She was right, of course; and yet what he saw in the net and in town tried his patience and his pride. It seemed that to be a soldier now was a disgrace. Government reports, the news and the analyses, constantly referred to the Army and particularly the veot class as fossils, costly and useless, Voe Deo's principal obstacle to full admission to the Ekumen. His own uselessness was made clear to him when his request for a posting was met by an indefinite extension of his leave on half pay. At thirty-two, they appeared to be telling him, he was superannuated.

Again he suggested to his mother that he should accept the situation, settle down, and look for a wife. "Talk to your father," she said. He did so; his father said, "Of course your help is welcome, but I can run the farm well enough for a while yet. Your mother thinks you should go to the capital, to Command. They can't ignore you if you're there. After all. After seven years' combat—your record—"

Teyeo knew what that was worth, now. But he was certainly not needed here, and probably irritated his father with his ideas of changing this or that way things were done. They were right: he should go to the capital and find out for himself what part he could play in the new world of peace.

His first half-year there was grim. He knew almost no one at Command or in the barracks; his generation was dead, or invalided out, or home on half pay. The younger officers, who had not been on Yeowe, seemed to him a cold, buttoned-up lot, always talking money and politics. Little businessmen, he privately thought them. He knew they were afraid of him—of his record, of his reputation. Whether he wanted to or not he reminded them that there had been a war that Werel had fought and lost, a civil war, their own race fighting against itself, class against class. They wanted to dismiss it as a meaningless quarrel on another world, nothing to do with them.

Teyeo walked the streets of the capital, watched the thousands of bondsmen and bondswomen hurrying about their owners' business, and wondered what they were waiting for.

"The Ekumen does not interfere with the social, cultural, or economic arrangements and affairs of any people," the Embassy and the government spokesmen repeated. "Full membership for any nation or people that wishes it is contingent only on absence, or renunciation, of certain specific methods and devices of warfare," and there followed the list of terrible weapons, most of them mere names to Teyeo, but a few of them inventions of his own country: the biobomb, as they called it, and the neuronics.

He personally agreed with the Ekumen's judgment on such devices, and respected their patience in waiting for Voe Deo and the rest of Werel to prove not only compliance with the ban, but acceptance of the principle. But he very deeply resented their condescension. They sat in judgment on everything Werelian, viewing from above. The less they said about the division of classes, the clearer their disapproval was. "Slavery is of very rare occurrence in Ekumenical worlds," said their books, "and disappears completely with full participation in the Ekumenical polity." Was that what the Alien Embassy was really waiting for?

"By our Lady!" said one of the young officers—many of them were Tualites, as well as businessmen—"the Aliens are going to admit the dusties before they admit us!" He was sputtering with indignant rage, like a red-faced old rega faced with an insolent bondsoldier. "Yeowe—a damned planet of savages, tribesmen, regressed into barbarism—preferred over us!"

"They fought well," Teyeo observed, knowing he should not say it as he said it, but not liking to hear the men and women he had fought against called dusties. Assets, rebels, enemies, yes.

The young man stared at him and after a moment said, "I suppose you love 'em, eh? The dusties?"

"I killed as many as I could," Teyeo replied politely, and then changed the conversation. The young man, though nominally Teyeo's superior at Command, was an oga, the lowest rank of veot, and to snub him further would be ill-bred.

They were stuffy, he was touchy; the old days of cheerful good fellowship were a faint, incredible memory. The bureau chiefs at Command listened to his request to be put back on active service and sent him endlessly on to another department. He could not live in barracks, but had to find an apartment, like a civilian. His half pay did not permit him indulgence in the expensive pleasures of the city. While waiting for appointments to see this or that official, he spent his days in the library net of the Officers' Academy. He knew his education had been incomplete and was out of date. If his country was going to join the Ekumen, in order to be useful he must know more about the Alien ways of thinking and the new technologies. Not sure what he needed to know, he floundered about in the network, bewildered by the endless information available, increasingly aware that he was no intellectual and no scholar and would never understand Alien minds, but doggedly driving himself on out of his depth.

A man from the Embassy was offering an introductory course in Ekumenical history in the public net. Teyeo joined it, and sat through eight or ten lecture-and-discussion periods, straight-backed and still, only his hands moving slightly as he took full and methodical notes. The lecturer, a Hainishman who translated his extremely long Hainish name as Old Music, watched Teyeo, tried to draw him out in discussion, and at last asked him to stay in after session. "I should like to meet you, Rega," he said, when the others had dropped out.

They met at a café. They met again. Teyeo did not like the Alien's manners, which he found effusive; he did not trust his quick, clever mind; he felt Old Music was using him, studying him as a specimen of The Veot, The Soldier, probably The Barbarian. The Alien, secure in his superiority, was indifferent to Teyeo's coldness, ignored his distrust, insisted on helping him with information and guidance, and shamelessly repeated questions Teyeo had avoided answering. One of these was, "Why are you sitting around here on half pay?"

"It's not by my own choice, Mr. Old Music," Teyeo finally answered, the third time it was asked. He was very angry at the man's impudence, and so spoke with particular mildness. He kept his eyes away from Old Music's eyes, bluish, with the whites showing like a scared horse. He could not get used to Aliens' eyes.

"They won't put you back on active service?"

Teyeo assented politely. Could the man, however alien, really be oblivious to the fact that his questions were grossly humiliating?

"Would you be willing to serve in the Embassy Guard?"

That question left Teyeo speechless for a moment; then he committed the extreme rudeness of answering a question with a question. "Why do you ask?"

"I'd like very much to have a man of your capacity in that corps," said Old Music, adding with his appalling candor, "Most of them are spies or blockheads. It would be wonderful to have a man I knew was neither. It's not just sentry duty, you know. I imagine you'd be asked by your government to give information; that's to be expected. And we would use you, once you had experience and if you were willing, as a liaison officer. Here or in other countries. We would not, however, ask you to give information to us. Am I clear, Teyeo? I want no misunderstanding between us as to what I am and am not asking of you."

"You would be able . . . ?" Teyeo asked cautiously.

Old Music laughed and said, "Yes. I have a string to pull in your Command. A favor owed. Will you think it over?"

Teyeo was silent a minute. He had been nearly a year now in the capital and his requests for posting had met only bureaucratic evasion and, recently, hints that they were considered insubordinate. "I'll accept now, if I may," he said, with a cold deference.

The Hainishman looked at him, his smile changing to a thoughtful, steady gaze. "Thank you," he said. "You should hear from Command in a few days."

So Teyeo put his uniform back on, moved back to the City Barracks, and served for another seven years on alien ground. The Ekumenical Embassy was, by diplomatic agreement, a part not of Werel but of the Ekumen—a piece of the planet that no longer belonged to it. The Guardsmen furnished by Voe Deo were protective and decorative, a highly visible presence on the Embassy grounds in their white-and-gold dress uniform. They were also visibly armed, since protest against the Alien presence still broke out erratically in violence.

Rega Teyeo, at first assigned to command a troop of these guards, soon was transferred to a different duty, that of accompanying members of the Embassy staff about the city and on journeys. He served as a bodyguard, in undress uniform. The Embassy much preferred not to use their own people and weapons, but to request and trust Voe Deo to protect them. Often he was also called upon to be a guide and interpreter, and sometimes a companion. He did not like it when visitors from somewhere in space wanted to be chummy and confiding, asked him about himself, invited him to come drinking with them. With perfectly concealed distaste, with perfect civility, he refused such offers. He did his job and kept his distance. He knew that that was precisely what the Embassy valued him for. Their confidence in him gave him a cold satisfaction.

His own government had never approached him to give information, though he certainly learned things that would have interested them. Voe Dean intelligence did not recruit their agents among veots. He knew who the agents in the Embassy Guard were; some of them tried to get information from him, but he had no intention of spying for spies.

Old Music, whom he now surmised to be the head of the Embassy's intelligence system, called him in on his return from a winter leave at home. The Hainishman had learned not to make emotional demands on Teyeo, but could not hide a note of affection in his voice greeting him. "Hullo, Rega! I hope your family's well? Good. I've got a particularly tricky job for you. Kingdom of Gatay. You were there with Kemehan two years ago, weren't you? Well, now they want us to send an Envoy. They say they want to join. Of course the old King's a puppet of your government; but there's a lot else going on there. A strong religious separatist movement. A Patriotic Cause, kick out all the foreigners, Voe Deans and Aliens alike. But the King and Council requested an Envoy, and all we've got to send them is a new arrival. She may give you some problems till she learns the ropes. I judge her a bit headstrong. Excellent material, but young, very young. And she's only been here a few weeks. I requested you, because she needs your experience. Be patient with her, Rega. I think you'll find her likable."

He did not. In seven years he had got accustomed to the Aliens' eyes and their various smells and colors and manners. Protected by his flawless courtesy and his stoical code, he endured or ignored their strange or shocking or troubling behavior, their ignorance and their different knowledge. Serving and protecting the foreigners entrusted to him, he kept himself aloof from them, neither touched nor touching. His charges learned to count on him and not to presume on him. Women were often quicker to see and respond to his Keep Out signs than men; he had an easy, almost friendly relationship with an old Terran Observer whom he had accompanied on several long investigatory tours. "You are as peaceful to be with as a cat, Rega," she told him once, and he valued the compliment. But the Envoy to Gatay was another matter.

She was physically splendid, with clear red-brown skin like that of a baby, glossy swinging hair, a free walk—too free: she flaunted her ripe, slender body at men who had no access to it, thrusting it at him, at everyone, insistent, shameless. She expressed her opinion on everything with coarse self-confidence. She could not hear a hint and refused to take an order. She was an aggressive, spoiled child with the sexuality of an adult, given the responsibility of a diplomat in a dangerously unstable country. Teyeo knew as soon as he met her that this was an impossible assignment. He could not trust her or himself. Her sexual immodesty aroused him as it disgusted him; she was a whore whom he must treat as a princess. Forced to endure and unable to ignore her, he hated her.

He was more familiar with anger than he had used to be, but not used to hating. It troubled him extremely. He had never in his life asked for a reposting, but on the morning after she had taken the makil into her room, he sent a stiff little appeal to the Embassy. Old Music responded to him with a sealed voice-message through the diplomatic link: "Love of god and country is like fire, a wonderful friend, a terrible enemy; only children play with fire. I don't like the situation. There's nobody here I can replace either of you with. Will you hang on a while longer?"

He did not know how to refuse. A veot did not refuse duty. He was ashamed at having even thought of doing so, and hated her again for causing him that shame.

The first sentence of the message was enigmatic, not in Old Music's usual style but flowery, indirect, like a coded warning. Teyeo of course knew none of the intelligence codes either of his country or of the Ekumen. Old Music would have to use hints and indirection with him. "Love of god and country" could well mean the Old Believers and the Patriots, the two subversive groups in Gatay, both of them fanatically opposed to foreign influence; the Envoy could be the child playing with fire. Was she being approached by one group or the other? He had seen no evidence of it, unless the man in the shadows that night had been not a knifeman but a messenger. She was under his eyes all day, her house watched all night by soldiers under his command. Surely the makil, Batikam, was not acting for either of those groups. He might well be a member of the Hame, the asset liberation underground of Voe Deo, but as such would not endanger the Envoy, since the Hame saw the Ekumen as their ticket to Yeowe and to freedom.

Teyeo puzzled over the words, replaying them over and over, knowing his own stupidity faced with this kind of subtlety, the ins and outs of the political labyrinth. At last he erased the message and yawned, for it was late; bathed, lay down, turned off the light, said under his breath, "Lord Kamye, let me hold with courage to the one noble thing!" and slept like a stone.

The makil came to her house every night after the theater. Teyeo tried to tell himself there was nothing wrong in it. He himself had spent nights with the makils, back in the palmy days before the war. Expert, artistic sex was part of their business. He knew by hearsay that rich city women often hired them to come supply a husband's deficiencies. But even such women did so secretly, discreetly, not in this vulgar, shameless way, utterly careless of decency, flouting the moral code, as if she had some kind of right to do whatever she wanted wherever and whenever she wanted it. Of course Batikam colluded eagerly with her, playing on her infatuation, mocking the Gatayans, mocking Teyeo—and mocking her, though she didn't know it. What a chance for an asset to make fools of all the owners at once!

Watching Batikam, Teyeo felt sure he was a member of the Hame. His mockery was very subtle; he was not trying to disgrace the Envoy. Indeed his discretion was far greater than hers. He was trying to keep her from disgracing herself. The makil returned Teyeo's cold courtesy in kind, but once or twice their eyes met and some brief, involuntary understanding passed between them, fraternal, ironic.

There was to be a public festival, an observation of the Tualite Feast of Forgiveness, to which the Envoy was pressingly invited by the King and Council. She was put on show at many such events. Teyeo thought nothing about it except how to provide security in an excited holiday crowd, until San told him that the festival day was the highest holy day of the old religion of Gatay, and that the Old Believers fiercely resented the imposition of the foreign rites over their own. The little man seemed genuinely worried. Teyeo worried too when next day San was suddenly replaced by an elderly man who spoke little but Gatayan and was quite unable to explain what had become of San Ubattat. "Other duties, other duties call," he said in very bad Voe Dean, smiling and bobbing, "very great relishes time, aha? Relishes duties call."

During the days that preceded the festival tension rose in the city; graffiti appeared, symbols of the old religion smeared across walls; a Tualite temple was desecrated, after which the Royal Guard was much in evidence in the streets. Teyeo went to the palace and requested, on his own authority, that the Envoy not be asked to appear in public during a ceremony that was "likely to be troubled by inappropriate demonstrations." He was called in and treated by a Court official with a mixture of dismissive insolence and conniving nods and winks, which left him really uneasy. He left four men on duty at the Envoy's house that night. Returning to his quarters, a little barracks down the street which had been handed over to the Embassy Guard, he found the window of his room open and a scrap of writing, in his own language, on his table: *Fest F is set up for assasnation.*

He was at the Envoy's house promptly the next morning and asked her asset to tell her he must speak to her. She came out of her bedroom pulling a white wrap around her naked body. Batikam followed her, half-dressed, sleepy, and amused. Teyeo gave him the eye-signal *go*, which he received with a serene, patronising smile, murmuring to the woman, "I'll go have some breakfast. Rewe? have you got something to feed me?" He followed the bondswoman out of the room. Teyeo faced the Envoy and held out the scrap of paper.

"I received this last night, ma'am," he said. "I must ask you not to attend the festival tomorrow."

She considered the paper, read the writing, and yawned. "Who's it from?"

"I don't know, ma'am."

"What's it mean? *Assassination?* They can't spell, can they?"

After a moment, he said, "There are a number of other indications—enough that I must ask you—"

"Not to attend the festival of Forgiveness, yes. I heard you." She went to a window seat and sat down, her robe falling wide to reveal her legs; her bare, brown feet were short and supple, the soles pink, the toes small and orderly. Teyeo looked fixedly at the air beside her head. She twiddled the bit of paper. "If you think it's dangerous, Rega, bring a guardsman or two with you," she said, with the faintest tone of scorn. "I really have to be there. The King requested it, you know. And I'm to light the big fire, or something. One of the few things women are allowed to do in public here. . . . I can't back out of it." She held out the paper, and after a moment he came close enough to take it. She looked up at him smiling; when she defeated him she always smiled at him. "Who do you think would want to blow me away, anyhow? The Patriots?"

"Or the Old Believers, ma'am. Tomorrow is one of their holidays."

"And your Tualites have taken it away from them? Well, they can't exactly blame the Ekumen, can they?"

"I think it possible that the government might permit violence in order to excuse retaliation, ma'am."

She started to answer carelessly, realised what he had said, and frowned. "You think the Council's setting me up? What evidence have you?"

After a pause he said, "Very little, ma'am. San Ubattat—"

"San's been ill. The old fellow they sent isn't much use, but he's scarcely dangerous! Is that all?" He said nothing, and she went on, "Until you have real evidence, Rega, don't interfere with my obligations. Your militaristic paranoia isn't acceptable when it spreads to the people I'm dealing with here. Control it, please! I'll expect an extra guardsman or two tomorrow, and that's enough."

"Yes, ma'am," he said, and went out. His head sang with anger. It occurred to him now that her new guide had told him San Ubattat had been kept away by religious duties, not by illness. He did not turn back. What was the use? "Stay on for an hour or so, will you, Seyem?" he said to the guard at her gate, and strode off down the street, trying to walk away from her, from her soft brown thighs and the pink soles of her feet and her stupid, insolent, whorish voice giving him orders. He tried to let the bright icy sunlit air, the stepped streets snapping with banners for the festival, the glitter of the great mountains and the clamor of the markets fill him, dazzle and distract him; but he walked seeing his own shadow fall in front of him like a knife across the stones, knowing the futility of his life.

"The veot looked worried," Batikam said in his velvet voice, and she laughed, spearing a preserved fruit from the dish and popping it, dripping, into his mouth.

"I'm ready for breakfast now, Rewe," she called, and sat down across from Batikam. "I'm starving! He was having one of his phallocratic fits. He hasn't saved me from anything lately. It's his only function, after all. So he has to invent occasions. I wish, I wish he was out of my hair. It's so nice not to have poor little old San crawling around like some kind of pubic infestation. If only I could get rid of the Major now!"

"He's a man of honor," the makil said; his tone did not seem ironical.

"How can an owner of slaves be an honorable man?"

Batikam watched her from his long, dark eyes. She could not read Werelian eyes, beautiful as they were, filling their lids with darkness.

"Male hierarchy members always yatter about their precious honor," she said. "And 'their' women's honor, of course."

"Honor is a great privilege," Batikam said. "I envy it. I envy him."

"Oh, the hell with all that phony dignity, it's just pissing to mark your territory. All you need envy him, Batikam, is his freedom."

He smiled. "You're the only person I've ever known who was neither owned nor owner. That is freedom. *That* is freedom. I wonder if you know it?"

"Of course I do," she said. He smiled, and went on eating his breakfast, but there had been something in his voice she had not heard before. Moved and a little troubled, she said after a while, "You're going away soon."

"Mind reader. Yes. In ten days, the troupe goes on to tour the Forty States."

"Oh, Batikam, I'll miss you! You're the only man, the only person here I can talk to—let alone the sex—"

"Did we ever?"

"Not often," she said, laughing, but her voice shook a little. He held out his hand; she came to him and sat on his lap, the robe dropping open. "Little pretty Envoy breasts," he said, lipping and stroking, "little soft Envoy belly . . ." Rewe came in with a tray and softly set it down. "Eat your breakfast, little Envoy," Batikam said, and she disengaged herself and returned to her chair, grinning.

"Because you're free you can be honest," he said, fastidiously peeling a pini fruit. "Don't be too hard on those of us who aren't and can't." He cut a slice and fed it to her across the table. "It has been a taste of freedom to know you," he said. "A hint, a shadow . . ."

"In a few years at most, Batikam, you will be free. This whole idiotic structure of masters and slaves will collapse completely when Werel comes into the Ekumen."

"If it does."

"Of course it will."

He shrugged. "My home is Yeowe," he said.

She stared, confused. "You come from Yeowe?"

"I've never been there," he said. "I'll probably never go there. What use have they got for makils? But it is my home. Those are my people. That is my freedom. When will you see . . ." His fist was clenched; he opened it with a soft gesture of letting something go. He smiled and returned to his breakfast. "I've got to get back to the theater," he said. "We're rehearsing an act for the Day of Forgiveness."

She wasted all day at court. She had made persistent attempts to obtain permission to visit the mines and the huge government-run farms on the far side of the mountains, from which Gatay's wealth flowed. She had been as persistently foiled—by the protocol and bureaucracy of the government, she had thought at first, their unwillingness to let a diplomat do anything but run round to meaningless events; but some businessmen had let something slip about conditions in the mines and on the farms that made her think they might be hiding a more brutal kind of slavery than any visible in the capital. Today she got nowhere, waiting for appointments that had not been made. The old fellow who was standing in for San misunderstood most of what she said in Voe Dean, and when she tried to speak Gatayan he misunderstood it all, through stupidity or intent. The Major was blessedly absent most of the morning, replaced by one of his soldiers, but turned up at court, stiff and silent and set-jawed, and attended her until she gave up and went home for an early bath.

Batikam came late that night. In the middle of one of the elaborate fantasy games and role reversals she had learned from him and found so exciting, his caresses grew slower and slower, soft, dragging across her like feathers, so that she shivered with unappeased desire and, pressing her body against his, realised that he had gone to sleep. "Wake up," she said, laughing and yet chilled, and shook him a little. The dark eyes opened, bewildered, full of fear.

"I'm sorry," she said at once, "go back to sleep, you're tired. No, no, it's all right, it's late." But he went on with what she now, whatever his skill and tenderness, had to see was his job.

In the morning at breakfast she said, "Can you see me as an equal, do you, Batikam?"

He looked tired, older than he usually did. He did not smile. After a while he said, "What do you want me to say?"

"That you do."

"I do," he said quietly.

"You don't trust me," she said, bitter.

After a while he said, "This is Forgiveness Day. The Lady Tual came to the men of Asdok, who had set their hunting cats upon her followers. She came among them riding on a great hunting cat with a fiery tongue, and they fell down in terror, but she blessed them, forgiving them." His voice and hands enacted the story as he told it. "Forgive me," he said.

"You don't need any forgiveness!"

"Oh, we all do. It's why we Kamyites borrow the Lady Tual now and then. When we need her. So, today you'll be the Lady Tual, at the rites?"

"All I have to do is light a fire, they said," she said anxiously, and he laughed. When he left she told him she would come to the theater to see him, tonight, after the festival.

The horse-race course, the only flat area of any size anywhere near the city, was thronged, vendors calling, banners waving; the Royal motorcars drove straight into the crowd, which parted like water and closed behind. Some rickety-looking bleachers had been erected for lords and owners, with a curtained section for ladies. She saw a motorcar drive up to the bleachers; a figure swathed in red cloth was bundled out of it and hurried between the curtains, vanishing. Were there peepholes for them to watch the ceremony through? There were women in the crowds, but bondswomen only, assets. She realised that she, too, would be kept hidden until her moment of the ceremony arrived: a red tent awaited her, alongside the bleachers, not far from the roped enclosure where priests were chanting. She was rushed out of the car and into the tent by obsequious and determined courtiers.

Bondswomen in the tent offered her tea, sweets, mirrors, makeup, and hair oil, and helped her put on the complex swathing of fine red-and-yellow cloth, her costume for her brief enactment of Lady Tual. Nobody had told her very clearly what she was to do, and to her questions the women said, "The priests will show you, Lady, you just go with them. You just light the fire. They have it all ready." She had the impression that they knew no more than she did; they were pretty girls, court assets, excited at being part of the show, indifferent to the religion. She knew the symbolism of the fire she was to light: into it faults and transgressions could be cast and burnt up, forgotten. It was a nice idea.

The priests were whooping it up out there; she peeked out—there were indeed peepholes in the tent fabric—and saw the crowd had thickened. Nobody except in the bleachers and right against the enclosure ropes could possibly see anything, but everybody was waving red-and-yellow banners, munching fried food, and making a day of it, while the priests kept up their deep chanting. In the far right of the little, blurred field of vision through the peephole was a familiar arm: the Major's, of course. They had not let him get into the motorcar with her. He must have been furious. He had got here, though, and stationed himself on guard. "Lady, Lady," the court girls were saying, "here come the priests now," and they buzzed around her making sure her headdress was on straight and the damnable, hobbling skirts fell in the right folds. They were still plucking and patting as she stepped out of the tent, dazzled by the daylight, smiling and trying to hold herself very straight and dignified as a Goddess ought to do. She really didn't want to fuck up their ceremony.

Two men in priestly regalia were waiting for her right outside the tent door. They stepped forward immediately, taking her by the elbows and saying, "This way, this way, Lady." Evidently she really wouldn't have to figure out what to do. No doubt they considered women incapable of it, but in the circumstances it was a relief. The priests hurried her along faster than she could comfortably walk in the tight-drawn skirt. They were behind the bleachers now; wasn't the enclosure in the other direction? A car was coming straight at them, scattering the few people who were in its way. Somebody was shouting; the priests suddenly began yanking her, trying to run; one of them yelled and let go her arm, felled by a flying darkness that had hit him with a jolt—she was in the middle of a melee, unable to break the iron hold on her arm, her legs imprisoned in the skirt, and there was a noise, an enormous noise, that hit her head and bent it down, she couldn't see or hear, blinded, struggling, shoved face first into some dark place with her face pressed into a stifling, scratchy darkness and her arms held locked behind her.

A car, moving. A long time. Men, talking low. They talked in Gatayan. It was very hard to breathe. She did not struggle; it was no use. They had taped her arms and legs, bagged her head. After a long time she was hauled out like a corpse and carried quickly, indoors, down stairs, set down on a bed or couch, not roughly though with the same desperate haste. She lay still. The men talked, still almost in whispers. It made no sense to her. Her head was still hearing that enormous noise, had it been real? had she been struck? She felt deaf, as if inside a wall of cotton. The cloth of the bag kept getting stuck on her mouth, sucked against her nostrils as she tried to breathe.

It was plucked off; a man stooping over her turned her so he could untape her arms, then her legs, murmuring as he did so, "Don't to be scared, Lady, we don't to hurt you," in Voe Dean. He backed away from her quickly. There were four or five of them; it was hard to see, there was very little light. "To wait here," another said, "everything all right. Just to keep happy." She was trying to sit up, and it made her dizzy. When her head stopped spinning, they were all gone. As if by magic. Just to keep happy.

A small very high room. Dark brick walls, earthy air. The light was from a little bi-olume plaque stuck on the ceiling, a weak, shadowless glow. Probably quite sufficient for Werelian eyes. Just to keep happy. I have been kidnapped. How about that. She inventoried: the thick mattress she was on; a blanket; a door; a small pitcher and a cup; a drainhole, was it, over in the corner? She swung her legs off the mattress and her feet struck something lying on the floor at the foot of it—she coiled up, peered at the dark mass, the body lying there. A man. The uniform, the skin so black she could not see the features, but she knew him. Even here, even here, the Major was with her.

She stood up unsteadily and went to investigate the drainhole, which was simply that, a cement-lined hole in the floor, smelling slightly chemical, slightly foul. Her head hurt, and she sat down on the bed again to massage her arms and ankles, easing the tension and pain and getting herself back into herself by touching and confirming herself, rhythmically, methodically. I have been kidnapped. How about that. Just to keep happy. What about him?

Suddenly knowing that he was dead, she shuddered and held still.

After a while she leaned over slowly, trying to see his face, listening. Again she had the sense of being deaf. She heard no breath. She reached out, sick and shaking, and put the back of her hand against his face. It was cool, cold. But warmth breathed across her fingers, once, again. She crouched on the mattress and studied him. He lay absolutely still, but when she put her hand on his chest she felt the slow heartbeat.

"Teyeo," she said in a whisper. Her voice would not go above a whisper.

She put her hand on his chest again. She wanted to feel that slow, steady beat, the faint warmth; it was reassuring. Just to keep happy.

What else had they said? Just to wait. Yes. That seemed to be the program. Maybe she could sleep. Maybe she could sleep and when she woke up the ransom would have come. Or whatever it was they wanted.

She woke up with the thought that she still had her watch, and after sleepily studying the tiny silver readout for a while decided she had slept three hours; it was still the day of the Festival, too soon for ransom probably, and she wouldn't be able to go to the theater to see the makils tonight. Her eyes had grown accustomed to the low light and when she looked she could see, now, that there was dried blood all over one side of the man's head. Exploring, she found a hot lump like a fist above his temple, and her fingers came away smeared. He had got himself crowned. That must have been him, launching himself at the priest, the fake priest, all she could remember was a flying shadow and a hard thump and an ooof! like an aiji attack, and then there had been the huge noise that confused everything. She clicked her tongue, tapped the wall, to check her hearing. It seemed to be all right; the wall of cotton had disappeared. Maybe she had been crowned herself? She felt her head, but found no lumps. The man must have a concussion, if he was still out after three hours. How bad? When would the men come back?

She got up and nearly fell over, entangled in the damned Goddess skirts. If only she was in her own clothes, not this fancy dress, three pieces of flimsy stuff you had to have servants to put on you! She got out of the skirt piece, and used the scarf piece to make a kind of tied skirt that came to her knees. It wasn't warm in this basement or whatever it was; it was dank and rather cold. She walked up and down, four steps turn, four steps turn, four steps turn, and did some warm-ups. They had dumped the man onto the floor. How cold was it? Was shock part of concussion? People in shock needed to be kept warm. She dithered a long time, puzzled at her own indecision, at not knowing what to do. Should she try to heave him up onto the mattress? Was it better not to move him? Where the hell were the men? Was he going to die?

She stooped over him and said sharply, "Rega! Teyeo!" and after a moment he caught his breath.

"Wake up!" She remembered now, she thought she remembered, that it was important not to let concussed people lapse into a coma. Except he already had.

He caught his breath again, and his face changed, came out of the rigid immobility, softened; his eyes opened and closed, blinked, unfocused. "Oh Kamye," he said very softly.

She couldn't believe how glad she was to see him. Just to keep happy. He evidently had a blinding headache, and admitted that he was seeing double. She helped him haul himself up onto the mattress and covered him with the blanket. He asked no questions, and lay mute, lapsing back to sleep soon. Once he was settled she went back to her exercises, and did an hour of them. She looked at her watch. It was two hours later, the same day, the Festival day. It wasn't evening yet. When were the men going to come?

They came early in the morning, after the endless night that was the same as the afternoon and the morning. The metal door was unlocked and thrown clanging open, and one of them came in with a tray while two of them stood with raised, aimed guns in the doorway. There was nowhere to put the tray but the floor, so he shoved it at Solly, said, "Sorry, Lady!" and backed out; the door clanged shut, the bolts banged home. She stood holding the tray. "Wait!" she said.

The man had waked up and was looking groggily around. After finding him in this place with her she had somehow lost his nickname, did not think of him as the Major, yet shied away from his name. "Here's breakfast, I guess," she said, and sat down on the edge of the mattress. A cloth was thrown over the wicker tray; under it was a pile of Gatayan grainrolls stuffed with meat and greens, several pieces of fruit, and a capped water carafe of thin, fancily beaded metal alloy. "Breakfast, lunch, and dinner, maybe," she said. "Shit. Oh well. It looks good. Can you eat? Can you sit up?"

He worked himself up to sit with his back against the wall, and then shut his eyes. "You're still seeing double?"

He made a small noise of assent.

"Are you thirsty?"

Small noise of assent.

"Here." She passed him the cup. By holding it in both hands he got it to his mouth, and drank the water slowly, a swallow at a time. She meanwhile devoured three grainrolls one after the other, then forced herself to stop, and ate a pini fruit. "Could you eat some fruit?" she asked him, feeling guilty. He did not answer. She thought of Batikam feeding her the slice of pini at breakfast, when, yesterday, a hundred years ago.

The food in her stomach made her feel sick. She took the cup from the man's relaxed hand—he was asleep again—and poured herself water, and drank it slowly, a swallow at a time.

When she felt better she went to the door and explored its hinges, lock, and surface. She felt and peered around the brick walls, the poured concrete floor, seeking she knew not what, something to escape with, something. . . . She should do exercises. She forced herself to do some, but the queasiness returned, and a lethargy with it. She went back to the mattress and sat down. After a while she found she was crying. After a while she found she had been asleep. She needed to piss. She squatted over the hole and listened to her urine fall into it. There was nothing to clean herself with. She came back to the bed and sat down on it, stretching out her legs, holding her ankles in her hands. It was utterly silent.

She turned to look at the man; he was watching her. It made her start. He looked away at once. He still lay half-propped up against the wall, uncomfortable, but relaxed.

"Are you thirsty?" she asked.

"Thank you," he said. Here where nothing was familiar and time was broken off from the past, his soft, light voice was welcome in its familiarity. She poured him a cup full and gave it to him. He managed it much more steadily, sitting up to drink. "Thank you," he whispered again, giving her back the cup.

"How's your head?"

He put up his hand to the swelling, winced, and sat back.

"One of them had a stick," she said, seeing it in a flash in the jumble of her memories—"a priest's staff. You jumped the other one."

"They took my gun," he said. "Festival." He kept his eyes closed.

"I got tangled in those damn clothes. I couldn't help you at all. Listen. Was there a noise, an explosion?"

"Yes. Diversion, maybe."

"Who do you think these boys are?"

"Revolutionaries. Or . . ."

"You said you thought the Gatayan government was in on it."

"I don't know," he murmured.

"You were right, I was wrong, I'm sorry," she said with a sense of virtue at remembering to make amends.

He moved his hand very slightly in an it-doesn't-matter gesture.

"Are you still seeing double?"

He did not answer; he was phasing out again.

She was standing, trying to remember Selish breathing exercises, when the door crashed and clanged, and the same three men were there, two with guns, all young, black-skinned, short-haired, very nervous. The lead one stooped to set a tray down on the floor, and without the least premeditation Solly stepped on his hand and brought her weight down on it. "You wait!" she said. She was staring straight into the faces and gun muzzles of the other two. "Just wait a moment, listen! He has a head injury, we need a doctor, we need more water, I can't even clean his wound, there's no toilet paper, who the hell are you people anyway?"

The one she had stomped was shouting, "Get off! Lady to get off my hand!" but the others heard her. She lifted her foot and got out of his way as he came up fast, backing into his buddies with the guns. "All right, Lady, we are sorry to have trouble," he said, tears in his eyes, cradling his hand. "We are Patriots. You send messish to this Pretender, like our messish. Nobody is to hurt. All right?" He kept backing up, and one of the gunmen swung the door to. Crash, rattle.

She drew a deep breath and turned. Teyeo was watching her. "That was dangerous," he said, smiling very slightly.

"I know it was," she said, breathing hard. "It was stupid. I can't get hold of myself.
I feel like pieces of me. But they shove stuff in and run, damn it! We have to have
some water!" She was in tears, the way she always was for a moment after violence or
a quarrel. "Let's see, what have they brought this time." She lifted the tray up onto
the mattress; like the other, in a ridiculous semblance of service in a hotel or a house
with slaves, it was covered with a cloth. "All the comforts," she murmured. Under
the cloth was a heap of sweet pastries, a little plastic hand mirror, a comb, a tiny pot
of something that smelled like decayed flowers, and a box of what she identified after a while as Gatayan tampons.

"It's things for the lady," she said, "God damn them, the stupid Goddamn pricks!
A mirror!" She flung the thing across the room. "Of course I can't last a day without
looking in the mirror! God *damn* them!" She flung everything else but the pastries
after the mirror, knowing as she did so that she would pick up the tampons and keep
them under the mattress and, oh, God forbid, use them if she had to, if they had to
stay here, how long would it be? ten days or more—"Oh, God," she said again. She
got up and picked everything up, put the mirror and the little pot, the empty water
jug and the fruit skins from the last meal, onto one of the trays and set it beside the
door. "Garbage," she said in Voe Dean. Her outburst, she realised, had been in another language; Alterran, probably. "Have you any idea," she said, sitting down on
the mattress again, "how hard you people make it to be a woman? You could turn a
woman against being one!"

"I think they meant well," Teyeo said. She realised that there was not the faintest
shade of mockery, even of amusement in his voice. If he was enjoying her shame, he
was ashamed to show her that he was. "I think they're amateurs," he said.

After a while she said, "That could be bad."

"It might." He had sat up and was gingerly feeling the knot on his head. His
coarse, heavy hair was blood-caked all around it. "Kidnapping," he said. "Ransom
demands. Not assassins. They didn't have guns. Couldn't have got in with guns. I
had to give up mine."

"You mean these aren't the ones you were warned about?"

"I don't know." His explorations caused him a shiver of pain, and he desisted.
"Are we very short of water?"

She brought him another cupful. "Too short for washing. A stupid Goddamn
mirror when what we need is water!"

He thanked her and drank and sat back, nursing the last swallows in the cup.
"They didn't plan to take me," he said.

She thought about it and nodded. "Afraid you'd identify them?"

"If they had a place for me, they wouldn't put me in with a lady." He spoke without irony. "They had this ready for you. It must be somewhere in the city."

She nodded. "The car ride was half an hour or less. My head was in a bag,
though."

"They've sent a message to the Palace. They got no reply, or an unsatisfactory
one. They want a message from you."

"To convince the government they really have me? Why do they need convincing?"

They were both silent.

"I'm sorry," he said, "I can't think." He lay back. Feeling tired, low, edgy after her adrenaline rush, she lay down alongside him. She had rolled up the Goddess's skirt to make a pillow; he had none. The blanket lay across their legs.

"Pillow," she said. "More blankets. Soap. What else?"

"Key," he murmured.

They lay side by side in the silence and the faint unvarying light.

Next morning about eight, according to Solly's watch, the Patriots came into the room, four of them. Two stood on guard at the door with their guns ready; the other two stood uncomfortably in what floor space was left, looking down at their captives, both of whom sat cross-legged on the mattress. The new spokesman spoke better Voe Dean than the others. He said they were very sorry to cause the lady discomfort and would do what they could to make it comfortable for her, and she must be patient and write a message by hand to the Pretender King, explaining that she would be set free unharmed as soon as the King commanded the Council to rescind their treaty with Voe Deo.

"He won't," she said. "They won't let him."

"Please do not discuss," the man said with frantic harshness. "This is writing materials. This is the message." He set the papers and a stylo down on the mattress, nervously, as if afraid to get close to her.

She was aware of how Teyeo effaced himself, sitting without a motion, his head lowered, his eyes lowered; the men ignored him.

"If I write this for you, I want water, a lot of water, and soap and blankets and toilet paper and pillows and a doctor, and I want somebody to come when I knock on that door, and I want some decent clothes. Warm clothes. Men's clothes."

"No doctor!" the man said. "Write it! Please! Now!" He was jumpy, twitchy, she dared push him no further. She read their statement, copied it out in her large, childish scrawl—she seldom handwrote anything—and handed both to the spokesman. He glanced over it and without a word hurried the other men out. Clash went the door.

"Should I have refused?"

"I don't think so," Teyeo said. He stood up and stretched, but sat down again looking dizzy. "You bargain well," he said.

"We'll see what we get. Oh, God. What is going *on?*"

"Maybe," he said slowly, "Gatay is unwilling to yield to these demands. But when Voe Deo—and your Ekumen—get word of it, they'll put pressure on Gatay."

"I wish they'd get moving. I suppose Gatay is horribly embarrassed, saving face by trying to conceal the whole thing—is that likely? How long can they keep it up? What about your people? Won't they be hunting for you?"

"No doubt," he said, in his polite way.

It was curious how his stiff manner, his manners, which had always shunted her aside, cut her out, here had quite another effect: his restraint and formality reassured her that she was still part of the world outside this room, from which they came and to which they would return, a world where people lived long lives.

What did long life matter? she asked herself, and didn't know. It was nothing she had ever thought about before. But these young Patriots lived in a world of short lives. Demands, violence, immediacy, and death, for what? for a bigotry, a hatred, a rush of power.

"Whenever they leave," she said in a low voice, "I get really frightened."

Teyeo cleared his throat and said, "So do I."

Exercises.

"Take hold—no, take *hold*, I'm not made of glass!—Now—"

"Ha!" he said, with his flashing grin of excitement, as she showed him the break, and he in turn repeated it, breaking from her.

"All right, now you'd be waiting—here"—thump—"see?"

"Ai!"

"I'm sorry—I'm sorry, Teyeo—I didn't think about your head—Are you all right? I'm really sorry—"

"Oh, Kamye," he said, sitting up and holding his black, narrow head between his hands. He drew several deep breaths. She knelt penitent and anxious.

"That's," he said, and breathed some more, "that's not, not fair play."

"No of course it's not, it's aiji—all's fair in love and war, they say that on Terra—Really, I'm sorry, I'm terribly sorry, that was so stupid of me!"

He laughed, a kind of broken and desperate laugh, shook his head, shook it again. "Show me," he said. "I don't know what you did."

Exercises.

"What do you do with your mind?"

"Nothing."

"You just let it wander?"

"No. Am I and my mind different beings?"

"So . . . you don't focus on something? You just wander with it?"

"No."

"So you *don't* let it wander."

"Who?" he said, rather testily.

A pause.

"Do you think about—"

"No," he said. "Be still."

A very long pause, maybe a quarter hour.

"Teyeo, I can't. I itch. My mind itches. How long have you been doing this?"

A pause, a reluctant answer: "Since I was two."

He broke his utterly relaxed motionless pose, bent his head to stretch his neck and shoulder muscles. She watched him.

"I keep thinking about long life, about living long," she said. "I don't mean just being alive a long time, hell, I've been alive about eleven hundred years, what does that mean, nothing. I mean . . . Something about thinking of life as long makes a difference. Like having kids does. Even thinking about having kids. It's like it changes some balance. It's funny I keep thinking about that now, when my chances for a long life have kind of taken a steep fall. . . ."

He said nothing. He was able to say nothing in a way that allowed her to go on talking. He was one of the least talkative men she had ever known. Most men were so wordy. She was fairly wordy herself. He was quiet. She wished she knew how to be quiet.

"It's just practice, isn't it?" she asked. "Just sitting there."

He nodded.

"Years and years and years of practice. . . . Oh, God. Maybe . . ."

"No, no," he said, taking her thought immediately.

"But why don't they *do* something? What are they *waiting* for? It's been nine *days*!"

From the beginning, by unplanned, unspoken agreement, the room had been divided in two: the line ran down the middle of the mattress and across to the facing wall. The door was on her side, the left; the shit-hole was on his side, the right. Any invasion of the other's space was requested by some almost invisible cue and permitted the same way. When one of them used the shit-hole the other unobtrusively faced away. When they had enough water to take cat-baths, which was seldom, the same arrangement held. The line down the middle of the mattress was absolute. Their voices crossed it, and the sounds and smells of their bodies. Sometimes she felt his warmth; Werelian body temperature was somewhat higher than hers, and in the dank, still air she felt that faint radiance as he slept. But they never crossed the line, not by a finger, not in the deepest sleep.

Solly thought about this, finding it, in some moments, quite funny. At other moments it seemed stupid and perverse. Couldn't they both use some human comfort? The only time she had touched him was the first day, when she had helped him get onto the mattress, and then when they had enough water she had cleaned his scalp wound and little by little washed the clotted, stinking blood out of his hair, using the comb, which had after all been a good thing to have, and pieces of the Goddess's skirt, an invaluable source of washcloths and bandages. Then once his head healed, they practiced aiji daily; but aiji had an impersonal, ritual purity to its clasps and grips that was a long way from creature comfort. The rest of the time his bodily presence was clearly, invariably uninvasive and untouchable.

He was only maintaining, under incredibly difficult circumstances, the rigid restraint he had always shown. Not just he, but Rewe, too; all of them, all of them but Batikam; and yet was Batikam's instant yielding to her whim and desire the true contact she had thought it? She thought of the fear in his eyes, that last night. Not restraint, but constraint.

It was the mentality of a slave society: slaves and masters caught in the same trap of radical distrust and self-protection.

"Teyeo," she said, "I don't understand slavery. Let me say what I mean," though he had shown no sign of interruption or protest, merely civil attention. "I mean, I do understand how a social institution comes about and how an individual is simply part of it—I'm not saying why don't you agree with me in seeing it as wicked and unprofitable, I'm not asking you to defend it or renounce it. I'm trying to understand what it feels like to believe that two-thirds of the human beings in your world are actually, rightfully your property. Five-sixths, in fact, including women of your caste."

After a while he said, "My family owns about twenty-five assets."

"Don't quibble."

He accepted the reproof.

"It seems to me that you cut off human contact. You don't touch slaves and slaves don't touch you, in the way human beings ought to touch, in mutuality. You have to keep yourselves separate, always working to maintain that boundary. Because it isn't a natural boundary—it's totally artificial, manmade. I can't tell owners and assets apart physically. Can you?"

"Mostly."

"By cultural, behavioral clues—right?"

After thinking a while, he nodded.

"You are the same species, race, people, exactly the same in every way, with a slight selection towards color. If you brought up an asset child as an owner it would *be* an owner in every respect, and vice versa. So you spend your lives keeping up this tremendous division that doesn't exist. What I don't understand is how you can fail to see how appallingly wasteful it is. I don't mean economically!"

"In the war," he said, and then there was a very long pause; though Solly had a lot more to say, she waited, curious. "I was on Yeowe," he said, "you know, in the civil war."

That's where you got all those scars and dents, she thought; for however scrupulously she averted her eyes, it was impossible not to be familiar with his spare, onyx body by now, and she knew that in aiji he had to favor his left arm, which had a considerable chunk out of it just above the bicep.

"The slaves of the Colonies revolted, you know, some of them at first, then all of them. Nearly all. So we Army men there were all owners. We couldn't send asset soldiers, they might defect. We were all veots and volunteers. Owners fighting assets. I was fighting my equals. I learned that pretty soon. Later on I learned I was fighting my superiors. They defeated us."

"But that—" Solly said, and stopped; she did not know what to say.

"They defeated us from beginning to end," he said. "Partly because my government didn't understand that they could. That they fought better and harder and more intelligently and more bravely than we did."

"Because they were fighting for their freedom!"

"Maybe so," he said in his polite way.

"So . . ."

"I wanted to tell you that I respect the people I fought."

"I know so little about war, about fighting," she said, with a mixture of contrition and irritation. "Nothing, really. I was on Kheakh, but that wasn't war, it was racial suicide, mass slaughter of a biosphere. I guess there's a difference. . . . That was when the Ekumen finally decided on the Arms Convention, you know. Because of Orint and then Kheakh destroying themselves. The Terrans had been pushing for the Convention for ages. Having nearly committed suicide themselves a while back. I'm half-Terran. My ancestors rushed around their planet slaughtering each other. For millennia. They were masters and slaves, too, some of them, a lot of them. . . . But I don't know if the Arms Convention was a good idea. If it's right. Who are we to tell anybody what to do and not to do? The idea of the Ekumen was to offer a way. To open it. Not to bar it to anybody."

He listened intently, but said nothing until after some while. "We learn to . . . close ranks. Always. You're right, I think, it wastes . . . energy, the spirit. You are open."

His words cost him so much, she thought, not like hers that just came dancing out of the air and went back into it. He spoke from his marrow. It made what he said a solemn compliment, which she accepted gratefully, for as the days went on she realized occasionally how much confidence she had lost and kept losing: self-confidence, confidence that they would be ransomed, rescued, that they would get out of this room, that they would get out of it alive.

"Was the war very brutal?"

"Yes," he said. "I can't . . . I've never been able to—to see it—Only something comes like a flash—" He held his hands up as if to shield his eyes. Then he glanced at her, wary. His apparently cast-iron self-respect was, she knew now, vulnerable in many places.

"Things from Kheakh that I didn't even know I saw, they come that way," she said. "At night." And after a while, "How long were you there?"

"A little over seven years."

She winced. "Were you lucky?"

It was a queer question, not coming out the way she meant, but he took it at value. "Yes," he said. "Always. The men I went there with were killed. Most of them in the first few years. We lost three hundred thousand men on Yeowe. They never talk about it. Two-thirds of the veot men in Voe Deo were killed. If it was lucky to live, I was lucky." He looked down at his clasped hands, locked into himself.

After a while she said softly, "I hope you still are."

He said nothing.

"How long has it been?" he asked, and she said, clearing her throat, after an automatic glance at her watch, "Sixty hours."

Their captors had not come yesterday at what had become a regular time, about eight in the morning. Nor had they come this morning.

With nothing left to eat and now no water left, they had grown increasingly silent and inert. It was hours since either had said anything. He had put off asking the time as long as he could prevent himself.

"This is horrible," she said, "this is so horrible. I keep thinking . . ."

"They won't abandon you," he said. "They feel a responsibility."

"Because I'm a woman?"

"Partly."

"Shit."

He remembered that in the other life her coarseness had offended him.

"They've been taken, shot. Nobody bothered to find out where they were keeping us," she said.

Having thought the same thing several hundred times, he had nothing to say.

"It's just such a horrible *place* to die," she said. "It's sordid. I stink. I've stunk for twenty days. Now I have diarrhea because I'm scared. But I can't shit anything. I'm thirsty and I can't drink."

"Solly," he said sharply. It was the first time he had spoken her name. "Be still. Hold fast."

She stared at him.

"Hold fast to what?"

He did not answer at once and she said, "You won't let me touch you!"

"Not to me—"

"Then to what? There isn't anything!" He thought she was going to cry, but she stood up, took the empty tray, and beat it against the door till it smashed into fragments of wicker and dust. "Come! God damn you! Come, you bastards!" she shouted. "Let us out of here!"

After that she sat down again on the mattress. "Well," she said.

"Listen," he said.

They had heard it before: no city sounds came down to this cellar, wherever it was, but this was something bigger, explosions, they both thought.

The door rattled.

They were both afoot when it opened: not with the usual clash and clang, but slowly. A man waited outside; two men came in. One, armed, they had never seen; the other, the tough-faced young man they called the spokesman, looked as if he had been running or fighting, dusty, worn-out, a little dazed. He closed the door. He had some papers in his hand. The four of them stared at one another in silence for a minute.

"Water," Solly said. "You bastards!"

"Lady," the spokesman said, "I'm sorry." He was not listening to her. His eyes were not on her. He was looking at Teyeo, for the first time. "There is a lot of fighting," he said.

"Who's fighting?" Teyeo asked, hearing himself drop into the even tone of authority, and the young man respond to it as automatically: "Voe Deo. They sent troops. After the funeral, they said they would send troops unless we surrendered. They came yesterday. They go through the city killing. They know all the Old Believer centers. Some of ours." He had a bewildered, accusing note in his voice.

"What funeral?" Solly said.

When he did not answer, Teyeo repeated it: "What funeral?"

"The lady's funeral, yours. Here—I brought net prints—A state funeral. They said you died in the explosion."

"What Goddamned explosion?" Solly said in her hoarse, parched voice, and this time he answered her: "At the Festival. The Old Believers. The fire, Tual's fire, there were explosives in it. Only it went off too soon. We knew their plan. We rescued you from that, Lady," he said, suddenly turning to her with that same accusatory tone.

"Rescued me, you asshole!" she shouted, and Teyeo's dry lips split in a startled laugh, which he repressed at once.

"Give me those," he said, and the young man handed him the papers.

"Get us water!" Solly said.

"Stay here, please. We need to talk," Teyeo said, instinctively holding on to his ascendancy. He sat down on the mattress with the net prints. Within a few minutes he and Solly had scanned the reports of the shocking disruption of the Festival of Forgiveness, the lamentable death of the Envoy of the Ekumen in a terrorist act executed by the cult of Old Believers, the brief mention of the death of a Voe Dean Embassy guard in the explosion, which had killed over seventy priests and onlookers, the long descriptions of the state funeral, reports of unrest, terrorism, reprisals, then reports of the Palace gratefully accepting offers of assistance from Voe Deo in cleaning out the cancer of terrorism. . . .

"So," he said finally. "You never heard from the Palace. Why did you keep us alive?"

Solly looked as if she thought the question lacked tact, but the spokesman answered with equal bluntness, "We thought your country would ransom you."

"They will," Teyeo said. "Only you have to keep your government from knowing we're alive. If you—"

"Wait," Solly said, touching his hand. "Hold on. I want to think about this stuff. You'd better not leave the Ekumen out of the discussion. But getting in touch with them is the tricky bit."

"If there are Voe Dean troops here, all I need is to get a message to anyone in my command, or the Embassy Guards."

Her hand was still on his, with a warning pressure. She shook the other one at the spokesman, finger outstretched:"You kidnapped an Envoy of the Ekumen, you asshole! Now you have to do the thinking you didn't do ahead of time. And I do too, because I don't want to get blown away by your Goddamned little government for turning up alive and embarrassing them. Where are you hiding, anyhow? Is there any chance of us getting out of this room, at least?"

The man, with that edgy, frantic look, shook his head. "We are all down here now," he said. "Most of the time. You stay here safe."

"Yes, you'd better keep your passports safe!" Solly said. "Bring us some water, damn it! Let us talk a while. Come back in an hour."

The young man leaned towards her suddenly, his face contorted. "What the hell kind of lady you are," he said. "You foreign filthy stinking cunt."

Teyeo was on his feet, but her grip on his hand had tightened: after a moment of silence, the spokesman and the other man turned to the door, rattled the lock, and were let out.

"Ouf," she said, looking dazed.

"Don't," he said, "don't—" He did not know how to say it. "They don't understand," he said. "It's better if I talk."

"Of course. Women don't give orders. Women don't talk. Shitheads! I thought you said they felt so responsible for me!"

"They do," he said. "But they're young men. Fanatics. Very frightened." And you talk to them as if they were assets, he thought, but did not say.

"Well so am I frightened!" she said, with a little spurt of tears. She wiped her eyes and sat down again among the papers. "God," she said. "We've been dead for twenty days. Buried for fifteen. Who do you think they buried?"

Her grip was powerful; his wrist and hand hurt. He massaged the place gently, watching her.

"Thank you," he said. "I would have hit him."

"Oh, I know. Goddamn chivalry. And the one with the gun would have blown your head off. Listen, Teyeo. Are you sure all you have to do is get word to somebody in the Army or the Guard?"

"Yes, of course."

"You're sure your country isn't playing the same game as Gatay?"

He stared at her. As he understood her, slowly the anger he had stifled and denied, all these interminable days of imprisonment with her, rose in him, a fiery flood of resentment, hatred, and contempt.

He was unable to speak, afraid he would speak to her as the young Patriot had done.

He went around to his side of the room and sat on his side of the mattress, somewhat turned from her. He sat cross-legged, one hand lying lightly in the other.

She said some other things. He did not listen or reply.

After a while she said, "We're supposed to be talking, Teyeo. We've only got an hour. I think those kids might do what we tell them, if we tell them something plausible—something that'll work."

He would not answer. He bit his lip and held still.

"Teyeo, what did I say? I said something wrong. I don't know what it was. I'm sorry."

"They would—" He struggled to control his lips and voice. "They would not betray us."

"Who? The Patriots?"

He did not answer.

"Voe Deo, you mean? Wouldn't betray us?"

In the pause that followed her gentle, incredulous question, he knew that she was right; that it was all collusion among the powers of the world; that his loyalty to his country and service was wasted, as futile as the rest of his life. She went on talking, palliating, saying he might very well be right. He put his head into his hands, longing for tears, dry as stone.

She crossed the line. He felt her hand on his shoulder.

"Teyeo, I am very sorry," she said. "I didn't mean to insult you! I honor you. You've been all my hope and help."

"It doesn't matter," he said. "If I—If we had some water."

She leapt up and battered on the door with her fists and a sandal.

"Bastards, bastards," she shouted.

Teyeo got up and walked, three steps and turn, three steps and turn, and halted on his side of the room. "If you're right," he said, speaking slowly and formally, "we and our captors are in danger not only from Gatay but from my own people, who may . . . who have been furthering these anti-Government factions, in order to make an excuse to bring troops here . . . to *pacify* Gatay. That's why they know where to find the factionalists. We are . . . we're lucky our group were . . . were genuine."

She watched him with a tenderness that he found irrelevant.

"What we don't know," he said, "is what side the Ekumen will take. That is . . . There really is only one side."

"No, there's ours, too. The underdogs. If the Embassy sees Voe Deo pulling a takeover of Gatay, they won't interfere, but they won't approve. Especially if it involves as much repression as it seems to."

"The violence is only against the anti-Ekumen factions."

"They still won't approve. And if they find out I'm alive, they're going to be quite pissed at the people who claimed I went up in a bonfire. Our problem is how to get word to them. I was the only person representing the Ekumen in Gatay. Who'd be a safe channel?"

"Any of my men. But . . ."

"They'll have been sent back; why keep Embassy Guards here when the Envoy's dead and buried? I suppose we could try. Ask the boys to try, that is." Presently she said wistfully, "I don't suppose they'd just let us go—in disguise? It would be the safest for them."

"There is an ocean," Teyeo said.

She beat her head. "Oh, why don't they bring some *water*. . . ." Her voice was like paper sliding on paper. He was ashamed of his anger, his grief, himself. He wanted to tell her that she had been a help and hope to him too, that he honored her, that she was brave beyond belief; but none of the words would come. He felt empty, worn-out. He felt old. If only they would bring water!

Water was given them at last; some food, not much and not fresh. Clearly their captors were in hiding and under duress. The spokesman—he gave them his war-name, Kergat, Gatayan for Liberty—told them that whole neighborhoods had been cleared out, set afire, that Voe Dean troops were in control of most of the city including the Palace, and that almost none of this was being reported in the net. "When this is over Voe Deo will own my country," he said with disbelieving fury.

"Not for long," Teyeo said.

"Who can defeat them?" the young man said.

"Yeowe. The idea of Yeowe."

Both Kergat and Solly stared at him.

"Revolution," he said. "How long before Werel becomes New Yeowe?"

"The assets?" Kergat said, as if Teyeo had suggested a revolt of cattle or of flies. "They'll never organise."

"Look out when they do," Teyeo said mildly.

"You don't have any assets in your group?" Solly asked Kergat, amazed. He did not bother to answer. He had classed her as an asset, Teyeo saw. He understood why; he had done so himself, in the other life, when such distinctions made sense.

"Your bondswoman, Rewe," he asked Solly—"was she a friend?"

"Yes," Solly said, then, "No. I wanted her to be."

"The makil?"

After a pause she said, "I think so."

"Is he still here?"

She shook her head. "The troupe was going on with their tour, a few days after the Festival."

"Travel has been restricted since the Festival," Kergat said. "Only government and troops."

"He's Voe Dean. If he's still here, they'll probably send him and his troupe home. Try and contact him, Kergat."

"A makil?" the young man said, with that same distaste and incredulity. "One of your Voe Dean homosexual clowns?"

Teyeo shot a glance at Solly: Patience, patience.

"Bisexual actors," Solly said, disregarding him, but fortunately Kergat was determined to disregard her.

"A clever man," Teyeo said, "with connections. He could help us. You and us. It could be worth it. If he's still here. We must make haste."

"Why would he help us? He is Voe Dean."

"An asset, not a citizen," Teyeo said. "And a member of Hame, the asset underground, which works against the government of Voe Deo. The Ekumen admits the legitimacy of Hame. He'll report to the Embassy that a Patriot group has rescued the Envoy and is holding her safe, in hiding, in extreme danger. The Ekumen, I think, will act promptly and decisively. Correct, Envoy?"

Suddenly reinstated, Solly gave a short, dignified nod. "But discreetly," she said. "They'll avoid violence, if they can use political coercion."

The young man was trying to get it all into his mind and work it through. Sympathetic to his weariness, distrust, and confusion, Teyeo sat quietly waiting. He noticed that Solly was sitting equally quietly, one hand lying in the other. She was thin and dirty and her unwashed, greasy hair was in a lank braid. She was brave, like a brave mare, all nerve. She would break her heart before she quit.

Kergat asked questions; Teyeo answered them, reasoning and reassuring. Occasionally Solly spoke, and Kergat was now listening to her again, uneasily, not wanting to, not after what he had called her. At last he left, not saying what he intended to do; but he had Batikam's name and an identifying message from Teyeo to the Embassy: "Half-pay veots learn to sing old songs quickly."

"What on earth!" Solly said when Kergat was gone.

"Did you know a man named Old Music, in the Embassy?"

"Ah! Is he a friend of yours?"

"He has been kind."

"He's been here on Werel from the start. A First Observer. Rather a powerful man—Yes, and 'quickly,' all right. . . . My mind really isn't working at all. I wish I could lie down beside a little stream, in a meadow, you know, and drink. All day. Every time I wanted to, just stretch my neck out and slup, slup, slup. . . . Running water . . . In the sunshine . . . Oh God, oh God, sunshine. Teyeo, this is very difficult. This is harder than ever. Thinking that there maybe is really a way out of here. Only not knowing. Trying not to hope and not to not hope. Oh, I am so tired of sitting here!"

"What time is it?"

"Half past twenty. Night. Dark out. Oh God, darkness! Just to be in the darkness . . . Is there any way we could cover up that damned biolume? Partly? To pretend we had night, so we could pretend we had day?"

"If you stood on my shoulders, you could reach it. But how could we fasten a cloth?"

They pondered, staring at the plaque.

"I don't know. Did you notice there's a little patch of it that looks like it's dying? Maybe we don't have to worry about making darkness. If we stay here long enough. Oh, God!"

"Well," he said after a while, curiously self-conscious, "I'm tired." He stood up, stretched, glanced for permission to enter her territory, got a drink of water, returned to his territory, took off his jacket and shoes, by which time her back was turned, took off his trousers, lay down, pulled up the blanket, and said in his mind, "Lord Kamye, let me hold fast to the one noble thing." But he did not sleep.

He heard her slight movements; she pissed, poured a little water, took off her sandals, lay down.

A long time passed.

"Teyeo."

"Yes."

"Do you think . . . that it would be a mistake . . . under the circumstances . . . to make love?"

A pause.

"Not under the circumstances," he said, almost inaudibly. "But—in the other life—"

A pause.

"Short life versus long life," she murmured.

"Yes."

A pause.

"No," he said, and turned to her. "No, that's wrong." They reached out to each other. They clasped each other, cleaved together, in blind haste, greed, need, crying out together the name of God in their different languages and then like animals in the wordless voice. They huddled together, spent, sticky, sweaty, exhausted, reviving, rejoined, reborn in the body's tenderness, in the endless exploration, the ancient discovery, the long flight to the new world.

He woke slowly, in ease and luxury. They were entangled, his face was against her arm and breast; she was stroking his hair, sometimes his neck and shoulder. He lay for a long time aware only of that lazy rhythm and the cool of her skin against his face, under his hand, against his leg.

"Now I know," she said, her half whisper deep in her chest, near his ear, "that I don't know you. Now I need to know you." She bent forward to touch his face with her lips and cheek.

"What do you want to know?"

"Everything. Tell me who Teyeo is. . . ."

"I don't know," he said. "A man who holds you dear."

"Oh, God," she said, hiding her face for a moment in the rough, smelly blanket.

"Who is God?" he asked sleepily. They spoke Voe Dean, but she usually swore in

Terran or Alterran; in this case it had been Alterran, *Seyt*, so he asked, "Who is Seyt?"

"Oh—Tual—Kamye—what have you. I just say it. It's just bad language. Do you believe in one of them? I'm sorry! I feel like such an oaf with you, Teyeo. Blundering into your soul, invading you—We *are* invaders, no matter how pacifist and priggish we are—"

"Must I love the whole Ekumen?" he asked, beginning to stroke her breasts, feeling her tremor of desire and his own.

"Yes," she said, "yes, yes."

It was curious, Teyeo thought, how little sex changed anything. Everything was the same, a little easier, less embarrassment and inhibition; and there was a certain and lovely source of pleasure for them, when they had enough water and food to have enough vitality to make love. But the only thing that was truly different was something he had no word for. Sex, comfort, tenderness, love, trust, no word was the right word, the whole word. It was utterly intimate, hidden in the mutuality of their bodies, and it changed nothing in their circumstances, nothing in the world, even the tiny wretched world of their imprisonment. They were still trapped. They were getting very tired and were hungry most of the time. They were increasingly afraid of their increasingly desperate captors.

"I will be a lady," Solly said. "A good girl. Tell me how, Teyeo."

"I don't want you to give in," he said, so fiercely, with tears in his eyes, that she went to him and held him in her arms.

"Hold fast," he said.

"I will," she said. But when Kergat or the others came in she was sedate and modest, letting the men talk, keeping her eyes down. He could not bear to see her so, and knew she was right to do so.

The doorlock rattled, the door clashed, bringing him up out of a wretched, thirsty sleep. It was night or very early morning. He and Solly had been sleeping close entangled for the warmth and comfort of it; and seeing Kergat's face now he was deeply afraid. This was what he had feared, to show, to prove her sexual vulnerability. She was still only half-awake, clinging to him.

Another man had come in. Kergat said nothing. It took Teyeo some time to recognise the second man as Batikam.

When he did, his mind remained quite blank. He managed to say the makil's name. Nothing else.

"Batikam?" Solly croaked. "Oh, my God!"

"This is an interesting moment," Batikam said in his warm actor's voice. He was not transvestite, Teyeo saw, but wore Gatayan men's clothing. "I meant to rescue you, not to embarrass you, Envoy, Rega. Shall we get on with it?"

Teyeo had scrambled up and was pulling on his filthy trousers. Solly had slept in the ragged pants their captors had given her. They both had kept on their shirts for warmth.

"Did you contact the Embassy, Batikam?" she was asking, her voice shaking, as she pulled on her sandals.

"Oh, yes. I've been there and come back, indeed. Sorry it took so long. I don't think I quite realised your situation here."

"Kergat has done his best for us," Teyeo said at once, stiffly.

"I can see that. At considerable risk. I think the risk from now on is low. That is . . ." He looked straight at Teyeo. "Rega, how do you feel about putting yourself in the hands of Hame?" he said. "Any problems with that?"

"Don't, Batikam," Solly said. "Trust him!"

Teyeo tied his shoe, straightened up, and said, "We are all in the hands of the Lord Kamye."

Batikam laughed, the beautiful full laugh they remembered.

"In the Lord's hands, then," he said, and led them out of the room.

In the *Arkamye* it is said, "To live simply is most complicated."

Solly requested to stay on Werel, and after a recuperative leave at the seashore was sent as Observer to South Voe Deo. Teyeo went straight home, being informed that his father was very ill. After his father's death, he asked for indefinite leave from the Embassy Guard, and stayed on the farm with his mother until her death two years later. He and Solly, a continent apart, met only occasionally during those years.

When his mother died, Teyeo freed his family's assets by act of irrevocable manumission, deeded over their farms to them, sold his now almost valueless property at auction, and went to the capital. He knew Solly was temporarily staying at the Embassy. Old Music told him where to find her. He found her in a small office of the palatial building. She looked older, very elegant. She looked at him with a stricken and yet wary face. She did not come forward to greet or touch him. She said, "Teyeo, I've been asked to be the first Ambassador of the Ekumen to Yeowe."

He stood still.

"Just now—I just came from talking on the ansible with Hain—"

She put her face in her hands. "Oh, my God!" she said.

He said, "My congratulations, truly, Solly."

She suddenly ran at him, threw her arms around him, and cried, "Oh, Teyeo, and your mother died, I never thought, I'm so sorry, I never, I never do—I thought we could—What are you going to do? Are you going to stay there?"

"I sold it," he said. He was enduring rather than returning her embrace. "I thought I might return to the service."

"You sold your *farm?* But I never saw it!"

"I never saw where you were born," he said.

There was a pause. She stood away from him, and they looked at each other.

"You would come?" she said.

"I would," he said.

Several years after Yeowe entered the Ekumen, Mobile Solly Agat Terwa was sent as an Ekumenical liaison to Terra; later she went from there to Hain, where she served with great distinction as a Stabile. In all her travels and posts she was accompanied by her husband, a Werelian army officer, a very handsome man, as reserved as she was outgoing. People who knew them knew their passionate pride and trust in each other. Solly was perhaps the happier person, rewarded and fulfilled in her work; but Teyeo had no regrets. He had lost his world, but he had held fast to the one noble thing.

The cost to be wise

MAUREEN F. MCHUGH

Maureen F. McHugh made her first sale in 1989, and has since made a powerful impression on the SF world with a relatively small body of work, becoming one of today's most respected writers. In 1992, she published one of the year's most widely acclaimed and talked-about first novels, *China Mountain Zhang*, which won the Locus Award for Best First Novel, the Lambda Literary Award, and the James Tiptree Jr. Memorial Award, and was named a *New York Times* Notable Book as well as being a finalist for the Hugo and Nebula Awards. Her other books, including the novels *Half the Day Is Night, Mission Child,* and *Nekropolis,* have been greeted with similar enthusiasm. Her powerful short fiction has appeared in *Asimov's Science Fiction, SCI FICTION, The Magazine of Fantasy and Science Fiction, Starlight, Alternate Warriors, Polyphony, The Infinite Matrix, Killing Me Softly,* and other markets, and has been assembled in a collection called *The Lincoln Train.* She has had stories in our tenth through fourteenth, and our nineteenth and twentieth annual collections. Her most recent book is a major new collection, *Mothers and Other Monsters.* She lives in Twinsburg, Ohio, with her husband, her son, and a golden retriever named Smith.

In the quiet but powerful story that follows, she tells the story of a young woman who learns the painful lesson that wisdom has a price. And that sometimes that price is more than you were willing to *pay.*

i

The sun was up on the snow and everything was bright to look at when the skimmer landed. It landed on the long patch of land behind the schoolhouse, dropping down into the snow like some big bug. I was supposed to be down at the distillery helping my mam but we needed water and I had to get an ice ax so I was outside when the offworlders came.

The skimmer was from Barok. Barok was a city. It was so far away that no one I knew in Sckarline had ever been there (except for the teachers, of course) but for the offworlders the trip was only a few hours. The skimmer came a couple of times a year to bring packages for the teachers.

The skimmer sat there for a moment—long time waiting while nothing happened except people started coming to watch—and then the hatch opened out and an offworlder stepped gingerly out on the snow. The offworlder wasn't a skimmer pilot though, it was a tall, thin boy. I shaded my eyes and watched. My hands were cold but I wanted to see.

The offworlder wore strange colors for the snow. Offworlders always wore unnatural colors. This boy wore purples and oranges and black, all shining as if they were wet and none of them thick enough to keep anyone warm. He stood with his knees stiff and his body rigid because the snow was packed to flat, slick ice by the skimmer and he wasn't sure of his balance. But he was tall and I figured he was as old as I am so it looked odd that he still didn't know how to walk on snow. He was beardless, like a boy. Darker than any of us.

Someone inside the skimmer handed him a bag. It was deep red and shined as if it were hard and wrinkled as if it were felt. My father crossed to the skimmer and took the bag from the boy because it was clear that the boy might fall with it and it made a person uncomfortable to watch him try to balance and carry something.

The dogs were barking, and more Sckarline people were coming because they'd heard the skimmer.

I wanted to see what the bags were made of so I went to the hatch of the skimmer to take something. We didn't get many things from the offworlders because they weren't appropriate, but I liked offworlder things. I couldn't see much inside the skimmer because it was dark and I had been out in the sun, but standing beside the seat where the pilot was sitting was an old white-haired man, all straight-legged and tall. As tall as Ayudesh the teacher, which is to say taller than anyone else I knew. He handed the boy a box, though, not a bag, a bright blue box with a thick white lid. A plastic box. An offworlder box. The boy handed it to me.

"Thanks," the boy said in English. Up close I could see that the boy was really a girl. Offworlders dress the same both ways, and they are so tall it's hard to tell sometimes, but this was a girl with short black hair and skin as dark as wood.

My father put the bag in the big visitors' house and I put the box there, too. It was midday at winterdark, so the sun was a red glow on the horizon. The bag looked black except where it fell into the red square of sunlight from the doorway. It shone like metal. So very fine. Like nothing we had. I touched the bag. It was plastic, too. I liked the feeling of plastic. I liked the sound of the word in lingua. If someday I had a daughter, maybe I'd name her Plastic. It would be a rich name, an exotic name. The teachers wouldn't like it, but it was a name I wished I had.

Ayudesh was walking across the snow to the skimmer when I went back outside. The girl (I hadn't shaken free from thinking of her as a boy) stuck out her hand to him. Should I have shaken her hand? No, she'd had the box, I couldn't have shaken her hand. So I had done it right. Wanji, the other teacher, was coming, too.

I got wood from the pile for the boxstove in the guest house, digging it from under the top wood because the top wood would be damp. It would take a long time to heat up the guest house, so the sooner I got started the sooner the offworlders would be comfortable.

There was a window in the visitor's house, fat-yellow above the purple-white snow.

Inside everyone was sitting around on the floor, talking. None of the teachers were there, were they with the old man? I smelled whisak but I didn't see any, which meant that the men were drinking it outside. I sat down at the edge of the group, where it was dark, next to Dirtha. Dirtha was watching the offworld girl who was shaking her head at Harup to try to tell him she didn't understand what he was asking. Harup pointed at her blue box again. "Can I see it?" he asked. Harup was my father's age so he didn't speak any English.

It was warming up in here, although when the offworlder girl leaned forward and breathed out, her mouth in an O, her breath smoked the air for an instant.

It was too frustrating to watch Harup try to talk to the girl. "What's your kinship?" he asked. "I'm Harup Sckarline." He thumped his chest with his finger. "What's your kinship?" When she shook her head, not understanding all these words, he looked around and grinned. Harup wouldn't stop until he was bored, and that would take a long time.

"I'm sorry," the girl said, "I don't speak your language." She looked unhappy.

Ayudesh would be furious with us if he found out that none of us would try and use our English.

I had to think about how to ask. Then I cleared my throat, so people would know I was going to talk from the back of the group. "He asks what is your name," I said.

The girl's chin came up like a startled animal. "What?" she said.

Maybe I said it wrong? Or my accent was so bad she couldn't understand? I looked at my boots; the stitches around the toes were fraying. They had been my mother's. "Your name," I said to the boots.

The toes twitched a little, sympathetic. Maybe I should have kept quiet.

"My name is Veronique," she said.

"What is she saying?" asked Harup.

"She says her kinship is Veronique," I said.

"That's not a kinship," said Little Shemus. Little Shemus wasn't old enough to have a beard, but he was old enough to be critical of everything.

"Offworlders don't have kinship like we do," I said. "She gave her front name."

"Ask her her kinship name," Little Shemus said.

"She just told you," Ardha said, taking the end of her braid out of her mouth. Ardha was a year younger than me. "They don't have kinship names. Ayudesh doesn't have a kinship name. Wanji doesn't."

"Sure they do," Shemus said. "Their kinship name is Sckarlineclan."

"We give them that name," said Ardha and pursed her round lips. Ardha was always bossy.

"What are they saying?" asked the girl.

"They say, err, they ask, what is your," your what? How would I even ask what her kinship name was in English? There was a word for it, but I couldn't think of it. "Your other name."

She frowned. Her eyebrows were quite black. "You mean my last name? It's Veronique Twombly."

What was so hard about 'last name'? I remembered it as soon as she said it. "Tawomby," I said. "Her kinship is Veronique Tawomby."

"Tawomby," Harup said. "Amazing. It doesn't sound like a word. It sounds made-up, like children do. What's in her box?"

"I know what's in her box," said Erip. Everybody laughed except for Ardha and me. Even Little Sherep laughed and he didn't really understand.

The girl was looking at me to explain.

"He asks inside, the box is." I had gotten tangled up. Questions were hard.

"Is the box inside?" she asked.

I nodded.

"It's inside," she said.

I didn't understand her answer, so I waited for her to explain.

"I don't know what you mean," she said. "Did someone bring the box inside?"

I nodded, because I wasn't sure exactly what she'd said, but she didn't reach for the box or open it or anything. I tried to think of how to say it.

"Inside," Ardha said, tentative. "What is?"

"The box," she said. "Oh wait, you want to know what's in the box?"

Ardha looked at the door so she wouldn't have to look at the offworlder. I wasn't sure so I nodded.

She pulled the box over and opened it up. Something glimmered hard and green and there were red and yellow boxes covered in lingua and she said, "Presents for Ayudesh and Wanji." Everybody stood up to see inside, so I couldn't see, but I heard her say things. The words didn't mean anything. Tea, that I knew. Wanji talked about tea. "These are sweets," I heard her say. "You know, candy." I knew the word 'sweet,' but I didn't know what else she meant. It was so much harder to speak English to her than it was to do it in class with Ayudesh.

Nobody was paying any attention to what she said but me. They didn't care as long as they could see. I wished I could see.

Nobody was even thinking about me, or that if I hadn't been there she never would have opened the box. But that was the way it always was. If I only lived somewhere else, my life would be different. But Sckarline was neither earth nor sky, and I was living my life in-between. People looked and fingered, but she wouldn't let them take things out, not even Harup, who was as tall as she was and a lot stronger. The younger people got bored and sat down and finally I could see Harup poking something with his finger, and the outland girl watching. The she looked at me.

"What's your name?" she asked.

"Me?" I said. "Umm, Janna."

She said my name. "What's your last name, Janna?"

"Sckarline," I said.

"Oh," she said, "like the settlement."

I just nodded.

"What is his name?" She pointed.

"Harup," I said. He looked up and grinned.

"What's your name?" she asked him and I told him what she had said.

"Harup," he said. Then she went around the room, saying everybody's names. It made everyone pleased to be noticed. She was smart that way. And it was easy. Then she tried to remember all their names, which had everyone laughing and correcting her so I didn't have to talk at all.

Ayudesh came in, taller than anyone, and I noticed, for the first time in my life, that he was really an offworlder. Ayudesh had been there all my life, and I knew he was an offworlder, but to me he had always been just Ayudesh.

Then they were talking about me and Ayudesh was just Ayudesh again. "Janna?" he said. "Very good. I'll tell you what, you take care of Veronique, here. You're her translator, all right?"

I was scared, because I really couldn't understand when she talked, but I guessed I was better than anybody else.

Veronique unpacked, which was interesting, but then she just started putting things here and there and everybody else drifted off until it was just her and me.

Veronique did a lot of odd things. She used a lot of water. The first thing I did for her was get water. She followed me out and watched me chip the ice for water and fill the bucket. She fingered the wooden bucket and the rope handle.

She said something I didn't understand because it had 'do' in it and a lot of pronouns and I have trouble following sentences like that. I smiled at her but I think she realized I didn't understand. Her boots were purple. I had never seen purple boots before.

"They look strange," she said. I didn't know what looked strange. "I like your boots," she said, slowly and clearly. I did understand, but then I didn't know what to do, did she want me to give her my boots? They were my mother's old boots and I wouldn't have minded giving them to her except I didn't have anything to take their place.

"It is really cold," she said.

Which seemed very odd to say, except I remembered that offworlders talk about the weather, Ayudesh had made us practice talking about the weather. He said it was something strangers talked about. "It is," I said. "But it will not snow tonight." That was good, it made her happy.

"And it gets dark so early," she said. "It isn't even afternoon and it's like night."

"Where you live, it is cold as this, umm," I hadn't made a question right.

But she understood. "Oh no," she said, "where I live is warm. It is hot, I mean. There is snow only on the mountains."

She wanted to heat the water so I put it on the stove, and then she showed me pictures of her mother and father and her brother at her house. It was summer and they were wearing only little bits of clothes.

Then she showed me a picture of herself and a man with a beard. "That's my boyfriend," she said. "We're getting married."

He looked old. Grown up. In the picture Veronique looked older, too. I looked at her again, not sure how old she was. Maybe older than me? Wanji said offworlders got married when they were older, not like the clans.

"I have boyfriend," I said.

"You do?" She smiled at me. "What's his name?"

"Tuuvin," I said.

"Was he here before?"

I shook my head.

Then she let me see her bag. The dark red one. I loved the color. I stroked it, as slick as leather and shining. "Plastic?" I said.

She nodded.

"I like plastic," I said.

She smiled a little, like I'd said something wrong. But it was so perfect, so even in color.

"Do you want it?" she asked. Which made me think of my boots and whether she had wanted them. I shook my head.

"You can have it," she said. "I can get another one."

"No," I said. "It isn't appropriate."

She laughed, a startled laugh. I didn't understand what I'd done and the feeling that I was foolish sat in my stomach, but I didn't know what was so foolish.

She said something I didn't understand, which made me feel worse. "What did you say?" she said. "'Appropriate'?"

I nodded. "It's not appropriate," I said.

"I don't understand," she said.

Our lessons in appropriate development used lots of English words because it was hard to say these things any other way, so I found the words to tell her came easily. "Plastic," I said, "it's not appropriate. Appropriate technologies are based on the needs and capacities of people, they must be sustainable without outside support. Like the distillery is. Plastic isn't appropriate to Sckarline's economy because we can't create it and it replaces things we can produce, like skin bags." I stroked the bag again. "But I like plastic. It's beautiful."

"Wow," Veronique said. She was looking at me sharp, all alert like a stabros smelling a dog for the first time. Not afraid, but not sure what to think. "To me," she said slowly, "your skin bags are beautiful. The wooden houses," she touched the black slick wood wall, "they are beautiful."

Ayudesh and Wanji were always telling us that offworlders thought our goods were wonderful, but how could anyone look at a skin bag and then look at plastic and not see how brilliant the colors were in plastic? Dye a skin bag red and it still looked like a skin bag, like it came from dirt.

"How long you, um, you do stay?" I asked.

"Fourteen days," she said. "I'm a student, I came with my teacher."

I nodded. "Ayudesh, he is a teacher."

"My teacher, he's a friend of Ayudesh. From years ago," she said. "Have you always lived here? Were you born here?"

"Yes," I said. "I am born here. My mother and father are born in Tentas clan, but they come here."

"Tentas clan is another settlement?" she asked.

I shook my head. "No," I said. "No. Sckarline only is a settlement."

"Then, what is Tentas clan?"

"It is people." I didn't know how to explain clans to her at all. "They have kinship, and they have stabros, and they are together—"

"Stabros, those are animals," she said.

I nodded. "Sckarline, uh . . . is an appropriate technology mission."

"Right, that Ayudesh and Wanji started. Tentas clan is a clan, right?"

I nodded. I was worn out from talking to her.

After that she drank tea and then I took her around to show her Sckarline. It was already almost dark. I showed her the generator where we cooked stabros manure to make electricity. I got a lantern there.

I showed her the stabros pens and the dogs, even though it wasn't really very interesting. Tuuvin was there, and Gerdor, my little uncle, leaning and watching the stabros who were doing nothing but rooting at the mud in the pen and hoping someone would throw them something to eat. The stabros shook their heads and dug with their long front toes.

"This is Tuuvin?" Veronique said.

I was embarrassed. One of the stabros, a gelding with long feathery ears, craned his head toward me. I reached out and pulled on the long guard hairs at the tips of his ears and he lipped at my hand. He had a long purple tongue. He breathed out steam. Their breath always reminded me of the smell of whisak mash.

"Do you ride them?" Veronique asked.

"What?" I asked.

"Do you, um, get on their backs?" She made a person with her fingers walking through the air, then the fingers jumped on the other hand.

"A stabros?" I asked. Tuuvin and Gerdor laughed. "No," I said. "They have no like that. Stabros angry, very much." I pretended to kick. "They have milk, sometimes. And sleds," I said triumphantly, remembering the word.

She leaned on the fence. "They are pretty," she said. "They have pretty eyes. They look so sad with their long drooping ears."

"What?" Tuuvin asked. "What's pretty?"

"She says they have pretty eyes," I said.

Gerdor laughed but Tuuvin and I gave him a sharp look.

The dogs were leaping and barking and clawing at the gate. She stopped and reached a hand out to touch them. "Dogs are from Earth," she said.

"Dogs are *aufwurld*," I said. "Like us. Stabros are *util*."

"What's that mean?" she asked.

"Stabros can eat food that is *aunwurld*," I said. "We can't, dogs can't. But we can eat stabros so they are between."

"Are stabros from Earth?" Veronique asked.

I didn't know, but Tuuvin did, which surprised me. "Stabros are from here," he said. "Ayudesh explained where it all came from, remember? *Util* animals and plants were here but we could use them. *Aunwurld* animals and plants make us sick."

"I know they make us sick," I snapped. But I translated as best I could.

Veronique was looking at the dogs. "Do they bite?" she asked. Bite? "You mean," I clicked my teeth, "like eat? Sometimes. Mostly if they're fighting."

She took her hand back.

"I'll get a puppy," Tuuvin said, and swung a leg over the side of the pen and waded through the dogs. Tuuvin took care of the dogs a lot so he wasn't afraid of them. I didn't like them much. I liked stabros better.

"There's a winter litter?" I said.

"Yeah," he said. "but it hasn't been too cold, they might be okay. If it gets cold we can always eat 'em."

The puppy looked like a little sausage with short arms and legs and a pink nose. Veronique cooed and took it from Tuuvin and cradled it in her arms. She talked to it, but she talked in a funny way, like baby talk, and I couldn't understand anything she said. "What's its name?" she asked.

"Its name?" I said.

"Do you name them?" she asked.

I looked at Tuuvin. Even Tuuvin should have been able to understand that, the first thing anybody learned in lingua was 'What's your name?' But he wasn't paying any attention. I asked him if any of the dogs had names.

He nodded. "Some of them do. The dark male, he's a lead dog, he's called Bigman. And that one is Yellow Dog. The puppies don't have names, though."

"I think this one should have a name," Veronique said, when I told her. "I think he'll be a mighty hunter, so call him Hunter."

I didn't understand what hunting had to do with dogs, and I thought it was a bitch puppy anyway, but I didn't want to embarrass her, so I told Tuuvin. I was afraid he would laugh but he didn't.

"How do you say that in English?" he asked. "Hunter? Okay, I'll remember." He smiled at Veronique and touched the puppy's nose. "Hunter," he said. The puppy licked him with a tiny pink tongue.

Veronique smiled back. And I didn't like it.

Veronique went to find her teacher. I went down to the distillery to tell Mam why I wasn't there helping. Tuuvin followed me down the hill. The distillery stank so it was down below Sckarline in the trees, just above the fields.

He caught me by the waist and I hung there so he could brush his lips across my hair.

"It's too cold out here," I said and broke out of his arms.

"Let's go in the back," he said.

"I've got to tell Mam," I said.

"Once you tell your mam, there'll be all these things to do and we won't get any time together," he said.

"I can't," I said, but I let him make up my mind for me.

We went around the side, tracking through the dry snow where no one much walked, through the lacey wintertrees to the door to the storage in the back. It was as cold in the back as it was outside, and it was dark. It smelled like mash and whisak and the faint charcoal smell of the charred insides of the kegs. Brass whisak, Sckarline whisak.

He boosted me on a stack of kegs and kissed me.

It wasn't that I really cared so much about kissing. It was nice, but Tuuvin would have kissed and kissed for hours if I would let him and if we would ever find a place where we could be alone for hours. Tuuvin would kiss long after my face felt over-used and bruised from kissing. But I just wanted to be with Tuuvin so much. I wanted to talk with him, and have him walk with me. I would let him kiss me if I could whisper to him. I liked the way he pressed against me now, he was warm and I was cold.

He kissed me with little kisses; kiss, kiss, kiss. I liked the little kisses. It was almost like he was talking to me in kisses. Then he kissed me hard, and searched around with his tongue. I never knew what to do with my tongue when he put his in my mouth, so I just kept mine still. I could feel the rough edge of the keg beneath my legs, and if I shifted my weight it rocked on the one below it. I turned my face side-ways to get my nose out of the way and opened my eyes to look past Tuuvin. In the dark I could barely make out Uukraith's eye burned on all the kegs, to keep them from going bad. Uukraith was the door witch. Uukraith's sister Ina took souls from their mother and put them in seeds, put the seed in women to make babies. The kegs were all turned different directions, eyes looking everywhere. I closed mine again. Uukraith was also a virgin.

"Ohhhh, Heth! Eeeuuuu!"

I jumped, but Tuuvin didn't, he just let go of my waist and stepped back and crossed his arms the way he did when he was uncomfortable. The air felt cold where he had just been warm.

My little sister, Bet, shook her butt at us. "Kissy, kissy, kissy," she said. "MAM, JANNA'S BACK IN THE KEGS WITH TUUVIN!"

"Shut up, Bet," I said. Not that she would stop.

"Slobber, slobber," she said, like we were stabros trading cud. She danced around, still shaking her butt. She puckered up her lips and made wet, smacking noises.

"Fucking little bitch," I said.

Tuuvin frowned at me. He liked Bet. She wasn't his little sister.

"MAM," Bet hollered, "JANNA SAID 'FUCKING'!"

"Janna," my mother called, "come here."

I tried to think of what to do to Bet. I'd have liked to slap her silly. But she'd go crying to Mam and I'd really be in trouble. It was just that she thought she was so smart and she was really being so stupid.

Mam was on her high stool, tallying. My mam wore trousers most often, and she was tall and man-faced. Still and all, men liked her. I took after her so I was secretly glad that men watched her walk by, even if she never much noticed.

"Leave your little sister alone," she said.

"Leave her alone!" I said. "She came and found me."

"Don't swear at her. You talk like an old man." Mam was acting like a headman, her voice even and cool.

"If she hadn't come looking—"

"If you had been working as you're supposed to, she'd have had no one to look for, would she."

"I went out to see the visitors," I said. "There are two. An old man and a girl. I helped Da carry their things to the visitors' house."

"So that means it is okay to swear at your sister."

It was the same words we always traded. The same arguments, all worn smooth and shining like the wood of a yoke. The brand for the kegs was heating in the fire and I could smell the tang of hot iron in the dung.

"You treat me like a child," I said.

She didn't even answer, but I knew what she would say, that I acted like a child. As if what Tuuvin and I were doing had anything to do with being a child.

I was so tired of it I thought I would burst.

"Go back to work," Mam said, turning on her stool. Saying, 'this talk is done' with her shoulders and her eyes.

"It's wrong to live this way," I said.

She looked back at me.

"If we lived with the clans, Tuuvin and I could be together."

That made her angry. "This is a better life than the clans," she said. "You don't know what you're talking about. Go back to work."

I didn't say anything. I just hated her. She didn't understand anything. She and my Da hadn't waited until they were old. They hadn't waited for anything, and they'd left their clan to come to Sckarline when it was new. I stood in front of her, making her feel me standing there, all hot and silent.

"Janna," she said, "I'll not put up with your sullenness—" It made her furious when I didn't talk.

So she slapped me, and then I ran out, crying, past Bet who was delighted, and past Tuuvin, who had his mouth open and a stupid look on his face. And I wished they would all disappear.

Veronique sat with Tuuvin and me at dinner in the guesthouse. The guesthouse was full of smoke. We all sat down on the floor with felt and blankets. I looked to see what Veronique would be sitting on and it was wonderful. It was dark, dark blue and clean on the outside, and inside it was red and black squares. I touched it. It had a long metal fastener, a cunning thing that locked teeth together, that Veronique had unfastened so she could sit on the soft red and black inside. Dark on the outside, red on the inside; it was as if it represented some strange offworld beast. My felt blanket was red but it was old and the edges were gray with dirt. Offworlders were so clean, as if they were always new.

Ayudesh was with the old man who had come with Veronique. Wanji was there, but she was being quiet and by herself, the way Wanji did.

Tuuvin had brought the puppy into the guesthouse. "She asked me to," he said when I asked him what he was doing.

"She did not," I said. "People are watching a dog in this house. Besides, you don't understand her when she talks."

"I do, too," he said. "I was in school, too."

I rolled my eyes. He was when he was little but he left as soon as he was old enough to hunt. Men always left as soon as they were old enough to hunt. And he hated it anyway.

Veronique squealed when she saw the puppy and took it from Tuuvin as if it were a baby. Everyone watched out of the corner of their eyes. Ayudesh thought it was funny. We were all supposed to be equal in Sckarline, but Ayudesh was really like a headman.

She put the puppy on her offworld blanket and it rolled over on its back, showing her its tan belly. It would probably pee on her blanket.

My da leaned over. "I hope it isn't dinner." My da hated dog.

"No," I said. "She just likes it."

My dad said to her, "Hie." Then to me he said, "What is she called?"

"Veronique," I said.

"Veronique," he said. Then he pointed to himself. "Guwk."

"Hello Guwk," Veronique said.

"Hello Veronique," said my da, which surprised me because I had never heard him say anything in English before. "Ask her for her cup," he said to me.

She had one; bright yellow and smooth. But my da handled it matter-of-factly, as if he handled beautiful things every day. He had a skin and he poured whisak into her cup. "My wife," he waved at mam, "she makes whisak for Sckarline."

I tried to translate but I didn't know what 'whisak' was in English.

Veronique took the cup. My da held his hand up for her to wait and poured himself a cup. He tossed it back. Then he nodded at her for her to try.

She took a big swallow. She hadn't expected the burn, you could see. She choked and her face got red. Tuuvin patted her on the back while she coughed. "Oh my God," she said. "That's strong!" I didn't think I needed to translate that.

ii

The sound of the guns is like the cracking of whips. Like the snapping of bones. The outrunners for the Scathalos High-on came into Sckarline with a great deal of racket; brass clattering, the men singing and firing their guns into the air. It started the dogs barking and scared our stabros and brought everyone outside.

Scathalos dyed the toes and ridgeline manes of their stabros kracken yellow. They hung brass clappers in the harnesses of their caravan animals and bits of milky blue glass from the harnesses of their dogs. On this sunny day everything winked. Only their milking does were plain, and that's only because even the will of a hunter can't make a doe stabros tractable.

Veronique came out with me. "Who are they?" she asked.

Even after just three days I could understand Veronique a lot better. "They are from a great clan, Scathalos," I said. "They come to buy whisak." We hoped they would buy it. Sometimes, when Scathalos outrunners came, they just took it.

"They're another clan?" she asked. "Where are the women?"

"They're outrunners," I said. "They go out and hunt and trade. Outrunners are not-married men."

"They have a lot of guns," she said.

They had more guns than I had ever seen. Usually when outrunners came they had one or two guns. Guns are hard to get. But it looked as if almost every outrunner had a gun.

"Does Sckarline have guns?" Veronique asked.

"No," I said.

"They're not appropriate, right?"

A lot of people said we should have guns, whether Ayudesh and Wanji thought they were appropriate or not. They had to buy the clips that go with them. Ayudesh said that the offworlders used the need of the clips to control the clans. He said that it wasn't appropriate because we couldn't maintain it ourselves.

My da said that maybe some things we should buy. We bought things from other clans, that was trade. Maybe guns were trade, too.

The dogs nipped at the doe stabros, turning them, making them stop until outrunners could slip hobbles on them. The stabros looked pretty good. They were mostly dun, and the males were heavy in the shoulders, with heads set low and forward on their necks. Better than most of our animals. The long hairs on their ears were braided with red and yellow threads. Handlers unhooked the sleds from the pack stabros.

Two of them found the skimmer tracks beyond the schoolhouse. They stopped and looked around. They saw Veronique. Then another stared at her, measuring her.

"Come with me," I said.

Our dogs barked and their dogs barked. The outrunner men talked loudly. Sckarline people stood at the doors of their houses and didn't talk at all.

"What's wrong?" Veronique asked.

"Come help my mam and me." She would be under the gaze of them in the distillery, too, but I suspected she would be under their gaze anywhere. And this way Mam would be there.

"Scathalos come here for whisak," I said to my mam, even though she could see for herself. Mam was at the door, shading her eyes and watching them settle in. Someone should have been telling them we had people in the guesthouse and offering to put their animals up, but no one was moving.

"Tuuvin is in back," Mam said, pointing with her chin. "Go back and help him."

Tuuvin was hiding the oldest whisak, what was left of the three-year-old brass whisak. Scathalos had come for whisak two years ago and taken what they wanted and left us almost nothing but lame stabros. They said it was because we had favored Toolie Clan in trade. The only reason we had any three-year-old whisak left was because they couldn't tell what was what.

So my da and some of the men had dug a cellar in the distillery. Tuuvin was standing in the cellar, taking kegs he had stacked at the edge and pulling them down. It wasn't very deep, not much over his chest, but the kegs were heavy. I started stacking more for him to hide.

I wondered what the outrunners would do if they caught us at our work. I wondered if Tuuvin was thinking the same thing. We'd hidden some down there in the spring before the stabros went up to summer grazing but then we'd taken some of the oldest kegs to drink when the stabros came back down in the fall.

"Hurry," Tuuvin said softly.

My hands were slick. Veronique started taking kegs, too. She couldn't lift them, so she rolled them on their edge. Her hands were soft and pretty, not used to rough kegs. It seemed like it took a long time. Tuuvin's hands were rough and red. I'd never thought about how hard his hands were. Mine were like his, all red. My hands were ugly compared to Veronique's. Surely he was noticing that, too, since every time Veronique rolled a keg over her hands were right there.

And then the last keg was on the edge. Uukraith's eye looked at me, strangely unaffected. Or maybe amused. Or maybe angry. Da said that spirits do not feel the way we feel. The teachers never said anything at all about spirits, which was how we knew that they didn't listen to them. There was not much space in the cellar, just enough for Tuuvin to stand and maybe a little more.

Tuuvin put his hands on the edge and boosted himself out of the cellar. In front of the store we heard the crack of the door on its hinges and we all three jumped.

Tuuvin slid the wooden cover over the hole in the floor. "Move those," he said, pointing at empty kegs.

I didn't hear voices.

"Are you done yet?" Mam said, startling us again.

"Are they here?" I asked.

"No," she said. "Not yet." She didn't seem afraid. I had seen my mam afraid, but not very often. "What is she doing here?" Mam asked, looking at Veronique.

"I thought she should be here, I mean, I was afraid to leave her by herself."

"She's not a child," Mam said. But she said it mildly, so I knew she didn't really mind. Then Mam helped us stack kegs. We all tried to be quiet but they thumped like hollow drums. They filled the space around us with noise. It seemed to me that the outrunners could hear us thumping away from outside. I kept looking at Mam, who was stacking kegs as if we hid whisak all the time. Tuuvin was nervous, too. His shoulders were tense. I almost said to him, 'you're up around the ears, boy,' the way the hunters did, but right now I didn't think it would make him smile.

Mam scuffed the dirt around the kegs.

"Will they find them?" I asked.

Mam shrugged. "We'll see."

There was a lot to do to get ready for the outrunners besides hiding the best whisak. Mam had us count the kegs, even Veronique. Then when we all three finally agreed on a number she wrote it in her tally book. "So we know how much we sell," she said.

We were just finishing counting when outrunners came with Ayudesh. They came into the front. First the wind like a wild dog sliding around the door and making the fires all sway. Then Ayudesh and then the outrunners. The outrunners looked short compared to Ayudesh. And they looked even harder than we did. Their cheeks were winter red. Their felts were all dark with dirt, like they'd been out for a long time.

"Hie," said one of the men, seeing my mother. They all grinned. People always seemed surprised that they were going to trade with my mam. The outrunners already smelled of whisak so people had finally made them welcome. Or maybe someone had the sense to realize that if they gave them drink we'd have time to get things ready. Maybe my da.

My mam stood as she always did, with her arms crossed, tall as any of them. Waiting them out.

"What's this," said the man, looking around. "Eh? What's this? It stinks in here." The distillery always stank.

They walked around, looked at the kegs, poked at the copper tubing and the still. One stuck his finger under the drip and tasted the raw stuff and grimaced. Ayudesh looked uncomfortable, but the teachers always said that the distillery was ours and they didn't interfere with how we ran it. Mam was in charge here.

Mam just stood and let them walk all around her. She didn't turn her head to watch them.

They picked up the brand. "What's this?" the man said again.

"We mark all our kegs with the eye of Uukraith," Mam said.

"Woman's work," he said.

He stopped and looked at Veronique. He studied her for a moment, then frowned. "You're no boy," he said.

Veronique looked at me, the whites of her eyes bright even in the dimness, but she didn't say anything.

He grinned and laughed. The other two outrunners crowded close to her and fingered the slick fabric of her sleeve, touched her hair. Veronique pulled away.

The first outrunner got bored and walked around the room some more.

He tapped a keg. Not like Mam thumped them, listening, but just as if everything here were his. He had dirty brown hair on the backs of his hands. Everywhere I looked I was seeing people's hands. I didn't like the way he put his hands on things.

Then he pointed to a keg, not the one he was tapping on but a different one, and one of the other men picked it up. "Is it good?" he asked.

My mam shrugged.

He didn't like that. He took two steps forward and hit her across the face. I looked at the black packed dirt floor.

Ayudesh made a noise.

"It's good," my mam said. I looked up and she had a red mark on the side of her face. Ayudesh looked as if he would speak but he didn't.

The outrunner grabbed her braid—she flinched as he reached past her face—and yanked her head. "It's good, woman?" he asked.

"Yes," she said, her voice coming almost airless, like she could not breathe.

He yanked her down to her knees. Then he let go and they all went out with the keg.

Ayudesh said, "Are you all right?" Mam stood back up again and touched her braid, then flipped it back over her neck. She didn't look at any of us.

People were in the schoolhouse. Ayudesh sat on the table at the front and people were sitting on the floor talking as if it were a meeting. Veronique's teacher was sitting next to Ayudesh and Veronique started as if she was going to go sit with him. Then she looked around and sat down with Mam and Tuuvin and me.

"So we should just let them take whatever they want?" Harup said. He wasn't clowning now, but talking as a senior hunter. He sat on his heels, the way hunters do when they're waiting.

Ayudesh said, "Even if we could get guns, they're used to fighting and we aren't. What do you think would happen?"

Veronique was very quiet. She sat down between Tuuvin and me.

"If we don't stand up for ourselves, what will happen?" Harup said.

"If you provoke them they'll destroy us," Ayudesh said.

"Teacher," Harup said, spreading his hands as if he was telling a story. "Stabros are not hunting animals, eh. They are not sharp toothed like haunds or dogs. Haunds are hunters, packs of hunters, who do nothing but hunt stabros. There are more stabros than all the haunds could eat, eh. So how do they choose? They don't kill the buck stabros with their hard toes and heads, they take the young, the old, the sick, the helpless. We do not want to be haunds, teacher. We just want the haunds to go elsewhere for easy prey."

Wanji came in behind us, and the fire in the boxstove ducked and jumped in the draft. Wanji didn't sit down on the table, but as was her custom, lowered herself to the floor. "Old hips," she muttered as if everyone in the room wasn't watching her. "Old women have old hips."

When I thought of Kalky, the old woman who makes the souls of everything, I thought of her as looking like Wanji. Wanji had a little face and a big nose and deep lines down from her nose to her chin. "What happened to you, daughter?" she asked my mam.

"The outrunners came to the distillery to take a keg," Mam said.

I noticed that now the meeting had turned around, away from Ayudesh on the table towards us in the back. Wanji always said that Ayudesh was vain and liked to sit high. Sometimes she called him 'High-on.' "And so," Wanji said.

My mother's face was still red from the blow, but it hadn't yet purpled. "I don't think the outrunners like to do business with me," Mam said.

"One of them hit her," I said, because Mam wasn't going to. Mam never talked about it when my da hit her, either. Although he didn't do it as much as he used to when I was Bet's age.

Mam looked at me, but I couldn't tell if she was angry with me or not.

Harup spread his hands to say, 'See?'

Wanji clucked.

"We got the three-year-old whisak in the cellar," Mam said.

I was looking but I didn't see my da.

"What are they saying," Veronique asked.

"They are talking," I said, and had to think how to say it, "about what we do, but they, eh, not, do not know? Do not know what is right. Harup want guns. Wants guns. Ayudesh says guns are bad."

"Wanji," Tuuvin whispered, "Wanji, she ask—eh," and then in our own tongue, "tell her she was asking your mam what happened."

"Wanji ask my mother what is the matter," I said.

Veronique looked at Tuuvin and then at me.

"Guns are bad," Veronique said.

Tuuvin scowled. "She doesn't understand," he said.

"What?" Veronique said, but I just shook my head rather than tell her what Tuuvin had said.

Some of the men were talking about guns. Wanji was listening without saying anything, resting her chin on her head. Sometimes it seemed like Wanji didn't even blink, that she just turned into stone and you didn't know what she was thinking.

Some of the other men were talking to Ayudesh about the whisak. Yet, Harup's wife, got up and put water on the boxstove for the men to drink and Big Sherep went out the men's door in the back of the schoolhouse, which meant he was going to get whisak or beer.

"Nothing will get done now," Tuuvin said, disgusted. "Let's go."

He stood up and Veronique looked up at him, then scrambled to her feet.

"Now they talk, talk, talk," I said in English. "Nothing to say, just talk, you know?"

Outside there were outrunners. It seemed as if they were everywhere, even though there were really not that many of them. They watched Veronique.

Tuuvin scowled at them and I looked at their guns. Long black guns slung over their backs. I had never seen a gun close. And there was my da, standing with three outrunners, holding a gun in his hands as if it were a fishing spear, admiring it. He was nodding and grinning, the way he did when someone told a good hunting story. Of course, he didn't know that one of these people had hit Mam.

Still, it made me mad that he was being friendly.

"We should go somewhere," Tuuvin said.

"The distillery?" I asked.

"No," he said, "they'll go back there." And he looked at Veronique. Having Veronique around was like having Bet, you always had to be thinking about her. "Take her to your house."

"And do what?" I asked. A little angry at him because now he had decided he wasn't going back with us.

"I don't know, teach her to sew or something," he said. He turned and walked across to where my dad was standing.

The outrunners took two more kegs of whisak and got loud. They stuck torches in the snow, so the dog's harnesses were all glittering and winking, and we gave them a stabros to slaughter and they roasted that. Some of the Sckarline men like my da— and even Harup—sat with them and drank and talked and sang. I didn't understand why Harup was there, but there he was, laughing and telling stories about the time my da got dumped out of the boat fishing.

Ayudesh was there, just listening. Veronique's grandfather was out there, too, even though he couldn't understand what they were saying.

"When will they go?" Veronique asked.

I shrugged.

She asked something I didn't understand.

"When you trade," she said, "trade?"

"Trade," I said, "trade whisak, yes?"

"Yes," she said. "When you trade whisak, men come? Are you afraid when you trade whisak?"

"Afraid?" I asked. "When Scathalos come, yes."

"When other people come, are you afraid?" she asked.

"No," I said. "Just Scathalos."

She sat on my furs. My mam was on the bed and Bet had gone to sleep. Mam watched us talk, sitting cross-legged and mending Bet's boots. She didn't understand any English. It felt wrong to talk when Mam didn't understand, but Veronique couldn't understand when I talked to Mam, either.

"I have to go back to my hut," Veronique said. "Ian will come back and he'll worry about me."

Outside the air was so cold and dry that the inside of our noses felt it.

"Don't you get tired of being cold?" Veronique asked.

The cold made people tired, I thought, yes. That was why people slept so much during winterdark. I didn't always know what to say when Veronique talked about the weather.

"We tell your teacher, you sleep in our house, yes?" I offered.

"Who?" she said. "You mean Ian? He isn't really my teacher like you mean it. He's my professor."

I tried to think of what a professor might be, maybe the person who took you when your father died? It always seemed English didn't have enough words for different relatives, but now here was one I didn't know.

The outrunners and the Sckarline hunters were singing about Fhidrhin the hunter and I looked up to see if I could make out the stars that formed him, but the sky had drifting clouds and I couldn't find the stars.

I couldn't see well enough, the light from the bonfire made everyone else just shadows. I took Veronique's hand and started around the outside of the circle of singers, looking for Ayudesh and Veronique's teacher or whatever he was. Faces glanced up, spirit faces in the firelight. The smoke blew our way and then shifted, and I smelled the sweat smell that came from the men's clothes as they warmed by the fire. And whisak, of course. The stabros was mostly bones.

"Janna," said my da. His face was strange, too, not human, like a mask. His eyes looked unnaturally light. "Go on back to your mother."

"Veronique needs to tell the offworlder that she's staying with us."

"Go on back to the house," he said again. I could smell whisak on him, too. Whisak sometimes made him mean. My da used to drink a lot of whisak when I was young, but since Bet was born he didn't drink it very often at all. He said the mornings were too hard when you got old.

I didn't know what to do. If I kept looking for Veronique's grandfather and he got angry he would probably hit me. I nodded and backed away, pulling Veronique with me, then when he stopped watching me, I started around the fire the other way.

One of the outrunners stumbled up and into us before we could get out of the way. "Eh—?"

I pulled Veronique away but he gripped her arm. "Boy?"

His breath in her face made her close her eyes and turn her head.

"No boy," he said. He was drunk, probably going to relieve himself. "No boy, outsider girl, pretty as a boy," he said. "Outsider, they like that? Eh?"

Veronique gripped my hand. "Let go," she said in English.

He didn't have to speak English to see she was afraid of him.

"I'm not pretty enough for you?" he said. "Eh? Not pretty enough?" He wasn't pretty, he was wiry and had teeth missing on one side of his mouth. "Not Sckarline? With their pretty houses like offworlders? Not pretty, eh?"

Veronique drew a breath like a sob.

"Let go of her, please," I said, "we have to find her teacher."

"Look at the color of her," he said, "does that wash off? Eh?"

"Do you know where her teacher is?" I asked.

"Shut up, girl," he said to me. He licked his thumb and reached towards her face. Veronique raised her hand and drew back, and he twisted her arm. "Stand still." He rubbed her cheek with his thumb and peered closely at her.

"Damn," he said, pleased. "How come the old man isn't dark?"

"Maybe they are different clans," I said.

He stared at her as if weighing what I'd said. As if thinking. Although he actually looked too drunk to do much thinking. Then he leaned forward and tried to kiss her.

Veronique pushed him away with her free arm. He staggered and fell, pulling her down, too.

"Let go!" she shrieked.

Shut up, I thought, shut up, shut up! Give in, he's too drunk to do much. I tried to pull his arm off, but his grip was too strong.

"What's this?" another outrunner was saying.

"Fohlder's found some girl."

"It would be fucking Fohlder!"

Veronique slapped at him and struggled, trying to get away.

"Hey now," Ayudesh was saying, "hey now, she's a guest, an offworlder." But nobody was paying attention. Everybody was watching the outrunner wrestle with her. He pinned her with her arms over her head and kissed her.

Veronique was crying and slapping. Stop it, I kept thinking, just stop it, or he won't let you alone.

Her grandfather tried to pull the outrunner off. I hadn't even seen him come up. "No no no no no," he was saying as if scolding someone. "No no no no no—"

"Get off him," another outrunner hauled him away.

Ayudesh said, "Stop! She is our guest!"

"She's yours, eh?" someone said.

"No," Ayudesh said, "she should be left alone. She's a guest."

"Your guest, right. Not interested in the likes of us."

Someone else grunted and laughed.

"She likes Sckarline better, eh?"

"That's because she doesn't know better."

"Fohlder'll show her."

You all stink like drunks, I wanted to scream at them, because they did.

"Think she's dark inside like she is outside?"

"Have to wait until morning to see."

Oh, my da would be so mad at me, the stupid bitch, why didn't she stop, he was drunk, he was drunk, why had she slapped at him, stupider than Bet, she was as stupid as Bet my little sister, I was supposed to be taking care of her, I was supposed to be watching out for her, my da would be so mad—

There was the bone crack of gunfire and everybody stopped.

Harup was standing next to the fire with an outrunner gun pointed up, as if he were shooting at Fhidrhin up there in the stars. His expression was mild and he was studying the gun as if he hadn't even noticed what was going on.

"Hey," an outrunner said, "put that down!"

Harup looked around at the outrunners, at us. He looked slowly. He didn't look like he usually did, he didn't look funny or angry, he looked as if he were out on a boat in the ice. Calm, far away. Cold as the stars. He could kill someone.

The outrunners felt it too. They didn't move. If he shot one of them, the others would kill him, but the one he shot would still be dead. No one wanted to be the one that might be dead.

"It's a nice piece," Harup said, "but if you used it for hunting you'd soon be so deaf you couldn't hear anything moving." Then he grinned.

Someone laughed.

Everybody laughed.

"Janna," Harup said, "take your friend and get us more whisak."

"Fohlder, you old walking dick, get up from that girl." One of them reached down and pulled him off. He looked mad.

"What," he said, "what."

"Go take a piss," the outrunner said.

Everyone laughed.

iii

Veronique stayed with me that night, lying next to me in my blankets and furs. She didn't sleep. I don't think. I was listening to her breath. I felt as if I should help her sleep. I lay there and tried to think if I should put my arm around her, but I didn't know. Maybe she didn't want to be touched.

And she had been a stupid girl, anyway.

She lay tense in the dark. "Are you going to be a teacher?" I asked.

She laughed. "If I get out of here."

I waited for her to say more, but she didn't. 'Get out of here' meant to make someone leave. Maybe she meant if she made herself.

"You come here from Earth?" I asked. To get her to talk, although I was tired of lingua and I didn't really want to think about anything.

"My family came here from Earth," she said.

"Why?"

"My father, he's an anthropologist," she said. "Do you know anthropologist?"

"No," I said.

"He is a person who studies the way people live. And he is a teacher."

All the offworlders I had ever met were teachers. I wondered who did all the work on Earth.

"Because Earth lost touch with your world, the people here are very interesting to my father," she said. Her voice was listless in the dark and she was even harder to understand when I couldn't see her properly. I didn't understand so I didn't say anything. I was sorry I'd started her talking.

"History, do you know the word 'history'?" she asked.

Of course I knew the word 'history.' "I study history in school," I said. Anneal and Kumar taught it.

"Do you know the history of this world?"

It took my tired head a long time to sort that out. "Yes," I said. "We are a colony. People from Earth come here to live. Then there is a big problem on Earth, and the people of Earth forget we are here. We forget we are from Earth. Then Earth finds us again."

"Some people have stories about coming from the Earth," Veronique said. "My father is collecting those stories from different peoples. I'm a graduate student."

The clans didn't have any stories about coming from Earth. We said the first people came out of the sun. This somehow seemed embarrassing. I didn't understand what kind of student she was.

"Are you here for stories?" I asked.

"No," she said. "Ian is old friends with your teacher, from back when they were both with the survey. We just came to visit."

I didn't understand what she'd said except that they were visiting.

We were quiet after that. I pretended to sleep. Sometimes there was gunfire outside and we jumped, even Mam on the bed. Everyone but Bet. Once Bet was asleep it was impossible to wake her up.

I fell asleep thinking about how I wished that the Scathalos outrunners were gone. I dreamed that I was at the offworlders' home, where it was summer but no one was taking care of the stabros, and I said I could take care of the stabros, and they were all glad, and so I was a hero—and I was startled awake by gunfire.

Just more drinking and shooting.

I wished my da would come home. It didn't seem fair that we should lie there and be afraid while the men were getting drunk and singing.

The outrunners stayed the next day, taking three more kegs of whisak but not talking about trade. The following day they sent out hunters but didn't find their own meat and so took another stabros, the gelding I'd shown to Veronique. And more whisak.

I went down to the distillery after they took more whisak. It was already getting dark. The dark comes so early at this time of year. The door was left open and the fire was out. Mam wasn't coming anymore. There was no work being done. Kegs had been taken down and some had been opened and left open. Some had been spilled. They had started on the green stuff, not knowing what was what and had thrown most of it in the snow, probably thinking it was bad. Branded eyes on the kegs looked everywhere.

I thought maybe they wouldn't leave until all the whisak was gone. For one wild moment I thought about taking an ax to the kegs. Give them no reason to stay.

Instead I listened to them singing, their voices far away. I didn't want to walk back towards the voices, but I didn't want to be outside in the dark, either. I walked until I could see the big fire they had going, and smell the stabros roasting. Then I stood for a while, because I didn't want to cross the light more than I wanted to go home. Maybe someone was holding me back, maybe my spirit knew something.

I looked for my father. I saw Harup on the other side of the fire. His face was in the light. He wasn't singing, he was just watching. I saw Gerdor, my little uncle, my father's half brother. I did not see my father anywhere.

Then I saw him. His back was to me. He was just a black outline against the fire. He had his hands open wide, as if he was explaining. He had his empty hands open. Harup was watching my father explaining something to some of the outrunners and something was wrong.

One of the outrunners turned his head and spat.

My father, I couldn't hear his voice, but I could see his body, his shoulders moving as he explained. His shoulders working, working hard as if he were swimming. Such hard work, this talking with his hands open, talking, talking.

The outrunner took two steps, bent down and pulled his rifle into the light. It was a dark thing there, a long thing against the light of the fire. My father took a step back and his hands came up, pushing something back.

And then the outrunner shot my father.

All the singing stopped. The fire cracked and the sparks rose like stars while my father struggled in the snow. He struggled hard, fighting and scraping back through the snow. Elbow-walking backwards. The outrunner was looking down the long barrel of the rifle.

Get up, I thought. Get up. For a long time it seemed I thought, Get up, get up. Da, get up! But no sound came out of my mouth and there was black on the snow in the trampled trail my father left.

The outrunner shot again.

My father flopped into the snow and I could see the light on his face as he looked up. Then he stopped.

Harup watched. No one moved except the outrunner who put his rifle away.

I could feel the red meat, the hammering muscle in my chest. I could feel it squeezing, squeezing. Heat flowed in my face. In my hands.

Outrunners shouted at outrunners. "You shit," one shouted at the one who shot my father. "You drunken, stupid shit!" The one who shot my father shrugged at first, as if he didn't care, and then he became angry, too, shouting.

My breath was in my chest, so full. If I breathed out loud the outrunners would hear me out here. I tried to take small breaths, could not get enough air. I did not remember when I had been holding my breath.

Harup and the hunters of Sckarline sat, like prey, hiding in their stillness. The arguing went on and on, until it wasn't about my father at all and his body was forgotten in the dirty snow. They argued about who was stupid and who had the High-on's favor. The whisak was talking.

I could think of nothing but air.

I went back through the dark, out of Sckarline, and crept around behind the houses, in the dark and cold until I could come to our house without going past the fire. I took great shuddering breaths of cold air, breathed out great gouts of fog.

My mother was trying to get Bet quiet when I came in. "No," she was saying, "stop it now, or I'll give you something to cry about."

"Mam," I said, and I started to cry.

"What," she said. "Janna, your face is all red." She was my mam, with her face turned towards me, and I had never seen her face so clearly.

"They're going to kill all of us," I said. "They killed Da with a rifle."

She never said a word but just ran out and left me there. Bet started to cry although she didn't really know what I was crying about. Just that she should be scared. Veronique was still. As still as Harup and all the hunters.

Wanji came and got me and brought me to Ayudesh's house because our house is small and Ayudesh's house had enough room for some people. Snow was caked in the creases of my father's pants. It was in his hands, too, unmelted. I had seen dead people before, and my father looked like all of them. Not like himself at all.

My mother had followed him as far as the living can go, or at least as someone untrained in spirit journeys, and she was not herself. She was sitting on the floor next to his body, rocking back and forth with her arms crossed in her lap. I had seen women like that before, but not my mother. I didn't want to look. It seemed indecent. Worse than the body of my father, since my father wasn't there at all.

Bet was screaming. Her face was red from the effort. I held her even though she was heavy and she kept arching away from me like a toddler in a tantrum. "MAM! MAM!" she kept screaming.

People came in and squatted down next to the body for a while. People talked about guns. It was important that I take care of Bet so I did, until finally she wore herself out from crying and fell asleep. I held her on my lap until the blood was out of my legs and I couldn't feel the floor and then Wanji brought me a blanket and I wrapped Bet in it and let her sleep.

Wanji beckoned me to follow. I could barely stand, my legs had so little feeling. I held the wall and looked around, at my mother sitting next to the vacant body, at my sister, who though asleep was still alive. Then I tottered after Wanji as if I was the old woman.

"Where is the girl?" Wanji said.

"Asleep," I said. "On the floor."

"No, the girl," Wanji said, irritated. "Ian's girl. From the university."

"I don't know," I said.

"You're supposed to be watching her. Didn't Ayudesh tell you to watch her?"

"You mean Veronique? She's back at my house. In my bed."

Wanji nodded and sucked on her teeth. "Okay," she said. And then again to herself, "Okay."

Wanji took me to her house, which was little and dark. She had a lamp shaped like a bird. It had been in her house as long as I could remember. It didn't give very much light, but I had always liked it. We sat on the floor. Wanji's floor was always piled high with rugs from her home and furs and blankets. It made it hard to walk but nice to sit. Wanji got cold and her bones hurt, so she always made a little nest when she sat down. She pulled a red and blue rug across her lap. "Sit, sit, sit," she said.

I was cold, but there was a blanket to wrap around my shoulders and watch Wanji make hot tea. I couldn't remember being alone with Wanji before. But everything was so strange it didn't seem to make any difference and it was nice to have Wanji deciding what to do and me not having to do anything.

Wanji made tea over her little bird lamp. She handed me a cup and I sipped it. Tea was a strange drink. Wanji and Ayudesh liked it and hoarded it. It was too bitter to be very good, but it was warm and the smell of it was always special. I drank it and held it against me. I started to get warm. The blanket got warm from me and smelled faintly of Wanji, an old dry smell.

I was sleepy. It would have been nice to go to sleep right there in my little nest on Wanji's floor.

"Girl," Wanji said. "I must give you something. You must take care of Veronique."

I didn't want to take care of anybody. I wanted someone to take care of me. My eyes started to fill up and in a moment I was crying salt tears into my tea.

"No time for that, Janna," Wanji said. Always sharp with us. Some people were afraid of Wanji. I was. But it felt good to cry, and I didn't know how to stop it so I didn't.

Wanji didn't pay any attention. She was hunting through her house, checking in a chest, pulling up layers of rugs to peer in a corner. Was she going to give me a gun? I couldn't think of anything else that would help very much right now, but I couldn't imagine that Wanji owned a gun.

She came back with a dark blue plastic box not much bigger than the span of my spread hand. That was almost as astonishing as a gun. I wiped my nose on my sleeve. I was warm and tired. Would Wanji let me sleep right here on her floor?

Wanji opened the plastic box, but away from me so I couldn't see inside it. She picked at it as if she were picking at a sewing kit, looking for something. I wanted to look in it but I was afraid that if I tried she'd snap at me.

She looked at me. "This is mine," she said. "We both got one and we decided that if the people who settled Sckarline couldn't have it, we wouldn't either."

I didn't care about that. That was old talk. I wanted to know what it was.

Wanji wasn't ready to tell me what it was. I had the feeling that Ayudesh didn't know about this, and I was afraid she would talk herself out of it. She looked at it and thought. If I thought, I thought about my father being dead. I sipped tea and tried to think about being warm, about sleeping but that feeling had passed. I wondered where Tuuvin was.

I thought about my da and I started to cry again.

I thought that would really get Wanji angry so I tried to hide it, but she didn't pay any attention at all. The shawl she wore over her head slipped halfway down so when I glanced up I could see where her hair parted and the line of pale skin. It looked so bare that I wanted it covered up again. It made me think of the snow in my father's hands.

"It was a mistake," Wanji said.

I thought she meant the box, and I felt a terrible disappointment that I wouldn't get to see what was inside it.

"You understand what we were trying to do?" she asked me.

With the box? Not at all.

"What are the six precepts of development philosophy?" she asked.

I had to think. "One," I said, "that economic development should be gradual. Two, that analyzing economic growth by the production of goods rather than the needs and capacities of people leads to displacement and increased poverty. Three, that economic development should come from the integrated development of rural areas with the traditional sector—"

"It's just words," she snapped at me.

I didn't know what I had done wrong so I ducked my head and sniffed and waited for her to get angry because I couldn't stop crying.

Instead she stroked my hair. "Oh, little girl. Oh, Janna. You are one of the bright ones. If you aren't understanding it, then we really haven't gotten it across, have we?" Her hand was nice on my hair, and it seemed so unlike Wanji that it scared me into stillness. "We were trying to help, you know," she said. "We were trying to do good. We gave up our lives to come here. Do you realize?"

Did she mean that they were going to die? Ayudesh and Wanji?

"This," she said, suddenly brisk. "This is for, what would you call them, runners. Foreign runners. It is to help them survive. I am going to give it to you so that you will help Veronique, understood?"

I nodded.

But she didn't give it to me. She just sat holding the box, looking in it. She didn't want to give it up. She didn't feel it was appropriate.

She sighed again, a terrible sound. Out of the box she pulled shiny foil packets, dark blue, red, and yellow. They were the size of the palm of her hand. Her glasses were around her neck. She put them on like she did in the schoolroom, absent from the gesture. She studied the printing on the foil packets.

I loved foil. Plastic was beautiful, but foil, foil was something unimaginable. Tea came in foil packets. The strange foods that the teachers got off the skimmer came in foil.

My tea was cold.

"This one," she said, "it is a kind of signal." She looked over her glasses at me. "Listen to me Janna. Your life will depend on this. When you have this, you can send a signal that the outsiders can hear. They can hear it all the way in Bashtoy. And after you send it, if you can wait in the same place, they will send someone out to get you and Veronique."

"They can hear it in Bashtoy?" I said. I had never even met anyone other than Wanji and the teachers who had ever been to Bashtoy.

"They can pick it up on their instruments. You send it every day until someone comes."

"How do I send it?"

She read the packet. "We have to set the signal, you and I. First we have to put it in you."

I didn't understand, but she was reading, so I waited.

"I'm going to put it in your ear," she said. "From there it will migrate to your brain."

"Will it hurt?" I asked.

"A little," she said. "But it has its own way of taking pain away. Now, what should be the code?" She studied the packet. She pursed her lips.

A thing in my ear. I was afraid and I wanted to say no, but I was more afraid of Wanji so I didn't.

"You can whistle, can't you?" she asked.

I knew how to whistle, yes.

"Okay," she said, "here it is. I'll put this in your ear, and then we'll wait for a while. Then when everything is ready we'll set the code."

She opened up the packet and inside was another packet and a little metal fork. She opened the inside packet and took out a tiny little disk, a soft thing almost like egg white or like a fish egg. She leaned forward and put it in my left ear. Then she pushed it in hard and I jerked.

"Hold still," she said.

Something was moving and making noise in my ear and I couldn't be still. I pulled away and shook my head. The noise in my ear was loud, a sort of rubbing, oozing sound. I couldn't hear normal things out of my left ear. It was stopped up with whatever was making the oozing noise. Then it started to hurt. A little at first, then more and more.

I put my hand over my ear, pressing against the pain. Maybe it would eat through my ear? What would stop it from eating a hole in my head?

"Stop it," I said to Wanji. "Make it stop!"

But she didn't, she just sat there, watching.

The pain grew sharp, and then suddenly it stopped. The sound, the pain, everything.

I took my hand away. I was still deaf on the left side but it didn't hurt.

"Did it stop?" Wanji asked.

I nodded.

"Do you feel dizzy? Sick?"

I didn't.

Wanji picked up the next packet. It was blue. "While that one is working, we'll do this one. Then the third one, which is easy. This one will make you faster when you are angry or scared. It will make time feel slower. There isn't any code for it. Something in your body starts it."

I didn't have any idea what she was talking about.

"After it has happened, you'll be tired. It uses up your energy." She studied the back of the packet, then she scooted closer to me, so we were both sitting cross-legged with our knees touching. Wanji had hard, bony knees, even through the felt of her dress.

"Open your eye, very wide," she said.

"Wait," I said. "Is this going to hurt?"

"No," she said.

I opened my eyes as wide as I could.

"Look down, but keep your eyes wide open," she said.

I tried.

"No," she said, irritated, "keep your eyes open."

"They are open," I said. I didn't think she should treat me this way. My da had just died. She should be nice to me. I could hear her open the packet. I wanted to blink but I was afraid to. I did, because I couldn't help it.

She leaned forward and spread my eye open with thumb and forefinger. Then she swiftly touched my eye.

I jerked back. There was something in my eye, I could feel it, up under my eyelid. It was very uncomfortable. I blinked and blinked and blinked. My eye filled up with tears, just the one eye, which was very very strange.

My eye socket started to ache. "It hurts," I said.

"It won't last long," she said.

"You said it wouldn't hurt!" I said, startled.

"I lied," Wanji said, matter-of-fact.

It hurt more and more. I moaned. "You're hateful," I said.

"That's true," she said, unperturbed.

She picked up the third packet, the red one.

"No," I said, "I won't! I won't! You can't do it!"

"Hush," she said, "this one won't hurt. I saved it until last on purpose."

"You're lying!" I scrambled away from her. The air was cold where the nest of rugs and blankets had been wrapped around me. My head ached. It just ached. And I still couldn't hear anything out of my left ear.

"Look," she said, "I will read you the lingua. It is a patch, nothing more. It says it will feel cold, but that is all. See, it is just a square of cloth that will rest on your neck. If it hurts you can take it off."

I scrambled backwards away from her.

"Janna," she said. "Enough!" She was angry.

I was afraid of it, but I was still more afraid of Wanji. So I hunched down in front of her. I was so afraid that I sobbed while she peeled the back off the square and put it on me.

"See," she said, still sharp with me, "it doesn't hurt at all. Stop crying. Stop it. Enough is enough." She waved her hands over her head in disgust. "You are hysterical."

I held my hand over the patch. It didn't hurt but it did feel cold. I scrunched up and wrapped myself in a rug and gave myself over to my misery. My head hurt and my ear still ached faintly and I was starting to feel dizzy.

"Lie down," Wanji said. "Go on, lie down. I'll wake you when we can set the signal."

I made myself a nest in the mess of Wanji's floor and piled a blanket and a rug on top of me. Maybe the dark made my head feel better, I didn't know. But I fell asleep.

Wanji shook me awake. I hadn't been asleep long, and my head still ached. She had the little metal fork from the ear packet, the yellow packet. It occurred to me that she might stick it in my ear.

I covered my ear with my hand. My head hurt enough. I wasn't going to let Wanji stick a fork in my ear.

"Don't scowl," she said.

"My head hurts," I said.

"Are you dizzy?" she asked.

I felt out of sorts, unbalanced, but not dizzy, not really.

"Shake your head," Wanji said.

I shook my head. Still the same, but no worse. "Don't stick that in my ear," I said.

"What? I'm not going to stick this in your ear. It's a musical fork. I'm going to make a sound with it and hold it to your ear. When I tell you to I want you to whistle something, okay?"

"Whistle what?" I said.

"Anything," she said, "I don't care. Whistle something for me now."

I couldn't think of anything to whistle. I couldn't think of anything at all except that I wished Wanji would leave me alone and let me go back to sleep.

Wanji squatted there. Implacable old bitch.

I finally thought of something to whistle, a crazy dog song for children. I started whistling—

"That's enough," she said. "Now don't say anything else, but when I nod my head you whistle that. Don't say anything to me. If you do, it will ruin everything. Nod your head if you understand."

I nodded.

She slapped the fork against her hand and I could see the long tines vibrating. She held it up to my ear, the one I couldn't hear anything out of. She held it there, concentrating fiercely. Then she nodded.

I whistled.

"Okay," she said. "Good. That is how you start it. Now whistle it again."

I whistled.

Everything went dark and then suddenly my head got very hot. Then I could see again.

"Good," Wanji said. "You just sent a signal."

"Why did everything get dark?" I asked.

"All the light got used in the signal," Wanji said. "It used all the light in your head so you couldn't see."

My head hurt even worse. Now besides my eye aching, my temples were pounding. I had a fever. I raised my hand and felt my hot cheek.

Wanji picked up the blue packet. "Now we have to figure out about the third one, the one that will let you hibernate."

I didn't want to learn about hibernating. "I feel sick," I said.

"It's probably too soon, anyway," Wanji said. "Sleep for a while."

I felt so awful I didn't know if I could sleep. But Wanji brought me more tea and I drank that and lay down in my nest and presently I was dreaming.

iv

There was a sound of gunfire, far away, just a pop. And then more pop-pop-pop.

It startled me, although I had been hearing the outrunners' guns at night since they got here. I woke with a fever and everything felt as if I were still dreaming. I was alone in Wanji's house. The lamp was still lit but I didn't know if it had been refilled or how long I had slept. During the long night of winterdark it is hard to know when you are. I got up, put out the lamp and went outside.

Morning cold is worst when you are warm from sleep. The dry snow crunched in the dark. Nothing was moving except the dogs were barking, their voices coming at me from every way.

The outrunners were gone from the center of town, nothing there but the remains of their fire and the trampled slick places where they had walked. I slid a bit as I walked there. My head felt light and I concentrated on my walking because if I did not think about it I didn't know what my feet would do. I had to pee.

Again I heard the pop-pop-pop. I could not tell where it was coming from because it echoed off the buildings around me. I could smell smoke and see the dull glow of fire above the trees. It was down from Sckarline, the fire. At first I thought they had gotten a really big fire going, and then I thought they had set fire to the distillery. I headed for home.

Veronique was asleep in a nest of blankets, including some of my parent's blankets from their bed.

"They set fire to the distillery," I said. I didn't say it in English, but she sat up and rubbed her face.

"It's cold," she said.

I could not think of anything to respond.

She sat there, holding her head.

"Come," I said, working into English. "We go see your teacher." I pulled on her arm.

"Where is everybody," she said.

"My father die, my mother is, um, waiting with the die."

She frowned at me. I knew I hadn't made any sense. I pulled on her again and she got up and stumbled around, putting on boots and jacket.

Outside I heard the pop-pop-pop again. This time I thought maybe it was closer.

"They're shooting again?" she asked.

"They shoot my father," I said.

"Oh God," she said. She sat down on the blankets. "Oh God."

I pulled on her arm.

"Are you all right?" she asked.

"Hurry," I said. I made a pack of blankets. I found my ax and a few things and put them in the bundle, then slung it all over my shoulders. I didn't know what we would do, but if they were shooting people we should run away. I had to pee really bad.

She did hurry, finally awake. When we went outside and the cold hit her she shuddered and shook off the last of the sleep. I saw the movement of her shoulders against the glow of the fire on the horizon, against the false dawn.

People were moving, clinging close to houses where they were invisible against the black wood, avoiding the open spaces. We stayed close to my house, waiting to see whose people were moving. Veronique held my arm. A dog came past the schoolhouse into the open area where the outrunners' fire had been and stopped and sniffed — maybe the place where my father had died.

I drew Veronique back, along to the back of the house. The spirit door was closed and my father was dead. I crouched low and ran, holding her arm, until we were in the trees and then she slipped and fell and pulled me down, too. We slid feet first in the snow, down the hill between the tree trunks, hidden in the pools of shadow under the trees. Then we were still, waiting.

I still felt feverish and nothing was real.

The snow under the trees was all powder. It dusted our leggings and clung in clumps in the wrinkles behind my knees.

Nothing came after us that we could see. We got up and walked deeper into the trees and then uphill, away from the distillery but still skirting the village. I left her for a moment to pee, but she followed me and we squatted together. We should run, but I didn't know where to run to and the settlement pulled at me. I circled around it as if on a tether, pulling in closer and closer as we got to the uphill part of town. Coming back around we hung in the trees beyond the field behind the schoolhouse. I could see the stabros pens and see light. The outrunners were in the stabros pens and the stabros were down. A couple of the men were dressing the carcasses.

We stumbled over Harup in the darkness. Literally fell over him in the bushes.

He was dead. His stomach was ripped by rifle fire and his eyes were open. I couldn't tell in the darkness if he had dragged himself out here to die or if someone had thrown the body here. We were too close.

I started backing away. Veronique was stiff as a spooked stabros. She lifted her feet high out of the snow, coming down hard and loud. One of the dogs at the stabros pen heard us and started to bark. I could see it in the light, its ears up and its tail curled over its back. The others barked, too, ears towards us in the dark. I stopped and Veronique stopped, too. Men in the pen looked out in the dark. A couple of them picked up rifles, and cradling them in their arms walked out towards us from the light.

I backed up, slowly. Maybe they would find Harup's body and think that the dogs were barking at that. But they were hunters and they would see the marks of our boots in the snow and follow us. If we ran they would hear us. I was not a hunter. I did not know what to do.

We backed up, one slow step and then another, while the outrunners walked out away from the light. They were not coming straight at us, but they were walking side by side and they would spread out and find us. I had my knife. There was cover around, mostly trees, but I didn't know what I could do against a hunter with a rifle, and even if I could stop one the others would hear us.

There were shouts over by the houses.

The outrunners kept walking but the shouts did not stop, and then there was the pop of guns. That stopped one and then the other and they half-turned.

The dogs turned barking towards the shouts.

The outrunners started to jog towards the schoolhouse.

We walked backward in the dark.

There were flames over there, at the houses. I couldn't tell whose house was on fire. It was downhill from the schoolhouse, which meant it might be our house. People were running in between the schoolhouse and Wanji's house and the outrunners lifted their guns and fired. People, three of them, kept on running.

The outrunners fired again and again. One of the people stumbled but they all kept running. They were black shapes skimming on the field. The snow on the field was not deep because the wind blew it into the trees. Then one was in the trees. The outrunners fired again, but the other two made the trees as well.

There was a summer camp out this way, down by the river, for drying fish.

I pulled on Veronique's arm and we picked our way through the trees.

There were people at the summer camp and we waited in the trees to make sure they were Sckarline people. It was gray, false dawn by the time we got there. I didn't remember ever having seen the summer camp in the winter before. The drying racks were bare poles with a top covering of snow, and the lean-to was almost covered in drifted snow. There was no shelter here.

There were signs of three or four people in the trampled snow. I didn't think it would be the outrunners down there because how would they even know where the summer camp was but I was not sure of anything. I didn't know if I was thinking right or not.

Veronique leaned close to my ear and whispered so softly I could barely hear. "We have to go back."

I shook my head.

"Ian is there."

Ian. Ian. She meant her teacher.

She had a hood on her purple clothing and I pulled it back to whisper, "Not now. We wait here." So close to the brown shell of her ear. Like soft dark leather. Not like a real, people's ear. She was shivering.

I didn't feel too cold. I still had a fever—I felt as if everything were far from me, as if I walked half in this world. I sat and looked at the snow cupped in a brown leaf and my mind was empty and things did not seem too bad. I don't know how long we sat.

Someone walked in the summer camp. I thought it was Sored, one of the boys.

I took Veronique's arm and tugged her up. I was stiff from sitting and colder than I had noticed but moving helped. We slid down the hill into the summer camp.

The summer camp sat in a V that looked at the river frozen below. Sored was already out of the camp when we got there, but he waved at us from the trees and we scrambled back up there. Veronique slipped and used her hands.

There were two people crouched around a fire so tiny it was invisible and one of them was Tuuvin.

"Where is everyone else?" Sored asked.

"I don't know," I said. Tuuvin stood up.

"Where's your mother and your sister?" he asked.

"I was at Wanji's house all night," I said. "Where's your family?"

"My da and I were at the stabros pen this morning with Harup," he said.

"We found Harup," I said.

"Did you find my da?" he asked.

"No. Was he shot?"

"I don't know. I don't think so."

"We saw some people running across the field behind the schoolhouse. Maybe one of them was shot."

He looked down at Gerda, crouched by the fire. "None of us were shot."

"Did you come together?"

"No," Sored said. "I found Gerda here and Tuuvin here."

He had gone down to see the fire at the distillery. The outrunners had taken some of the casks. He didn't know how the fire had started, if it was an accident or if they'd done it on purpose. It would be easy to start if someone spilled something too close to the fire.

Veronique was crouched next to the tiny fire. "Janna," she said, "has anyone seen Ian?"

"Did you see the offworlder teacher?" I asked.

No one had.

"We have to find him," she said.

"Okay," I said.

"What are you going to do with her?" Sored asked, pointing at Veronique with his chin. "Is she ill?"

She crouched over the fire like someone who was sick.

"She's not sick," I said. "We need to see what is happening at Sckarline."

"I'm not going back," Gerda said, looking at no one. I did not know Gerda very well. She was old enough to have children but she had no one. She lived by herself. She had her nose slit by her clan for adultery but I never knew if she had a husband with her old clan or not. Some people came to Sckarline because they didn't want to be part of their clan anymore. Most of them went back, but Gerda had stayed.

Tuuvin said, "I'll go."

Sored said he would stay in case anyone else came to the summer camp. In a day or two they were going to head towards the west and see if they could come across the winter pastures of Haufsdaag Clan. Sored had kin there.

"That's pretty far," Tuuvin said. "Toolie clan would be closer."

"You have kin with Toolie Clan," Sored said.

Tuuvin nodded.

"We go to Sckarline," I said to Janna.

She stood up. "It's so damn cold," she said. Then she said something about wanting coffee. I didn't understand a lot of what she said. Then she laughed and said she wished she could have breakfast.

Sored looked at me. I didn't translate what she had said. He turned his back on her, but she didn't notice.

It took us through the sunrise and beyond the short midwinter morning and into afternoon to get to Sckarline. The only good thing about winterdark is that it would be dark for the outrunners, too.

Only hours of daylight.

Nothing was moving when we got back to Sckarline. From the back the school-house looked all right, but the houses were all burned. I could see where my house had been. Charred logs standing in the red afternoon sun. The ground around them was wet and muddy from the heat of the fires.

Tuuvin's house. Ayudesh's house and Wanji's house.

In front of the schoolhouse there were bodies. My da's body, thrown back in the snow. My mam and my sister. My sister's head was broken in. My mam didn't have her pants on. The front of the schoolhouse had burned but the fire must have burned out before the whole building was gone. The dogs were moving among the bodies, sniffing, stopping to tug on the freezing flesh.

Tuuvin shouted at them to drive them off.

My mam's hip bones were sharp under the bloody skin and her sex was there for everyone to see but I kept noticing her bare feet. The soles were dark. Her toenails were thick and her feet looked old, an old old woman's feet. As if she were as old as Wanji.

I looked at people to see who else was there. I saw Wanji, although she had no face but I knew her from her skin. Veronique's teacher was there, his face red and peeled from fire and his eyes baked white like a smoked fish. Ayudesh had no ears and no sex. His clothes had been taken.

The dogs were circling back, watching Tuuvin.

He screamed at them. Then he crouched down on his heels and covered his eyes with his arm and cried.

I did not feel anything. Not yet.

I whistled the tune that Wanji had taught me to send out the message, and the world went dark. It was something to do, and for a moment, I didn't have to look at my mother's bare feet.

The place for the Sckarline dead was up the hill beyond the town, away from the river, but without stabros I couldn't think of how we could get all these bodies there. We didn't have anything for the bodies, either. Nothing for the spirit journey, not even blankets to wrap them in.

I could not bear to think of my mother without pants. There were lots of dead women in the snow and many of them did have pants. It may not have been fair that my mother should have someone else's but I could not think of anything else to do so I took the leggings off of Maitra and tried to put them on my mother. I could not really get them right—my mother was tall and her body was stiff from the cold and from death. I hated handling her.

Veronique asked me what I was doing but even if I knew enough English to an-swer, I was too embarrassed to really try to explain.

My mother's flesh was white and odd to touch. Not like flesh at all. Like plastic. Soft looking but not to touch.

Tuuvin watched me without saying anything. I thought he might tell me not to, but he didn't. Finally he said, "We can't get them to the place for the dead."

I didn't know what to say to that.

"We don't have anyone to talk to the spirits," he said. "Only me."

He was the man here. I didn't know if Tuuvin had talked with spirits or not, people didn't talk about that with women.

"I say that this place is a place of the dead, too," he said. His voice was strange. "Sckarline is a place of the dead now."

"We leave them here?" I asked.

He nodded.

He was beardless, but he was a boy and he was old enough that he had walked through the spirit door. I was glad that he had made the decision.

I looked in houses for things for the dead to have with them, but most things were burned. I found things half-burned and sometimes not burned at all. I found a fur, and used that to wrap the woman whose leggings I had stolen. I tried to make sure that everybody got something—a bit of stitching or a cup or something, so they would not be completely without possessions. I managed to find something for almost everybody, and I found enough blankets to wrap Tuuvin's family and Veronique's teacher. I wrapped Bet with my mother. I kept blankets separate for Veronique, Tuuvin, and me and anything I found that we could use I didn't give to the dead, but everything else I gave to them.

Tuuvin sat in the burned-out schoolhouse and I didn't know if what he did was a spirit thing or if it was just grief, but I didn't bother him. He kept the dogs away. Veronique followed me and picked through the blackened sticks of the houses. Both of us had black all over our gloves and our clothes and black marks on our faces.

We stopped when it got too dark, and then we made camp in the schoolhouse next to the dead. Normally I would not have been able to stay so close to the dead, but now I felt part of them.

Tuuvin had killed and skinned a dog and cooked that. Veronique cried while she ate. Not like Tuuvin had cried. Not sobs. Just helpless tears that ran down her face. As if she didn't notice.

"What are we going to do?" she asked.

Tuuvin said, "We will try for Toolie Clan."

I didn't have any idea where their winter pastures were, much less how to find them, and I almost asked Tuuvin if he did, but I didn't want to shame his new manhood, so I didn't.

"The skimmer will come back here," Veronique said. "I have to wait here."

"We can't wait here," Tuuvin said. "It is going to get darker, winter is coming and we'll have no sun. We don't have any animals. We can't live here."

I told her what Tuuvin said. "I have, in here," I pointed to my head, "I call your people. Wanji give to me."

Veronique didn't understand and didn't even really try.

I tried not to think about the dogs wandering among the dead. I tried not to think about bad weather. I tried not to think about my house or my mam. It did not leave much to think about.

Tuuvin had kin with Toolie Clan but I didn't. Tuuvin was my clankin, though, even if he wasn't a cousin or anything. I wondered if he would still want me after we got to Toolie Clan. Maybe there would be other girls. New girls, that he had never talked to before. They would be pretty, some of them.

My kin were Lagskold. I didn't know where their pastures were, but someone would know. I could go to them if I didn't like Toolie Clan. I had met a couple of my cousins when they came and brought my father's half brother, my little uncle.

"Listen," Tuuvin said, touching my arm.

I didn't hear it at first, then I did.

"What?" Veronique said. "Are they coming back?"

"Hush," Tuuvin snapped at her, and even though she didn't understand the word she did.

It was a skimmer.

It was far away. Skimmers didn't land at night. They didn't even come at night. It had come to my message, I guessed.

Tuuvin got up, and Veronique scrambled to her feet and we all went out to the edge of the field behind the schoolhouse.

"You can hear it?" I asked Veronique.

She shook her head.

"Listen," I said. I could hear it. Just a rumble. "The skimmer."

"The skimmer?" she said. "The skimmer is coming? Oh God. Oh God. I wish we had lights for them. We need light, to signal them that someone is here."

"Tell her to hush," Tuuvin said.

"I send message," I said. "They know someone is here."

"We should move the fire."

I could send them another message, but Wanji had said to do it one time a day until they came and they were here.

Dogs started barking.

Finally we saw lights from the skimmer, strange green and red stars. They moved against the sky as if they had been shaken loose.

Veronique stopped talking and stood still.

The lights came towards us for a long time. They got bigger and brighter, more than any star. It seemed as if they stopped but the lights kept getting brighter and I finally decided that they were coming straight towards us and it didn't look as if they were moving but they were.

Then we could see the skimmer in its own lights.

It flew low over us and Veronique shouted, "I'm here! I'm here!"

I shouted, and Tuuvin shouted, too, but the skimmer didn't seem to hear us. But then it turned and slowly curved around, the sound of it going farther away and then just hanging in the air. It got to where it had been before and came back. This time it came even lower and it dropped red lights. One. Two. Three.

Then a third time it came around and I wondered what it would do now. But this time it landed, the sound of it so loud that I could feel it as well as hear it. It was a different skimmer from the one we always saw. It was bigger, with a belly like it was pregnant. It was white and red. It settled easily on the snow. Its engines, pointed down, melted snow underneath them.

And then it sat. Lights blinked. The red lights on the ground flickered. The dogs barked.

Veronique ran towards it.

The door opened and a man called out to watch something but I didn't understand. Veronique stopped and from where I was she was a black shape against the lights of the skimmer.

Finally a man jumped down, and then two more men and two women and they ran to Veronique.

She gestured and the lights flickered in the movements of her arms until my eyes hurt and I looked away. I couldn't see anything around us. The offworlders' lights made me quite nightblind.

"Janna," Veronique called. "Tuuvin!" She waved at us to come over. So we walked out of the dark into the relentless lights of the skimmer.

I couldn't understand what anyone was saying in English. They asked me questions, but I just kept shaking my head. I was tired and now, finally, I wanted to cry.

"Janna," Veronique said. "You called them. Did you call them?"

I nodded.

"How?"

"Wanji give me . . . In my head . . ." I had no idea how to explain. I pointed to my ear.

One of the women came over, and handling my head as if I were a stabros, turned it so she could push my hair out of the way and look in my ear. I still couldn't hear very well out of that ear. Her handling wasn't rough, but it was not something people do to each other.

She was talking and nodding, but I didn't try to understand. The English washed over us and around us.

One of the men brought us something hot and bitter and sweet to drink. The drink was in blue plastic cups, the same color as the jackets that they all wore except for one man whose jacket was red with blue writing. Pretty things. Veronique drank hers gratefully. I made myself drink mine. Anything this black and bitter must have been medicine. Tuuvin just held his.

Then they got hand lights and we all walked over and looked at the bodies. Dogs ran from the lights, staying at the edges and slinking as if guilty of something.

"Janna," Veronique said. "Which one is Ian? Which is my teacher?"

I had to walk between the bodies. We had laid them out so their heads all faced the schoolhouse and their feet all faced the center of the village. They were more bundles than people. I could have told her in the light, but in the dark, with the hand lights making it hard to see anything but where they were pointed, it took me a while. I found Harup by mistake. Then I found the teacher.

Veronique cried and the woman who had looked in my ear held her like she was her child. But that woman didn't look dark like Veronique at all and I thought she was just kin because she was an offworlder, not by blood. All the offworlders were like Sckarline; kin because of where they were, not because of family.

The two men in blue jackets picked up the body of the teacher. With the body they were clumsy on the packed snow. The man holding the teacher's head slipped and fell. Tuuvin took the teacher's head and I took his feet. His boots were gone. His feet were as naked as my mother's. I had wrapped him in a skin but it wasn't very big so his feet hung out. But they were so cold they felt like meat, not like a person.

We walked right up to the door of the skimmer and I could look in. It was big inside. Hollow. It was dark in the back. I had thought it would be all lights inside and I was disappointed. There were things hanging on the walls but mostly it was empty. One of the offworld men jumped up into the skimmer and then he was not clumsy at all. He pulled the body to the back of the skimmer.

They were talking again. Tuuvin and I stood there. Tuuvin's breath was an enormous white plume in the lights of the skimmer. I stamped my feet. The lights were bright but they were a cheat. They didn't make you any warmer.

The offworlders wanted to go back to the bodies, so we did. "Your teachers," Veronique said. "Where are your teachers?"

I remembered Wanji's body. It had no face, but it was easy to tell it was her. Ayudesh's body was still naked under the blanket I had found. The blanket was burned along one side and didn't cover him. Where his sex had been, the frozen blood shone in the hand lights. I thought the dogs might have been at him, but I couldn't tell.

They wanted to take Wanji's and Ayudesh's bodies back to the skimmer. They motioned for us to pick up Ayudesh.

"Wait," Tuuvin said. "They shouldn't do that."

I squatted down.

"They are Sckarline people," Tuuvin said.

"Their spirit is already gone," I said.

"They won't have anything," he said.

"If the offworlders take them, won't they give them offworld things?"

"They didn't want offworld things," Tuuvin said. "That's why they were here."

"But we don't have anything to give them. At least if the offworlders give them things they'll have something."

Tuuvin shook his head. "Harup—" he started to say but stopped. Harup talked to spirits more than anyone. He would have known. But I didn't know how to ask him and I didn't think Tuuvin did either. Although I wasn't sure. There wasn't any drum or anything for spirit talk anyway.

The offworlders stood looking at us.

"Okay," Tuuvin said. So I stood up and we picked up Ayudesh's body and the two offworld men picked up Wanji's body and we took them to the skimmer.

A dog followed us in the dark.

The man in the red jacket climbed up and went to the front of the skimmer. There were chairs there and he sat in one and talked to someone on a radio. I could remember the word for radio in English. Ayudesh used to have one until it stopped working and he didn't get another.

My thoughts rattled through my empty head.

They put the bodies of the teachers next to the body of Veronique's teacher. Tuuvin and I stood outside the door, leaning in to watch them. The floor of the skimmer was metal.

One of the blue jacket men brought us two blankets. The blankets were the same blue as his jacket and had a red symbol on them. A circle with words. I didn't pay much attention to them. He brought us foil packets. Five. Ten of them.

"Food," he said, pointing to the packets.

I nodded. "Food," I repeated.

"Do they have guns?" Tuuvin asked harshly.

"Guns?" I asked. "You have guns?"

"No guns," the blue jacket said. "No guns."

I didn't know if we were supposed to get in the skimmer or if the gifts meant to go. Veronique came over and sat down in the doorway. She hugged me. "Thank you, Janna," she whispered. "Thank you."

Then she got up.

"Move back," said the red jacket, shooing us.

We trotted back away from the skimmer. Its engines fired and the ground underneath them steamed. The skimmer rose, and then the engines turned from pointing down to pointing back and it moved off. Heavy and slow at first, but then faster and faster. Higher and higher.

We blinked in the darkness, holding our gifts.

oceanic

GREG EGAN

Looking back at the century that's just ended, it's obvious that Australian writer Greg Egan was one of the big new names to emerge in SF in the '90s, and is probably one of the most significant talents to enter the field in the last several decades. Already one of the most widely known of all Australian genre writers, Egan may well be the best new "hard-science" writer to enter the field since Greg Bear, and is still growing in range, power, and sophistication. In the last few years, he has become a frequent contributor to *Interzone* and *Asimov's Science Fiction,* and has made sales to *Pulphouse, Analog, Aurealis, Eidolon,* and elsewhere; many of his stories have also appeared in various "Best of the Year" series, and he was on the Hugo Final Ballot in 1995 for his story "Cocoon," which won the Ditmar Award and the Asimov's Readers Award. He won the Hugo Award in 1999 for his novella "Oceanic." His first novel, *Quarantine,* appeared in 1992; his second novel, *Permutation City,* won the John W. Campbell Memorial Award in 1994. His other books include the novels *Distress, Diaspora,* and *Teranesia,* and three collections of his short fiction, *Axiomatic, Luminous,* and *Our Lady of Chernobyl.* His most recent book is a new novel *Schild's Ladder.* He has a Web site at http://www.netspace .netau/^gregegan/.

Here he takes us into the far-future and across the Galaxy for a powerful, evocative, and compelling study of a young boy's coming-of-age, as that boy struggles to understand the world and his place in it, and grapples with controversial and perhaps potentially deadly issues of faith and acceptance and God's Plan For The World, as well as diving deep into a literal ocean of mystery in search of answers to the kinds of questions it's always been dangerous to ask, in any age and on any world.

ONE

The swell was gently lifting and lowering the boat. My breathing grew slower, falling into step with the creaking of the hull, until I could no longer tell the difference between the faint rhythmic motion of the cabin and the sensation of filling and emptying my lungs. It was like floating in darkness: every inhalation buoyed me up, slightly; every exhalation made me sink back down again.

In the bunk above me, my brother Daniel said distinctly, "Do you believe in God?"

My head was cleared of sleep in an instant, but I didn't reply straight away. I'd never closed my eyes, but the darkness of the unlit cabin seemed to shift in front of me, grains of phantom light moving like a cloud of disturbed insects.

"Martin?"

"I'm awake."

"Do you believe in God?"

"Of course." Everyone I knew believed in God. Everyone talked about Her, everyone prayed to Her. Daniel most of all. Since he'd joined the Deep Church the previous summer, he prayed every morning for a kilotau before dawn. I'd often wake to find myself aware of him kneeling by the far wall of the cabin, muttering and pounding his chest, before I drifted gratefully back to sleep.

Our family had always been Transitional, but Daniel was fifteen, old enough to choose for himself. My mother accepted this with diplomatic silence, but my father seemed positively proud of Daniel's independence and strength of conviction. My own feelings were mixed. I'd grown used to swimming in my older brother's wake, but I'd never resented it, because he'd always let me in on the view ahead: reading me passages from the books he read himself, teaching me words and phrases from the languages he studied, sketching some of the mathematics I was yet to encounter first-hand. We used to lie awake half the night, talking about the cores of stars or the hierarchy of transfinite numbers. But Daniel had told me nothing about the reasons for his conversion, and his ever-increasing piety. I didn't know whether to feel hurt by this exclusion, or simply grateful; I could see that being Transitional was like a pale imitation of being Deep Church, but I wasn't sure that this was such a bad thing if the wages of mediocrity included sleeping until sunrise.

Daniel said, "Why?"

I stared up at the underside of his bunk, unsure whether I was really seeing it or just imagining its solidity against the cabin's ordinary darkness. "Someone must have guided the Angels here from Earth. If Earth's too far away to see from Covenant . . . how could anyone find Covenant from Earth, without God's help?"

I heard Daniel shift slightly. "Maybe the Angels had better telescopes than us. Or maybe they spread out from Earth in all directions, launching thousands of expeditions without even knowing what they'd find."

I laughed. "But they had to come *here*, to be made flesh again!" Even a less-than-devout ten-year-old knew that much. God prepared Covenant as the place for the Angels to repent their theft of immortality. The Transitionals believed that in a million years we could earn the right to be Angels again; the Deep Church believed that we'd remain flesh until the stars fell from the sky.

Daniel said, "What makes you so sure that there were ever really Angels? Or that God really sent them Her daughter, Beatrice, to lead them back into the flesh?"

I pondered this for a while. The only answers I could think of came straight out of the Scriptures, and Daniel had taught me years ago that appeals to authority counted for nothing. Finally, I had to confess: "I don't know." I felt foolish, but I was grateful that he was willing to discuss these difficult questions with me. I wanted to believe in God for the right reasons, not just because everyone around me did.

He said, "Archaeologists have shown that we must have arrived about twenty thousand years ago. Before that, there's no evidence of humans, or any coecological plants and animals. That makes the Crossing older than the Scriptures say, but there are some dates that are open to interpretation, and with a bit of poetic license everything can be made to add up. And most biologists think the native microfauna could have formed by itself over millions of years, starting from simple chemicals, but that doesn't mean God didn't guide the whole process. Everything's compatible, really. Science and the Scriptures can both be true."

I thought I knew where he was headed, now. "So you've worked out a way to use science to prove that God exists?" I felt a surge of pride; my brother was a genius!

"No." Daniel was silent for a moment. "The thing is, it works both ways. Whatever's written in the Scriptures, people can always come up with different explanations for the facts. The ships might have left Earth for some other reason. The Angels might have made bodies for themselves for some other reason. There's no way to convince a non-believer that the Scriptures are the word of God. It's all a matter of faith."

"Oh."

"Faith's the most important thing," Daniel insisted. "If you don't have faith, you can be tempted into believing anything at all."

I made a noise of assent, trying not to sound too disappointed. I'd expected more from Daniel than the kind of bland assertions that sent me dozing off during sermons at the Transitional church.

"Do you know what you have to do to get faith?"

"No."

"Ask for it. That's all. Ask Beatrice to come into your heart and grant you the gift of faith."

I protested, "We do that every time we go to church!" I couldn't believe he'd forgotten the Transitional service already. After the priest placed a drop of seawater on our tongues, to symbolize the blood of Beatrice, we asked for the gifts of faith, hope, and love.

"But have you received it?"

I'd never thought about that. "I'm not sure." I believed in God, didn't I? "I might have."

Daniel was amused. "If you had the gift of faith, you'd *know*."

I gazed up into the darkness, troubled. "Do you have to go to the Deep Church, to ask for it properly?"

"No. Even in the Deep Church, not everyone has invited Beatrice into their hearts. You have to do it the way it says in the Scriptures: 'like an unborn child again, naked and helpless.'"

"I was Immersed, wasn't I?"

"In a metal bowl, when you were thirty days old. Infant Immersion is a gesture by the parents, an affirmation of their own good intentions. But it's not enough to save the child."

I was feeling very disoriented now. My father, at least, approved of Daniel's conversion . . . but now Daniel was trying to tell me that our family's transactions with God had all been grossly deficient, if not actually counterfeit.

Daniel said, "Remember what Beatrice told Her followers, the last time She appeared? 'Unless you are willing to drown in My blood, you will never look upon the face of My Mother.' So they bound each other hand and foot, and weighted themselves down with rocks."

My chest tightened. "And you've done that?"

"Yes."

"When?"

"Almost a year ago."

I was more confused than ever. "Did Ma and Fa go?"

Daniel laughed. "No! It's not a public ceremony. Some friends of mine from the Prayer Group helped; someone has to be on deck to haul you up, because it would be arrogant to expect Beatrice to break your bonds and raise you to the surface, like She did with Her followers. But in the water, you're alone with God."

He climbed down from his bunk and crouched by the side of my bed. "Are you ready to give your life to Beatrice, Martin?" His voice sent gray sparks flowing through the darkness.

I hesitated. "What if I just dive in? And stay under for a while?" I'd been swimming off the boat at night plenty of times, there was nothing to fear from that.

"No. You have to be weighted down." His tone made it clear that there could be no compromise on this. "How long can you hold your breath?"

"Two hundred tau." That was an exaggeration; two hundred was what I was aiming for.

"That's long enough."

I didn't reply. Daniel said, "I'll pray with you."

I climbed out of bed, and we knelt together. Daniel murmured, "Please, Holy Beatrice, grant my brother Martin the courage to accept the precious gift of Your blood." Then he started praying in what I took to be a foreign language, uttering a rapid stream of harsh syllables unlike anything I'd heard before. I listened apprehensively; I wasn't sure that I wanted Beatrice to change my mind, and I was afraid that this display of fervor might actually persuade Her.

I said, "What if I don't do it?"

"Then you'll never see the face of God."

I knew what that meant: I'd wander alone in the belly of Death, in darkness, for eternity. And even if the Scriptures weren't meant to be taken literally on this, the reality behind the metaphor could only be worse. Indescribably worse.

"But . . . what about Ma and Fa?" I was more worried about them, because I knew they'd never climb weighted off the side of the boat at Daniel's behest.

"That will take time," he said softly.

My mind reeled. He was absolutely serious.

I heard him stand and walk over to the ladder. He climbed a few rungs and opened the hatch. Enough starlight came in to give shape to his arms and shoulders, but as he turned to me I still couldn't make out his face. "Come on, Martin!" he whispered. "The longer you put it off, the harder it gets." The hushed urgency of his voice was familiar: generous and conspiratorial, nothing like an adult's impatience: He might almost have been daring me to join him in a midnight raid on the pantry—not because he really needed a collaborator, but because he honestly didn't want me to miss out on the excitement, or the spoils.

I suppose I was more afraid of damnation than drowning, and I'd always trusted Daniel to warn me of the dangers ahead. But this time I wasn't entirely convinced that he was right, so I must have been driven by something more than fear, and blind trust.

Maybe it came down to the fact that he was offering to make me his equal in this. I was ten years old, and I ached to become something more than I was; to reach, not my parents burdensome adulthood, but the halfway point, full of freedom and secrets, that Daniel had reached. I wanted to be as strong, as fast, as quick-witted and widely read as he was. Becoming as certain of God would not have been my first choice, but there wasn't much point hoping for divine intervention to grant me anything else.

I followed him up onto the deck.

He took cord, and a knife, and four spare weights of the kind we used on our nets from the toolbox. He threaded the weights onto the cord, then I took off my shorts and sat naked on the deck while he knotted a figure-eight around my ankles. I raised my feet experimentally; the weights didn't seem all that heavy. But in the water, I knew, they'd be more than enough to counteract my body's slight buoyancy.

"Martin? Hold out your hands."

Suddenly I was crying. With my arms free, at least I could swim against the tug of the weights. But if my hands were tied, I'd be helpless.

Daniel crouched down and met my eyes. "Ssh. It's all right."

I hated myself. I could feel my face contorted into the mask of a blubbering infant.

"Are you afraid?"

I nodded.

Daniel smiled reassuringly. "You know why? You know who's doing that? Death doesn't want Beatrice to have you. He wants you for himself. So he's here on this boat, putting fear into your heart, because he *knows* he's almost lost you."

I saw something move in the shadows behind the toolbox, something slithering into the darkness. If we went back down to the cabin now, would Death follow us? To wait for Daniel to fall asleep? If I'd turned my back on Beatrice, who could I ask to send Death away?

I stared at the deck, tears of shame dripping from my cheeks. I held out my arms, wrists together.

When my hands were tied—not palm-to-palm as I'd expected, but in separate loops joined by a short bridge—Daniel unwound a long stretch of rope from the winch at the rear of the boat, and coiled it on the deck. I didn't want to think about how long it was, but I knew I'd never dived to that depth. He took the blunt hook at the end of the rope, slipped it over my arms, then screwed it closed to form an unbroken ring. Then he checked again that the cord around my wrists was neither so tight as to burn me, nor so loose as to let me slip. As he did this, I saw something creep over his face: some kind of doubt or fear of his own. He said, "Hang on to the hook. Just in case. Don't let go, no matter what. Okay?" He whispered something to Beatrice, then looked up at me, confident again.

He helped me to stand and shuffle over to the guard rail, just to one side of the winch. Then he picked me up under the arms and lifted me over, resting my feet on the outer hull. The deck was inert, a mineralized endoshell, but behind the guard rails the hull was palpably alive: slick with protective secretions, glowing softly. My toes curled uselessly against the lubricated skin; I had no purchase at all. The hull was supporting some of my weight, but Daniel's arms would tire eventually. If I wanted to back out, I'd have to do it quickly.

A warm breeze was blowing. I looked around, at the flat horizon, at the blaze of stars, at the faint silver light off the water. Daniel recited: "Holy Beatrice, I am ready to die to this world. Let me drown in Your blood, that I might be redeemed, and look upon the face of Your Mother."

I repeated the words, trying hard to mean them.

"Holy Beatrice, I offer You my life. All I do now, I do for You. Come into my heart, and grant me the gift of faith. Come into my heart, and grant me the gift of hope. Come into my heart, and grant me the gift of love."

"And grant me the gift of love."

Daniel released me. At first, my feet seemed to adhere magically to the hull, and I pivoted backward without actually falling. I clung tightly to the hook, pressing the cold metal against my belly, and willed the rope of the winch to snap taut, leaving me dangling in midair. I even braced myself for the shock. Some part of me really did believe that I could change my mind, even now.

Then my feet slipped and I plunged into the ocean and sank straight down.

It was not like a dive—not even a dive from an untried height, when it took so long for the water to bring you to a halt that it began to grow frightening. I was falling through the water ever faster, as if it was air. The vision I'd had of the rope keeping me above the water now swung to the opposite extreme: my acceleration seemed to prove that the coil on the deck was attached to nothing, that its frayed end was already beneath the surface. *That's what the followers had done, wasn't it? They'd let themselves be thrown in without a lifeline.* So Daniel had cut the rope, and I was on my way to the bottom of the ocean.

Then the hook jerked my hands up over my head, jarring my wrists and shoulders, and I was motionless.

I turned my face toward the surface, but neither starlight nor the hull's faint phosphorescence reached this deep. I let a stream of bubbles escape from my mouth; I felt them slide over my upper lip, but no trace of them registered in the darkness.

I shifted my hands warily over the hook. I could still feel the cord fast around my wrists, but Daniel had warned me not to trust it. I brought my knees up to my chest, gauging the effect of the weights. If the cord broke, at least my hands would be free, but even so I wasn't sure I'd be able to ascend. The thought of trying to unpick the knots around my ankles as I tumbled deeper filled me with horror.

My shoulders ached, but I wasn't injured. It didn't take much effort to pull myself up until my chin was level with the bottom of the hook. Going further was awkward—with my hands so close together I couldn't brace myself properly—but on the third attempt I managed to get my arms locked, pointing straight down.

I'd done this without any real plan, but then it struck me that even with my hands and feet tied, I could try shinning up the rope. It was just a matter of getting started. I'd have to turn upside-down, grab the rope between my knees, then curl up— dragging the hook—and get a grip with my hands at a higher point.

And if I couldn't reach up far enough to right myself?

I'd ascend feet-first.

I couldn't even manage the first step. I thought it would be as simple as keeping my arms rigid and letting myself topple backward, but in the water even two-thirds of my body wasn't sufficient to counterbalance the weights.

I tried a different approach: I dropped down to hang at arm's length, raised my legs as high as I could, then proceeded to pull myself up again. But my grip wasn't tight enough to resist the turning force of the weights; I just pivoted around my center of gravity—which was somewhere near my knees—and ended up, still bent double, but almost horizontal.

I eased myself down again, and tried threading my feet through the circle of my arms. I didn't succeed on the first attempt, and then on reflection it seemed like a bad move anyway. Even if I managed to grip the rope between my bound feet— rather than just tumbling over backward, out of control, and dislocating my shoulders—climbing the rope *upside-down with my hands behind my back* would either be impossible, or so awkward and strenuous that I'd run out of oxygen before I got a tenth of the way.

I let some more air escape from my lungs. I could feel the muscles in my diaphragm reproaching me for keeping them from doing what they wanted to do; not urgently yet, but the knowledge that I had no control over when I'd be able to draw breath again made it harder to stay calm. I knew I could rely on Daniel to bring me to the surface on the count of two hundred. But I'd only ever stayed down for a hundred and sixty. Forty more tau would be an eternity.

I'd almost forgotten what the whole ordeal was meant to be about, but now I started praying. *Please Holy Beatrice, don't let me die. I know You drowned like this to save me, but if I die it won't help anyone. Daniel would end up in the deepest shit . . . but that's not a threat, it's just an observation.* I felt a stab of anxiety; on top of everything else, had I just offended the Daughter of God? I struggled on, my confidence waning. *I don't want to die. But You already know that. So I don't know what You want me to say.*

I released some more stale air, wishing I'd counted the time I'd been under: you weren't supposed to empty your lungs too quickly—when they were deflated it was even harder not to take a breath—but holding all the carbon dioxide in too long wasn't good either.

Praying only seemed to make me more desperate, so I tried to think other kinds of holy thoughts. I couldn't remember anything from the Scriptures word for word, but the gist of the most important part started running through my mind.

After living in Her body for thirty years, and persuading all the Angels to become mortal again, Beatrice had gone back up to their deserted spaceship and flown it straight into the ocean. When Death saw Her coming, he took the form of a giant serpent, coiled in the water, waiting. And even though She was the Daughter of God, with the power to do anything, She let Death swallow Her.

That's how much She loved us.

Death thought he'd won everything. Beatrice was trapped inside him, in the darkness, alone. The Angels were flesh again, so he wouldn't even have to wait for the stars to fall before he claimed them.

But Beatrice was part of God. Death had swallowed part of God. This was a mistake. After three days, his jaws burst open and Beatrice came flying out, wreathed in fire. Death was broken, shriveled, diminished.

My limbs were numb but my chest was burning. Death was still strong enough to hold down the damned. I started thrashing about blindly, wasting whatever oxygen was left in my blood, but desperate to distract myself from the urge to inhale.

Please Holy Beatrice—

Please Daniel—

Luminous bruises blossomed behind my eyes and drifted out into the water. I watched them curling into a kind of vortex, as if something was drawing them in.

It was the mouth of the serpent, swallowing my soul. I opened my own mouth and made a wretched noise, and Death swam forward to kiss me, to breathe cold water into my lungs.

Suddenly, everything was seared with light. The serpent turned and fled, like a pale timid worm. A wave of contentment washed over me, as if I was an infant again and my mother had wrapped her arms around me tightly. It was like basking in sunlight, listening to laughter, dreaming of music too beautiful to be real. Every muscle in my body was still trying to prize my lungs open to the water, but now I found myself fighting this almost absentmindedly while I marveled at my strange euphoria.

Cold air swept over my hands and down my arms. I raised myself up to take a mouthful, then slumped down again, giddy and spluttering, grateful for every breath but still elated by something else entirely. The light that had filled my eyes was gone, but it left a violet afterimage everywhere I looked. Daniel kept winding until my head was level with the guard rail, then he clamped the winch, bent down, and threw me over his shoulder.

I'd been warm enough in the water, but now my teeth were chattering. Daniel wrapped a towel around me, then set to work cutting the cord. I beamed at him. "I'm so happy!" He gestured to me to be quieter, but then he whispered joyfully, "That's the love of Beatrice. She'll always be with you now, Martin."

I blinked with surprise, then laughed softly at my own stupidity. Until that moment, I hadn't connected what had happened with Beatrice at all. But of course it was Her. I'd asked Her to come into my heart, and She had.

And I could see it in Daniel's face: a year after his own Drowning, he still felt Her presence.

He said, "Everything you do now is for Beatrice. When you look through your telescope, you'll do it to honor Her creation. When you eat, or drink, or swim, you'll do it to give thanks for Her gifts." I nodded enthusiastically.

Daniel tidied everything away, even soaking up the puddles of water I'd left on the deck. Back in the cabin, he recited from the Scriptures, passages that I'd never really understood before, but which now all seemed to be about the Drowning, and the way I was feeling. It was as if I'd opened the book and found myself mentioned by name on every page.

When Daniel fell asleep before me, for the first time in my life I didn't feel the slightest pang of loneliness. The Daughter of God was with me: I could feel Her presence, like a flame inside my skull, radiating warmth through the darkness behind my eyes.

Giving me comfort, giving me strength.

Giving me faith.

TWO

The monastery was almost four milliradians northeast of our home grounds. Daniel and I took the launch to a rendezvous point, and met up with three other small vessels before continuing. It had been the same routine every tenth night for almost a year—and Daniel had been going to the Prayer Group himself for a year before that—so the launch didn't need much supervision. Feeding on nutrients in the ocean, propelling itself by pumping water through fine channels in its skin, guided by both sunlight and Covenant's magnetic field, it was a perfect example of the kind of legacy of the Angels that technology would never be able to match.

Bartholomew, Rachel, and Agnes were in one launch, and they traveled beside us while the others skimmed ahead. Bartholomew and Rachel were married, though they were only seventeen, scarcely older than Daniel. Agnes, Rachel's sister, was sixteen. Because I was the youngest member of the Prayer Group, Agnes had fussed over me from the day I'd joined. She said, "It's your big night tonight, Martin, isn't it?" I nodded, but declined to pursue the conversation, leaving her free to talk to Daniel.

It was dusk by the time the monastery came into sight, a conical tower built from at least ten thousand hulls, rising up from the water in the stylized form of Beatrice's spaceship. Aimed at the sky, not down into the depths. Though some commentators on the Scriptures insisted that the spaceship itself had sunk forever, and Beatrice had risen from the water unaided, it was still the definitive symbol of Her victory over Death. For the three days of Her separation from God, all such buildings stood in darkness, but that was half a year away, and now the monastery shone from every porthole.

There was a narrow tunnel leading into the base of the tower; the launches detected its scent in the water and filed in one by one. I knew they didn't have souls, but I wondered what it would have been like for them if they'd been aware of their actions. Normally they rested in the dock of a single hull, a pouch of boatskin that secured them but still left them largely exposed. Maybe being drawn instinctively into this vast structure would have felt even safer, even more comforting, than docking with their home boat. When I said something to this effect, Rachel, in the launch behind me, sniggered. Agnes said, "Don't be horrible."

The walls of the tunnel phosphoresced pale green, but the opening ahead was filled with white lamplight, dazzlingly richer and brighter. We emerged into a canal circling a vast atrium, and continued around it until the launches found empty docks.

As we disembarked, every footstep, every splash, echoed back at us. I looked up at the ceiling, a dome spliced together from hundreds of curved triangular hull sections, tattooed with scenes from the Scriptures. The original illustrations were more than a thousand years old, but the living boatskin degraded the pigments on a time scale of decades, so the monks had to constantly renew them.

"Beatrice Joining the Angels" was my favorite. Because the Angels weren't flesh, they didn't grow inside their mothers; they just appeared from nowhere in the streets of the Immaterial Cities. In the picture on the ceiling, Beatrice's immaterial body was half-formed, with cherubs still working to clothe the immaterial bones of Her legs and arms in immaterial muscles, veins, and skin. A few Angels in luminous robes were glancing sideways at Her, but you could tell they weren't particularly impressed. They'd had no way of knowing, then, who She was.

A corridor with its own smaller illustrations led from the atrium to the meeting room. There were about fifty people in the Prayer Group—including several priests and monks, though they acted just like everyone else. In church, you followed the liturgy; the priest slotted in his or her sermon, but there was no room for the worshippers to do much more than pray or sing in unison and offer rote responses. Here it was much less formal. There were two or three different speakers every night—sometimes guests who were visiting the monastery, sometimes members of the group—and after that anyone could ask the group to pray with them, about whatever they liked.

I'd fallen behind the others, but they'd saved me an aisle seat. Agnes was to my left, then Daniel, Bartholomew and Rachel. Agnes said, "Are you nervous?"

"No."

Daniel laughed, as if this claim was ridiculous.

I said, "I'm not." I'd meant to sound loftily unperturbed, but the words came out sullen and childish.

The first two speakers were both lay theologians, Firmlanders who were visiting the monastery. One gave a talk about people who belonged to false religions, and how they were all—in effect—worshipping Beatrice, but just didn't know it. He said they wouldn't be damned, because they'd had no choice about the cultures they were born into. Beatrice would know they'd meant well, and forgive them.

I wanted this to be true, but it made no sense to me. Either Beatrice *was* the Daughter of God, and everyone who thought otherwise had turned away from Her into the darkness, or . . . there was no "or." I only had to close my eyes and feel Her presence to know that. Still, everyone applauded when the man finished, and all the questions people asked seemed sympathetic to his views, so perhaps his arguments had simply been too subtle for me to follow.

The second speaker referred to Beatrice as "the Holy Jester," and rebuked us severely for not paying enough attention to Her sense of humor. She cited events in the Scriptures which she said were practical jokes, and then went on at some length about "the healing power of laughter." It was all about as gripping as a lecture on nutrition and hygiene; I struggled to keep my eyes open. At the end, no one could think of any questions.

Then Carol, who was running the meeting, said, "Now Martin is going to give witness to the power of Beatrice in his life."

Everyone applauded encouragingly. As I rose to my feet and stepped into the aisle, Daniel leaned toward Agnes and whispered sarcastically, "This should be good."

I stood at the lectern and gave the talk I'd been rehearsing for days. Beatrice, I said, was beside me now whatever I did: whether I studied or worked, ate or swam, or just sat and watched the stars. When I woke in the morning and looked into my heart, She was there without fail, offering me strength and guidance. When I lay in bed at night, I feared nothing, because I knew She was watching over me. Before my Drowning, I'd been unsure of my faith, but now I'd never again be able to doubt that the Daughter of God had become flesh, and died, and conquered Death, because of Her great love for us.

It was all true, but even as I said these things I couldn't get Daniel's sarcastic words out of my mind. I glanced over at the row where I'd been sitting, at the people I'd traveled with. What did I have in common with them, really? Rachel and Bartholomew were married. Bartholomew and Daniel had studied together, and still played on the same dive-ball team. Daniel and Agnes were probably in love. And Daniel was my brother . . . but the only difference that seemed to make was the fact that he could belittle me far more efficiently than any stranger.

In the open prayer that followed, I paid no attention to the problems and blessings people were sharing with the group. I tried silently calling on Beatrice to dissolve the knot of anger in my heart. But I couldn't do it; I'd turned too far away from Her.

When the meeting was over, and people started moving into the adjoining room to talk for a while, I hung back. When the others were out of sight, I ducked into the corridor, and headed straight for the launch.

Daniel could get a ride home with his friends; it wasn't far out of their way. I'd wait a short distance from the boat until he caught up; if my parents saw me arrive on my own I'd be in trouble. Daniel would be angry, of course, but he wouldn't betray me.

Once I'd freed the launch from its dock, it knew exactly where to go: around the canal, back to the tunnel, out into the open sea. As I sped across the calm, dark water, I felt the presence of Beatrice returning, which seemed like a sign that She understood that I'd had to get away.

I leaned over and dipped my hand in the water, feeling the current the launch was generating by shuffling ions in and out of the cells of its skin. The outer hull glowed a phosphorescent blue, more to warn other vessels than to light the way. In the time of Beatrice, one of her followers had sat in the Immaterial City and designed this creature from scratch. It gave me a kind of vertigo, just imagining the things the Angels had known. I wasn't sure why so much of it had been lost, but I wanted to rediscover it all. Even the Deep Church taught that there was nothing wrong with that, so long as we didn't use it to try to become immortal again.

The monastery shrank to a blur of light on the horizon, and there was no other beacon visible on the water, but I could read the stars, and sense the field lines, so I knew the launch was heading in the right direction.

When I noticed a blue speck in the distance, it was clear that it wasn't Daniel and the others chasing after me; it was coming from the wrong direction. As I watched the launch drawing nearer I grew anxious; if this was someone I knew, and I couldn't come up with a good reason to be traveling alone, word would get back to my parents.

Before I could make out anyone on board, a voice shouted, "Can you help me? I'm lost!"

I thought for a while before replying. The voice sounded almost matter-of-fact, making light of this blunt admission of helplessness, but it was no joke. If you were sick, your diurnal sense and your field sense could both become scrambled, making the stars much harder to read. It had happened to me a couple of times, and it had been a horrible experience—even standing safely on the deck of our boat. This late at night, a launch with only its field sense to guide it could lose track of its position, especially if you were trying to take it somewhere it hadn't been before.

I shouted back our coordinates, and the time. I was fairly confident that I had them down to the nearest hundred microradians, and few hundred tau.

"That can't be right! Can I approach? Let our launches talk?"

I hesitated. It had been drummed into me for as long as I could remember that if I ever found myself alone on the water, I should give other vessels a wide berth unless I knew the people on board. But Beatrice was with me, and if someone needed help it was wrong to refuse them.

"All right!" I stopped dead, and waited for the stranger to close the gap. As the launch drew up beside me, I was surprised to see that the passenger was a young man. He looked about Bartholomew's age, but he'd sounded much older.

We didn't need to tell the launches what to do; proximity was enough to trigger a chemical exchange of information. The man said, "Out on your own?"

"I'm traveling with my brother and his friends. I just went ahead a bit."

That made him smile. "Sent you on your way, did they? What do you think they're getting up to, back there?" I didn't reply; that was no way to talk about people you didn't even know. The man scanned the horizon, then spread his arms in a gesture of sympathy. "You must be feeling left out."

I shook my head. There was a pair of binoculars on the floor behind him; even before he'd called out for help, he could have seen that I was alone.

He jumped deftly between the launches, landing on the stern bench. I said, "There's nothing to steal." My skin was crawling, more with disbelief than fear. He was standing on the bench in the starlight, pulling a knife from his belt. The details—the pattern carved into the handle, the serrated edge of the blade—only made it seem more like a dream.

He coughed, suddenly nervous. "Just do what I tell you, and you won't get hurt."

I filled my lungs and shouted for help with all the strength I had; I knew there was no one in earshot, but I thought it might still frighten him off. He looked around, more startled than angry, as if he couldn't quite believe I'd waste so much effort. I jumped backward, into the water. A moment later I heard him follow me.

I found the blue glow of the launches above me, then swam hard, down and away from them, without wasting time searching for his shadow. Blood was pounding in my ears, but I knew I was moving almost silently; however fast he was, in the darkness he could swim right past me without knowing it. If he didn't catch me soon he'd probably return to the launch and wait to spot me when I came up for air. I had to surface far enough away to be invisible — even with the binoculars.

I was terrified that I'd feel a hand close around my ankle at any moment, but Beatrice was with me. As I swam, I thought back to my Drowning, and Her presence grew stronger than ever. When my lungs were almost bursting. She helped me to keep going, my limbs moving mechanically, blotches of light floating in front of my eyes. When I finally knew I had to surface, I turned face-up and ascended slowly, then lay on my back with only my mouth and nose above the water, refusing the temptation to stick my head up and look around.

I filled and emptied my lungs a few times, then dived again.

The fifth time I surfaced, I dared to look back. I couldn't see either launch. I raised myself higher, then turned a full circle in case I'd grown disoriented, but nothing came into sight.

I checked the stars, and my field sense. The launches should *not* have been over the horizon. I trod water, riding the swell, and tried not to think about how tired I was. It was at least two milliradians to the nearest boat. Good swimmers — some younger than I was — competed in marathons over distances like that, but I'd never even aspired to such feats of endurance. Unprepared, in the middle of the night, I knew I wouldn't make it.

If the man had given up on me, would he have taken our launch? When they cost so little, and the markings were so hard to change? That would be nothing but an admission of guilt. *So why couldn't I see it?* Either he'd sent it on its way, or it had decided to return home itself.

I knew the path it would have taken; I would have seen it go by, if I'd been looking for it when I'd surfaced before. But I had no hope of catching it now.

I began to pray. I knew I'd been wrong to leave the others, but I asked for forgiveness, and felt it being granted. I watched the horizon almost calmly — smiling at the blue flashes of meteors burning up high above the ocean — certain that Beatrice would not abandon me.

I was still praying — treading water, shivering from the cool of the air — when a blue light appeared in the distance. It disappeared as the swell took me down again, but there was no mistaking it for a shooting star. *Was this Daniel and the others — or the stranger?* I didn't have long to decide; if I wanted to get within earshot as they passed, I'd have to swim hard.

I closed my eyes and prayed for guidance. *Please Holy Beatrice, let me know.* Joy flooded through my mind, instantly: it was them, I was certain of it. I set off as fast as I could.

I started yelling before I could see how many passengers there were, but I knew Beatrice would never allow me to be mistaken. A flare shot up from the launch, revealing four figures standing side by side, scanning the water. I shouted with jubilation, and waved my arms. Someone finally spotted me, and they brought the launch around toward me. By the time I was on board I was so charged up on adrenaline and relief that I almost believed I could have dived back into the water and raced them home.

I thought Daniel would be angry, but when I described what had happened all he said was, "We'd better get moving."

Agnes embraced me. Bartholomew gave me an almost respectful look, but Rachel muttered sourly, "You're an idiot, Martin. You don't know how lucky you are."

I said, "I know."

Our parents were standing on deck. The empty launch had arrived some time ago; they'd been about to set out to look for us. When the others had departed I began recounting everything again, this time trying to play down any element of danger.

Before I'd finished, my mother grabbed Daniel by the front of his shirt and started slapping him. "I trusted you with him! *You maniac!* I trusted you!" Daniel half raised his arm to block her, but then let it drop and just turned his face to the deck.

I burst into tears. "It was my fault!" Our parents never struck us; I couldn't believe what I was seeing.

My father said soothingly, "Look . . . he's home now. He's safe. No one touched him." He put an arm around my shoulders and asked warily. "That's right, Martin, isn't it?"

I nodded tearfully. This was worse than anything that had happened on the launch, or in the water; I felt a thousand times more helpless, a thousand times more like a child.

I said, "Beatrice was watching over me."

My mother rolled her eyes and laughed wildly, letting go of Daniel's shirt. "Beatrice? *Beatrice?* Don't you know what could have happened to you? You're too young to have given him what he wanted. He would have had to use the knife."

The chill of my wet clothes seemed to penetrate deeper. I swayed unsteadily, but fought to stay upright. Then I whispered stubbornly, "Beatrice was there."

My father said, "Go and get changed, or you're going to freeze to death."

I lay in bed listening to them shout at Daniel. When he finally came down the ladder I was so sick with shame that I wished I'd drowned.

He said, "Are you all right?"

There was nothing I could say. I couldn't ask him to forgive me.

"Martin?" Daniel turned on the lamp. His face was streaked with tears: he laughed softly, wiping them away. "Fuck, you had me worried. Don't ever do anything like that again."

"I won't."

"Okay." That was it; no shouting, no recriminations. "Do you want to pray with me?"

We knelt side by side, praying for our parents to be at peace, praying for the man who'd tried to hurt me. I started trembling; everything was catching up with me. Suddenly, words began gushing from my mouth—words I neither recognized nor understood, though I knew I was praying for everything to be all right with Daniel, praying that our parents would stop blaming him for my stupidity.

The strange words kept flowing out of me, an incomprehensible torrent somehow imbued with everything I was feeling. I knew what was happening: *Beatrice had given me the Angels' tongue.* We'd had to surrender all knowledge of it when we became flesh, but sometimes. She granted people the ability to pray this way, because the language of the Angels could express things we could no longer put into words. Daniel had been able to do it ever since his Drowning, but it wasn't something you could teach, or even something you could ask for.

When I finally stopped, my mind was racing. "Maybe Beatrice planned everything that happened tonight? Maybe She arranged it all, to lead up to this moment!"

Daniel shook his head, wincing slightly. "Don't get carried away. You have the gift; just accept it." He nudged me with his shoulder. "Now get into bed, before we're both in more trouble."

I lay awake almost until dawn, overwhelmed with happiness. Daniel had forgiven me. Beatrice had protected and blessed me. I felt no more shame, just humility and amazement. I knew I'd done nothing to deserve it, but my life was wrapped in the love of God.

THREE

According to the Scriptures, the oceans of Earth were storm-tossed, and filled with dangerous creatures. But on Covenant, the oceans were calm, and the Angels created nothing in the ecopoiesis that would harm their own mortal incarnations. The four continents and the four oceans were rendered equally hospitable, and just as women and men were made indistinguishable in the sight of God, so were Freelanders and Firmlanders. (Some commentators insisted that this was literally true: God chose to blind Herself to where we lived, and whether or not we'd been born with a penis. I thought that was a beautiful idea, even if I couldn't quite grasp the logistics of it.)

I'd heard that certain obscure sects taught that half the Angels had actually become embodied as a separate people who could live in the water and breathe beneath the surface, but then God destroyed them because they were a mockery of Beatrice's death. No legitimate church took this notion seriously, though, and archaeologists had found no trace of these mythical doomed cousins. Humans were humans, there was only one kind. Freelanders and Firmlanders could even intermarry—if they could agree where to live.

When I was fifteen, Daniel became engaged to Agnes from the Prayer Group. That made sense: they'd be spared the explanations and arguments about the Drowning that they might have faced with partners who weren't so blessed. Agnes was a Freelander, of course, but a large branch of her family, and a smaller branch of ours, were Firmlanders, so after long negotiations it was decided that the wedding would be held in Ferez, a coastal town.

I went with my father to pick a hull to be fitted out as Daniel and Agnes's boat. The breeder, Diana, had a string of six mature hulls in tow, and my father insisted on walking out onto their backs and personally examining each one for imperfections.

By the time we reached the fourth I was losing patience. I muttered, "It's the skin underneath that matters." In fact, you could tell a lot about a hull's general condition from up here, but there wasn't much point worrying about a few tiny flaws high above the waterline.

My father nodded thoughtfully. "That's true. You'd better get in the water and check their undersides."

"I'm not doing that." We couldn't simply trust this woman to sell us a healthy hull for a decent price; that wouldn't have been sufficiently embarrassing.

"Martin! This is for the safety of your brother and sister-in-law."

I glanced at Diana to show her where my sympathies lay, then slipped off my shirt and dived in. I swam down to the last hull in the row, then ducked beneath it. I began the job with perverse thoroughness, running my fingers over every square nanoradian of skin. I was determined to annoy my father by taking even longer than he wanted—and determined to impress Diana by examining all six hulls without coming up for air.

An unfitted hull rode higher in the water than a boat full of furniture and junk, but I was surprised to discover that even in the creature's shadow there was enough light for me to see the skin clearly. After a while I realized that, paradoxically, this was because the water was slightly cloudier than usual, and whatever the fine particles were, they were scattering sunlight into the shadows.

Moving through the warm, bright water, feeling the love of Beatrice more strongly than I had for a long time, it was impossible to remain angry with my father. He wanted the best hull for Daniel and Agnes, and so did I. As for impressing Diana . . . who was I kidding? She was a grown woman, at least as old as Agnes, and highly unlikely to view me as anything more than a child. By the time I'd finished with the third hull I was feeling short of breath, so I surfaced and reported cheerfully, "No blemishes so far!"

Diana smiled down at me. "You've got strong lungs."

All six hulls were in perfect condition. We ended up taking the one at the end of the row, because it was easiest to detach.

Ferez was built on the mouth of a river, but the docks were some distance upstream. That helped to prepare us; the gradual deadening of the waves was less of a shock than an instant transition from sea to land would have been. When I jumped from the deck to the pier, though, it was like colliding with something massive and unyielding, the rock of the planet itself. I'd been on land twice before, for less than a day on both occasions. The wedding celebrations would last ten days, but at least we'd still be able to sleep on the boat.

As the four of us walked along the crowded streets, heading for the ceremonial hall where everything but the wedding sacrament itself would take place, I stared uncouthly at everyone in sight. Almost no one was barefoot like us, and after a few hundred tau on the paving stones—much rougher than any deck—I could understand why. Our clothes were different, our skin was darker, our accent was unmistakably foreign . . . but no one stared back. Freelanders were hardly a novelty here. That made me even more self-conscious; the curiosity I felt wasn't mutual.

In the hall, I joined in with the preparations, mainly just lugging furniture around under the directions of one of Agnes's tyrannical uncles. It was a new kind of shock to see so many Freelanders together in this alien environment, and stranger still when I realized that I couldn't necessarily spot the Firmlanders among us; there was no sharp dividing line in physical appearance, or even clothing. I began to feel slightly guilty; if God couldn't tell the difference, what was I doing hunting for the signs?

At noon, we all ate outside, in a garden behind the hall. The grass was soft, but it made my feet itch. Daniel had gone off to be fitted for wedding clothes, and my parents were performing some vital task of their own; I only recognized a handful of the people around me. I sat in the shade of a tree, pretending to be oblivious to the plant's enormous size and bizarre anatomy. I wondered if we'd take a siesta; I couldn't imagine falling asleep on the grass.

Someone sat down beside me, and I turned.

"I'm Lena. Agnes's second cousin."

"I'm Daniel's brother, Martin." I hesitated, then offered her my hand; she took it, smiling slightly. I'd awkwardly kissed a dozen strangers that morning, all distant prospective relatives, but this time I didn't dare.

"Brother of the groom, doing grunt work with the rest of us." She shook her head in mocking admiration.

I desperately wanted to say something witty in reply, but an attempt that failed would be even worse than merely being dull. "Do you live in Ferez?"

"No, Mitar. Inland from here. We're staying with my uncle." She pulled a face. "Along with ten other people. No privacy. It's awful."

I said, "It was easy for us. We just brought our home with us." *You idiot. As if she didn't know that.*

Lena smiled. "I haven't been on a boat in years. You'll have to give me a tour sometime."

"Of course. I'd be happy to." I knew she was only making small talk; she'd never take me up on the offer.

She said, "Is it just you and Daniel?"

"Yes."

"You must be close."

I shrugged. "What about you?"

"Two brothers. Both younger. Eight and nine. They're all right, I suppose." She rested her chin on one hand and gazed at me coolly.

I looked away, disconcerted by more than my wishful thinking about what lay behind that gaze. Unless her parents had been awfully young when she was born, it didn't seem likely that more children were planned. So did an odd number in the family mean that one had died, or that the custom of equal numbers carried by each parent wasn't followed where she lived? I'd studied the region less than a year ago, but I had a terrible memory for things like that.

Lena said, "You looked so lonely, off here on your own."

I turned back to her, surprised. "I'm never lonely."

"No?"

She seemed genuinely curious. I opened my mouth to tell her about Beatrice, but then changed my mind. The few times I'd said anything to friends—ordinary friends, not Drowned ones—I'd regretted it. Not everyone had laughed, but they'd all been acutely embarrassed by the revelation.

I said, "Mitar has a million people, doesn't it?"

"Yes."

"An area of ocean the same size would have a population of ten."

Lena frowned. "That's a bit too deep for me, I'm afraid." She rose to her feet. "But maybe you'll think of a way of putting it that even a Firmlander can understand." She raised a hand goodbye and started walking away.

I said, "Maybe I will."

The wedding took place in Ferez's Deep Church, a spaceship built of stone, glass, and wood. It looked almost like a parody of the churches I was used to, though it probably bore a closer resemblance to the Angels' real ship than anything made of living hulls.

Daniel and Agnes stood before the priest, beneath the apex of the building. Their closest relatives stood behind them in two angled lines on either side. My father—Daniel's mother—was first in our line, followed by my own mother, then me. That put me level with Rachel, who kept shooting disdainful glances my way. After my misadventure, Daniel and I had eventually been allowed to travel to the Prayer Group meetings again, but less than a year later I'd lost interest, and soon after I'd also stopped going to church. Beatrice was with me, constantly, and no gatherings or ceremonies could bring me any closer to Her. I knew Daniel disapproved of this attitude, but he didn't lecture me about it, and my parents had accepted my decision without any fuss. If Rachel thought I was some kind of apostate, that was her problem.

The priest said, "Which of you brings a bridge to this marriage?"

Daniel said, "I do." In the Transitional ceremony, they no longer asked this; it was really no one else's business—and in a way the question was almost sacrilegious. Still, Deep Church theologians had explained away greater doctrinal inconsistencies than this, so who was I to argue?

"Do you, Daniel and Agnes, solemnly declare that this bridge will be the bond of your union until death, to be shared with no other person?"

They replied together, "We solemnly declare."

"Do you solemnly declare that as you share this bridge, so shall you share every joy and every burden of marriage—equally?"

"We solemnly declare."

My mind wandered; I thought of Lena's parents. Maybe one of the family's children was adopted. Lena and I had managed to sneak away to the boat three times so far, early in the evenings while my parents were still out. We'd done things I'd never done with anyone else, but I still hadn't had the courage to ask her anything so personal.

Suddenly the priest was saying, "In the eyes of God, you are one now." My father started weeping softly. As Daniel and Agnes kissed, I felt a surge of contradictory emotions. I'd miss Daniel, but I was glad that I'd finally have a chance to live apart from him. And I wanted him to be happy—I was jealous of his happiness already—but at the same time, the thought of marrying someone like Agnes filled me with claustrophobia. She was kind, devout, and generous. She and Daniel would treat each other, and their children, well. But neither of them would present the slightest challenge to the other's most cherished beliefs.

This recipe for harmony terrified me. Not least because I was afraid that Beatrice approved, and wanted me to follow it myself.

Lena put her hand over mine and pushed my fingers deeper into her, gasping. We were sitting on my bunk, face to face, my legs stretched out flat, hers arching over them.

She slid the palm of her other hand over my penis. I bent forward and kissed her, moving my thumb over the place she'd shown me, and her shudder ran through both of us.

"Martin?"

"What?"

She stroked me with one fingertip; somehow it was far better than having her whole hand wrapped around me.

"Do you want to come inside me?"

I shook my head.

"Why not?"

She kept moving her finger, tracing the same line; I could barely think. Why *not?* "You might get pregnant."

She laughed. "Don't be stupid. I can control that. You'll learn, too. It's just a matter of experience."

I said. "I'll use my tongue, You liked that."

"I did. But I want something more now. And you do, too. I can tell." She smiled imploringly. "It'll be nice for both of us, I promise. Nicer than anything you've done in your life."

"Don't bet on it."

Lena made a sound of disbelief, and ran her thumb around the base of my penis. "I can tell you haven't put this inside anyone before. But that's nothing to be ashamed of."

"Who said I was ashamed?"

She nodded gravely. "All right. Frightened."

I pulled my hand free, and banged my head on the bunk above us. Daniel's old bunk.

Lena reached up and put her hand on my cheek.

I said. "I can't. We're not married."

She frowned. "I heard you'd given up on all that."

"All what?"

"Religion."

"Then you were misinformed."

Lena said, "This is what the Angels made our bodies to do. How can there be anything sinful in that?" She ran her hand down my neck, over my chest.

"But the bridge is meant to . . ." *What?* All the Scriptures said was that it was meant to unite men and women, equally. And the Scriptures said God couldn't tell women and men apart, but in the Deep Church, in the sight of God, the priest had just made Daniel claim priority. So why should I care what any priest thought?

I said, "All right."

"Are you sure?"

"Yes." I took her face in my hands and started kissing her. After a while, she reached down and guided me in. The shock of pleasure almost made me come, but I stopped myself somehow. When the risk of that had lessened, we wrapped our arms around each other and rocked slowly back and forth.

It wasn't better than my Drowning, but it was so much like it that it had to be blessed by Beatrice. And as we moved in each other's arms, I grew determined to ask Lena to marry me. She was intelligent and strong. She questioned everything. It didn't matter that she was a Firmlander; we could meet halfway, we could live in Ferez.

I felt myself ejaculate. "I'm sorry."

Lena whispered, "That's all right, that's all right. Just keep moving."

I was still hard; that had never happened before. I could feel her muscles clenching and releasing rhythmically, in time with our motion, and her slow exhalations. Then she cried out, and dug her fingers into my back. I tried to slide partly out of her again, but it was impossible, she was holding me too tightly. This was it. There was no going back.

Now I was afraid. "I've never—" Tears were welling up in my eyes; I tried to shake them away.

"I know. And I know it's frightening." She embraced me more tightly. "Just feel it, though. Isn't it wonderful?"

I was hardly aware of my motionless penis anymore, but there was liquid fire flowing through my groin, waves of pleasure spreading deeper. I said, "Yes. Is it like that for you?"

"It's different. But it's just as good. You'll find out for yourself, soon enough."

"I hadn't been thinking that far ahead," I confessed.

Lena giggled. "You've got a whole new life in front of you, Martin. You don't know what you've been missing."

She kissed me, then started pulling away. I cried out in pain, and she stopped. "I'm sorry. I'll take it slowly." I reached down to touch the place where we were joined; there was a trickle of blood escaping from the base of my penis.

Lena said, "You're not going to faint on me, are you?"

"Don't be stupid." I did feel queasy, though. "What if I'm not ready? What if I can't do it?"

"Then I'll lose my hold in a few hundred tau. The Angels weren't completely stupid."

I ignored this blasphemy, though it wasn't just any Angel who'd designed our bodies—it was Beatrice Herself. I said, "Just promise you won't use a knife."

"That's not funny. That really happens to people."

"I know." I kissed her shoulder. "I think—"

Lena straightened her legs slightly, and I felt the core break free inside me. Blood flowed warmly from my groin, but the pain had changed from a threat of damage to mere tenderness; my nervous system no longer spanned the lesion. I asked Lena, "Do you feel it? Is it part of you?"

"Not yet. It takes a while for the connections to form." She ran her fingers over my lips. "Can I stay inside you, until they have?"

I nodded happily. I hardly cared about the sensations anymore; it was just contemplating the miracle of being able to give a part of my body to Lena that was wonderful. I'd studied the physiological details long ago, everything from the exchange of nutrients to the organ's independent immune system—and I knew that Beatrice had used many of the same techniques for the bridge as She'd used with gestating embryos—but to witness Her ingenuity so dramatically at work in my own flesh was both shocking and intensely moving. Only giving birth could bring me closer to Her than this.

When we finally separated, though, I wasn't entirely prepared for the sight of what emerged. "Oh, that is disgusting!"

Lena shook her head, laughing. "New ones always look a bit . . . encrusted. Most of that stuff will wash away, and the rest will fall off in a few kilotau."

I bunched up the sheet to find a clean spot, then dabbed at my—her—penis. My newly formed vagina had stopped bleeding, but it was finally dawning on me just how much mess we'd made. "I'm going to have to wash this before my parents get back. I can put it out to dry in the morning, after they're gone, but if I don't wash it now they'll smell it."

We cleaned ourselves enough to put on shorts, then Lena helped me carry the sheet up onto the deck and drape it in the water from the laundry hooks. The fibers in the sheet would use nutrients in the water to power the self-cleaning process.

The docks appeared deserted; most of the boats nearby belonged to people who'd come for the wedding. I'd told my parents I was too tired to stay on at the celebrations; tonight they'd continue until dawn, though Daniel and Agnes would probably leave by midnight. To do what Lena and I had just done.

"Martin? Are you shivering?"

There was nothing to be gained by putting it off. Before whatever courage I had could desert me, I said, "Will you marry me?"

"Very funny. Oh—" Lena took my hand. "I'm sorry, I never know when you're joking."

I said, "We've exchanged the bridge. It doesn't matter that we weren't married first, but it would make things easier if we went along with convention."

"Martin—"

"Or we could just live together, if that's what you want. I don't care. We're already married in the eyes of Beatrice."

Lena bit her lip. "I don't want to live with you."

"I could move to Mitar. I could get a job."

Lena shook her head, still holding my hand. She said firmly, "No. You knew, before we did anything, what it would and wouldn't mean. You don't want to marry me, and I don't want to marry you. So snap out of it."

I pulled my hand free, and sat down on the deck. *What had I done?* I'd thought I'd had Beatrice's blessing, I'd thought this was all in Her plan . . . but I'd just been fooling myself.

Lena sat beside me. "What are you worried about? Your parents finding out?"

"Yes." That was the least of it, but it seemed pointless trying to explain the truth. I turned to her. "When could we—?"

"Not for about ten days. And sometimes it's longer after the first time."

I'd known as much, but I'd hoped her experience might contradict my theoretical knowledge. *Ten days.* We'd both be gone by then.

Lena said, "What do you think, you can never get married now? How many marriages do you imagine involve the bridge one of the partners was born with?"

"Nine out of ten. Unless they're both women."

Lena gave me a look that hovered between tenderness and incredulity. "My estimate is about one in five."

I shook my head. "I don't care. We've exchanged the bridge, we have to be together." Lena's expression hardened, then so did my resolve. "Or I have to get it back."

"Martin, that's ridiculous. You'll find another lover soon enough, and then you won't even know what you were worried about. Or maybe you'll fall in love with a nice Deep Church boy, and then you'll both be glad you've been spared the trouble of getting rid of the extra bridge."

"Yeah? Or maybe he'll just be disgusted that I couldn't wait until I really *was* doing it for him!"

Lena groaned, and stared up at the sky. "Did I say something before about the Angels getting things right? Ten thousand years without bodies, and they thought they were qualified—"

I cut her off angrily. "Don't be so fucking blasphemous! Beatrice knew exactly what. She was doing. If we mess it up, that's our fault!"

Lena said, matter-of-factly. "In ten years' time, there'll be a pill you'll be able to take to keep the bridge from being passed, and another pill to make it pass when it otherwise wouldn't. We'll win control of our bodies back from the Angels, and start doing exactly what we like with them."

"That's sick. That really is sick."

I stared at the deck, suffocating in misery. *This was what I'd wanted, wasn't it? A lover who was the very opposite of Daniel's sweet, pious Agnes?* Except that in my fantasies, we'd always had a lifetime to debate our philosophical differences. Not one night to be torn apart by them.

I had nothing to lose, now. I told Lena about my Drowning. She didn't laugh; she listened in silence.

I said, "Do you believe me?"

"Of course." She hesitated. "But have you ever wondered if there might be another explanation for the way you felt, in the water that night? You were starved of oxygen—"

"People are starved of oxygen all the time. Freelander kids spend half their lives trying to stay underwater longer than the last time."

Lena nodded. "Sure. But that's not quite the same, is it? You were pushed beyond the time you could have stayed under by sheer willpower. And . . . you were cued, you were told what to expect."

"That's not true. Daniel never told me what it would be like. I was *surprised* when it happened." I gazed back at her calmly, ready to counter any ingenious hypothesis she came up with. I felt chastened, but almost at peace now. This was what Beatrice had expected of me, before we'd exchanged the bridge: not a dead ceremony in a dead building, but the honesty to tell Lena exactly who she'd be making love with.

We argued almost until sunrise; neither of us convinced the other of anything. Lena helped me drag the clean sheet out of the water and hide it below deck. Before she left, she wrote down the address of a friend's house in Mitar, and a place and time we could meet.

Keeping that appointment was the hardest thing I'd ever done in my life. I spent three solid days ingratiating myself with my Mitar-based cousins, to the point where they would have had to be openly hostile to get out of inviting me to stay with them after the wedding. Once I was there, I had to scheme and lie relentlessly to ensure that I was free of them on the predetermined day.

In a stranger's house, in the middle of the afternoon, Lena and I joylessly reversed everything that had happened between us. I'd been afraid that the act itself might rekindle all my stupid illusions, but when we parted on the street outside, I felt as if I hardly knew her.

I ached even more than I had on the boat, and my groin was palpably swollen, but in a couple of days, I knew, nothing less than a lover's touch or a medical examination would reveal what I'd done.

In the train back to the coast, I replayed the entire sequence of events in my mind, again and again. *How could I have been so wrong?* People always talked about the power of sex to confuse and deceive you, but I'd always believed that was just cheap cynicism. Besides, I hadn't blindly surrendered to sex; I'd thought I'd been guided by Beatrice.

If I could be wrong about that—

I'd have to be more careful. Beatrice always spoke clearly, but I'd have to listen to. Her with much more patience and humility.

That was it. That was what She'd wanted me to learn. I finally relaxed and looked out the window, at the blur of forest passing by, another triumph of the ecopoiesis. If I needed proof that there was always another chance, it was all around me now. The Angels had traveled as far from God as anyone could travel, and yet God had turned around and given them Covenant.

FOUR

I was nineteen when I returned to Mitar, to study at the city's university. Originally, I'd planned to specialize in the ecopoiesis—and to study much closer to home—but in the end I'd had to accept the nearest thing on offer, geographically and intellectually: working with Barat, a Firmlander biologist whose real interest was native microfauna. "Angelic technology is a fascinating subject in its own right," he told me. "But we can't hope to work backward and decipher terrestrial evolution from anything the Angels created. The best we can do is try to understand what Covenant's own biosphere was like, before we arrived and disrupted it."

I managed to persuade him to accept a compromise: my thesis would involve the impact of the ecopoiesis on the native microfauna. That would give me an excuse to study the Angels' inventions, alongside the drab unicellular creatures that had inhabited Covenant for the last billion years.

"The impact of the ecopoiesis" was far too broad a subject, of course; with Barat's help, I narrowed it down to one particular unresolved question. There had long been geological evidence that the surface waters of the ocean had become both more alkaline, and less oxygenated, as new species shifted the balance of dissolved gases. Some native species must have retreated from the wave of change, and perhaps some had been wiped out completely, but there was a thriving population of zooytes in the upper layers at present. So had they been there all along, adapting in *situ*? Or had they migrated from somewhere else?

Mitar's distance from the coast was no real handicap in studying the ocean; the university mounted regular expeditions, and I had plenty of library and lab work to do before embarking on anything so obvious as gathering living samples in their natural habitat. What's more, river water, and even rainwater, was teeming with closely related species, and since it was possible that these were the reservoirs from which the "ravaged" ocean had been recolonized, I had plenty of subjects worth studying close at hand.

Barat set high standards, but he was no tyrant, and his other students made me feel welcome. I was homesick, but not morbidly so, and I took a kind of giddy pleasure from the vivid dreams and underlying sense of disorientation that living on land induced in me. I wasn't exactly fulfilling my childhood ambition to uncover the secrets of the Angels—and I had fewer opportunities than I'd hoped to get side-tracked on the ecopoiesis itself—but once I started delving into the minutiae of Covenant's original, wholly undesigned biochemistry, it turned out to be complex and elegant enough to hold my attention.

I was only miserable when I let myself think about sex. I didn't want to end up like Daniel, so seeking out another Drowned person to marry was the last thing on my mind. But I couldn't face the prospect of repeating my mistake with Lena: I had no intention of becoming physically intimate with anyone unless we were already close enough for me to tell them about the most important thing in my life. But that wasn't the order in which things happened here. After a few humiliating attempts to swim against the current, I gave up on the whole idea, and threw myself into my work instead.

Of course, it was possible to socialize at Mitar University without actually exchanging bridges with anyone. I joined an informal discussion group on Angelic culture, which met in a small room in the students' building every tenth night—just like the old Prayer Group though I was under no illusion that this one would be stacked with believers. It hardly needed to be. The Angels' legacy could be analyzed perfectly well without reference to Beatrice's divinity. The Scriptures were written long after the Crossing by people of a simpler age: there was no reason to treat them as infallible. If non-believers could shed some light on any aspect of the past, I had no grounds for rejecting their insights.

"It's obvious that only one faction came to Covenant!" That was Céline, an anthropologist, a woman so much like Lena that I had to make a conscious effort to remind myself, every time I set eyes on her, that nothing could ever happen between us. "*We're* not so homogeneous that we'd all choose to travel to another planet and assume a new physical form, whatever cultural forces might drive one small group to do that. So why should the Angels have been unanimous? The other factions must still be living in the Immaterial Cities, on Earth, and on other planets."

"Then why haven't they contacted us? In twenty thousand years, you'd think they'd drop in and say hello once or twice." David was a mathematician, a Freelander from the southern ocean.

Céline replied, "The attitude of the Angels who came here wouldn't have encouraged visitors. If all we have is a story of the Crossing in which Beatrice persuades every last Angel in existence to give up immortality—a version that simply erases everyone else from history—that doesn't suggest much of a desire to remain in touch."

A woman I didn't know interjected, "It might not have been so clear-cut from the start, though. There's evidence of settler-level technology being deployed for more than three thousand years after the Crossing, long after it was needed for the ecopoiesis. New species continued to be created, engineering projects continued to use advanced materials and energy sources. But then in less than a century, it all stopped. The Scriptures merge three separate decisions into one: renouncing immortality, migrating to Covenant, and abandoning the technology that might have provided an escape route if anyone changed their mind. But we *know* it didn't happen like that. Three thousand years after the Crossing, something changed. The whole experiment suddenly became irreversible."

These speculations would have outraged the average pious Freelander, let alone the average Drowned one, but I listened calmly, even entertaining the possibility that some of them could be true. The love of Beatrice was the only fixed point in my cosmology; everything else was open to debate.

Still, sometimes the debate was hard to take. One night, David joined us straight from a seminar of physicists. What he'd heard from the speaker was unsettling enough, but he'd already moved beyond it to an even less palatable conclusion.

"Why did the Angels choose mortality? After ten thousand years without death, why did they throw away all the glorious possibilities ahead of them, to come and die like animals on this ball of mud?" I had to bite my tongue to keep from replying to his rhetorical question: because God is the only source of eternal life, and Beatrice showed them that all they really had was a cheap parody of that divine gift.

David paused, then offered his own answer—which was itself a kind of awful parody of Beatrice's truth. "Because they discovered that they weren't immortal, after all. They discovered that *no one can be*. We've always known, as they must have, that the universe is finite in space and time. It's destined to collapse eventually: 'the stars will fall from the sky.' But it's easy to *imagine* ways around that." He laughed. "We don't know enough physics yet, ourselves, to rule out anything. I've just heard an extraordinary woman from Tia talk about coding our minds into waves that would orbit the shrinking universe so rapidly that we could think *an infinite number of thoughts* before everything was crushed!" David grinned joyfully at the sheer audacity of this notion. I thought primly: what blasphemous nonsense.

Then he spread his arms and said, "Don't you see, though? If the Angels *had* pinned their hopes on something like that—some ingenious trick that would keep them from sharing the fate of the universe—*but then they finally gained enough knowledge to rule out every last escape route*, it would have had a profound effect on them. Some small faction could then have decided that since they were mortal after all, they might as well embrace the inevitable, and come to terms with it on the way their ancestors had. In the flesh."

Céline said thoughtfully, "And the Beatrice myth puts a religious gloss on the whole thing, but that might be nothing but a *post hoc* reinterpretation of a purely secular revelation."

This was too much; I couldn't remain silent. I said, "If Covenant really was founded by a pack of terminally depressed atheists, what could have changed their minds? Where did the desire to impose a '*post hoc* reinterpretation' *come from?* If the revelation that brought the Angels here was 'secular,' why isn't the whole planet still secular today?"

Someone said snidely, "Civilization collapsed. What do you expect?"

I opened my mouth to respond angrily, but Céline got in first. "No, Martin has a point. If David's right, the rise of religion needs to be explained more urgently than ever. And I don't think anyone's in a position to do that yet."

Afterward, I lay awake thinking about all the other things I should have said, all the other objections I should have raised. (And thinking about Céline.) Theology aside, the whole dynamics of the group was starting to get under my skin; maybe I'd be better off spending my time in the lab, impressing Barat with my dedication to his pointless fucking microbes.

Or maybe I'd be better off at home. I could help out on the boat; my parents weren't young anymore, and Daniel had his own family to look after.

I climbed out of bed and started packing, but halfway through I changed my mind. I didn't really want to abandon my studies. And I'd known all along what the antidote was for all the confusion and resentment I was feeling.

I put my rucksack away, switched off the lamp, lay down, closed my eyes, and asked Beatrice to grant me peace.

I was awakened by someone banging on the door of my room. It was a fellow boarder, a young man I barely knew. He looked extremely tired and irritable, but something was overriding his irritation.

"There's a message for you."

My mother was sick, with an unidentified virus. The hospital was even further away than our home grounds; the trip would take almost three days.

I spent most of the journey praying, but the longer I prayed, the harder it became. I *knew* that it was possible to save my mother's life with one word in the Angels' tongue to Beatrice, but the number of ways in which I could fail, corrupting the purity of the request with my own doubts, my own selfishness, my own complacency, just kept multiplying.

The Angels created nothing in the ecopoiesis that would harm their own mortal incarnations. The native life showed no interest in parasitizing us. But over the millennia, our own DNA had shed viruses. And since Beatrice Herself chose every last base pair, that must have been what She intended. Aging was not enough. Mortal injury was not enough. Death had to come without warning, silent and invisible.

That's what the Scriptures said.

The hospital was a maze of linked hulls. When I finally found the right passageway, the first person I recognized in the distance was Daniel. He was holding his daughter Sophie high in his outstretched arms, smiling up at her. The image dispelled all my fears in an instant, I almost fell to my knees to give thanks.

Then I saw my father. He was seated outside the room, his head in his hands. I couldn't see his face, but I didn't need to. He wasn't anxious, or exhausted. He was crushed.

I approached in a haze of last-minute prayers, though I knew I was asking for the past to be rewritten. Daniel started to greet me as if nothing was wrong, asking about the trip—probably trying to soften the blow—then he registered my expression and put a hand on my shoulder.

He said, "She's with God now."

I brushed past him and walked into the room. My mother's body was lying on the bed, already neatly arranged: arms straightened, eyes closed. Tears ran down my cheeks, angering me. Where had my love been when it might have prevented this? When Beatrice might have heeded it?

Daniel followed me into the room, alone. I glanced back through the doorway and saw Agnes holding Sophie.

"She's with God, Martin." He was beaming at me as if something wonderful had happened.

I said numbly, "She wasn't Drowned." I was almost certain that she hadn't been a believer at all. She'd remained in the Transitional church all her life—but that had long been the way to stay in touch with your friends when you worked on a boat nine days out of ten.

"I prayed with her, before she lost consciousness. She accepted Beatrice into her heart."

I stared at him. Nine years ago he'd been certain: you were Drowned, or you were damned. It was as simple as that. My own conviction had softened long ago; I couldn't believe that Beatrice really was so arbitrary and cruel. But I knew my mother would not only have refused the full-blown ritual; the whole philosophy would have been as nonsensical to her as the mechanics.

"Did she say that? Did she tell you that?"

Daniel shook his head. "But it was clear." Filled with the love of Beatrice, he couldn't stop smiling.

A wave of revulsion passed through me; I wanted to grind his face into the deck. *He didn't care what my mother had believed*. Whatever eased his *own* pain, whatever put his own doubts to rest, had to be the case. To accept that she was damned—or even just dead, gone, erased—was unbearable; everything else flowed from that. *There was no truth in anything he said, anything he believed. It was all just an expression of his own needs*.

I walked back into the corridor and crouched beside my father. Without looking at me, he put an arm around me and pressed me against his side. I could feel the blackness washing over him, the helplessness, the loss. When I tried to embrace him he just clutched me more tightly, forcing me to be still. I shuddered a few times, then stopped weeping. I closed my eyes and let him hold me.

I was determined to stay there beside him, facing everything he was facing. But after a while, unbidden, the old flame began to glow in the back of my skull: the old warmth, the old peace, the old certainty. Daniel was right, my mother was with God. *How could I have doubted that?* There was no point asking how it had come about; Beatrice's ways were beyond my comprehension. But the one thing I knew firsthand was the strength of Her love.

I didn't move, I didn't free myself from my father's desolate embrace. But I was an impostor now, merely praying for his comfort, interceding from my state of grace. Beatrice had raised me out of the darkness, and I could no longer share his pam.

FIVE

After my mother's death, my faith kept ceding ground, without ever really wavering. Most of the doctrinal content fell away, leaving behind a core of belief that was a great deal easier to defend. It didn't matter if the Scriptures were superstitious non-sense or the Church was full of fools and hypocrites; Beatrice was still Beatrice, the way the sky was still blue. Whenever I heard debates between atheists and believers, I found myself increasingly on the atheists' side — not because I accepted their con-clusion for a moment, but because they were so much more honest than their op-ponents. Maybe the priests and theologians arguing against them had the same kind of direct, personal experience of God as I did — or maybe not, maybe they just des-perately needed to believe. But they never disclosed the true source of their convic-tion; instead, they just made laughable attempts to "prove" God's existence from the historical record, or from biology, astronomy, or mathematics. Daniel had been right at the age of fifteen — you couldn't prove any such thing — and listening to these people twist logic as they tried made me squirm.

I felt guilty about leaving my father working with a hired hand, and even guiltier when he moved onto Daniel's boat a year later, but I knew how angry it would have made him if he thought I'd abandoned my career for his sake. At times, that was the only thing that kept me in Mitar: even when I honestly wanted nothing more than to throw it all in and go back to hauling nets, I was afraid that my decision would be misinterpreted.

It took me three years to complete my thesis on the migration of aquatic zooytes in the wake of the ecopoiesis. My original hypothesis, that freshwater species had re-plenished the upper ocean, turned out to be false. Zooytes had no genes as such, just families of enzymes that resynthesized each other after cell division, but com-parisons of these heritable molecules showed that, rather than rain bringing new life from above, an ocean-dwelling species from a much greater depth had moved steadily closer to the surface, as the Angels' creations drained oxygen from the water. That wouldn't have been much of a surprise, if the same techniques hadn't also shown that several species found in river water were even closer relatives of the sur-face dwellers. But those freshwater species weren't anyone's ancestors; they were the newest migrants. Zooytes that had spent a billion years confined to the depths had suddenly been able to survive (and reproduce, and mutate) closer to the surface than ever before, and when they'd stumbled on a mutation that let them thrive in the presence of oxygen, they'd finally been in a position to make use of it. The ecopoiesis might have driven other native organisms into extinction, but the invasion from Earth had enabled this ancient benthic species to mount a long overdue invasion of its own. Unwittingly or not, the Angels had set in motion the sequence of events that had released it from the ocean to colonize the planet.

So I proved myself wrong, earned my degree, and became famous amongst a circle of peers so small that we were all famous to each other anyway. Vast new territories did not open up before me. Anything to do with native biology was rapidly becoming an academic cul-de-sac; I'd always suspected that was how it would be, but I hadn't fought hard enough to end up anywhere else.

For the next three years, I clung to the path of least resistance: assisting Barat with his own research, taking the teaching jobs no one else wanted. Most of Barat's other students moved on to better things, and I found myself increasingly alone in Mitar. But that didn't matter; I had Beatrice.

At the age of twenty-five, I could see my future clearly. While other people deciphered—and built upon—the Angels' legacy, I'd watch from a distance, still messing about with samples of seawater from which all Angelic contaminants had been scrupulously removed.

Finally, when it was almost too late, I made up my mind to jump ship. Barat had been good to me, but he'd never expected loyalty verging on martyrdom. At the end of the year, a bi-ecological (native and Angelic) microbiology conference was being held in Tia, possibly the last event of its kind. I had no new results to present, but it wouldn't be hard to find a plausible excuse to attend, and it would be the ideal place to lobby for a new position. My great zooyte discovery hadn't been entirely lost on the wider community of biologists; I could try to rekindle the memory of it. I doubted there'd be much point offering to sleep with anyone; ethical qualms aside, my bridge had probably rusted into place.

Then again, maybe I'd get lucky. Maybe I'd stumble on a fellow Drowned Freelander who'd ended up in a position of power, and all I'd have to do was promise that my work would be for the greater glory of Beatrice.

Tia was a city of ten million people on the east coast. New towers stood side-by-side with empty structures from the time of the Angels, giant gutted machines that might have played a role in the ecopoiesis. I was too old and proud to gawk like a child, but for all my provincial sophistication I wanted to. These domes and cylinders were twenty times older than the illustrations tattooed into the ceiling of the monastery back home. They bore no images of Beatrice; nothing of the Angels did. But why would they? They predated Her death.

The university, on the outskirts of Tia, was a third the size of Mitar itself. An underground train ringed the campus; the students I rode with eyed my unstylish clothes with disbelief. I left my luggage in the dormitory and headed straight for the conference center. Barat had chosen to stay behind; maybe he hadn't wanted to witness the public burial of his field. That made things easier for me; I'd be free to hunt for a new career without rubbing his face in it.

Late additions to the conference program were listed on a screen by the main entrance. I almost walked straight past the display; I'd already decided which talks I'd be attending. But three steps away, a title I'd glimpsed in passing assembled itself in my mind's eye, and I had to backtrack to be sure I hadn't imagined it.

Carla Reggia: "Euphoric Effects of Z/12/80 Excretions"

I stood there laughing with disbelief. I recognized the speaker and her coworkers by name, though I'd never had a chance to meet them. If this wasn't a hoax . . . what had they done? Dried it, smoked it, and tried writing that up as research? Z/12/80 was one of "my" zooytes, one of the escapees from the ocean; the air and water of Tia were swarming with it. If its excretions were euphoric, the whole city would be in a state of bliss.

I knew, then and there, what they'd discovered. I knew it, long before I admitted it to myself. I went to the talk with my head full of jokes about neglected culture flasks full of psychotropic breakdown products, but for two whole days, I'd been steeling myself for the truth, finding ways in which it didn't have to matter.

Z/12/80, Carla explained, excreted among its waste products an amine that was able to bind to receptors in our Angel-crafted brains. Since it had been shown by other workers (no one recognized me; no one gave me so much as a glance) that Z/12/80 hadn't existed at the time of the ecopoiesis, this interaction was almost certainly undesigned, and unanticipated. "It's up to the archaeologists and neurochemists to determine what role, if any, the arrival of this substance in the environment might have played in the collapse of early settlement culture. But for the past fifteen to eighteen thousand years, we've been swimming in it. Since we still exhibit such a wide spectrum of moods, we're probably able to compensate for its presence by down-regulating the secretion of the endogenous molecule that was designed to bind to the same receptor. That's just an educated guess, though. Exactly what the effects might be from individual to individual, across the range of doses that might be experienced under a variety of conditions, is clearly going to be a matter of great interest to investigators with appropriate expertise."

I told myself that I felt no disquiet. Beatrice acted on the world through the laws of nature; I'd stopped believing in supernatural miracles long ago. The fact that someone had now identified the way in which She'd acted on *me*, that night in the water, changed nothing.

I pressed ahead with my attempts to get recruited. Everyone at the conference was talking about Carla's discovery, and when people finally made the connection with my own work, their eyes stopped glazing over halfway through my spiel. In the next three days, I received seven offers—all involving research into *zooyte biochemistry*. There was no question, now, of side-stepping the issue, of escaping into the wider world of Angelic biology. One man even came right out and said to me: "You're a Freelander, and you know that the ancestors of Z/12/80 live in much greater numbers in the ocean. Don't you think *oceanic* exposure is going to be the key to understanding this?" He laughed. "I mean, you swam in the stuff as a child, didn't you? And you seem to have come through unscathed."

"Apparently."

On my last night in Tia, I couldn't sleep. I stared into the blackness of the room, watching the gray sparks dance in front of me. (Contaminants in the aqueous humor? Electrical noise in the retina? I'd heard the explanation once, but I could no longer remember it.)

I prayed to Beatrice in the Angels' tongue; I could still feel Her presence, as strongly as ever. The effect clearly wasn't just a matter of dosage, or trans-cutaneous absorption: merely swimming in the ocean at the right depth wasn't enough to make anyone feel Drowned. But in combination with the stress of oxygen starvation, and all the psychological build-up Daniel had provided, the jolt of zooyte piss must have driven certain neuroendocrine subsystems into new territory—or old territory, by a new path. *Peace, joy, contentment, the feeling of being loved* weren't exactly unknown emotions. But by short-circuiting the brain's usually practice of summoning those feelings only on occasions when there was a reason for them, I'd been "blessed with the love of Beatrice." I'd found happiness on demand.

And I still possessed it. That was the eeriest part. Even as I lay there in the dark, on the verge of reasoning everything I'd been living for out of existence, my ability to work the machinery was so ingrained that I felt as loved, as blessed as ever.

Maybe Beatrice was offering me another chance, making it clear that She'd still forgive this blasphemy and welcome me back. But why did I believe that there was anyone there to "forgive me"? You couldn't reason your way to God; there was only faith. And I knew, now, that the source of my faith was a meaningless accident an unanticipated side-effect of the ecopoiesis.

I still had a choice. I could, still, decide that the love of Beatrice was immune to all logic, a force beyond understanding, untouched by evidence of any kind.

No, I couldn't. I'd been making exceptions for Her for too long. Everyone lived with double standards—but I'd already pushed mine as far as they'd go.

I started laughing and weeping at the same time. It was almost unimaginable: all the millions of people who'd been misled the same way. All because of the zooytes, and . . . what? One Freelander; diving for pleasure, who'd stumbled on a strange new experience? Then tens of thousands more repeating it, generation after generation—until one vulnerable man or woman had been driven to invest the novelty with meaning. Someone who'd needed so badly to feel loved and protected that the illusion of a real presence behind the raw emotion had been impossible to resist. Or who'd desperately wanted to believe that—in spite of the Angels' discovery that they, too, were mortal—death could still be defeated.

I was lucky: I'd been born in an era of moderation. I hadn't killed in the name of Beatrice. I hadn't suffered for my faith. I had no doubt that I'd been far happier for the last fifteen years than I would have been if I'd told Daniel to throw his rope and weights overboard without me.

But that didn't change the fact that the heart of it all had been a lie.

I woke at dawn, my head pounding, after just a few kilotau's sleep. I closed my eyes and searched for Her presence, as I had a thousand times before. *When I woke in the morning and looked into my heart, She was there without fail, offering me strength and guidance. When I lay in bed at night, I feared nothing, because I knew She was watching over me.*

There was nothing. She was gone.

I stumbled out of bed, feeling like a murderer, wondering how I'd ever live with what I'd done.

SIX

I turned down every offer I'd received at the conference, and stayed on in Mitar. It took Barat and me two years to establish our own research group to examine the effects of the zooamine, and nine more for us to elucidate the full extent of its activity in the brain. Our new recruits all had solid backgrounds in neurochemistry, and they did better work than I did, but when Barat retired I found myself the spokesperson for the group.

The initial discovery had been largely ignored outside the scientific community; for most people, it hardly mattered whether our brain chemistry matched the Angels' original design, or had been altered fifteen thousand years ago by some unexpected contaminant. But when the Mitar zooamine group began publishing detailed accounts of the biochemistry of religious experience, the public at large rediscovered the subject with a vengeance.

The university stepped up security, and despite death threats and a number of unpleasant incidents with stone-throwing protesters, no one was hurt. We were flooded with requests from broadcasters—though most were predicated on the notion that the group was morally obliged to "face its critics," rather than the broadcasters being morally obliged to offer us a chance to explain our work, calmly and clearly, without being shouted down by enraged zealots.

I learned to avoid the zealots, but the obscurantists were harder to dodge. I'd expected opposition from the Churches—defending the faith was their job, after all—but some of the most intellectually bankrupt responses came from academics in other disciplines. In one televised debate, I was confronted by a Deep Church priest, a Transitional theologian, a devotee of the ocean god Marni, and an anthropologist from Tia.

"This discovery has no real bearing on any belief system," the anthropologist explained serenely. "All truth is local. Inside every Deep Church in Ferez. Beatrice *is* the daughter of God, and we're the mortal incarnations of the Angels, who traveled here from Earth. In a coastal village a few milliradians south, Mami is the supreme creator, and it was She who gave birth to us, right here. Going one step further and moving from the spiritual domain to the scientific might appear to 'negate' certain spiritual truths . . . but equally, moving from the scientific domain to the spiritual demonstrates the same limitations. We are nothing but the stories we tell ourselves, and no one story is greater than another." He smiled beneficently, the expression of a parent only too happy to give all his squabbling children an equal share in some disputed toy.

I said, "How many cultures do you imagine share your definition of 'truth'? How many people do you think would be content to worship a God who consisted of literally nothing but the fact of their belief?" I turned to the Deep Church priest. "Is that enough for you?"

"Absolutely not!" She glowered at the anthropologist. "While I have the greatest respect for my brother here," she gestured at the devotee of Marni, "you can't draw a line around those people who've been lucky enough to be raised in the true faith, and then suggest that *Beatrice's* infinite power and love is confined to that group of people . . . like some collection of folk songs!"

The devotee respectfully agreed. Marni had created the most distant stars, along with the oceans of Covenant. Perhaps some people called Her by another name, but if everyone on this planet was to die tomorrow, She would still be Mami: unchanged, undiminished.

The anthropologist responded soothingly, "Of course. But in context, and with a wider perspective—"

"I'm perfectly happy with a God who resides within us," offered the Transitional theologian. "It seems . . . *immodest* to expect more. And instead of fretting uselessly over these ultimate questions, we should confine ourselves to matters of a suitably human scale."

I turned to him. "So you're actually indifferent as to whether an infinitely powerful and loving being created everything around you, and plans to welcome you into Her arms after death . . . or if the universe is a piece of quantum noise that will eventually vanish and erase us all?"

He sighed heavily, as if I was asking him to perform some arduous physical feat just by responding. "I can summon no enthusiasm for these issues."

Later, the Deep Church priest took me aside and whispered, "Frankly, we're all very grateful that you've debunked that awful cult of the Drowned. They're a bunch of fundamentalist hicks, and the Church will be better off without them. But you mustn't make the mistake of thinking that your work has anything to do with ordinary, civilized believers!"

I stood at the back of the crowd that had gathered on the beach near the rock pool, to listen to the two old men who were standing ankle-deep in the milky water. It had taken me four days to get here from Mitar, but when I'd heard reports of a zooyte bloom washing up on the remote north coast, I'd had to come and see the results for myself. The zooamine group had actually recruited an anthropologist for such occasions—one who could cope with such taxing notions as the existence of objective reality, and a biochemical substrate for human thought—but Céline was only with us for part of the year, and right now she was away doing other research.

"This is an ancient, sacred place!" one man intoned, spreading his arms to take in the pool. "You need only observe the shape of it to understand that. It concentrates the energy of the stars, and the sun, and the ocean."

"The focus of power is there, by the inlet," the other added, gesturing at a point where the water might have come up to his calves. "Once, I wandered too close. I was almost lost in the great dream of the ocean, when my friend here came and rescued me!"

These men weren't devotees of Mami, or members of any other formal religion.

As far as I'd been able to tell from old news reports, the blooms occurred every eight or ten years, and the two had set themselves up as "custodians" of the pool more than fifty years ago. Some local villagers treated the whole thing as a joke, but others revered the old men. And for a small fee, tourists and locals alike could be chanted over, then splashed with the potent brew. Evaporation would have concentrated the trapped waters of the bloom; for a few days, before the zooytes ran out of nutrients and died *en masse* in a cloud of hydrogen sulphide, the amine would be present in levels as high as in any of our laboratory cultures back in Mitar.

As I watched people lining up for the ritual, I found myself trying to downplay the possibility that anyone could be seriously affected by it. It was broad daylight, no one feared for their life, and the old men's pantheistic gobbledy-gook carried all the gravitas of the patter of streetside scam merchants. Their marginal sincerity, and the money changing hands, would be enough to undermine the whole thing. This was a tourist trap, not a life-altering experience.

When the chanting was done, the first customer knelt at the edge of the pool. One of the custodians filled a small metal cup with water and threw it in her face. After a moment, she began weeping with joy. I moved closer, my stomach tightening. *It was what she'd known was expected of her, nothing more. She was playing along, not wanting to spoil the fun—like the good sports who pretended to have their thoughts read by a carnival psychic.*

Next, the custodians chanted over a young man. He began swaying giddily even before they touched him with the water; when they did, he broke into sobs of relief that racked his whole body.

I looked back along the queue. There was a young girl standing third in line now, looking around apprehensively; she could not have been more than nine or ten. Her father (I presumed) was standing behind her, with his hand against her back, as if gently propelling her forward.

I lost all interest in playing anthropologist. I forced my way through the crowd until I reached the edge of the pool, then turned to address the people in the queue. "These men are frauds! There's nothing mysterious going on here. I can tell you exactly what's in the water: it's just a drug, a natural substance given out by creatures that are trapped here when the waves retreat."

I squatted down and prepared to dip my hand in the pool. One of the custodians rushed forward and grabbed my wrist. He was an old man, I could have done what I liked, but some people were already jeering, and I didn't want to scuffle with him and start a riot. I backed away from him, then spoke again.

"I've studied this drug for more than ten years, at Mitar University. It's present in water all over the planet. We drink it, we bathe in it, we swim in it every day. But it's concentrated here, and if you don't understand what you're doing when you use it, that misunderstanding can harm you!"

The custodian who'd grabbed my wrist started laughing. "The dream of the ocean is powerful, yes, but we don't need your advice on that! For fifty years, my friend and I have studied its lore, until we were strong enough to *stand* in the sacred water!" He gestured at his leathery feet; I didn't doubt that his circulation had grown poor enough to limit the does to a tolerable level.

He stretched out his sinewy arm at me. "So fuck off back to Mitar, Inlander! Fuck off back to your books and your dead machinery! What would you know about the sacred mysteries? *What would you know about the ocean?*"

I said, "I think you're out of your depth."

I stepped into the pool. He started wailing about my unpurified body polluting the water, but I brushed past him. The other custodian came after me, but though my feet were soft after years of wearing shoes, I ignored the sharp edges of the rocks and kept walking toward the inlet. The zooamine helped. I could feel the old joy, the old peace, the old "love"; it made a powerful anesthetic.

I looked back over my shoulder. The second man had stopped pursuing me; it seemed he honestly feared going any further. I pulled off my shirt, bunched it up, and threw it onto a rock at the side of the pool. Then I waded forward, heading straight for the "focus of power."

The water came up to my knees. I could feel my heart pounding, harder than it had since childhood. People were shouting at me from the edge of the pool—some outraged by my sacrilege, some apparently concerned for my safety in the presence of forces beyond my control. Without turning, I called out at the top of my voice. "There is no 'power' here! There's nothing 'sacred'! There's nothing here but a drug—"

Old habits die hard; I almost prayed first. *Please, Holy Beatrice, don't let me regain my faith.*

I lay down in the water and let it cover my face. My vision turned white; I felt like I was leaving my body. The love of Beatrice flooded into me, and nothing had changed: Her presence was as palpable as ever, as undeniable as ever. I *knew* that I was loved, accepted, forgiven.

I waited, staring into the light, almost expecting a voice, a vision, detailed hallucinations. That had happened to some of the Drowned. How did anyone ever claw their way back to sanity, after that?

But for me, there was only the emotion itself, overpowering but unembellished. It didn't grow monotonous; I could have basked in it for days. But I understood, now, that it said no more about my place in the world than the warmth of sunlight on skin. I'd never mistake it for the touch of a real hand again.

I climbed to my feet and opened my eyes. Violet afterimages danced in front of me. It took a few tau for me to catch my breath, and feel steady on my feet again. Then I turned and started wading back toward the shore.

The crowd had fallen silent, though whether it was in disgust or begrudging respect I had no idea.

I said, "It's not just here. It's not just in the water. It's part of us now; it's in our blood." I was still half-blind; I couldn't see whether anyone was listening. "But as long as you know that, you're already free As long as you're ready to face the possibility that everything that makes your spirits soar, everything that lifts you up and fills your heart with joy, *everything that makes your life worth living* . . . is a lie, is corruption, is meaningless—then you can never be enslaved!"

They let me walk away unharmed. I turned back to watch as the line formed again; the girl wasn't in the queue.

I woke with a start, from the same old dream.

I was lowering my mother into the water from the back of the boat. Her hands were tied. Her feet weighted. She was afraid, but she'd put her trust in me. "You'll bring me up safely, won't you, Martin?"

I nodded reassuringly. But once she'd vanished beneath the waves, I thought: What am I doing? I don't believe in this shit any more.

So I took out a knife and started cutting through the rope—

I brought my knees up to my chest, and crouched on the unfamiliar bed in the darkness. I was in a small town on the railway line, halfway back to Mitar. Halfway between midnight and dawn.

I dressed, and made my way out of the hostel. The center of town was deserted, and the sky was thick with stars. Just like home. In Mitar, everything vanished in a fog of light.

All three of the stars cited by various authorities as the Earth's sun were above the horizon. If they weren't all mistakes, perhaps I'd live to see a telescope's image of the planet itself. But the prospect of seeking contact with the Angels—if there really was a faction still out there, somewhere—left me cold. I shouted silently up at the stars: *Your degenerate offspring don't need your help! Why should we rejoin you? We're going to surpass you!*

I sat down on the steps at the edge of the square and covered my face. Bravado didn't help. Nothing helped. Maybe if I'd grown up facing the truth, I would have been stronger. But when I woke in the night, knowing that my mother was simply dead, that everyone I'd ever loved would follow her, that I'd vanish into the same emptiness myself, it was like being buried alive. It was like being back in the water, bound and weighted, with the certain knowledge that there was no one to haul me up.

Someone put a hand on my shoulder. I looked up, startled. It was a man about my own age. His manner wasn't threatening; if anything, he looked slightly wary of me.

He said, "Do you need a roof? I can let you into the Church if you want." There was a trolley packed with cleaning equipment a short distance behind him.

I shook my head. "It's not that cold." I was too embarrassed to explain that I had a perfectly good room nearby. "Thanks."

As he was walking away, I called after him, "Do you believe in God?"

He stopped and stared at me for a while, as if he was trying to decide if this was *a* trick question—as if I might have been hired by the local parishioners to vet him for theological soundness. Or maybe he just wanted to be diplomatic with anyone desperate enough to be sitting in the town square in the middle of the night, begging a stranger for reassurance.

He shook his head. "As a child I did. Not anymore. It was a nice idea . . . but it made no sense." He eyed me skeptically, still unsure of my motives.

I said, "Then isn't life unbearable?"

He laughed. "Not all the time!"

He went back to his trolley, and started wheeling it toward the Church.

I stayed on the steps, waiting for dawn.

Tendeléo's Story

IAN MCDONALD

British author Ian McDonald is an ambitious and daring writer with a wide range and an impressive amount of talent. His first story was published in 1982, and since then he has appeared with some frequency in *Interzone*, *Asimov's Science Fiction*, *New Worlds*, *Zenith*, *Other Edens*, *Amazing*, and elsewhere. He was nominated for the John W. Campbell Award in 1985, and in 1989 he won the *Locus* Best First Novel Award for his novel *Desolation Road*. He won the Philip K. Dick Award in 1992 for his novel *King of Morning, Queen of Day*. His other books include the novels *Out on Blue Six*, *Hearts, Hands and Voices*, *Terminal Cafe*, *Sacrifice of Fools*, *Evolution's Shore*, *Kirinya*, a chapbook novella *Tendeléo's Story*, *Ares Express*, and *Cyberabad*, as well as two collections of his short fiction, *Empire Dreams* and *Speaking in Tongues*. His most recent novel, *River of Gods*, was a finalist for both the Hugo Award and the Arthur C. Clarke Award in 2005. Coming up is another new novel, *Brazil*. His stories have appeared in our eighth through tenth, fourteenth through sixteenth, nineteenth, twentieth, and twenty-third annual collections. Born in Manchester, England, in 1960, McDonald has spent most of his life in Northern Ireland, and now lives and works in Belfast. He has a Web site at http://www.lysator.liu.se/^unicorn/mcdonald/.

Here's a powerful, compassionate, and darkly lyrical story of a young girl's coming-of-age in a future Africa that is literally being eaten by an alien invader, and, after passing through that invader's alien guts, as it were, is being transformed into something rich and strange and totally unexpected. A sea-change that extends as well to the lives of the people who find themselves in its way.

I shall start my story with my name. I am Tendeléo. I was born here, in Gichichi. Does that surprise you? The village has changed so much that no one born then could recognize it now, but the name is still the same. That is why names are important. They remain.

I was born in 1995, shortly after the evening meal and before dusk. That is what

Tendeléo means in my language, Kalenjin: early-evening-shortly-after-dinner. I am
the oldest daughter of the pastor of St. John's Church. My younger sister was born in
1998, after my mother had two miscarriages, and my father asked the congregation
to lay hands on her. We called her Little Egg. That is all there are of us, two. My father felt that a pastor should be an example to his people, and at that time the government was calling for smaller families.

My father had cure of five churches. He visited them on a red scrambler bike the
bishop at Nakuru had given him. It was good motorbike, a Yamaha. Japanese. My father loved riding it. He practiced skids and jumps on the back roads because he
thought a clergyman should not be seen stunt-riding. Of course, people did, but they
never said to him. My father built St. John's. Before him, people sat on benches under trees. The church he made was sturdy and rendered in white concrete. The roof
was red tin, trumpet vine climbed over it. In the season flowers would hang down
outside the window. It was like being inside a garden. When I hear the story of Adam
and Eve, that is how I think of Eden, a place among the flowers. Inside there were
benches for the people, a lectern for the sermon and a high chair for when the
bishop came to confirm children. Behind the altar rail was the holy table covered
with a white cloth and an alcove in the wall for the cup and holy communion plate.
We didn't have a font. We took people to the river and put them under. I and my
mother sang in the choir. The services were long and, as I see them now, quite boring, but the music was wonderful. The women sang, the men played instruments.
The best was played by a tall Luo, a teacher in the village school we called, rather
blasphemously, Most High. It was a simple instrument: a piston ring from an old
Peugeot engine which he hit with a heavy steel bolt. It made a great, ringing
rhythm.

What was left over from the church went into the pastor's house. It had poured
concrete floors and louvre windows, a separate kitchen and a good charcoal stove a
parishioner who could weld had made from a diesel drum. We had electric light,
two power sockets and a radio/cassette player, but no television. It was inviting the
devil to dinner, my father told us. Kitchen, living room, our bedroom, my mother's
bedroom, and my father's study. Five rooms. We were people of some distinction in
Gichichi; for Kalenjin.

Gichichi was a thin, straggly sort of village; shops, school, post-office, matatu office, petrol station and mandazi shop up on the main road, with most of the houses
set off the footpaths that followed the valley terraces. On one of them was our
shamba, half a kilometer down the valley. The path to it went past the front door of
the Ukerewe family. They had seven children who hated us. They threw dung or
stones and called us see-what-we-thought-of-ourselves-Kalenjin and hated-of-God-
Episcopalians. They were African Inland Church Kikuyu, and they had no respect
for the discipline of the bishop.

If the church was my father's Eden, the shamba was my mother's. The air was
cool in the valley and you could hear the river over the stones down below. We grew
maize and gourds and some sugar-cane, which the local rummers bought from my
father and he pretended not to know. Beans and chillis. Onions and potatoes. Two
trees of finger bananas, though M'zee Kipchobe maintained that they sucked the
life out of the soil. The maize grew right over my head, and I would run into the

sugar-cane and pretend that two steps had taken me out of this world into another. There was always music there; the solar radio, or the women singing together when they helped each other turn the soil or hoe the weeds. I would sing with them, for I was considered good at harmonies. The shamba too had a place where the holy things were kept. Among the thick, winding tendrils of an old tree killed by strangling fig the women left little wooden figures gifts of money, Indian-trader jewelry and beer.

You are wondering, what about the Chaga? You've worked out from the dates that I was nine when the first package came down on Kilimanjaro. How could such tremendous events, a thing like another world taking over our own, have made so little impression on my life? It is easy, when it is no nearer to you than another world. We were not ignorant in Gichichi. We had seen the pictures from Kilimanjaro on the television, read the articles in the Nation about the thing that is like a coral reef and a rainforest that came out of the object from the sky. We had heard the discussions on the radio about how fast it was growing—fifty meters every day, it was ingrained on our minds—and what it might be and where it might come from. Every morning the vapor trails of the big UN jets scored our sky as they brought more men and machines to study it, but it was another world. It was not our world. Our world was church, home, shamba, school. Service on Sunday, Bible Study on Monday. Singing lessons, homework club. Sewing, weeding, stirring the ugali. Shooing the goats out of the maize. Playing with Little Egg and Grace and Ruth from next door in the compound: not too loud, Father's working. Once a week, the mobile bank. Once a fortnight, the mobile library. Mad little matatus dashing down, overtaking everything they could see, people hanging off every door and window. Big dirty country buses winding up the steep road like oxen. Gikombe, the town fool, if we could have afforded one, wrapped in dung-colored cloth sitting down in front of the country buses to stop them moving. Rains and hot seasons and cold fogs. People being born, people getting married, people running out on each other, or getting sick, or dying in accidents. Kilimanjaro, the Chaga? Another picture in a world where all pictures come from the same distance.

I was thirteen and just a woman when the Chaga came to my world and destroyed it. That night I was at Grace Muthiga's where she and I had a homework club. It was an excuse to listen to the radio. One of the great things about the United Nations taking over your country is the radio is very good. I would sing with it. They played the kind of music that wasn't approved of in our house.

We were listening to trip hop. Suddenly the record started to go all phasey, like the radio was tuning itself on and off the station. At first we thought the disc was slipping or something, then Grace got up to fiddle with the tuning button. That only made it worse. Grace's mother came in from the next room and said she couldn't get a picture on the battery television. It was full of wavy lines. Then we heard the first boom. It was far away and hollow and it rolled like thunder. Most nights up in the Highlands we get thunder. We know very well what it sounds like. This was something else. Boom! Again. Closer now. Voices outside, and lights. We took torches and went out to the voices. The road was full of people; men, women, children. There were torch beams weaving all over the place. Boom! Close now, loud enough to rattle the windows. All the people shone their torches straight up into the sky, like spears of light. Now the children were crying and I was afraid. Most High had the answer: "Sonic booms! There's something up there." As he said those words, we saw it. It was so slow. That was the amazing thing about it. It was like a child drawing a chalk line across a board. It came in from the south east, across the hills east of Kiriani, straight as an arrow, a little to the south of us. The night was such as we often get in late May, clear after evening rains, and very full of stars. We all saw a glowing dot cut across the face of the stars. It seemed to float and dance, like illusions in the eye if you look into the sun. It left a line behind it like the trails of the big UN jets, only pure, glowing blue, drawn on the night. Double-boom now, so close and loud it hurt my ears. At that, one of the old women began wailing. The fear caught, and soon whole families were looking at the line of light in the sky with tears running down their faces, men as well as women. Many sat down and put their torches in their laps, not knowing what they should do. Some of the old people covered their heads with jackets, shawls, newspapers. Others saw what they were doing, and soon everyone was sitting on the ground with their heads covered. Not Most High. He stood looking up at the line of light as it cut his night in half. "Beautiful!" he said. "That I should see such things, with these own eyes!"

He stood watching until the object vanished in the dark of the mountains to the west. I saw its light reflected in his eyes. It took a long time to fade.

For a few moments after the thing went over, no one knew what to do. Everyone was scared, but they were relieved at the same time because, like the angel of death, it had passed over Gichichi. People were still crying, but tears of relief have a different sound. Someone got a radio from a house. Others fetched theirs, and soon we were all sitting in the middle of the road in the dark, grouped around our radios. An announcer interrupted the evening music show to bring a news flash. At twenty twenty eight a new biological package had struck in Central Province. At those words, a low keen went up from each group.

"Be quiet!" someone shouted, and there was quiet. Though the words would be terrible, they were better than the voices coming out of the dark.

The announcer said that the biological package had come down on the eastern slopes of the Nyandarua near to Tusha, a small Kikuyu village. Tusha was a name we knew. Some of us had relatives in Tusha. The country bus to Nyeri went through Tusha. From Gichichi to Tusha was twenty kilometers. There were cries. There were prayers. Most said nothing. But we all knew time had run out. In four years the Chaga had swallowed up Kilimanjaro, and Amboseli, and the border country of Namanga and was advancing up the A104 on Kajiado and Nairobi. We had ignored it and gone on with our lives, believing that when it finally came, we would know what to do. Now it had dropped out of the sky twenty kilometers north of us and said, Twenty kilometers, four hundred days: that's how long you've got to decide what you're going to do.

Then Jackson who ran the Peugeot Service Office stood up. He cocked his head to one side. He held up a finger. Everyone fell silent. He looked to the sky. "Listen!" I could hear nothing. He pointed to the south, and we all heard it: aircraft engines. Flashing lights lifted out of the dark tree-line on the far side of the valley. Behind it came others, then others, then ten, twenty, thirty, more. Helicopters swarmed over Gichichi like locusts. The sound of their engines filled the whole world. I wrapped my school shawl around my head and put my hands over my ears and yelled over the noise but it still felt like it would shatter my skull like a clay pot. Thirty-five helicopters: They flew so low their down-wash rattled our tin roofs and sent dust swirling up around our faces. Some of the teenagers cheered and waved their torches and white school shirts to the pilots. They cheered the helicopters on, right over the ridge. They cheered until the noise of their engines was lost among the night-insects. Where the Chaga goes, the United Nations comes close behind, like a dog after a bitch.

A few hours later the trucks came through. The grinding of engines as they toiled up the winding road woke all Gichichi. "It's three o'clock in the morning!" Mrs. Kuria shouted at the dusty white trucks with the blue symbol of UNECTA on the doors, but no one would sleep again. We lined the main road to watch them go through our village. I wonder what the drivers thought of all those faces and eyes suddenly appearing in their headlights as they rounded the bend. Some waved. The children waved back. They were still coming through as we went down to the shamba at dawn to milk the goats. They were a white snake coiling up and down the valley road as far as I could see. As they reached the top of the pass the low light from the east caught them and burned them to gold.

The trucks went up the road for two days. Then they stopped and the refugees started to come the other way, down the road. First the ones with the vehicles: matatus piled high with bedding and tools and animals, trucks with the family balanced in the back on top of all the things they had saved. A Toyota microbus, bursting with what looked like bolts of colored cloth but which were women, jammed in next to each other. Ancient cars, motorbikes and mopeds vanishing beneath sagging bales of possessions. It was a race of poverty; the rich ones with machines took the lead. After motors came animals; donkey carts and ox-wagons, pedal-rickshaws. Most came in the last wave, the ones on foot. They pushed handcarts laden with pots and bedding rolls and boxes lashed with twine, or dragged trolleys on ropes or shoved frightened-faced old women in wheelbarrows. They struggled their burdens down the steep valley road. Some broke free and bounced over the edge down across the terraces, strewing clothes and tools and cooking things over the fields. Last of all came hands and heads. These people carried their possessions on their heads and backs and children's shoulders.

My father opened the church to the refugees. There they could have rest, warm chai, some ugali, some beans. I helped stir the great pots of ugali over the open fire. The village doctor set up a treatment center. Most of the cases were for damaged feet and hands, and dehydrated children. Not everyone in Gichichi agreed with my father's charity. Some thought it would encourage the refugees to stay and take food from our mouths. The shopkeepers said he was ruining their trade by giving away what they should be selling. My father told them he was just trying to do what he thought Jesus would have done. They could not answer that, but I know he had another reason. He wanted to hear the refugee's stories. They would be his story, soon enough.

What about Tusha?

The package missed us by a couple of kilometers. It hit a place called Kombé;

two Kikuyu farms and some shit-caked cows. There was a big bang. Some of us from Tusha took a matatu to see what had happened to Kombé. They tell us there is nothing left. There they are, go, ask them.

This nothing, my brothers, what was it like? A hole?

No, it was something, but nothing we could recognize. The photographs? They only show the thing. They do not show how it happens. The houses, the fields, the fields and the track, they run like fat in a pan. We saw the soil itself melt and new things reach out of it like drowning men's fingers.

What kind of things?

We do not have the words to describe them. Things like you see in the television programs about the reefs on the coast, only the size of houses, and striped like zebras. Things like fists punching out of the ground, reaching up to the sky and opening like fingers. Things like fans, and springs, and balloons, and footballs.

So fast?

Oh yes. So fast that even as we watched, it took our matatu. It came up the tires and over the bumper and across the paintwork like a lizard up a wall and the whole thing came out in thousands of tiny yellow buds.

What did you do?

What do you think we did? We ran for our lives.

The people of Kombé?

When we brought back help from Tusha, we were stopped by helicopters. Soldiers, everywhere. Everyone must leave, this is a quarantine area. You have twenty four hours.

Twenty four hours!

Yes, they order you to pack up a life in twenty four hours. The Blue Berets brought in all these engineers who started building some great construction, all tracks and engines. The night was like day with welding torches. They plowed Kiyamba under with bulldozers to make a new airstrip. They were going to bring in jets there. And before they let us go they made everyone take medical tests. We lined up and went past these men in white coats and masks at tables.

Why?

I think they were testing to see if the Chaga-stuff had got into us.

What did they do, that you think that?

Pastor, some they would tap on the shoulder, just like this. Like Judas and the Lord, so gentle. Then a soldier would take them to the side.

What then?

I do not know, pastor. I have not seen them since. No one has.

These stories troubled my father greatly. They troubled the people he told them to, even Most High, who had been so thrilled by the coming of the alien to our land. They especially troubled the United Nations. Two days later a team came up from Nairobi in five army hummers. The first thing they did was tell my father and the doctor to close down their aid station. The official UNHCR refugee center was Muranga. No one could stay here in Gichichi, everyone must go.

In private they told my father that a man of his standing should not be sowing rumors and half truths in vulnerable communities. To make sure that we knew the real truth, UNECTA called a meeting in the church. Everyone packed onto the benches, even the Muslims. People stood all the way around the walls; others outside lifted out the louvres to listen in at the windows. My father sat with the doctor and our local chief at a table. With them was a government man, a white soldier and an Asian woman in civilian dress who looked scared. She was a scientist, a xenologist. She did most of the talking; the government man from Nairobi twirled his pencil between his fingers and tapped it on the table until he broke the point. The soldier, a French general with experience of humanitarian crises, sat motionless.

The xenologist told us that the Chaga was humanity's first contact with life from beyond the Earth. The nature of this contact was unclear; it did not follow any of the communication programs we had predicted. This contact was the physical transformation of our native landscape and vegetation. But what was in the package was not seeds and spores. The things that had consumed Kombé and were now consuming Tusha were more like tiny machines, breaking down the things of this world to pieces and rebuilding them in strange new forms. The Chaga responded to stimuli and adapted to counterattacks on itself. UNECTA had tried fire, poison, radioactive dusting, genetically modified diseases. Each had been quickly routed by the Chaga. However, it was not apparent if it was intelligent, or the tool of an as-yet unseen intelligence.

"And Gichichi?" Ismail the barber asked.

The French general spoke now.

"You will all be evacuated in plenty of time."

"But what if we do not want to be evacuated?" Most High asked. "What if we decide we want to stay here and take our chances with the Chaga?"

"You will all be evacuated," the general said again.

"This is our village, this is our country. Who are you to tell us what we must do in our own country?" Most High was indignant now. We all applauded, even my father up there with the UNECTA people. The Nairobi political looked vexed.

"UNECTA, UNHCR and the UN East Africa Protection Force operate with the informed consent of the Kenyan government. The Chaga has been deemed a threat to human life. We're doing this for your own good."

Most High drove on. "A threat? Who 'deems' it so? UNECTA? An organization that is eighty percent funded by the United States of America? I have heard different, that it doesn't harm people or animals. There are people living inside the Chaga; it's true, isn't it?"

The politician looked at the French general, who shrugged. The Asian scientist answered.

"Officially, we have no data."

Then my father stood up and cut her short.

"What about the people who are being taken away?"

"I don't know anything. . . ." the UNECTA scientist began but my father would not be stopped.

"What about the people from Kombé? What are these tests you are carrying out?"

The woman scientist looked flustered. The French general spoke.

"I'm a soldier, not a scientist. I've served in Kosovo and Iraq and East Timor. I can only answer your questions as a soldier. On the fourteenth of June next year, it will come down that road. At about seven thirty in the evening, it will come through this church. By Tuesday night, there will be no sign that a place called Gichichi ever existed."

And that was the end of the meeting. As the UNECTA people left the church, the Christians of Gichichi crowded around my father. What should they believe? Was Jesus come again, or was it anti-Christ? These aliens, were they angels, or fallen creatures like ourselves? Did they know Jesus? What was God's plan in this? Question after question after question.

My father's voice was tired and thin and driven, like a leopard harried by beaters toward guns. Like that leopard, he turned on his hunters.

"I don't know!" he shouted. "You think I have answers to all these things? No. I have no answers. I have no authority to speak on these things. No one does. Why are you asking these silly silly questions? Do you think a country pastor has the answers that will stop the Chaga in its tracks and drive it back where it came from? No. I am making them up as I go along, like everyone else."

For a moment the whole congregation was silent. I remember feeling that I must die from embarrassment. My mother touched my father's arm. He had been shaking. He excused himself to his people. They stood back to let us out of the church. We stopped on the lintel, amazed. A rapture had indeed come. All the refugees were gone from the church compound. Their goods, their bundles, their carts and animals: Even their excrement had been swept away.

As we walked back to the house, I saw the woman scientist brush past Most High as she went to the UNECTA hummer. I heard her whisper, "About the people. It's true. But they're changed."

"How?" Most High asked but the door was closed. Two blue berets lifted mad Gikombe from in front of the hummer and it drove off slowly through the throng of people. I remembered that the UNECTA woman looked frightened.

That afternoon my father rode off on the red Yamaha and did not come back for almost a week.

I learned something about my father's faith that day. It was that it was strong in the small, local questions because it was weak in the great ones. It believed in singing and teaching the people and the disciplines of personal prayer and meditation, because you could see them in the lives of others. In the big beliefs, the ones you could not see, it fell.

That meeting was the wound through which Gichichi slowly bled to death. "This is our village, this is our country." Most High had declared, but before the end of the week the first family had tied their things onto the back of their pickup and joined the flow of refugees down the road to the south. After that a week did not pass that someone from our village would not close their doors a last time and leave Gichichi. The abandoned homes soon went to ruin. Water got in, roofs collapsed, then rude boys set fire to them. The dead houses were like empty skulls. Dogs fell into toilet pits and drowned. One day when we went down to the shamba there were no names and stones from the Ukerewe house. Within a month its windows were empty, smoke-stained sockets.

With no one to tend them, the shambas went to wild and weeds. Goats and cows grazed where they would, the terrace walls crumbled, the rains washed the soil down the valley in great red tears. Fields that had fed families for generations vanished in a night. No one cared for the women's tree anymore, to give the images their cups of beer. Hope stopped working in Gichichi. Always in the minds of the ones who remained was the day when we would look up the road and see the spines and fans and twisted spites of the Chaga standing along the ridge-line like warriors.

I remember the morning I was woken by the sound of voices from the Muthiga house. Men's voices, speaking softly so as not to waken anyone, for it was still dark, but they woke me. I put on my things and went out into the compound. Grace and Ruth were carrying cardboard boxes from the house, their father and a couple of other men from the village were loading them onto a Nissan pick-up. They had started early, and the pick-up was well laden. The children were gathering up the last few things.

"Ah, Tendeléo," Mr. Muthiga said, sadly. "We had hoped to get away before anyone was around."

"Can I talk to Grace?" I asked.

I did not talk to her. I shouted at her. I would be all alone when she went. I would be abandoned. She asked me a question. She said, "You say we must not go. Tell me, Tendeléo, why must you stay?"

I did not have an answer to that. I had always presumed that it was because a pastor must stay with his people, but the bishop had made several offers to my father to relocate us to a new parish in Eldoret.

Grace and her family left as it was getting light. Their red tail lights swung into the slow stream of refugees. I heard the horn hooting to warn stragglers and animals all the way down the valley. I tried to keep the house good and safe but two weeks later a gang of rude boys from another village broke in, took what they could and burned the rest. They were a new thing in what the radio called the "sub-terminum," gangs of raiders and looters stripping the corpses of the dead towns.

"Vultures, is what they are," my mother said.

Grace's question was a dark parting gift to me. The more I thought about it, the more I became convinced that I must see this thing that had forced such decisions on us. The television and newspaper pictures were not enough. I had to see it with my own eyes. I had to look at its face and ask it its reasons. Little Egg became my lieutenant. We slipped money from the collection plate, and we gathered up secret bundles of food. A schoolday was the best to go. We did not go straight up the road, where we would have been noticed. We caught a matatu to Kinangop in the Nyandarua valley where nobody knew us. There was still a lively traffic; the matatu was full of country people with goods to sell and chickens tied together by the feet stowed under the bench. We sat in the back and ate nuts from a paper cone folded from a page of the Bible. Everywhere were dirty white United Nations vehicles. One by one the people got out and were not replaced. By Ndunyu there was only me and Little Egg, jolting around in the back of the car.

The driver's mate turned around and said, "So, where for, girls?"

I said, "We want to look at the Chaga."

"Sure, won't the Chaga be coming to look at you soon enough?"

"Can you take us there?" I showed him Church shillings.

"It would take a lot more than that." He talked to the driver a moment. "We can drop you at Njeru. You can walk from there, it's under seven kilometers."

Njeru was what awaited Gichichi, when only the weak and poor and mad remained. I was glad to leave it. The road to the Chaga was easy to find, it was the direction no one else was going in. We set off up the red dirt road toward the mountains. We must have looked very strange, two girls walking through a ruined land with their lunches wrapped in kangas. If anyone had been there to watch.

The soldiers caught us within two kilometers of Njeru. I had heard the sound of their engine for some minutes, behind us. It was a big eight wheeled troop carrier of the South African army.

The officer was angry, but I think a little impressed. What did we think we were doing? There were vultures everywhere. Only last week an entire bus had been massacred, five kilometers from here. Not one escaped alive. Two girls alone, they would rob us and rape us, hang us up by our heels and cut our throats like pigs. All the time he was preaching, a soldier in the turret swept the countryside with a big heavy machine gun.

"So, what the hell are you doing here?"

I told him. He went to talk on the radio. When he came back, he said, "In the back."

The carrier was horribly hot and smelled of men and guns and diesel. When the door clanged shut on us I thought we were going to suffocate.

"Where are you taking us?" I asked, afraid.

"You came to see the Chaga," the commander said. We ate our lunch meekly and tried not to stare at the soldiers. They gave us water from their canteens and tried to make us laugh. The ride was short but uncomfortable. The door clanged open. The officer helped me out and I almost fell over with shock.

I stood in a hillside clearing. Around me were tree stumps, fresh cut, sticky with sap. From behind came the noise of chain saws. The clearing was full of military vehicles and tents. People hurried every way. Most of them were white. At the center of this activity was what I can only call a city on wheels. I had not yet been to Nairobi, but I knew it from photographs, a forest of beautiful towers rising out of a circle of townships. That was how the base seemed to me when I first saw it. Looking closer, I saw that the buildings were portable cabins stacked up on big tracked flatbeds, like the heavy log-carriers up in Eldoret. The tractors and towers were joined together with walkways and loops of cable. I saw people running along the high walkways. I would not have done that, not for a million shillings.

I tell you my first impressions, of a beautiful white city—and you may laugh because you know it was only a UNECTA mobile base—that they put together as fast and cheap as they could. But there is a truth here; seeing is magical. Looking kills. The longer I looked, the more the magic faded.

The air in the clearing smelled as badly of diesel smoke as it had in the troop carrier. Everywhere was engine-noise. A path had been slashed through the forest, as if the base had come down it. I looked at the tracks. The big cog wheels were turning. The base was moving, slowly and heavily, like the hands of a clock, creaking backward on its tracks in pace with the advance of the Chaga. Little Egg took my hand. I think my mouth must have been open in wonder for some time.

"Come on then," said the officer. He was smiling now. "You wanted to see the Chaga."

He gave us over to a tall American man with red hair and a red beard and blue eyes. His name was Byron and he spoke such bad Swahili that he did not understand when Little Egg said to me, "he looks like a vampire."

"I speak English," I told him and he looked relieved.

He took us through the tractors to the tower in the middle, the tallest. It was painted white, with the word UNECTA big in blue on the side, and beneath it, the name, Nyandarua Station. We got into a small metal cage. Byron closed the door and pressed a button. The cage went straight up the side of the building. I tell you this, that freight elevator was more frightening than any stories about murdering gangs of vultures. I gripped the handrail and closed my eyes. I could feel the whole base swaying below me.

"Open your eyes," Byron said. "You wouldn't want to come all this way and miss it."

As we rose over the tops of the trees the land opened before me. Nyandarua Station was moving down the eastern slopes of the Aberdare range: the Chaga was spread before me like a wedding kanga laid out on a bed.

It was as though someone had cut a series of circles of colored paper and let them fall on the side of the mountains. The Chaga followed the ridges and the valleys, but that was all it had to do with our geography. It was completely something else. The colors were so bright and silly I almost laughed: purples, oranges, lots of pink and deep red. Veins of bright yellow. Real things, living things were not these colors. This was a Hollywood trick, done with computers for a film. I guessed we were a kilometer from the edge. It was not a very big Chaga, not like the Kilimanjaro Chaga that had swallowed Moshi and Arusha and all the big Tanzanian towns at the foot of the mountain and was now halfway to Nairobi. Byron said this Chaga was about five kilometers across and beginning to show the classic form, a series of circles. I tried to make out the details. I thought details would make it real to me. I saw jumbles of reef-stuff the color of wiring. I saw a wall of dark crimson trees rise straight for a tremendous height. The trunks were as straight and smooth as spears. The leaves joined together like umbrellas. Beyond them, I saw things like icebergs tilted at an angle, things like open hands, praying to the sky, things like oil refineries made out of fungus, things like brains and fans and domes and footballs. Things like other things. Nothing that seemed a thing in itself. And all this was reaching toward me. But, I realized, it would never catch me. Not while I remained here, on this building that was retreating from it down the foothills of the Aberdares, fifty meters every day.

We were close to the top of the building. The cage swayed in the wind. I felt sick and scared and grabbed the rail and that was when it became real for me. I caught the scent of the Chaga on the wind. False things have no scent. The Chaga smelled of cinnamon and sweat and soil new turned up. It smelled of rotting fruit and diesel and concrete after rain. It smelled like my mother when she had The Visit. It smelled like the milk that babies spit out of their mouths. It smelled like televisions and the stuff the Barber Under the Tree put on my father's hair and the women's holy place in the shamba. With each of these came a memory of Gichichi and my life and people. The scent stirred the things I had recently learned as a woman. The Chaga became real for me there, and I understood that it would eat my world.

While I was standing, putting all these things that were and would be into circles within circles inside my head, a white man in faded jeans and Timberland boots rushed out of a sliding door onto the elevator.

"Byron," he said, then noticed that there were two little Kenyan girls there with him. "Who're these?"

"I'm Tendeléo and this is my sister," I said. "We call her Little Egg. We've come to see the Chaga."

This answer seemed to please him.

"I'm called Shepard." He shook our hands. He also was American. "I'm a Peripatetic Executive Director. That means I rush around the world finding solutions to the Chaga."

"And have you?"

For a moment he was taken aback, and I felt bold and rude. Then he said, "come on, let's see."

"Shepard." Byron the vampire said. "It'll wait."

He took us in to the base. In one room were more white people than I had seen in the whole of my life. Each desk had a computer but the people—most of them were men dressed very badly in shorts, with beards—did not use them. They preferred to sit on each other's desks and talk very fast with much gesturing.

"Are African people not allowed in here?" I asked.

The man Shepard laughed. Everything I said that tour he treated as if it had come from the lips of a wise old m'zee. He took us down into the Projection Room where computers drew huge plans on circular tables: of the Chaga now, the Chaga in five years time and the Chaga when it met with its brother from the south and both of them swallowed Nairobi like two old men arguing over a stick of sugar cane.

"And after Nairobi is gone?" I asked. The maps showed the names of all the old towns and villages, under the Chaga. Of course. The names do not change. I reached out to touch the place that Gichichi would become.

"We can't project that far," he said. But I was thinking of an entire city, vanished beneath the bright colors of the Chaga like dirt trodden into carpet. All those lives and histories and stories. I realized that some names can be lost, the names of big things, like cities, and nations, and histories.

Next we went down several flights of steep steel stairs to the "lab levels." Here samples taken from the Chaga were stored inside sealed environments. A test tube might hold a bouquet of delicate fungi, a cylindrical jar a fistful of blue spongy fingers, a tank a square meter of Chaga, growing up the walls and across the ceiling. Some of the containers were so big people could walk around inside. They were dressed in bulky white suits that covered every part of them and were connected to the wall with pipes and tubes so that it was hard to tell where they ended and alien Chaga began. The weird striped and patterned leaves looked more natural than the UNECTA people in their white suits. The alien growing things were at least in their right world.

"Everything has to be isolated." Mr. Shepard said.

"Is that because even out here, it will start to attack and grow?" I asked.

"You got it."

"But I heard it doesn't attack people or animals," I said.

"Where did you hear that?" this man Shepard asked.

"My father told me," I said mildly.

We went on down to Terrestrial Cartography, which was video-pictures the size of a wall of the world seen looking down from satellites. It is a view that is familiar to everyone of our years, though there were people of my parents' generation who laughed when they heard that the world is a ball, with no string to hold it up. I looked for a long time—it is the one thing that does not pale for looking—before I saw that the face of the world was scarred, like a Giriama woman's. Beneath the clouds, South America and South Asia and mother Africa were spotted with dots of lighter color than the brown-green land. Some were large, some were specks, all were precise circles. One, on the eastern side of Africa, identified this disease of continents to me. Chagas. For the first time I understood that this was not a Kenyan thing, not even an African thing, but a whole world thing.

"They are all in the south," I said. "There is not one in the north."

"None of the biological packages have seeded in the northern hemisphere. This is what makes us believe that there are limits to the Chaga. That it won't cover our whole world, pole to pole. That it might confine itself only to the southern hemisphere."

"Why do you think that?"

"No reason at all."

"You just hope."

"Yeah. We hope."

"Mr. Shepard," I said. "Why should the Chaga take away our lands here in the south and leave you rich people in the north untouched? It does not seem fair."

"The universe is not fair, kid. Which you probably know better than me."

We went down then to Stellar Cartography, another dark room, with walls full of stars. They formed a belt around the middle of the room, in places so dense that individual stars blurred into masses of solid white.

"This is the Silver River," I said. I had seen this on Grace's family's television, which they had taken with them.

"Silver river. It is that. Good name."

"Where are we?" I asked.

Shepard went over to the wall near the door and touched a small star down near his waist. It had a red circle around it. Otherwise I do not think even he could have picked it out of all the other small white stars. I did not like it that our sun was so small and common. I asked, "And where are they from?"

The UNECTA man drew a line with his finger along the wall. He walked down one side of the room, halfway along the other, before he stopped. His finger stopped in a swirl of rainbow colors, like a flame.

"Rho Ophiuchi. It's just a name, it doesn't matter. What's important is that it's a long long way from us . . . so far it takes light—and that's as fast as anything can go—eight hundred years to get there, and it's not a planet, or even a star. It's what we call a nebula, a huge cloud of glowing gas."

"How can people live in a cloud?" I asked. "Are they angels?"

The man laughed at that.

"Not people," he said. "Not angels either. Machines. But not like you or I think of machines. Machines more like living things, and very very much smaller. Smaller even than the smallest cell in your body. Machines the size of chains of atoms, that can move other atoms around and so build copies of themselves, or copies of anything else they want. And we think those gas clouds are trillions upon trillions of those tiny, living machines."

"Not plants and animals," I said.

"Not plants and animals, no."

"I have not heard this theory before." It was huge and thrilling, but like the sun, it hurt if you looked at it too closely. I looked again at the swirl of color, colored like the Chaga scars on Earth's face, and back at the little dot by the door that was my light and heat. Compared to the rest of the room, they both looked very small. "Why should things like this, from so far away, want to come to my Kenya?"

"That's indeed the question."

That was all of the science that the UNECTA man was allowed to show us, so he took us down through the areas where people lived and ate and slept, where they watched television and films and drank alcohol and coffee, the places where they exercised, which they liked to do a lot, in immodest costumes. The corridors were full of them, immature and loosely put together, like leggy puppies.

"This place stinks of wazungu," Little Egg said, not thinking that maybe this m'zungu knew more Swahili than the other one. Mr. Shepard smiled.

"Mr. Shepard," I said. "You still haven't answered my question."

He looked puzzled a moment, then remembered.

"Solutions. Oh yes. Well, what do you think?"

Several questions came into my head but none as good, or important to me, as the one I did ask.

"I suppose the only question that matters, really, is can people live in the Chaga?"

Shepard pushed open a door and we were on a metal platform just above one of the big track sets.

"That, my friend, is the one question we aren't even allowed to consider." Shepard said as he escorted us onto a staircase.

The tour was over. We had seen the Chaga. We had seen our world and our future and our place among the stars; things too big for country church children, but which even they must consider, for unlike most of the wazungu here, they would have to find answers.

Down on the red dirt with the diesel stink and roar of chain-saws, we thanked Dr. Shepard. He seemed touched. He was clearly a person of power in this place. A word, and there was a UNECTA Landcruiser to take us home. We were so filled up with what we had seen that we did not think to tell the driver to let us off at the next village down so we could walk. Instead we went landcruising right up the main road, past Haran's shop and the Peugeot Service Station and all the Men Who Read Newspapers under the trees.

Then we faced my mother and father. It was bad. My father took me into his study. I stood. He sat. He took his Kalenjin Bible, that the Bishop gave him on his ordination so that he might always have God's word in his own tongue, and set it on the desk between himself and me. He told me that I had deceived my mother and him, that I had led Little Egg astray, that I had lied; that I had stolen, not God's money, for God had no need of money, but the money that people I saw every day, people I sang and prayed next to every Sunday, gave in their faith. He said all this in a very straightforward, very calm way, without ever raising his voice. I wanted to tell him all the things I said seen, offer them in trade, yes, I have cheated, I have lied, I have stolen from the Christians of Gichichi, but I have learned. I have seen. I have seen our sun lost among a million other suns. I have seen this world, that God is supposed to have made most special of all worlds, so small it cannot even be seen. I have seen men, that God is supposed to have loved so much that he died for their evils, try to understand living machines, each smaller than the smallest living thing, but together, so huge it takes light years to cross their community. I know how different things are from what we believe, I wanted to say, but I said nothing, for my father did an unbelievable thing. He stood up. Without sign or word or any display of strength, he hit me across the face. I fell to the ground, more from the unexpectedness than the hurt. Then he did another unbelievable thing. He sat down. He put his head in his hand. He began to cry. Now I was very scared, and I ran to my mother.

"He is a frightened man," she said. "Frightened men often strike out at the thing they fear."

"He has his church, he has his collar, he has his Bible, what can frighten him?"

"You," she said. This answer was as stunning as my father hitting me. My mother asked me if I remembered the time, after the argument outside the church, when my father had disappeared on the red Yamaha for a week. I said I did, yes.

"He went down south, to Nairobi, and beyond. He went to look at the thing he feared, and he saw that, with all his faith, he could not beat the Chaga."

My father stayed in his study a long time. Then he came to me and went down on his knees and asked me to forgive him. It was a Biblical principle, he said. Do not let the sun go down on your anger. But though Bible principles lived, my father died a little to me that day. This is life: a series of dyings and being born into new things and understandings.

Life by life, Gichichi died too. There were only twenty families left on the morning when the spines of the alien coral finally reached over the treetops up on the pass. Soon after dawn the UNECTA trucks arrived. They were dirty old Sudanese Army things, third hand Russian, badly painted and billowing black smoke. When we saw the black soldiers get out we were alarmed because we had heard bad things about Africans at the hands of other Africans. I did not trust their officer; he was too thin and had an odd hollow on the side of his shaved head, like a crater on the moon. We gathered in the open space in front of the church with our things piled around us. Ours came to twelve bundles wrapped up in kangas. I took the radio and a clatter of pots. My father's books were tied with string and balanced on the petrol tank of his red scrambler.

The moon-headed officer waved and the first truck backed up and let down its tail. A soldier jumped out, set up a folding beach-chair by the tail-gate and sat with a clip-board and a pencil. First went the Kurias, who had been strong in the church. They threw their children up into the truck, then passed up their bundles of belongings. The soldier in the beach-chair watched for a time, then shook his head.

"Too much, too much," he said in bad Swahili. "You must leave something."

Mr. Kuria frowned, measuring all the space in the back of the truck with his eyes. He lifted off a bundle of clothes.

"No no no," the soldier said, and stood up and tapped their television with his pencil. Another soldier came and took it out of Mr. Kuria's arms to a truck at the side of the road, the tithe truck.

"Now you get on," the soldier said, and made a check on his clip-board.

It was as bold as that. Wide-open crime under the blue sky. No one to see. No one to care. No one to say a word.

Our family's tax was the motorbike. My father's face had gone tight with anger and offense to God's laws, but he gave it up without a whisper. The officer wheeled it away to a group of soldiers squatting on their heels by a smudge-fire. They were very pleased with it, poking and teasing its engine with their long fingers. Every time since that I have heard a Yamaha engine I have looked to see if it is a red scrambler, and what thief is riding it.

"On, on," said the tithe-collector.

"My church," my father said and jumped off the truck. Immediately there were a dozen Kalashnikovs pointing at him. He raised his hands, then looked back at us.

"Tendeléo, you should see this."

The officer nodded. The guns were put down and I jumped to the ground. I walked with my father to the church. We proceeded up the aisle. The prayer books were on the bench seats, the woven kneelers set square in front of the pews. We went into the little vestry, where I had stolen the money from the collection. There were other dark secrets here. My father took a battered red petrol can from his robing cupboard and carried it to the communion table. He took the chalice, offered it to God, then filled it with petrol from the can. He turned to face the holy table.

"The blood of Christ keep you in eternal life," he said, raising the cup high. The he poured it out onto the white altar cloth. A gesture too fast for me to see; he struck fire. There was an explosion of yellow flame. I cried out. I thought my father had gone up in the gush of fire. He turned to me. Flames billowed behind him.

"Now do you understand?" he said.

I did. Sometimes it is better to destroy a thing you love than have it taken from you and made alien. Smoke was pouring from under the roof by the time we climbed back onto the truck. The Sudanese soldiers were only interested in that it was fire, and destruction excites soldiers. Ours was the church of an alien god.

Old Gikombe, too old and stupid to run away, did his "sitting in front of the trucks" trick. Every time the soldiers moved him, he scuttled back to his place. He did it once too often. The truck behind us had started to roll, and the driver did not see the dirty, rag-wrapped thing dart in under his wing. With a cry, Gikombe fell under the wheels and was crushed.

A wind from off the Chaga carried the smoke from the burning church over us as we went down the valley road. The communion at Gichichi was broken.

I think time changes everything into its opposite. Youth into age, innocence into experience, certainty into uncertainty. Life into death. Long before the end, time was changing Nairobi into the Chaga. Ten million people were crowded into the shanties that ringed the towers of downtown. Every hour of every day, more came. They came from north and south, from Rift Valley and Central Province, from Il-bisil and Naivasha, from Makindu and Gichichi.

Once Nairobi was a fine city. Now it was a refugee camp. Once it had great green parks. Now they were trampled dust between packing-case homes. The trees had all been hacked down for firewood. Villages grew up on road roundabouts, like cast-aways on coral islands, and in the football stadiums and sports grounds. Armed pa-trols daily cleared squatters from the two airport runways. The railway had been abandoned, cut south and north. Ten thousand people now lived in abandoned car-riages and train sheds and between the tracks. The National Park was a dust bowl, ravaged for fuel and building material, its wildlife fled or slaughtered for food. Nairobi air was a smog of wood smoke, diesel and sewage. The slums spread for twenty kilometers on every side. It was an hour's walk to fetch water, and that was stinking and filthy. Like the Chaga, the shanties grew, hour by hour, family by fam-ily. String up a few plastic sheets here, shove together some cardboard boxes there, set up home where a matatu dies, pile some stolen bricks and sacking and tin. City and Chaga reached out to each other, and came to resemble each other.

I remember very little of those first days in Nairobi. It was too much, too fast—it numbed my sense of reality. The men who took our names, the squatting people watching us as we walked up the rows of white tents looking for our number, were things done to us that we went along with without thinking. Most of the time I had that high-pitched sound in my ear when you want to cry but cannot.

Here is an irony: we came from St. John's, we went to St. John's. It was a new camp, in the south close by the main airport. One eight three two. One number, one tent, one oil lamp, one plastic water bucket, one rice scoop. Every hundred tents there was a water pipe. Every hundred tents there was a shit pit. A river of sewage ran past our door. The stench would have stopped us sleeping, had the cold not done that first. The tent was thin and cheap and gave no protection from the night. We huddled together under blankets. No one wanted to be the first to cry, so no one did. Between the big aircraft and people crying and fighting, there was no quiet, ever. The first night, I heard shots. I had never heard them before but I knew exactly what they were.

In this St. John's we were no longer people of consequence. We were no longer anything. We were one eight three two. My father's collar earned no respect. The first day he went to the pipe for water he was beaten by young men, who stole his plastic water pail. The collar was a symbol of God's treachery. My father stopped wearing his collar; soon after, he stopped going out at all. He sat in the back room listening to the radio and looking at his books, which were still in their tied-up bun-dles. St. John's destroyed the rest of the things that had bound his life together. I think that if we had not been rescued, he would have gone under. In a place like St. John's, that means you die. When you went to the food truck you saw the ones on the way to death, sitting in front of their tents, holding their toes, rocking, looking at the soil.

We had been fifteen days in the camp—I kept a tally on the tent wall with a burned-out match—when we heard the vehicle pull up and the voice call out,

"Jonathan Bi. Does anyone know Pastor Jonathan Bi?" I do not think my father could have looked anymore surprised if Jesus had called his name. Our savior was the Pastor Stephen Elezeke, who ran the Church Army Centre on Jogoo Road. He and my father had been in theological college together; they had been great foot-balling friends. My father was godfather to Pastor Elezeke's children; Pastor Elezeke, it seemed, was my godfather. He piled us all in the back of a white Nissan minibus with Praise Him on the Trumpet written on one side and Praise Him with the Psaltery and Harp, rather squashed up, on the other. He drove off hooting at the crowds of young men, who looked angrily at church men in a church van. He explained that he had found us through the net. The big churches were flagging certain clergy names. Bi was one of them.

So we came to Jogoo Road. Church Army had once been an old, pre-Independence teaching center with a modern, two-level accommodation block. These had overflowed long ago; now every open space was crowded with tents and wooden shanties. We had two rooms beside the metal working shop. They were comfortable but cramped, and when the metal workers started, noisy. There was no privacy.

The heart of Church Army was a little white chapel, shaped like a drum, with a thatched roof. The tents and lean-tos crowded close to the chapel but left a respect-ful distance. It was sacred. Many went there to pray. Many went to cry away from others, where it would not infect them like dirty water. I often saw my father go into the chapel. I thought about listening at the door to hear if he was praying or crying, but I did not. Whatever he looked for there, it did not seem to make him a whole man again.

My mother tried to make Jogoo Road Gichichi. Behind the accommodation block was a field of dry grass with an open drain running down the far side. Beyond the drain was a fence and a road, then the Jogoo Road market with its name painted on its rusting tin roof, then the shanties began again. But this field was untouched and open. My mother joined a group of women who wanted to turn the field into shambas. Pastor Elezeke agreed and they made mattocks in the workshops from bits of old car, broke up the soil and planted maize and cane. That summer we watched the crops grow as the shanties crowded in around the Jogoo Road market, and stifled it, and took it apart for roofs and walls. But they never touched the shambas. It was as if they were protected. The women hoed and sang to the radio and laughed and talked women-talk, and Little Egg and the Chole girls chased enormous sewer rats with sticks. One day I saw little cups of beer and dishes of maize and salt in a corner of the field and understood how it was protected.

My mother pretended it was Gichichi but I could see it was not. In Gichichi, the men did not stand by the fence wire and stare so nakedly. In Gichichi the helicopter gunships did not wheel overhead like vultures. In Gichichi the brightly painted matatus that roared up and down did not have heavy machine guns bolted to the roof and boys in sports fashion in the back looking at everything as if they owned it. They were a new thing in Nairobi, these gun-gangs: the Tacticals. Men, usually young, organized into gangs, with vehicles and guns, dressed in anything they could make a uniform. Some were as young as twelve. They gave themselves names like the Black Simbas and the Black Rhinos and the Ebonettes and the United Christian Front and the Black Taliban. They liked the word black. They thought it sounded threatening. These Tacticals had as many philosophies and beliefs as names, but they all owned territory, patrolled their streets and told their people they were the law. They enforced their law with kneecappings and burning car tires, they defended their streets with AK47s. We all knew that when the Chaga came, they would fight like hyenas over the corpse of Nairobi. The Soca Boys was our local army. They wore sports fashion and knee-length Manager's coats and had football team logos painted in the sides of their picknis, as the armed matatus were called. On their banners they had a black-and-white patterned ball on a green field. Despite their name, it was not a football. It was a buckyball, a carbon fullerene molecule, the half-living, half-machine building-brick of the Chaga. Their leader, a rat-faced boy in a Manchester United coat and shades that kept sliding down his nose, did not like Christians, so on Sundays he would send his picknis up and down Jogoo Road, roaring their engines and shooting into the air, but because they could.

The Church Army had its own plans for the coming time of changes. A few nights later, as I went to the choo, I overheard Pastor Elezeke and my father talking in the Pastor's study. I put my torch out and listened at the louvres.

"We need people like you, Jonathan," Elezeke was saying. "It is a work of God, I think. We have a chance to build a true Christian society."

"You cannot be certain."

"There are Tacticals . . ."

"They are filth. They are vultures."

"Hear me out, Jonathan. Some of them go into the Chaga. They bring things out—for all their quarantine, there are things the Americans want very much from the Chaga. It is different from what we are told is in there. Very very different. Plants that are like machines, that generate electricity, clean water, fabric, shelter, medicines. Knowledge. There are devices, the size of this thumb, that transmit information directly into the brain. And more; there are people living in there, not like primitives, not, forgive me, like refugees. It shapes itself to them, they have learned to make it work for them. There are whole towns—towns, I tell you—down there under Kilimanjaro. A great society is rising."

"It shapes itself to them," my father said. "And it shapes them to itself."

There was a pause.

"Yes. That is true. Different ways of being human."

"I cannot help you with this, my brother."

"Will you tell me why?"

"I will," my father said, so softly I had to press close to the window to hear. "Because I am afraid, Stephen. The Chaga has taken everything from me, but that is still not enough for it. It will only be satisfied when it has taken me, and changed me, and made me alien to myself."

"Your faith, Jonathan. What about your faith?"

"It took that first of all."

"Ah," Pastor Elezeke sighed. Then, after a time, "You understand you are always welcome here?"

"Yes, I do. Thank you, but I cannot help you."

That same night I went to the white chapel—my first and last time—to force issues with God. It was a very beautiful building, with a curving inner wall that made you walk halfway around the inside before you could enter. I suppose you could say it was spiritual, but the cross above the table angered me. It was straight and true and did not care for anyone or anything. I sat glaring at it some time before I found the courage to say, "You say you are the answer."

I am the answer, said the cross.

"My father is destroyed by fear. Fear of the Chaga, fear of the future, fear of death, fear of living. What is your answer?"

I am the answer.

"We are refugees, we live on wazungu's charity, my mother hoes corn, my sister roasts it at the roadside; tell me your answer."

I am the answer.

"An alien life has taken everything we ever owned. Even now, it wants more, and nothing can stop it. Tell me, what is your answer?"

I am the answer.

"You tell me you are the answer to every human need and question, but what does that mean? What is the answer to your answer?"

I am the answer, the silent, hanging cross said.

"That is no answer!" I screamed at the cross. "You do not even understand the questions, how can you be the answer? What power do you have? None. You can do nothing! They need me, not you. I am going to do what you can't."

I did not run from the chapel. You do not run from gods you no longer believe in. I walked, and took no notice of the people who stared at me.

The next morning, I went into Nairobi to get a job. To save money I went on foot. There were men everywhere, walking with friends, sitting by the roadside selling sheet metal charcoal burners or battery lamps, or making things from scrap metal and old tires, squatting together outside their huts with their hands draped over their knees. There must have been women, but they kept themselves hidden. I did not like the way the men worked me over with their eyes. They had shanty-town eyes, that see only what they can use in a thing. I must have appeared too poor to rob and too hungry to sexually harass, but I did not feel safe until the downtown towers rose around me and the vehicles on the streets were diesel-stained green and yellow buses and quick white UN cars.

I went first to the back door of one of the big tourist hotels.

"I can peel and clean and serve people," I said to an undercook in dirty whites. "I work hard and I am honest. My father is a pastor."

"You and ten million others," the cook said. "Get out of here."

Then I went to the CNN building. It was a big, bold idea. I slipped in behind a motorbike courier and went up to a good-looking Luo on the desk.

"I'm looking for work," I said. "Any work, I can do anything. I can make chai, I can photocopy, I can do basic accounts. I speak good English and a little French. I'm a fast learner."

"No work here today," the Luo on the desk said. "Or any other day. Learn that, fast."

I went to the Asian shops along Moi Avenue.

"Work?" the shopkeepers said. "We can't even sell enough to keep ourselves, let alone some up-country refugee."

I went to the wholesalers on Kimathi Street and the City Market and the stall traders and I got the same answer from each of them: no economy, no market, no work. I tried the street hawkers, selling liquidated stock from tarpaulins on the pavement, but their bad mouths and lewdness sickened me. I walked the five kilometers along Uhuru Highway to the UN East Africa Headquarters on Chiromo Road. The soldier on the gate would not even look at me. Cars and hummers he could see. His own people, he could not. After an hour I went away.

I took a wrong turn on the way back and ended up in a district I did not know, of dirty-looking two-story buildings that once held shops, now burned out or shuttered with heavy steel. Cables dipped across the street, loop upon loop upon loop, sagging and heavy. I could hear voices but see no one around. The voices came from an alley behind a row of shops. An entire district was crammed into this alley. Not even in St. John's camp have I seen so many people in one place. The alley was solid with bodies, jammed together, moving like one thing, like a rain cloud. The noise was incredible. At the end of the alley I glimpsed a big black foreign car, very shiny, and a man standing on the roof. He was surrounded by reaching hands, as if they were worshipping him.

"What's going on?" I shouted to whoever would hear. The crowd surged. I stood firm.

"Hiring," a shaved-headed boy as thin as famine shouted back. He saw I was puzzled. "Watekni. Day jobs in data processing. The UN treats us like shit in our own country, but we're good enough to do their tax returns."

"Good money?"

"Money." The crowd surged again, and made me part of it. A new car arrived behind me. The crowd turned like a flock of birds on the wing and pushed me toward the open doors. Big men with dark glasses got out and made a space around the watekni broker. He was a small Luhya in a long white jellaba and the uniform shades. He had a mean mouth. He fanned a fistful of paper slips. My hand went out by instinct and I found a slip in it. A single word was printed on it: Nimepata.

"Password of the day," my thin friend said. "Gets you into the system."

"Over there, over there," one of the big men said, pointing to an old bus at the end of the alley. I ran to the bus. I could feel a hundred people on my heels. There was another big man at the bus door.

"What're your languages?" the big man demanded.

"English and a bit of French," I told him.

"You waste my fucking time, kid," the man shouted. He tore the password slip from my hand, pushed me so hard, with two hands, I fell. I saw feet, crushing feet, and I rolled underneath the bus and out the other side. I did not stop running until I was out of the district of the watekni and into streets with people on them. I did not see if the famine-boy got a slip. I hope he did.

Singers wanted, said the sign by the flight of street stairs to an upper floor. So, my skills had no value in the information technology market. There were other markets. I climbed the stairs. They led to a room so dark I could not at first make out its dimensions. It smelled of beer, cigarettes and poppers. I sensed a number of men.

"Your sign says you want singers," I called into the dark.

"Come in then." The man's voice was low and dark, smoky, like an old hut. I ventured in. As my eyes grew used to the dark, I saw tables, chairs upturned on them, a bar, a raised stage area. I saw a number of dark figures at a table, and the glow of cigarettes.

"Let's have you."

"Where?"

"There."

I got up on the stage. A light stabbed out and blinded me.

"Take your top off."

I hesitated, then unbuttoned my blouse. I slipped it off, stood with my arms loosely folded over my breasts. I could not see the men, but I felt the shanty-eyes.

"You stand like a Christian child," smoky voice said. "Let's see the goods."

I unfolded my arms. I stood in the silver light for what seemed like hours.

"Don't you want to hear me sing?"

"Girl, you could sing like an angel, but if you don't have the architecture . . ."

I picked up my blouse and rebuttoned it. It was much more shaming putting it on than taking it off. I climbed down off the stage. The men began to talk and laugh. As I reached the door, the dark voice called me.

"Can you do a message?"

"What do you want?"

"Run this down the street for me right quick."

I saw fingers hold up a small glass vial. It glittered in the light from the open door.

"Down the street."

"To the American Embassy."

"I can find that."

"That's good. You give it to a man."

"What man?"

"You tell the guard on the gate. He'll know."

"How will he know me?"

"Say you're from Brother Dust."

"And how much will Brother Dust pay me?"

The men laughed.

"Enough."

"In my hand?"

"Only way to do business."

"We have a deal."

"Good girl. Hey."

"What?"

"Don't you want to know what it is?"

"Do you want to tell me?"

"They're fullerenes. They're from the Chaga. Do you understand that? They are alien spores. The Americans want them. They can use them to build things, from nothing up. Do you understand any of this?"

"A little."

"So be it. One last thing."

"What?"

"You don't carry it in your hand. You don't carry it anywhere on you. You get my meaning?"

"I think I do."

"There are changing rooms for the girls back of the stage. You can use one of them."

"Okay. Can I ask a question?"

"You can ask anything you like."

"These . . . fullerenes. These Chaga things . . . What if they; go off, inside?"

"You trust the stories that they never touch human flesh. Here. You may need this." An object flipped through the air toward me. I caught it . . . a tube of KY jelly. "A little lubrication."

I had one more question before I went backstage area.

"Can I ask, why me?"

"For a Christian child, you've a decent amount of dark," the voice said. "So, you've a name?"

"Tendeléo."

Ten minutes later I was walking across town, past all the UN checkpoints and security points, with a vial of Chaga fullerenes slid into my vagina. I walked up to the gate of the American Embassy. There were two guards with white helmets and white gaiters. I picked the big black one with the very good teeth.

"I'm from Brother Dust," I said.

"One moment please," the marine said. He made a call on his PDU. One minute later the gates swung open and a small white man with sticking-up hair came out.

"Come with me," he said, and took me to the guard unit toilets, where I extracted the consignment. In exchange he gave me a playing card with a portrait of a President of the United States on the back. The President was Nixon.

"You ever go back without one of these, you die," he told me. I gave the Nixon card to the man who called himself Brother Dust. He gave me a roll of shillings and told me to come back on Tuesday.

I gave two thirds of the roll to my mother.

"Where did you get this?" she asked, holding the notes in her hands like blessings.

"I have a job," I said, challenging her to ask. She never did ask. She bought clothes for Little Egg and fruit from the market. On the Tuesday, I went back to the upstairs club that smelled of beer and smoke and come and took another load inside me to the spikey-haired man at the Embassy.

So I became a runner. I became a link in a chain that ran from legendary cities under the clouds of Kilimanjaro across terminum, past the UN Interdiction Force, to an upstairs club in Nairobi, into my body, to the US Embassy. No, I do not have that right. I was a link in a chain that started eight hundred years ago, as light flies, in a gas cloud called Rho Ophiuchi, that ran from US Embassy to US Government, and on to a man whose face was on the back on one of my safe-conduct cards and from him into a future no one could guess.

"It scares them, that's why they want it," Brother Dust told me. "Americans are always drawn to things that terrify them. They think these fullerenes will give the edge to their industries, make the economy indestructible. Truth is, they'll destroy their industries, wreck their economy. With these, anyone can make anything they want. Their free market can't stand up to that."

I did not stay a runner long. Brother Dust liked my refusal to be impressed by what the world said should impress me. I became his personal assistant. I made appointments, kept records. I accompanied him when he called on brother Sheriffs. The Chaga was coming closer, the Tacticals were on the streets; old enemies were needed as allies now.

One such day, Brother Dust gave me a present wrapped in a piece of silk. I unwrapped it, inside was a gun. My first reaction was fear; that a sixteen year-old girl should have the gift of life or death in her hand. Would I, could I, ever use it on living flesh? Then a sense of power crept through me. For the first time in my life, I had authority.

"Don't love it too much," Brother Dust warned. "Guns don't make you safe. Nowhere in this world is safe, not for you, not for anyone."

It felt like a sin, like a burn on my body as I carried it next to my skin back to Jogoo Road. It was impossible to keep it in our rooms, but Simeon in the metal shop had been stashing my roll for some time now and he was happy to hide the gun behind the loose block. He wanted to handle it. I would not let him, though I think he did when I was not around. Every morning I took it out, some cash for lunch and bribes, and went to work.

With a gun and money in my pocket, Brother Dust's warning seemed old and full of fear. I was young and fast and clever. I could make the world as safe or as dangerous as I liked. Two days after my seventeenth birthday, the truth of what he said arrived at my door.

It was late, it was dark and I was coming off the matatu outside Church Army. It was a sign of how far things had gone with my mother and father that they no longer asked where I was until so late, or how the money kept coming. At once I could tell something was wrong; a sense you develop when you work on the street. People were milling around in the compound, needing to do something, not knowing what they could do. Elsewhere, women's voices were shouting. I found Simeon.

"What's happening, where is my mother?"

"The shambas. They have broken through into the shambas."

I pushed my way through the silly, mobbing Christians. The season was late, the corn over my head, the cane dark and whispering. I strayed off the shamba paths in moments. The moon ghosted behind clouds, the air-glow of the city surrounded me but cast no light. The voices steered me until I saw lights gleaming through the stalks: torches and yellow naphtha flares. The voices were loud now, close. There were now men, loud men. Loud men have always frightened me. Not caring for the crop; I charged through the maize, felling rich, ripe heads.

The women of Church Army stood at the edge of the crushed crop. Maize, potatoes, cane, beans had been trodden down, ripped out, torn up. Facing them was a mob of shanty-town people. The men had torches and cutting tools. The women's kangas bulged with stolen food. The children's baskets and sacks were stuffed with bean pods and maize cobs. They faced us shamelessly. Beyond the flattened wire fence, a larger crowd was waiting in front of the market; the hyenas, who if the mob won, would go with them, and if it lost, would sneak back to their homes. They out-numbered the women twenty to one. But I was bold. I had the authority of a gun.

"Get out of here," I shouted at them. "This is not your land."

"And neither is it yours," their leader said, a man thin as a skeleton, barefoot, dressed in cut-off jeans and a rag of a fertilizer company T-shirt. He held a tin-can oil-lamp in his left hand, in his right a machete. "It is all borrowed from the Chaga. It will take it away, and none of us will have it. We want what we can take, before it is lost to all of us."

"Go to the United Nations," I shouted.

The leader shook his head. The men stepped forward. The women murmured, gripped their mattocks and hoes firmly.

"The United Nations? Have you not heard? They are scaling down the relief ef-fort. We are to be left to the mercy of the Chaga."

"This is our food. We grew it, we need it. Get off our land!"

"Who are you?" the leader laughed. The men hefted their pangas and stepped forward. The laughter lit the dark inside me that Brother Dust had recognized, that made me a warrior. Light-headed with rage and power, I pulled out my gun. I held it over my head. One, two, three shots cracked the night. The silence after was more shocking than the shots.

"So. The child has a gun," the hungry man said.

"The child can use it too. And you will be first to die."

"Perhaps." the leader said. "But you have three bullets. We have three hundred hands."

My mother pulled me to one side as the shanty men came through. Their pangas caught the yellow light as they cut their way through our maize and cane. After them came the women and the children, picking, sifting; gleaning. The three hundred hands stripped our fields like locusts. The gun pulled my arm down like an iron weight. I remember I cried with frustration and shame. There were too many of them. My power, my resolve, my weapon, were nothing. False bravery. Boasting. Show.

By morning the field was a trampled mess of stalks, stems and shredded leaves. Not a grain worth eating remained. By morning I was waiting on the Jogoo Road, my thumb held out for a matatu, my possessions in a sports bag on my back. A refugee again. The fight had been brief and muted.

"What is this thing?" My mother could not touch the gun. She pointed at it on the bed. My father could not even look. He sat hunched up in a deep, old armchair, staring at his knees. "Where did you get such a thing?"

The dark thing was still strong in me. It had failed against the mob, but it was more than enough for my parents.

"From a Sheriff," I said. "You know what a sheriff is? He is a big man. For him I stick Chaga-spores up my crack. I give them to Americans, Europeans, Chinese, anyone who will pay."

"Do not speak to us like that!"

"Why shouldn't I? What have you done, but sit here and wait for something to happen? I'll tell the only thing that is going to happen. The Chaga is going to come and destroy everything. At least I have taken some responsibility for this family, at least I have kept us out of the sewer! At least we have not had to steal other people's food!"

"Filth money! Dirt money, sin money!"

"You took that money readily enough."

"If we had known . . ."

"Did you ever ask?"

"You should have told us."

"You were afraid to know."

My mother could not answer that. She pointed at the gun again, as if it were the proof of all depravity.

"Have you ever used it?"

"No," I said, challenging her to call me a liar.

"Would you have used it, tonight?"

"Yes," I said. "I would, if I thought it would have worked."

"What has happened to you?" my mother said. "What have we done?"

"You have done nothing," I said. "That's what's wrong with you. You give up. You sit there, like him." My father had not yet said a word. "You sit there, and you do nothing. God will not help you. If God could, would he have sent the Chaga? God has made you beggars."

Now my father got up out of his deep chair.

"Leave this house," he said in a very quiet voice. I stared. "Take your things. Go on. Go now. You are no longer of this family. You will not come here again."

So I walked out with my things in my bag and my gun in my pants and my roll in my shoe and I felt the eyes in every room and lean-to and shack and I learned Christians can have shanty-eyes too. Brother Dust found me a room in the back of the club. I think he hoped it would give him a chance to have sex with me. It smelled and it was noisy at night and I often had to quit it to let the prostitutes do their business; but it was mine, and I believed I was free and happy. But his words were a curse on me. Like Evil Eye, I knew no peace. You do nothing, I had accused my parents but what had I done? What was my plan for when the Chaga came? As the months passed and the terminum was now at Muranga, now at Ghania Falls, now at Thika, Brother Dust's curse accused me. I watched the Government pull out for Mombasa in a convoy of trucks and cars that took an hour and a half to go past the Haile Selassie Avenue cafe where I bought my runners morning coffee. I saw the gangs of picknis race through the avenues, loosing off tracer like firecrackers, until the big UN troop carriers drove them before them like beggars. I crouched in roadside ditches from terrible fire-fights over hijacked oil tankers. I went up to the observation deck of the Moi Telecom Tower and saw the smoke from battles out in the suburbs, and beyond, on the edge of the heat-haze, to south and north, beyond the mottled duns and dusts of the squatter towns, the patterned colors of the Chaga. I saw the newspapers announce that on July 18th, 2013, the walls of the Chaga would meet and Nairobi cease to exist. Where is safe? Brother Dust said in my spirit. What are you going to do?

———

A man dies, and it is easy to say when the dying ends. The breath goes out and does not come in again. The heart stills. The blood cools and congeals. The last thought fades from the brain. It is not so easy to say when a dying begins. Is it, for example, when the body goes into the terminal decline? When the first cell turns black and cancerous? When we pass our DNA to a new human generation, and become genetically redundant? When we are born? A civil servant once told me that when they make out your birth certificate, they also prepare your death certificate.

It was the same for the big death of Nairobi. The world saw the end of the end from spy satellites and camera-blimps. When the end for a city begins is less clear. Some say it was when the United Nations pulled out and left Nairobi open. Others, when the power plants at Embakasi went down and the fuel and telephone lines to the coast were cut. Some trace it to the first Hatching Tower appearing over the avenues of Westlands; some to the pictures on the television news of the hexagon pattern of Chaga-moss slowly obliterating a "Welcome to Nairobi" road sign. For me it was when I slept with Brother Dust in the back room of the upstairs club.

I told him I was a virgin.

"I always pegged you for a Christian child," he said, and though my virginity excited him, he did not try and take it from me forcefully or disrespectfully. I was fumbling and dry and did not know what to do and pretended to enjoy it more than I did. The truth was that I did not see what all the fuss was about. Why did I do it? It was the seal that I had become a fine young criminal, and tied my life to my city.

Though he was kind and gentle, we did not sleep together again.

They were bad times, those last months in Nairobi. Some times, I think, are so bad that we can only deal them with by remembering what is good, or bright. I will try and look at the end days straight and honestly. I was now eighteen, it was over a year since I left Jogoo Road and I had not seen my parents or Little Egg since. I was proud and angry and afraid. But a day had not passed that I had not thought about them and the duty I owed them. The Chaga was advancing on two fronts, marching up from the south and sweeping down from the north through the once-wealthy suburbs of Westlands and Garden Grove. The Kenyan Army was up there, firing mortars into the cliff of vegetation called the Great Wall, taking out the Hatching Towers with artillery. As futile as shelling the sea. In the south the United Nations was holding the international airport open at every cost. Between them, the Tacticals tore at each other like street dogs. Alliances formed and were broken in the same day. Neighbor turned on neighbor, brother killed brother. The boulevards of downtown Nairobi were littered with bullet casings and burned out picknis. There was not one pane of glass whole on all of Moi Avenue, nor one shop that was not looted. Between them were twelve million civilians, and the posses.

We too made and dissolved our alliances. We had an arrangement with Mombi, who had just bloodily ended an agreement with Haran, one of the big sheriffs, to make a secret deal with the Black Simbas, who intended to be a power in the new order after the Chaga. The silly, vain Soca Boys had been swept away in one night by the Simbas East Starehe Division. Custom matatus and football managers' coats were no match for Russian APCs and light-scatter combat-suits. Brother Dust's associations were precarious: the posses had wealth and influence but no power. Despite our AK47s and street cool uniforms—in the last days, everyone had a uniform—even the Soca Boys could have taken us out. We were criminals, not warriors.

Limuru, Tigani, Kiambu, in the north. Athi River, Matathia, Embakasi to the south. The Chaga advanced a house here, a school there, half a church, a quarter of a street. Fifty meters every day. Never slower, never faster. When the Supreme Commander East African Protection Force announced terminum at Ngara, I made my move. In my Dust Girl uniform of street-length, zebra-stripe PVC coat over short-shorts, I took a taxi to the Embassy of the United States of America. The driver detoured through Riverside.

"Glider come down on Limuru Road," the driver explained. The gliders scared me, hanging like great plastic bats from the hatching towers, waiting to drop, spread their wings and sail across the city sowing Chaga spores. To me they were dark death on wings. I have too many Old Testament images still in me. The army took out many on the towers, the helicopters the ones in the air, but some always made it down. Nairobi was being eaten away from within.

Riverside had been rich once. I saw a tank up-ended in a swimming pool, a tennis court strewn with swollen bodies in purple combats. Chaga camouflage. Beyond the trees I saw fans of lilac land-coral.

I told the driver to wait outside the Embassy. The grounds were jammed with trucks. Chains of soldiers and staff were loading them with crates and machinery. The black marine knew me by now.

"You're going?" I asked.

"Certainly are, ma'am," the marine said. I handed him my gun. He nodded me through. People pushed through the corridors under piles of paper and boxes marked Property of the United States Government. Everywhere I heard shredders. I found the right office. The spikey-haired man, whose name was Knutson, was piling cardboard boxes on his desk.

"We're not open for business."

"I'm not here to trade." I said. I told him what I was here for. He looked at me as if I had said that the world was made of wool, or the Chaga had reversed direction. So I cleared a space on his desk and laid out the photographs I had brought.

"Please tell me, because I don't understand this attraction," I said. "Is it that, when they are that young, you cannot tell the boys from the girls? Or is it the tightness?"

"Fuck you. You'll never get these public."

"They already are. If the Diplomatic Corps Personnel Section does not receive a password every week, the file will download."

If there had been a weapon to hand, I think Knutson would have killed me where I stood.

"I shouldn't have expected any more from a woman who sells her cunt to aliens."

"We are all prostitutes, Mr. Knutson. So?"

"Wait there. To get out you need to be chipped." In the few moments he was out of the room I studied the face of the President on the wall. I was familiar with Presidential features; is it something in the nature of the office, I wondered, that gives them all the same look? Knutson returned with a metal and plastic device like a large hypodermic. "Name, address, Social Security Number." I gave them to him.

He tapped tiny keys on the side of the device, then he seized my wrist, pressed the nozzle against forearm. There was click, I felt a sharp pain but I did not cry out.

"Congratulations, you're an employee of US Military Intelligence. I hope that fucking hurt."

"Yes it did." Blood oozed down my wrist. "I need three more. These are the names."

Beside the grainy snaps of Knutson on the bed with the naked children, I laid out my family. Knutson thrust the chip gun at me.

"Here. Take it. Take the fucking thing. They'll never miss it, not in all this. It's easy to use, just dial it in there. And those."

I scooped up the photographs and slid them with the chip gun into my inside pocket. The freedom chip throbbed under my skin as I walked through the corridors full of people and paper into the light.

Back at the club I paid the driver in gold. It and cocaine were the only universally acceptable street currencies. I had been converting my roll to Kruger rands for some months now. The rate was not good. I jogged up the stairs to the club, and into slaughter.

Bullets had been poured into the dark room. The bar was shattered glass, stinking of alcohol. The tables were spilled and splintered. The chairs were overturned, smashed. Bodies lay among them, the club men, sprawled inelegantly. The carpet was sticky with blood. Flies buzzed over the dead. I saw the Dust Girls, my sisters, scattered across the floor, hair and bare skin and animal prints drenched with blood. I moved among them. I thought of zebras on the high plains, hunted down by lions, limbs and muscle and skin torn apart. The stench of blood is an awful thing. You never get it out of you. I saw Brother Dust on his back against the stage. Someone had emptied a clip of automatic fire into his face.

Our alliances were ended.

A noise; I turned. I drew my gun. I saw it in my hand, and the dead lying with their guns in their hands. I ran from the club. I ran down the stairs onto the street. I was a mad thing, screaming at the people in the street, my gun in hand, my coat flying out behind me. I ran as fast as I could. I ran for home, I ran for Jogoo Road. I ran for the people I had left there. Nothing could stop me. Nothing dared, with my gun in my hand. I would go home and I would take them away from this insanity. The last thing the United Nations will ever do for us is fly us out of here, I would tell them. We will fly somewhere we do not need guns or camps or charity, where we will again be what we were. In my coat and stupid boots, I ran, past the plastic city at the old country bus terminal, around the metal barricades on Landhies Road, across the waste ground past the Lusaka Road roundabout where two buses were burning. I ran out into Jogoo Road.

There were people right across the road. Many many people, with vehicles, white UN vehicles. And soldiers, a lot of soldiers. I could not see Church Army. I slammed into the back of the crowd, I threw people out of my way, hammered at them with the side of my gun.

"Get out of my way, I have to get to my family!"

Hands seized me, spun me around. A Kenyan Army soldier held me by the shoulders.

"You cannot get through."

"My family lives here. The Church Army Centre, I need to see them."

"No one goes through. There is no Church Army."

"What do you mean? What are you saying?"

"A glider came down."

I tore away from him, fought my way through the crowd until I came to the cordon of soldiers. A hundred meters down the road was a line of hummers and APCs. A hundred yards beyond them, the alien infection. The glider had crashed into the accommodation block. I could still make out the vile bat-shape among the crust of fungus and sponge spreading across the white plaster. Ribs of Chagacoral had burst the tin roof of the teaching hall, the shacks were a stew of dissolving plastic and translucent bubbles that burst in a cloud of brown dust. Where the dust touched, fresh bubbles grew. The chapel had vanished under a web of red veins. Even Jogoo Road was blistered by yellow flowers and blue barrel-like objects. Fingers of the hexagonal Chaga moss were reaching toward the road block. As I watched, one of the thorn trees outside the center collapsed into the sewer and sent up a cloud of buzzing silver mites.

"Where are the people?" I asked a soldier.

"Decontamination," he said.

"My family was in there!" I screamed at him. He looked away. I shouted at the crowd. I shouted my father's name, my mother's name, Little Egg's, my own name. I pushed through the people, trying to look at the faces. Too many people, too many faces. The soldiers were looking at me. They were talking on radios, I was disturbing them. At any moment they might arrest me. More likely, they would take me to a quiet place and put a bullet in the back of my skull. Too many people, too many faces. I put the gun away, ducked down, slipped between the legs to the back of the crowd. Decontamination. A UN word, that. Headquarters would have records of the contaminated. Chiromo Road. I would need transport. I came out of the crowd and started to run again. I ran up Jogoo Road, past the sports stadium, around the roundabout onto Landhies Road. There were still a few civilian cars on the street. I ran up the middle of the road, pointing my gun at every car that came toward me.

"Take me to Chiromo Road!" I shouted. The drivers would veer away, or hoot and swear. Some even aimed at me. I sidestepped them, I was too fast for them. "Chiromo Road, or I will kill you!" Tacticals laughed and yelled as they swept past in their picknis. Not one stopped. Everyone had seen too many guns.

There was a Kenyan Army convoy on Pumwani Road, so I cut up through the cardboard cities into Kariokor. As long as I kept the Nairobi River, a swamp of refuse and sewage, to my left, I would eventually come out onto Ngara Road. The shanty people fled from the striped demon with the big gun.

"Get out of my way!" I shouted. And then, all at once, the alley people disobeyed me. They stood stock still. They looked up.

I felt it before I saw it. Its shadow was cold on my skin. I stopped running. I too looked up and it swooped down on me. That is what I thought, how I felt—this thing had been sent from the heart of the Chaga to me alone. The glider was bigger than I had imagined, and much much darker. It swept over me. I was paralyzed with dread, then I remembered what I held in my hand. I lifted my gun and fired at the dark bat-thing. I fired and fired and fired until all I heard was a stiff click. I stood, shaking, as the glider vanished behind the plastic shanty roofs. I stood, staring at my hand holding the gun. Then the tiniest yellow buds appeared around the edge of the cylinder. The buds unfolded into crystals, and the crystals spread across the black, oiled metal like scale. More buds came out of the muzzle and grew back down the barrel. Crystals swelled up and choked the cocked hammer.

I dropped the gun like a snake. I tore at my hair, my clothes, I scrubbed at my skin. My clothes were already beginning to change. My zebra-striped coat was blistering. I pulled out the chip injector. It was a mess of yellow crystals and flowers. I could not hope to save them now. I threw it away from me. The photographs of Knutson with the children fell to the earth. They bubbled up and went to dust. I tore at my coat; it came apart in my fingers into tatters of plastic and spores. I ran. The heel of one knee-boot gave way. I fell, rolled, recovered, and stripped the foolish things off me. All around me, the people of Kariokor were running, ripping at their skin and their clothes with their fingers. I ran with them, crying with fear. I let them lead me. My finery came apart around me. I ran naked, I did not care. I had nothing now. Everything had been taken from me, everything but the chip in my arm. On every side the plastic and wood shanties sent up shoots and stalks of Chaga.

We crashed up against the UN emergency cordon at Kariokor Market. Wicker shields pushed us back; rungu clubs went up, came down. People fell, clutching smashed skulls. I threw myself at the army line.

"Let me through!"

I thrust my arm between the riot shields.

"I'm chipped! I'm chipped!"

Rungus rose before my face.

"UN pass! I'm chipped!"

The rungus came down, and something whirled them away. A white man's voice shouted.

"Jesus fuck, she is! Get her out of there! Quick!"

The shield wall parted, hands seized me, pulled me through.

"Get something on her!"

A combat jacket fell on my shoulders. I was taken away very fast through the lines of soldiers to a white hummer with a red cross on the side. A white man with a red cross vest sat me on the back step and ran a scanner over my forearm. The wound was livid now, throbbing.

"Tendeléo Bi. US Embassy Intelligence Liaison. Okay Tendeléo Bi, I've no idea what you were doing in there, but it's decontam for you."

A second soldier—an officer, I guessed—had come back to the hummer.

"No time. Civs have to be out by twenty three hundred."

The medic puffed his cheeks.

"This is not procedure . . ."

"Procedure?" the officer said. "With a whole fucking city coming apart around us? But I guarantee you this, the Americans will go fucking ballistic if we fuck with one of their spooks. A surface scrub'll do . . ."

They took me over to a big boxy truck with a biohazard symbol on the side. It was parked well away from the other vehicles. I was shivering from shock. I made no complaint as they shaved all hair from my body. Someone gently took away the army jacket and showed me where to stand. Three men unrolled high-pressure hoses from the side of the truck and worked me from top to bottom. The water was cold, and hard enough to be painful. My skin burned. I twisted and turned to try to keep it away from my nipples and the tender parts of my body. On the third scrub, I realized what they were doing, and remembered.

"Take me to decontam!" I shouted. "I want to go to decontam! My family's there, don't you realize?" The men would not listen to me. I do not think they even knew it was a young woman's body they were hosing down. No one listened to me. I was dried with hot air guns, given some loose fatigues to wear, then put in the back of a diplomatic hummer that drove very fast through the streets to the airport. We did not go to the terminal building. There, I might have broken and run. We went through the wire gates, and straight to the open back of a big Russian transport plane. A line of people was going up the ramp into the cavern of its belly. Most of them were white, many had children, and all were laden with bags and goods. All were refugees, too . . . like me.

"My family is back there, I have to get them," I told the man with the security scanner at the foot of the ramp.

"We'll find them," he said as he checked off my Judas chip against the official database. "That's you. Good luck." I went up the metal ramp into the plane. A Russian woman in uniform found me a seat in the middle block, far from any window. Once I was belted in I sat trembling until I heard the ramp close and the engines start up. Then I knew I could do nothing, and the shaking stopped. I felt the plane bounce over the concrete and turn onto the runway. I hoped a terrible hope: that something would go wrong and the plane would crash and I would die. Because I needed to die. I had destroyed the thing I meant to save and saved the thing that was worthless. Then the engines powered up and we made our run and though I could see only the backs of seats and the gray metal curve of the big cabin, I knew when we left the ground because I felt my bond with Kenya break and my home fall away beneath me as the plane took me into exile.

I pause now in my story now, for where it goes now is best told by another voice.

My name is Sean. It's an Irish name. I'm not Irish. No bit of Irish in me, as you can probably see. My mum liked the name. Irish stuff was fashionable, thirty years ago. My telling probably won't do justice to Tendeléo's story; I apologize. My gift's numbers. Allegedly. I'm a reluctant accountant. I do what I do well, I just don't have a gut feel for it. That's why my company gave me all the odd jobs. One of them was this African-Caribbean-World restaurant just off Canal Street. It was called I-Nation—the menu changed every week, the ambience was great and the music was mighty. The first time I wore a suit there, Wynton the owner took the piss so much I never dressed up for them again. I'd sit at a table and poke at his VAT returns and find myself nodding to the drum and bass. Wynton would try out new grooves on me and I'd give them thumbs up or thumbs down. Then he'd fix me coffee with this liqueur he imported from Jamaica and that was the afternoon gone. It seemed a shame to invoice him.

One day Wynton said to me, "You should come to our evening sessions. Good music. Not this fucking bang bang bang. Not fucking deejays. Real music. Live music."

However, my mates liked fucking deejays and bang bang bang so I went to I-Nation on my own. There was a queue but the door staff nodded me right in. I got a seat at the bar and a Special Coffee, compliments of the house. The set had already begun, the floor was heaving. That band knew how to get a place moving. After the dance set ended, the lead guitarist gestured offstage. A girl got up behind the mic. I recognized her—she waitressed in the afternoons. She was a small, quiet girl, kind of unnoticeable, apart from her hair which stuck out in spikes like it was growing back after a Number Nought cut with the razor.

She got up behind that mic and smiled apologetically. Then she began to sing, and I wondered how I had never thought her unnoticeable. It was a slow, quiet song. I couldn't understand the language. I didn't need to, her voice said it all: loss and hurt and lost love. Bass and rhythm felt out the depth and damage in every syllable. She was five foot nothing and looked like she would break in half if you blew on her, but her voice had a stone edge that said, I've been where I'm singing about. Time stopped, she held a note then gently let it go. I-Nation was silent for a moment. Then it exploded. The girl bobbed shyly and went down through the cheering and whistling. Two minutes later she was back at work, clearing glasses. I could not take my eyes off her. You can fall in love in five minutes. It's not hard at all.

When she came to take my glass, all I could say was, "that was . . . great."

"Thank you."

And that was it. How I met Ten, said three shit words to her, and fell in love.

I never could pronounce her name. On the afternoons when the bar was quiet and we talked over my table she would shake her head at my mangling the vowel sounds.

"Eh-yo."

"Ay-oh?"

The soft spikes of hair would shake again. Then, she never could pronounce my name either. Shan, she would say.

"No, Shawn."

"Shone . . ."

So I called her Ten, which for me meant Il Primo, Top of the Heap, King of the Hill, A-Number-One. And she called me Shone. Like the sun. One afternoon when she was off shift, I asked Boss Wynton what kind of name Tendeléo was.

"I mean, I know it's African, I can tell by the accent, but it's a big continent."

"It is that. She not told you?"

"Not yet."

"She will when she's ready. And Mr. Accountant, you fucking respect her."

Two weeks later she came to my table and laid a series of forms before me like tarot cards. They were Social Security applications, Income Support, Housing Benefit.

"They say you're good with numbers."

"This isn't really my thing, but I'll take a look." I flipped through the forms. "You're working too many hours . . . they're trying to cut your benefits. It's the classic welfare trap. It doesn't pay you to work."

"I need to work," Ten said.

Last in line was a Home Office Asylum Seeker's form. She watched me pick it up and open it. She must have seen my eyes widen.

"Gichichi, in Kenya."

"Yes."

I read more.

"God. You got out of Nairobi."

"I got out of Nairobi, yes."

I hesitated before asking, "Was it bad?"

"Yes," she said. "I was very bad."

"I?" I said.

"What?"

"You said 'I.' I was very bad."

"I meant it, it was very bad."

The silence could have been uncomfortable, fatal even. The thing I had wanted to say for weeks rushed into the vacuum.

"Can I take you somewhere? Now? Today? When you finish? Would you like to eat?"

"I'd like that very much," she said.

Wynton sent her off early. I took her to a great restaurant in Chinatown where the waiters ask you before you go in how much you'd like to spend.

"I don't know what this is," she said as the first of the courses arrived.

"Eat it. You'll like it."

She toyed with her wontons and chopsticks.

"Is something wrong with it?"

"I will tell you about Nairobi now," she said. The food was expensive and lavish and exquisitely presented and we hardly touched it. Course after course went back to the kitchen barely picked over as Ten told me the story of her life, the church in Gichichi, the camps in Nairobi, the career as a posse girl, and of the Chaga that destroyed her family, her career, her hopes, her home, and almost her life. I had seen the coming of the Chaga on the television. Like most people, I had tuned it down to background muzak in my life; oh, wow, there's an alien life-form taking over the southern hemisphere. Well, it's bad for the safari holidays and carnival in Rio is fucked and you won't be getting the Brazilians in the next World Cup, but the Cooperage account's due next week and we're pitching for the Maine Road job and interest rates have gone up again. Aliens schmaliens. Another humanitarian crisis. I had followed the fall of Nairobi, the first of the really big cities to go, trying to make myself believe that this was not Hollywood, this was not Bruce Willis versus the CGI. This was twelve million people being swallowed by the dark. Unlike most of my friends and work mates. I had felt something move painfully inside me when I saw the walls of the Chaga close on the towers of downtown Nairobi. It was like a kick in my heart. For a moment I had gone behind the pictures that are all we are allowed to know of our world, to the true lives. And now the dark had spat one of these true lives up onto the streets of Manchester. We were on the last candle at the last table by the time Ten got around to telling me how she had been dumped out with the other Kenyans at Charles de Gaulle and shuffled for months through EU refugee quotas until she arrived, jet-lagged, culture-shocked and poor as shit, in the gray and damp of an English summer.

Afterward, I was quiet for some time. Nothing I could have said was adequate to what I had heard. Then I said, "would you like to come home with me for a drink, or a coffee, or something?"

"Yes," she said. Her voice was husky from much talking, and low, and unbearably attractive. "I would, very much."

I left the staff a big tip for above-and-beyondness.

Ten loved my house. The space astonished her. I left her curled up on my sofa savoring the space as I went to open wine.

"This is nice," she said. "Warm. Big. Nice. Yours."

"Yes," I said and leaned forward and kissed her. Then, before I could think about what I had done, I took her arm and kissed the round red blemish of her chip. Ten slept with me that night, but we did not make love. She lay, curled and chaste, in the hollow of my belly until morning. She cried out in her sleep often. Her skin smelled of Africa.

The bastards cut her housing benefit. Ten was distraught. Home was everything to her. Her life had been one long search for a place of her own; safe, secure, stable.

"You have two options," I said. "One, give up working here."

"Never," she said. "I work. I like to work." I saw Wynton smile, polishing the glasses behind the bar.

"Option two, then."

"What's that?"

"Move in with me."

It took her a week to decide. I understood her hesitation. It was a place, safe, secure, stable, but not her own. On the Saturday I got a phone call from her. Could I help her move? I went around to her flat in Salford. The rooms were tatty and cold, the furniture charity-shop fare, and the decor ugly. The place stank of dope. The television blared, unwatched; three different boomboxes competed with each other. While Ten fetched her stuff, her flatmates stared at me as if I were something come out of the Chaga. She had two bags—one of clothes, one of music and books. They went in the back of the car and she came home with me.

Life with Ten. She put her books on a shelf and her clothes in a drawer. She improvised harmonies to my music. She would light candles on any excuse. She spent hours in the bathroom and used toilet paper by the roll. She was meticulously tidy. She took great care of her little money. She would not borrow from me. She kept working at I-Nation, she sang every Friday. She still killed me every time she got up on that stage.

She said little, but it told. She was dark and intensely beautiful to me. She didn't smile much. When she did it was a knife through the heart of me. It was a sharp joy. Sex was a sharpness of a different kind—it always seemed difficult for her. She didn't lose herself in sex. I think she took a great pleasure from it, but it was controlled . . . it was owned, it was hers. She never let herself make any sound. She was a little afraid of the animal inside. She seemed much older than she was; on the times we went dancing, that same energy that lit her up in singing and sex burned out of her.

It was then that she surprised me by being a bright, energetic, sociable eighteen-year-old. She loved me. I loved her so hard it felt like sickness. I would watch her unaware I was doing it . . . watch the way she moved her hands when she talked on the phone, how she curled her legs under her when she watched television, how she brushed her teeth in the morning. I would wake up in the night just to watch her sleep. I would check she was still breathing. I dreaded something insane, something out of nowhere, taking her away.

She stuck a satellite photograph of Africa on the fridge. She showed me how to trace the circles of the Chaga through the clouds. Every week she updated it. Week by week, the circles merging. That was how I measured our life together, by the circles, merging. Week by week, her home was taken away. Her parents and sister were down there, under those blue and white bars of cloud; week by week the circles were running them out of choices.

She never let herself forget she had failed them. She never let herself forget she was a refugee. That was what made her older, in ways, than me. That was what all her tidiness and orderliness around the house were about. She was only here for a little time. It could all be lifted at a moment's notice.

She liked to cook for me on Sundays, though the kitchen smelled of it for a week afterward. I never told her her cooking gave me the shits. She was chopping something she had got from the Caribbean stores and singing to herself. I was watching from the hall, as I loved to watch her without being watched. I saw her bring the knife down, heard a Kalenjin curse, saw her lift her hand to her mouth. I was in like a shot.

"Shit shit shit shit," she swore. It was a deep cut, and blood ran freely down her forefinger. I rushed her to the tap, stuck it under the cold, then went for the medical bag. I returned with gauze, plasters and a heal-the-world attitude.

"It's okay," she said, holding the finger up. "It's better."

The cut had vanished. No blood, no scab. All that remained was a slightly raised red weal. As I watched, even that faded.

"How?"

"I don't know," Ten said. "But it's better."

I didn't ask. I didn't want to ask. I didn't want there to be anything more difficult or complex in Ten's life. I wanted what she had from her past to be enough, to be all. I knew this was something alien; no one healed like that. I thought that if I let it go, it would never trouble us again. I had not calculated on the bomb.

Some fucking Nazis or other had been blast-bombing gay bars. London, Edinburgh, Dublin so far, always a Friday afternoon, work over, weekend starting. Manchester was on the alert. So were the bombers. Tuesday, lunch time, half a kilo of semtex with nails and razor blades packed around it went off under a table outside a Canal Street bar. No one died, but a woman at the next table lost both legs from the knees down and there were over fifty casualties. Ten had been going in for the afternoon shift. She was twenty meters away when the bomb went off. I got the call from the hospital same time as the news broke on the radio.

"Get the fuck over there," Willy the boss ordered. I didn't need ordering. Manchester Royal Infirmary casualty was bedlam. I saw the doctors going around in a slow rush and the people looking up at everyone who came in, very very afraid and the police taking statements and the trolleys in the aisles and I thought: It must have been something like this in Nairobi, at the end. The receptionist showed me to a room where I was to wait for a doctor. I met her in the corridor, a small, harassed-looking Chinese girl.

"Ah, Mr. Giddens. You're with Ms. Bi, that's right?"

"That's right, how is she?"

"Well, she was brought in with multiple lacerations, upper body, left side of face, left upper arm and shoulder . . ."

"Oh Jesus God. And now?"

"See for yourself."

Ten walked down the corridor. If she had not been wearing a hospital robe, I would have sworn she was unchanged from how I had left her that morning.

"Shone."

The weals were already fading from her face and hands. A terrible prescience came over me, so strong and cold I almost threw up.

"We want to keep her in for further tests, Mr. Giddens," the doctor said. "As you can imagine, we've never seen anything quite like this before."

"Shone, I'm fine, I want to go home."

"Just to be sure, Mr. Giddens."

When I brought Ten back a bag of stuff, the receptionist directed me to Intensive Care. I ran the six flights of stairs to ICU, burning with dread. Ten was in a sealed room full of white equipment. When she saw me, she ran from her bed to the window, pressed her hands against it.

"Shone!" Her words came through a speaker grille. "They won't let me out!"

Another doctor led to me a side room. There were two policemen there, and a man in a suit.

"What the hell is this?"

"Mr. Giddens. Ms. Bi, she is a Kenyan refugee?"

"You fucking know that."

"Easy. Mr. Giddens. We've been running some tests on Ms. Bi, and we've discovered the presence in her bloodstream of fullerene nanoprocessors."

"Nanowhat?"

"What are commonly know as Chaga spores."

Ten, Dust Girl, firing and firing and firing at the glider, the gun blossoming in her hand, the shanty town melting behind her as her clothes fell apart, her arm sticking through the shield wall as she shouted, I'm chipped, I'm chipped! The soldiers shaving her head, hosing her down. Those things she had carried inside her. All those runs for the Americans.

"Oh my God."

There was a window in the little room. Through it I saw Ten sitting on a plastic chair by the bed, hands on her thighs, head bowed.

"Mr. Giddens." The man in the suit flashed a little plastic wallet. "Robert Mc-Glennon, Home Office Immigration. Your, ah . . ." He nodded at the window.

"Partner."

"Partner. Mr. Giddens, I have to tell you, we cannot be certain that Ms. Bi's continued presence is not a public health risk. Her refugee status is dependent on a number of conditions, one of which is that . . ."

"You're fucking deporting her . . ."

The two policemen stirred. I realized then that they were not there for Ten. There were there for me.

"It's a public health issue, Mr. Giddens. She should never have been allowed in in the first place. We have no idea of the possible environmental impact. You, of all people, should be aware what these things can do. Have done. Are still doing. I have to think of public safety."

"Public safety, fuck!"

"Mr. Giddens . . ."

I went to the window. I beat my fists on the wired glass.

"Ten! Ten! They're trying to deport you! They want to send you back!"

The policemen prised me away from the window. On the far side, Ten yelled silently.

"Look, I don't like having to do this," the man in the suit said.

"When?"

"Mr. Giddens."

"When? Tell me, how long has she got?"

"Usually there'd be a detention period, with limited rights of appeal. But as this is a public health issue . . ."

"You're going to do it right now."

"The order is effective immediately, Mr. Giddens. I'm sorry. These officers will go with you back to your home. If you could gather up the rest of her things . . ."

"At least let me say goodbye, Jesus, you owe me that!"

"I can't allow that, Mr. Giddens. There's a contamination risk."

"Contamination? I've only been fucking her for the past six months."

As the cops marched me out, the doctor came up for a word.

"Mr. Giddens, these nanoprocessors in her bloodstream . . ."

"That are fucking getting her thrown out of the country."

"The fullerenes . . ."

"She heals quick. I saw it."

"They do much more than that, Mr. Giddens. She'll probably never get sick again. And there's some evidence that they prevent telomere depletion in cell division."

"What does that mean?"

"It means, she ages very much more slowly than we do. Her life expectancy may be, I don't know, two, three hundred years."

I stared. The policemen stared.

"There's more. We observed unfamiliar structures in her brain; the best I can describe them is, the nanoprocessors seem to be re-engineering dead neurons into a complementary neural network."

"A spare brain?"

"An auxiliary brain."

"What would you do with that?"

"What wouldn't you do with that, Mr. Giddens." He wiped his hand across his mouth. "This bit is pure speculation, but . . ."

"But."

"But in some way, she's in control of it all. I think—this is just a theory—that through this auxiliary brain she's able to interact with the nanoprocessors. She might be able to make them do what she wants. Program them."

"Thank you for telling me that," I said bitterly. "That makes it all so much easier."

I took the policemen back to my house. I told them to make themselves tea. I took Ten's neatly arranged books and CDs off my shelves and her neatly folded clothes out of my drawers and her toilet things out of my bathroom and put them back in the two bags in which she had brought them. I gave the bags to the policemen, they took them away in their car. I never got to say goodbye. I never learned what flight she was on, where she flew from, when she left this country. A face behind glass. That was my last memory. The thing I feared—insane, out of nowhere—had taken her away.

After Ten went, I was sick for a long time. There was no sunshine, no rain, no wind. No days or time, just a constant, high-pitched, quiet whine in my head. People at work played out a slightly amplified normality for my benefit. Alone, they would ask, very gently. How do you feel?

"How do I feel?" I told them. "Like I've been shot with a single, high velocity round, and I'm dead, and I don't know it."

I asked for someone else to take over the I-Nation account. Wynton called me but I could not speak with him. He sent around a bottle of that good Jamaican import liqueur, and a note, "Come and see us, any time." Willy arranged me a career break and a therapist.

His name was Greg, he was a client-centered therapist, which meant I could talk for as long as I liked about whatever I liked and he had to listen. I talked very little, those first few sessions. Partly I felt stupid, partly I didn't want to talk, even to a stranger. But it worked, little by little, without my knowing. I think I only began to be aware of that the day I realized that Ten was gone, but not dead. Her last photo of Africa was still on the fridge and I looked at it and saw something new: down there, in there, somewhere, was Ten. The realization was vast and subtle at the same time. I think of it like a man who finds himself in darkness. He imagines he's in a room, no doors, no windows, and that he'll never find the way out. But then he hears noises, feels a touch on his face, smells a subtle smell, and he realizes that he is not in a room at all—he is outside: the touch on his face is the wind, the noises are night birds, the smell is from night-blooming flowers, and above him, somewhere, are stars.

Greg said nothing when I told him this—they never do, these client-centered boys, but after that session I went to the net and started the hunt for Tendeléo Bi. The Freedom of Information Act got me into the Immigration Service's databases. Ten had been flown out on a secure military transport to Mombasa. UNHCR in Mombasa had assigned her to Likoni Twelve, a new camp to the south of the city. She was transferred out on November Twelfth. It took two days searching to pick up a Tendeléo Bi logged into a place called Samburu North three months later. Medical records said she was suffering from exhaustion and dehydration, but responding to sugar and salt treatment. She was alive.

On the first Monday of winter, I went back to work. I had lost a whole season. On the first Friday, Willy gave me print-out from an on-line recruitment agency.

"I think you need a change of scene," he said. "These people are looking for a stock accountant."

These people were Medecins Sans Frontiers. Where they needed a stock accountant was their East African theater.

Eight months after the night the two policemen took away Ten's things, I stepped off the plane in Mombasa. I think hell must be like Mombasa in its final days as capital of the Republic of Kenya, infrastructure unravelling, economy disintegrating, the harbor a solid mass of boat people and a million more in the camps in Likoni and Shimba Hills, Islam and Christianity fighting a new Crusade for control of this chaos and the Chaga advancing from the west and now the south, after the new impact at Tanga. And in the middle of it all, Sean Giddens, accounting for stock. It was good, hard, solid work in MSF Sector Headquarters, buying drugs where, when, and how we could; haggling down truck drivers and Sibirsk jet-jockeys; negotiating service contracts as spare parts for the Landcruisers gradually ran out, every day juggling budgets always too small against needs too big. I loved it more than any work I've ever done. I was so busy I sometimes forgot why I was there. Then I would go in the safe bus back to the compound and see the smoke going up from the other side of the harbor, hear the gunfire echo off the old Arat houses, and the memory of her behind that green wired glass would gut me.

My boss was a big bastard Frenchman, Jean-Paul Gastineau. He had survived wars and disasters on every continent except Antarctica. He liked Cuban cigars and wine from the valley where he was born and opera, and made sure he had them, never mind distance or expense. He took absolutely no shit. I liked him immensely. I was a fucking thin-blooded number-pushing black rosbif, but he enjoyed my creative accounting. He was wasted in Mombasa. He was a true front-line medic. He was itching for action.

One lunchtime, as he was opening his red wine, I asked him how easy it would to find someone in the camps. He looked at me shrewdly, then asked, "Who is she?"

He poured two glasses, his invitation to me. I told him my history and her history over the bottle. It was very good.

"So, how do I find her?"

"You'll never get anything through channels," Jean-Paul said. "Easiest thing to do is go there yourself. You have leave due."

"No I don't."

"Yes you do. About three weeks of it. Ah. Yes." He poked about in his desk drawers. He threw me a black plastic object like a large cell-phone.

"What is it?"

"US ID chips have a PS transponder. They like to know where their people are. Take it. If she is chipped, this will find her."

"Thanks."

He shrugged.

"I come from a nation of romantics. Also, you're the only one in this fucking place appreciates a good Beaune."

I flew up north on a Sibirsk charter. Through the window I could see the edge of the Chaga. It was too huge to be a feature of the landscape, or even a geographical entity. It was like a dark sea. It looked like what it was . . . another world, that had pushed up against our own. Like it, some ideas are too huge to fit into our everyday worlds. They push up through it, they take it over, and they change it beyond recognition. If what the doctor at Manchester Royal Infirmary had said about the things in Ten's blood were true, then this was not just a new world. This was a new humanity. This was every rule about how we make our livings, how we deal with each other, how we lead our lives, all overturned.

The camps, also, are too big to take in. There is too much there for the world we've made for ourselves. They change everything you believe. Mombasa was no preparation. It was like the end of the world up there on the front line.

"So, you're looking for someone," Heino Rautavana said. He had worked with Jean-Paul through the fall of Nairobi; I could trust him, Jay-Pee said, but I think he thought I was a fool, or, all at best, a romantic. "No shortage of people here."

Jean-Paul had warned the records wouldn't be accurate. But you hope. I went to Samburu North, where my search in England had last recorded Ten. No trace of her. The UNHCR warden, a grim little American woman, took me up and down the rows of tents. I looked at the faces and my tracker sat silent on my hip. I saw those faces that night in the ceiling, and for many nights after.

"You expect to hit the prize first time?" Heino said as we bounced along the dirt track in an MSF Landcruiser to Don Dul.

I had better luck in Don Dul, if you can call it that. Ten had definitely been here two months ago. But she had left eight days later. I saw the log in, the log out, but there was no record of where she had gone.

"No shortage of camps either," Heino said. He was a dour bastard. He couldn't take me any further but he squared me an authorization to travel on Red Cross/Crescent convoys, who did a five hundred mile run through the camps along the northern terminum. In two weeks I saw more misery than I ever thought humanity could take. I saw the faces and the hands and the bundles of scavenged things and I thought, why hold them here? What are they saving them from? Is it so bad in the Chaga? What is so terrible about people living long lives, being immune from sickness, growing extra layers in their brains? What is so frightening about people being able to go into that alien place, and take control of it, and make it into what they want?

I couldn't see the Chaga, it lay just below the southern horizon, but I was constantly aware of its presence, like they say people who have plates in their skulls always feel a slight pressure. Sometimes, when the faces let me sleep, I would be woken instead by a strange smell, not strong, but distinct; musky and fruity and sweaty, sexy, warm. It was the smell of the Chaga, down there, blowing up from the south.

Tent to truck to camp to tent. My three weeks were running out and I had to arrange a lift back along the front line to Samburu and the flight to Mombasa. With three days left, I arrived in Eldoret, UNECTA's Lake Victoria regional center. It gave an impression of bustle, the shops and hotels and cafés were busy, but the white faces and American accents and dress sense said Eldoret was a company town. The Rift Valley Hotel looked like heaven after eighteen days on the front line. I spent an hour in the pool trying to beam myself into the sky. A sudden rain-storm drove everyone from the water but me. I floated there, luxuriating in the raindrops splashing around me. At sunset I went down to the camps. They lay to the south of the town, like a line of cannon-fodder against the Chaga. I checked the records, a matter of form. No Tendeléo Bi. I went in anyway. And it was another camp, and after a time, anyone can become insulated to suffering. You have to. You have to book into the big hotel and swim in the pool and eat a good dinner when you get back; in the camps you have to look at the faces just as faces and refuse to make any connection with the stories behind them. The hardest people I know work in the compassion business. So I went up and down the faces and somewhere halfway down some row I remembered this toy Jean-Paul had given me. I took it out. The display was flashing green. There was a single word: lock.

I almost dropped it.

I thought my heart had stopped. I felt shot between the eyes. I forgot to breathe. The world reeled sideways. My fucking stupid fingers couldn't get a precise reading. I ran down the row of tents, watching the figures. The digits told me how many meters I was to north and east. Wrong way. I doubled back, ducked right at the next opening and headed east. Both sets of figures were decreasing. I overshot, the cast reading went up. Back again. This row. This row. I peered through the twilight. At the far end was a group of people talking outside a tent lit by a yellow petrol lamp. I started to run, one eye on the tracker. I stumbled over guy-ropes, kicked cans, hurdled children, apologized to old women. The numbers clicked down, thirty five, thirty, twenty five meters . . . I could see this one figure in the group, back to me, dressed in purple combat gear. East zero, North twenty, eighteen . . . Short, female, Twelve, ten. Wore its hair in great soft spikes. Eight, six. I couldn't make it past four. I couldn't move. I couldn't speak. I was shaking.

Sensing me, the figure turned. The yellow light caught her.

"Ten," I said. I saw fifty emotions on that face. Then she ran at me and I dropped the scanner and I lifted her and held her to me and no words of mine, or anyone else's, I think, can say how I felt then.

Now our lives and stories and places come together, and my tale moves to its conclusion.

I believe that people and their feelings write themselves on space and time. That is the only way I can explain how I knew, even before I turned and saw him there in that camp, that it was Sean, that he had searched for me, and found me. I tell you, that is something to know that another person has done for you. I saw him, and it was like the world had set laws about how it was to work for me, and then suddenly it said, no. I break them now, for you Tendeléo, because it pleases me. He was impossible, he changed everything I knew, he was there.

Too much joy weeps. Too much sorrow laughs.

He took me back to his hotel. The staff looked hard at me as he picked up his keycard from the lobby. They knew what I was. They did not dare say anything. The white men in the bar also turned to stare. They too knew the meaning of the colors I wore.

He took me to his room. We sat on the verandah with beer. There was a storm that night—there is a storm most nights, up in the high country—but it kept itself in the west among the Nandi Hills. Lightning crawled between the clouds, the distant thunder rattled our beer bottles on the iron table. I told Sean where I had been, what I had done, how I had lived. It was a story long in the telling. The sky had cleared, a new day was breaking by the time I finished it. We have always told each other stories, and each other's stories.

He kept his questions until the end. He had many, many of them.

"Yes, I suppose, it is like the old slave underground railroads," I answered one.

"I still don't understand why they try to stop people going in."

"Because we scare them. We can build a society in there that needs nothing from them. We challenge everything they believe. This is the first century we have gone into where we have no ideas, no philosophies, no beliefs. Buy stuff, look at stuff. That's it. We are supposed to build a thousand years on that? Well, now we do. I tell you, I've been reading, learning stuff, ideas, politics. Philosophy. It's all in there. There are information storage banks the size of skyscrapers. Sean. And not just our history. Other people, other races. You can go into them, you can become them, live their lives, see things through their senses. We are not the first. We are part of a long, long chain, and we are not the end of it. The world will belong to us; we will control physical reality as easily as computers control information."

"Hell, never mind the UN . . . you scare me, Ten!"

I always loved it when he called me Ten. Il Primo, Top of the Heap, King of the Hill, A-Number-One.

Then he said, "and your family?"

"Little Egg is in a place called Kilandui. It's full of weavers, she's a weaver. She makes beautiful brocades. I see her quite often."

"And your mother and father?"

"I'll find them."

But to most of his questions, there was only one answer: "Come, and I will show you." I left it to last. It rocked him as if he had been struck.

"You are serious."

"Why not? You took me to your home once. Let me take you to mine. But first, it's a year . . . And so so much . . ."

He picked me up.

"I like you in this combat stuff," he said.

We laughed a lot and remembered old things we had forgotten. We slowly shook off the rust and the dust, and it was good, and I remember the room maid opening the door and letting out a little shriek and going off giggling.

Sean once told me that one of his nation's greatest ages was built on those words, why not? For a thousand years Christianity had ruled England with the question: "Why?" Build a cathedral, invent a science, write a play, discover a new land, start a business: "why?" Then came the Elizabethans with the answer: "Why not?"

I knew the old Elizabethan was thinking, why not? There are only numbers to go back to, and benefit traps, and an old, gray city, and an old, gray dying world, a safe world with few promises. Here there's a world to be made. Here there's a future of a million years to be shaped. Here there are a thousand different ways of living together to be designed, and if they don't work, roll them up like clay and start again.

I did not hurry Sean for his answer. He knew as well as I that it was not a clean decision. It was lose a world, or lose each other. These are not choices you make in a day. So, I enjoyed the hotel. One day I was having a long bath. The hotel had a great bathroom and there was a lot of free stuff you could play with, so I abused it. I heard Sean pick up the phone. I could not make out what he was saying, but he was talking for some time. When I came out he was sitting on the edge of the bed with the telephone beside him. He sat very straight and formal.

"I called Jean-Paul," he said. "I gave him my resignation."

Two days later, we set out for the Chaga. We went by matatu. It was a school holiday, the Peugeot Services were busy with children on their way back to their families. They made a lot of noise and energy. They looked out the corners of their eyes at us and bent together to whisper. Sean noticed this.

"They're talking about you," Sean said.

"They know what I am, what I do."

One of the schoolgirls, in a black and white uniform, understood our English. She fixed Sean a look. "She is a warrior," she told him. "She is giving us our nation back."

We left most of the children in Kapsabet to change onto other matatus; ours drove on into the heart of the Nandi Hills. It was a high, green rolling country, in some ways like Sean's England. I asked the driver to stop just past a metal cross that marked some old road death.

"What now?" Sean said. He sat on the small pack I had told him was all he could take.

"Now, we wait. They won't be long."

Twenty cars went up the muddy red road, two trucks, a country bus and medical convoy went down. Then they came out of the darkness between the trees on the other side of the road like dreams out of sleep: Meji, Naomi and Hamid. They beckoned; behind them came men, women, children . . . entire families, from babes in arms to old men; twenty citizens, appearing one by one out of the dark, looking nervously up and down the straight red road, then crossing to the other side.

I fived with Meji, he looked Sean up and down.

"This is the one?"

"This is Sean."

"I had expected something, um . . ."

"Whiter?"

He laughed. He shook hands with Sean and introduced himself. Then Meji took a tube out of his pocket and covered Sean in spray. Sean jumped back, choking.

"Stay there, unless you want your clothes to fall off you when you get inside," I said.

Naomi translated this for the others. They found it very funny. When he had immunized Sean's clothes. Meji sprayed his bag.

"Now, we walk," I told Sean.

We spent the night in the Chief's house in the village of Senghalo. He was the last station on our railroad. I know from my Dust Girl days you need as good people on the outside as the inside. Folk came from all around to see the black Englishman. Although he found being looked at intimidating, Sean managed to tell his story. I translated. At the end the crowd outside the Chief's house burst into spontaneous applause and finger-clicks.

"Aye, Tendeléo, how can I compete?" Meji half-joked with me.

I slept fitfully that night, troubled by the sound of aircraft moving under the edge of the storm.

"Is it me?" Sean said.

"No, not you. Go back to sleep."

Sunlight through the bamboo wall woke us. While Sean washed outside in the bright, cold morning, watched by children curious to see if the black went all the way down, Chief and I tuned his shortwave to the UN frequencies. There was a lot of chatter in Klingon. You Americans think we don't understand Star Trek?

"They've been tipped off," Chief said. We fetched the equipment from his souterrain. Sean watched Hamid, Naomi, Meri and I put on the communicators. He said nothing as the black-green knob of cha-plastic grew around the back of my head, into my ear, and sent a tendril to my lips. He picked up my staff.

"Can I?"

"It won't bite you."

He looked closely at the fist-sized ball of amber at its head, and the skeleton outline of a sphere embedded in it.

"It's a buckyball," I said. "The symbol of our power."

He passed it to me without comment. We unwrapped our guns, cleaned them, checked them and set off. We walked east that day along the ridges of the Nandi Hills, through ruined fields and abandoned villages. Helicopter engines were our constant companions. Sometimes we glimpsed them through the leaf cover, tiny in the sky like black mosquitoes. The old people and the mothers looked afraid. I did not want them to see how nervous they were making me. I called my colleagues apart.

"They're getting closer."

Hamid nodded. He was a quiet, thin twenty-two year old ... Ethiopian skin, goatee, a political science graduate from the university of Nairobi.

"We choose a different path every time," he said. "They can't know this."

"Someone's selling us," Meji said.

"Wouldn't matter. We pick one at random."

"Unless they're covering them all."

In the afternoon we began to dip down toward the Rift Valley and terminum. As we wound our way down the old hunters' paths, muddy and slippery from recent rain, the helicopter came swooping in across the hillside. We scrambled for cover. It turned and made another pass, so low I could see the light glint from the pilot's heads-up visor.

"They're playing with us," Hamid said. "They can blow us right off this hill any time they want."

"How?" Naomi asked. She said only what was necessary, and when.

"I think I know," Sean said. He had been listening a little away. He slithered down to join us as the helicopter beat over the hillside again, flailing the leaves, showering us with dirt and twigs. "This." He tapped my forearm. "If I could find you, they can find you."

I pulled up my sleeve. The Judas chip seemed to throb under my skin, like poison.

"Hold my wrist," I said to Sean. "Whatever happens, don't let it slip."

Before he could say a word, I pulled my knife. These things must be done fast. If you once stop to think, you will never do it. Make sure you have it straight. You won't get another go. A stab down with the tip, a short pull, a twist, and the traitor thing was on the ground, greasy with my blood. It hurt. It hurt very much, but the blood had staunched, the wound was already closing.

"I'll just have to make sure not to lose you again," Sean said.

Very quietly, very silently, we formed up the team and one by one slipped down the hillside, out from under the eyes of the helicopter. For all I know, the stupid thing is up there still, keeping vigil over a dead chip. We slept under the sky that night, close together for warmth and on the third day we came to Tinderet and the edge of the Chaga.

Ten had been leading us a cracking pace, as if she were impatient to put Kenya behind us. Since mid-morning, we had been making our way up a long, slow hill. I'd done some hill-walking, I was fit for it, but the young ones and the women with babies found it tough going. When I called for a halt, I saw a moment of anger cross Ten's face. As soon as she could, we upped packs and moved on. I tried to catch up with her, but Ten moved steadily ahead of me until, just below the summit, she was almost running.

"Shone!" she shouted back. "Come with me!"

She ran up through the thinning trees to the summit. I followed, went bounding down a slight dip, and suddenly, the trees opened and I was on the edge.

The ground fell away at my feet into the Rift Valley, green on green on green, sweeping to the valley floor where the patterns of the abandoned fields could still be made out in the patchwork of yellows and buffs and earth tones. Perspective blurred the colors—I could see at least fifty miles—until, suddenly, breathtakingly, they changed. Browns and dry-land beiges blended into burgundies and rust reds, were shot through with veins of purple and white, then exploded into chaos, like a bed of flowers of every conceivable color, a jumble of shapes and colors like a mad coral reef, like a box of kiddie's plastic toys spilled out on a Chinese rug. It strained the eyes, it hurt the brain. I followed it back, trying to make sense of what I was seeing. A sheer wall, deep red, rose abruptly out of the chaotic landscape, straight up, almost as high as the escarpment I was standing on. It was not a solid wall, it looked to me to be made up of pillars or, I thought, tree trunks. They must have been of titanic size to be visible from this distance. They opened into an unbroken, flat crimson canopy. In the further distance, the flat roof became a jumble of dark greens, broken by what I can only describe as small mesas, like the Devil's Tower in Wyoming or the old volcanoes in Puy de Dome. But these glittered in the sun like glass. Beyond them, the landscape was striped like a tiger, yellow and dark brown, and formations like capsizing icebergs, pure white, lifted out of it. And beyond that, I lost the detail, but the colors went on and on, all the way to the horizon.

I don't know how long I stood, looking at the Chaga. I lost all sense of time. I became aware at some point that Ten was standing beside me. She did not try to move me on, or speak. She knew that the Chaga was one of these things that must just be experienced before it can be interpreted. One by one the others joined us. We stood in a row along the bluffs, looking at our new home.

Then we started down the path to the valley below.

Half an hour down the escarpment, Meji up front called a halt.

"What is it?" I asked Ten. She touched her fingers to her communicator, a half-eggshell of living plastic unfolded from the headset and pressed itself to her right eye.

"This is not good," she said. "Smoke, from Menengai."

"Menengai?"

"Where we're going. Meji is trying to raise them on the radio."

I looked over Ten's head to Meji, one hand held to his ear, looking around him. He looked worried.

"And?"

"Nothing."

"And what do we do?"

"We go on."

We descended through microclimates. The valley floor was fifteen degrees hotter than the cool, damp Nandi Hills. We toiled across brush and overgrown scrub, along abandoned roads, through deserted villages. The warriors held their weapons at the slope. Ten regularly scanned the sky with her all-seeing eye. Now even I could see the smoke, blowing toward us on a wind from the east, and smell it. It smelled like burned spices. I could make out Meji trying to call up Menengai. Radio silence.

In the early afternoon, we crossed terminum. You can see these things clearly from a distance. At ground level, they creep up on you. I was walking through tough valley grasses and thorn scrub when I noticed lines of blue moss between the roots. Oddly regular lines of moss, that bent and forked at exactly one hundred and twenty degrees, and joined up into hexagons. I froze. Twenty meters ahead of me, Ten stood in one world . . . I stood in another.

"Even if you do nothing, it will still come to you," she said. I looked down. The blue lines were inching toward my toes. "Come on." Ten reached out her hand. I took it, and she led me across. Within two minutes walk, the scrub and grass had given way entirely to Chaga vegetation. For the rest of the afternoon we moved through the destroying zone. Trees crashed around us, shrubs were devoured from the roots down, grasses fell apart and dissolved; fungus fingers and coral fans pushed up on either side, bubbles blew around my head. I walked through it untouched like a man in a furnace.

Meji called a halt under an arch of Chaga-growth like a vault in a medieval cathedral. He had a report on his earjack.

"Menengai has been attacked."

Everyone started talking asking question, jabbering. Meji held up his hand.

"They were Africans. Someone had provided them with Chaga-proof equipment, and weapons. They had badges on their uniforms: KLA."

"Kenyan Liberation Army," the quiet one, Naomi said.

"We have enemies," the clever one, Hamid said. "The Kenyan Government still claims jurisdiction over the Chaga. Every so often, they remind us who's in charge. They want to keep us on the run, stop us getting established. They're nothing but contras with western money and guns and advisers."

"And Menengai?" I asked. Meji shook his head.

"Most High is bringing the survivors to Ol Punyata."

I looked at Ten.

"Most High?"

She nodded.

We met up with Most High under the dark canopy of the Great Wall. It was an appropriately somber place for the meeting: the smooth soaring trunks of the trees; the canopy of leaves, held out like hands, a kilometer over our heads; the splashes of light that fell through the gaps to the forest floor; survivors and travelers, dwarfed by it all. Medieval peasants must have felt like this, awestruck in their own cathedrals.

It's an odd experience, meeting someone you've heard of in a story. You want to say, I've heard about you, you haven't heard about me, you're nothing like I imagined. You check them out to make sure they're playing true to their character. His story was simple and grim.

A village, waking, going about its normal business, people meeting and greeting, walking and talking, gossiping and idling, talking the news, taking coffee. Then, voices, strange voices, and shots, and people looking up wondering. What is going on here? and while they are caught wondering, strangers running at them, running through, strangers with guns, shooting at anything in front of them, not asking questions, not looking or listening, shooting and running on. Shooting, and burning. Bodies left where they lay, homes like blossoming flowers going up in gobs of flame. Through, back, and out. Gone. As fast, as off-hand as that. Ten minutes, and Menengai was a morgue. Most High told it as casually as it had been committed, but I saw his knuckles whiten as he gripped his staff.

To people like me, who come from a peaceful, ordered society, violence like that is unimaginable.

I've seen fights and they scared me, but I've never experienced the kind of violence. Most High was describing, where people's pure intent is to kill other people. I could see the survivors—dirty, tired, scared, very quiet—but I couldn't see what had been done to them. So I couldn't really believe it. And though I'd hidden up there on the hill from the helicopter, I couldn't believe it would have opened up those big gatlings on me, and I couldn't believe now that the people who attacked Menengai, this Kenyan Liberation Army, whose only purpose was to kill Chaga-folk and destroy their lives, were out there somewhere, probably being resupplied by airdrop, reloading, and going in search of new targets. It seemed wrong in a place as silent and holy as this . . . like a snake in the garden.

Meji and Ten believed it. As soon as we could, they moved us on and out.

"Where now?" I asked Ten.

She looked uncertain.

"East. The Black Simbas have a number of settlements on Kirinyaga. They'll defend them."

"How far?"

"Three days?"

"That woman back there, Hope. She won't be able to go on very much longer." I had been speaking to her, she was heavily pregnant. Eight months, I reckoned. She had no English, and I had Aid-Agency Swahili, but she appreciated my company, and I found her big belly a confirmation that life was strong, life went on.

"I know," Ten said. She might wear the gear and carry the staff and have a gun at her hip, but she was facing decisions that told her, forcefully, You're still in your teens, little warrior.

We wound between the colossal buttressed roots of the roof-trees. The globes on the tops of the staffs gave off a soft yellow light—bioluminescence. Ten told me.

We followed the bobbing lights through the dark, dripping wall-forest. The land rose, slowly and steadily. I fell back to walk with Hope. We talked. It passed the time. The Great Wall gave way abruptly to an ecosystem of fungi. Red toadstools towered over my head, puff-balls dusted me with yellow spores, trumpetlike chanterelles dripped water from their cups, clusters of pin-head mushrooms glowed white like corpses. I saw monkeys, watching from the canopy.

We were high now, climbing up ridges like the fingers of a splayed out hand. Hope told me how her husband had been killed in the raid on Menengai. I did not know what to say. Then she asked me my story. I told it in my bad Swahili. The staffs led us higher.

"Ten."

We were taking an evening meal break. That was one thing about the Chaga, you could never go hungry. Reach out, and anything you touched would be edible. Ten had taught me that if you buried your shit, a good-tasting tuber would have grown in the morning. I hadn't had the courage yet to try it. For an alien invasion, the Chaga seemed remarkably considerate of human needs.

"I think Hope's a lot further on than we thought."

Ten shook her head.

"Ten, if she starts, will you stop?"

She hesitated a moment.

"Okay. We will stop."

She struggled for two days, down into a valley, through terribly tough terrain of great spheres of giraffe-patterned moss, then up, into higher country than any we had attempted before.

"Ten, where are we?" I asked. The Chaga had changed our geography, made all our maps obsolete. We navigated by compass, and major, geophysical land-marks.

"We've passed through the Nyandarua Valley, now we're going up the east side of the Aberdares."

The line of survivors became strung out. Naomi and I struggled at the rear with the old and the women with children, and Hope. We fought our way up that hill-side, but Hope was flagging, failing.

"I think . . . I feel . . ." she said, hand on her belly.

"Call Ten on that thing," I ordered Naomi. She spoke into her mouthpiece.

"No reply."

"She what?"

"There is no reply."

I ran. Hands, knees, belly, whatever way I could, I made it up that ridge, as fast as I could. Over the summit the terrain changed, as suddenly as Chaga landscapes do, from the moss maze to a plantation of regularly spaced trees shaped like enormous ears of wheat.

Ten was a hundred meters downslope. She stood like a statue among the wheat-trees. Her staff was planted firmly on the ground. She did not acknowledge me when I called her name. I ran down through the trees to her.

"Ten, Hope can't go on. We have to stop."

"No!" Ten shouted. She did not look at me, she stared down through the rows of trees.

"Ten!" I seized her, spun her round. Her face was frantic, terrified, tearful, joyful, as if in this grove of alien plants was something familiar and absolutely agonizing. "Ten! You promised!"

"Shone! Shone! I know where I am! I know where this is! That is the pass, and that is where the road went, this is the valley, that is the river, and down there, is Gichichi!" She looked back up to the pass, called to the figures on the tree-line. "Most High! Gichichi! This is Gichichi! We are home!"

She took off. She held her staff in her hand like a hunter's spear, she leaped rocks and fallen trunks, she hurdled streams and run-offs; bounding down through the trees. I was after her like a shot but I couldn't hope to keep up. I found Ten standing in an open space where a falling wheat-tree had brought others down like dominoes. Her staff was thrust deep into the earth. I didn't interrupt. I didn't say a word. I knew I was witnessing something holy.

She went down on her knees. She closed her eyes. She pressed her hands to the soil. And I saw dark lines, like slow, black lightning, go out from her fingertips across the Chaga-cover. The lines arced and intersected, sparked out fresh paths.

The carpet of moss began to resemble a crackle-glazed Japanese bowl. But they all focused on Ten. She was the source of the pattern. And the Chaga-cover began to flow toward the lines of force. Shapes appeared under the moving moss, like ribs under skin. They formed grids and squares, slowly pushing up the Chaga-cover. I understood what I was seeing. The lines of buried walls and buildings were being exhumed. Molecule by molecule, centimeter by centimeter, Gichichi was being drawn out of the soil.

By the time the others had made it down from the ridge, the walls stood waist-high and service units were rising out of the earth, electricity generators, water pumps, heat-exchangers, nanofacturing cells. Refugees and warriors walked in amazement among the slowly rising porcelain walls.

Then Ten chose to recognize me.

She looked up. Her teeth were clenched, her hair was matted, sweat dripped from her chin and cheekbones. Her face was gaunt, she was burning her own body-mass, ramming it through that mind/Chaga interface in her brain to program nanoprocessors on a massive scale.

"We control it, Shone," she whispered. "We can make the world any shape we want it to be. We can make a home for ourselves."

Most High laid his hand on her shoulder.

"Enough, child. Enough. It can make itself now."

Ten nodded. She broke the spell. Ten rolled onto her side, gasping, shivering.

"It's finished," she whispered. "Shone . . ."

She still could not say my name right. I went to her, I took her in my arms while around us Gichichi rose, unfolded roofs like petals, grew gardens and tiny, tangled lanes. No words. No need for words. She had done all her saying, but close at hand. I heard the delighted, apprehensive cry of a woman entering labor.

We begin with a village, and we end with a village. Different villages, a different world, but the name remains the same. Did I not tell you that names are important? Ojok, Hope's child, is our first citizen. He is now two, but every day people come over the pass or up from the valley, to stay, to make their homes here. Gichichi is now two thousand souls strong. Five hundred houses straggle up and down the valley side, each with its own garden-shamba and nanofactory, where we can make whatever we require. Gichichi is famous for its nanoprocessor programmers. We earn much credit hiring them to the towns and villages that are growing up like mushrooms down in the valley of Nyeri and along the foothills of Mt. Kenya. A great city is growing there, I have heard, and a mighty culture developing; but that is for the far future. Here in Gichichi, we are wealthy in our own way; we have a community center, three bars, a mandazi shop, even a small theater. There is no church, yet. If Christians come, they may build one. If they do, I hope they call it St. John's. The vine-flowers will grow down over the roof again.

Life is not safe. The KLA have been joined by other contra groups, and we have heard through the net that the West is tightening its quarantine of the Chaga zones. There are attacks all along the northern edge. I do not imagine Gichichi is immune. We must scare their powerful ones very much, now. But the packages keep coming down, and the world keeps changing. And life is never safe. Brother Dust's lesson is the truest I ever learned, and I have been taught it better than many. But I trust in the future. Soon there will be a new name among the citizens of Gichichi, this fine, fertile town in the valleys of the Aberdares. Of course, Sean and I cannot agree what it should be. He wants to call her after the time of day she is born, I want something Irish.

"But you won't be able to pronounce it!" he says. We will think of something. That is the way we do things here. Whatever her name, she will have a story to tell, I am sure, but that is not for me to say. My story ends here, and our lives go on. I take up mine again, as you lift yours. We have a long road before us.

New Light on the Drake Equation
IAN R. MACLEOD

British writer Ian R. MacLeod was one of the hottest new writers of the '90s, and, as we travel further into the new century ahead, his work continues to grow in power and deepen in maturity. MacLeod has published a slew of strong stories in *Interzone, Asimov's Science Fiction, SCI FICTION, Weird Tales, Amazing,* and *The Magazine of Fantasy and Science Fiction,* among other markets. Several of these stories made the cut for one or another of the various "Best of the Year" anthologies; in 1990, in fact, he appeared in *three* different "Best of the Year" anthologies with three different stories, certainly a rare distinction. His stories have appeared in our eighth through thirteenth, fifteenth, sixteenth, nineteenth, and twentieth annual collections. His first novel, *The Great Wheel,* was published to critical acclaim in 1997, followed by a collection of his short work, *Voyages by Starlight.* In 1999, he won the World Fantasy Award with his novella "The Summer Isles," and followed it up in 2000 by winning another World Fantasy Award for his novelette "The Chop Girl." In 2004 he published a major new novel, *The Light Ages,* which finally garnered MacLeod some of the wide audiences he so richly deserves, and a new collection, *Breathmoss and Other Exhalations.* His most recent books are the sequel to *The Light Ages, The House of Storms,* and the long-overdue novel version of *The Summer Isles.* Coming up is a new collection, *Past Magic.* MacLeod lives with his wife and young daughter in the West Midlands of England and is at work on several new novels.

Here he paints a brilliant and moving portrait of one man's persistent belief in his vision across the span of an entire lifetime, in the face of mounting odds and a dream that seems to be dying.

A s he did on the first Wednesday of every month, after first finishing off the bottle of wine he'd fallen asleep with, then drinking three bleary fingers of absinthe, and with an extra slug for good measure, Tom Kelly drove down into St. Hilaire to collect his mail and provisions. The little town was red-brown, shimmering in the depths of the valley, flecked with olive trees, as he slewed the old Citröen around the hairpins from his mountain. Up to the east, where the karst rose in a mighty crag, he could just make out the flyers circling against the sheer, white drop if he rubbed his eyes and squinted, and the glint of their wings as they caught the morning thermals. But Tom felt like a flyer of sorts himself, now that the absinthe was fully in his bloodstream. He let the Citröen's piebald tyres, the skid of the grit, and the pull of the mountain take him endlessly downward. Spinning around the bends blind and wrong-side with the old canvas roof flapping, in and out of the shadows, scattering sheep in the sweet, hot roar of the antique motor, Tom Kelly drove down from his mountain toward the valley.

In the *Bureau de poste*, Madame Brissac gave him a smile that seemed even more patronising than usual.

"Any messages?" he croaked.

She blinked slowly. "One maybe two." Bluebottles circled the close air, which smelled of boiled sweets and Gitanes and Madame Brissac. Tom swayed slightly in his boots. He wiped off some of the road grit, which had clung to the stubble on his face. He picked a stain from his T-shirt, and noticed as he did so that a fresh age spot was developing on the back of his right hand. It would disappoint her, really, if he took a language vial and started speaking fluent French after all these years—or even if he worked at it the old way, using bookplates and audio samples, just as he'd always been promising himself. It would deprive her of their small monthly battle.

"Then, ah, *je voudrais* . . ." He tried waving his arms.

"You would like to have?"

"Yes please. *Oui*. Ah—*s'il vous plaît* . . ."

Still the tepid pause, the droning bluebottles. Or Madame Brissac could acquire English, Tom thought, although she was hardly likely to do it for his sake.

"You late." She said eventually.

"You mean—"

Then the door banged open in a crowded slab of shadows and noise and a cluster of flyers, back from their early morning spin on the thermals, bustled up behind Tom with skinsuits squealing, the folded tips of their wings bumping against the brown curls of sticky flypaper which the bluebottles had been scrupulously avoiding. These young people, Tom decided as he glanced back at them, truly were like bright, alien insects in their gaudy skinsuits, their thin bodies garishly striped with the twisting logos of sports companies and their wings, a flesh of fine silk stretched between feathery bones, folded up behind their backs like delicate umbrellas. And they were speaking French, too; speaking it in loud, high voices, but overdoing every phrase and gesture and emphasis in the way that people always did when they were new to a language. They thought that just because they could understand each other and talk sensibly to their flying instructor and follow the tour guide and order a drink at the bar that they were jabbering away like natives, but then they hadn't yet come up against Madame Brissac, who would be bound to devise some bureaucratic twist or incomprehension which would send them away from here without whatever particular form or permission it was that they were expecting. Tom turned back to Madame Brissac and gave her a grin from around the edges of his gathering absinthe headache. She didn't bother to return it. Instead, she muttered something that sounded like *I'm Judy*.

"What? *Voulez-vous repeter?*"

"Is Thursday."

"Ah. *Je comprends*. I see . . ." Not that he did quite, but the flyers were getting impatient and crowding closer to him, wings rustling with echoes of the morning air that had recently been filling them and the smell of fresh sweat, clean endeavour. How was it, Tom wondered, that they could look so beautiful from a distance, and so stupid and ugly close up? But *Thursday*—and he'd imagined it was Wednesday. Of course he'd thought that it was Wednesday, otherwise he wouldn't be here in St. Hilaire, would he? He was a creature of habit, worn in by the years like the grain of the old wood of Madame Brissac's counter. So he must have lost track, or not bothered to check his calendar back up on the mountain, or both. An easy enough mistake to make, living the way he did. Although . . .

"You require them? Yes?"

"*S'il vous plait* . . ."

At long last, Madame Brissac was turning to the pigeonholes where she kept his and a few other message cards filed according to her own alchemic system. Putting them in one place, labelled under Kelly, Tom—or American, Drunk; Elderly, Stupid—was too simple for her. Neither had Tom ever been able to see a particular pattern that would relate to the source of the cards, which were generally from one or another of his various academic sponsors and came in drips and drabs and rushes, but mostly drabs. Those old, brown lines of wooden boxes, which looked as if they had probably once held proper, old-fashioned letters and telegrams, and perhaps messages and condolences from the World Wars, and the revolutionary proclamations of the *sans-culottes*, and decrees from the Sun King, and quite possibly even the odd pigeon, disgorged their contents to Madame Brissac's quick hands in no way that Tom could ever figure. He could always ask, of course, but that would just be an excuse for a raising of Gallic eyebrows and shoulders in mimed incomprehension. After all, Madame Brissac was Madame Brissac, and the flyers behind him were whispering, fluttering, trembling like young egrets, and it was none of his business.

There were market stalls lined across the Place de Revolution, which had puzzled Tom on his way into the *Bureau de poste*, but no longer. The world was right and he was wrong. This was Thursday. And his habitual café was busier than usual, although the couple who were occupying his table got up at his approach and strolled off, hand in hand, past the heaped and shadowed displays of breads and fruits and cheeses. The girl had gone for an Audrey Hepburn look, but the lad had the muscles of a paratrooper beneath his sleeveless T-shirt, and his flesh was green and lightly scaled. To Tom, it looked like a skin disease. He wondered, as lonely men gazing at young couples from café tables have wondered since time immemorial, what the hell she saw in him.

The waiter Jean-Benoît was busier than usual, and, after giving Tom a glance that almost registered surprise, took his time coming over. Tom, after all, would be going nowhere in any hurry. And he had his cards—all six of them—to read. They lay there, face down on the plastic tablecloth; a hand of poker he had to play. But he knew already what the deal was likely to be. One was blue and almost plain, with a pattern like rippled water, which was probably some kind of junk mail, and another looked suspiciously like a bill for some cyber-utility he probably wasn't even using, and the rest, most undoubtedly, were from his few remaining sponsors. Beside them on the table, like part of a fine still life into which he and these cards were an unnecessary intrusion, lay the empty carafe and the wineglasses from which the lovers had been drinking. Wine at ten in the morning! That was France for you. *This* was France. And he could do with a drink himself, could Tom Kelly. Maybe just a *pastis*, which would sit nicely with the absinthe he'd had earlier—just as a bracer, mind. Tom sighed and rubbed his temples and looked about him in the morning brightness. Up at the spire of St. Marie rising over the awnings of the market, then down at the people, gaudily, gorgeously fashionable in their clothes, their skins, their faces. France, this real France of the living, was a place he sometimes felt he only visited on these Wednesday—this Thursday—mornings. He could have been anywhere for the rest of the time, up with the stars there on his mountain, combing his way through eternity on the increasing off chance of an odd blip. That was why he was who he was—some old gook whom people like Madame Brissac and Jean-Benoît patronised without ever really knowing. That was why he'd never really got around to mastering this language which was washing all around him in persibilant waves. Jean-Benoît was still busy, flipping his towel and serving up crepes with an on-off smile of his regulation-handsome features, his wings so well tucked away that no one would ever really know he had them. Like a lot of the people who worked here, he did the job so he could take to the air in his free time. Tom, with his *trois diget pastis merci*, was never going to be much of a priority.

Tom lifted one of the cards and tried to suppress a burp as the bitter residue of absinthe flooded his mouth. The card was from the University of Aston, in Birmingham, England, of all places. Now, he'd forgotten *they* were even sponsoring him. He ran his finger down the playline, and half-closed his eyes to witness a young man he'd never seen before in his life sitting at the kind of impressively wide desk that only people, in Tom's experience, who never did any real work possessed.

"Mister Kelly, it's a real pleasure to make your acquaintance . . ." The young man paused. He was clearly new to whatever it was he was doing, and gripping that desk as if it was perched at the top of a roller-coaster ride. "As you may have seen in the academic press, I've now taken over from Doctor Sally Normanton. I didn't know her personally, but I know that all of you who did valued her greatly, and I, too, feel saddened by the loss of a fine person and physicist . . ."

Tom withdrew his finger from the card for a moment, and dropped back into France. He'd only ever met the woman once. She'd been warm and lively and sympathetic, he remembered, and had moved about on autolegs because of the advanced arthritis which, in those days at least, the vials hadn't been able to counteract. They'd sat under the mossy trees and statues in Birmingham's Centenary Square, which for him had held other memories, and she'd sighed and smiled and explained how the basic policy of her institution had gone firmly against any positive figure to the Drake Equation several decades before, but Sally Normanton herself had always kept a soft spot for that kind of stuff, and she'd really got into physics in the first place on the back of reading Clarke and Asimov. Not that she imagined Tom had heard of them? But Tom had, of course. They were almost of the same generation. He'd developed a dust allergy from hunching over those thrilling, musty, analogue pages as a kid. They chatted merrily, and on the walk back to the campus Sally Normanton had confided, as she heaved and clicked on her legs, that she had control of a smallish fund. It was left over from some government work, and was his to have for as long as it took the accountants to notice. And that was more than twenty years ago. And now she was dead.

". . . physicist. But in clearing out and revising her responsibilities, it's come to my attention that monies have been allocated to your project which, I regret to say . . ."

Tom spun the thing forward until he came to the bit at the end when the young man, who had one eye green and one eye blue—and nails like talons, so perhaps he too was a flyer, although he didn't look quite thin enough and seemed too easily scared—announced that he'd left a simulacrum AI of his business self on the card, which would be happy to answer any pertinent questions, although the decision to withdraw funds was, regrettably, quite irrevocable. The AI was there, of course, to save the chance that Tom might try to bother this man of business with feeble pleas. But Tom knew he was lucky to have got what he got from that source, and even luckier that they weren't talking about suing him to take it all back.

Aston University. England. The smell of different air. Different trees. If there was one season that matched the place, a mood that always seemed to be hanging there in the background, even on the coldest or hottest or wettest of days, it had to be fall, autumn. How long had it been now? Tom tried not to think—that was one equation which even to him always came back as a recurring nothing. He noticed instead that the wineglass that the pretty, young girl had been drinking bore the red imprint of her lipstick, and was almost sad to see it go, and with it the better memories he'd been trying to conjure, when Jean-Benoît finally bustled up and plonked a glass of cloudy, yellow liquid, which Tom wasn't really sure that he wanted any longer, down in front of him. *Voilà. Merci.* Pidgin French as he stared at the cards from Madame Brissac's incomprehensible pigeonholes. But he drank it anyway, the *pastis*. Back in one. At least it got rid of the taste of the absinthe.

And the day was fine, the market was bustling. It would be a pity to spoil this frail, good mood he was building with messages which probably included the words *regret, withdraw,* or at the very least, *must query* . . . This square, it was baguettes and Edith Piaf writ large, it was the Eiffel Tower in miniature. The warm smells of garlic and slightly dodgy drains and fine, dark coffee. And those ridiculous little poodles dragged along by those long-legged women. The shouts and the gestures, the black, old widows, who by now were probably younger than he was, muttering to themselves and barging along with their stripy shopping bags like extras from the wrong film and scowling at this or that vial-induced wonder. And a priest in his cassock stepping from the church, pausing in the sunlight at the top of the steps to take in the scene, although he had wings behind him which he stretched as if to yawn, and his hair was scarlet. Another flyer. Tom smiled to think how he got on with his congregation, which was mostly those scowling old women, and thought about ordering—why not?—another *pastis.* . . .

Then he noticed a particular figure wandering beside the stalls at the edge of the market where displays of lace billowed in the wind, which blew off the karst and squeezed in a warm, light breeze down between the washing-strung tenements. It couldn't be, of course. Couldn't be. It was just that lipstick on the edge of that glass which had prickled that particular memory. That, and getting a message from England, and that woman dying, and losing another income source, all of which, if he'd have let them, would have stirred up a happy-sad melange of memories. She was wearing a dark blue, sleeveless dress and was standing in a bright patch of sunlight which flamed on her blonde hair and made it hard for him to see her face. She could have been anyone, but in that moment, she could have been Terr, and Tom felt the strangely conflicting sensations of wanting to run over and embrace her, and also to dig a hole for himself where he could hide forever right here beneath this café paving. He blinked. His head swam. By the time he'd refocused, the girl, the woman, had moved on. A turn of bare arm, a flash of lovely calf. Why *did* they have to change themselves like they did now? Women were perfect as they were. Always had been, as far as Tom was concerned—or as best he could remember. Especially Terr. But then perhaps that had been an illusion, too.

Tom stood up and dropped a few francs on the table and blundered off between the market stalls. That dark blue, sleeveless dress, those legs, that hair. His heart was pounding as it hadn't done in years from some strange inner exertion of memory. Even if it *wasn't* her, which it obviously wasn't, he still wanted to know, to see. But St. Hilaire was Thursday-busy. The teeming market swallowed him up and spat him out again downhill where the steps ran beside the old battlements and the river flashed under the willow trees, then uphill by the bright, expensive shops along the Rue de Commerce, which offered in their windows designer clothes, designer vials, designer lives. Fifteen different brands of colloquial French in bottles like costly perfumes and prices to match. Only you crushed them between your teeth and the glass tasted like spun sugar and tiny miracles of lavish engineering poured down your throat and through the walls of your belly and into your bloodstream where they shed their protective coating and made friends with your immune system and hitched a ride up to your brain. Lessons were still necessary (they played that down on the packaging) but only one or two, and they involved little more than sitting in flashing darkness in a Zenlike state of calm induced by various drug suppositories (this being France) whilst nanomolecules fiddled with your sites of language and cognition until you started *parlez vous*-ing like a native. Or you could grow wings, although the vials in the sports shops were even more expensive. But the dummies beyond the plateglass whispered and beckoned to Tom and fluttered about excitedly; Day-Glo fairies, urging him to make the investment in a fortnight's experience that would last a lifetime.

Tom came to an old square at the far end of the shops. The Musée de Masque was just opening, and a group of people who looked like late revellers from the night before were sitting on its steps and sharing a bottle of neat Pernod. The women had decorated their wings with silks and jewels; although by now they looked like tired hatstands. The men, but for the pulsing tattoo-like adornments they'd woven into their flesh and the pouchlike g-strings around their crotches which spoke, so to speak, volumes, were virtually naked. Their skin was heliotrope. Tom guessed it was the colour for this season. To him, though, they looked like a clutch of malnourished, crash-landed gargoyles. He turned back along the street, and found his Citröen pretty much where he thought he'd left it by the *alimentation générale* where he'd already purchased next month's supplies, and turned the old analogue key he'd left in the ignition, and puttered slowly out across the cobbles, supplies swishing and jingling in their boxes, then gave the throttle an angry shove, and roared out toward midday, the heat, the scattered olive trees, and the grey-white bulk of his mountain.

Dusk. The coming stars. His time. His mountain. Tom stood outside his sparse wooden hut, sipping coffee and willing the sun to unravel the last of her glowing clouds from the horizon. Around him on the large, flat, mile-wide, slightly west-tilted slab of pavement limestone glittered the silver spiderweb of his tripwires, which were sheening with dew as the warmth of the day evaporated, catching the dying light as they and he waited for the stars.

He amazed himself sometimes, the fact that he was up here doing this, the fact that he was still searching for anything at all at the ripe, nearly old age of near-seventy, let alone for something as wild and extravagant as intelligent extra-terrestrial life. Where had it began? What had started him on this quest of his? Had it really been those SF stories—dropping through the Stargate with Dave Bowman, or staggering across the sandworm deserts of Arrakis with Paul Atreides? Was it under rocks in Eastport when he was a kid raising the tiny translucent crabs to the light, or was it down the wires on the few remaining SETI websites when he wasn't that much older? Was it pouring through the library screens at college, or was it now as he stood looking up at the gathering stars from his lonely hut on this lonely French mountain? Or was it somewhere else? Somewhere out there, sweet and glorious and imponderable?

Most of the people he still knew, or at least maintained a sort of long-distance touch with, had given up with whatever had once bugged them some time ago; the ones, in fact, who seemed the happiest, the most settled, the most at ease with their lives—and thus generally had the least to do with him—had never really started worrying about such things in the first place. They took vacations in places like St. Hilaire, they grew wings or gills just like the kids did, and acquired fresh languages and outlooks as they swallowed their vials and flew or dived in their new element. He put down his cup of coffee, which was already skinned and cold, and then he smiled to himself—he still couldn't help it—as he watched more of the night come in. Maybe it was that scene in *Fantasia*, watching it on video when he was little more than a baby. The one set to the music he recognised later as Beethoven's *Pastoral*. Those cavorting cherubs and centaurs, and then at the end, after Zeus has packed away his thunderbolts, the sun sets, and over comes Morpheus in a glorious cloak of night. The idea of life amid the stars had already been with him then, filling him as he squatted entranced before the screen and the Baltimore traffic buzzed by outside unnoticed, filled with something that was like a sweet sickness, like his mother's embrace when she thought he was sleeping, like the ache of cola and ice cream. That sweet ache had been with him, he decided as he looked up and smiled as the stars twinkled on and goosebumps rose on his flesh, ever since.

So Tom had become a nocturnal beast, a creature of twilights and dawns. He supposed that he'd become so used to his solitary life up here on this wide and empty mountain that he'd grown a little agora—or was it claustro?—phobic. Hence the need for the absinthe this morning—or at least the extra slug of it. The Wednesdays, the bustle of the town, had become quite incredible to him, a blast of light and smell and sound and contact, almost like those VR suites where you tumbled through huge fortresses on strange planets and fought and cannon-blasted those ever-imaginary aliens. Not that Tom had ever managed to bring himself to do such a thing. As the monsters glowered over him, jaws agape and fangs dripping, all he'd wanted to do was make friends and ask them about their customs and religions and mating habits. He'd never got through many levels on those VR games, the few times he'd tried them. Now he thought about it, he really hadn't got through so very many levels of the huge VR game known as life, either.

Almost dark. A time for secrets and lovers and messages. A time for the clink of wineglasses and the soft puck of opening bottles. The west was a faint, red blush of clouds and mountains, which caught glimmering in a pool on the fading slope of the mountain. Faint, grey shapes were moving down there; from the little Tom could see now from up here, they could have been stray flares and impulses from the failing remaining rods and cones in his weary eyes—random scraps of data—but he knew from other nights and mornings that they were the shy ibex which grazed this plateau, and were drawn here from miles around along with many other creatures simply because most of the moisture that fell here in the winter rains and summer storms drained straight through the cave-riddled limestone. Sometimes, looking that way on especially clear nights, Tom would catch the glimmer of stars as if a few had fallen there, although on the rare occasions he'd trekked to the pool down across difficult slopes, he'd found that, close to, it was a disappointment. A foul, brown oval of thick amoebic fluid surrounded by cracked and caked mud, it was far away from the sweet oasis he'd imagined, where bright birds and predators and ruminants all bowed their heads to sip the silver, cool liquid and forget, in the brief moments of their parched and mutual need, their normal animosities. But it was undeniably a waterhole, and as such important to the local fauna. It had even been there on the map all those years ago, when he'd been looking for somewhere to begin what he was sure was to be the remainder of his life's work. A blue full stop, a small ripple of hope and life. He'd taken it as a sign.

Tom went inside his hut and spun the metal cap off one of the cheap but decent bottles of *vin de table* with which he generally started the evenings. He took a swig from it, looked around without much hope for a clean glass, then took another swig. One handed, he tapped up the keys of one of his bank of machines. Lights stuttered, cooling fans chirruped like crickets or groaned like wounded bears. It was hot in here from all this straining antique circuitry. There was the strong smell of singed dust and warm wires, and a new, dim, fizzing sound which could have been a spark which, although he turned his head this way and that, as sensitive to the changes in this room's topography as a shepherd to the moods of his flock, Tom couldn't quite locate. But no matter. He'd wasted most of last night fiddling and tweaking to deal with the results of a wine spillage, and didn't want to waste this one doing the same. There was something about today, this not-Wednesday known as Thursday, which filled Tom with an extra sense of urgency. He'd grounded himself far too firmly on the side of science and logic to believe in such rubbish as premonitions, but still he couldn't help but wonder if this wasn't how they felt, the Hawkings and the Einsteins and the Newtons—the Cooks and the Columbuses, for that matter—in the moment before they made their Big Discovery, their final break. Of course, any such project, viewed with hindsight, could be no more than a gradual accumulation of knowledge, a hunch that a particular area of absent knowledge might be fruitfully explored, followed generally by years of arse-licking and fund-searching and peer-group head shaking and rejected papers and hard work during which a few extra scraps of information made that hunch seem more and more like a reasonably intelligent guess, even if everyone else was heading in the opposite direction and thought that you were, to coin a phrase once used by Tom's cosmology professor, barking up the wrong fucking tree in the wrong fucking forest. In his bleaker moments, Tom sometimes wondered if there was a tree there at all.

But not now. The data, of course, was processed automatically, collected day and night according to parameters and wavelengths he'd predetermined but at a speed which, even with these processors, sieved and reamed out information by the giga-byte per second. He'd set up the search systems to flash and bleep and make whatever kind of electronic racket they were capable of if they ever came upon any kind of anomaly. Although he was routinely dragged from his bleary daytime slumbers by a surge in power or a speck of fly dirt or a rabbit gnawing the tripwires or a stray cosmic ray, it was still his greatest nightmare that they would blithely ignore the one spike, the one regularity or irregularity, that might actually mean something—or that he'd be so comatose he'd sleep through it. And then of course the computers couldn't look everywhere. By definition, with the universe being as big as it was, they and Tom were always missing something. The something, in fact, was so large it was close to almost everything. Not only was there all the data collected for numerous other astronomical and non-astronomical purposes which he regularly downloaded from his satellite link and stored on the disks which, piled and waiting in one corner, made a silvery pillar almost to the ceiling, but the stars themselves were always out there, the stars and their inhabitants. Beaming down in real-time. Endlessly.

So how to sort, where to begin? Where was the best place on all the possible radio wavelengths to start looking for messages from little green men? It was a question which had first been asked more than a century before, and to which, of all the many, many guesses, one still stood out as the most reasonable. Tom turned to that frequency now, live through the tripwires out on the karst, and powered up the speakers and took another slug of *vin de table* and switched on the monitor and sat there listening, watching, drinking. That dim hissing of microwaves, the cool dip of interstellar quietude amid the babble of the stars and the gas clouds and the growl of the big bang and the spluttering quasars, not to mention all the racket that all the other humans on Earth and around the solar system put out. The space between the emissions of interstellar hydrogen and hydroxyl radical at round about 1420 MHz, which was known as the waterhole; a phrase which reflected not only the chemical composition of water, but also the idea of a place where, just as the shy ibex clustered to quench themselves at dusk and dawn, all the varied species of the universe might gather after a weary day to exchange wondrous tales.

Tom listened to the sound of the waterhole. What were the chances, with him sitting here, of anything happening right now? Bleep, bleep. Bip, bip. Greetings from the planet Zarg. Quite, quite impossible. But then, given all the possibilities in the universe, what were the chances of him, Tom Kelly, sitting here on this particular mountain at this particular moment with this particular bank of equipment and this particular near-empty bottle of *vin de table* listening to this frequency in the first place? That was pretty wild in itself. Wild enough, in fact—he still couldn't help it—to give him goosebumps. Life itself was such an incredible miracle. In fact, probably unique, if one was to believe the figure of which was assigned to it by the few eccentric souls who still bothered to tinker with the Drake Equation. That was the problem.

He forced himself to stand up, stretch, leave the room, the speakers still hissing with a soft sea-roar, the monitor flickering and jumping. The moment when the transmission finally came through was bound to be when you turned your back. It stood to reason. A watched kettle, after all . . . And not that he was superstitious. So he wandered out into the night again, which was now starry and marvellous and moonless and complete, and he tossed the evening's first empty into the big skip and looked up at the heavens, and felt that swell in his chest and belly he'd felt those more than sixty years ago, which was still like the ache of cola and ice cream. And had he eaten? He really couldn't remember, although he was pretty sure he'd fixed some coffee. This darkness was food enough for him, all the pouring might of the stars. Odd to say, but on nights like this the darkness had a glow to it like something finely wrought, finally polished, a lustre and a sheen. You could believe in God. You could believe in anything. And the tripwires were still just visible, the vanishing trails like tiny shooting stars crisscrossing this arid, limestone plain as they absorbed the endless transmission. They flowed toward the bowl of darkness that was the hidden valley, the quiet waterhole, the flyers sleeping in their beds in St. Hilaire, dreaming of thermals, twitching their wings. Tom wondered if Madame Brissac slept. It was hard to imagine her anywhere other than standing before her pigeonholes in the *Bureau de poste*, waiting for the next poor sod she could make life difficult for. The pigeonholes themselves, whatever code it was that she arranged them in, really would be worth making the effort to find out about on the remote chance that, Madame Brissac being Madame Brissac, the information was sorted in a way that Tom's computers, endlessly searching the roar of chaos for order, might have overlooked. And he also wondered if it wasn't time already for another bottle, one of the plastic litre ones, which tasted like shit if you started on them, but were fine if you had something half-decent first to take off the edge. . . .

A something—a figure—was walking up the track toward him. No, not a fluke, and not random data, and certainly not an ibex. Not Madame Brissac either, come to explain her pigeonholes and apologise for her years of rudeness. Part of Tom was watching the rest of Tom in quiet amazement as his addled mind and tired eyes slowly processed the fact that he wasn't alone, and that the figure was probably female, and could almost have been, no looked like, in fact was, the woman in the dark blue dress he'd glimpsed down by the lace stalls in the market that morning. And she really did bear a remarkable resemblance to Terr, at least in the sole dim light, which emanated from the monitors inside his hut. The way she walked. The way she was padding across the bare patch of ground in front of the tripwires. That same lightness. And then her face. And her voice.

"Why do you have to live so bloody far up here Tom? The woman I asked in the post office said it was just up the road. . . ."

He shrugged. He was floating. His arms felt light, his hands empty. "That would be Madame Brissac."

"Would it? Anyway, she was talking rubbish."

"You should have tried asking in French."

"I *was* speaking French. My poor feet. It's taken me bloody hours."

Tom had to smile. The stars were behind Terr, and they were shining on her once-blonde hair, which the years had silvered to the gleam of those tripwires, and touched the lines around her mouth as she smiled. He felt like crying and laughing. Terr. "Well, that's Madame Brissac for you."

"So? Are you going to invite me inside?"

"There isn't much of an inside."

Terr took another step forward on her bare feet. She was real. So close to him. He could smell the dust on her salt flesh. Feel and hear her breathing. She was Terr alright. He wasn't drunk or dreaming, or at least not that drunk yet; he'd only had— what?—two bottles of wine so far all evening. And she had and hadn't changed.

"Well," she said, "that's Tom Kelly for you, too, isn't it?"

The idea of sitting in the hut was ridiculous on a night like this. And the place, as Tom stumbled around in it and slewed bottles off the table and shook rubbish off the chairs, was a dreadful, terrible mess. So he hauled two chairs out into the night for them to sit on, and the table to go between, and found unchipped glasses from somewhere, and gave them a wipe to get rid of the mould, and ferreted around in the depths of his boxes until he found the solitary bottle of Santernay le Chenay 2058 he'd been saving for First Contact—or at least until he felt too depressed—and lit one of the candles he kept for when the generator went down. Then he went searching for a corkscrew, ransacking cupboards and drawers and cursing under his breath at the ridiculousness of someone who goes through as much wine as he did not being able to lay his hands upon one—but then the cheaper bottles were all screw-capped, and the really cheap plastic things had tops a blind child could pop off one-handed. He was breathless when he finally sat down. His heart ached. His face throbbed. His ears were singing.

"How did you find me, Terr?"

"I told you, I asked that woman in the post office. Madame Brissac.

"I mean . . ." He used both hands to still the shaking as he sloshed wine from the bottle. ". . . here in France, in St. Hilaire, on this mountain."

She chuckled. She sounded like the Terr of old speaking to him down the distance of an antique telephone line. "I did a search for you. One of those virtual things, where you send an AI out like a genie from a bottle. But would you believe I had to explain to it that SETI meant the Search for Extra-Terrestrial Intelligence? It didn't have the phrase in its standard vocabulary. But it found you anyway, once I'd sorted that out. You have this old-fashioned website-thingy giving information on your project here and inviting new sponsors. You say it will be a day-by-day record of setbacks, surprises, and achievements. You even offer T-shirts. By the look of it, it was last updated about twenty years ago. You can virtually see the dust on it through the screen. . . ."

Tom laughed. Sometimes, you have to. "The T-shirts never really took off . . ." He studied his glass, which also had a scum of dust floating on it, like most of his life. The taste of this good wine—sitting here—everything—was strange to him.

"Oh, and she sent me across the square to speak to this incredibly handsome waiter who works in this café. Apparently, you forgot these . . ." Terr reached into the top of her dress, and produced the cards he must have left on the table. They were warm when he took them, filled with a sense of life and vibrancy he doubted was contained in any of the messages. Terr. And her own personal filing system.

"And what about you, Terr?"

"What do you mean?"

"All these years, I mean I guess it's pretty obvious what *I've* been doing—"

"—which was what you always said . . ."

"Yes. But you, Terr. I've thought about you once or twice. Just occasionally . . ."

"Mmmm." She smiled at him over her glass, through the candlelight. "Let's just talk about *now* for a while, shall we, Tom? That is, if you'll put up with me?"

"Fine." His belly ached. His hands, as he took another long slug of this rich, good wine, were still trembling.

"Tom, you haven't said the obvious thing yet."

"Which is?"

"That I've changed. Although we both have, I suppose. Time being time."

"You look great."

"You were always good at compliments."

"That was because I always meant them."

"And you're practical at the bottom of it, Tom. Or at least you were. I used to like that about you, too. Even if we didn't always agree about it. . . ."

With Tom it had always been one thing, one obsession. With Terr, it had to be everything. She'd wanted the whole world, the universe. And it was there even now, Tom could feel it quivering in the night between them, that division of objectives, a loss of contact, as if they were edging back toward the windy precipice which had driven them apart in the first place.

"Anyway," he said stupidly, just to fill the silence, "if you don't like how you look these days, all you do is take a vial."

"What? And be ridiculous—like those women you see along Oxford Street and Fifth Avenue, with their fake furs, their fake smiles, their fake skins? Youth is for the young, Tom. Always was, and always will be. Give them their chance, is what I say. After all, we had ours. And they're so much better at it than we are."

Terr put down her glass on the rough table, leaned back, and stretched on the rickety chair. Her hair sheened back from her shoulders, and looked almost blonde for a moment. Darkness hollowed in her throat. "When you get to my age, Tom— *our* age. It just seems . . . Looking back is more important than looking forward. . . ."

"Is that why you're here?"

A more minor stretch and shrug. Her flesh whispered and seemed to congeal around her throat in stringy clumps. Her eyes hollowed, and the candlelight went out in them. Her arms thinned. Tom found himself wishing there were either more illumination, or less. He wanted to see Terr as she was, or cloaked in total darkness; not like this, twisting and changing like the ibex at the twilight waterhole. So perhaps candlelight was another thing that the young should reserve for themselves, like the vials, like flying, like love and faith and enthusiasm. Forget about romance — what you needed at his, at their, ages, was to *know*. You wanted certainty. And Tom himself looked, he knew, from his occasional forays in front of a mirror, like a particularly vicious cartoon caricature of the Tom Kelly that Terr remembered; the sort of thing that Gerald Scarfe had done to Reagan and Thatcher in the last century. The ruined veins in his cheeks and eyes. The bruises and swellings. Those damn age spots that had recently started appearing — gravestone marks, his grandmother had once called them. He was like Tom Kelly hungover after a fight in a bar, with a bout of influenza on top of that, and then a bad case of sunburn, and struggling against the influence of the gravity of a much larger planet. That was pretty much what ageing felt like, too, come to think of it.

Flu, and too much gravity.

He'd never been one for chat-up lines. He'd had the kind of natural, not-quite regular looks when he was young which really didn't need enhancing — which was good, because he'd never have bothered, or been able to afford it — but he had a shyness which came out mostly like vague disinterest when he talked to girls. The lovelier they were, the more vague and disinterested Tom became. But this woman or girl he happened to find himself walking beside along the canals of this old and once-industrial city called Birmingham after one of those parties when the new exchange students were supposed to meet up, she was different. She was English for a start, which to Tom, a little-traveled American on this foreign shore, seemed both familiar and alien. Everything she said, every gesture, had a slightly different slant to it, which he found strange, intriguing . . .

She'd taken him around the canals to Gas Street Basin, the slick waters sheened with antique petrol, antique fog, and along the towpath to the Sealife Centre, where deepsea creatures out of Lovecraft mouthed close to the tripleglass of their pressurised tanks. Then across the iron bridges of the Worcester and Birmingham Canal to a pub. Over her glass of wine, Terr had explained that an American president had once sat here in this pub and surprised the locals and drunk a pint of bitter during some world conference. Her hair was fine blonde. Her eyes were stormy green. She'd shrugged off the woollen coat with a collar that had brushed the exquisite line of her neck and jaw as she walked in a way that had made Tom envy it. Underneath, she was wearing a sleeveless, dark blue dress, which was tight around her hips and smallish breasts, and showed her fine legs. Of course, he envied that dress as well. There was a smudged red crescent at the rim of the glass made by her lipstick. Terr was studying literature then, an arcane enough subject in itself, and for good measure she'd chosen as her special field the kind of stories of the imaginary future which had been popular for decades, until the real and often quite hard to believe present had finally extinguished them. Tom, who'd been immersed in such stuff for much of his teenage years, almost forgot his reticence as he recommended John Varley, of whom she hadn't even heard, and that she avoid the late-period Heinlein, and then to list his own particular favourites, which had mostly been Golden Age writers (yes, yes, she knew the phrase) like Simak and Van Vogt and Wyndham and Sheckley. And then there was Lafferty, and Cordwainer Smith. . . .

Eventually, sitting at a table in the top room in that bar where an American president might once have sat and overlooking the canal where the long boats puttered past with their antique, petrol motors, bleeding their colours into the mist, Terr had steered Tom away from science fiction, and nudged him into talking about himself. He found out later that the whole genre of SF was already starting to bore her in any case. And he discovered that Terr had already worked her way through half a dozen courses, and had grown bored with all of them. She was bright enough to get a feel of any subject very quickly, and in the process to convince some new senior lecturer that, contrary to all the evidence on file, she finally had found her true focus in medieval history or classics or economics. And she was quick—incredibly so, by Tom's standards—at languages. That would have given her a decent career in any other age; even as she sat there in her blue dress in that Birmingham pub, he could picture her beside that faceless American president, whispering words in his ears. But by then it was already possible for any normally intelligent human to acquire any new language in a matter of days. Deep therapy. Bio-feedback. Nano-enhancement. Out in the real world, those technologies that Tom had spent his teenage years simply dreaming about, as he wondered over those dusty, analogue pages, had been growing at an exponential rate.

But Terr, she fluttered from enthusiasm to enthusiasm, flower to flower, sipping its nectar, then once again spreading her wings and wafting off to some other faculty. And people, too. Terr brought that same incredible focus to bear on everyone she met as well—or at least those who interested her—understanding, absorbing, taking everything in.

She was even doing it now, Tom decided as they sat outside all these years later together by his hut on this starlit French mountain. This Terr who changed and unchanged in the soft flood of candlelight across this battered table was reading him like a book. Every word, every gesture: the way this bottle of wine, good though it was, wouldn't be anything like enough to see him through the rest of this night. She was feeling the tides of the world which had borne him here with all his hopes still somehow intact like Noah in his Ark, and then withdrawn and left him waiting, beached, dry, and drowning.

"What are you thinking?"

He shrugged. But for once, the truth seemed easy. "That pub you took me to, the first time we met."

"You mean the Malt House?"

Terr was bright, quick. Even now. Of course she remembered.

"And you went on and on about SF," she added.

"Did I? I suppose I did. . . ."

"Not really, Tom, but I'd sat through a whole bloody lecture of the stuff that morning, and I'd decided I'd had enough of it—of any kind of fiction. I realised I wanted something that was fabulous, but real."

"That's always been a tall order . . ." Terr had been so lovely back then. That blue dress, the shape of her lips on the wineglass she'd been drinking. Those stormy green eyes. Fabulous, but real. But it was like the couple he'd seen that morning. What had she ever seen in him?

"But then you told me you planned to prove that there was other intelligent life in the universe, Tom. Just like that. I don't know why, but it just sounded so wonderful. Your dream, and then the way you could be so matter-of-fact about it. . . ."

Tom gripped his glass a little tighter, and drank the last of it. His dream. He could feel it coming, the next obvious question.

"So did it ever happen?" Terr was now asking. "Did you ever find your little, green men, Tom? But then I suppose I'd have heard. Remember, how you promised to tell me? Or at least it might have roused you to post some news on that poor, old website of yours." She chuckled with her changed voice, slightly slurring the words. But Terr, Tom remembered, could get drunk on half a glass of wine. She could get drunk on nothing. Anything. "I'm sorry, Tom. It's your life, isn't it? And what the hell do I know? It was one of the things I always liked about you, your ability to dream in that practical way of yours. Loved . . ."

Loved? Had she said that? Or was that another blip, stray data?

"So you must tell me, Tom. How's it going? After I've come all this way. You and your dream."

The candle was sinking. The stars were pouring down on him. And the wine wasn't enough, he needed absinthe—but his dream. And where to begin? *Where* to begin?

"D'you remember the Drake Equation?" Tom asked.

"Yes, I remember," Terr said. "I remember the Drake Equation. You told me all about the Drake Equation that first day on our walk from that pub . . ." She tilted her head to one side, studying the glimmer of Aries in the west as if she was trying to remember the words of some song they'd once shared. "Now, how exactly did it go?"

Until that moment, none of it had yet seemed quite real to Tom. This night, and Terr being here. And, as the candle flickered, she still seemed to twist and change from Terr as he remembered to the Terr she was now in each quickening pulse of the flame. But with the Drake Equation, with that Tom Kelly was anchored. And how *did* it go, in any case?

That long and misty afternoon. Walking beside the canal towpaths from that pub and beneath the dripping tunnels and bridges all the way past the old factories and the smart houses to the city's other university out in Edgbaston as the streetlights came on. He'd told Terr about a radio astronomer named Frank Drake who—after all the usual false alarms and funding problems which, even in its embryonic stage back in the middle of the last century, had beset SETI—had tried to narrow the whole question down to a logical series of parameters, which could then be brought together in an equation which, if calculated accurately, would neatly reveal a figure N which would represent a good estimate for the number of intelligent and communicating species currently in our galaxy. If the figure was found to be high, then space would be aswarm with the signals of sentient species anxious to talk to each other. If the figure was found to be one, then we were, to all intents and purposes, alone in the universe. Drake's equation involved the number of stars in our galaxy, and chances of those stars having habitable planets, and then those planets actually bearing life, and of that life evolving into intelligence, and of that intelligence wanting to communicate with other intelligences, and of that communication happening in an era in human history when we humans were capable of listening—which amounted to a microscopic *now*.

And they *had* listened, at least those who believed, those who wanted that number N at the end of the Drake Equation to be up in the tens or hundreds or thousands. They skived spare radiotelescopy and mainframe processing time and nagged their college principals and senators and fellow dreamers for SETI funding. Some, like a project at Arecibo, had even beamed out messages, although the message was going out in any cause, the whole babble of radio communications had been spreading out into space from Earth at the speed of light since Marconi's first transmission . . . *We are here. Earth is alive.* And they listened. They listened for a reply. Back then, when he had met Terr, Tom had still believed in the Drake Equation with a near-religious vehemence, even if many others were beginning to doubt it and funding was getting harder to maintain. As he walked with her beneath the clocktower through the foggy lights of Birmingham's other campus, his PC at his college digs in Erdington was chewing through the data he'd downloaded from a SETI website whilst his landlord's cat slept on it. Tom was sure that, what with the processing technology that was becoming available, and then the wide-array radio satellites, it was only a matter of time and persistence before that first wonderful spike of First Contact came through. And it had stood him in good stead, now that he came to think of it, had the Drake Equation, as he walked with Terr on that misty English autumn afternoon. One of the most convoluted chat-up lines in history. But, at least that once, it had worked.

They took the train back to the city and emerged onto New Street as the lights and the traffic fogged the evening, and at some point on their return back past the big shops and the law courts to the campus Terr had leaned against him and he had put his arm around her. First contact, and the tension between them grew sweet and electric and a wonderful ache had swelled in his throat and belly, until they stopped and kissed in the dank quietude of one of the old subways whilst the traffic swept overhead like a distant sea. Terr. The taste of her mouth, and at last he got to touch that space between her jaw and throat that he had been longing to touch all afternoon. Terr, who was dark and alive in his arms and womanly and English and alien. Terr, who closed her stormy eyes as he kissed her and then opened them again and looked at him with a thrilling candour. After that, everything was different.

Terr had a zest for life, an enthusiasm for everything. And she had an old car, a nondescript Japanese thing with leaky sills, a corrupted GPS, and a badly botched hydrogen conversion. Tom often fiddled under the bonnet to get the thing started before they set out on one of their ambitious weekend trips across the cool and misty country of love and life called England he suddenly found himself in. South to the biscuit-coloured villages of the Cotswolds, north to the grey hills of the Peak District, and then further, further up the map as autumn—he could no longer think of it as fall—rattled her leaves and curled up her smoky clouds and faded and winter set in, juddering for hours along the old public lanes of the motorways as the sleek, new transports swept past outside them with their occupants teleconferencing or asleep. But Tom liked the sense of effort, the sense of getting there, the rumble of the tyres and the off-centre pull of the steering, swapping over with Terr every hour or two, and the way the hills rose and fell but always got bigger as they headed north. And finally stepping out, and seeing the snow and the sunlight on the high flanks, and feeling the clean bite of the wind. They climbed fells where the tracks had long vanished and the sheep looked surprised at these humans who had invaded their territory. Hot and panting, they stopped in the lee of cols, and looked down at all the tiny details of the vast world they had. made. By then; Terr had changed options from SF to the early romantics, poets such as Wordsworth and Coleridge, and she would chant from the *Prelude* in her lovely voice as they clambered up Scarfell and the snow and the lakes gleamed around them and Tom struggled, breathless, to keep up until they finally rested, sweating and freezing, and Terr sat down and smiled at him and pulled off her top layers of fleece and Gore-Tex and began to unlace her boots. It was ridiculous, the feel of snow and her body intermingled, and the chant of her breath in his ear, urging him on as the wind and her fingers and the shadows of the clouds swept over his naked back. Dangerous, too, in the mid of winter—you'd probably die from exposure here if you lapsed into a post-coital sleep. But it was worth it. Everything. He'd never felt more alive.

Terr huddled against him in a col. Her skin was taut, freezing, as the sweat evaporated from between them. Another hour, and the sun would start to set. Already, it was sinking down through the clouds over Helvellyn with a beauty that Tom reckoned even old Wordsworth would have been hard put to describe. His fingers played over the hardness of Terr's right nipple, another lovely peak Wordsworth might have struggled to get over in words. It was totally, absolutely cold, but, to his pleasant surprise, Tom found that he, too, was getting hard. He pressed his mouth against Terr's shoulder, ran his tongue around that lovely hollow beneath her ear. She was shivering already, but he felt her give a shiver within the shiver, and traced his fingers down her belly, and thought of the stars which would soon be coming, and perhaps of finding one of those abandoned farmhouses where they could spend the night, and of Terr's sweet moisture, and of licking her there. She tensed and shivered again, which he took as encouragement, even though he was sure, as the coat slid a few inches from his shoulder, that he felt a snowflake settle on his bare back. Then, almost abruptly, she drew away.

"Look over there, Tom. Can you see them—those specks, those colours?"

Tom looked, and sure enough, across in the last, blazing patch of sunlight, a few people were turning like birds. They could have been using microlites, but on a day like this, the sound of their engines would have cut through the frozen air. But Tom had a dim recollection of reading of a new craze, still regarded as incredibly dangerous, both physically and mentally, whereby you took a gene-twist in a vial, and grew wings, just like in a fairy tale, or an SF story.

Tom had dreamed, experienced, all the possibilities. He'd loved those creatures in *Fantasia*, half-human, half-faun; those beautiful, winged horses. And not much later, he'd willed the green-eyed monsters and robots that the cartoon superheroes battled to put their evil plans into practise at least once. Then there were the old episodes of *Star Trek*—the older, the better—and all those other series where the crews of warp-driven starships calmly conversed around long florescent-lit tables with computer-generated aliens and men with rubber masks. By the age of eight, he'd seen galaxy-wide empires rise and fall, and tunnelled through ice planets, he'd battled with the vast and still-sentient relics of ancient conflicts . . . And he found the pictures he could make in his head from the dusty books he discovered for sale in an old apple box when they were closing down the local library were better than anything billion-dollar Hollywood could generate. And it seemed to him that the real technology which he had started to study at school and to mug up on in his spare time was always just a breakthrough or two away from achieving one or other of the technological feats which would get the future, the real future for which he felt an almost physical craving, up and spinning. The starships would soon be ready to launch, even if NASA was running out of funding. The photon sails were spreading, although most of the satellites spinning around the Earth seemed to be broadcasting virtual shopping and porn. The wormholes through time and dimension were just a quantum leap away. And the marvellous worlds, teeming with emerald clouds and sentient crimson oceans, the vast diamond cities and the slow beasts of the gas clouds with their gaping mouths spanning fractions of a light year, were out there waiting to be found. So, bright kid that he was, walking the salt harbours of Baltimore with his mother and gazing at the strange star-creatures in their luminous tanks at the National Aquarium long before he met Terr, he'd gone to sleep at nights with the radio on, but tuned between the station to the billowing hiss of those radio waves, spreading out. *We are here. Earth is alive.* Tom was listening, and waiting for a reply.

Doing well enough at exams and aptitudes at school to get to the next level without really bothering, he toyed with the cool physics of cosmology and the logic of the stars, and followed the tangled paths of life through chemistry and biology, and listened to the radio waves, and tinkered with things mechanical and electrical and gained a competence at computing and engineering, and took his degree in Applied Physics at New Colombia, where he had an on-off thing with a psychology undergrad, during which he'd finally got around to losing his virginity before—as she herself put it the morning after; as if, despite all the endearments and promises, she was really just doing him a favour—*it* lost him.

Postgrad time, and the cosmology weirdoes went one way, and the maths bods another, and the computer nerds went thataway, and physics freaks like Tom got jobs in the nano-technology companies which were then creating such a buzz on the World Stock Exchange. But Tom found the same problem at the interviews he went to that he still often found with girls, at least when he was sober—which was that people thought him vague and disinterested. But it was true in any case. His heart really wasn't in it—whatever it was. So he did what most shiftless, young academics with a good degree do when they can't think of anything else. He took a postgrad course in another country, which, pin in a map time, really, happened to be at Aston in Birmingham, England. And there he got involved for the first time in the local SETI project, which of course was shoestring and voluntary, but had hooked on to some spare radio time that a fellow-sympathiser had made available down the wire from Jodrell Bank. Of course, he'd known about SETI for ages; his memory of the Drake Equation went so far back into his childhood that, like Snow

White or the songs of the Beatles, he couldn't recall when he had first stumbled across it. But to be involved at last, to be one of the ones who were listening. And then persuading his tutor that he could twist around his work on phase-shift data filtering to incorporate SETI work into his dissertation. He was with fellow dreamers at last. It all fitted. What Tom Kelly could do on this particular planet orbiting this common-or-garden sun, and what was actually possible. Even though people had already been listening for a message from the stars for more than fifty years and the politicians and the bureaucrats and the funding bodies—even Tom's ever-patient tutor—were shaking their heads and frowning, he was sure it was just a matter of time. One final push to get there.

There was a shop in Kendal, at the edge of the Lake District. It was on a corner where the cobbled road sloped back and down, and it had, not so many years before, specialised in selling rock-climbing and fell-walking gear, along with the mint cake for which the town was justly famous and which tasted, as Terr had memorably said to Tom when she'd first got him to try it, like frozen toothpaste. You still just about see the old name of the shop—Peak and Fell, with a picture of a couple of hikers— beneath the garish orange paintwork of the new name that had replaced it. EXTREME LAKES.

There were people going in and out, and stylish couples outside posing beneath the bubble hoods of their pristine, lime-green, balloon-tyred off-roaders. Even on this day of freezing rain, but there was no doubt that the new, bodily enhanced sports for which this shop was now catering were good for business. Stood to reason, really. Nobody simply looked up at one of those rounded, snowy peaks and consulted an old edition of Wainwright and then put one booted foot in front of another and walked up them any longer. Nobody except Tom and Terr, scattering those surprised, black-legged sheep across the frozen landscape, finding abandoned farmhouses, making sweet, freezing love which was ice cream and agony on the crackling ice of those frozen cols. Until that moment, Tom had been entirely grateful for it.

The people themselves had an odd look about them. Tom, who had rarely done more than take the autotram to and from the campus and his digs in England until he met Terr, and since had noticed little other than her, was seeing things here he'd only read about; and barely that, seeing as he had little time for newspapers. Facial enhancements, not just the subtle kind that made you look handsomer or prettier, but things, which turned your eyebrows into blue ridges, or widened your lips into pillowy creations, which would had surprised Salvador Dali, let alone Mick Jagger. Breasts on the women like airbags, or nothing but roseate nipples, which of course they displayed teasingly beneath outfits which changed transparency according to the pheromones the smart fabrics detected. One creature, Tom was almost sure, had a threesome, a double-cleavage, although it was hard to tell just by glancing, and he really didn't want to give her the full-bloodied stare she so obviously craved. But most of them were so *thin*. That was the thing, which struck him the most strongly. They were thin as birds, and had stumpy, quill-like appendages sticking from their backs. They were angels or devils, these people, creatures of myth whose wings God had clipped after they had committed some terrible, theological crime, although the wings themselves could be purchased once you went inside the shop. Nike and Reebok and Shark and Microsoft and Honda at quite incredible prices. Stacked in steel racks like ski poles.

The assistant swooped on them from behind her glass counter. She had green hair, which even to Tom seemed reasonable enough, nothing more than a playful use of hair dye, but close-up it didn't actually appear to be hair at all, but some sort of sleek curtain which reminded him of cellophane. It crackled when she touched it, which she did often, as if she couldn't quite believe it was there, the way men do when they have just grown a moustache or beard. She and Terr were soon gabbling about brands and tensile strength and power-to-weight ratios and cold-down and thrillbiting and brute thermals and cloud virgins—which Tom guessed was them. But Terr was soaking it all up in the way that she soaked up anything that was new and fresh and exciting. He watched her in the mirror behind the counter, and caught the amazing flash of those storm green eyes. She looked so beautiful when she was like this; intent and surprised. And he longed to touch that meeting of her throat and jaw just beneath her ear, which was still damp from the rain and desperately needed kissing, although this was hardly the appropriate time. And those eyes. He loved the way Terr gazed right back at him when she was about to come; that look itself was enough to send him tumbling, falling into those gorgeous, green nebulae, down into the spreading dark core of her pupils which were like forming stars.

"Of course, it'll take several weeks, just to make the basic bodily adjustments . . ."

Was the assistant talking to him? Tom didn't know or care. He edged slightly closer to the counter to hide the awkward bulge of his erection, and studied the Kendal Mint Cake, which they still had for sale. The brown and the chocolate-coated, and the standard white blocks, which did indeed taste like frozen toothpaste, but much, much sweeter. A man with jade skin and dreadfully thin arms excused-me past Tom to select a big bar, and then another. Tom found it encouraging, to think that Kendal Mint Cake was still thriving in this new age. There were medals and awards on the old-fashioned wrapping, which commemorated expeditions and treks from back in the times when people surmounted physical challenges with their unaided bodies because, as Mallory had said before he disappeared into the mists of the last ridge of Everest, they were there. But it stood to reason that you needed a lot of carbohydrate if your body was to fuel the changes which would allow you to, as the adverts claimed, fly like a bird. Or at least flap around like a kite. Pretty much, anyway.

This was the new world of extreme sports, where, if you wanted to do something that your body wasn't up to, you simply had your body changed. Buzzing between channels awhile back in search of a site which offered Carl Sagan's Cosmos, which to Tom, when he was feeling a bit down, was the equivalent of a warm malt whisky, he'd stumbled across a basketball match, and had paused the search engine, imagining for a moment he'd stumbled across a new version of *Fantasia*, then wondering at the extraordinary sight of these ten-and twelve-foot giants swaying between each other on their spindly legs, clumsy and graceful as new-born fawns. But this, after all, was the future. It was the world he was in. And Terr was right when she urged him to accept it, and with it this whole idea of flying, and then offered to help with the money, which Tom declined, ridiculously excessive though the cost of it was. He lived cheaply enough most of the time, and the bank was always happy to add more to his student loan so that he could spend the rest of his life repaying it. And not that he and Terr were going the whole way, in any case. They were on the nursery slopes, they were ugly chicks still trembling in their nest, they were Dumbo teetering atop that huge ladder in the circus tent. They were cloud virgins. So the heart and circulatory enhancements, and the bone-thinning and the flesh-wasting and the new growth crystals which sent spiderwebs of carbon fibre teasing their way through your bone marrow, the Kevlar skin which the rapids surfers used, all the stuff which came stacked with health warnings and disclaimers which would have made the Surgeon General's warning on a packet of full-strength Camels look like a nursery tale: all of that they passed on. They simply went for the bog-standard Honda starter kits of vials and Classic (*Classic* meant boring and ordinary; even Tom had seen enough adverts to know that) wings. That would do—at least for a beginning, Terr said ominously, between humming to herself and swinging the elegant, little bag which contained the first installment of their vials as they headed out from the shop into the driving, winter rain.

It was January already, and the weather remained consistently foul for weeks in its own unsettled English way, which was cold and damp, and billows and squalls, and chortling gutters and rainswept parks, and old leaves and dog mess on the slippery Birmingham pavements. The Nissan packed up again too, but in a way whichwas beyond Tom's skill to repair, and a part was sent off for which might as well have been borne over from China on a none-too-fast sea clipper, the time it took to come. Days and weekends, they were grounded, and sort-of living together in Tom's digs, or in the pounding, smoky, Rastafarian fug of Terr's shared house in Handsworth. But Tom liked the Rastas; they took old-fashioned chemicals, they worshipped an old-fashioned God, and talked in their blurred and rambling way of a mythic Africa which would never exist beyond the haze of their dreams. Tom did a little ganja himself, and he did a fair amount of wine, and he lay in bed with Terr back in his digs in Erdington one night when the first men landed on Mars, and they watched the big screen on the wall from the rucked and damp sheets whilst the landlord's cat slept on the purring computer.

"Hey, look . . ." Terr squirmed closer to him. "Roll over. I want to see. I was *sure* I could feel something just then . . ."

"I should hope so."

Terr chuckled, and Tom rolled over. He stared at the face in the woodgrain of the old mahogany headboard. She drew back the sheets from him. The cold air. The rain at the window. The murmuring of the astronauts as they undocked and began the last, slow glide. Her fingers on his bare shoulders, then on his spine. It hurt there. It felt as if her nails were digging.

"Hey!!!"

"No no no no no . . ." She pressed him there, her fingers tracing the source of the pain. A definite lump was rising. An outgrowth which, in another age, would have sent you haring to the doctor thinking, *cancer*. . . .

"I'm jealous Tom. I thought I was going to be the first. It's like when I was a kid, and I concentrated hard on growing breasts."

"And it happened?"

"Obviously . . . cheeky sod . . . a bit, anyway . . ." Slim and warm and womanly, she pressed a little closer. He felt her breath, her lips, down on his back where the quills were growing. She kissed him there. "I check in the mirror every morning. I try to feel there . . ." he felt her murmur. "It's like a magic spell, isn't it? Waiting for the vials to work. You haven't noticed anything on me yet, have you, Tom?"

"No." He turned his head and looked at Terr. She was lying on her front too, and the red light of rising Mars on the screen was shining on the perfect skin of her thighs, her buttocks, her spine, her shoulders.

"You must have been waiting for this to happen for a long time," she said.

"What?"

Her blonde hair swayed as she tipped her head toward the screen. "Men landing on Mars."

He nodded.

"Will it take much longer before they actually touch down?"

"I suppose a few minutes."

"Well, that's good news . . ." Terr's hand traveled down his spine. Her knuckles brushed his buttocks, raising the goosebumps. Her fingers explored him there. "Isn't it . . . ?"

So they missed the actual instant when the lander kicked up the rusty dust of the surface, but were sharing a celebratory bottle of Asti Spumante an hour or so later when, after an interminable string of adverts, the first ever human being stepped onto the surface of another planet and claimed all its ores and energies and secrets for the benefit of the mission's various sponsors. Another figure climbed out. Amid the many logos on this one's suit there was a Honda one, which sent Tom's mind skittering back toward the growing lump on his back, which he could feel like a bad spot no matter how he laid the pillows now that Terr had mentioned it. How would he *sleep* from now on? How would they make *love?* Terr on top, fluttering her Honda wings like a predator as she bowed down to eat him? It was almost a nice idea, but not quite. And the Mars astronauts, even in their suits, didn't look quite right to Tom either. The suits themselves were okay—they were grey-white, and even had the sort of longer-at-top faceplates he associated with 2001 and Hal and Dave Poole and Kubrick's incredible journey toward the alien monolith—but they were the wrong shape in the body; too long and thin. It was more like those bad, old films; you half expected something horrible and inhuman to slither out of them once they got back into the lander, where it turned out to have crossed light years driven by nothing more than a simple desire to eat people's brains. . . .

Tom poured out the rest of the Asti into his glass.

"Hey!" Terr gave him a playful push. He slopped some of it. "What about me? You've had almost all of that. . . ."

He ambled off into the cupboard, which passed for his kitchen to get another bottle of something, and stroked the landlord's cat and gave the keyboard of his PC a tweak on the way. It was processing a search in the region of Cygnus, and not on the usual waterhole wavelength. Somebody's hunch. Not that the PC had found anything; even in those days, he had the bells and whistles rigged for *that* event. But what *was* the problem with him, he wondered, as he raked back the door of the fridge and studied its sparse contents? He was watching the first Mars landing, in bed with a naked, beautiful, and sexually adventurous woman, whilst his PC diligently searched the stars for the crucial first sign of intelligent life. If this wasn't his dream of the future, what on Earth was? And even this flying gimmick which Terr was insisting they try together—that fitted in as well, didn't it? In many ways, the technology that was causing his back to grow spines was a whole lot more impressive than the brute force and money and Newtonian physics which had driven that Martian lander from one planet to another across local space.

The problem with this manned Mars landing, as Tom had recently overheard someone remark in the university refectory, was that it had come at least four decades too late. Probably more, really. NASA could have gone pretty much straight from Apollo to a Mars project, back at the end of the delirious 1960s. Even then, the problems had been more of money than of science. Compared to politics, compared to getting the right spin and grip on the public's attention and then seeing the whole thing through Congress before something else took the headlines or the next recession or election came bounding along, the science and the engineering had been almost easy. But a first landing by 1995 at the latest, which had once seemed reasonable—just a few years after establishing the first permanent moonbase. And there really had been Mariner and Viking back in those days of hope and big-budget NASA: technically successful robot probes which had nevertheless demystified Mars and finished off H. G. Wells's Martians and Edgar Rice Burrows's princesses and Lowell's canals in the popular mind, and which, despite Sagan's brave talk about Martian giraffes wandering by when the camera wasn't looking, had scuppered any realistic sense that there might be large and complex Martian life-forms waiting to be fought against, interviewed, studied, dissected, argued over by theologians, or fallen in love with. Still, there were hints that life might exist on Mars at a microscopic level; those tantalisingly contradictory results from the early Viking landers, and the micro-bacteria supposedly found on Martian meteorites back on Earth. But, as the probes had got more advanced and the organic tests more accurate, even those possibilities had faded. Tom, he'd watched Mars become a dead planet both in the real world, and in the books he loved reading. The bulge-foreheaded Martians faded to primitive cave-dwellers, then to shy kangaroo-like creatures of the arid plains, until finally they became bugs dwelling around vents deep in the hostile Martian soil, then anaerobic algae, until they died out entirely.

Mars was a dead planet.

Tom unscrewed the bottle of slivovitz that was the only thing he could find, and went back to bed with Terr, and they watched the figures moving about on the Martian landscape between messages from their sponsors. They were half Martians already. Not that they could breathe the emaciated atmosphere, or survive without their suits on, but nevertheless they had been radically transformed before the launch. Up in space, in null gravity, their bones and their flesh and their nutritional requirements had been thinned down to reduce the payload, then boosted up just a little as they approached Mars a year and a half later so they could cope with the planet's lesser pull. They were near-sexless creatures with the narrow heads and bulging eyes of a thyroid complaint, fingers as long and bony as ET's. The way they looked, far worse than any flyers, Tom figured that you really didn't need to search further than these telecasts to find aliens to Mars. Or Belsen victims.

The slivovitz and the whole thing got to him. He had a dim recollection of turning off the screen at some point, and of making love to Terr, and touching the hollow of her back and feeling a tiny, sharp edge there sliding beneath her skin; although he wasn't quite sure about that, or whether he'd said anything to her afterward about growing bigger breasts, which had been a joke in any case. In the morning, when she had gone, he also discovered that he had broken up the Honda vials and flushed them down the communal toilet. Bits of the spun glass stuff were still floating there. He nearly forgot his slivovitz headache as he pissed them down. This was one thing he'd done when he was drunk he was sure he'd never regret.

The winter faded. Terr went flying. Tom didn't. The spines on her back really weren't so bad; the wings themselves were still inorganic in those days, carbon fibre and smart fabric, almost like the old microlites, except you bonded them to the quills with organic superglue just before you took the leap, and unbonded them again and stacked them on the roof rack of your car at the end of the day. Terr's were sensitive enough when Tom touched them, licked them, risked brushing their sharp edges against his penis to briefly add a new and surprising spice to their love making, although if he grew too rough, too energetic, both he and they were prone to bleed.

Terr was unbothered about his decision to stop taking the vials. After all, it was his life. *And why do something you don't want to do just to please me?* she'd said with her characteristic logic. But Terr was moving with a different set now, with the flyers, and their relationship, as spring began and the clean thermals started to rise on the flanks of Skiddaw and Helvellyn and Ben Nevis, began to have that ease and forgetfulness which Tom, little versed though he was in the ways of love, still recognised as signaling the beginning of the end. Terr had always been one for changing enthusiasms in any case. At university, she was now talking of studying creative writing, or perhaps dropping the literature thing entirely and swapping over to cultural studies, whatever the hell that was. It would be another one of Terr's enthusiasms, just, as Tom was coming to realise, had been Tom Kelly.

He still saw plenty of Terr for a while, although it was more often in groups. He enjoyed the jazz with her at Ronnie Scott's and sat around florescent tables in the smart bars along Broad Street with people whose faces often reminded him of those rubber-masked creatures you used to get in *Star Trek*. The world was changing—just like Terr, it didn't feel like it was quite *his* any longer, even though he could reach out and touch it, taste it, smell it. He drove up with her once or twice to the Lakes, and watched her make that first incredible leap from above the pines on Skiddaw and across the wind-rippled, grey expanse of Bassenthwaite Lake. He felt nothing but joy and pride at that moment, and almost wished that he, too, could take to the air, but soon, Terr was just another coloured dot, swooping and circling in the lemony, spring sunlight on her Honda-logoed wings, and no longer a cloud virgin. He could block her out with the finger of one hand.

So they drifted apart, Tom and Terr, and part of Tom accepted this fact—it seemed like a natural and organic process; you meet, you exchange signals of mutual interest, you fall in love and fuck each other brainless for a while and live in each other's skin and hair, then you get to know your partner's friends and foibles and settle into a warmer and easier affection as you explore new hobbies and positions and fetishes until the whole thing becomes just a little stale—and part of Tom screamed and hollered against the loss, and felt as if he was drowning as the sounds, the desperate, pleading signals he wanted to make, never quite seemed to reach the surface. He had, after all, always been shy and diffident with women. Especially the pretty ones. Especially, now, Terr.

At the end of the summer term, Tom got his postgrad diploma based around his SETI work and Terr didn't get anything. Just as she'd done with Tom, she'd worn Aston University out as she explored its highways and byways and possibilities with that determination that was so uniquely Terr. Next year, if any would take her and she could gather up the money, she'd have to try another enthusiasm at another university. They hadn't been lovers for months, which seemed to Tom like years, and had lost regular contact at the time, by pure chance, he last saw her. Tom, he needed to get on with his life, and had already booked a flight to spend some time at home with his parents in the States whilst he decided what *getting on with life* might actually involve for him.

It was after the last, official day of term, and the wine bars around the top of the city were busy with departing students and the restaurants contained the oddly sombre family groups who had come up to bear a sibling and their possessions back home. The exams had been and gone, the fuss over the assessments and dissertations and oral hearings had faded. There was both a sense of excitement and anticlimax, and beneath that an edge of sorrow and bone-aching tiredness which came from too many—or not enough—nights spent revising, screwing, drinking . . . Many, many people had already left, and hallways in the North Wing rang hollow and the offices were mostly empty as Tom called in to pick up his provisional certificate, seeing as he wouldn't be here for the award ceremonies in the autumn, and he didn't attend such pompous occasions in any case.

There was no obvious reason for Terr to be around. Her friends by now were mostly flyers, non-students, and she hadn't sat anything remotely resembling an exam. The season wasn't a Terr season in Tom's mind, either. A late afternoon, warm and humid as a dishrag, uncomfortable and un-English, when the T-shirt clung to his back and a bluish smog, which even the switch from petrol to hydrogen hadn't been able to dissolve, hung over the city. Put this many people together, he supposed, holding his brown envelope by the tips of this fingers so that he didn't get sweat onto it, this much brick and industry, and you'd always get city air. Even now. In this future world. He caught a whiff of curry-house cooking, and of beer-infused carpets from the open doorways of the stifling Yate's Wine Lodge, and of hot pavements, and of warm tar and of dog mess and rank canals, and thought of the packing he'd left half finished in his room, and of the midnight flight he was taking back to the States, and of the last SETI download his PC would by now have probably finished processing, and decided he would probably miss this place.

Characteristically, Terr was walking one way up New Street as Tom was heading the other. Characteristically, Terr was with a group of gaudy fashion victims; frail waifs and wasp-waisted freaks. Many of them looked Japanese, although Tom knew not to read too much into that, when a racial look was as easy to change as last season's shoes if you had the inclination and the money. In fact, Terr rather stood out, in that she really hadn't done anything that freakish to herself, although the clothes she wore—and sensibly enough, really, in this weather—were barebacked and scanty, to display the quills of those wings. And her hair was red; not the red of a natural redhead, or even the red of someone who had dyed it that colour in the old-fashioned way. But crimson; for a moment, she almost looked to Tom as if her head was bleeding. But he recognised her instantly. And Terr, Tom being Tom and thus unchanged, probably even down to his T-shirt, instantly recognised him.

She peeled off from the arm-in-arm group she was swaying along with, and he stopped and faced her as they stood in the shadow of the law courts whilst the pigeons cluttered up around them and the bypass traffic swept by beyond the tall buildings like the roar of the sea. He'd given a moment such as this much thought and preparation. He could have been sitting an exam. A thousand different scenarios, but none of them now quite seemed to fit. Terr had always been hard to keep up with, the things she talked about, the way she dressed. And those storm green eyes, which were the one thing about her that he hoped she would never change, they were a shock to him now as well.

They always had been.

"I thought you weren't going to notice, Tom. You looked in such a hurry. . . ."

"Just this . . ." He waved the limp, brown envelope as if it was the reason for everything. "And I've got a plane to catch."

She nodded, gazing at him. Tom gazed back—those green nebulae—and instantly he was falling. "I'd heard that you were leaving."

"What about you, Terr?"

She shrugged. The people behind her were chattering in a language Tom didn't recognise. His eyes traveled quickly over them, wondering which of them was now screwing Terr, and which were male—as if that would matter, Terr being Terr. . . .

"Well, actually, it's a bit of a secret, and quite illegal probably, but we're going to try to get onto the roof of one of the big halls of residence and—"

"—fly?"

She grinned. Her irises were wide. Those dark stars. She was high on something. Perhaps it was life. "Obviously. Can you imagine what the drift will be like, up there, with all these cliff-face buildings, on an afternoon like this?"

"Drift?"

"The thermals."

He smiled. "Sounds great."

One of those pauses, a slow, roaring beat of city silence, as one human being gazes at another and wonders what to say to them next. How to make contact—or how to regain it. That was always the secret, the thing for which Tom was searching. And he had a vision, ridiculous in these circumstances, of clear, winter daylight on a high fell. He and Terr . . .

"That dress you used to wear," he heard himself saying, "the blue one—"

"—Have you had any luck yet, Tom?" It was a relief, really, that she cut across his rambling. "With that SETI work you were doing? All that stuff about . . ." She paused. Her hands touched her hair, which didn't seem like hair at all, not curtains of blood, but of cellophane. It whispered and rustled in her fingers, and then parted, and he glimpsed in the crimson shade beneath that space at the join of her jaw and neck, just beneath her ear, before she lowered her hand and it was gone again. He wondered if he would ever see it again; that place which—of all the glories in the universe, the dark light years and the sentient oceans and the ice planets and the great beasts of the stellar void—was the one he now most longed to visit. Then she remembered the phrase for which she'd been searching, which was one Tom had explained, when they'd walked that first day by the canals in fall, in English autumn. ". . . the Drake Equation."

"I'm still looking."

"That's good." She nodded and smiled at him in a different way, as if taking in the full implications of this particular that's-goodness, and what it might mean one great day to all of mankind. "You're not going to give up on it, are you?"

"No."

"You're going to keep looking?"

"Of course I will. It's my life."

As he said it, he wondered if it was. But the creatures, the flyers, behind Tom and Terr, were twitching and twittering; getting restless. And one or two of the things they were saying Tom now recognised as having the cadence of English. There was just so much jargon thrown in there.

"And you'll let me know, won't you? You'll let me know as soon as you get that first message." Terr's tongue moistened her lower lip. "And I don't mean ages later, Tom. I want you to call me the moment it happens, wherever you are, up in what-ever observatory. Will you do that for me? I want to be the first to hear. . . ."

Tom hesitated, then nodded. Hesitated not because of the promise itself, which seemed sweet and wonderful, but because of the way that she'd somehow made this chance meeting, this short conversation, into an almost final parting. Or entirely fi-nal. It all now really depended on the outcome of the Drake Equation. Life out there, or endless barren emptiness. Terr, or no Terr.

"And I'll let you know, too, Tom," she said, and gave him a kiss that was half on his cheek, half on the side of his mouth, "I'll let you know if I hear anything as well . . ." But it was too quick for him to really pay attention to this strange thing she was saying. He was just left with a fading impression of her lips, her scent, the coolly different feel of her hair.

"You'd better be going," he said.

"Yes! While we've still got the air. Or before the Provost finds us. And you've got that plane to catch. . . ."

Terr gave him a last smile, and touched the side of his face with her knuckles al-most where she'd kissed it, and traced the line of his jaw with fingernails which were now crimson. Then she turned and rejoined the people she was with. Tom thought she looked thinner as he watched the departing sway of her hips, and the way a satyr-like oaf put his arm around her in what might or might not have been a normally friendly manner. And narrower around the shoulders, too. Almost a waif. Not quite the fully rounded Terr he'd loved through the autumn and winter, although her breasts seemed to be bigger. Another few months, and he'd probably barely recognise her, which was a comfort of sorts. Things changed. You moved on. Like it or not, the tide of the future was always rushing over you.

Determined not to look back, Tom headed briskly on down New Street. Then, when he did stop and swallow the thick choking in his throat, which was like gritty phlegm and acid, and turn around for a last, anguished glimpse of Terr, she and her friends had already gone from sight beyond the law courts. *I'll let you know if I hear anything, Tom . . .* What a strange, ridiculous idea! But at least the incident had helped him refine his own feelings, and put aside that hopeful longing which he realised had been dogging him like a cloud in a cartoon. As he strode down New Street to catch the autotram back to Erdington and finish his packing, Tom had a clear, almost Biblical certainty about his life, and the direction in which it would lead him. It was—how could he ever have doubted it?—the Drake Equation.

"So how does it work out?" Terr said to him now, up on his mountain. "That Drake fellow must have been around more than a century ago. So much has changed— even in the time since we were . . . since England, since Birmingham. We've progressed as a race, haven't we, us humans? The world hasn't quite disintegrated. The sun hasn't gone out. So surely you must have a better idea by now, surely you must know?"

"Nobody knows for sure, Terr. I wouldn't be here if I did. The Drake Equation is still just a series of guesses."

"But *we're* here on Earth, aren't we, Tom? Us humans and apes and bugs and cockroaches and dolphins. We must have somehow got started."

He nodded. Even now. Terr was so right. "Exactly."

"And we're still listening, and we want to hear . . ." She chuckled. "Or at least *you're* still listening, Tom. So all you have to hope for is another Tom Kelly out in space, up there amid all those stars. It's that simple, isn't it?"

"Can you imagine that?"

Terr thought for a moment. She thought for a long time. The wine bottle was empty. The candle was guttering. "Does he have to have the same colour skin, this alien Tom Kelly? Does he have to have four purple eyes and wings like a flyer?"

"That's up to you, Terr."

Then she stood up, and the waft of her passage toward him blew out the candle and brightened the stars and brought her scent, which was sweet and dusty and as utterly unchanged as the taste of her mouth, as she leaned down out of the swarming night and kissed him.

"I think you'll do as you are," she said, and traced her finger around his chin, just as she'd used to do, and down his nose and across his lips, as if he was clay, earth, and she was sculpting him. "One Tom Kelly. . . ."

In the years after he left Aston and split with Terr, Tom had found that he was able to put aside his inherent shyness, and go out in the big, bad world of academic science, and smile and press the flesh with administrators and business suits and dinosaur heads-of-department, and develop a specialisation of sorts which combined data analysis with radio astronomy. He knew he was able enough—somehow, his ability was the only thing about himself that he rarely doubted—and he found to his surprise that he was able to move from commercial development contracts to theoretical work to pure research without many of the problems of job security and unemployment which seemed to plague his colleagues. Or perhaps he just didn't care. He was prepared to go anywhere, do anything. He lived entirely in his head, as a brief womanfriend had said to him. Which was probably true, for Tom knew that he was never that sociable. Like the essential insecurity of research work, he simply didn't let it worry him. It helped, often, that there was a ready supply of drinks at many of the conferences and seminars he attended—not perhaps in the actual lecture halls and conference suites, but afterward, in the bars and rooms where the serious science of self-promotion went on. It helped, too, that at the back of it all, behind all the blind alleys and government cuts and flurries of spending, he had one goal.

It had surprised Tom that that first Martian landing should have had such a depressing effect on SETI research, when any sensible interpretation of the Drake Equation had always allowed for the fact that Earth was the only planet likely to harbour life in this particular solar system. Even he was disappointed, though, when the Girouard probe finally put the kibosh on any idea of life existing in what had once seemed like the potentially warm and habitable waters of Jupiter's satellite Europa. Still, the Principal of Mediocrity, which is that this sun, this solar system, this planet, and even the creatures which dwell upon it, are all common-or-garden phenomena, and thus likely to be repeated in similar form all over the galaxy, remained entirely undamaged by such discoveries, at least in Tom's mind. But in the mind of the general public (in that the general public has a mind to care about such things) and in the minds of the politicians and administrators who controlled scientific funding (ditto), it was a turning point, and began to confirm the idea that there really wasn't much out there in space apart from an endless vacuum punctuated a few aggregations of rocks, searing temperatures, hostile chemicals.

Funnily enough, this recession of the tides in SETI funding worked in Tom's favour. Like a collector of a type of objet d'art which was suddenly no longer fashionable, he was able to mop up the data, airtime, and hardware of several abandoned projects at bargain prices, sometimes using his own money, sometimes by tapping the enthusiasm of the few remaining SETI-freaks, sometimes by esoteric tricks of funding. Now that the big satellite telescopes could view and analyse stars and their orbital perturbation with a previously unheard-of accuracy, a few other solar systems had come out of the woodwork, but they were astonishingly rare, and mostly seemed to consist either of swarms of asteroids and dust clouds or huge near-stella aggregations of matter, which would fuse and crush anything resembling organic life. So f_p in the Drake Equation—the fraction of stars to likely have a planetary system—went down to something like 0.0001, and n_e—the number of those planets which could bear life—fell to the even lower 0.0000-somethings unless you happened to think that life was capable of developing using a different chemical basis to carbon, as Tom, reared as he was on a diet of incredible starbeasts, of course did. f_l the probability that life would then develop on a suitable planet—

also took a downturn, thanks to lifeless Mars and dead Europa, and then as every other potential niche in the solar system that some hopeful scientist had posited was probed and explored and spectrum analysed out of existence. The stock of SETI was as low as it had ever been, and Tom really didn't care. In fact, he relished it.

He wrote a paper entitled "New Light on the Drake Equation," and submitted it to *Nature*, and then, as the last SETI journal had recently folded, to the *Radio Astronomy Bulletin* and, without any more success, and with several gratuitously sneering remarks from referees, to all the other obvious and then the less obvious journals. In the paper, he analysed each element of the equation in turn, and explained why what had become accepted as the average interpretation of it was in fact deeply pessimistic. Taking what he viewed as the true middle course of balance and reason, and pausing only to take a few telling swipes at the ridiculous idea that computer simulations could provide serious data on the likelihood of life spontaneously developing, and thus on f_l, he concluded that the final N figure in the Drake Equation was, by any balanced interpretation, still in the region 1,000–10,000, and that it was thus really only a matter of time before contact was made. That was, as long as people were still listening. . . .

He didn't add it to the versions of the paper he submitted, but he also planned to ask whoever finally published the thing to place a dedication when it was printed: *For Terr*. That, at least, was the simplest variant of a text he spent many wall-staring hours expanding, cutting, revising. But the paper never did get published, although a much shortened work, stripped of its maths by Tom and then of a lot of its sense by the copy editor, finally did come out in a popular science comic, beside an article about a man who was growing a skein of his own nerve tissue to a length of several hundred feet so that he could bungee jump with it from the Victoria Falls. Still, the response was good, even if many of the people who contacted Tom were of a kind he felt reluctant to give out his email, let alone his home, address to.

The years passed. Through a slow process of hard work, networking, and less-than-self-aggrandisement, Tom became Mr SETI. There always was, he tended to find, at least one member of the astronomy or the physics or even the biology faculty of most institutes of learning who harboured a soft spot for his topic. Just as Sally Normanton had done when he returned to Aston on that autumn, when the air had smelled cleaner and different and yet was in so many ways the same, they found ways of getting him small amounts of funding. Slowly, Tom was able to bow out of his other commitments, although he couldn't help noticing how few attempts were made to dissuade him. Perhaps he'd lost his youthful zest, perhaps it was the smell on his breath of whatever he'd drank the night before, which now seemed to carry over to the morning. He was getting suprisingly near to retirement age, in any case. And the thought, the ridiculous idea that he'd suddenly been on the planet for *this long*, scared him, and he needed something that would carry him through the years ahead. What scared him even more, though, like a lottery addict who's terrified that their number will come up on exactly the week that they stop buying the tickets, was what would happen to SETI if he stopped listening. Sometimes, looking up at the night sky as the computers at whatever faculty he was now at pounded their way through the small hours with his latest batch of star data, gazing at those taunting pinpricks with all their mystery and promise, he felt as if he was bearing the whole universe up by the effort of his mind, and that the stars themselves would go out, just as they did in that famous Clarke story, the moment he turned his back on them. It was about then that he generally thought about having another drink, just to see him through the night, just to keep up his spirits. It was no big deal. A drink was a drink. Everyone he knew did it.

So Tom finally got sufficient funds and bluff together to set up his own specialised SETI project, and then settled on France for reasons he couldn't now quite remember, except that it was a place he hadn't been to where they still spoke a language which wasn't English, and then chose the karst area of the Massif Central because it gave the sort of wide, flat planes which fitted with the technology of his tripwire receivers, and was high up and well away from the radio babble of the cities. The choice was semi-symbolic—as well as the tripwires, he planned to borrow and buy-in as much useful data as he could from all possible sources, and process it there with whatever equipment he could borrow or cannibalise. Then he saw the waterhole, a tiny, blue dot on the map of this otherwise desolate mountain plateau above a small place called St. Hilaire, and that settled it. He hadn't even known that the place was a flying resort, until he'd signed all the necessary legal papers and hitched his life to it. And even that, in its way—those rainbow butterflies and beetles, those prismatic famine victims clustering around their smart bars and expensive shops, queuing with their wings whispering to take the cable lifts to the high peaks in the sun-struck south each morning—seemed appropriate. It made him think of Terr, and how her life had been, and it reminded him—as if he'd ever forgotten—of his, of *their* promise.

But it had never happened. There'd never been a reason to let her know.

Tom wrestled with the memories, the feelings, as Terr touched him, and closed her hands around his with fingers that seemed to have lost all their flesh. She was tunneling down the years to him, kissing him from the wide sweep of some incredible distance. He tried closing his eyes, and felt the jagged rim of teeth and bone beneath her lips. He tried opening them, and he saw her flesh streaked and lined against the stars, as if the Terr of old was wearing a mask made of paper. And her eyes had gone out. All the storms had faded. She touched him, briefly, intimately, but he knew that it was useless.

She stood back from him and sighed, scarecrow figure in her scarecrow dress, long hair in cobwebs around her thin and witchy face.

"I'm sorry, Tom—"

"No, it isn't—"

"—I was making presumptions."

But Tom knew who and what was to blame. Too many years of searching, too many years of drink. He sat outside his hut, frozen in his chair with his tripwires glimmering, and watched as Terr wandered off. He heard the clink of bottles as she inspected his skip. He heard the shuffle of rubbish as she picked her way around indoors. He should have felt ashamed, but he didn't. He was past that, just as he was past, he realised, any approximation of the act of love.

When Terr came out again into the starlight, she was carrying a bottle. It was the absinthe.

"Is this what you want?" she said, and unstoppered it. She poured a slug of the stuff into her own empty wineglass, and raised it to her thin lips, and sipped. Even under this starlight, her face grew wrinkled, ugly. "God, it's *so bitter. . . .*"

"Perhaps that's why I like it."

"You know, you could get rid of this habit, Tom. It's like you said to me—if there's something about yourself you don't like, all you need do is take a vial."

Tom shrugged, wondering whether she was going to pour some absinthe out into his glass or just stand there, waving the bottle at him. Was he being deliberately taunted? But Terr was right, of course. You took a vial, and you were clean. The addiction was gone. Everything about you was renewed, apart from the fact that you were who you were, and still driven by the same needs and contradictions that had given you the craving in the first place. So you went back to the odd drink, because you knew you were clean now, you were safe. And the odd drink became a regular habit again, and you were back where you started again, only poorer and older, and filled with an even deeper self-contempt. And worse headaches. Yes, Tom had been there.

"It's like you say, Terr. We are as we are. A few clever chemicals won't change that."

"You're going to be telling me next that you're an addictive personality."

"I wouldn't be here otherwise would I, doing this?"

She nodded and sat down again. She tipped some absinthe into his glass, and Tom stared at it, and at the faintly glowing message cards which he still hadn't read which lay beside it on the table, allowing a slight pause to elapse before he drank the absinthe, just to show her that he could wait. Then the taste of anise and wormwood, which was the name of the star, as he recalled, which had fallen from the heavens and seared the rivers and fountains in the Book of Revelation. It had all just been a matter of belief, back then.

"You still haven't told me how things have been for you, Terr."

"They've been okay. On and off . . ." Terr considered, her head in shade and edged with starlight. Tom told himself that the skull he could now see had always been there, down beneath Terr's skin that he had once so loved to touch and taste. Nothing was really that different. "With a few regrets."

"Did you really get into flying? That was how I always pictured you, up in the skies. Like the kids you see now down in this valley."

"Yes! I was a flyer, Tom. Not quite the way they are now—I'm sure they'd think the stuff we used then was uselessly heavy and clumsy. But it was great while it lasted. I made a lot of friends."

"Did you ever go back to your studies?"

She gave that dry chuckle again; the rustle of wind through old telephone wires. "I don't think I ever had *studies*, Tom. No, I got a job. Worked in public relations. Built up this company I was involved in very well for a while, sold other people's projects and ideas, covered up other people's mistakes—"

"—We could have used you for SETI."

"I thought of that, Tom—or of you, at least. But you had your own life. I didn't want to seem patronising. And then I got sick of being slick and enthusiastic about other people's stuff, and I got involved in this project of my own. Basically, it was a gallery, a sort of art gallery, except the exhibits were people. I was . . ."

"You were one of them?"

"Of course I was, Tom! What do you expect? But it plays havoc with your immune system after a while. You hurt and ache and bleed. It's something for the very fit, the very young, or the very dedicated. And then I tried being normal and got married and unmarried, and then married again."

"Not to the same person?"

"Oh no. Although they made friends, funnily enough, did my two ex's. Last time I heard from one of them, they were both still keeping in touch. Probably still are. Then I got interested in religion. *Religions*, being me . . ."

"Any kids?"

"Now never quite seemed the time. I wish there had been a *now*, though, but on the other hand perhaps I was always too selfish."

"You were never selfish, Terr."

"Too unfocussed then."

"You weren't that either." Tom took another slug of absinthe, and topped up the glass. He could feel the bitter ease of it seeping into him. It was pleasant to sit talking like this. Sad, but pleasant. He realised he hadn't just missed Terr. These last few years up on his mountain, he'd missed most kinds of human company. "But I know what you mean. Even when I used to dream about us staying together, I could never quite manage the idea of kids. . . ."

"How can two people be so different, and so right for each other?"

"Is that what you really think?"

"I loved you more than I loved anyone, Tom. All the time since, I often got this feeling you were watching, listening. Like that afternoon when I jumped with my wings from that tower in Aston and then got arrested. And the body art. You were like a missing guest at the weddings. I was either going for or against you in whatever I did—and sort of wondering how you'd react. And then I went to the Moon, and your ghost seemed to follow me there, too. Have you ever been off-planet?"

He shook his head. He hadn't—or at least not in the obvious physical sense, although he'd traveled with Kubrick over the Moon's craters a thousand times to the thrilling music of Ligeti.

"Thought not. It was the most expensive thing I ever did."

"What's it like?"

"That's just about it with the moon, Tom—it's expensive. The place you stay in is like one of those cheap, old, Japanese hotels. Your room's a pod you can't even sit up in. Who'd ever have thought space could be so claustrophobic!"

"All these things you've done, Terr. They sound so fascinating."

"Do, don't they—saying them like I'm saying them now? But it was always like someone else's life that I seemed to be stuck in. Like wearing the wrong clothes. I was always looking for my own. And then you get older—God, you know what it's like! And there are so many *choices* nowadays. So many different ways of stretching things out, extending the years, but the more you stretch them, the thinner they get. I always knew that I never wanted to live to some great age. These one-and-a-half centenarians you see, they seem to be there just to prove a point. Tortoises in an endless race. Or animals in a grotty zoo. Minds in twisted rusty cages . . ."

"I'd never really thought—"

"—You'll just go on until the bang, won't you Tom? Until the booze finally wreaks some crucial organ or busts a capillary in your head. Or until the Vesuvians land over there, on those funny wires, in a flying saucer and take you away with them. Although you'd probably say no because they aren't quite the aliens you expected."

"What do you mean?"

"Nothing, Tom. It's just the way you are. And you've been lucky, really, to have managed to keep your dream intact, despite all the evidence. I read that article you did, years ago in that funny little paper with all the flashing adverts for body-changing. 'New Light on the Drake Equation.' I had to smile. You still sounded so positive. But don't you think we'd have heard from them by now, if they really were out there? Think of all the millions of stars, all these millions of years, and all those galactic civilisations you used to read about. It wouldn't be a whisper, would it, Tom, something you needed all this fiddly technology to pick up on? It would be all around us, and unavoidable. If the aliens wanted us to hear from them, it would be an almighty roar. . . ."

The stars were just starting to fade now at the edge of the east; winking out one by one in the way that Tom had always feared. Taurus, Orion . . . the first hint of light as this part of the planet edged its face toward the sun was always grey up here on the karst, oddly wan and depressing. It was the colour, he often felt as the night diluted and the optimism that the booze inspired drained out of him in torrents of piss and the occasional worrying hawk of bloody vomit, that his whole world would become—if he lost SETI. And the argument which Terr had so cannily absorbed, was, he knew, the most damning of all the arguments against his dream. The odd thing was, it lay outside the Drake Equation entirely, which was probably why that dumb article of his had avoided mentioning it. What Terr was saying was a version of a question that the founding father of the nuclear chain reaction Enrico Fermi had once asked in the course of a debate about the existence of extraterrestrial intelligence nearly a century and half—and how time flew!—ago. The question was simply this: "Where are they?"

There were these things called von Neumann machines; perhaps Terr knew that as well. They'd once been a theory, and stalwarts of the old tales of the future Tom had loved reading, but now they were out working in the asteroid belt and on Jupiter's lesser moons, and down in deep mines on Earth and the sea trenches and on Terr's moon and any other place where mankind wanted something but didn't want to risk its own skin getting it. They were robots, really, but they were able to manufacture new versions of themselves—reproduce, if you wanted to make the obvious biological comparison—using the available local materials. They were smart, too. They could travel and adapt to new environments. They could do pretty much anything you wanted of them. So surely, went the argument, which sometimes crept along with the depression and the morning hangover into Tom's head, any other intelligent lifeform would have come up with a similar invention? Even with the staggering distance involved in travel between the stars, all you had to do was launch some into space, wait a few million years—a mere twitch of God's eye, by any cosmological timescale—and the things would be colonising this entire galaxy. So where were they?

The answer was as simple as Fermi's question: *They aren't here.* And mankind was a freak; he and his planet were a fascinating outrage against all the laws of probability. The rest of the universe was either empty, or any other dim glimmerings of life were so distant and faint as to be unreachable in all the time remaining until the whole shebang collapsed again. Better luck next time, perhaps. Or the time after that. By one calculation of the Drake Equation Tom had read, life of some kind was likely to appear somewhere in the entire universe once in every 10^{10} big bangs, and even that was assuming the physical laws remained unchanged. The guy hadn't bothered to put the extra spin on the figure, which would involve two communicating intelligences arising at the same time and in the same corner of the same galaxy. Probably hadn't wanted to wreck his computer.

Half the sky was greying out now. Star by star by star. At least he'd soon get a proper look at Terr, and she'd get a proper look at him, although he wasn't sure that that was what either of them wanted. Perhaps there was something to be said for the grey mists of uncertainty, after all.

"I always said—didn't I, Tom?—that I'd bring you a message."

"And *this* is it? You saying I should give up on the one thing that means something to me?"

"Don't look at it like that, Tom. Think of it as . . ." A faint breeze had sprung up, the start of the wind that would soon lift the flyers as the temperature gradients hit the valley. Tom thought for a moment that they must still have a candle burning on the table between them, the way Terr seemed to flicker and sway beyond it. She was like smoke. Her hair, her face. He poured himself some more absinthe, which he decided against drinking. "The thing is, Tom, that you've got yourself into this state where you imagine that whether or not you listen in itself proves something. It doesn't, Tom. They're out there—they're not out there. Either way, it's a fact already isn't it? It's just one we don't happen to know the answer to . . . and wouldn't it be a pity, if we knew the answer to everything? Where would your dreams be then?"

"Science is all about finding out the truth—"

"—And this life of yours Tom! I mean, why on Earth do you have to go down to the village to pick up those messages? Can't you communicate with people from up here? It looks like you've got enough equipment in that hut to speak to the entire world if you wanted to. But I suppose that doesn't interest you."

"I find personal messages . . ." He gazed as the hills in the east as a questing spear of light rose over them, then down at the cards she'd brought up to him. "I find them distracting."

"I'm sorry, Tom. I don't want to distract you."

"I didn't mean . . ." There he went again. Terr in tears, just the way she'd been, in a memory he'd suppressed for so long, in his bed in Erdington on that night of the Mars landing when the booze first started to get the better of him. But this was different. Terr was different. She was twisting, writhing. And the wind, the dawn, was rising.

"And I always felt responsible for you in a way, Tom. It was probably just a sort of vanity, but I felt as if I'd given you some final push along a path down which you might not otherwise have taken. You were charming, Tom. You were handsome and intelligent. You could have made a fortune and had a happy life doing anything other than SETI. Is that true Tom? Does that make any sense to you?"

He didn't reply, which he knew in itself was a positive answer. The truth was always out there in any case, with or without him. What was the point in denying anything?

"And that promise I made you make, that last day when we were standing outside the law courts with all those stupid flyer friends of mine. It seemed clever, somehow. I knew how much you still loved me and I wanted to leave my mark on you, just to prove it. I'm sorry, Tom. It was another one of my stupid, stupid projects. . . ."

"You can't hold yourself responsible for someone else's life, Terr."

"I know, Tom. It didn't even feel like I was responsible for my own."

Tom looked away from Terr, and back at his ragged hut. But for the fine-spun silver of his field of tripwires, but for the faint glow of his computers, but for the bottle-filled skip and the old Citröen beside it, it could have been the dwelling of a medieval hermit. He sighed and looked down the slope of his mountain. In this gathering light, the whole world looked frail as a spiderweb. And down there—he could just see it—lay his waterhole, and the flickering movement of the shy mountain ibex who gathered dawn and dusk to drink there.

"The sun's coming up, Tom. I'll have to be going soon. . . ."

"But you haven't . . ." The words froze in his mouth as he looked back at Terr. Even as the light strengthened, the substance was draining from her. ". . . can't you stay . . . ?"

"I'm sorry, Tom. I've said all there is to be said. . . ."

She stood up and moved, floated, toward him. Changed and not changed. Terr and not Terr. What few stars remained in the west were now shining right through her. But Tom felt no fear as she approached him. All he felt, welling up in his heart, was that childhood ache, that dark sweetness which was cola and ice cream and his mother's embrace. All he felt was a glorious, exquisite sense of wonder.

The rim of the sun gilded the edge of those ranged peaks. Terr broke and shimmered. She was like her eyes now; a beautiful, swarming nebula. But the sun was brightening, the wind was still rising. She was fading, fading. Tom stretched out a hand to touch whatever it was she had become, and found only morning coolness, the air on his flesh.

Remember, Tom.

Terr had no voice now, no substance. She was just a feeling, little more than the sad and happy memory he had carried with him through all these years into this dim and distant age. But he felt also that she was moving, turning away from him, and he smiled as he watched her in that dark blue dress, as beautiful as she had always been, walking away down the silvered turf of his mountain toward the waterhole. Terr with her blonde hair. Terr with her beautiful eyes. Terr with the mist on her flesh in that place where her jaw met her throat beneath her earlobe. She turned and gave him a smile and a wave as the sun sent a clear spine of light up from the cleft between two mountains. Terr in her dark blue dress, heading down toward that waterhole where all the shy creatures of the universe might gather at the beginning or end of the longest of days. Then she was gone.

Tom sat there for a long while. It was, after all, his time of day for doing nothing. And the sun rose up, brightening the world, corkscrewing the spirals beside the lime-stone crags. He thought he caught the flash of wings, but the light, his whole world and mountain, was smeared and rainbowed. He thought that he had probably been crying.

The cards on the table before him had lost most of their glow. And they were cold and slickly damp when he turned them over. He selected the one card he didn't recognise, the one that was blue and almost plain, with a pattern on its surface like rippled water. He was sure now that it was more than just spam, junk mail. He ran his finger across the message strip to activate it, and closed his eyes, and saw a man standing before him in a fountained garden which was warm and afternoon-bright and almost Moorish; it could have been Morocco, Los Angeles, Spain. The man was good looking, but no longer young. He had allowed the wrinkles to spread over his face, his hair to grey and recede. There was something, Tom found himself thinking, about himself, about his face, or at least the self he thought he remem-bered once seeing in a mirror. But the man was standing with the fixedness of some-one preparing for a difficult moment. His face was beyond ordinary sadness. His eyes were grave.

Tom waited patiently through the you-don't-know-me-and-I-don't-know-you part of the message, and the birds sang and the bees fumbled for pollen amid deep red and purple tropic flowers as the man gave Tom his name, and explained the one thing about their backgrounds which they had in common, which was that they had both loved Terr. They'd loved Terr, and then of course they'd lost her, because Terr was impossible to keep—it was in her nature; it was why they'd made the glorious leap of loving her in the first place. But this man was aware of Tom Kelly in a way that Tom wasn't aware of him. Not that Terr had ever said much about her past be-cause she lived so much in the present, but he'd known that Tom was there, and in a way he'd envied him, because love for Terr was a first and only thing, glorious in its moment, then impossible to ever quite recapture in the same way. So he and Terr had eventually parted, and their marriage—which was her second, in any case—had ended as, although he'd hoped against hope, he'd always known it would. And Terr had gone on with her life, and he'd got on with his, and he'd followed her sometimes through the ether, her new friends, her new discoveries, and fresh obsessions, until he heard this recent news, which was terrible, and yet for him, not quite unex-pected, Terr being Terr.

There was a ridge on a peak in the Andes known as Catayatauri. It sounded like a newly discovered star to Tom, and was almost as distant and as hostile. The ridge leading up to it was incredible; in the east, it dropped nearly ten thousand sheer feet, and it took a week of hard walking and another week of hard climbing to reach it, that was, if the winds and the treacherous séracs let you get there at all. But it had ac-quired a near-mythic reputation amongst a certain kind of flyer, a reputation which went back to the time of the Incas, when human sacrifices were thrown from that ridge to placate Viracocha, the old man of the sky.

So picture Terr making that climb alone in the brutal cold, no longer as young or as fit as she might once have been, but still as determined. She left messages in the village, which lay in Catayatauri's permanent shadow. If she didn't come back, she didn't want anyone risking their lives trying to find her. The Incas had held Catayatauri with a deep, religious intensity, and so had the climbers who came after, and so must Terr, alone up in those godly mountains. She climbed unaided; no wings, no muscle or lung enhancements, no crampon claws on her feet or hands, no ropes, and no oxygen. The fact that she made it there at all was incredible, clinging to that ridge at the roof of the world. From Catayatauri, from that drop, nothing else was comparable. And Terr had stood there alone, a nearly old woman at the edge of everything. She'd bought vials at a shop in Lima. She'd emptied what little she had left in her accounts to get hold of them. These weren't like the vials they sold along the Rue de Commerce in St. Hilaire. Scarcely legal, they were the quickest acting, the most radical, the most expensive. They tore through your blood and veins by the nano-second, they burned you up and twisted your body inside out like a storm-wrecked umbrella. And Terr had purchased three times the usual dosage.

And she probably did get there, and make the leap from the ridge on Catayatauri. It seemed like the most likely explanation, even though her body hadn't been found. Terr had thrown herself from the precipice with the vials singing in her body, her bones twisting, the wings breaking out from her like a butterfly emerging from a chrysalis, although they would have been too damp and frail to do more than be torn to shreds in the brutal torrents of air. And then, finally, finally, she would have been buffeted on the rocks. Terr, it seemed, had chosen the most extreme of all possible ways of dying. . . .

Was it like her, to do this, Tom wondered? Terr plummeting, twisting and writhing? Had she meant to kill herself, or just wanted to take the risk, and lived the moment, and not really cared about the next? The man in the Moorish garden was as lost and puzzled by all these questions as Tom was himself. But the thing about Terr, as they both realised, was that she had always changed moment by moment, hour by hour, year by year. The thing about Terr was that you could never really know her. Tom, he had always been steady and purposeful; long ago, he had laid down the tracks of his life. Terr was different. Terr was always different. She'd never been troubled as Tom had been most of his life by that sense of missed appointments, unfinished business, time slipping by; of a vital message which he had never quite heard. Terr had always leapt without looking back.

The man gave a smile and signed off. The Moorish garden, the dense scent of the flowers, faded. Tom Kelly was back in the morning as the shadows raced the clouds over his mountain; and he was wondering, like a character in a fairy story, just where he had been this previous night, and exactly what it was that he had witnessed. And if he could have been granted one wish—which was something that Terr, whatever she had been, hadn't even offered to him—it would still be the thing for which he had always been hoping. He was nearly seventy, after all. He was Tom Kelly; Mr SETI. No matter what happened to you, no matter what wonders you witnessed, people his age didn't change. He was still sure of that, at least.

Tom Kelly, speeding down his mountain. The sun is blazing and the chairlifts are still and the flyers are resting as shadow lies down next to shadow for the long, slumberous afternoon. He parks in the near-empty Place de Revolution, and climbs out from his Citröen, and waves to Jean-Benoît wiping his tables, and then bangs on the door of the *Bureau de poste*. The sign says *fermé*, but Madame Brissac slides back the bolts. She seems almost pleased to see him. She nearly gives him a smile. Then they spend their hour together, seated beside the counter as bluebottles buzz and circle by her pigeonholes in the warm, intensely odorous air. Tom's got as far as transitive verbs, and here he's struggling. But after all, French is a foreign language, and you don't learn such things in a day—at least, not the way Tom's learning. It will be some months, he reckons late autumn at least—*l'automne*, and perhaps even winter, whatever that's called—before he's got enough of a grip to ask her about how she sorts the mail in those pigeonholes. And he suspects she'll think it's a stupid question in any case. Madame Brissac is, after all, Madame Brissac. But who'd have thought that she was once a teacher, back in the days when people still actually needed to be taught things? For every person, it seems to Tom, who gains something in this future age, there's someone else who makes a loss from it.

Things are just starting to reawaken when he emerges into the blazing Place de Revolution, and he has to move his Citröen and park it round the corner to make room for the evening's festivities. It's the *Foire aux Sorcières* tonight, which a few months ago would have meant nothing to him, and still means little enough. But the French like a good festival, he knows that much now at least. They have them here in St. Hilaire regularly—in fact, almost every week, seeing as there's such a regular throughput of new flyers needing to have their francs taken from them. But this festival is special. Tom knows that, too.

Drinking sweet, hot coffee at his usual table, he passes the necessary hour whilst the market stalls and the stage for the evening pageant assemble themselves to the attentions of robot crabs and the clang of poles and the shouts of a few, largely unnecessary artisans. The town, meanwhile, stretches itself and scratches its belly, emerges from its long meals and lovers' slumbers. The girl with that Audrey Hepburn look, whom he now knows is called Jeannette, gives him a smile and goes over to say hi, *boujour*. She thinks it's sweet, that a mad, old mountain goat like Tom should take the long way around to learning her language. And so does Michel, her boyfriend, who is as urbane and charming as anyone can be who's got the muscles of a cartoon god and the green, scaly skin of a reptile. They even help Tom carry his few boxes of stuff from the boot of his Citröen to the stall he's booked, and wish him luck, and promise to come back and buy something later on in the evening, although Tom suspects they'll be having too much fun by then to remember him.

But it turns out that business at his stall is surprisingly brisk in any case. It's been this way for a couple of weeks now, and if it continues, Tom reckons he'll have to order some new SETI T-shirts and tea towels to replace his lost stock, although the tea towels in particular will be hard to replace after all these years, seeing as people don't seem to have any proper use for them any longer. They ask him what they're for, these big SETI handkerchiefs, and then tie them around their necks like flags. Who'd have thought it—that tea towels would be a casualty of this future he finds himself in? But bargaining, setting a price for something and then dropping it to make the sale; that's no problem for Tom. The numbers of another language come almost easily to him; he supposes his brain dimly remembers it once had an aptitude for maths.

The *Foire aux Sorcières* seems an odd festival for summer, but, even before the darkness has settled, the children are out, dressed as witches, ghosts, goblins, and waving lanterns that cast, through some technical trick Tom can't even guess at, a night-murk across their faces. Still, the whole occasion, with those sweet and ghastly faces, the trailing sheets with cut eye-holes, the shrieking, cackling devices, has a pleasantly old-fashioned feel about it to Tom. Even the flyers, when they emerge, have done nothing more to change themselves than put on weird costumes and make-ups, although, to Tom's mind at least, many of them had looked the part already. The scene, as the sun finally sinks behind the tenements and a semblance of cool settles over the hot and frenzied square, is incredible. Some of the people wandering the stalls have even dressed themselves up as old-fashioned aliens. He spots a bulge-headed Martian, then a cluster of those slim things with slanted eyes which were always abducting people in the Midwest, and even someone dressed as that slippery grey thing that used to explode out of people's stomachs in the films, although the guy's taken the head off and is mopping his face with one of Tom's SETI tea towels because he's so hot inside it. If you half closed your eyes, Tom thinks, it really could be market day on the planet Zarg, or anywhere else of a million places in this universe which he suspects that humanity will eventually get around to colonising, when it stops having so much fun here on Earth. Look at Columbus, look at Cook, look at Einstein, look at NASA. Look at Terr. We are, in the depths of our hearts, a questing, dreaming race.

Small demons, imps, and several ghosts cluster around him now, and ask him *quel est SETI?* which Tom attempts to explain in French. They nod and listen and gaze up at him with grave faces. He's almost thinking he's starting to get somewhere, when they all dissolve into gales of laughter and scatter off through the crowds. He watches them go, smiling, those ghosts, those flapping sheets. When he returns his gaze, Madame Brissac has materialised before him. She is dressed as an old-fashioned witch. But she seems awkward beneath her stick-on warts and green make-up, shorn of the usual wooden counter which, even now that they're attempting to talk to each other in the same language, still separates Tom and her. Still, she politely asks the price of his SETI paperweights, and rummages in her witchy bag and purchases one from him, and then comments on the warmth and the beauty of this evening, and how pretty and amusing the children are. And Tom agrees with her in French, and offers Madame Brissac a SETI tea towel at no extra cost, which she declines. Wishing him a good evening, she turns and walks away. But Tom still feels proud of himself, and he knows that she's proud of him to. It's an achievement for them both, that they can talk to each other now in the same language, although, being Madame Brissac, she'll never quite let it show.

The music rides over him. The crowds whoop and sing. The lanterns sway. Down the slope toward the river, the lace-draped stalls look almost cool in the soft breeze, which plays down from the hills and over the tenements as Tom sweats in his SETI T-shirt. Jean-Benoît's down there, dressed red as fallen Lucifer and surrounded by lesser demons, and looking most strange and splendid for his evening off. There's no sign, though, of the woman in the dark blue dress whom Tom glimpsed standing in the sunlight all those weeks ago. He knows that Terr's dead now, although the thought still comes as a cold, blunt shock to him. So how could there ever be any sign of Terr?

Tom's got his days better sorted now. He's never got so drunk as to lose one whole day and imagine Thursday is Wednesday. In fact, nowadays, Tom never has a drink at all. It would be nice to say that he's managed it through pure willpower. But he's old, and a creature of habit, even when the habits are the wrong ones. And this is the future, after all. So Tom's taken a vial, just as he had done several times before, and the need, the desire, the welling emptiness, faded so completely that he found himself wondering for the first few days what all the trouble and fuss had been about. But that was two months ago, and he still rarely entertains the previous stupid thoughts about how a social drink, a sip and a glass here and there, would be quite safe for someone like him. Even on a night such as this, when the air smells of wine and sweat and Pernod and coffee and Gitanes, and he can hear bottles popping and glasses clinking and liquid choruses of laughter all around the square, he doesn't feel the usual emptiness. Or barely. Or at least he's stopped kidding himself that it's something the alcohol will ever fill, and decided to get on with the rest of his life unaided.

He sometimes wonders during the long, hot afternoons of his lessons with Madame Brissac whether a woman in a blue dress and grey or blonde hair really did enter the *Bureau de poste* to enquire about an elderly American called Tom Kelly on that magical Thursday. Sometimes, he's almost on the brink of interrupting her as she forces him through the endless twists and turns of French grammar, although he knows she'd probably regard it as an unnecessary distraction. He's thought of asking Jean-Benoît, too—at least, when he's not dressed up as Lucifer—if he remembers a woman who could have been old or might have been young coming to his café, and who undertook to pass on the message cards he'd forgotten to take with him. Would they remember Terr? Would they deny that they'd ever seen her at all? More likely, Tom has decided, they'll have long forgotten such a trivial incident amid the stream of faces and incidents that populate their lives.

Tom glances up from the bright Place de Revolution at the few, faint stars which have managed to gather over the rooftops and spires of St. Hilaire. Like Terr—or the ghost of her—he suspects they'll remain a mystery that he'll have to carry to his grave. But there's nothing so terrible about mysteries. It was mystery, after all, which drew him to the stars in the first place. Wonder and mystery. He smiles to himself, and waves to Jeannette and Michel as they pass through the crowds. Then Jean-Benoît, amid great cheers, flaps his crimson wings and rises over the stalls and hovers floodlit above the church spire to announce the real beginning of the night's festivities, which will involve fireworks, amazing pageants, dancing. . . .

This *Foire aux Sorcières* will probably still be going on at sunrise, but Tom Kelly knows it will be too much for him. He's getting too old for this world he finds himself in. He can barely keep pace. But he permits himself another smile as he starts to pack up his stall of SETI memorabilia, the T-shirts and paperweights, the lapel pins embossed with a tiny representations of the Drake Equation which not a single person who's bought one of the things has ever asked him to explain. He's looking forward to the midnight drive back up his mountain in his old Citröen, and the way the stars will blossom on when he finally turns off the headlights and steps into the cool darkness outside his hut, with the glitter of his tripwires, the hum and glow of his machines. Who knows what messages might be up there?

He's Tom Kelly, after all.

And this might be the night.

He's still listening, waiting.

Turquoise Days

ALASTAIR REYNOLDS

Alastair Reynolds is a frequent contributor to *Interzone*, and has also sold to *Asimov's Science Fiction*, *Spectrum SF*, and elsewhere. His first novel, *Revelation Space*, was widely hailed as one of the major SF books of the year; it was quickly followed by *Chasm City*, *Redemption Ark*, *Absolution Gap*, and *Century Rain*, all big books that were big sellers as well, establishing Reynolds as one of the best and most popular new SF writers to enter the field in many years. His other books include a novella collection, *Diamond Dogs, Turquoise Days*. His most recent book is a new novel, *Pushing Ice*. Coming up are two new collections, *Galactic North* and *Zima Blue and Other Stories*. A professional scientist with a Ph.D. in astronomy, he comes from Wales, but lives in the Netherlands, where he works for the European Space Agency.

Here's a visit to a serene, peaceful, quiet little planet, a sea-world, an idyllic world nearly covered by tropical turquoise oceans. But as we shall see, placid as things seem, you never know what's lurking beneath the surface. Or when it's going to come out to get you.

I

Naqi Okpik waited until her sister was safely asleep before she stepped onto the railed balcony that circled the gondola.

It was the most perfectly warm and still summer night in months. Even the breeze caused by the airship's motion was warmer than usual, as soft against her cheek as the breath of an attentive lover. Above, yet hidden by the black curve of the vacuum bladder, the two moons were nearly at their fullest. Microscopic creatures sparkled a hundred metres under the airship, great schools of them daubing galaxies against the profound black of the sea. Spirals, flukes and arms of luminescence wheeled and coiled as if in thrall to secret music.

Naqi looked to the rear, where the airship's ceramic-jacketed sensor pod carved a twinkling furrow. Pinks and rubies and furious greens sparkled in the wake. Occasionally they darted from point to point with the nervous motion of kingfishers. As ever she was alert to anything unusual in movements of the messenger sprites, anything that might merit a note in the latest circular, or even a full-blown article in one of the major journals of Juggler studies. But there was nothing odd happening tonight; no yet-to-be-catalogued forms or behaviour patterns, nothing that might indicate more significant Pattern Juggler activity.

She walked around the airship's balcony until she had reached the stem, where the submersible sensor pod was tethered by a long fibre-optic dragline. Naqi pulled a long hinged stick from her pocket, flicked it open in the manner of a courtesan's fan, and then waved it close to the winch assembly. The default watercoloured lilies and sea serpents melted away, replaced by tables of numbers, sinuous graphs and trembling histograms. A glance established that there was nothing surprising here either, but the data would still form a useful calibration set for other experiments.

As she closed the fan—delicately, for it was worth almost as much as the airship itself—Naqi reminded herself that it was a day since she had gathered the last batch of incoming messages. Rot had taken out the connection between the antenna and the gondola during the last expedition, and since then collecting the messages had become a chore, to be taken in turns or traded for less tedious tasks.

Naqi gripped a handrail and swung out behind the airship. Here the vacuum bladder overhung the gondola by only a metre, and a grilled ladder allowed her to climb around the overhang and scramble onto the flat top of the bag. She moved gingerly, bare feet against rusting rungs, doing her best not to disturb Mina. The airship rocked and creaked a little as she found her balance on the top and then was again silent and still. The churning of its motors was so quiet that Naqi had long ago filtered the sound from her experience.

All was calm, beautifully so.

In the moonlight the antenna was a single dark flower rising from the broad back of the bladder. Naqi started moving along the railed catwalk that led to it, steadying herself as she went but feeling much less vertigo than would have been the case in daytime.

Then she froze, certain that she was being watched.

Just within Naqi's peripheral vision appeared a messenger sprite. It had flown to the height of the airship and was now shadowing it from a distance of ten or twelve metres. Naqi gasped, delighted and unnerved at the same time. Apart from dead specimens this was the first time Naqi had ever seen a sprite this close. The organism had the approximate size and morphology of a terrestrial hummingbird, yet it glowed like a lantern. Naqi recognised it immediately as a long-range packet carrier. Its belly would be stuffed with data coded into tightly packed wads of RNA, locked within microscopic protein capsomeres. The packet carrier's head was a smooth teardrop, patterned with luminous pastel markings but lacking any other detail save for two black eyes positioned above the midline. Inside the head was a cluster of neurones, which encoded the positions of the brightest circumpolar stars. Other than that, sprites had only the most rudimentary kind of intelligence. They existed only to shift information between nodal points in the ocean when the usual chemical signalling pathways were deemed too slow or imprecise. The sprite would die when it reached its destination, consumed by microscopic organisms that would unravel and process the information stored in the capsomeres.

And yet Naqi had the acute sense that it was watching her. Not just the airship, but *her*, with a kind of watchful curiosity that made the hairs on the back of her neck bristle. And then—just at the point when the feeling of scrutiny had become unsettling—the sprite whipped sharply away from the airship. Naqi watched it descend back toward the ocean and then coast above the surface, bobbing now and then like a skipping stone. She remained still for several more minutes, convinced that something of significance had happened and yet also aware of how subjective the experience had been; how unimpressive it would seem if she tried to explain it to Mina tomorrow. Anyway, Mina was the one with the special bond to the ocean, wasn't she? Mina was the one who scratched her arms at night; Mina was the one who had too high a conformal index to be allowed into the swimmer corps. It was always Mina.

It was never Naqi.

The antenna's metre wide dish was anchored to a squat plinth inset with weatherproofed controls and readouts. It was century-old *Pelican* technology, like the airship and the fan. Many of the controls and displays were dead, but the unit was still able to lock onto the functioning satellites. Naqi flicked open the fan and copied the latest feeds into the fan's remaining memory. Then she knelt down next to the plinth, propped the fan on her knees and sifted through the messages and news summaries of the last day. A handful of reports had arrived from friends in Prachuap-Pangnirtung and Umingmaktok snowflake cities, another from an old boyfriend in the swimmer corps station on Narathiwat atoll. He had sent her a list of jokes that were already in wide circulation. She scrolled down the list, grimacing more than grinning, before finally managing a half-hearted chuckle at one that had escaped her. Then there were a dozen digests from various special interest groups related to the Jugglers, along with a request from a journal editor that she critique a paper. Naqi skimmed the paper's abstract, judging that she was probably capable of reviewing it.

She scrolled through the remaining messages. There was a note from Dr Sivaraksa saying that her formal application to work on the Moat project had been received and was now under consideration. There had been no official interview, but Naqi had met Sivaraksa a few weeks earlier when the two of them happened to be in Umingmaktok. Sivaraksa had been in an encouraging mood during the meeting, though Naqi couldn't say whether that was due to her having given a good impression or the fact that Sivaraksa had just had his tapeworm swapped for a nice new one. But Sivaraksa's message said she could expect to hear the result in a day or two. Idly, Naqi wondered how she would break the news to Mina if she was offered the job. Mina was critical of the whole idea of the Moat and would probably take a dim view of her sister having anything to do with it.

Scrolling down farther, she read another message from a scientist in Qaanaaq requesting access to some calibration data she had obtained earlier in the summer. Then there were four or five automatic weather advisories, drafts of two papers she was contributing to, and an invitation to attend the amicable divorce of Kugluktuk and Gjoa, scheduled to take place in three weeks time. Following that there was a summary of the latest worldwide news—an unusually bulky file—and then there was nothing. No further messages had arrived for eight hours.

There was nothing particularly unusual about that—the ailing network was always going down—but for the second time that night the back of Naqi's neck tingled. Something must have happened, she thought.

She opened the news summary and started reading. Five minutes later she was waking Mina.

"I don't think I want to believe it," Mina Okpik said.

Naqi scanned the heavens, dredging childhood knowledge of the stars. With some minor adjustment to allow for parallax, the old constellations were still more or less valid when seen from Turquoise.

"That's it, I think."

"What?" Mina said, still sleepy.

Naqi waved her hand at a vague area of the sky, pinned between Scorpius and Hercules. "Ophiuchus. If our eyes were sensitive enough, we'd be able to see it now; a little prick of blue light."

"I've had enough of little pricks for one lifetime," Mina said, tucking her arms around her knees. Her hair was the same pure black as Naqi's, but trimmed into a severe, spiked crop which made her look younger or older depending on the light. She wore black shorts and a shirt that left her arms bare. Luminous tattoos, in emerald and indigo, spiralled around the piebald marks of random fungal invasion that covered her arms, thighs, neck and cheeks. The fullness of the moons caused the fungal patterns to glow a little themselves, shimmering with the same emerald and indigo hues. Naqi had no tattoos and scarcely any fungal patterns of her own, and could not help feel slightly envious of her sister's adornments.

Mina continued: "But seriously, you don't think it might be a mistake?"

"I don't think so, no. See what it says there? They detected it weeks ago, but they kept quiet until now so that they could make more measurements."

"I'm surprised there wasn't a rumour."

Naqi nodded. "They kept the lid on it pretty well. Which doesn't mean there isn't going to be a lot of trouble."

"Mm. And they think this blackout is going to help?"

"My guess is official traffic's still getting through. They just don't want the rest of us clogging up the network with endless speculation."

"Can't blame us for that, can we? I mean, everyone's going to be guessing, aren't they?"

"Maybe they'll announce themselves before very long," Naqi said doubtfully.

While they had been speaking the airship had passed into a zone of the sea largely devoid of bioluminescent surface life. Such zones were almost as common as the nodal regions where the network was thickest, like the gaping voids between clusters of galaxies. The wake of the sensor pod was almost impossible to pick out, and the darkness around them was absolute, only occasionally relieved by the mindless errand of a solitary messenger sprite.

Mina said: "And if they don't?"

"Then I guess we're all in a lot more trouble than we'd like."

For the first time in a century a ship was approaching Turquoise, commencing its deceleration from interstellar cruise speed. The flare of the lighthugger's exhaust was pointed straight at the Turquoise system. Measurement of the Doppler shift of the flame showed that the vessel was still two years out, but that was hardly any time at all on Turquoise. The ship had yet to announce itself, but even if it turned out to have nothing but benign intentions—a short trade stopover, perhaps—the effect on Turquoise society would be incalculable. Everyone knew of the troubles that followed the arrival of the *Pelican in Impiety*. When the Ultras moved into orbit there had been much unrest below. Spies had undermined lucrative trade deals. Cities had jockeyed for prestige, competing for technological tidbits. There had been hasty marriages and equally hasty separations. A century later, old enmities smouldered just beneath the surface of cordial intercity politics.

It wouldn't be any better next time.

"Look," Mina said. "It doesn't have to be all that bad. They might not even want to talk to us. Didn't a ship pass through the system about seventy years ago, without so much as a by-your-leave?"

Naqi nodded—it was mentioned in a sidebar to one of the main articles. "They had engine trouble, or something. But the experts say there's no sign of anything like that this time."

"So they've come to trade. What have we got to offer them that we didn't have last time?"

"Not much, I suppose."

Mina nodded knowingly. "A few works of art that probably won't travel very well. Ten-hour-long nose-flute symphonies, anyone?" She pulled a face. "That's supposedly my culture, and even I can't stand it. What else? A handful of discoveries about the Jugglers, which have more than likely been replicated elsewhere a dozen times. Technology, medicine? Forget it."

"They must think we have something worth coming here for," Naqi said. "Whatever it is, we'll just have to wait and see, won't we? It's only two years."

"I expect you think that's quite a long time," Mina said.

"Actually . . ."

Mina froze.

"Look!"

Something whipped past in the night, far below, then a handful of them, then a dozen, and then a whole bright squadron. Messenger sprites. Naqi diagnosed. But she had never seen so many of them moving at once, and on what was so evidently the same errand. Against the darkness of the ocean the lights were mesmerising: curling and weaving, swapping positions and occasionally veering far from the main pack before arcing back toward the swarm. Again one of the sprites climbed to the altitude of the airship, loitering for a few moments on fanning wings before whipping off to rejoin the others. The swarm receded, becoming a tight ball of fireflies and then only a pale globular smudge. Naqi watched until she was certain that the last sprite had vanished into the night.

"Wow," Mina said quietly.

"Have you ever seen anything like that?"

"Never."

"Bit funny that it should happen tonight, wouldn't you say?"

"Don't be silly," Mina said. "The Jugglers can't possibly know about the ship."

"We don't know that for sure. Most people heard about this ship hours ago. That's more than enough time for someone to have swum."

Mina conceded her younger sister's point with a delicate provisional nod of the head. "Still, information flow isn't usually that clear-cut. The Jugglers store patterns, but they seldom show any sign of comprehending actual content. We're dealing with a mindless biological archiving system, a museum without a curator."

"That's one view."

Mina shrugged. "I'd love to be proved otherwise."

"Well, do you think we should try following them? I know we can't track sprites over any distance, but we might be able to keep up for a few hours before we drain the batteries."

"We wouldn't learn much."

"We wouldn't know until we tried," Naqi said, gritting her teeth. "Come on—it's got to be worth a go, hasn't it? I reckon that swarm moved a bit slower than a single sprite. We'd at least have enough for a report, wouldn't we?"

Mina shook her head. "All we'd have is a single observation with a little bit of speculation thrown in. You know we can't publish that sort of thing. And anyway— assuming that sprite swarm did have something to do with the ship—there are going to be hundreds of similar sightings tonight."

"I was just hoping it might take our minds off the news."

"Perhaps it would. But it would also make us unforgivably late for our target." Mina dropped the tone of her voice, making an obvious effort to sound reasonable. "Look—I understand your curiosity. I feel it as well. But the chances are it was either a statistical fluke or part of a global event everyone else will have had a much better chance to study. Either way we can't contribute anything useful, so we might as well just forget about it." She rubbed at the marks on her forearm, tracing the paisley-patterned barbs and whorls of glowing colouration. "And I'm tired, and we have several busy days ahead of us. I think we just need to put this one down to experience, all right?"

"Fine," Naqi said.

"I'm sorry, but I just know we'd be wasting our time."

"I said fine." Naqi stood up and steadied herself on the railing that traversed the length of the airship's back.

"Where are you going?"

"To sleep. Like you said, we've got a busy day coming up. We'd be fools to waste time chasing a fluke, wouldn't we?"

———

An hour after dawn they crossed out of the dead zone. The sea below began to thicken with floating life, becoming soupy and torpid. A kilometre or so farther in and the soup showed ominous signs of structure: a blue-green stew of ropy strands and wide kelplike plates. They suggested the floating, half-digested entrails of embattled sea monsters.

Within another kilometre the floating life had become a dense vegetative raft, stinking of brine and rotting cabbage. Within another kilometre of that the raft had thickened to the point where the underlying sea was only intermittently visible. The air above the raft was humid, hot and pungent with microscopic irritants. The raft itself was possessed of a curiously beguiling motion, bobbing and writhing and gyring according to the ebb and flow of weirdly localised current systems. It was as if many invisible spoons stirred a great bowl of spinach. Even the shadow of the airship—pushed far ahead of it by the low sun—had some influence on the movement of the material. The Pattern Juggler biomass scurried and squirmed to evade the track of the shadow, and the peculiar purposefulness of the motion reminded Naqi of an octopus she had seen in the terrestrial habitats aquarium on Umingmaktok, squeezing its way through impossibly small gaps in the glass prison of its tank.

Presently they arrived at the precise centre of the circular raft. It spread away from them in all directions, hemmed by a distant ribbon of sparkling sea. It felt as if the airship had come to rest above an island, as fixed and ancient as any geological feature. The island even had a sort of geography: humps and ridges and depressions sculpted into the cloying texture of layered biomass. But there were few islands on Turquoise, especially at this latitude, and the Juggler node was only a few days old. Satellites had detected its growth a week earlier, and Mina and Naqi had been sent to investigate. They were under strict instructions simply to hover above the island and deploy a handful of tethered sensors. If the node showed any signs of being unusual, a more experienced team would be sent out from Umingmaktok by highspeed dirigible. Most nodes dispersed within twenty to thirty days, so there was always a sense of urgency. They might even send trained swimmers, eager to dive into the sea and open their minds to alien communion. Ready to—as they said—*ken* the ocean.

But first things first. Chances were this node would turn out to be interesting rather than exceptional.

"Morning," Mina said, when Naqi approached her. Mina was swabbing the sensor pod she had reeled in earlier, collecting green mucous that had adhered to its ceramic teardrop. All human artifacts eventually succumbed to biological attack from the ocean, although ceramics were the most resilient.

"You're cheerful," Naqi said, trying to make the statement sound matter-of-fact rather than judgmental.

"Aren't you? It's not everyone gets a chance to study a node up this close. Make the most of it, sis. The news we got last night doesn't change what we have to do today."

Naqi scraped the back of her hand across her nose. Now that the airship was above the node she was breathing vast numbers of aerial organisms into her lungs with each breath. The smell was redolent of ammonia and decomposing vegetation. It required an intense effort of will not to keep rubbing her eyes more raw than was already the case. "Do you see anything unusual?"

"Bit early to say."

"So that's a 'no.' then."

"You can't learn much without probes, Naqi." Mina dipped a swab into a collection bag, squeezing tight the plastic seal. Then she dropped the bag into a bucket between her feet. "Oh, wait. I saw another of those swarms, after you'd gone to sleep."

"I thought you were the one complaining about being tired."

Mina dug out a fresh swab and rubbed vigorously at a deep olive smear on the side of the sensor. "I picked up my messages, that's all. Tried again this morning, but the blackout still hadn't been lifted. I picked up a few shortwave radio signals from the closest cities, but they were just transmitting a recorded message from the Snowflake Council: stay tuned and don't panic."

"So let's hope we don't find anything significant here," Naqi said, "because we won't be able to report it if we do."

"They're bound to lift the blackout soon. In the meantime I think we have enough measurements to keep us busy. Did you find that spiral sweep program in the airship's avionics box?"

"I haven't looked for it," Naqi said, certain that Mina had never mentioned such a thing before. "But I'm sure I can program something from scratch in a few minutes."

"Well, let's not waste any more time than necessary. Here." Smiling, she offered Naqi the swab, its tip laden with green slime. "You take over this, and I'll go and dig out the program."

Naqi took the swab after a moment's delay.

"Of course. Prioritise tasks according to ability, right?"

"That's not what I meant," Mina said soothingly. "Look. Let's not argue, shall we? We were best friends until last night. I just thought it would be quicker . . ." She trailed off and shrugged. "You know what I mean. I know you blame me for not letting us follow the sprites, but we had no choice but to come here. Understand that, will you? Under any other circumstances . . ."

"I understand," Naqi said, realising as she did how sullen and childlike she sounded; how much she was playing the petulant younger sister. The worst of it was that she knew Mina was right. At dawn it all seemed much clearer.

"Do you? Really?"

Naqi nodded, feeling the perverse euphoria that came with an admission of defeat. "Yes. Really. We'd have been wrong to chase them."

Mina sighed. "I was tempted, you know. I just didn't want you to see how tempted I was, or else you'd have found a way to convince me."

"I'm that persuasive?"

"Don't underestimate yourself, sis. I know I never would." Mina paused and took back the swab. "I'll finish this. Can you handle the sweep program?"

Naqi smiled. She felt better now. The tension between them would still take a little while to lift, but at least things were easier now. Mina was right about something else: they were best friends, not just sisters.

"I'll handle it," Naqi said.

Naqi stepped through the hermetic curtain into the air-conditioned cool of the gondola. She closed the door, rubbed her eyes, and then sat down at the navigator's station. The airship had flown itself automatically from Umingmaktok, adjusting its course to take cunning advantage of jet streams and weather fronts. Now it was in hovering mode: once or twice a minute the electrically driven motors purred, stabilising the craft against gusts of wind generated by the microclimate above the Juggler node. Naqi called up the current avionics program, a menu of options appearing on a flat screen. The options quivered; Naqi thumped the screen with the back of her hand until the display behaved itself. Then she scrolled down through the other flight sequences, but there was no preprogrammed spiral loaded into the current avionics suite. Naqi rummaged around in the background files, but there was nothing to help her there either. She was about to start hacking something together—at a push it would take her half an hour to assemble a routine—when she remembered that she had once backed up some earlier avionics files onto the fan. She had no idea if they were still there, or even if there was anything useful among the cache, but it was probably worth taking the time to find out. The fan lay closed on a bench, where Mina must have left it after she verified that the blackout was still in force.

Naqi grabbed the fan and spread it open across her lap. To her surprise, it was still active: instead of the usual watercolour patterns the display showed the messages she had been scrolling through earlier.

She looked closer and frowned. These were not her messages at all. She was looking at the messages Mina had copied onto the fan during the night. At this realisation Naqi felt an immediate prickle of guilt. She knew that she should snap the fan shut, or at the very least close her sister's mail and delve into her own area of the fan. But she did neither of those things. Telling herself that it was only what anyone else would have done, she accessed the final message in the list and examined its incoming time-stamp. To within a few minutes, it had arrived at the same time as the final message Naqi had received.

Mina had been telling the truth when she said that the blackout was continuing.

Naqi glanced up. Through the window of the gondola she could see the back of her sister's head, bobbing up and down as she checked winches along the side.

Naqi looked at the body of the message. It was nothing remarkable, just an automated circular from one of the Juggler special-interest groups. Something about neurotransmitter chemistry.

She exited the circular, getting back to the list of incoming messages. She told herself that she had done nothing shameful so far. If she closed Mina's mail now, she would have nothing to feel guilty about.

But a name she recognized jumped out at her from the list of messages: Dr Jotah Sivaraksa, manager of the Moat project. The man she had met in Umingmaktok, glowing with renewed vitality after his yearly worm change. What could Mina possibly want with Sivaraksa?

She opened the message, read it.

It was exactly as she had feared, and yet not dared to believe.

Sivaraksa was responding to Mina's request to work on the Moat. The tone of the message was conversational, in stark contrast to the businesslike response Naqi had received. Sivaraksa informed her sister that her request had been appraised favourably, and that while there were still one or two other candidates to be considered, the expectation was that Mina would emerge as the most convincing applicant. Even if this turned out not to be the case. Sivaraksa continued—and that outcome was not thought very likely—Mina's name would be at the top of the list when further vacancies became available. In short, she was more or less guaranteed a chance to work on the Moat within the year.

Naqi read the message again, just in case there was some highly subtle detail that threw the entire thing into a different, more benign light.

Then she snapped shut the fan with a sense of profound fury. She placed it back where it was, exactly as it had been.

Mina pushed her head through the hermetic curtain.

"How's it coming along?"

"Fine . . ." Naqi said. Her voice sounded drained of emotion even to herself.

"Got that routine cobbled together?"

"Coming along," Naqi said.

"Something the matter?"

"No . . ." Naqi forced a smile. "No. Just working through the details. Have it ready in a few minutes."

"Good. Can't wait to start the sweep. We're going to get some beautiful data, sis. And I think this is going to be a significant node. Maybe the largest this season. Aren't you glad it came our way?"

"Thrilled," Naqi said, before returning to her work.

Thirty specialised probes hung on telemetric cables from the underside of the gondola, dangling like the venom-tipped stingers of some grotesque aerial jellyfish. The probes sniffed the air metres above the Juggler biomass, or skimmed the fuzzy green surface of the formation. Weighted plumb lines penetrated to the sea beneath the raft, sipping the organism-infested depths dozens of metres under the node. Radar mapped larger structures embedded within the node—dense kernels of compacted biomass, or huge cavities and tubes of implacable function—while sonar graphed the topology of the many sinewy organic cables which plunged into darkness, umbilicals anchoring the node to the seabed. Smaller nodes drew most of their energy from sunlight and the breakdown of sugars and fats in the sea's other floating microorganisms but the larger formations—which had a vastly higher information-processing burden—needed to tap belching aquatic fissures, active rifts in the ocean bed kilometres under the waves. Cold water was pumped down each umbilical by peristaltic compression waves, heated by being circulated in the superheated thermal environment of the underwater volcanoes, and then pumped back to the surface.

In all this sensing activity, remarkably little physical harm was done to the extended organism itself. The biomass sensed the approach of the probes and rearranged itself so that they passed through with little obstruction, even those scything lines that reached into the water. Energy was obviously being consumed to avoid the organism sustaining damage, and by implication the measurements must therefore have had some effect on the node's information processing efficiency. The effect was likely to be small, however, and since the node was already subject to constant changes in its architecture—some probably intentional, and some probably forced on it by other factors in its environment—there appeared to be little point in worrying about the harm caused by the human investigators. Ultimately, so much was still guesswork. Although the swimmer teams had learned a great deal about the Pattern Jugglers' encoded information, almost everything else about them—how and why they stored the neural patterns, and to what extent the patterns were subject to subsequent postprocessing—remained unknown. And those were merely the immediate questions. Beyond that were the real mysteries, which everyone wanted to solve, but were simply beyond the scope of immediate academic study. What they would learn today could not be expected to shed any light on those profundities. A single data point—even a single clutch of measurements—could not usually prove or disprove anything. But nonetheless it might later turn out to play a vital role in some chain of argument, even if it was only in the biasing of some statistical distribution closer to one hypothesis than another. Science, as Naqi had long since realised, was as much a swarming, social process as it was something driven by ecstatic moments of personal discovery.

It was something she was proud to be part of.

The spiral sweep continued uneventfully, the airship chugging around in a gently widening circle. Morning shifted to early afternoon, and then the sun began to climb down toward the horizon, bleeding pale orange into the sky through soft-edged cracks in the cloud cover. For hours Naqi and Mina studied the incoming results, the ever-sharper scans of the node appearing on screens throughout the gondola. They discussed the results cordially enough, but Naqi could not stop thinking about Mina's betrayal. She took a spiteful pleasure in testing the extent to which her sister would lie, deliberately forcing the conversation around to Dr Sivaraksa and the project he steered.

"I hope I don't end up like one of those deadwood bureaucrats," Naqi said, when they were discussing the way their careers might evolve. "You know, like Sivaraksa." She observed Mina pointedly, yet giving nothing away. "I read some of his old papers; he used to be pretty good once. But now look at him."

"It's easy to say that," Mina said. "But I bet he doesn't like being away from the frontline any more than we would. But someone has to manage these big projects. Wouldn't you rather it was someone who'd at least been a scientist?"

"You sound like you're defending him. Next you'll be telling me you think the Moat is a good idea."

"I'm not defending Sivaraksa," Mina said. "I'm just saying . . ." She eyed her sister with a sudden glimmer of suspicion. Had she guessed that Naqi knew? "Never mind. Sivaraksa can fight his own battles. We've got work to do."

"Anyone would think you were changing the subject," Naqi said. But Mina was already on her way out of the gondola to check the equipment again.

At dusk the airship arrived at the perimeter of the node, completed one orbit, then began to track inward again. As it passed over the parts of the node previously mapped, time-dependent changes were highlighted on the displays: arcs and bands of red superimposed against the lime and turquoise false-colour of the mapped structures. Most of the alterations were minor: a chamber opening here or closing there, or a small alteration in the network topology to ease a bottleneck between the lumpy subnodes dotted around the floating island. Other changes were more mysterious in function, but conformed to types seen in other studies. They were studied at enhanced resolution, the data prioritised and logged.

It looked as if the node was large but in no way unusual.

Then night came, as swiftly as it always did at those latitudes. Mina and Naqi took turns sleeping for two or three hour stretches while the other kept an eye on the readouts. During a lull Naqi climbed up onto the top of the airship and tried the antenna again, and for a moment was gladdened when she saw that a new message had arrived. But the message itself turned out to be a statement from the Snowflake Council stating that the blackout on civilian messages would continue for at least another two days, until the current "crisis" was over. There were allusions to civil disturbances in two cities, with curfews being imposed, and imperatives to ignore all unofficial news sources concerning the nature of the approaching ship.

Naqi wasn't surprised that there was trouble, though the extent of it took her aback. Her instincts were to believe the government line. The problem—from the government's point of view—was that nothing was known for certain about the nature of the ship, and so by being truthful they ended up sounding like they were keeping something back. They would have been far better off making up a plausible lie, which could be gently moulded toward accuracy as time passed.

Mina rose after midnight to begin her shift. Naqi went to sleep and dreamed fitfully, seeing in her mind's eye red smears and bars hovering against amorphous green. She had been staring at the readouts too intently, for too many hours.

Mina woke her excitedly before dawn.

"Now I'm the one with the news," she said.

"What?"

"Come and see for yourself."

Naqi rose from her hammock, neither rested nor enthusiastic. In the dim light of the cabin Mina's fungal patterns shone with peculiar intensity, abstract detached shapes that only implied her presence.

Naqi followed the shapes onto the balcony.

"What," she said again, not even bothering to make it sound like a question.

"There's been a development," Mina said.

Naqi rubbed the sleep from her eyes. "With the node?"

"Look. Down below. Right under us."

Naqi pressed her stomach hard against the railing and leaned over as far as she dared. She had felt no real vertigo until they had lowered the sensor lines, and then suddenly there had been a physical connection between the airship and the ground. But was it her imagination or had the airship lowered itself to about half its previous altitude, reeling in the lines at the same time?

The midnight light was all spectral shades of milky gray. The creased and crumpled landscape of the node reached away into midgray gloom, merging with the slate of the overlying cloud deck. Naqi saw nothing remarkable, other than the surprising closeness of the surface.

"I mean *really* look down," Mina said.

Naqi pushed herself against the railing more than she had dared before, until she was standing on the very tips of her toes. Only then did she see it. Directly below them was a peculiar circle of darkness, almost as if the airship was casting a distinct shadow beneath itself. It was a circular zone of exposed seawater, like a lagoon enclosed by the greater mass of the node. Steep banks of Juggler biomass, its heart a deep charcoal gray, rimmed the lagoon. Naqi studied it quietly, sensing that her sister might judge her on any remark she made.

"How did you see it?" she asked eventually.

"See it?"

"It can't be more than twenty metres wide. A dot like that would have hardly shown up on the topographic map."

"Naqi, you don't understand. I didn't steer us over the hole. It appeared below us, as we were moving. Listen to the motors. We're *still* moving. The hole's shadowing us. It follows us precisely."

"Must be reacting to the sensors," Naqi said.

"I've hauled them in. We're not trailing anything within thirty metres of the surface. The node's reacting to us, Naqi—to the presence of the airship. The Jugglers know we're here, and they're sending us a signal."

"Maybe they are. But it isn't our job to interpret that signal. We're just here to take measurements, not to interact with the Jugglers."

"So whose job is it?" Mina asked.

"Do I have to spell it out? Specialists from Umingmaktok."

"They won't get here in time. You know how long nodes last. By the time the blackout's lifted, by the time the swimmer corps hotshots get here, we'll be sitting over a green smudge and not much more. This is a significant find, Naqi. It's the largest node this season and it's making a deliberate and clear attempt to invite swimmers."

She stepped back from the railing. "Don't even think about it."

"I've been thinking about it all night. This isn't just a large node, Naqi. Something's happening—that's why there's been so much sprite activity. If we don't swim here, we might miss something unique."

"And if we do swim, we'll be violating every rule in the book. We're not trained, Mina. Even if we learned something—even if the Jugglers deigned to communicate with us—we'd be ostracised from the entire scientific community."

"That would depend on what we learned, wouldn't it?"

"Don't do this, Mina. It isn't worth it."

"We won't know if it's worth it or not until we try, will we?" Mina extended a hand. "Look. You're right in one sense. Chances are pretty good nothing will happen. Normally you have to offer them a gift—a puzzle, or something rich in information. We haven't got anything like that. What'll probably happen is we hit the water and there won't be any kind of biochemical interaction. In which case, it doesn't matter. We don't have to tell anyone. And if we do learn something, but it isn't significant—well, we don't have to tell anyone about that either. Only if we learn something major. Something so big that they'll have to forget about a minor violation of protocol."

"A minor violation . . . ?" Naqi began, almost laughing at Mina's audacity.

"The point is, sis, we have a win-win situation here. And it's been handed to us on a plate."

"You could also argue that we've been handed a major chance to fuck up spectacularly."

"You read it whichever way you like. I know what I see."

"It's too dangerous, Mina. People have died . . ." Naqi looked at Mina's fungal patterns, enhanced and emphasised by her tattoos. "You flagged high for conformality. Doesn't that worry you slightly?"

"Conformality's just a fairy tale they use to scare children into behaving," said Mina. " 'Eat all your greens or the sea will swallow you up forever.' I take it about as seriously as I take the Thule kraken, or the drowning of Arviat. I'm fully aware of the risk."

"The Thule kraken is a joke, and Arviat never existed in the first place. But the last time I checked, conformality was an accepted phenomenon."

"It's an accepted research topic. There's a distinction."

"Don't split hairs . . ." Naqi began.

Mina gave every indication of not having heard Naqi speak. Her voice was distant, as if she were speaking to herself. It had a lilting, singsong quality. "Too late to even think about it now. But it isn't long until dawn. I think it'll still be there at dawn."

She pushed past Naqi.

"Where are you going now?"

"To catch some sleep. I need to be fresh for this. So will you."

They hit the lagoon with two gentle, anticlimactic splashes. Naqi was underwater for a moment before she bobbed to the surface, holding her breath. At first she had to make a conscious effort to start breathing again: the air immediately above the water was so saturated with microscopic organisms that choking seemed a real possibility. Mina, surfacing next to her, drew in gulps with wild enthusiasm, as if willing the tiny creatures to invade her lungs. She shrieked delight at the sudden cold. When they had both gained equilibrium, treading with their shoulders above water, Naqi was finally able to take stock. She saw everything through a stinging haze of tears. The gondola hovered above them, poised beneath the larger mass of the vacuum bladder. The life raft that it had deployed was sparkling new, rated for one hundred hours against moderate biological attack. But that was for mid-ocean, where the density of Juggler organisms would be much less than in the middle of a major node. Here, the hull might only endure a few tens of hours before it was consumed.

Once again, Naqi wondered if she should withdraw. There was still time. No real damage had yet been done. She could be back in the boat and back aboard the airship in a minute or so. Mina might not follow her, but she did not have to be complicit in her sister's actions. But Naqi knew she would not be able to turn back. She could not show weakness now that she had come this far.

"Nothing's happening . . ." she said.

"We've only been in the water a minute," Mina said.

The two of them wore black wetsuits. The suits themselves could become buoyant if necessary—all it would take would be the right sequence of tactile commands and dozens of tiny bladders would inflate around the chest and shoulder area—but it was easy enough to tread water. In any case, if the Jugglers initiated contact the suits would probably be eaten away in minutes. The swimmers who had made repeated contact often swam naked or near naked, but Naqi was not prepared for that level of abject surrender to the ocean's assault. Nor was Mina.

After another minute the water no longer seemed as cold. Through gaps in the cloud cover the sun was harsh on Naqi's cheek. It etched furiously bright lines in the bottle-green surface of the lagoon, lines that coiled and shifted into fleeting calligraphic shapes as if conveying secret messages. The calm water lapped gently against their upper bodies. The walls of the lagoon were metre-high masses of fuzzy vegetation, like the steep banks of a river. Now and then Naqi felt something brush gently against her feet, like a passing frond or strand of seaweed. The first few times she flinched at the contact, but after a while it became strangely soothing. Occasionally something stroked one or other hand, then moved playfully away. When she lifted her hands from the sea, mats of gossamer green draped from her fingers like the tattered remains of expensive gloves. The green material slithered free and slipped back into the sea. It tickled between her fingers.

"Nothing's still happened," Naqi said, more quietly this time.

"You're wrong. The shoreline's moved closer."

Naqi looked at it. "It's a trick of perspective."

"I assure you it isn't."

Naqi looked back at the raft. They had drifted five or six metres from it. It might as well have been a kilometre for all the sense of security that the raft now offered. Mina was right: the lagoon was closing in on them, gently, slowly. If the lagoon had been twenty metres wide when they had entered it must now be a third smaller. There was still time to escape before the hazy green walls squeezed in on them, but only if they moved now, back to the raft, back into the safety of the gondola.

"Mina . . . I want to go. We're not ready for this."

"We don't need to be ready. It's going to happen."

"We're not trained!"

"Call it learning on the job, in that case." Mina was still trying to sound outrageously calm, but it wasn't working. Naqi heard the flaw in her voice. She was either terribly frightened or terribly excited.

"You're more scared than I am," she said.

"I am scared," said Mina. "Scared we'll screw this up. Scared we'll blow this opportunity. Understand? I'm *that* kind of scared."

Either Naqi was treading water less calmly, or the water itself had become visibly more agitated in the last few moments. The green walls were perhaps ten metres apart, and now were not quite the sheer vertical structures they had appeared before. They had taken on form and design, growing and complexifying by the second. It was akin to watching a distant city emerge from fog, the revealing of bewildering, plunging layers of mesmeric detail, more than the eye or the mind could process.

"It doesn't look as if they're expecting a gift this time," Mina said.

Veined tubes and pipes coiled and writhed around each other in constant sinuous motion, making Naqi think of some hugely magnified circuitry formed from
plant parts. It was restless living circuitry that never quite settled into one configura-
tion. Now and then chequer-board designs appeared, or intricately interlocking
runes. Sharply geometric patterns flickered from point to point, echoed, amplified
and subtly iterated at each move. Distinct three-dimensional shapes assumed brief
solidity, carved from greenery as if by the deft hand of a topiarist. Naqi glimpsed unsettling anatomies; the warped memories of alien bodies that had once entered the
ocean, a million or a billion years ago. Here a three-jointed limb, here the shieldlike
curve of an exoskeletal plaque. The head of something that was almost equine
melted into a goggling mass of faceted eyes. Fleetingly, a human form danced from
the chaos. But only once. Alien swimmers outnumbered human swimmers vastly.

Here were the Pattern Jugglers, Naqi knew. The first explorers had mistaken these
remembered forms for indications of actual sentience, thinking that the oceanic
mass was a kind of community of intelligences. It was an easy mistake to have made,
but it was some way from the truth. These animate shapes were enticements, like
the gaudy covers of books. The minds themselves were captured only as frozen
traces. The only living intelligence within the ocean lay in its own curatorial system.

To believe anything else was heresy.

The dance of bodies became too rapid to follow. Pastel-coloured lights glowed
from deep within the green structure, flickering and stuttering. Naqi thought of
lanterns burning from the depths of a forest. Now the edge of the lagoon had become irregular, extending peninsulas toward the centre of the dwindling circle of
water, while narrow bays and inlets fissured back into the larger mass of the node.
The peninsulas sprouted grasping tendrils, thigh-thick at the trunk but narrowing to
the dimensions of plant fronds, and then narrowing further, bifurcating into lacy,
fernlike hazes of awesome complexity. They diffracted light like the wings of drag-
onflies. They were closing over the lagoon, forming a shimmering canopy. Now and
then a sprite—or something smaller but equally bright—arced from one bank of the
lagoon to another. Brighter things moved through the water like questing fish. Microscopic organisms were detaching from the larger fronds and tendrils, swarming
in purposeful clouds. They batted against her skin, against her eyelids. Every breath
that she took made her cough. The taste of the Pattern Jugglers was sour and medic-
inal. They were in her, invading her body.

She panicked. It was as if a tiny switch had flipped in her mind. Suddenly all
other concerns melted away. She had to get out of the lagoon immediately, no matter what Mina would think of her.

Thrashing more than swimming, Naqi tried to push herself toward the raft. But as
soon as the panic reaction had kicked in she had felt something else slide over her.
It was not so much paralysis as an immense sense of inertia. Moving, even breathing, became problematic. The boat was impossibly distant. She was no longer capable of treading water. She felt heavy, and when she looked down she saw that a green
haze enveloped the parts of her body that she could see above water. The organisms
were adhering to the fabric of her wetsuit.

"Mina . . ." she called. "Mina!"

But Mina only looked at her. Naqi sensed that her sister was experiencing the

600 | the best of the best, volume 2

same sort of paralysis. Mina's movements had become languid, and yet instead of panic what Naqi saw on her face was profound resignation and acceptance. It was dangerously close to serenity.

Mina wasn't frightened at all.

The patterns on her neck were flaring vividly. Her eyes were closed. Already the organisms had begun to attack the fabric of her suit, stripping it away from her flesh. Naqi could feel the same thing happening to her own suit. There was no pain, for the organisms stopped short of attacking her skin. With a mighty effort she hoisted her forearm from the water, studying the juxtaposition of pale flesh and dissolving black fabric. Her fingers were as stiff as iron.

But—and Naqi clung to this—the ocean recognised the sanctity of organisms, or at least thinking organisms. Strange things might happen to people who swam with the Jugglers, things that might be difficult to distinguish from death or near death. But people always emerged afterward, changed perhaps, but essentially whole. No matter what happened now, they would survive. The Jugglers always returned those who swam with them, and even when they did effect changes they were seldom permanent.

Except, of course, for those who didn't return.

No, Naqi told herself. What they were doing was foolish, and might perhaps destroy their careers. But they would survive. Mina had flagged high on the conformality index when she had applied to join the swimmer corps, but that didn't mean she was necessarily at risk. Conformality merely implied a rare connection with the ocean. It verged on the glamorous.

Now Mina was going under. She had stopped moving entirely. Her eyes were blankly ecstatic.

Naqi wanted to resist that same impulse to submission. But the strength had flown away from her. She felt herself commence the same descent. The water closed over her mouth, then her eyes, and in a moment she was under. She felt herself a toppled statue sliding toward the seabed. Her fear reached a crescendo and then passed. She was not drowning. The froth of green organisms had forced itself down her throat, down her nasal passage. She felt no fright. There was nothing except a profound feeling that this was what she had been born to do.

Naqi knew what was happening, what was going to happen. She had studied enough reports on swimmer missions. The tiny organisms were infiltrating her entire body, creeping into her lungs and bloodstream. They were keeping her alive, while at the same time flooding her with chemical bliss. Droves of the same tiny creatures were seeking routes to her brain, inching along the optic nerve, the aural nerve, or crossing the blood-brain barrier itself. They were laying tiny threads behind them, fibres that extended back into the larger mass of organisms suspended in the water around her. In turn, these organisms established data-carrying channels back into the primary mass of the node. . . . And the node itself was connected to other nodes, both chemically and via the packet-carrying sprites. The green threads bound Naqi to the entire ocean. It might take hours for a signal to reach her mind from halfway around Turquoise, but it didn't matter. She was beginning to think on Juggler time, her own thought processes seeming pointlessly quick, like the motion of bees.

She sensed herself becoming vaster.

She was no longer just a pale, hard-edged thing labelled *Naqi*, suspended in the lagoon like a dying starfish. Her sense of self was rushing out toward the horizon in all directions, encompassing first the node and then the empty oceanic waters around it. She couldn't say precisely how this information was reaching her. It wasn't through visual imagery, but more an intensely detailed spatial awareness. It was as if spatial awareness had suddenly become her most vital sense.

She supposed this was what swimmers meant when they spoke of *kenning*.

She kenned the presence of other nodes over the horizon, their chemical signals flooding her mind, each unique, each bewilderingly rich in information. It was like hearing the roar of a hundred crowds. And at the same time she kenned the ocean depths, the cold fathoms of water beneath the node, the life-giving warmth of the crustal vents. Closer, too, she kenned Mina. They were two neighbouring galaxies in a sea of strangeness. Mina's own thoughts were bleeding into the sea, into Naqi's mind, and in them Naqi felt the reflected echo of her own thoughts, picked up by Mina. . . .

It was glorious.

For a moment their minds orbited each other, kenning each other on a level of intimacy neither had dreamed possible.

Mina . . . Can you feel me?

I'm here, Naqi. Isn't this wonderful?

The fear was gone, utterly. In its place was a marvellous feeling of immanence. They had made the right decision, Naqi knew. She had been right to follow Mina. Mina was deliciously happy, basking in the same hopeful sense of security and promise.

And then they began to sense other minds.

Nothing had changed, but it was suddenly clear that the roaring signals from the other nodes were composed of countless individual voices, countless individual streams of chemical information. Each stream was the recording of a mind that had entered the ocean at some point. The oldest minds—those that had entered the ocean in the deep past—were the faintest ones, but they were also the most numerous. They had begun to sound alike, the shapes of their stored personalities blurring into each other, no matter how alien they had been to start with. The minds that had been captured more recently were sharper and more variegated, like oddly shaped pebbles on a beach. Naqi kenned brutal alienness, baroque architectures of mind shaped by outlandish chains of evolutionary contingency. The only thing any of them had in common was that they had all reached a certain threshold of tool-using intelligence, and had all—for one reason or another—been driven into interstellar space, where they had encountered the Pattern Jugglers. But that was like saying the minds of sharks and leopards were alike because they had both evolved to hunt. The differences between the minds were so cosmically vast that Naqi felt her own mental processes struggling to accommodate them.

Even that was becoming easier. Subtly—slowly enough that from moment to moment she was not aware of it—the organisms in her skull were retuning her neural connections, and allowing more and more of her consciousness to seep out into the extended processing loom of the sea.

She sensed the most recent arrivals.

They were all human minds, each a glittering gem of distinctness. Naqi sensed a great gulf in time between the earliest human mind and the last recognisably alien one. She had no idea if it was a million or a billion years, but it felt immense. At the same time she grasped that the ocean had been desperate for newness, and that while these human minds were welcome, they were barely sufficient.

The minds were snapshots, frozen in the conception of a single thought. It was like an orchestra of instruments, all sustaining a single unique note. Perhaps there was a grindingly slow evolution in those minds—she sensed the merest subliminal hint of change—but if that was the case it would take centuries to complete a thought . . . thousands of years to complete the simplest internalised statement. The newest minds might not even have come to the realisation that they had been swallowed by the sea.

Yet now Naqi sensed a single mind flaring louder than the others.

It was recent and human, and yet there was something about it that struck her as discordant. The mind was damaged, as if it had been captured imperfectly. It was disfigured, giving off squalls of hurt. It had suffered dreadfully. It was reaching out to her, craving love and affection; something to cling to in the abyssal loneliness it now knew.

Images ghosted through her mind. Something was burning. Flames licked through the interstitial gaps in a great black structure. She couldn't tell if it was a building or a vast, pyramidal bonfire.

She heard screams, and then something hysterical, which she at first took for more screaming, until she realised that it was something far, far worse. It was laughter, and as the flames roared higher, consuming the mass, smothering the screams, the laughter only intensified.

She thought it might be the laughter of a child.

Perhaps it was her imagination, but this mind appeared more fluid than the others. Its thoughts were still slow—far slower than Naqi's—but the mind appeared to have usurped more than its share of processing resources. It was stealing computational cycles from neighbouring minds, freezing them into absolute stasis while it completed a single sluggish thought.

The mind worried Naqi. Pain and fury was boiling off it.

Mina kenned it too. Naqi tasted Mina's thoughts and knew that her sister was equally disturbed by the mind's presence. Then she felt the mind's attention shift, drawn to the two inquisitive minds that had just entered the sea. It became aware of both of them, quietly watchful. A moment or two passed, and then the mind slipped away, back to wherever it had come from.

What was that . . .

She felt her sister's reply. *I don't know. A human mind. A conformal, I think. Someone who was swallowed by the sea. But it's gone now.*

No, it hasn't. It's still there. Just hiding.

Millions of minds have entered the sea, Naqi. Thousands of conformals, perhaps, if you think of all the aliens that came before us. There are bound to be one or two bad apples.

That wasn't just a bad apple. It was like touching ice. And it sensed us. It reacted to us. Didn't it?

She sensed Mina's hesitation.

We can't be sure. Our own perceptions of events aren't necessarily reliable. I can't even be certain we're having this conversation. I might be talking to myself . . .

Mina . . . Don't talk like that. I don't feel safe.

Me neither. But I'm not going to let one frightening thing unnecessarily affect me.

Something happened then. It was a loosening, a feeling that the ocean's grip on Naqi had just relented to a significant degree. Mina, and the roaring background of other minds, fell away to something much more distant. It was as if Naqi had just stepped out of a babbling party into a quiet adjacent room, and was even now moving farther and farther away from the door.

Her body tingled. She no longer felt the same deadening paralysis. Pearl-gray light flickered above. Without being sure whether she was doing it herself, she moved toward the surface. She was aware that she was moving away from Mina, but for now all that mattered was to escape the sea. She wanted to be as far from the mind as possible.

Her head rammed through a crust of green into air. At the same moment the Juggler organisms fled her body in a convulsive rush. She thrashed stiff limbs and took in deep, panicked breaths. The transition was horrible, but it was over in a few seconds. She looked around, expecting to see the sheer walls of the lagoon, but all she saw in one direction was open waters. Naqi felt panic rising again. Then she kicked herself around and saw a wavy line of bottle-green that had to be the perimeter of the node, perhaps half a kilometre away from her present position. The airship was a distant silvery teardrop that appeared to be perched on the surface of the node itself.

In her fear she did not immediately think of Mina. All she wanted to do was reach the safety of the airship, to be aloft. Then she saw the raft, bobbing only one or two hundred metres away. Somehow it had been transplanted to the open waters as well. It looked distant but reachable. She started swimming, the fear giving her strength and sense of purpose. In truth, she was still thick well within the true boundary of the node: the water was still thick with suspended microorganisms, so that it was more like swimming through cold green soup. It made each stroke harder, but by the same token she did not have to expend much effort to stay afloat.

Did she trust the Pattern Jugglers not to harm her? Perhaps. After all, she had not encountered *their* minds at all—if they even *had* minds. They were merely the archiving system. Blaming them for that one poisoned mind was like blaming a library for one hateful book.

But it had still unnerved her profoundly. She wondered why none of the other swimmers had ever communicated their encounters with the mind. After all, she remembered it well enough now, and she was nearly out of the ocean. She might forget shortly—there were bound to be subsequent neurological effects—but under other circumstances there would have been nothing to prevent her relating her experiences to a witness or inviolable recording system.

She kept swimming, and began to wonder why Mina hadn't emerged from the waters as well. Mina had been just as terrified. But Mina had also been more curious, and more willing to ignore her fears. Naqi had grasped the opportunity to leave the ocean when the Jugglers released their grip on her. But what if Mina had elected to remain?

What if Mina was still down there, still in communion with the Jugglers?

Naqi reached the raft and hauled herself aboard, being careful not to capsize it. She saw that the raft was still largely intact. It had been moved but not damaged, and although the ceramic sheathing was showing signs of attack, peppered here and there with scabbed green accretions, it was certainly good for another few hours. The rot-hardened control systems were still alive and still in telemetric connection with the distant airship.

Naqi had crawled from the sea naked. Now she felt cold and vulnerable. She pulled an aluminised quilt from the raft's supply box and wrapped it around herself. It did not stop her from shivering, did not make her feel any less nauseous, but at least it afforded some measure of symbolic barrier against the sea.

She looked around again, but there was still no sign of Mina.

Naqi folded aside the weatherproof control cover and tapped commands into the matrix of waterproofed keys. She waited for the response from the airship. The moment stretched. But there it was: a minute shift in the dull gleam on the silver back of the vacuum bladder. The airship was turning, pivoting like a great slow weather vane. It was moving, responding to the raft's homing command.

But where was Mina?

Now something moved in the water next to her, coiling in weak, enervated spasms. Naqi looked at it with horrified recognition. She reached over, still shivering, and with appalled gentleness fished the writhing thing from the sea. It lay in her fingers like a baby sea serpent. It was white and segmented, half a metre long. She knew exactly what it was.

It was Mina's worm. It meant Mina had died.

II

Two years later Naqi watched a spark fall from the heavens.

Along with many hundreds of spectators, she was standing on the railed edge of one of Umingmaktok's elegant cantilevered arms. It was afternoon. Every visible surface of the city had been scoured of rot and given a fresh coat of crimson on emerald paint. Amber bunting had been hung along the metal stay-lines that supported the tapering arms protruding from the city's towering commercial core. Most of the berthing slots around the perimeter were occupied with passenger or cargo craft, while many smaller vessels were holding station in the immediate airspace around Umingmaktok. The effect—which Naqi had seen on her approach to the city a day earlier—had been to turn the snowflake into a glittering, delicately ornamented vision. By night they had fireworks displays. By day, as now, conjurors and confidence tricksters wound their way through the crowds. Nose-flute musicians and drum dancers performed impromptu atop improvised podia. Kick-boxers were cheered on as they moved from one informal ring to another, pursued by whistle-blowing proctors. Hastily erected booths were marked with red and yellow pennants, selling refreshments, souvenirs or tattoo-work, while pretty costumed girls who wore back-packs equipped with tall flagstaffs sold drinks or ices. The children had balloons and rattles marked with the emblems of both Umingmaktok and the Snowflake Council, and many of them had had their faces painted to resemble stylised space travellers. Puppet theatres had been set up here and there, running through exactly the same small repertoire of stories that Naqi remembered from her childhood. The children were enthralled nonetheless; mouths agape at each miniature epic, whether it was a roughly accurate account of the world's settlement—with the colony ship being stripped to the bone for every gram of metal it held—or something altogether more fantastic, like the drowning of Arviat. It didn't matter to the children that the one was based in fact and the other pure mythology. To them the idea that every city they called home had been cannibalised from the belly of a four-kilometre-long ship was no more or less plausible than the idea that the living sea might occasionally snatch cities beneath the waves when they displeased it. At that age everything was both magical and mundane, and she supposed that the children were no more or less ex-cited by the prospect of the coming visitors than they were by the promised fireworks display, or the possibility of further treats if they were well behaved. Other than the children, there were animals—caged monkeys and birds—and the occasional ex-pensive pet, being shown off for the day. One or two servitors stalked through the crowd, and occasionally a golden float-cam would bob through the air, loitering over a scene of interest like a single detached eyeball. Turquoise had not seen this level of celebration since the last acrimonious divorce, and the networks were milk-ing it remorselessly, over-analysing the tiniest scrap of information.

This was, in truth, exactly the kind of thing Naqi would normally have gone to the other side of the planet to avoid. But something had drawn her this time, and made her wangle the trip out from the Moat at an otherwise critical time in the proj-ect. She could only suppose that it was a need to close a particular chapter in her life, one that had begun the night before Mina's death. The detection of the Ultra ship—they now knew that it was named the *Voice of Evening*—had been the event that triggered the blackout, and the blackout had been Mina's justification for the two of them attempting to swim with the Jugglers. Indirectly, therefore, the Ultras were "responsible" for whatever had happened to Mina. That was unfair, of course, but Naqi nonetheless felt the need to be here now, if only to witness the visitors' emergence with her own eyes and see if they really were the monsters of her imagi-nation. She had come to Umingmaktok with a stoic determination that she would not be swept up by the hysteria of the celebrations. Yet now that she had made the trip, now that she was amidst the crowd, drunk on the chemical buzz of human ex-citement with a nice fresh worm hooked onto her gut wall, she found herself in the perverse position of actually enjoying the atmosphere.

And now everyone had noticed the falling spark.

The crowd turned their heads into the sky, ignoring the musicians, conjurors and confidence tricksters. The backpacked girls stopped and looked aloft along with the others, shielding their eyes against the midday glare. The spark was the shuttle of the *Voice of Evening*, now parked in orbit around Turquoise.

Everyone had seen Captain Moreau's ship by now, either with their own eyes as a moving star or via the images captured by the orbiting cameras or ground-based telescopes. The ship was dark and sleek, outrageously elegant. Now and then its Conjoiner drives flickered on just enough to trim its orbit, those flashes like brief teasing windows into daylight for the hemisphere below.

A ship like that could do awful things to a world, and everyone knew it.

But if Captain Moreau and his crew meant ill of Turquoise, they'd had ample opportunity to do harm already. They had been silent at two years out, but at one year out, the *Voice of Evening* had transmitted the usual approach signals, requesting permission to stopover for three or four months. It was a formality—no one argued with Ultras—but it was also a gladdening sign that they intended to play by the usual rules.

Over the next year there had been a steady stream of communications between the ship and the Snowflake Council. The official word was that the messages had been designed to establish a framework for negotiation and person-to-person trade. The Ultras would need to update their linguistics software to avoid being confused by the subtleties of the Turquoise dialects, which, although based on Canasian, contained confusing elements of Inuit and Thai, relics of the peculiar social mix of the original settlement coalition.

The falling shuttle had slowed to merely supersonic speed now, shedding its plume of ionised air. Dropping speed with each loop, it executed a lazily contracting spiral above Umingmaktok. Naqi had rented cheap binoculars from one of the vendors. The lenses were scuffed, shimmering with the pink of fungal bloom. She visually locked onto the shuttle, its roughly delta shape wobbling in and out of sharpness. Only when it was two or three thousand metres above the Umingmaktok could she see it clearly. It was very elegant, a pure brilliant white like something carved from cloud. Beneath the mantalike hull, complex machines—fans and control surface—moved too rapidly to be seen as anything other than blurs of subliminal motion. She watched as the ship reduced speed until it hovered at the same altitude as the snowflake city. Above the roar of the crowd—an ecstatic, flag-waving mass—all Naqi heard was a shrill hum, almost too far into ultrasound to detect.

The ship approached slowly. It had been given instructions for docking with the arm adjacent to the one where Naqi and the other spectators gathered. Now that it was close it was apparent that the shuttle was larger than any of the dirigible craft normally moored to the city's arms; by Naqi's estimate it was at least half as wide as the city's central core. But it slid into its designated mooring point with exquisite delicacy. Bright red symbols flashed onto the otherwise blank white hull, signifying airlocks, cargo ports and umbilical sockets. Gangways were swung out from the arm to align with the doors and ports. Dockers—supervised by proctors and city officials—scrambled along the precarious connecting ways and attempted to fix magnetic berthing stays onto the shuttle's hull. The magnetics slid off the hull. They tried adhesive grips next, and these were no more successful. After that, the dockers shrugged their shoulders and made exasperated gestures in the direction of the shuttle.

The roar of the crowd had died down a little by now.

Naqi felt the anticipation as well. She watched as an entourage of VIPs moved to the berthing position, led by a smooth, faintly cherubic individual that Naqi recognised as Tak Thonburi, the mayor of Umingmaktok and presiding chair of the

Snowflake Council. Tak Thonburi was happily overweight and had a permanent cowlick of black hair, like an inverted question mark tattooed upon his forehead. His cheeks and brow were mottled with pale green. Next to him was the altogether leaner frame of Jotah Sivaraksa. It was no surprise that Dr Sivaraksa should be here today, for the Moat project was one of the most significant activities of the entire Snowflake Council. His iron-gray eyes flashed this way and that as if constantly triangulating the positions of enemies and allies alike. The group was accompanied by armed, ceremonially dressed proctors and a triad of martial servitors. Their articulation points and sensor apertures were lathered in protective sterile grease, to guard against rot.

Though they tried to hide it, Naqi could tell that the VIPs were nervous. They moved a touch too confidently, making their trepidation all the more evident.

The red door symbol at the end of the gangway pulsed brighter and a section of the hull puckered open. Naqi squinted, but even through the binoculars it was difficult to make out anything other than red-lit gloom. Tak Thonburi and his officials stiffened. A sketchy figure emerged from the shuttle, lingered on the threshold and then stepped with immense slowness into full sunlight.

The crowd's reaction—and to some extent Naqi's own—was double-edged. There was a moment of relief that the messages from orbit had not been outright lies. Then there was an equally brief tang of shock at the actual appearance of Captain Moreau. The man was at least a third taller than anyone Naqi had ever seen in her life, and yet commensurately thinner, his seemingly brittle frame contained within a jade-coloured mechanical exoskeleton of ornate design. The skeleton lent his movements something of the lethargic quality of a stick insect.

Tak Thonburi was the first to speak. His amplified voice boomed out across the six arms of Umingmaktok, echoing off the curved surfaces of the multiple vacuum bladders that held the city aloft. Float-cams jostled for the best camera angle, swarming around him like pollen-crazed bees.

"Captain Moreau . . . May I introduce myself? I am Tak Thonburi, mayor of Umingmaktok Snowflake City and incumbent chairman of the Snowflake Council of All Turquoise. It is my pleasure to welcome you, your crew and passengers to Umingmaktok, and to Turquoise itself. You have my word that we will do all in our power to make your visit as pleasant as possible."

The Ultra moved closer to the official. The door to the shuttle remained open behind him. Naqi's binocs picked out red hologram serpents on the jade limbs of the skeleton. The Ultra's own voice boomed at least as loud, but emanated from the shuttle rather than Umingmaktok's public address system.

"People of greenish-blue . . ." The captain hesitated, then tapped one of the stalks projecting from his helmet. "People of Turquoise . . . Chairman Thonburi . . . Thank you for your welcome, and for your kind permission to assume orbit. We have accepted it with gratitude. You have my word . . . as captain of the lighthugger *Voice of Evening* . . . that we will abide by the strict terms of your generous offer of hospitality." His mouth continued to move even during the pauses, Naqi noticed: the translation system was lagging. "You have my additional guarantee that no harm will be done to your world, and Turquoise law will be presumed to apply to the occupants . . . of all bodies and vessels in your atmosphere. All traffic between my ship and your world will be subject to the authorisation of the Snowflake Council, and any member of the council will—under the . . . auspices of the council—be permitted to visit the *Voice of Evening* at any time, subject to the availability of a . . . suitable conveyance."

The captain paused and looked at Tak Thonburi expectantly. The mayor wiped a nervous hand across his brow, smoothing his kiss-curl into obedience.

"Thank you . . . Captain." Tak Thonburi's eyes flashed to the other members of the reception party. "Your terms are of course more than acceptable. You have my word that we will do all in our power to assist you and your crew, and that we will do our utmost to ensure that the forthcoming negotiations of trade proceed in an equable manner . . . and in such a way that both parties will be satisfied upon their conclusion."

The captain did not respond immediately, allowing an uncomfortable pause to draw itself out. Naqi wondered if it was really the fault of the software, or whether Moreau was just playing on Tak Thonburi's evident nervousness.

"Of course," the Ultra said, finally. "Of course. My sentiments entirely . . . Chairman Thonburi. Perhaps now wouldn't be a bad time to introduce my guests?"

On his cue three new figures emerged from the *Voice of Evening*'s shuttle. Unlike the Ultra they could almost have passed for ordinary citizens of Turquoise. There were two men and one woman, all of approximately normal height and build. They all had long hair, tied back in elaborate clasps. Their clothes were brightly coloured, fashioned from many separate fabrics of yellow, orange, red and russet, and various permutations of the same warm sunset shades. The clothes billowed around them, rippling in the light afternoon breeze. All three members of the party wore silver jewellery, far more than was customary on Turquoise. They wore it on their fingers, in their hair, hanging from their ears.

The woman was the first to speak, her voice booming out from the shuttle's PA system.

"Thank you, Captain Moreau. Thank you also, Chairman Thonburi. We are delighted to be here. I am Amesha Crane, and I speak for the Vahishta Foundation. Vahishta's a modest scientific organisation with its origins in the cometary prefectures of the Haven Demarchy. Lately we have been expanding our realm of interest to encompass other solar systems, such as this one." Crane gestured at the two men who had accompanied her from the shuttle. "My associates are Simon Matsubara and Rafael Weir. There are another seventeen of us aboard the shuttle. Captain Moreau carried us here as paying passengers aboard the *Voice of Evening*, and as such Vahishta gladly accepts all the terms already agreed upon."

Tak Thonburi looked even less sure of himself. "Of course. We welcome your . . . interest. A scientific organisation, did you say?"

"One with a special interest in the study of the Jugglers," Amesha Crane answered. She was the most strikingly attractive member of the trio, with fine cheekbones and a wide, sensual mouth that always seemed on the point of smiling or laughing. Naqi felt that the woman was sharing something with her, something private and amusing. Doubtless everyone in the crowd felt the same vague sense of complicity.

Crane continued: "We have no Pattern Jugglers in our own system, but that hasn't stopped us from focussing our research on them, collating the data available from the worlds where Juggler studies are on-going. We've been doing this for decades, sifting inference and theory, guesswork and intuition. Haven't we, Simon?"

The man nodded. He had sallow skin and a fixed quizzical expression.

"No two Juggler worlds are precisely alike," Simon Matsubara said, his voice as clear and confident as the woman's. "And no two Juggler worlds have been studied by precisely the same mix of human socio-political factions. That means that we have a great many variables to take into consideration. Despite that, we believe we have identified similarities that may have been overlooked by the individual research teams. They may even be very important similarities, with repercussions for wider humanity. But in the absence of our own Jugglers, it is difficult to test our theories. That's where Turquoise comes in."

The other man—Naqi recalled his name as Rafael Weir—began to speak. "Turquoise has been largely isolated from the rest of human space for the better part of two centuries."

"We're aware of this," said Jotah Sivaraksa. It was the first time any member of the entourage other than Tak Thonburi had spoken. To Naqi he sounded irritated, though he was doing his best to hide it.

"You don't share your findings with the other Juggler worlds," said Amesha Crane. "Nor—to the best of our knowledge—do you intercept their cultural transmissions. The consequence is that your research on the Jugglers has been untainted by any outside considerations—the latest fashionable theory, the latest groundbreaking technique. You prefer to work in scholarly isolation."

"We're an isolationist world in other respects," Tak Thonburi said. "Believe it or not, it actually rather suits us."

"Quite," Crane said, with a hint of sharpness. "But the point remains. Your Jugglers are an uncontaminated resource. When a swimmer enters the ocean, their own memories and personality may be absorbed into the Juggler sea. The prejudices and preconceptions that swimmer carries inevitably enter the ocean in some shape or form—diluted, confused, but nonetheless present in some form. And when the next swimmer enters the sea, and opens their mind to communion, what they perceive— what they *ken*, in your own terminology—is irrevocably tainted by the preconceptions introduced by the previous swimmer. They may experience something that confirms their deepest suspicion about the nature of the Jugglers—but they can't be sure that they aren't simply picking up the mental echoes of the last swimmer, or the swimmer before that."

Jotah Sivaraksa nodded. "What you say is undoubtedly true. But we've had just as many cycles of fashionable theory as anyone else. Even within Umingmaktok there are a dozen different research teams, each with their own outlook."

"We accept that," Crane said, with an audible sigh. "But the degree of contamination is slight compared to other worlds. Vahishta lacks the resources for a trip to a previously unvisited Juggler world, so the next best thing is to visit one that has suffered the smallest degree of human cultural pollution. Turquoise fits the bill."

Tak Thonburi held the moment before responding, playing to the crowd again. Naqi rather admired the way he did it.

"Good. I'm very . . . pleased . . . to hear it. And might I ask just what it is about our ocean that we can offer you?"

"Nothing except the ocean itself," said Amesha Crane. "We simply wish to join you in its study. If you will allow it, members of the Vahishta Foundation will collaborate with native Turquoise scientists and study teams. They will shadow them and offer interpretation or advice when requested. Nothing more than that."

"That's all?"

Crane smiled. "That's all. It's not as if we're asking the world, is it?"

Naqi remained in Umingmaktok for three days after the arrival, visiting friends and taking care of business for the Moat. The newcomers had departed, taking their shuttle to one of the other snowflake cities—Prachuap or the recently married Qaanaaq-Pangnirtung, perhaps—where a smaller but no less worthy group of city dignitaries would welcome Captain Moreau and his passengers.

In Umingmaktok the booths and bunting were packed away and normal business resumed. Litter abounded. Worm dealers did brisk business, as they always did during times of mild gloom. There were far fewer transport craft moored to the arms, and no sign at all of the intense media presence of a few days before. Tourists had gone back to their home cities, and the children were safely back in school. Between meetings Naqi sat in the midday shade of half-empty restaurants and bars, observing the same puzzled disappointment in every face she encountered. Deep down she felt it herself. For two years they had been free to imprint every possible fantasy on the approaching ship. Even if the newcomers had arrived with less than benign intent, there would still have been something interesting to talk about; the possibility, however remote, that one's own life might be about to become drastically more exciting.

But now none of that was going to happen. Undoubtedly Naqi would be involved with the visitors at some point, allowing them to visit the Moat or one of the outlying research zones she managed, but there would be nothing life-changing.

She thought back to that night with Mina, when they had heard the news. Everything had changed then. Mina had died, and Naqi had found herself taking her sister's role in the Moat. She had risen to the challenge and promotions had followed with gratifying swiftness, until she was in effective charge of the Moat's entire scientific program. But that sense of closure she had yearned for was still absent. The men she had slept with—men who were almost always swimmers—had never provided it, and by turns they had each lost patience with her, realising that they were less important to her as people than what they represented, as connections to the sea. It had been months since her last romance, and once Naqi had recognised the way her own subconscious was drawing her back to the sea, she had drawn away from contact with swimmers. She had been drifting since then, daring to hope that the newcomers would allow her some measure of tranquillity.

But the newcomers had not supplied it.

She supposed she would have to find it elsewhere.

On the fourth day Naqi returned to the Moat on a high-speed dirigible. She arrived near sunset, dropping down from high altitude to see the structure winking back at her, a foreshortened ellipse of gray-white ceramic lying against the sea like some vast discarded bracelet. From horizon to horizon there were several Juggler nodes visible, webbed together by the faintest of filaments—to Naqi they looked like motes of ink spreading into blotting paper—but there were also smaller dabs of green within the Moat itself.

The structure was twenty kilometres wide and now it was nearly finished. Only a narrow channel remained where the two ends of the bracelet did not quite meet: a hundred-metre-wide shear-sided aperture flanked on either side by tall, ramshackle towers of accommodation modules, equipment sheds and construction cranes. To the north, strings of heavy cargo dirigibles ferried processed ore and ceramic cladding from Narathiwat atoll, lowering it down to the construction teams on the Moat.

They had been working here for nearly twenty years. The hundred metres of the Moat that projected above the water was only one tenth of the full structure—a kilometre high ring resting on the seabed. In a matter of months the gap—little more than a notch in the top of the Moat—would be sealed, closed off by immense hermetically tight sea-doors. The process would necessarily be slow and delicate, for what was being attempted here was not simply the closing-off of part of the sea. The Moat was an attempt to isolate a part of the living ocean, sealing off a community of Pattern Juggler organisms within its impervious ceramic walls.

The high-speed dirigible swung low over the aperture. The thick green waters streaming through the cut had the phlegmatic consistency of congealing blood. Thick, ropy tendrils permitted information transfer between the external sea and the cluster of small nodes within the Moat. Swimmers were constantly present, either inside or outside the Moat, *kenning* the state of the sea and establishing that the usual Juggler processes continued unabated.

The dirigible docked with one of the two flanking towers.

Naqi stepped out, back into the hectic corridors and office spaces of the project building. It felt distinctly odd to be back on absolutely firm ground. Although one was seldom aware of it, Umingmaktok was never quite still, no snowflake city or airship ever was. But she would get used to it; in a few hours she would be immersed in her work, having to think of a dozen different things at once, finessing solution pathways, balancing budgets against quality, dealing with personality clashes and minor turf wars, and perhaps—if she was very lucky—managing an hour or two of pure research. Aside from the science none of it was particularly challenging, but it kept her mind off other things. And after a few days of that, the arrival of the visitors would begin to seem like a bizarre, irrelevant interlude in an otherwise monotonous dream. She supposed that two years ago she would have been grateful for that. Life could indeed continue much as she had always imagined it would.

But when she arrived at her office there was a message from Dr Sivaraksa. He needed to speak to her urgently.

Dr Jotah Sivaraksa's office on the Moat was a good deal less spacious than his quarters in Umingmaktok, but the view was superb. His accommodation was perched halfway up one of the towers that flanked the cut through the Moat, buttressed out from the main mass of prefabricated modules like a partially opened desk drawer. Dr Sivaraksa was writing notes when she arrived. For long moments Naqi lingered at the sloping window, watching the construction activity hundreds of metres below. Railed machines and helmeted workers toiled on the flat upper surface of the Moat, moving raw materials and equipment to the assembly sites. Above, the sky was a perfect cobalt blue, marred now and then by the passing, green-stained hull of a cargo dirigible. The sea beyond the Moat had the dimpled texture of expensive leather.

Dr Sivaraksa cleared his throat, and when Naqi turned, he gestured at the vacant seat on the opposite side of his desk.

"Life treating you well?"

"Can't complain, sir."

"And work?"

"No particular problems that I'm aware of."

"Good. Good." Sivaraksa made a quick, cursive annotation in the notebook he had opened on his desk, then slid it beneath the smoky gray cube of a paperweight. "How long has it been now?"

"Since what, sir?"

"Since your sister . . . Since Mina . . ." He seemed unable to complete the sentence, substituting a spiralling gesture made with his index finger. His finely boned hands were marbled with veins of olive green.

Naqi eased into her seat. "Two years, sir."

"And you're . . . over it?"

"I wouldn't exactly say I'm over it, no. But life goes on, like they say. Actually I was hoping . . ." Naqi had been about to tell him how she had imagined the arrival of the visitors would close that chapter. But she doubted she would be able to convey her feelings in a way Dr Sivaraksa would understand. "Well, I was hoping I'd have put it all behind me by now."

"I knew another conformal, you know. Fellow from Gjoa. Made it into the elite swimmer corps before anyone had the foggiest idea. . . ."

"It's never been proven that Mina was conformal, sir."

"No, but the signs were there, weren't they? To one degree or another we're all subject to symbolic invasion by the ocean's microorganisms. But conformals show an unusual degree of susceptibility. On one hand it's as if their own bodies actively invite the invasion, shutting down the usual inflammatory or foreign cell rejection mechanisms. On the other, the ocean seems to tailor its messengers for maximum effectiveness, as if the Jugglers have selected a specific target they wish to absorb. Mina had very strong fungal patterns, did she not?"

"I've seen worse." Naqi said, which was not entirely a lie.

"But not, I suspect, in anyone who ever attempted to commune. I understand you had ambitions to join the swimmer corps yourself?"

"Before all that happened."

"I understand. And now?"

Naqi had never told anyone that she had joined Mina in the swimming incident. The truth was that even if she had not been present at the time of Mina's death, her encounter with the rogue mind would have put her off entering the ocean for life.

"It isn't for me. That's all."

Jotah Sivaraksa nodded gravely. "A wise choice. Aptitude or not, you'd have almost certainly been filtered out of the swimmer corps. A direct genetic connection to a conformal—even an unproven conformal—would be too much of a risk."

"That's what I assumed, sir."

"Does it . . . trouble you. Naqi?"

She was wearying of this. She had work to do—deadlines to meet that Sivaraksa himself had imposed.

"Does what trouble me?"

He nodded at the sea. Now that the play of light had shifted minutely, it looked less like dimpled leather than a sheet of beaten bronze. "The thought that Mina might still be out there . . . in some sense."

"It might trouble me if I were a swimmer, sir. Other than that . . . No. I can't say that it does. My sister died. That's all that mattered."

"Swimmers have occasionally reported encountering . . . minds . . . essences . . . of the lost, Naqi. The impressions are often acute. The conformed leave their mark on the ocean at a deeper, more permanent level than the impressions left behind by mere swimmers. One senses that there must be a purpose to this."

"That wouldn't be for me to speculate, sir."

"No." He glanced down at the compad and then tapped his forefinger against his upper lip. "No. Of course not. Well, to the matter at hand . . ."

She interrupted him. "You swam once, sir?"

"Yes. Yes, I did." The moment stretched. She was about to say something—anything—when Sivaraksa continued. "I had to stop for medical reasons. Otherwise I suppose I'd have been in the swimmer corps for a good deal longer, at least until my hands started turning green."

"What was it like?"

"Astonishing. Beyond anything I'd expected."

"Did they change you?"

At that he smiled. "I never thought that they did, until now. After my last swim I went through all the usual neurological and psychological tests. They found no anomalies; no indications that the Jugglers had imprinted any hints of alien personality or rewired my mind to think in an alien way."

Sivaraksa reached across the desk and held up the smoky cube that Naqi had taken for a paperweight. "This came down from the *Voice of Evening*. Examine it."

Naqi peered into the milky gray depths of the cube. Now that she saw it closely she realised that there were things embedded within the translucent matrix. There were chains of unfamiliar symbols, intersecting at right angles. They resembled the complex white scaffolding of a building.

"What is it?"

"Mathematics. Actually, a mathematical argument—a proof, if you like. Conventional mathematical notation—no matter how arcane—has evolved so that it can be written down, on a two-dimensional surface, like paper or a readout. This is a three-dimensional syntax, liberated from that constraint. It's enormously richer, enormously more elegant." The cube tumbled in Sivaraksa's hand. He was smiling.

"No one could make head or tail of it. Yet when I looked at it for the first time I nearly dropped it in shock. It made perfect sense to me. Not only did I understand the theorem, but I also understood the point of it. It's a joke, Naqi. A pun. This mathematics is rich enough to embody humour. And understanding *that* is the gift they left me. It was sitting in my mind for twenty-eight years, like an egg waiting to hatch."

Abruptly, Sivaraksa placed the cube back on the table.

"Something's come up," he said.

From somewhere came the distant, prolonged thunder of a dirigible discharging its cargo of processed ore. It must have been one of the last consignments.

"Something, sir?"

"They've asked to see the Moat."

"They?"

"Crane and her Vahishta mob. They've requested an oversight of all major scientific centres on Turquoise, and naturally enough we're on the list. They'll be visiting us, spending a couple of days seeing what we've achieved."

"I'm not too surprised that they've asked to visit, sir."

"No, but I was hoping we'd have a few months grace. We don't. They'll be here in a week."

"That's not necessarily a problem for us, is it?"

"It mustn't become one," Sivaraksa said. "I'm putting you in charge of the visit, Naqi. You'll be the interface between Crane's group and the Moat. That's quite a responsibility, you understand. A mistake—the tiniest gaff—could undermine our standing with the Snowflake Council." He nodded at the compad. "Our budgetary position is tenuous. Frankly, I'm in Tak Thonburi's lap. We can't afford any embarrassments."

"No sir."

She certainly did understand. The job was a poisoned chalice, or at the least a chalice with a strong potential to become poisoned. If she succeeded—if the visit went smoothly, with no hitches—Sivaraksa could still take much of the credit for it. If it went wrong, on the other hand, the fault would be categorically hers.

"One more thing." Sivaraksa reached under his desk and produced a brochure that he slid across to her. The brochure was marked with a prominent silver snowflake motif. It was sealed with red foil. "Open it; you have clearance."

"What is it, sir?"

"A security report on our new friends. One of them has been behaving a bit oddly. You'll need to keep an eye on him."

For inscrutable reasons of their own, the liaison committee had decided she would be introduced to Amesha Crane and her associates a day before the official visit, when the party was still in Sukhothai-Sanikiluaq. The journey there took the better part of two days, even allowing for the legs she took by high-speed dirigible or the ageing, unreliable trans-atoll railway line between Narathiwat and Cape Dorset. She arrived at Sukhothai-Sanikiluaq in a velvety purple twilight, catching the tail end of a fireworks display. The two snowflake cities had only been married three weeks, so the arrival of the off-worlders was an excellent pretext for prolonging the celebrations. Naqi watched the fireworks from a civic landing stage perched halfway up Sukhothai's core, starbursts and cataracts of scarlet, indigo and intense emerald green brightening the sky above the vacuum bladders. The colours reminded her of the organisms that she and Mina had seen in the wake of their airship. The recollection left her suddenly sad and drained, convinced that she had made a terrible mistake by accepting this assignment.

"Naqi?"

It was Tak Thonburi, coming out to meet her on the balcony. They had already exchanged messages during the journey. He was dressed in full civic finery and appeared more than a little drunk.

"Chairman Thonburi."

"Good of you to come here, Naqi." She watched his eyes map her contours with scientific rigour, lingering here and there around regions of particular interest. "Enjoying the show?"

"You certainly seem to be, sir."

"Yes, yes. Always had a thing about fireworks." He pressed a drink into her hand and together they watched the display come to its mildly disappointing conclusion. There was a lull then, but Naqi noticed that the spectators on the other balconies were reluctant to leave, as if waiting for something. Presently a stunning display of three-dimensional images appeared, generated by powerful projection apparatus in the *Voice of Evening*'s shuttle. Above Sukhothai-Sanikiluaq, Chinese dragons as large as mountains fought epic battles. Sea monsters convulsed and writhed in the night. Celestial citadels burned. Hosts of purple-winged fiery angels fell from the heavens in tightly knit squadrons, clutching arcane instruments of music or punishment.

A marbled giant rose from the sea, as if woken from some aeonslong slumber.

It was very, very impressive.

"Bastards," Thonburi muttered.

"Sir?"

"Bastards," he said, louder this time. "We know they're better than us. But do they have to keep reminding us?"

He ushered her into the reception chamber where the Vahishta visitors were being entertained. The return indoors had a magical sharpening effect on his senses. Naqi suspected that the ability to turn drunkenness on and off like a switch must be one of the most hallowed of diplomatic skills.

He leaned toward her, confidentially.

"Did Jotah mention any—"

"Security considerations, chairman? Yes, I think I got the message."

"It's probably nothing, only . . ."

"I understand. Better safe than sorry."

He winked, touching a finger against the side of his nose. "Precisely."

The interior was bright after the balcony. Twenty Vahishta delegates were standing in a huddle near the middle of the room. The captain was absent—little had been seen of Moreau since the shuttle's arrival in Umingmaktok—but the delegates were talking to a clutch of local bigwigs, none of whom Naqi recognised. Thonburi steered her into the fray, oblivious to the conversations that were taking place.

"Ladies and gentlemen . . . Might I introduce Naqi Okpik? Naqi oversees the scientific program on the Moat. She'll be your host for the visit to our project."

"Ah, Naqi." Amesha Crane leaned over and shook her hand. "A pleasure. I just read your papers on information propagation methods in class-three nodes. Erudite."

"They were collaborative works," Naqi said. "I really can't take too much credit."

"Ah, but you can. All of you can. You achieved those findings with the minimum of resources, and you made very creative use of some extremely simplistic numerical methods."

"We muddle through," Naqi said.

Crane nodded enthusiastically. "It must give you a great sense of satisfaction."

Tak Thonburi said: "It's a philosophy, that's all. We conduct our science in isolation, and we enjoy only limited communication with other colonies. As a social model it has its disadvantages, but it means we aren't forever jealous of what they're achieving on some other world that happens to be a few decades ahead of us because of an accident of history or location. We think that the benefits outweigh the costs."

"Well, it seems to work," Crane said. "You have a remarkably stable society here, Chairman. Verging on the utopian, some might say."

Tak Thonburi caressed his cowlick. "We can't complain."

"Nor can we," said the man Naqi recognised as quizzical-faced Simon Matsubara. "If you hadn't enforced this isolation, your own Juggler research would have been as hopelessly compromised as everywhere else."

"But the isolation isn't absolute, is it?"

The voice was quiet, but commanding.

Naqi followed the voice to the speaker. It was Rafael Weir, the man who had been identified as a possible security risk. Of the three who had emerged from Moreau's shuttle he was the least remarkable looking, possessing the kind of amorphous face that would allow him to blend in with almost any crowd. Had her attention not been drawn to him, he would have been the last one she noticed. He was not unattractive, but there was nothing particularly striking or charismatic about his looks. According to the security dossier, he had made a number of efforts to break away from the main party of the delegation while they had been visiting research stations. They could have been accidents—one or two other party members had become separated at other times—but it was beginning to look a little too deliberate.

"No," Tak Thonburi answered. "We're not absolute isolationists, or we'd never have given permission for the *Voice of Evening* to assume orbit around Turquoise. But we don't solicit passing traffic either. Our welcome is as warm as anyone's—we hope—but we don't encourage visitors."

"Are we the first to visit, since your settlement?" Weir asked.

"The first starship?" Tak Thonburi shook his head. "No. But it's been a number of years since the last one."

"Which was?"

"The *Pelican in Impiety*, a century ago."

"An amusing coincidence, then," Weir said.

Tak Thonburi narrowed his eyes. "Coincidence?"

"The *Pelican*'s next port of call was Haven, if I'm not mistaken. It was *en route* from Zion, but it made a trade stopover around Turquoise." He smiled. "And we have come from Haven, so history already binds our two worlds, albeit tenuously."

Thonburi's eyes narrowed. He was trying to read Weir and evidently failing. "We don't talk about the *Pelican* too much. There were technical benefits—vacuum bladder production methods, information technologies . . . but there was also a fair bit of unpleasantness. The wounds haven't entirely healed."

"Let's hope this visit will be remembered more fondly," Weir said.

Amesha Crane nodded, fingering one of the items of silver jewellery in her hair. "Agreed. All the indications are favourable, at the very least. We've arrived at a most auspicious time." She turned to Naqi. "I find the Moat project fascinating, and I'm sure I speak for the entire Vahishta delegation. I may as well tell you that no one else has attempted anything remotely like it. Tell me, scientist to scientist. Do you honestly think it will work?"

"We won't know until we try," Naqi said. Any other answer would have been politically hazardous: too much optimism and the politicians would have started asking just why the expensive project was needed in the first place. Too much pessimism and they would ask exactly the same question.

"Fascinating, all the same." Crane's expression was knowing, as if she understood Naqi's predicament perfectly. "I understand that you're very close to running the first experiment?"

"Given that it's taken us twenty years to get this far, yes—we're close. But we're still looking at three to four months, maybe longer. It's not something we want to rush."

"That's a great pity," Crane said, turning now to Thonburi. "In three to four months we might be on our way. Still, it would have been something to see, wouldn't it?"

Thonburi leaned toward Naqi. The alcohol on his breath was a fog of cheap vinegar. "I suppose there wouldn't be any chance of accelerating the schedule, would there?"

"Out of the question, I'm afraid," Naqi said

"That's just too bad," said Amesha Crane. Still toying with her jewellery, she turned to the others. "But we mustn't let a little detail like that spoil our visit, must we?"

They returned to the Moat using the *Voice of Evening*'s shuttle. There was another civic reception to be endured upon arrival, but it was a much smaller affair than the one in Sukhothai-Sanikiluaq. Dr Jotah Sivaraksa was there, of course, and once Naqi had dealt with the business of introducing the party to him she was able to relax for the first time in many hours, melting into the corner of the room and watching the interaction between visitors and locals with a welcome sense of detachment. Naqi was tired and had difficulty keeping her eyes open. She saw everything through a sleepy blur, the delegates surrounding Sivaraksa like pillars of fire, the fabric of their costumes rippling with the slightest movement, reds and russets and chrome yellows dancing like sparks or sheets of flame. Naqi left as soon as it was polite to do so, and when she reached her bed she fell immediately into troubled sleep, dreaming of squadrons of purple-winged angels falling from the skies and of the great giant rising from the depths, clawing the seaweed and kelp of ages from his eyes.

In the morning she awoke without really feeling refreshed. Anaemic light pierced the slats on her window. She was not due to meet the delegates again for another three or four hours, so there was time to turn over and try and catch some proper sleep. But she knew from experience that it would be futile.

She got up. To her surprise, there was a new message on her console from Jotah Sivaraksa. What, she wondered, did he have to say to her that he could not have said at the reception, or later this morning?

She opened the message and read.

"Sivaraksa," she said to herself. "Are you insane? It can't be done."

The message informed her that there had been a change of plan. The first closure of the sea-doors would be attempted in two days, while the delegates were still on the Moat.

It was pure madness. They were months away from that. Yes, the doors could be closed—the basic machinery for doing that was in place—and yes, the doors could be hermetically tight for at least one hundred hours after closure. But nothing else was ready. The sensitive monitoring equipment, the failsafe subsystems, the backups . . . None of that would be in place and operational for many weeks. Then there was supposed to be at least six weeks of testing, slowly building up to the event itself . . .

To do it in two days made no sense at all, except to a politician. At best all they would learn was whether or not the Jugglers had remained inside the Moat when the door was closed. They would learn nothing about how the data flow was terminated, or how the internal connections between the nodes adapted to the loss of contact with the wider ocean.

Naqi swore and hit the console. She wanted to blame Sivaraksa, but she knew that was unfair. Sivaraksa had to keep the politicians happy, or the whole project would be endangered. He was just doing what he had to do, and he almost certainly liked it even less than she did.

Naqi pulled on shorts and a T-shirt and found some coffee in one of the adjoining mess rooms. The Moat was deserted, quiet except for the womblike throb of generators and air-circulation systems. A week ago it would have been as noisy now as at any other time of day, for the construction had continued around the clock. But the heavy work was done now; the last ore dirigible had arrived while Naqi was away. All that remained was the relatively light work of completing the Moat's support subsystems. Despite what Sivaraksa had said in his message there was really very little additional work needed to close the doors. Even two days of frantic activity would make no difference to the usefulness of the stunt.

When she had judged her state of mind to be calmer, she returned to her room and called Sivaraksa. It was still far too early, but seeing as the bastard had already ruined her day she saw no reason not to reciprocate.

"Naqi." His silver hair was a sleep-matted mess on the screen. "I take it you got my message?"

"You didn't think I'd take it lying down, did you?"

"I don't like it anymore than you do. But I see the political necessity."

"Do you? This isn't like switching a light on and off, Jotah." His eyes widened at the familiarity, but she pressed on regardless. "If we screw up the first time, there might never be a second chance. The Jugglers have to play along. Without them all you've got here is a very expensive midocean refuelling point. Does that make political sense to you?"

He pushed green fingers through the mess of his hair. "Have some breakfast, get some fresh air, then come to my office. We'll talk about it then."

"I've had breakfast, thanks very much."

"Then get the fresh air. You'll feel better for it." Sivaraksa rubbed his eyes. "You're not very happy about this, are you?"

"It's bloody madness. And the worst thing is you know it."

"And my hands are tied. Ten years from now, Naqi, you'll be sitting in my place having to make similar decisions. And ten to one there'll be some idealistic young scientist telling you what a hopeless piece of deadwood you are." He managed a weary smile. "Mark my words, because I want you to remember this conversation when it happens."

"There's nothing I can do to stop this, is there?"

"I'll be in my office in . . ." Sivaraksa glanced at a clock. "Thirty minutes. We can talk about it properly then."

"There's nothing to talk about."

But even as she said that she knew she sounded petulant and inflexible. Sivaraksa was right: it was impossible to manage a project as complex and expensive as the Moat without a degree of compromise.

Naqi decided that Sivaraksa's advice—at least the part about getting some fresh air—was worth heeding. She descended a helical staircase until she reached the upper surface of the Moat's ring-shaped wall. The concrete was cold beneath her bare feet and a pleasant cool breeze caressed her legs and arms. The sky had brightened on one horizon. Machines and supplies were arranged neatly on the upper surface ready for use, although further construction would be halted until the delegates completed their visit. Stepping nimbly over the tracks, conduits and cables that crisscrossed each other on the upper surface, Naqi walked to the side. A high railing, painted in high-visibility rot-resistant sealer, fenced the inner part of the Moat. She touched it to make sure it was dry, then leaned over. The distant side of the Moat was a colourless thread, twenty kilometres away, like a very low wall of sea mist.

What could be done in two days? Nothing. Or at least nothing compared to what had always been planned. But if the new schedule was a *fait accompli*—and that was the message she was getting from Sivaraksa—then it was her responsibility to find a way to squeeze some scientific return from the event. She looked down at the cut, and at the many spindly gantries and catwalks that spanned the aperture or hung some way toward the centre of the Moat. Perhaps if she arranged for some standard-issue probes to be prepared today, the type dropped from dirigibles . . .

Naqi's eyes darted around, surveying fixtures and telemetry conduits.

It would be hard work to get them in place in time, and even harder to get them patched into some kind of real-time acquisition system. . . . But it *was* doable, just barely. The data quality would be laughable compared to the supersensitive instruments that were going to be installed over the next few months. . . . But crude was a lot better than nothing at all.

She laughed, aloud. An hour ago she would have stuck pins into herself rather than collaborate in this kind of fiasco.

Naqi walked along the railing until she reached a pair of pillar-mounted binoculars. They were smeared with rot-protection. She wiped the lens and eyepieces clean with a rag that was tied to the pedestal, then swung the binoculars in a slow arc, panning across the dark circle of water trapped within the Moat. Only vague patches of what Naqi would have called open water were visible. The rest was either a verdant porridge of Juggler organisms, or fully grown masses of organised floating matter, linked together by trunks and veins of the same green biomass. The latest estimate was that there were three small nodes within the ring. The smell was atrocious, but that was an excellent sign as well: it correlated strongly with the density of organisms in the nodes. She had experienced that smell many times, but it never failed to slam her back to that morning when Mina had died.

As much as the Pattern Jugglers "knew" anything, they were surely aware of what was planned here. They had drunk the minds of the swimmers who had already entered the sea near or within the Moat, and not one of those swimmers was ignorant of the project's ultimate purpose. It was possible that that knowledge simply couldn't be parsed into a form the aliens would understand, but Naqi considered that unlikely: the closure of the Moat would be about as stark a concept as one could imagine. If nothing else, geometry was the one thing the Jugglers did understand. And yet the aliens chose to remain within the closing Moat, hinting that they would tolerate the final closure that would seal them off from the rest of the ocean.

Perhaps they were not impressed. Perhaps they knew that the event would not rob them of every channel of communication, but only the chemical medium of the ocean. Sprites and other airborne organisms would still be able to cross the barrier. It was impossible to tell. The only way to know was to complete the experiment—to close the massive sea-doors—and see what happened.

She leaned back, taking her eyes from the binoculars.

Now Naqi saw something unexpected. It was a glint of hard white light, scudding across the water within the Moat.

Naqi squinted, but still she could not make out the object. She swung the binoculars hard around, got her eyes behind them and then zigzagged until something flashed through the field of view. She backed up and locked onto it.

It was a boat, and there was someone in it.

She keyed in the image zoom/stabilise function and the craft swelled to clarity across a clear kilometre of sea. The craft was a ceramic-hulled vessel of the type that the swimmer teams used, five or six metres from bow to stem. The person sat behind a curved spray shield, their hands on the handlebars of the control pillar. An inboard thruster propelled the boat without ever touching water.

The figure was difficult to make out, but the billowing orange clothes left no room for doubt. It was one of the Vahishta delegates. And Naqi fully expected it to be Rafael Weir.

He was headed toward the closest node.

For an agonising few moments she did not know what to do. He was going to attempt to swim, she thought, just like she and Mina had done. And he would be no better prepared for the experience. She had to stop him, somehow. He would reach the node in only a few minutes.

Naqi sprinted back to the tower, breathless when she arrived. She reached a communications post and tried to find the right channel for the boat. But either she was doing it wrong or Weir had sabotaged the radio. What next? Technically, there was a security presence on the Moat, especially given the official visit. But what did the security goons know about chasing boats? All their training was aimed at dealing with internal crises, and none of them were competent to go anywhere near an active node.

She called them anyway, alerting them to what had happened. Then she called Sivaraksa, telling him the same news. "I think it's Weir," she said. "I'm going to try and stop him."

"Naqi . . ." he said warningly.

"This is my responsibility, Jotah. Let me handle it."

Naqi ran back outside again. The closest elevator down to sea level was out of service; the next one was a kilometre farther around the ring. She didn't have that much time. Instead she jogged along the line of railings until she reached a break that admitted entry to a staircase that descended the steep inner wall of the Moat. The steps and handrails had been helpfully greased with antirot, just to make her descent more treacherous. There were five hundred steps down to sea level but she took them two or three at a time, sliding down the handrails until she reached the grilled platforms where the stairways reversed direction. All the while she watched the tiny white speck of the boat, seemingly immobile now that it was so far away, but undoubtedly narrowing the distance to the node with each minute. As she worked her way down she had plenty of time to think about what was going through the delegate's head. She was sure now that it was Weir. It did not really surprise her that he wanted to swim: it was what everyone who studied the Jugglers yearned for. But why make this unofficial attempt now when a little gentle persuasion would have made it possible anyway? Given Tak Thonburi's eagerness to please the delegates, it would not have been beyond the bounds of possibility for a swimming expedition to be organised. . . . The corps would have protested, but just like Naqi they would have been given a forceful lesson in the refined art of political compromise.

But evidently Weir hadn't been prepared to wait. It all made sense, at any rate: the times when he had dodged away from the party before must have all been abortive attempts to reach the Jugglers. But only now had he seen his opportunity.

Naqi reached the water level, where jetties floated on ceramic-sheathed pontoons. Most of the boats were suspended out of the water on cradles, to save their hulls from unnecessary degradation. Fortunately there was an emergency rescue boat already afloat. Its formerly white hull had the flaking, pea-green scab patterning of advanced rot, but it still had a dozen or so hours of seaworthiness in it. Naqi jumped aboard, released the boat from its moorings and fired up the thruster. In a moment she was racing away from the jetty, away from the vast stained edifice of the Moat itself. She steered a course through the least viscous stretches of water, avoiding conspicuous rafts of green matter.

She peered ahead, through the boat's spray-drenched shield. It had been easy to keep track of Weir's boat when she had been a hundred metres higher, but now she kept losing him behind swells or miniature islands of Juggler matter. After a minute or so she gave up trying to follow the boat, and instead diverted her concentration to finding the quickest route to the node.

She flipped on the radio. "Jotah? This is Naqi. I'm in the water, closing on Weir."

There was a pause, a crackle, then: "What's the status?"

She had to shout over the abrasive *thump, thump, thump* of the boat, even though the thruster was nearly silent.

"I'll reach the node in four or five minutes. Can't see Weir, but I don't think it matters."

"We can see him. He's still headed for the node."

"Good. Can you spare some more boats, in case he decides to make a run for another node?"

"They'll be leaving in a minute or so. I'm waking everyone I can."

"What about the other delegates?"

Sivaraksa did not answer her immediately. "Most are still asleep. I have Amesha Crane and Simon Matsubara in my office, however."

"Let me speak to them."

"Just a moment," he said, after the same brief hesitation.

"Crane here," said the woman.

"I think I'm chasing Weir. Can you confirm that?"

"He isn't accounted for," she told Naqi. "But it'll be a few minutes until we can be certain it's him."

"I'm not expecting a surprise. Weir already had a question mark over him, Amesha. We were waiting for him to try something."

"Were you?" Perhaps it was her imagination, but Crane sounded genuinely surprised. "Why? What had he done?"

"You don't know?"

"No . . ." Crane trailed off.

"He was one of us," Matsubara said. "A good . . . delegate. We had no reason to distrust him."

Perhaps Naqi was imagining this as well, but it almost sounded as if Matsubara had intended to say "disciple" rather than "delegate."

Crane came back on the radio. "Please do your best to apprehend him, Naqi. This is a source of great embarrassment to us. He mustn't do any harm."

Naqi gunned the boat harder, no longer bothering to avoid the smaller patches of organic matter. "No," she said. "He mustn't."

III

Something changed ahead.

"Naqi?" It was Jotah Sivaraksa's voice.

"What?"

"Weir's slowed his boat. From our vantage point it looks as if he's reached the perimeter of the node. He seems to be circumnavigating it."

"I can't see him yet. He must be picking the best spot to dive in."

"But it won't work, will it?" Sivaraksa asked. "There has to be an element of co-operation with the Jugglers. They have to invite the swimmer to enter the sea, or nothing happens."

"Maybe he doesn't realise that," Naqi said, under her breath. It was of no concern to her how closely Weir was adhering to the usual method of initiating Juggler communion. Even if the Jugglers did not cooperate—even if all Weir did was flounder in thick green water—there was no telling the hidden harm that might be done. She had already grudgingly accepted the acceleration of the closure operation. There was no way she was going to tolerate another upset, another unwanted perturbation of the experimental system. Not on her watch.

"He's stopped," Sivaraksa said excitedly. "Can you see him yet?"

Naqi stood up in her seat, even though she felt perilously out of balance. "Wait. Yes, I think so. I'll be there in a minute or so."

"What are you going to do?" Crane asked. "I hesitate to say it, but Weir may not respond to rational argument at this point. Simply requesting that he leave the water won't necessarily work. Um, do you have a weapon?"

"Yes," Naqi said. "I'm sitting in it."

She did not allow herself to relax, but at least now she felt that the situation was slipping back into her control. She would kill Weir rather than have him contaminate the node.

His boat was visible now only as a smudge of white, intermittently popping up between folds and hummocks of shifting green. Her imagination sketched in the details. Weir would be preparing to swim, stripping off until he was naked or nearly so. Perhaps he would feel some kind of erotic charge as he prepared for immersion. She did not doubt that he would be apprehensive, and perhaps he would hesitate on the threshold of the act, teetering on the edge of the boat before committing himself to the water. But a fanatic desire had driven him this far and she doubted that it would fail him.

"Naqi . . ."

"Jotah?"

"Naqi, he's moving again. He didn't enter the water. He didn't even look like he had any intention of swimming."

"He saw I was coming. I take it he's heading for the next closest node?"

"Perhaps . . ." But Jotah Sivaraksa sounded far from certain.

She saw the boat again. It was moving fast—much faster than it had appeared before—but that was only because she was now seeing lateral motion.

The next node was a distant island framed by the background of the Moat's encircling rim. If he headed that way she would be hard behind him all the way there as well. No matter his desire to swim, he must realise that she could thwart his every attempt.

Naqi looked back. The twin towers framing the cut were smothered in a haze of sea mist, their geometric details smeared into a vague suggestion of haphazard complexity. They suggested teetering, stratified sea-stacks, million-year-old towers of weathered and eroded rock guarding the narrow passage to the open ocean. Beneath them, winking in and out of clarity, she saw three or four other boats making their way into the Moat. The ponderous teardrop of a passenger dirigible was nosing away from the side of one of the towers, the low dawn sun throwing golden highlights along the fluted lines of its gondola. Naqi made out the sleek deltoid of the *Voice of Evening*'s shuttle, but it was still parked where it had landed.

She looked back to the node where Weir had hesitated.

Something was happening.

The node had become vastly more active than a minute earlier. It resembled a green, steep-sided volcanic island that was undergoing some catastrophic seismic calamity. The entire mass of the node was trembling, rocking and throbbing with an eerie regularity. Concentric swells of disturbed water raced away from it, sickening troughs that made the speeding boat pitch and slide. Naqi slowed her boat, some instinct telling her that it was now largely futile to pursue Weir. Then she turned around so that she faced the node properly, and, cautiously, edged closer, ignoring the nausea she felt as the boat ducked and dived from crest to trough.

The node, like all nodes, had always shown a rich surface topology; fused hummocks and tendrils; fabulous domes and minarets and helter-skelters of organised biomass, linked and entangled by a telegraphic system of draping aerial tendrils. In any instant it resembled a human city—or, more properly, a fairy-tale human city—that had been efficiently smothered in green moss. The bright moving motes of sprites dodged through the interstices, the portholes and arches of the urban mass. The metropolitan structure only hinted at the node's byzantine interior architecture, and much of that could only be glimpsed or implied.

But this node was like a city going insane. It was accelerating, running through cycles of urban renewal and redesign with indecent haste. Structures were evolving before Naqi's eyes. She had seen change this rapid just before Mina was taken, but normally those kinds of changes happened too slowly to be seen at all, like the daily movement of shadows.

The throbbing had decreased, but the flickering change was now throwing out a steady, warm, malodorous breeze. And when she stopped the boat—she dared come no closer now—Naqi heard the node. It was like the whisper of a billion forest leaves presaging a summer storm.

Whatever was happening here, it was about to become catastrophic.

Some fundamental organisation had been lost. The changes were happening too quickly, with too little central coordination. Tendrils thrashed like whips, unable to connect to anything. They flailed against each other. Structures were forming and collapsing. The node was fracturing, so that there were three, four, perhaps five distinct cores of flickering growth. As soon as she had the measure of it, the process shifted it all. Meagre light flickered within the epileptic mass. Sprites swarmed in confused flight patterns, orbiting mindlessly between foci. The sound of the node had become a distant shriek.

"It's dying . . ." Naqi breathed.

Weir had done something to it. What, she couldn't guess. But this could not be a coincidence.

The shrieking died down.

The breeze ceased.

The node had stopped its convulsions. She looked at it, hoping against hope that perhaps it had overcome whatever destabilising influence Weir had introduced. The structures were still misshapen, there was still an impression of incoherence, but the city was inert. The cycling motion of the sprites slowed, and a few of them dropped down into the mass, as if to roost.

A calm had descended.

Then Naqi heard another sound. It was lower than anything she had heard before—almost subsonic. It sounded less like thunder than like a very distant, very heated conversation.

It was coming from the approximate centre of the node.

She watched as a smooth green mound rose from the centre of the node, resembling a flattened hemisphere. It grew larger by the second, assimilating the malformed structures with quiet indifference. They disappeared into the surface of the mound as if into a wall of fog, but they did not emerge again. The mound only increased its size, rumbling toward Naqi. The entire mass of the node was changing into a single undifferentiated mass.

"Jotah . . ." she said.

"We see it, Naqi. We see it but we don't understand it."

"Weir must have used some kind of . . . weapon against it," she said.

"We don't know that he's harmed it. . . . He might just have precipitated a change to a state we haven't documented."

"That still makes it a weapon in my book. I'm scared, Jotah."

"You think I'm not?"

Around her the sea was changing. She had forgotten about the submerged tendrils that connected the nodes. They were as thick as hawsers, and now they were writhing and thrashing just beneath the surface of the water. Green-tinged spume lifted into the air. It was as if unseen aquatic monsters were wrestling, locked in some dire, to-the-death contest.

"Naqi . . . We're seeing changes in the closest of the two remaining nodes."

"No," she said, as if denying it would make any difference.

"I'm sorry . . ."

"Where is Weir?"

"We've lost him. There's too much surface disturbance."

She realised then what had to be done. The thought arrived in her head with a crashing urgency.

"Jotah . . . You have to close the sea-doors. Now. Immediately. Before whatever Weir's unleashed has a chance to reach open ocean. That also happens to be Weir's only escape route."

Sivaraksa, to his credit, did not argue. "Yes. You're right. I'll start closure. But it will take quite a few minutes. . . ."

"I know, Jotah!"

She cursed herself for not having thought of this sooner, and cursed Sivaraksa for the same error. But she could hardly blame either of them. Closure had never been something to take lightly. A few hours ago it had been an event months in the future—an experiment to test the willingness of the Jugglers to cooperate with human plans. Now it had turned into an emergency amputation, something to be done with brutal haste.

She peered at the gap between the towers. At the very least it would take several minutes for Sivaraksa to initiate closure. It was not simply a matter of pressing a button on his desk, but of rousing two or three specialist technicians, who would have to be immediately convinced that this was not some elaborate hoax. And then the machinery would have to work. The mechanisms that forced the sea-doors together had been tested numerous times. . . . But the machinery had never been driven to its limit; the doors had never moved more than a few metres together. Now they would have to work perfectly, closing with watchmaker precision.

And when had anything on Turquoise ever worked the first time?

There. The tiniest, least perceptible narrowing of the gap. It was all happening with agonising slowness.

She looked back to what remained of the node. The mound had consumed all the biomass available to it and had now ceased its growth. It was as if a child had sculpted in clay some fantastically intricate model of a city, which a callous adult had then squashed into a single blank mass, erasing all trace of its former complexity. The closest of the remaining nodes was showing something of the same transformation, Naqi saw: it was running through the frantic cycle that had presaged the emergence of the mound. She guessed now that the cycle had been the node's attempt to nullify whatever Weir had used against it, like a computer trying to reallocate resources to compensate for some crippling viral attack.

She could do nothing for the Jugglers now.

Naqi turned the boat around and headed back toward the cut. The sea-doors had narrowed the gap by perhaps a quarter.

The changes taking place within the Moat had turned the water turbulent, even at the jetty. She hitched the boat to a mooring point and then took the elevator up the side of the wall, preferring to sprint the distance along the top rather than face the climb. By the time she reached the cut the doors were three quarters of the way to closure, and to Naqi's immense relief the machinery had yet to falter.

She approached the tower. She had expected to see more people out on the top of the Moat, even if she knew that Sivaraksa would still be in his control centre. But no one was around. This was just beginning to register as a distinct wrongness when Sivaraksa emerged into daylight, stumbling from the door at the foot of the tower.

For an instant she was on the point of calling his name. Then she realised that he was stumbling because he had been injured — his fingers were scarlet with blood — and that he was trying to get away from someone or something.

Naqi dropped to the ground behind a stack of construction slabs. Through gaps between the slabs she observed Sivaraksa. He was swatting at something, like a man being chased by a persistent wasp. Something tiny and silver harried him. More than one thing, in fact: a small swarm of them, streaming out the open door. Sivaraksa fell to his knees with a moan, brushing ineffectually at his tormentors. His face was turning red, smeared with his own blood. He slumped on one side.

Naqi remained frozen with fear.

A person stepped from the open door.

The figure was garbed in shades of fire. It was Amesha Crane. For an absurd moment Naqi assumed that the woman was about to spring to Sivaraksa's assistance. It was something about her demeanour. Naqi found it hard to believe that someone so apparently serene could commit such a violent act.

But Crane did not step closer to Sivaraksa. She merely extended her arms before her, with her fingers outspread. She sustained the oddly theatrical gesture, the muscles in her neck standing proud and rigid.

The silver things departed Sivaraksa.

They swarmed through the air, slowing as they neared Crane. Then, with a startling degree of orchestrated obedience, they slid onto her fingers, locked themselves around her wrists, clasped onto the lobes of her ears.

Her jewellery had attacked Sivaraksa.

Crane glanced at the man one last time, spun on her heels and then retreated back into the tower.

Naqi waited until she was certain the woman was not coming back, then started to emerge from behind the pile of slabs. But Sivaraksa saw her. He said nothing, but his agonised eyes widened enough for Naqi to get the warning. She remained where she was, her heart hammering.

Nothing happened for another minute.

Then something moved above, changing the play of light across the surface of the Moat. The *Voice of Evening*'s shuttle was detaching from the tower, a flicker of white machinery beneath the manta curve of its hull.

The shuttle loitered above the cut, as if observing the final moment of closure. Naqi heard the huge doors grind shut. Then the shuttle banked, and headed over the circular sea, no more than two hundred metres above the waves. Some distance out it halted and executed a sharp right-angled turn. Then it resumed its flight, moving concentrically around the inner wall.

Sivaraksa closed his eyes. She thought he might have died, but then he opened them again and made the tiniest of nods. Naqi left her place of hiding. She crossed the open ground to Sivaraksa in a low, crablike stoop.

She knelt down by him, cradling his head in one hand and holding his own hand with the other. "Jotah . . . What happened?"

He managed to answer her. "They turned on us. The nineteen other delegates. As soon as . . ." He paused, summoning strength. "As soon as Weir made his move."

"I don't understand."

"Join the club," he said, managing a smile.

"I need to get you inside," she said.

"Won't help. Everyone else is dead. Or will be by now. They murdered us all."

"No."

"Kept me alive until the end. Wanted me to give the orders." He coughed. Blood spattered her hand.

"I can still get you . . ."

"Naqi. Save yourself. Get help."

She realised that he was about to die.

"The shuttle?"

"Looking for Weir. I think."

"They want Weir back?"

"No. Heard them talking. They want Weir dead. They have to be sure."

Naqi frowned. She understood none of this, or, at least, her understanding was only now beginning to crystallise. She had labelled Weir as the villain because he had harmed her beloved Pattern Jugglers. But Crane and her entourage had murdered people, dozens if what Sivaraksa said was correct. They appeared to want Weir dead as well. So what did that make Weir, now?

"Jotah . . . I have to find Weir. I have to find out why he did this." She looked back toward the centre of the Moat. The shuttle was continuing its search. "Did your security people get a trace on him again?"

Sivaraksa was near the end. She thought he was never going to answer her. "Yes," he said finally. "Yes, they found him again."

"And? Any idea where he is? I might still be able to reach him before the shuttle does."

"Wrong place."

She leaned closer. "Jotah?"

"Wrong place. Amesha's looking in the wrong place. Weir got through the cut. He's in the open ocean."

"I'm going after him. Perhaps I can stop him. . . ."

"Try," Sivaraksa said. "But I'm not sure what difference it will make. I have a feeling, Naqi. A very bad feeling. Things are ending. It was good, wasn't it? While it lasted?"

"I haven't given up just yet," Naqi said.

He found one last nugget of strength. "I knew you wouldn't. Right to trust you. One thing, Naqi. One thing that might make a difference . . . if it comes to the worst, that is . . ."

"Jotah?"

"Tak Thonburi told me this . . . the highest secret known to the Snowflake Council. Arviat, Naqi."

For a moment she thought she had misheard him, or that he was sliding into delirium. "Arviat? The city that sinned against the sea?"

"It was real," Sivaraksa said.

There were a number of lifeboats and emergency service craft stored at the top of near-vertical slipways, a hundred metres above the external sea. She took a small but fast emergency craft with a sealed cockpit, her stomach knotting as the vessel commenced its slide toward the ocean. The boat submerged before resurfacing, boosted up to speed and then deployed ceramic hydrofoils to minimise the contact between the hull and the water. Naqi had no precise heading to follow, but she believed. Weir would have followed a reasonably straight line away from the cut, aiming to get as far away from the Moat as possible before the other delegates realised their mistake. It would only require a small deviation from that course to take him to the nearest external node, which seemed as likely a destination as any.

When she was twenty kilometres from the Moat, Naqi allowed herself a moment to look back. The structure was a thin white line etched on the horizon, the towers and the now-sealed cut faintly visible as interruptions in the line's smoothness. Quills of dark smoke climbed from a dozen spots along the length of the structure. It was too far for Naqi to be certain that she saw flames licking from the towers, but she considered it likely.

The closest external node appeared over the horizon fifteen minutes later. It was nowhere as impressive as the one that had taken Mina, but it was still a larger, more complex structure than any of the nodes that had formed within the Moat—a major urban megalopolis, perhaps, rather than a moderately sized city. Against the skyline Naqi saw spires and rotunda and coronets of green, bridged by a tracery of elevated tendrils. Sprites were rapidly moving silhouettes. There was motion, but it was largely confined to the flying creatures. The node was not yet showing the frenzied changes she had witnessed within the Moat.

Had Weir gone somewhere else?

She pressed onward, slowing the boat slightly now that the water was thickening with microorganisms and it was necessary to steer around the occasional larger floating structure. The boat's sonar picked out dozens of submerged tendrils converging on the node, suspended just below the surface. The tendrils reached away in all directions, to the limits of the boat's sonar range. Most would have reached over the horizon, to nodes many hundreds of kilometres away. But it was a topological certainty that some of them had been connected to the nodes inside the Moat. Evidently, Weir's contagion had never escaped through the cut. Naqi doubted that the doors had closed in time to impede whatever chemical signals were transmitting the fatal message. It was more likely that some latent Juggler self-protection mechanism had cut in, the dying nodes sending emergency termination-of-connection signals that forced the tendrils to sever without human assistance.

Naqi had just decided that she had guessed wrongly about Weir's plan when she saw a rectilinear furrow gouged right through one of the largest subsidiary structures. The wound was healing itself as she watched—it would be gone in a matter of minutes—but enough remained for her to tell that Weir's boat must have cleaved through the mass very recently. It made sense. Weir had already demonstrated that he had no interest in preserving the Pattern Jugglers.

With renewed determination, Naqi gunned the boat forward. She no longer worried about inflicting local damage on the floating masses. There was a great deal more at stake than the well-being of a single node.

She felt a warmth on the back of her neck.

At the same instant the sky, sea and floating structures ahead of her pulsed with a cruel brightness. Her own shadow stretched forward ominously. The brightness faded over the next few seconds, and then she dared to look back, half-knowing what she would see.

A mass of hot, roiling gas was climbing into the air from the centre of the node. It hugged a column of matter beneath it, like the knotted and gnarled spinal column of a horribly swollen brain. Against the mushroom cloud she saw the tiny moving speck of the delegates' shuttle.

A minute later the sound of the explosion reached her, but although it was easily the loudest thing she had ever heard, it was not as deafening as she had expected. The boat lurched; the sea fumed and then was still again. She assumed that the Moat's wall had absorbed much of the energy of the blast.

Suddenly fearful that there might be another explosion, Naqi turned back toward the node. At the same instant she saw Weir's boat, racing perhaps three hundred metres ahead of her. He was beginning to curve and slow as he neared the impassable perimeter of the node. Naqi knew that she did not have time to delay.

That was when Weir saw her. His boat sped up again, arcing hard away. Naqi steered immediately, certain that her boat was faster and that it was now only a matter of time before she had him. A minute later Weir's boat disappeared around the curve of the node's perimeter. She might have stood a chance of getting an echo from his hull, but this close to the node all sonar returns were too garbled to be of any use. Naqi steered anyway, hoping that Weir would make the tactical mistake of striking for another node. In open water he stood no chance at all, but perhaps he understood that as well.

She had circumnavigated a third of the node's perimeter when she caught up with him again. He had not tried to run for it. Instead he had brought the boat to a halt within the comparative shelter of an inlet on the perimeter. He was standing up at the rear of the boat, with something small and dark in his hand.

Naqi slowed her boat as she approached him. She had popped back the canopy before it occurred to her that Weir might be equipped with the same weapons as Crane.

She stood up herself. "Weir?"

He smiled. "I'm sorry to have caused so much trouble. But I don't think it could have happened any other way."

She let this pass. "That thing in your hand?"

"Yes?"

"It's a weapon, isn't it?"

She could see it clearly now. It was merely a glass bauble, little larger than a child's marble. There was something opaque inside it, but she could not tell if it contained fluid or dark crystals.

"I doubt that a denial would be very plausible at this point." He nodded, and she sensed the lifting, partially at least, of some appalling burden. "Yes, it's a weapon. A Juggler killer."

"Until today, I'd have said no such thing was possible."

"I doubt that it was very easy to synthesize. Countless biological entities have entered their oceans, and none of them have ever brought anything with them that the Juggler couldn't assimilate in a harmless fashion. Doubtless some of those entities tried to inflict deliberate harm, if only out of morbid curiosity. None of them succeeded. Of course, you can kill Jugglers by brute force . . ." He glanced toward the Moat, where the mushroom cloud was dissipating. "But that isn't the point. Not subtle. But this is. It exploits a logical flaw in the Jugglers' own informational processing algorithms. It's insidious. And no, humans most certainly didn't invent it. We're clever, but we're not *that* clever."

Naqi strove to keep him talking. "Who made it, Weir?"

"The Ultras sold it to us in a presynthesized form. I've heard rumours that it was found inside the topmost chamber of a heavily fortified alien structure. . . . Another that it was synthesized by a rival group of Jugglers. Who knows? Who cares, even? It does what we ask of it. That's all that matters."

"Please don't use it, Rafael."

"I have to. It's what I came here to do."

"But I thought you all loved the Jugglers."

His fingers caressed the glass globe. It looked terribly fragile. "We?"

"Crane . . . Her delegates."

"They do. But I'm not one of them."

"Tell me what this is about, Rafael."

"It would be better if you just accepted what I have to do."

Naqi swallowed. "If you kill them, you will kill more than just an alien life form. You erase the memory of every sentient creature that's ever entered the ocean."

"Unfortunately, that rather happens to be the point."

Weir dropped the glass into the sea.

It hit the water, bobbed under and then popped back out again, floating on the surface. The small globe was already immersed in a brackish scum of gray-green microorganisms. They were beginning to lap higher up the sides of the globe, exploring it. A couple of millimetres of ordinary glass would succumb to Juggler erosion in perhaps thirty minutes. . . . But Naqi guessed that this was not ordinary glass, that it was designed to degrade much more rapidly.

She jumped back down into her control seat and shot her boat forward. She came alongside Weir's boat, trapping the globe between the two craft. Taking desperate care not to nudge the hulls together, she stopped her boat and leaned over as far as she could without falling in. Her fingertips brushed the glass. Maddeningly, she could not quite get a grip on it. She made one last valiant effort and it drifted beyond her reach. Now it was out of her range, no matter how hard she stretched. Weir watched impassively.

Naqi slipped into the water. The layer of Juggler organisms licked her chin and nose, the smell immediate and overwhelming now that she was in such close proximity. Her fear was absolute. It was the first time she had entered the water since Mina's death.

She caught the globe, taking hold of it with the exquisite care she might have reserved for a rare bird's egg.

Already the glass had the porous texture of pumice.

She held it up, for Weir to see.

"I won't let you do this, Rafael."

"I admire your concern."

"It's more than concern. My sister is here. She's in the ocean. And I won't let you take her away from me."

Weir reached inside a pocket and removed another globe.

They sped away from the node in Naqi's boat. The new globe rested in his hand like a gift. He had not yet dropped it in the sea, although the possibility was only ever an instant away. They were far from any node now, but the globe would be guaranteed to come into contact with Juggler matter sooner or later.

Naqi opened a watertight equipment locker, pushing aside the flare pistol and first-aid kit that lay within. Carefully she placed the globe inside, and then watched in horror as the glass immediately cracked and dissolved, releasing its poison: little black irregularly shaped grains like burnt sugar. If the boat sank, the locker would eventually be consumed into the ocean, along with its fatal contents. She considered using the flare pistol to incinerate the remains, but there seemed too much danger of dispersing it at the same time. Perhaps the toxin had a restricted life span once it came into contact with air, but that was nothing she could count on.

But Weir had not thrown the third globe into the sea. Not yet. Something she had said had made him hesitate.

"Your sister?"

"You know the story," Naqi said. "Mina was a conformal. The ocean assimilated her entirely, rather than just recording her neural patterns. It took her as a prize."

"And you believe that she's still present, in some sentient sense?"

"That's what I choose to believe, yes. And there's enough anecdotal evidence from other swimmers that conformals do persist, in a more coherent form than other stored patterns."

"I can't let anecdotal evidence sway me. Naqi. Have the other swimmers specifically reported encounters with Mina?"

"No . . ." Naqi said carefully. She was sure that he would see through any lie that she attempted. "But they wouldn't necessarily recognise her if they did."

"And you? Did you attempt to swim yourself?"

"The swimmer corps would never have allowed me."

"Not my question. Did you ever swim?"

"Once," Naqi said.

"And?"

"It didn't count. It was the same time that Mina died." She paused and then told him all that had happened. "We were seeing more sprite activity than we'd ever recorded. It seemed like coincidence. . . ."

"I don't think it was."

Naqi said nothing. She waited for Weir to collect his own thoughts, concentrating on the steering of the boat. Open sea lay ahead, but she knew that almost any direction would bring them to a cluster of nodes within a few hours.

"It began with the *Pelican in Impiety*," Weir said. "A century ago. There was a man from Zion on that ship. During the stopover he descended to the surface of Turquoise and swam in your ocean. He made contact with the Jugglers and then swam again. The second time the experience was even more affecting. On the third occasion, the sea swallowed him. He'd been a conformal, just like your sister. His name was Ormazd."

"It means nothing to me."

"I assure you that on his homeworld it means a great deal more. Ormazd was a failed tyrant, fleeing a political counter-revolution on Zion. He had murdered and cheated his way to power on Zion, burning his rivals in their houses while they slept. But there'd been a backlash. He got out just before the ring closed around him—him and a handful of his closest allies and devotees. They escaped aboard the *Pelican in Impiety*."

"And Ormazd died here?"

"Yes—but his followers didn't. They made it to Haven, our world. And once there they began to proliferate, spreading their word, recruiting new followers. It didn't matter that Ormazd was gone. Quite the opposite. He'd martyred himself; given them a saint figure to worship. It evolved from a political movement into a religious cult. The Vahishta Foundation's just a front for the Ormazd sect."

Naqi absorbed that, then asked: "Where does Amesha come into it?"

"Amesha was his daughter. She wants her father back."

Something lit the horizon, a pink-edged flash. Another followed a minute later, in nearly the same position.

"She wants to commune with him?"

"More than that," said Weir. "They all want to *become* him; to accept his neural patterns on their own. They want the Jugglers to imprint Ormazd's personality on all his followers, to remake them in his own image. The aliens will do that, if the right gifts are offered. And that's what I can't allow."

Naqi chose her words carefully, sensing that the tiniest thing could push Weir into releasing the globe. She had prevented his last attempt, but he would not allow her a second chance. All he would have to do would be to crush the globe in his fist before spilling the contents into the ocean. Then it would all be over. Everything she had ever known; everything she had ever lived for.

"But we're only talking about nineteen people," she said.

Weir laughed hollowly. "I'm afraid it's a little more than that. Why don't you turn on the radio and see what I mean?"

Naqi did as he suggested, using the boat's general communications console. The small, scuffed screen received television pictures beamed down from the comsat network. Naqi flicked through channels, finding static on most of them. The Snowflake Council's official news service was off the air and no personal messages were getting through. There were some suggestions that the comsat network itself was damaged. Yet finally Naqi found a few weak broadcast signals from the nearest snowflake cities. There was a sense of desperation in the transmissions, as if they expected to fall silent at any time.

Weir nodded with weary acceptance, as if he had expected this.

In the last six hours at least a dozen more shuttles had come down from the *Voice of Evening*. They had been packed with armed Vahishta disciples. The shuttles had attacked the planet's major snowflake cities and atoll settlements, strafing them into submission. Three cities had fallen into the sea, their vacuum bladders punctured by beam weapons. There could be no survivors. Others were still aloft, but had been set on fire. The pictures showed citizens leaping from the cities' berthing arms, falling like sparks. More cities had been taken bloodlessly, and were now under control of the disciples.

None of those cities were transmitting now.

It was the end of the world. Naqi knew that she should be weeping, or at the very least feel some writhing sense of loss in her stomach. But all she felt was a sense of denial; a refusal to accept that events could have escalated so quickly. This morning the only hint of wrongness had been a single absent disciple.

"There are tens of thousands of them up there," Weir said. "All that you've seen so far is the advance guard."

Naqi scratched her forearm. It was itching, as if she had caught a dose of sunburn.

"Moreau was in on this?"

"Captain Moreau's a puppet. Literally. The body you saw was just being teleoperated by orbital disciples. They murdered the Ultras; commandeered the ship."

"Rafael . . . Why didn't you tell us this before?"

"My position was too vulnerable. I was the only anti-Ormazd agent my movement managed to put aboard the *Voice of Evening*. If I'd attempted to warn the Turquoise authorities . . . Well, work it out for yourself. Almost certainly I wouldn't have been believed, and the disciples would have found a way to silence me before I became an embarrassment. And it wouldn't have made a difference to their takeover plans. My only hope was to destroy the ocean, to remove its usefulness to them. They might still have destroyed your cities out of spite, but at least they'd have lost the final thread that connected them to their martyr." Weir leaned closer to her. "Don't you understand? It wouldn't have stopped with the disciples aboard the *Voice*. They'd have brought more ships from Haven. Your ocean would have become a production line for despots."

"Why did they hesitate, if they had such a crushing advantage over us?"

"They didn't know about me, so they lost nothing by dedicating a few weeks to intelligence gathering. They wanted to know as much as possible about Turquoise and the Jugglers before they made their move. They're brutal, but they're not inefficient. They wanted their takeover to be as precise and surgical as possible."

"And now?"

"They've accepted that things won't be quite that neat and tidy." He flipped the globe from one palm to another, with a casual playfulness that Naqi found alarming. "They're serious, Naqi. Crane will stop at nothing now. You've seen those blast flashes. Pinpoint antimatter devices. They've already sterilised the organic matter within the Moat, to stop the effect of my weapon from reaching farther. If they know where we are, they'll drop a bomb on us as well."

"Human evil doesn't give us the excuse to wipe out the ocean."

"It's not an excuse, Naqi. It's an imperative."

At that moment something glinted on the horizon, something that was moving slowly from east to west.

"The shuttle," Weir said. "It's looking for us."

Naqi scratched her arm again. It was discoloured, itching.

Near local noon they reached the next node. The shuttle had continued to dog them, nosing to and fro along the hazy band where sea met sky. Sometimes it appeared closer, sometimes it appeared farther away. But it did not leave them alone, and Naqi knew that it would only be a matter of time before it detected a positive homing trace, a chemical or physical trace in the water that would lead to its quarry. The shuttle would cover the remaining distance in a matter of seconds, a minute at the most, and then all that she and Weir would know would be a moment of cleansing whiteness, a fire of holy purity. Even if Weir released his toxin just before the shuttle arrived it would not have time to dissipate into a wide enough volume of water to survive the fireball.

So why was he hesitating? It was Mina, of course. Naqi's sister had given a name to the faceless library of stored minds he was prepared to erase. She had removed the one-sidedness of the moral equation, and now Weir had to accept that his own actions could never be entirely blameless.

"I should just do this," he said. "By hesitating even for a second, I'm betraying the trust of the people who sent me here, people who have probably been tormented to extinction by Ormazd's followers."

Naqi shook her head. "If you didn't show doubt, you'd be as bad as the disciples."

"You almost sound as if you want me to do it."

She groped for something resembling the truth, as painful as that might be. "Perhaps I do."

"Even though it would mean killing whatever part of Mina survived?"

"I've lived in her shadow my entire life. Even after she died . . . I always felt she was still watching me: still observing my every mistake, still being faintly disappointed that I wasn't living up to all she had imagined I could be."

"You're being harsh on yourself. Harsh on Mina too, by the likes of things."

"I know," Naqi said angrily. "I'm just telling you how I feel."

The boat edged into a curving inlet that pushed deep into the node. Naqi felt less vulnerable now: there was a significant depth of organic matter to screen the boat from any sideways-looking sensors that the shuttle might have deployed, even though the evidence suggested that the shuttle's sensors were mainly focussed down from its hull. The disadvantage was that it was no longer possible to keep a constant vigil on the shuttle's movements. It could be on its way already.

She brought the boat to a halt and stood up from her control seat.

"What's happening?" Weir asked.

"I've come to a decision."

"Isn't that my job?"

Her anger—brief as it was, and directed less at Weir than the hopelessness of the situation—had evaporated. "I mean about swimming. It's what we haven't considered yet, Rafael. That there might be a third way; a choice between accepting the disciples and letting the ocean die."

"I don't see what that could be."

"Nor do I. But the ocean might find a way. It just needs the knowledge of what's at stake." She stroked her forearm again, marvelling at the sudden eruption of fungal patterns. They must have been latent for many years, but now something had caused them to flare up. Even in daylight, emeralds and blues shone against her skin. She suspected that the biochemical changes had been triggered when she entered the water to snatch the globe. Given that, she could not help but view it as a message. An invitation, perhaps. Or was it a warning, reminding her of the dangers of swimming?

She had no idea. For her peace of mind, however—and given the lack of alternatives—she chose to view it as an invitation.

But she did not dare wonder who was inviting her.

"You think the ocean can understand external events?" Weir asked.

"You said it yourself, Rafael. The night they told us the ship was coming? Somehow that information reached the sea. Via a swimmer's memories, perhaps. And the Jugglers knew then that this was something significant. Perhaps it was Ormazd's personality, rising to the fore."

Or maybe it was merely the vast, choral mind of the ocean, apprehending only that *something* was going to happen.

"Either way," Naqi said. "It still makes me think that there might be a chance."

"I only wish I shared your optimism."

"Give me this chance, Rafael. That's all I ask."

Naqi removed her clothes, less concerned that Weir would see her naked now than that she should have something to wear when she emerged. But although Weir studied her with unconcealed fascination, there was nothing prurient about it. What commanded his attention, Naqi realised, was the elaborate and florid patterning of the fungal markings. They curled and twined about her chest and abdomen and thighs, shining with a hypnotic intensity.

"You're changing," he said.

"We all change," Naqi answered.

Then she stepped from the side of the boat, into the water.

The process of descending into the ocean's embrace was much as she remembered it. She willed her body to submit to biochemical invasion, forcing down her fear and apprehension, knowing that she had been through this once before and that it was something that she could survive again. She did her best not to think about what it would mean to survive beyond this day, when all else had been shattered, every certainty crumbled.

Mina came to her with merciful speed.

Naqi?

I'm here: Oh, Mina, I'm here. There was terror and there was joy, alloyed together. *It's been so long.*

Naqi felt her sister's presence edge in and out of proximity and focus. Sometimes she appeared to share the same physical space. At other times she was scarcely more than a vague feeling of attentiveness.

How long?

Two years, Mina.

Mina's answer took an eternity to come. In that dreadful hiatus Naqi felt other minds crowd against her own, some of which were so far from human that she gasped at their oddity. Mina was only one of the conformal minds that had noticed her arrival, and not all were as benignly curious or glad.

It doesn't feel like two years to me.

How long?

Days . . . hours . . . It changes.

What do you remember?

Mina's presence danced around Naqi. *I remember what I remember. That we swam, when we weren't meant to. That something happened to me, and I never left the ocean.*

You became part of it, Mina.

The triumphalism of her answer shocked Naqi to the marrow. *Yes!*

You wanted this?

You would want it, if you knew what it was like. You could have stayed, Naqi. You could have let it happen to you, the way it happened to me. We were so alike.

I was scared.

Yes, I remember.

Naqi knew that she had to get to the heart of things. Time was passing differently here—witness Mina's confusion about how long she had been part of the ocean— and there was no telling how patient Weir would be. He might not wait until Naqi reemerged before deploying the Juggler killer.

There was another mind, Mina. We encountered it, and it scared me. Enough that I had to leave the ocean. Enough that I never wanted to go back.

You've come back now.

It's because of that other mind. It belonged to a man called Ormazd. Something very bad is going to happen because of him. One way or the other.

There was a moment then that transcended anything Naqi had experienced before. She felt herself and Mina become inseparable. She could not say where one began and the other ended, but it was entirely pointless to even think in those terms. If only fleetingly, Mina had become her. Every thought, every memory, was open to equal scrutiny by both of them.

Naqi understood what it was like for Mina. Her sister's memories were rapturous. She might only have sensed the passing of hours or days, but that belied the richness of her experience since merging with the ocean. She had exchanged experience with countless alien minds, drinking in entire histories beyond normal human comprehension. And in that moment of sharing, Naqi appreciated something of the reason for her sister having been taken in the first place. Conformals were the ocean's way of managing itself. Now and then the maintenance of the vaster archive of static minds required stewardship—the drawing in of independent intelligences. Mina had been selected and utilised, and given rewards beyond imagining for her efforts. The ocean had tapped the structure of her intelligence at a subconscious level. Only now and then had she ever felt that she was being directly petitioned on a matter of importance.

But Ormazd's mind . . . ?

Mina had seen Naqi's memories now. She would know exactly what was at stake, and she would know exactly what that mind represented.

I was always aware of him. He wasn't always there—he liked to hide himself—but even when he was absent, he left a shadow of himself. I even think he might be the reason the ocean took me as a conformal. It sensed a coming crisis. It knew Ormazd had something to do with it. It had made a terrible mistake by swallowing him. So it reached out for new allies, minds it could trust.

Minds like Mina, Naqi thought. In that instant she did not know whether to admire the Pattern Jugglers or detest them for their heartlessness.

Ormazd was contaminating it?

His influence was strong. His force of personality was a kind of poison in its own right. The Pattern Jugglers knew that, I think.

Why couldn't they just eject his patterns?

They couldn't. It doesn't work that way. The sea is a storage medium, but it has no self-censoring facility. If the individual minds detect a malign presence, they can resist it . . . But Ormazd's mind is human. There aren't enough of us here to make a difference, Naqi. The other minds are too alien to recognise Ormazd for what he is. They just see a sentience.

Who made the Pattern Jugglers, Mina? Answer me that, will you?

She sensed Mina's amusement.

Even the Jugglers don't know that. Naqi. Or why.

You have to help us, Mina. You have to communicate the urgency of this to the rest of the ocean.

I'm one mind among many, Naqi. One voice in the chorus.

You still have to find a way. Please, Mina. Understand this, if nothing else. You could die. You all could die. I lost you once, but now I know you never really went away. I don't want to have to lose you again, for good.

You didn't lose me, Naqi. I lost you.

She hauled herself from the water. Weir was waiting where she had left him, with the intact globe still resting in his hand. The daylight shadows had moved a little, but not as much as she had feared. She made eye contact with Weir, wordlessly communicating a question.

"The shuttle's come closer. It's flown over the node twice while you were under. I think I need to do this, Naqi."

He had the globe between thumb and forefinger, ready to drop it into the water.

She was shivering. Naqi pulled on her shorts and shirt, but she felt just as cold afterwards. The fungal marks were shimmering intensely, seeming to hover above her skin. If anything they were shining more furiously than before she had swum. Naqi did not doubt that if she had lingered—if she had stayed with Mina—she would have become a conformal as well. It had always been in her, but it was only now that her time had come.

"Please wait," Naqi said, her own voice sounding pathetic and childlike. "Please wait, Rafael."

"There it is again."

The shuttle was a fleck of white sliding over the top of the nearest wall of Juggler biomass. It was five or six kilometres away, much closer than the last time Naqi had seen it. Now it came to a sudden sharp halt, hovering above the surface of the ocean as if it had found something of particular interest.

"Do you think it knows we're here?"

"It suspects something," Weir said. The globe rolled between his fingers.

"Look," Naqi said.

The shuttle was still hovering. Naqi stood up to get a better view, nervous of making herself visible but desperately curious. Something was happening. She *knew* something was happening.

Kilometres away, the sea was bellying up beneath the shuttle. The water was the colour of moss, supersaturated with microorganisms. Naqi watched as a coil of solid green matter reached from the ocean, twisting and writhing. It was as thick as a building, spilling vast rivulets of water as it emerged. It extended upward with astonishing haste, bifurcating and flexing like a groping fist. For a brief moment it closed around the shuttle. Then it slithered back into the sea with a titanic splash; a prolonged roar of spent energy. The shuttle continued to hover above the same spot, as if oblivious to what had just happened. Yet the manta-shaped craft's white hull was lathered with various hues of green. And Naqi understood: what had happened to the shuttle was what had happened to Arviat, the city that drowned. She could not begin to guess the crime that Arviat had committed against the sea, the crime that had merited its destruction, but she could believe, now, at least, that the Jugglers had been capable of dragging it beneath the waves, ripping the main mass of the city away from the bladders that held it aloft. And of course such a thing would have to be kept maximally secret, known only to a handful of individuals. Otherwise no city would ever feel safe when the sea roiled and groaned beneath it.

But a city was not a shuttle.

Even if the Juggler material started eating away the fabric of the shuttle, it would still take hours to do any serious damage. . . . And that was assuming the Ultras had no better protection than the ceramic shielding used on Turquoise boats and machines. . . .

But the shuttle was already tilting over.

Naqi watched it pitch, attempt to regain stability and then pitch again. She understood, belatedly. The organic matter was clogging the shuttle's whisking propulsion systems, limiting its ability to hover. The shuttle was curving inexorably closer to the sea, spiralling steeply away from the node. It approached the surface, and then just before the moment of impact another misshapen fist of organised matter thrust from the sea, seizing the hull in its entirety. That was the last Naqi saw of it.

A troubled calm fell on the scene. The sky overhead was unmarred by questing machinery. Only the thin whisper of smoke rising from the horizon, in the direction of the Moat, hinted of the day's events.

Minutes passed, and then tens of minutes. Then a rapid series of bright flashes strobed from beneath the surface of the sea itself.

"That was the shuttle," Weir said, wonderingly.

Naqi nodded. "The Jugglers are fighting back. This is more or less what I hoped would happen."

"You asked for this?"

"I think Mina understood what was needed. Evidently she managed to convince the rest of the ocean, or at least this part of it."

"Let's see."

They searched the airwaves again. The comsat network was dead, or silent. Even fewer cities were transmitting now. But those that were—those that had not been overrun by Ormazd's disciples—told a frightening story. The ocean was clawing at them, trying to drag them into the sea. Weather patterns were shifting, entire storms being conjured into existence by the orchestrated circulation of vast ocean currents. It was happening in concentric waves, racing away from the precise point in the ocean where Naqi had swum. Some cities had already fallen into the sea, though it was not clear whether this had been brought about by the Jugglers themselves or because of damage to their vacuum bladders. There were people in the water: hundreds, thousands of them. They were swimming, trying to stay afloat, trying not to drown.

But what exactly did it mean to drown on Turquoise?

"It's happening all over the planet," Naqi said. She was still shivering, but now it was as much a shiver of awe as one of cold. "It's denying itself to us by smashing our cities."

"Your cities never harmed it."

"I don't think it's really that interested in making a distinction between one bunch of people and another, Rafael. It's just getting rid of us all, disciples or not. You can't really blame it for that, can you?"

"I'm sorry," Weir said.

He cracked the globe, spilled its contents into the sea.

Naqi knew there was nothing she could do now; there was no prospect of recovering the tiny black grains. She would only have to miss one, and it would be as bad as missing them all.

The little black grains vanished beneath the olive surface of the water.

It was done.

Weir looked at her, his eyes desperate for forgiveness.

"You understand that I had to do this, don't you? It isn't something I do lightly."

"I know. But it wasn't necessary. The ocean's already turned against us. Crane has lost. Ormazd has lost."

"Perhaps you're right," Weir said. "But I couldn't take the chance that we might be wrong. At least this way I know for sure."

"You've murdered a world."

He nodded. "It's exactly what I came here to do. Please don't blame me for it."

Naqi opened the equipment locker where she had stowed the broken vial of Juggler toxin. She removed the flare pistol, snatched away its safety pin and pointed it at Weir.

"I don't blame you, no. Don't even hate you for it."

He started to say something, but Naqi cut him off.

"But it's not something I can forgive."

She sat in silence, alone, until the node became active. The organic structures around her were beginning to show the same kinds of frantic rearrangement Naqi had seen within the Moat. There was a cold sharp breeze from the node's heart.

It was time to leave.

She steered the boat away from the node, cautiously, still not completely convinced that she was safe from the delegates even though the first shuttle had been destroyed. Undoubtedly the loss of that craft would have been communicated to the others, and before very long some of them would arrive, bristling with belligerence. The ocean might attempt to destroy the new arrivals, but this time the delegates would be profoundly suspicious.

She brought the boat to a halt when she was a kilometre from the fringe of the node. By then it was running through the same crazed alterations she had previously witnessed. She felt the same howling wind of change. In a moment the end would come. The toxin would seep into the node's controlling core, instructing the entire biomass to degrade itself to a lump of dumb vegetable matter. The same killing instructions would already be travelling along the internode tendril connections, winging their way over the horizon. Allowing for the topology of the network, it would only take fifteen or twenty hours for the message to reach every node on the planet. Within a day it would be over. The Jugglers would be gone, the information they'd encoded erased beyond recall. And Turquoise itself would begin to die at the same time; its oxygen atmosphere no longer maintained by the oceanic organisms.

Another five minutes passed, then ten.

The node's transformations were growing less hectic. She recalled this moment of false calm. It meant only that the node had given up trying to counteract the toxin, accepting the logical inevitability of its fate. A thousand times over this would be repeated around Turquoise. Toward the end, she guessed, there would be less resistance, for the sheer futility of it would have been obvious. The world would accept its fate.

Another five minutes passed.

The node remained. The structures were changing, but only gently. There was no sign of the emerging mound of undifferentiated matter she had seen before.

What was happening?

She waited another quarter of an hour and then steered the boat back toward the node, bumping past Weir's floating corpse on the way. Tentatively, an idea was forming in her mind. It appeared that the node had absorbed the toxin without dying. Was it possible that Weir had made a mistake? Was it possible that the toxin's effectiveness depended only on it being used once?

Perhaps.

There still had to be tendril connections between the Moat and the rest of the ocean at the time that the first wave of transformations had taken place. They had been severed later—either when the doors closed, or by some autonomic process within the extended organism itself—but until that moment, there would still have been informational links with the wider network of nodes. Could the dying nodes have sent sufficient warning that the other nodes were now able to find a strategy for protecting themselves?

Again, perhaps.

It never paid to take anything for granted where the Jugglers were concerned.

She parked the boat by the node's periphery. Naqi stood up and removed her clothes for the final time, certain that she would not need them again. She looked down at herself, astonished at the vivid tracery of green that now covered her body. On one level, the evidence of alien cellular invasion was quite horrific.

On another, it was startlingly beautiful.

Smoke licked from the horizon. Machines clawed through the sky, hunting nervously. She stepped to the edge of the boat, tensing herself at the moment of commitment. Her fear subsided, replaced by an intense, loving calm. She stood on the threshold of something alien, but in place of terror what she felt was only an imminent sense of homecoming. Mina was waiting for her below. Together nothing could stop them.

Naqi smiled, spread her arms and returned to the sea.